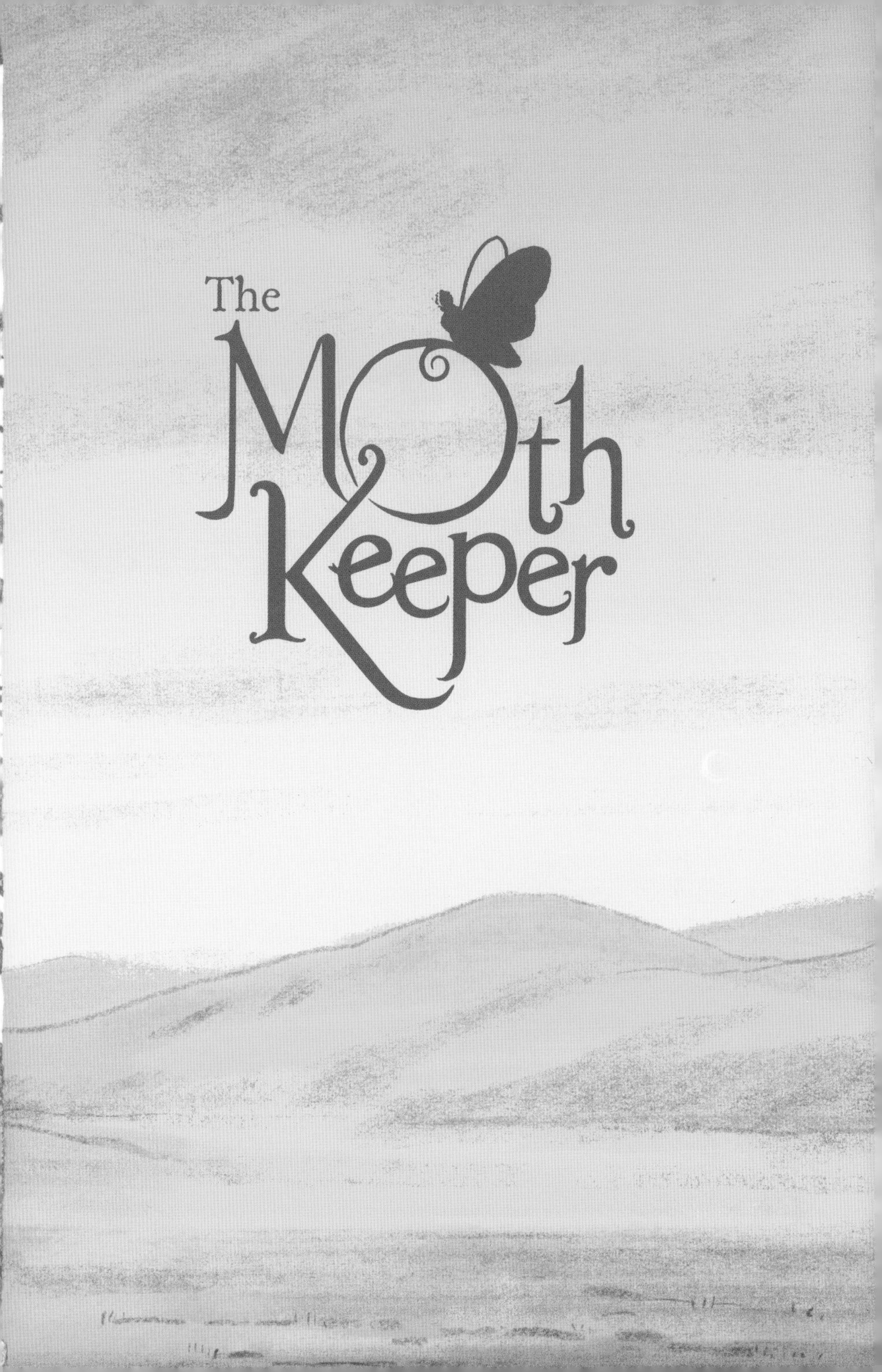
The
Moth
Keeper

Also by K. O'Neill

The Tea Dragon Society
The Tea Dragon Festival
The Tea Dragon Tapestry
Princess Princess Ever After
Aquicorn Cove
Dewdrop

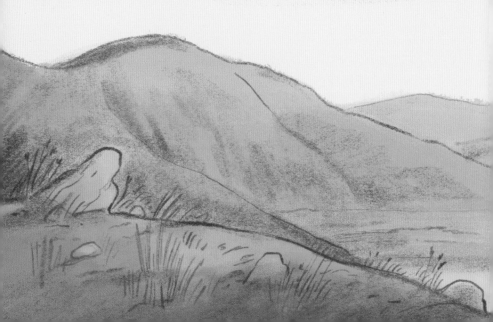

The Moth Keeper

K. O'Neill

RH
GRAPHIC

NEW YORK

The Moth Keeper was created on an iPad Pro with Procreate.

All rights reserved. Published in the United States by RH Graphic, an imprint of Random House Children's Books, a division of Penguin Random House LLC, New York.

RH Graphic with the book design is a trademark of Penguin Random House LLC.

Visit us on the web! RHKidsGraphic.com • @RHKidsGraphic

Educators and librarians, for a variety of teaching tools, visit us at RHTeachersLibrarians.com

Library of Congress Cataloging-in-Publication Data is available upon request.
ISBN 978-0-593-18227-7 (hardcover) — ISBN 978-0-593-18226-0 (paperback)
ISBN 978-0-593-18228-4 (library binding) — ISBN 978-0-593-18229-1 (ebook)

Designed by Patrick Crotty

MANUFACTURED IN CHINA
10 9 8 7 6 5 4 3 2
First Edition

A comic on every bookshelf.

For Alex

Chapter One

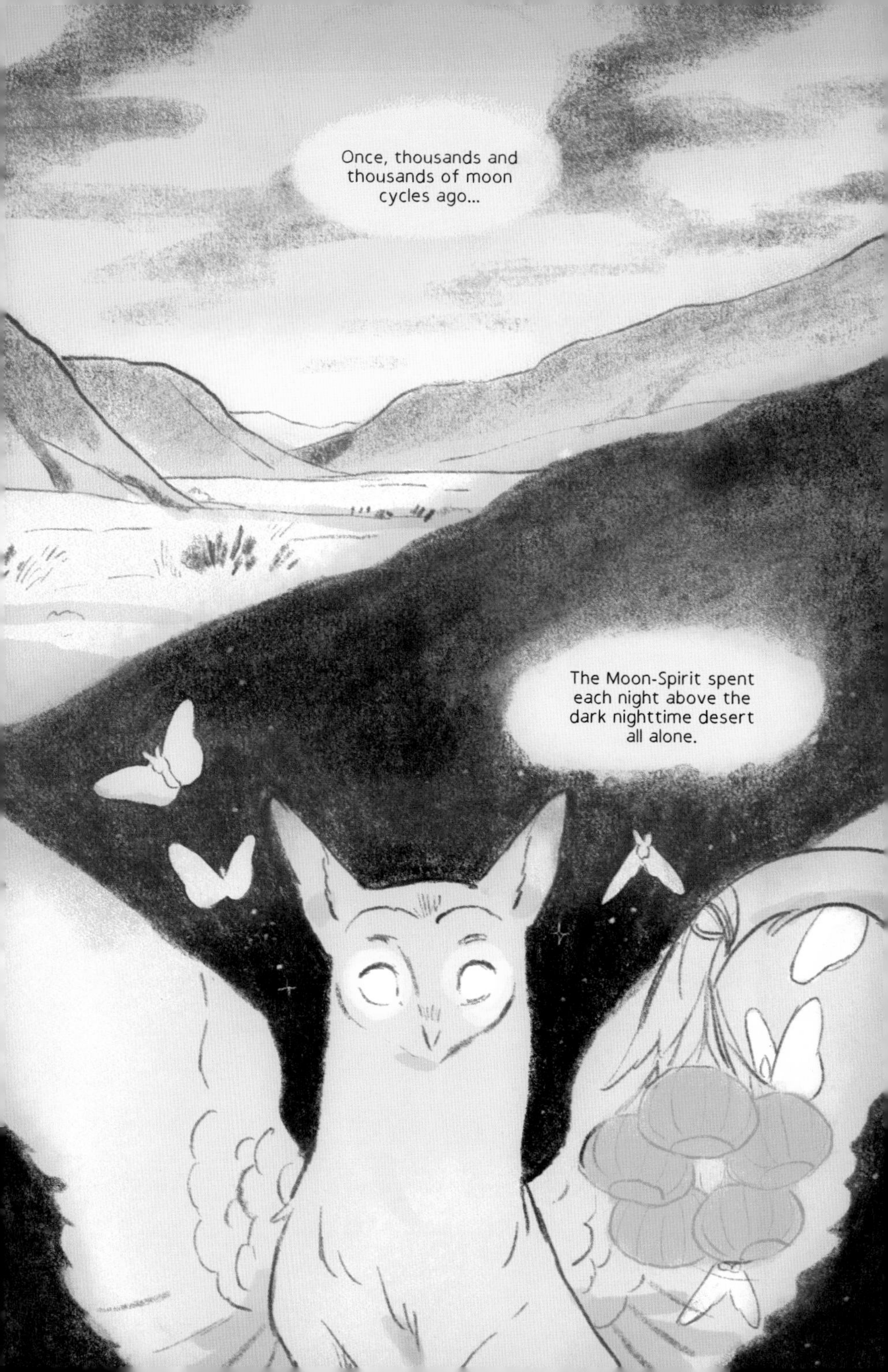
Once, thousands and thousands of moon cycles ago...
The Moon-Spirit spent each night above the dark nighttime desert all alone.

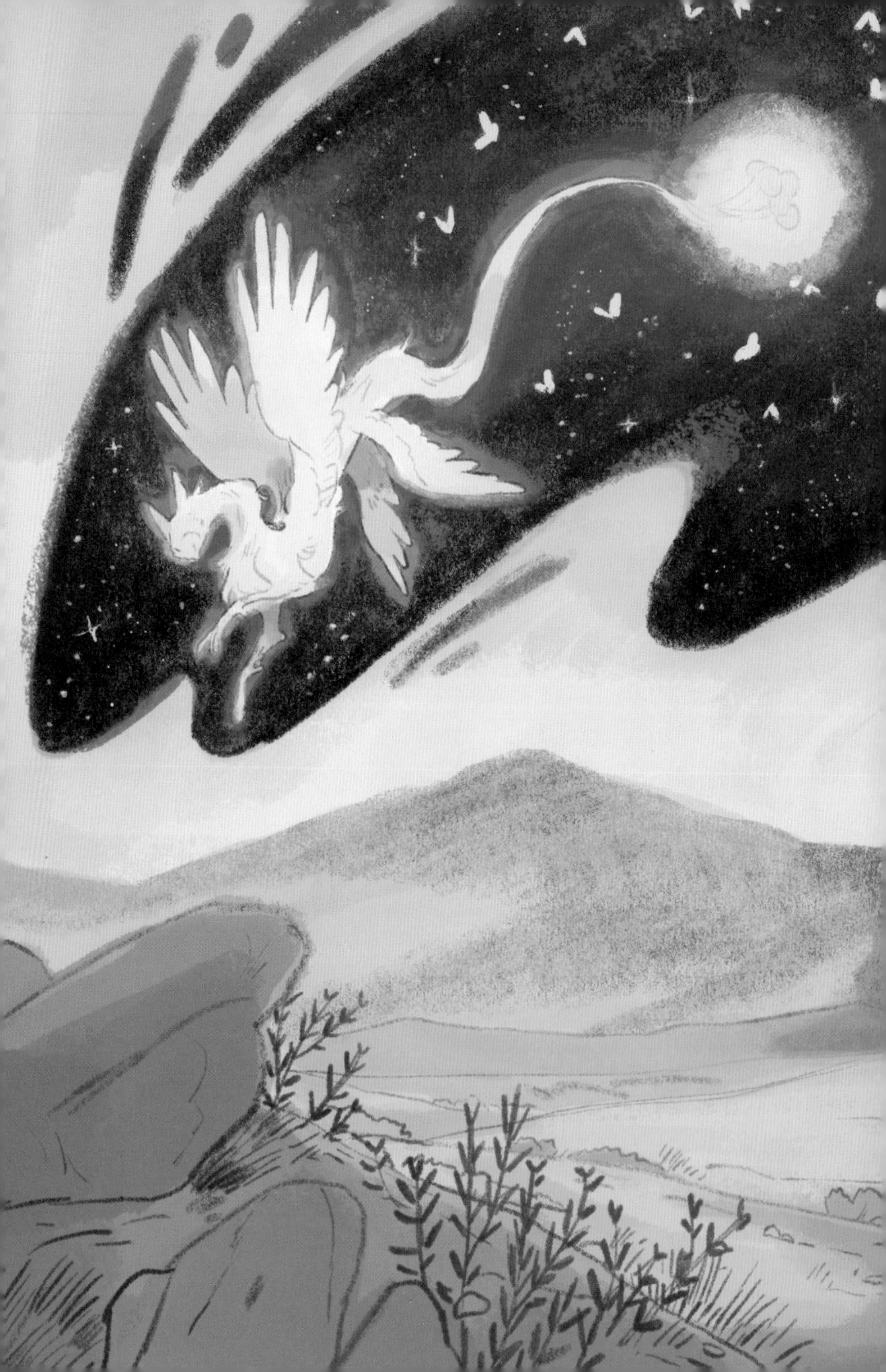

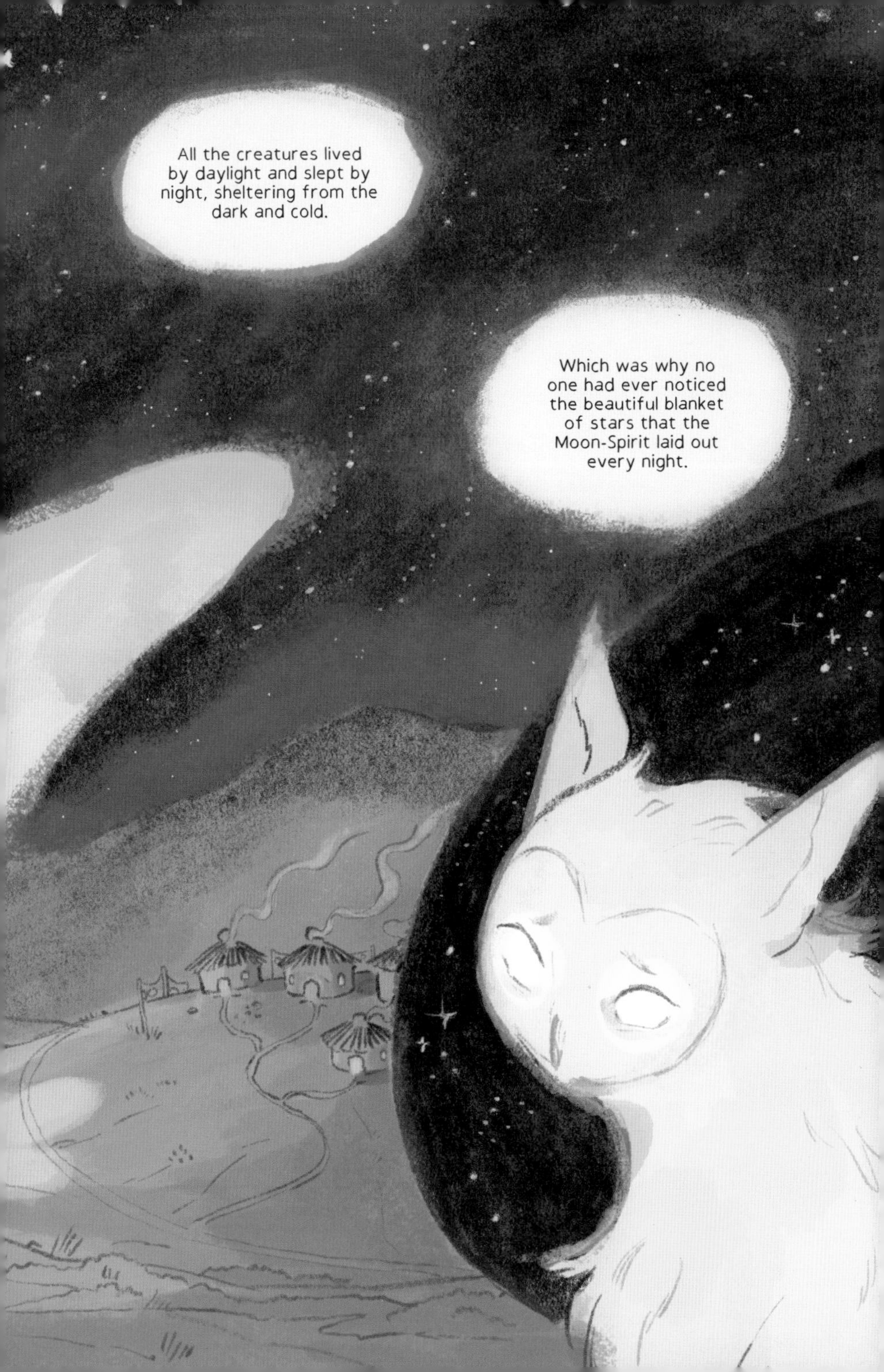
All the creatures lived by daylight and slept by night, sheltering from the dark and cold.
Which was why no one had ever noticed the beautiful blanket of stars that the Moon-Spirit laid out every night.

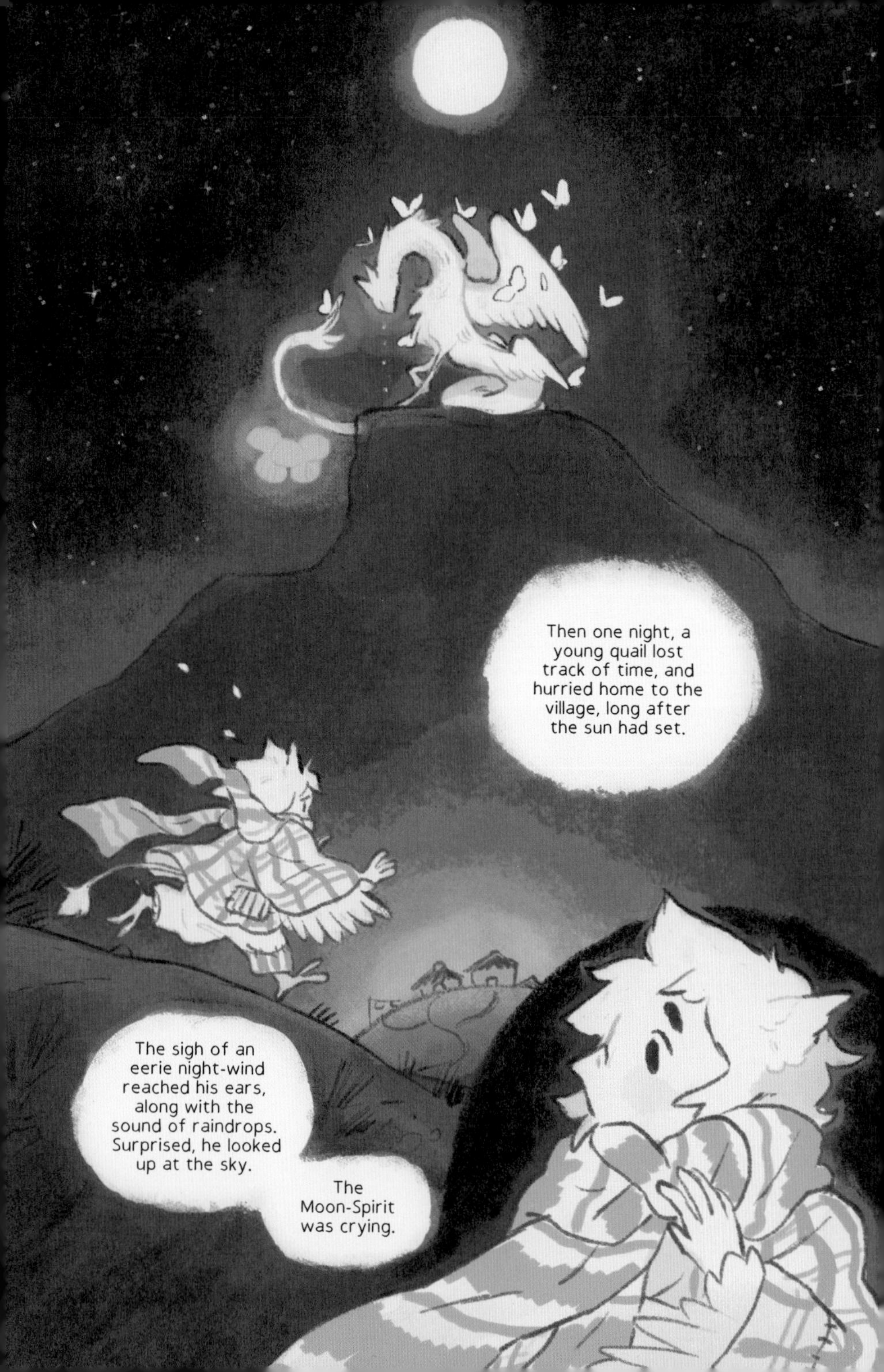
Then one night, a young quail lost track of time, and hurried home to the village, long after the sun had set.
The sigh of an eerie night-wind reached his ears, along with the sound of raindrops. Surprised, he looked up at the sky.
The Moon-Spirit was crying.

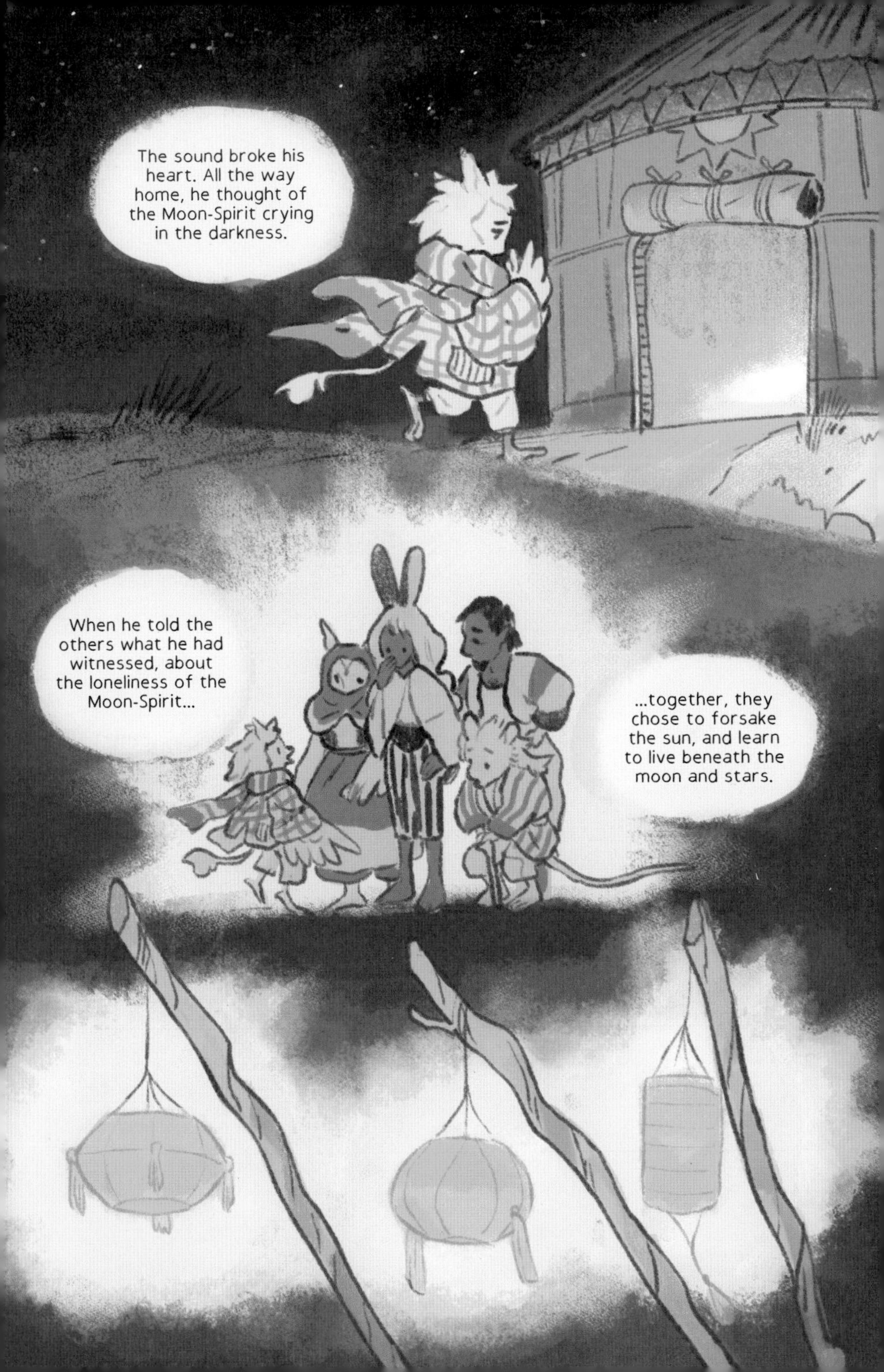
The sound broke his heart. All the way home, he thought of the Moon-Spirit crying in the darkness.
When he told the others what he had witnessed, about the loneliness of the Moon-Spirit...
...together, they chose to forsake the sun, and learn to live beneath the moon and stars.

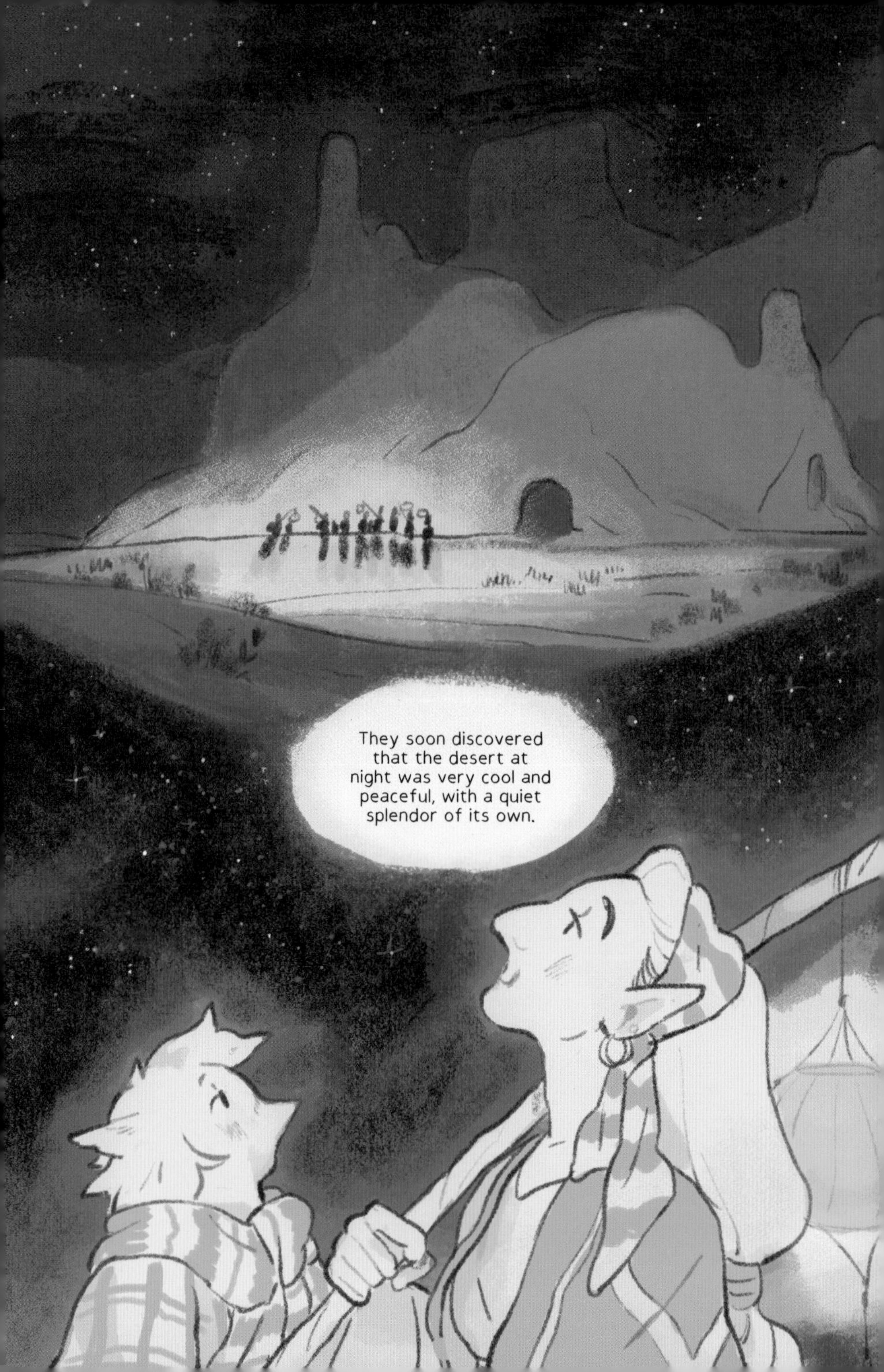
They soon discovered that the desert at night was very cool and peaceful, with a quiet splendor of its own.

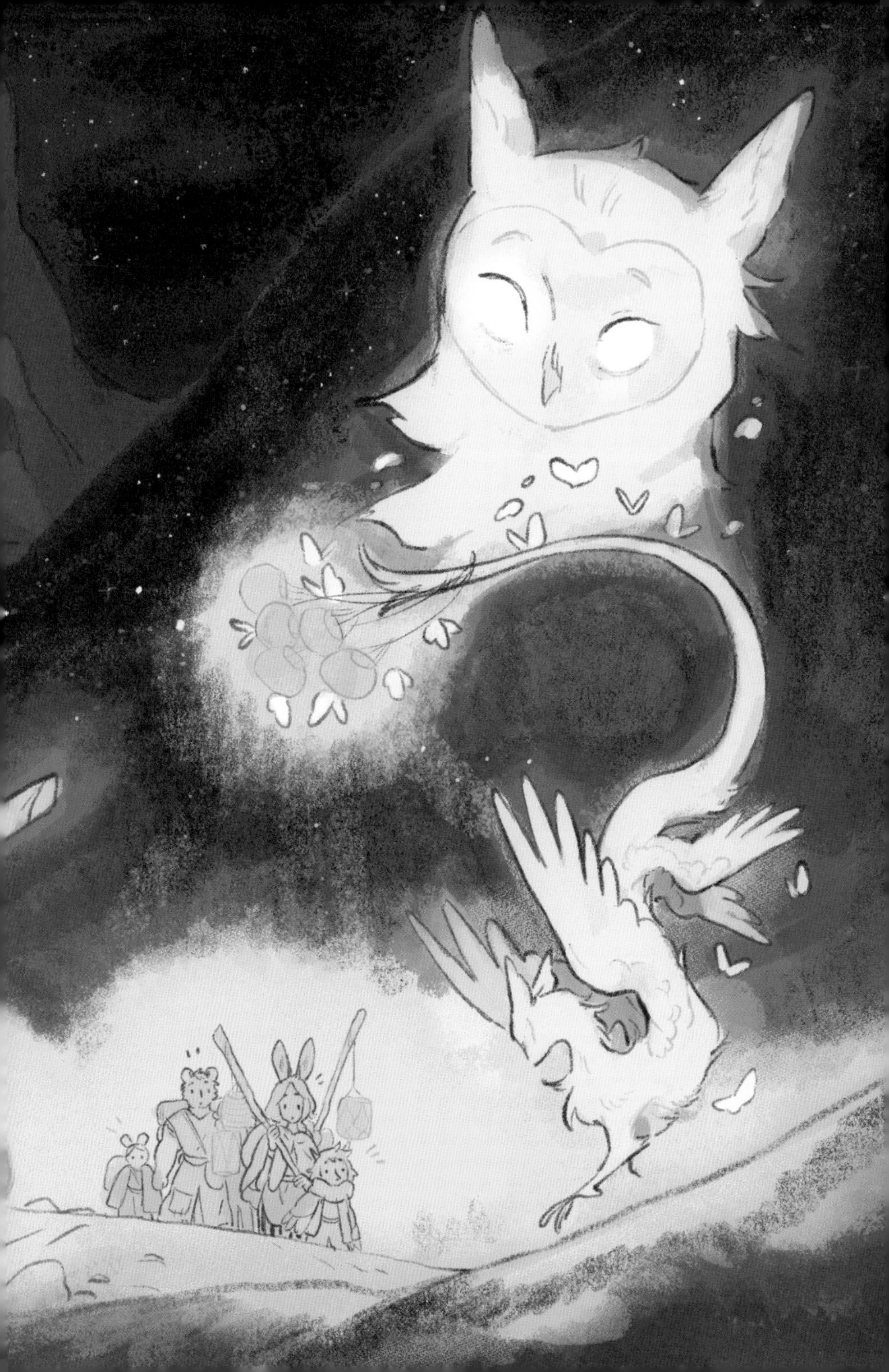

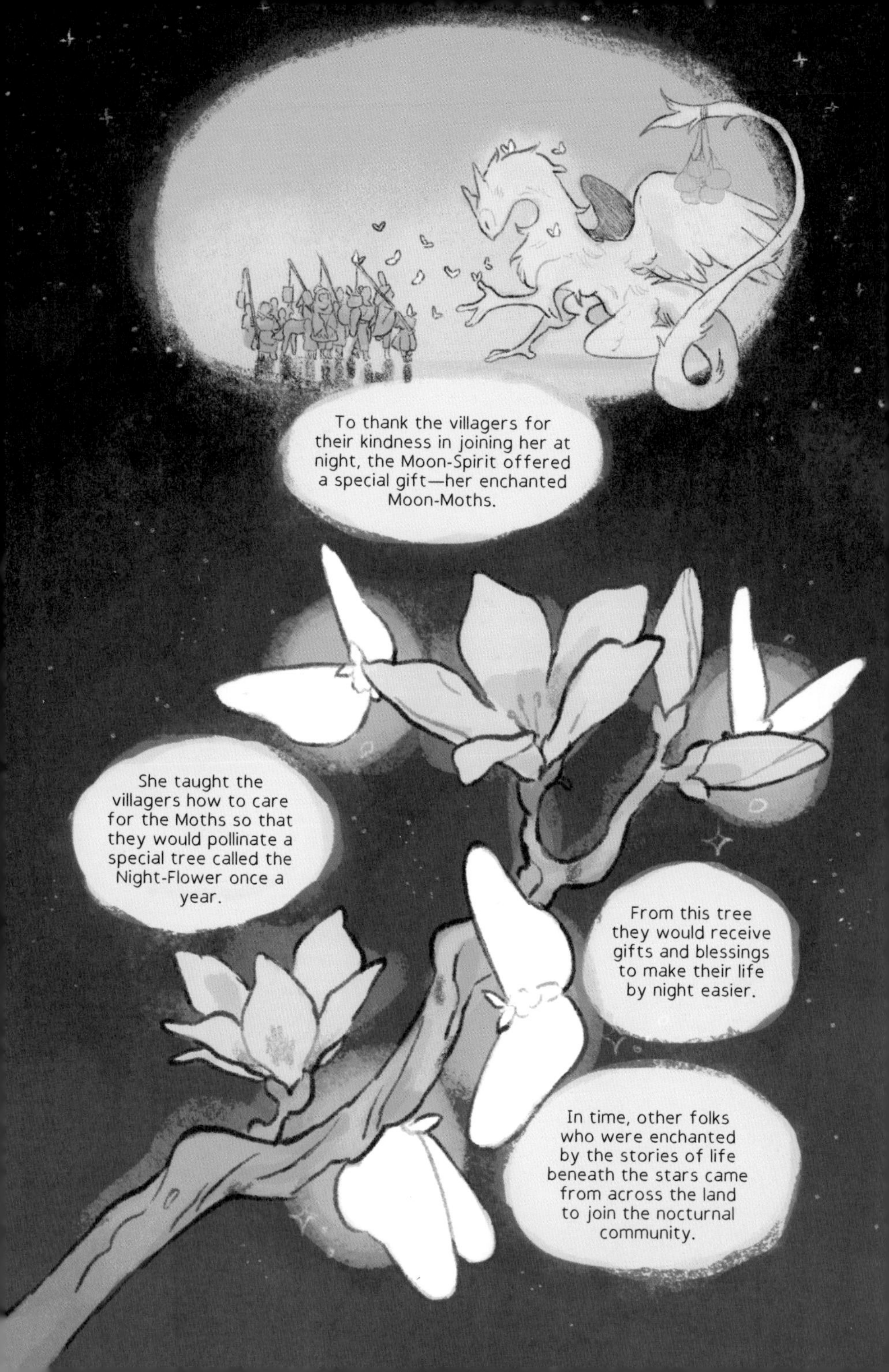

To thank the villagers for their kindness in joining her at night, the Moon-Spirit offered a special gift—her enchanted Moon-Moths.
She taught the villagers how to care for the Moths so that they would pollinate a special tree called the Night-Flower once a year.
From this tree they would receive gifts and blessings to make their life by night easier.
In time, other folks who were enchanted by the stories of life beneath the stars came from across the land to join the nocturnal community.

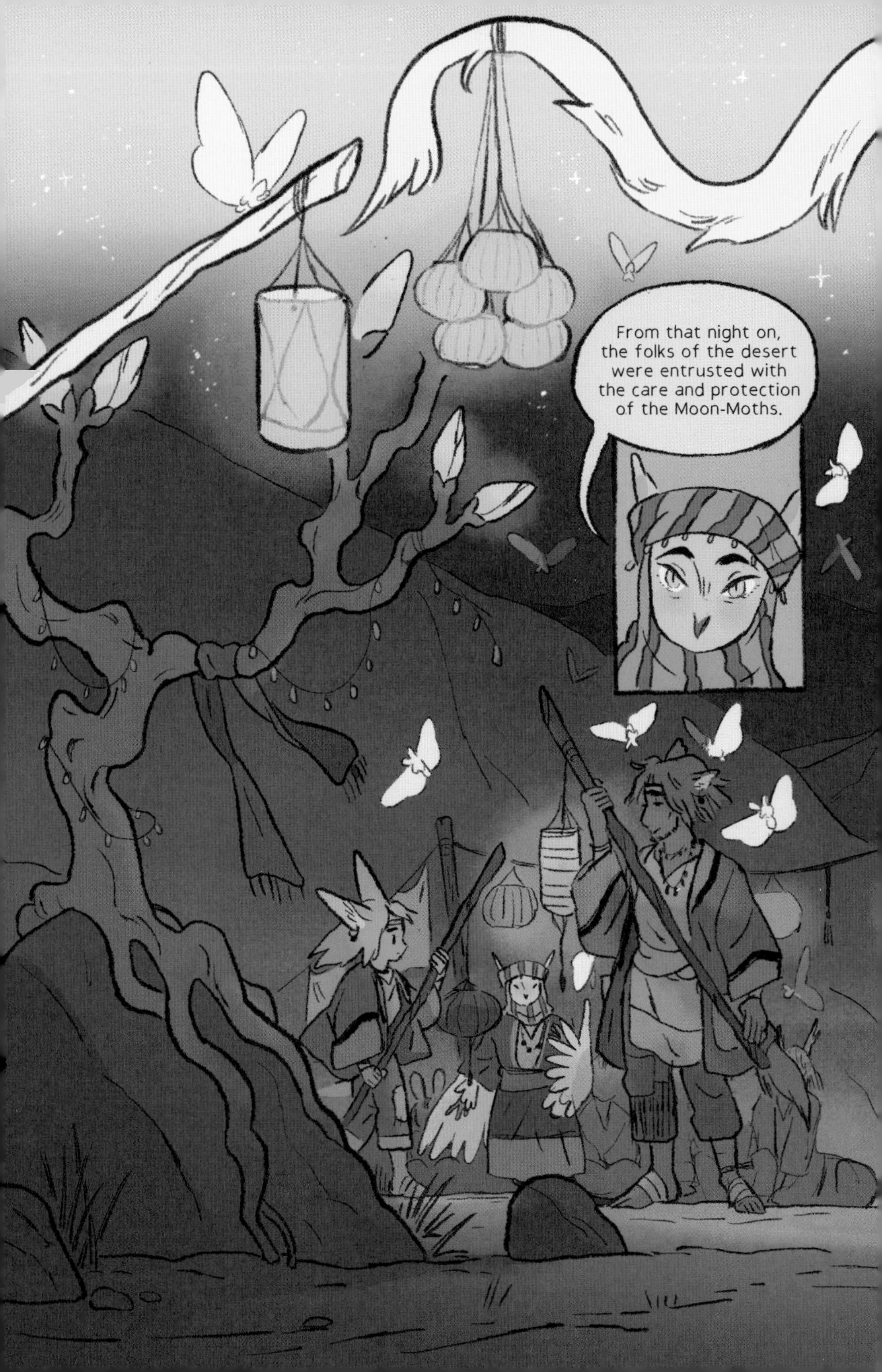
From that night on, the folks of the desert were entrusted with the care and protection of the Moon-Moths.

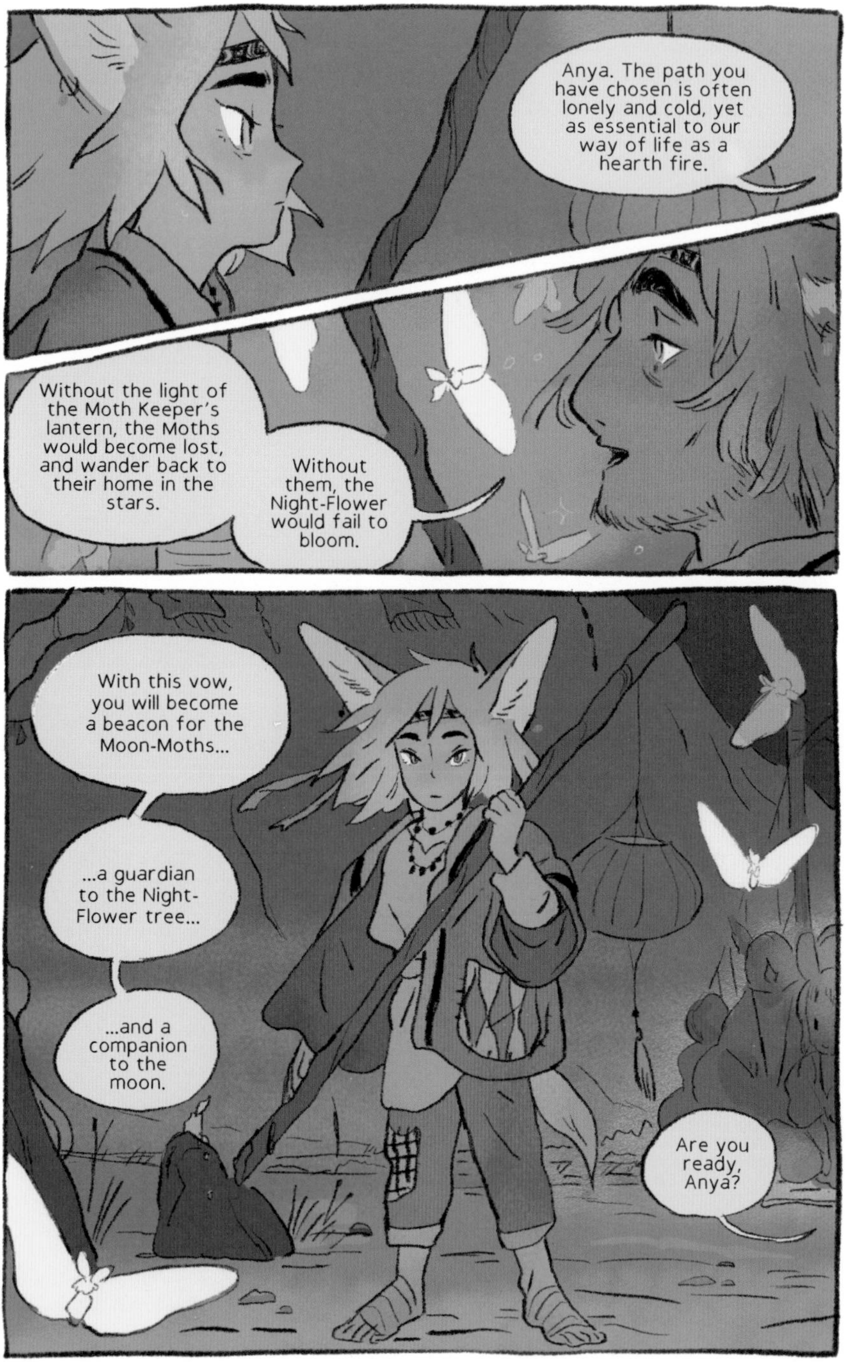
Anya. The path you have chosen is often lonely and cold, yet as essential to our way of life as a hearth fire.
Without the light of the Moth Keeper's lantern, the Moths would become lost, and wander back to their home in the stars.
Without them, the Night-Flower would fail to bloom.
With this vow, you will become a beacon for the Moon-Moths...
...a guardian to the Night-Flower tree...
...and a companion to the moon.
Are you ready, Anya?

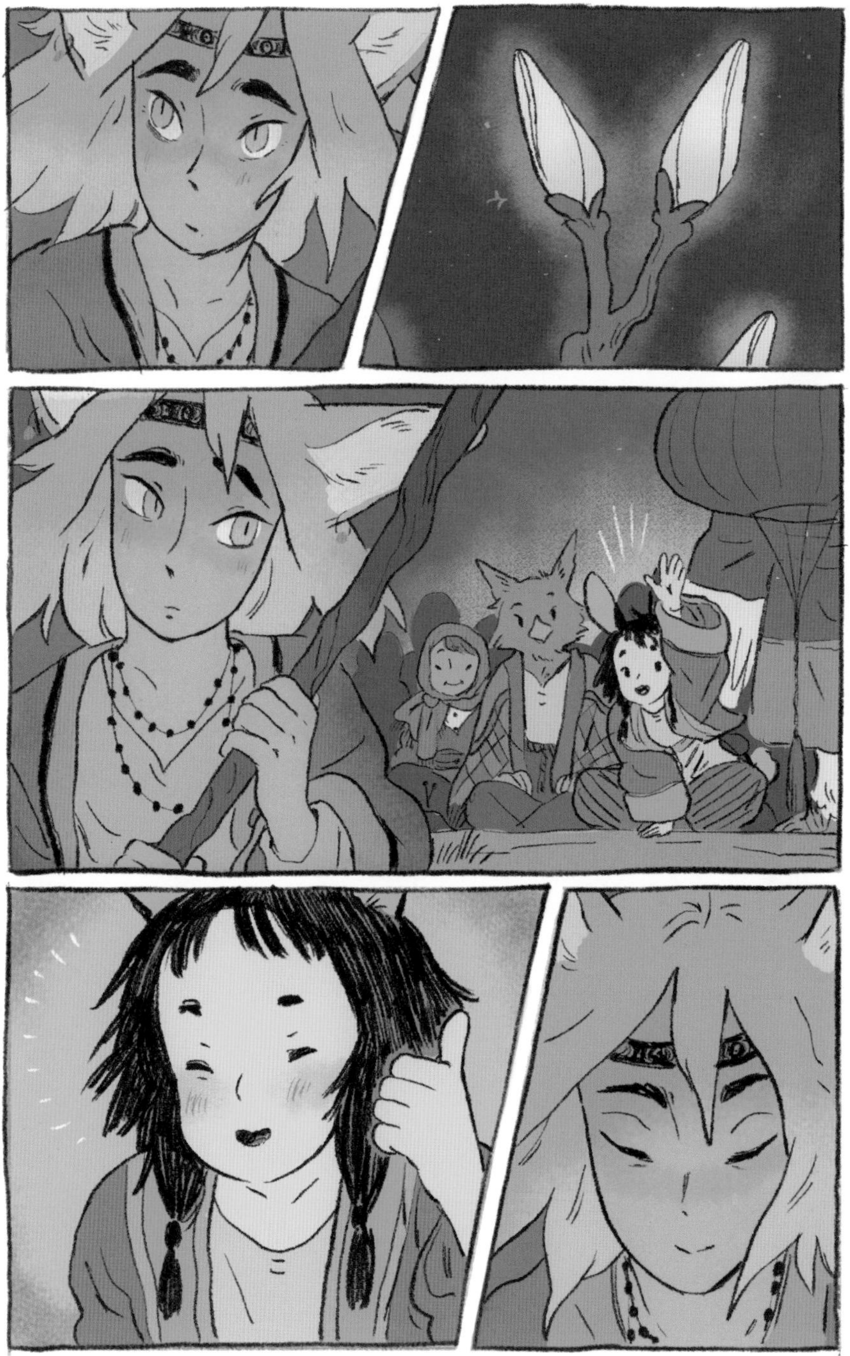

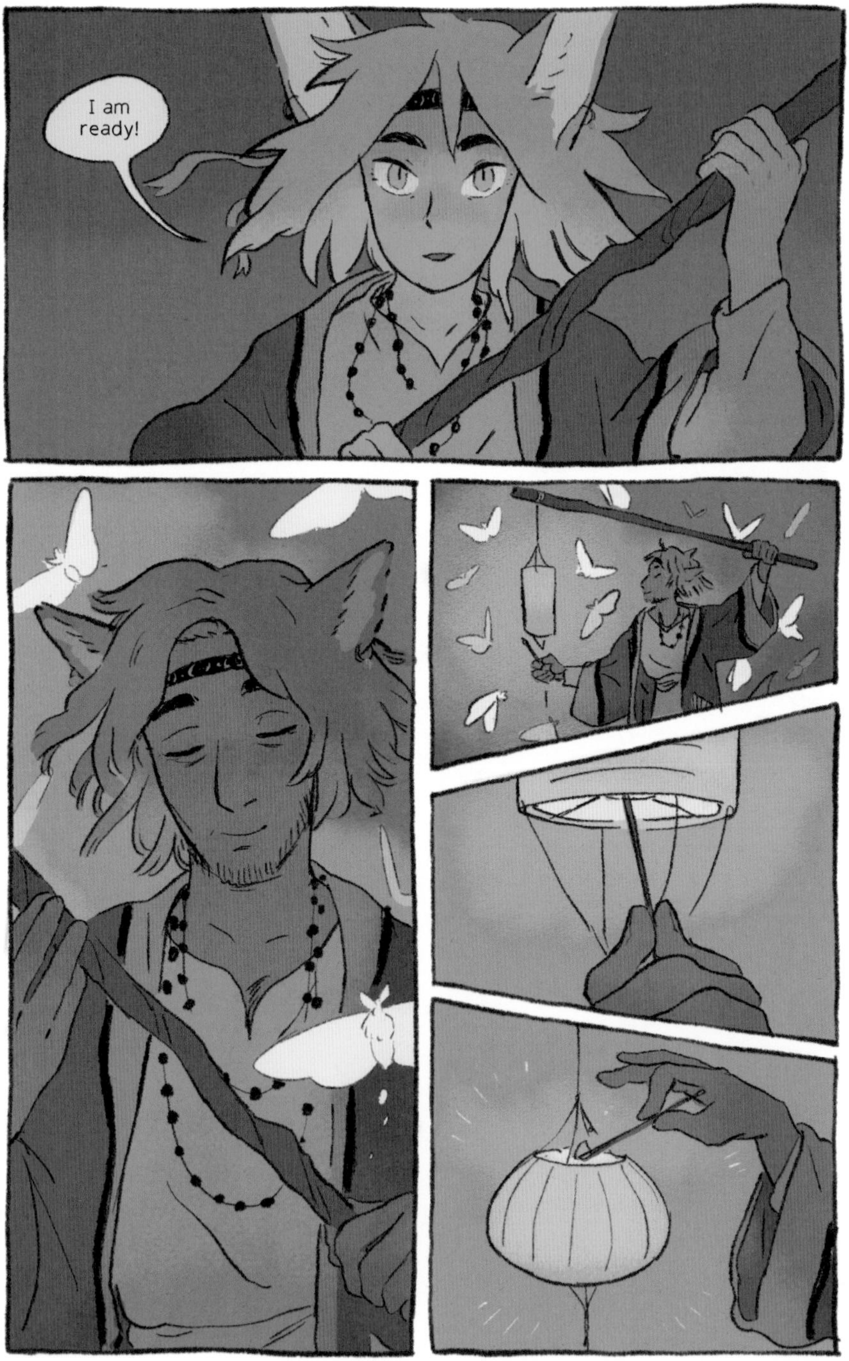
I am ready!

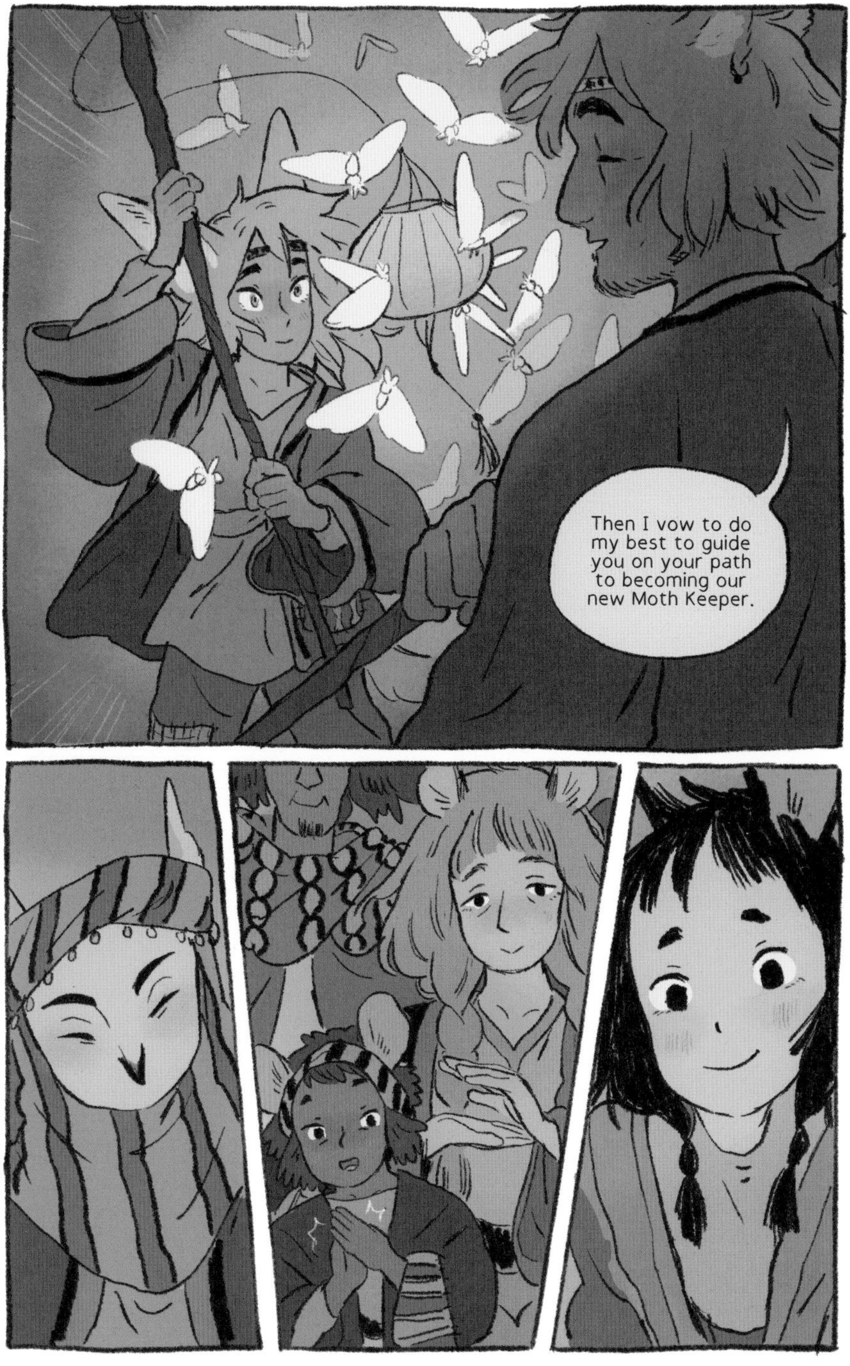
Then I vow to do my best to guide you on your path to becoming our new Moth Keeper.

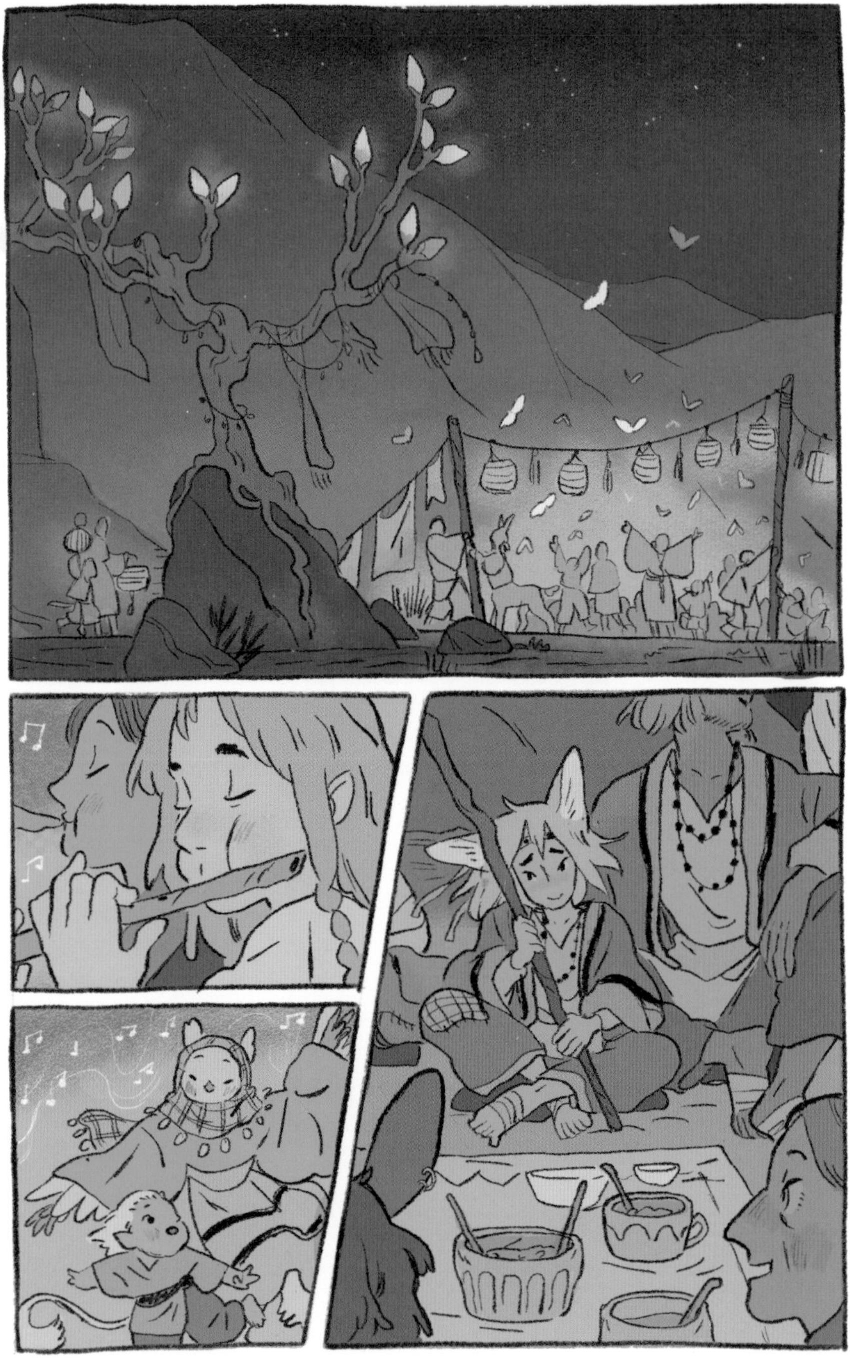

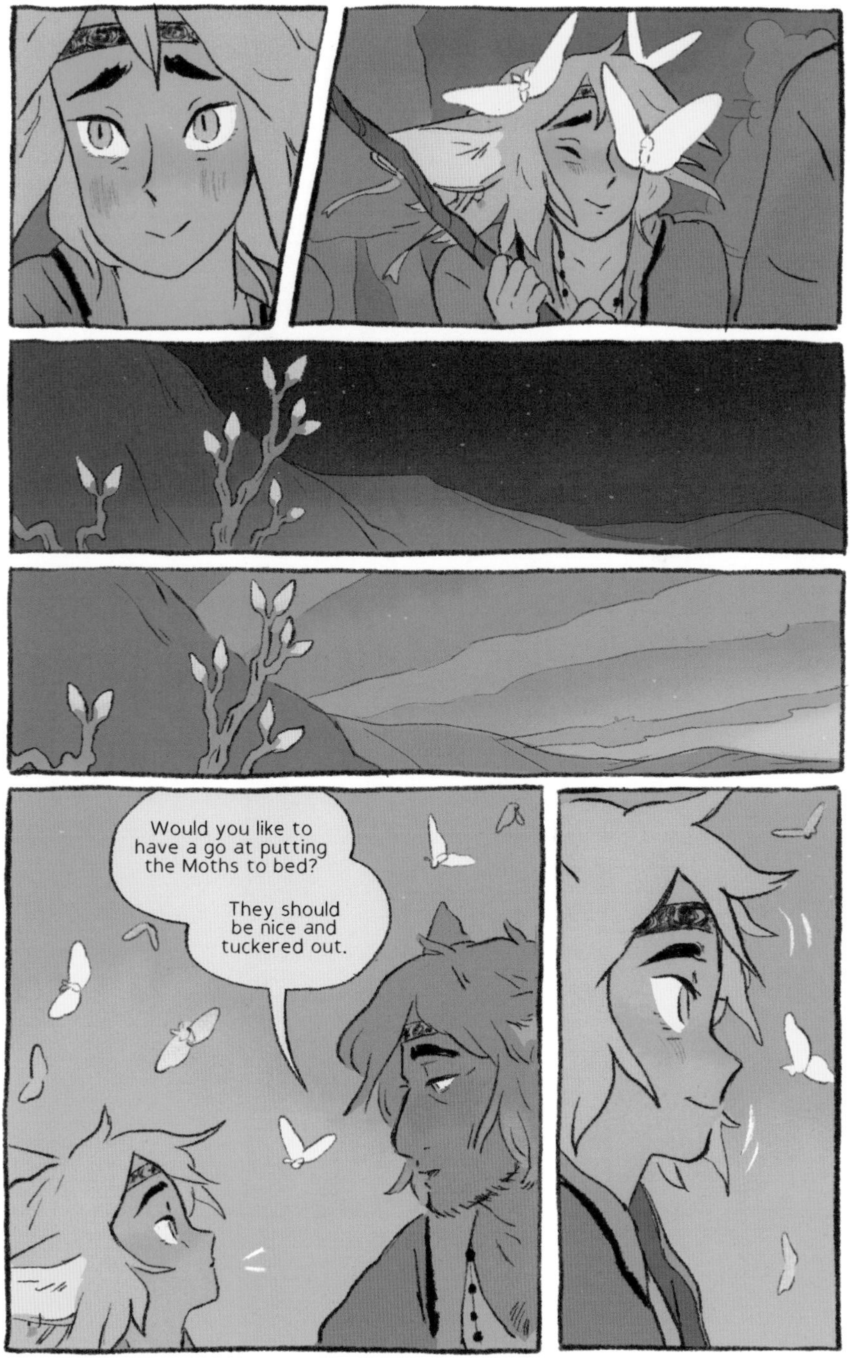
Would you like to have a go at putting the Moths to bed?
They should be nice and tuckered out.

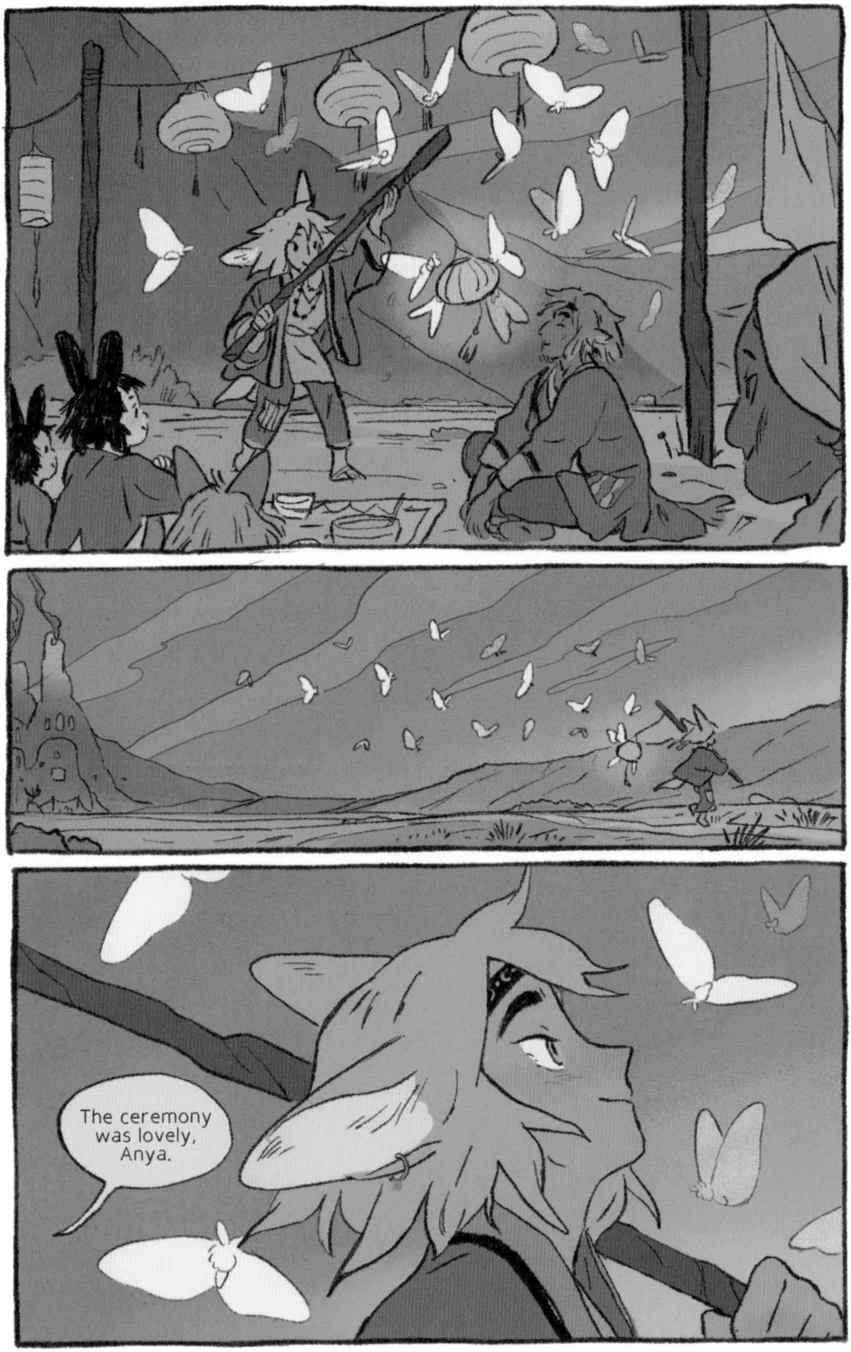
The ceremony was lovely, Anya.

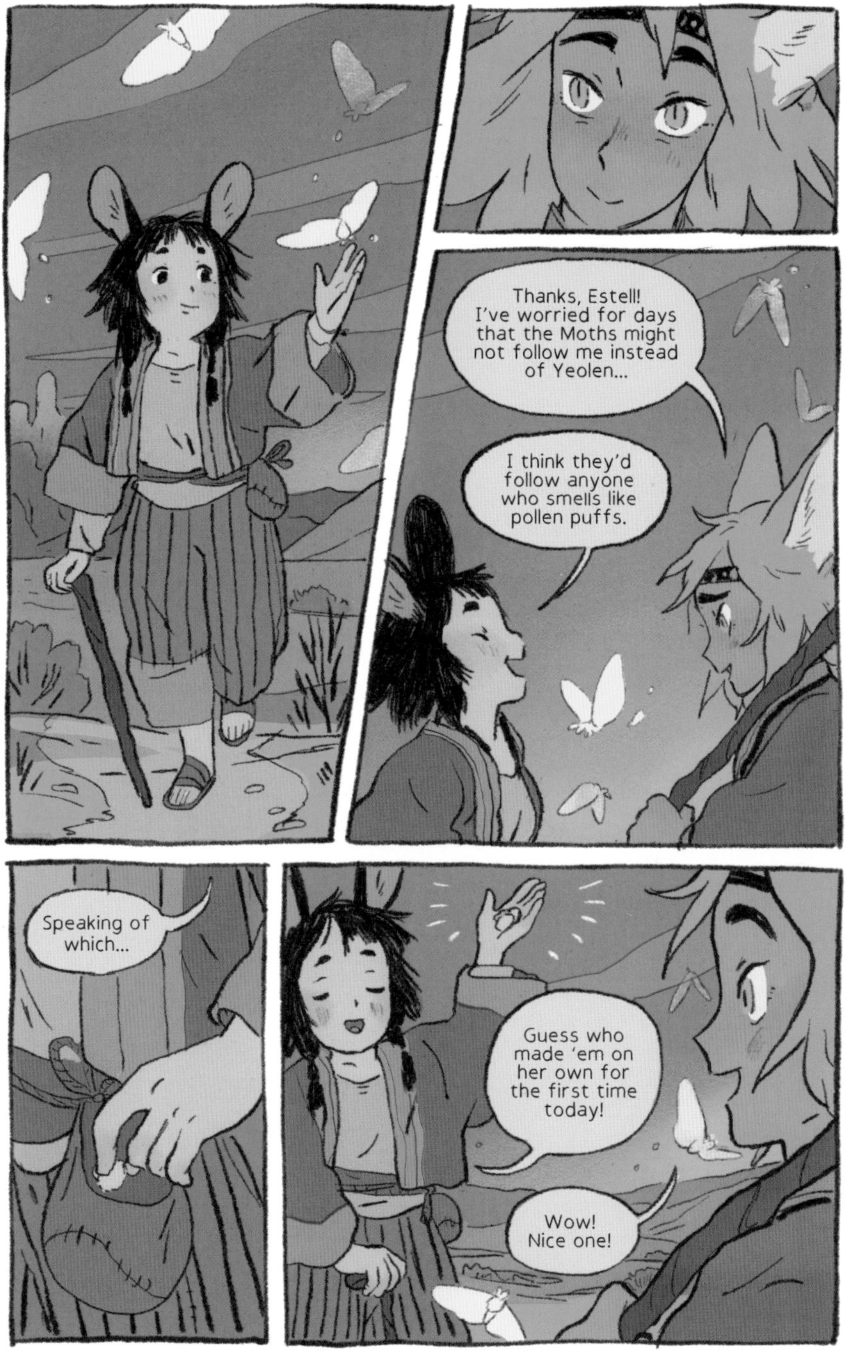
Thanks, Estell! I've worried for days that the Moths might not follow me instead of Yeolen...
I think they'd follow anyone who smells like pollen puffs.
Speaking of which...
Guess who made 'em on her own for the first time today!
Wow! Nice one!

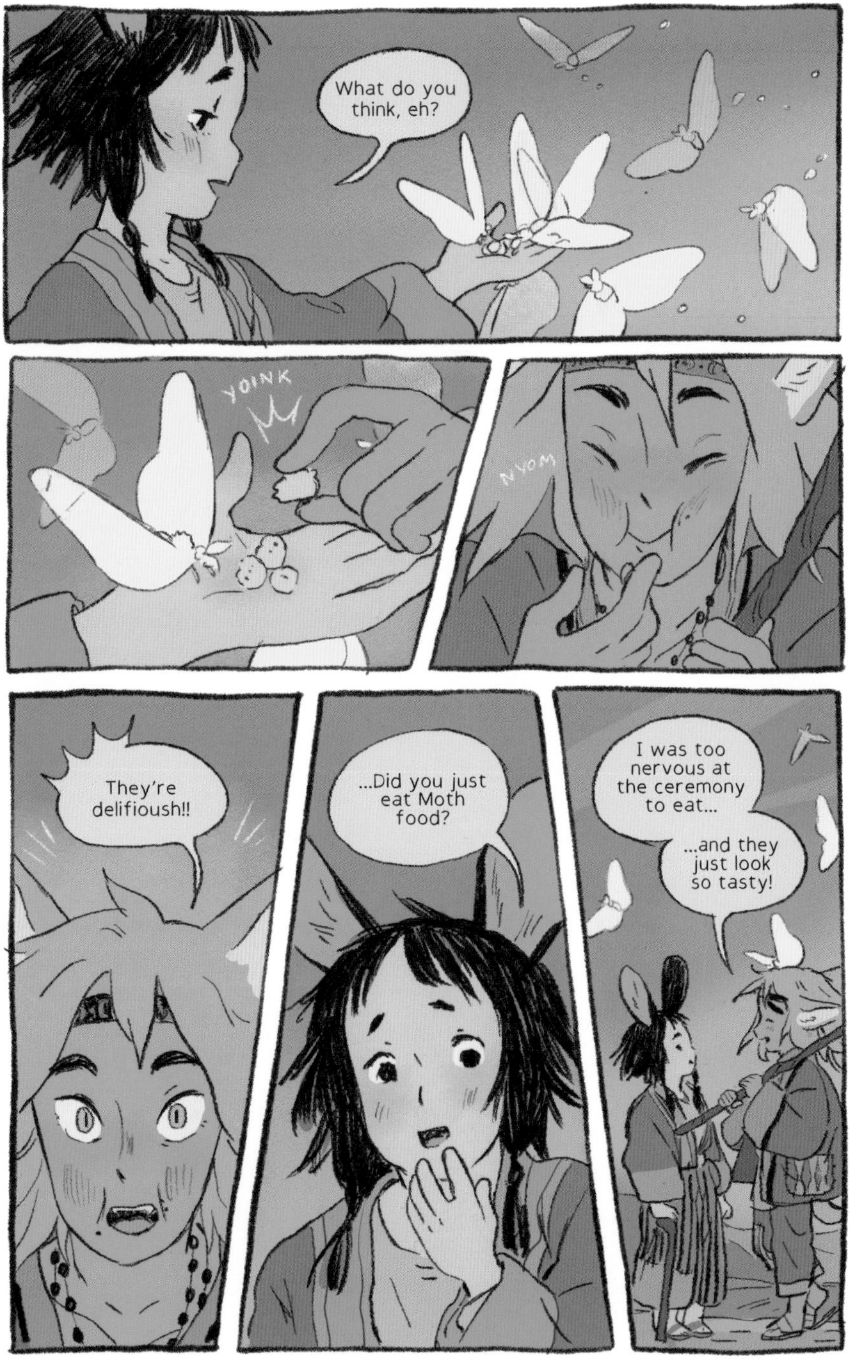
What do you think, eh?
YOINK
NYOM
They're delifioush!!
...Did you just eat Moth food?
I was too nervous at the ceremony to eat...
...and they just look so tasty!

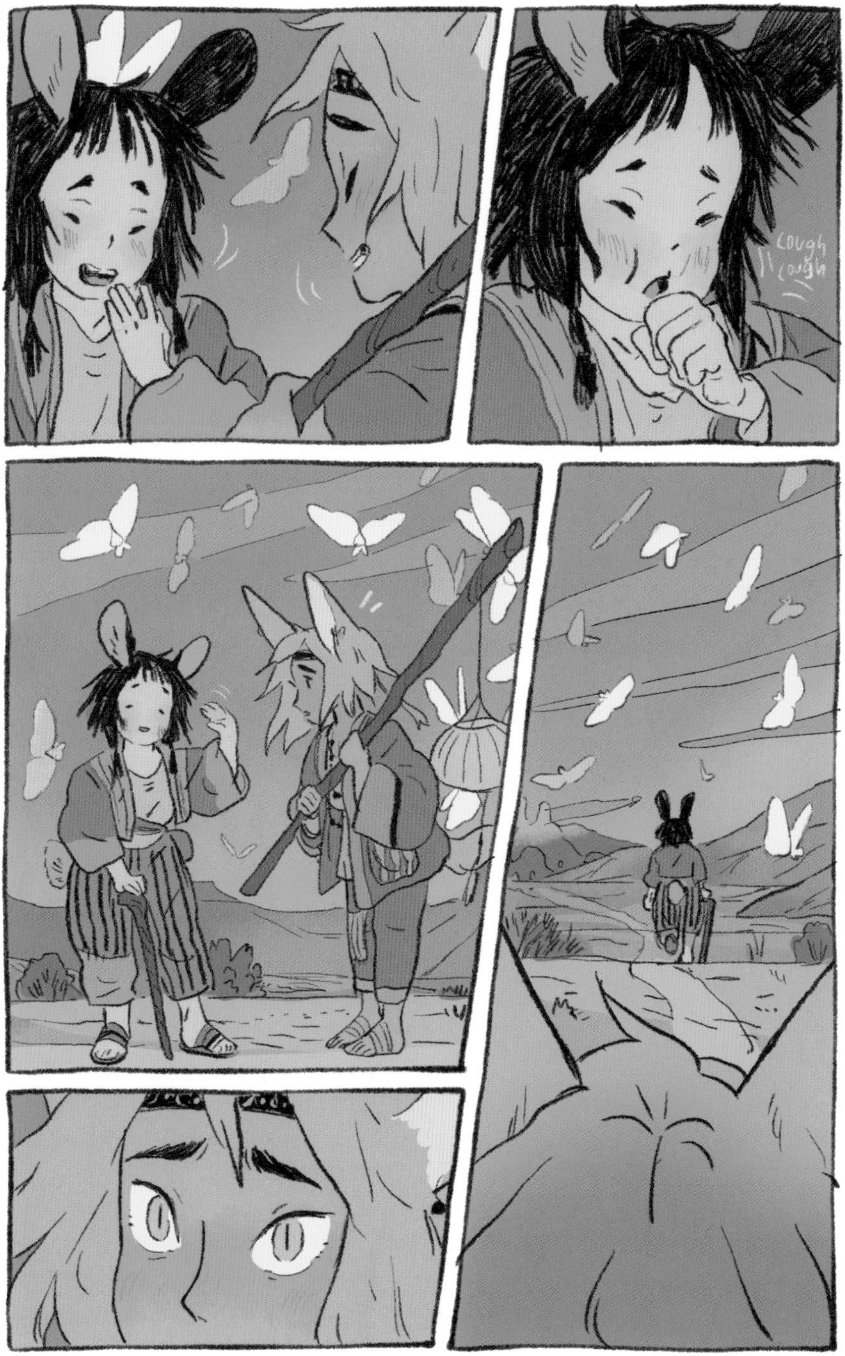
cough
cough

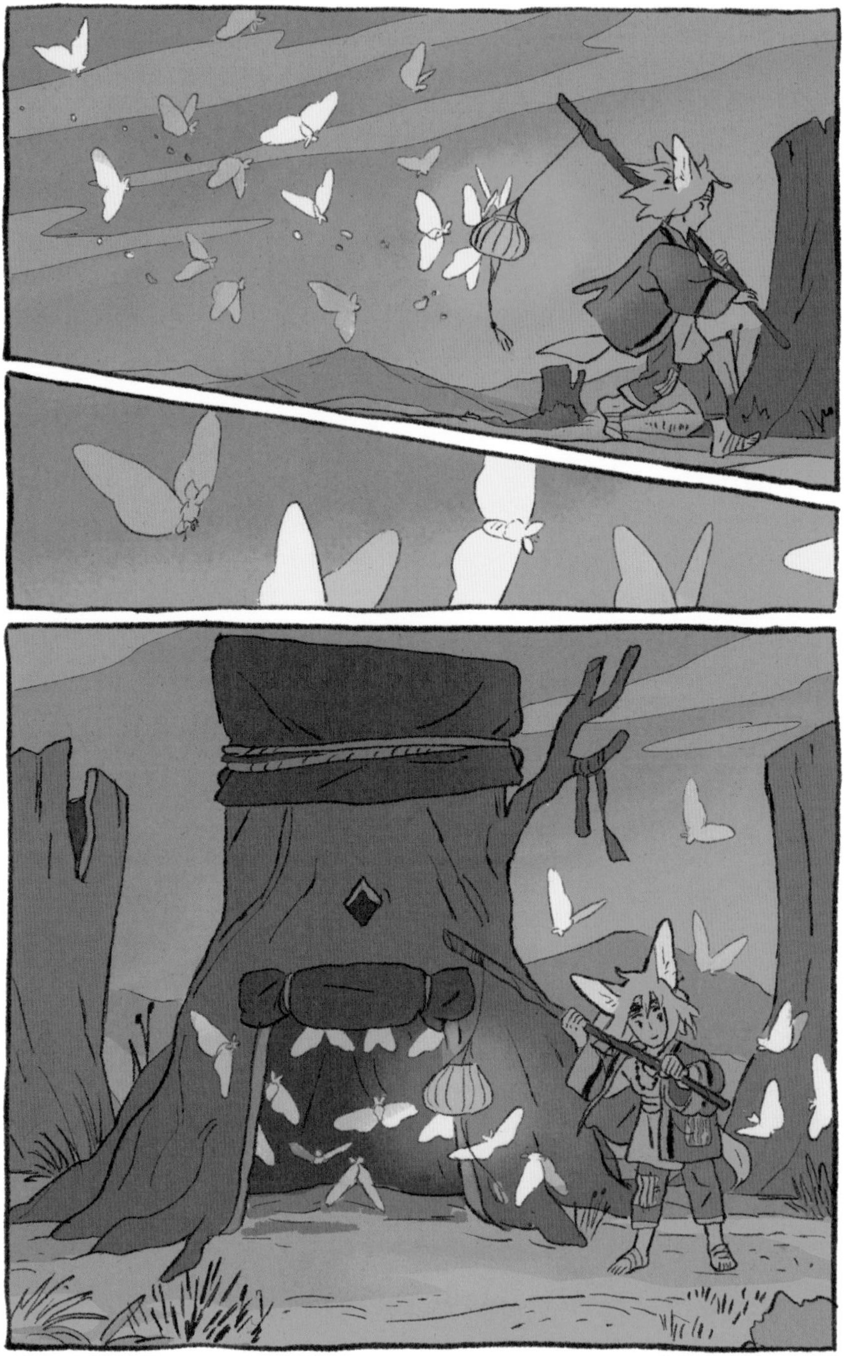

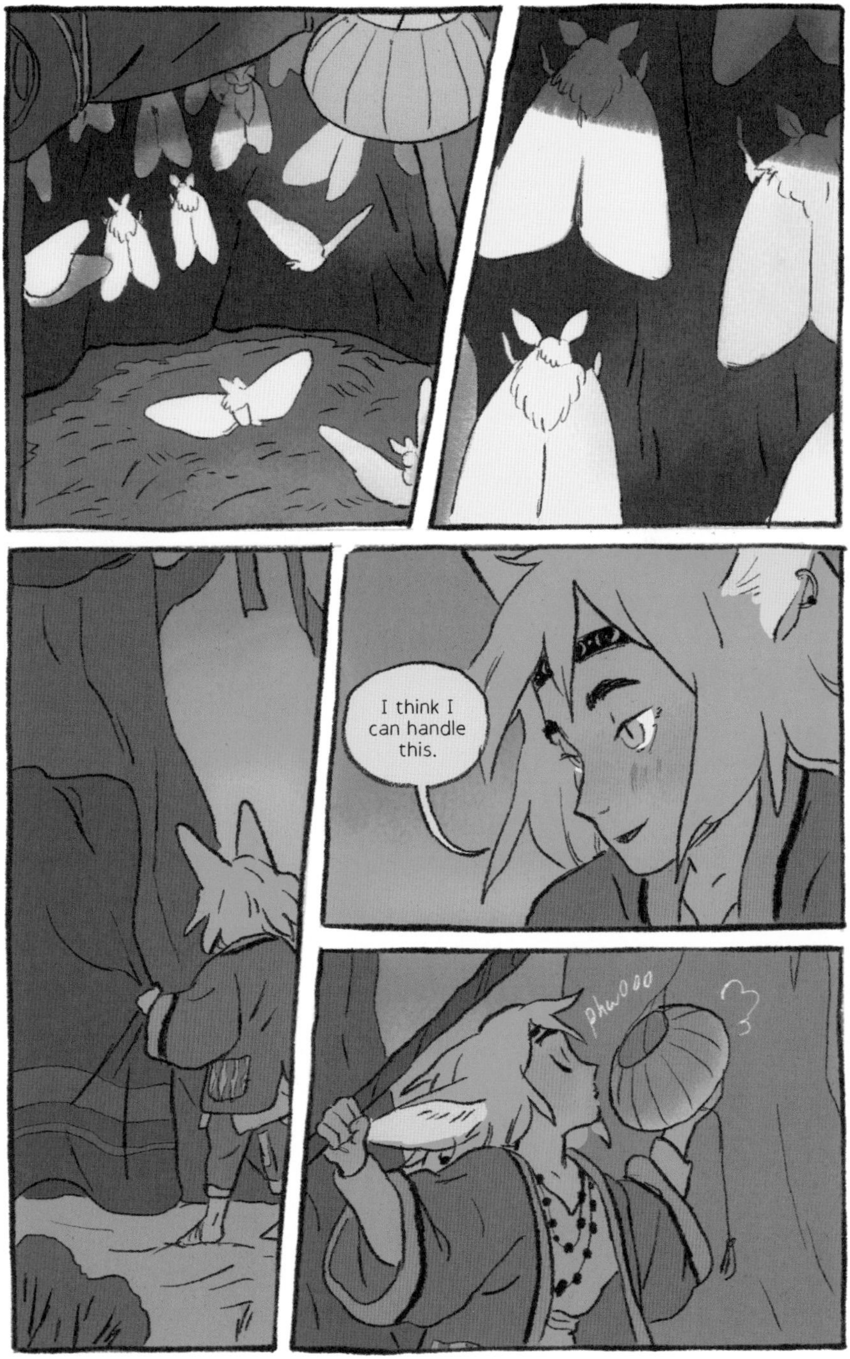
I think I can handle this.
phwooo

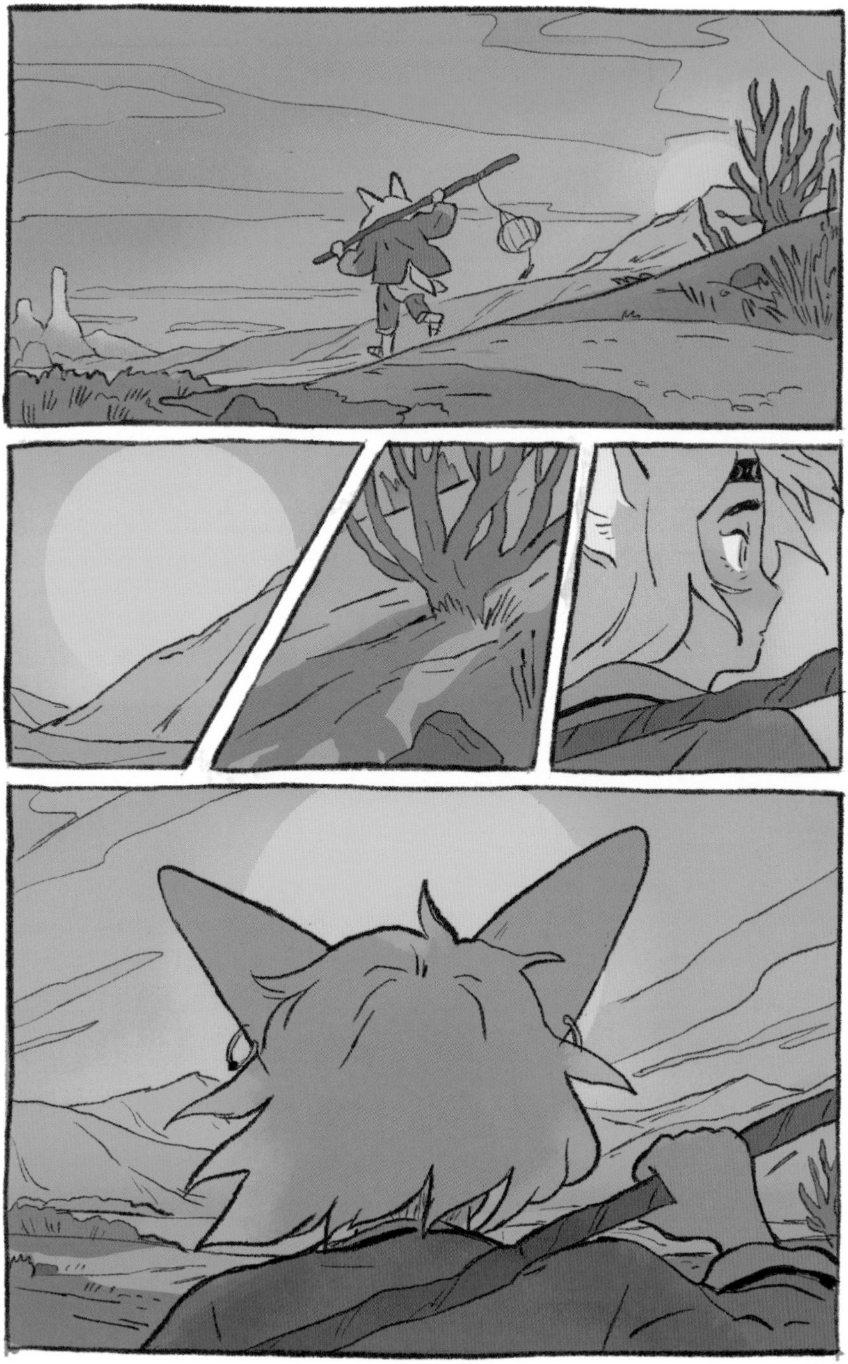

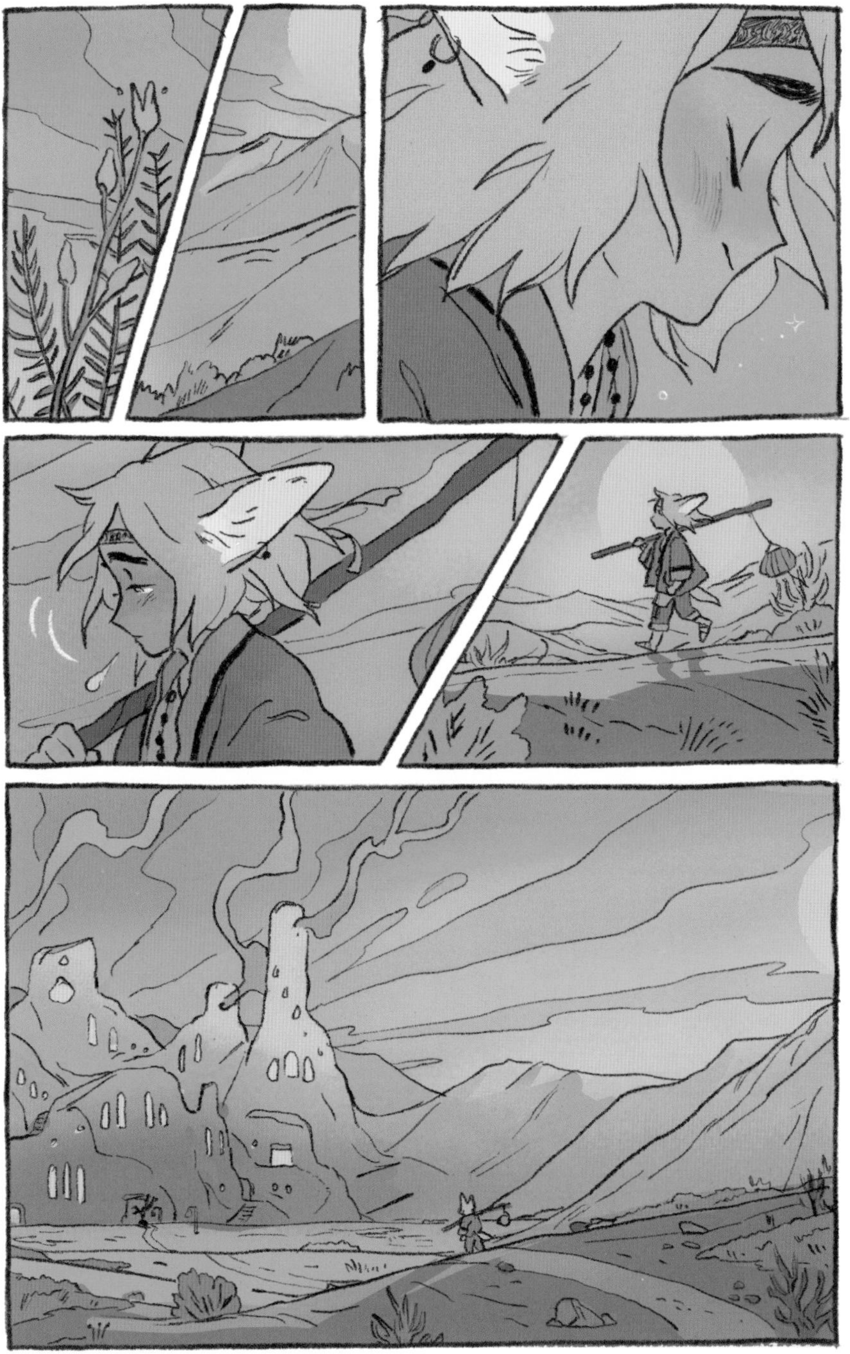

Chapter Two

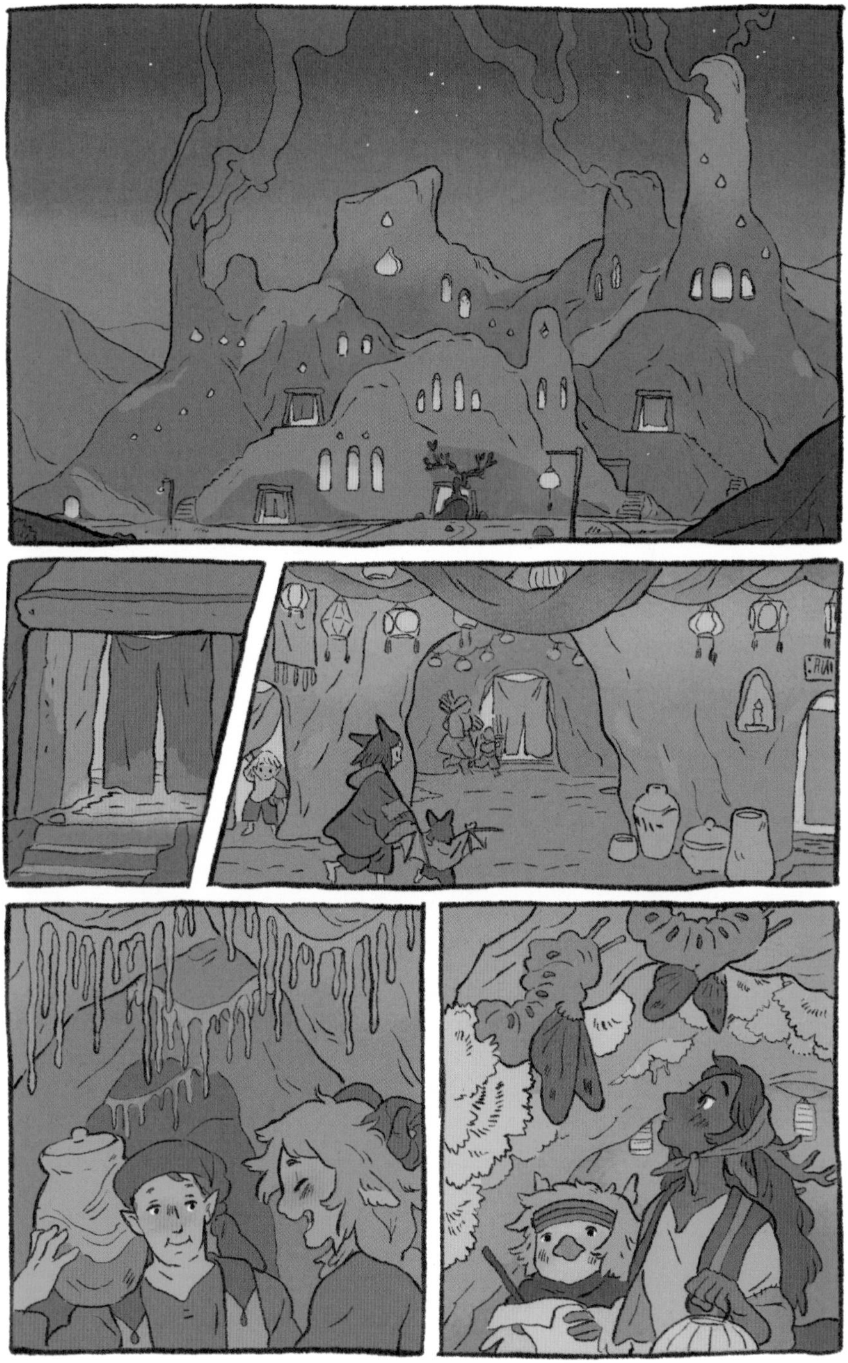

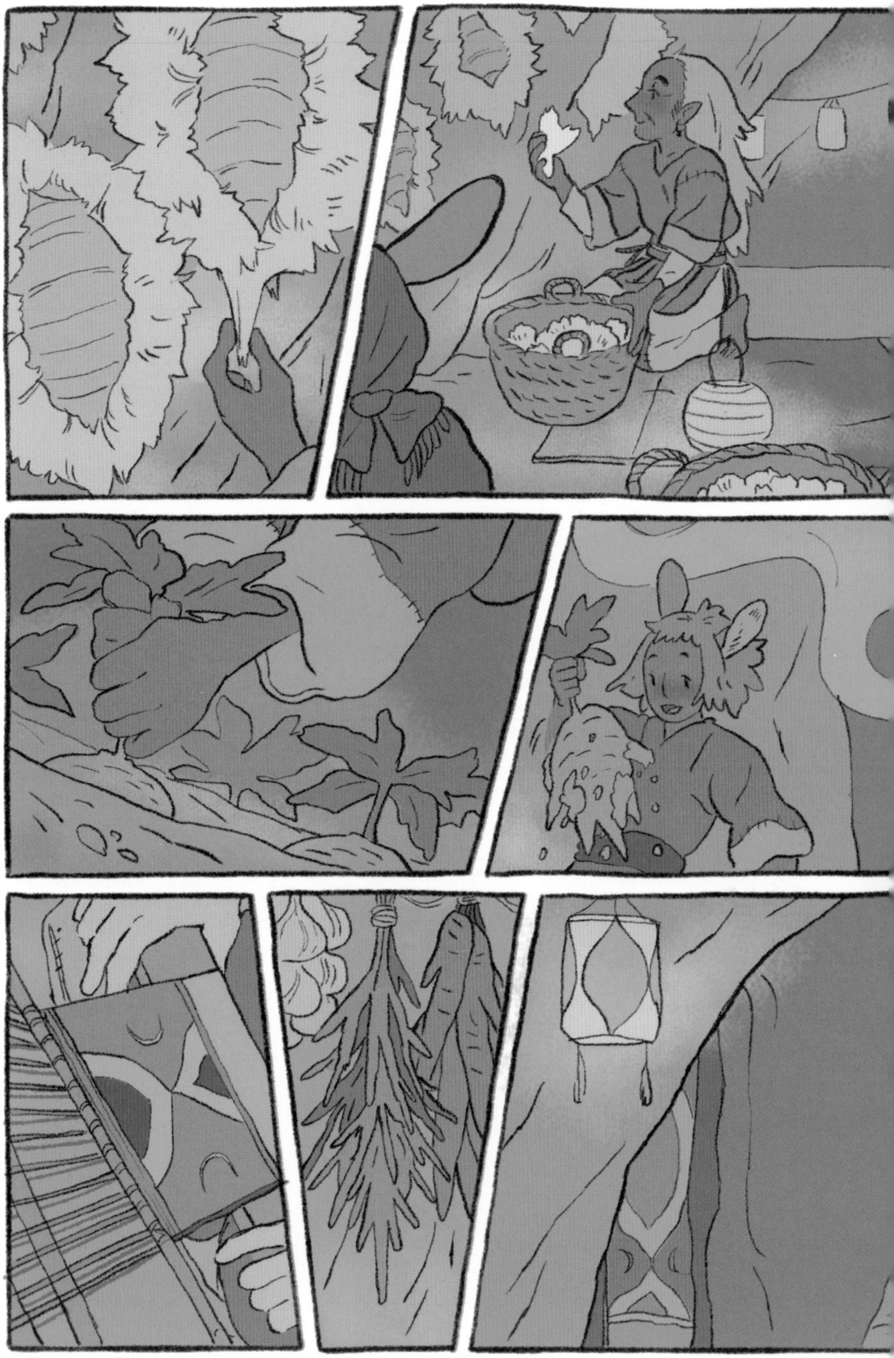

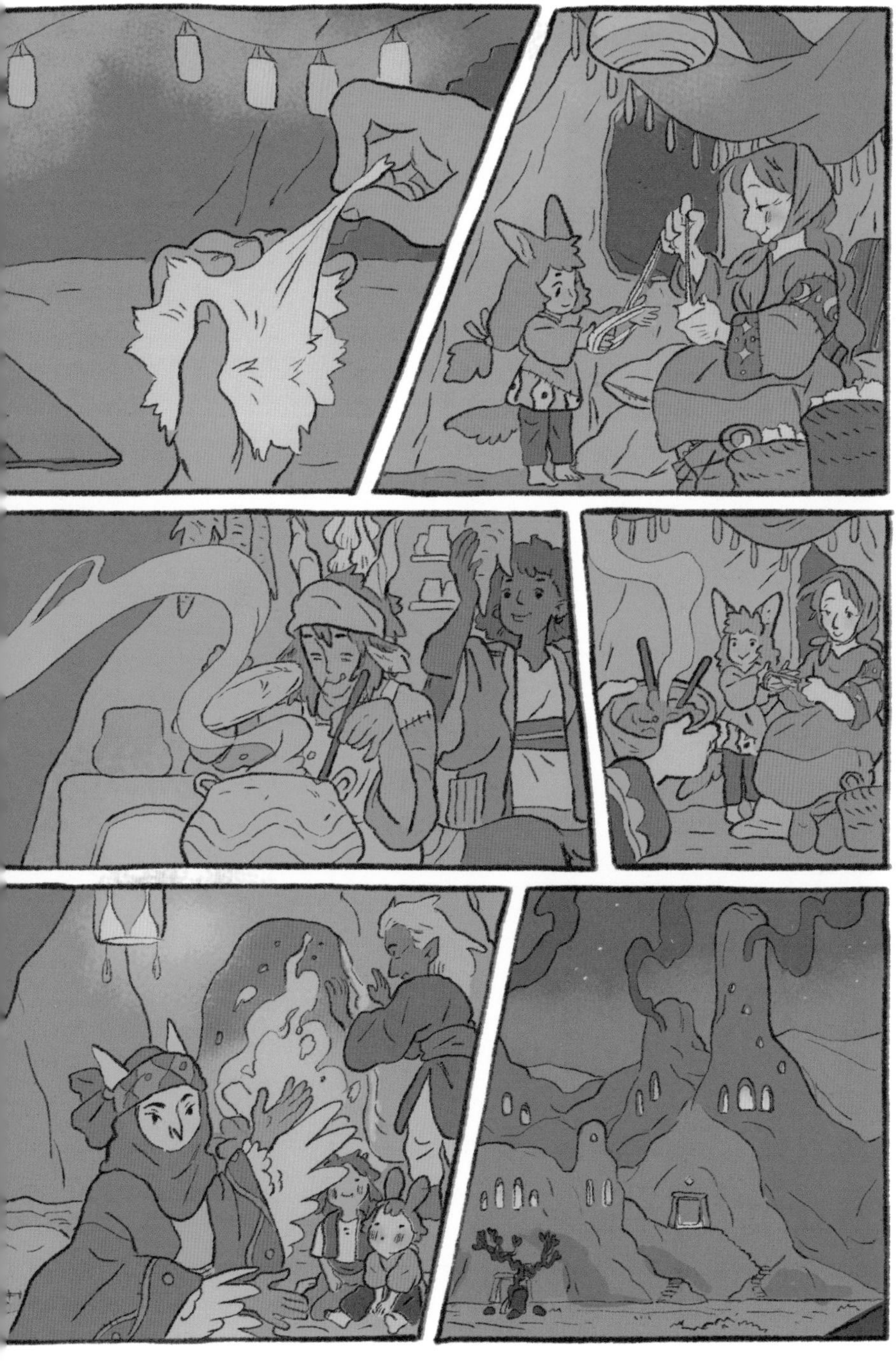

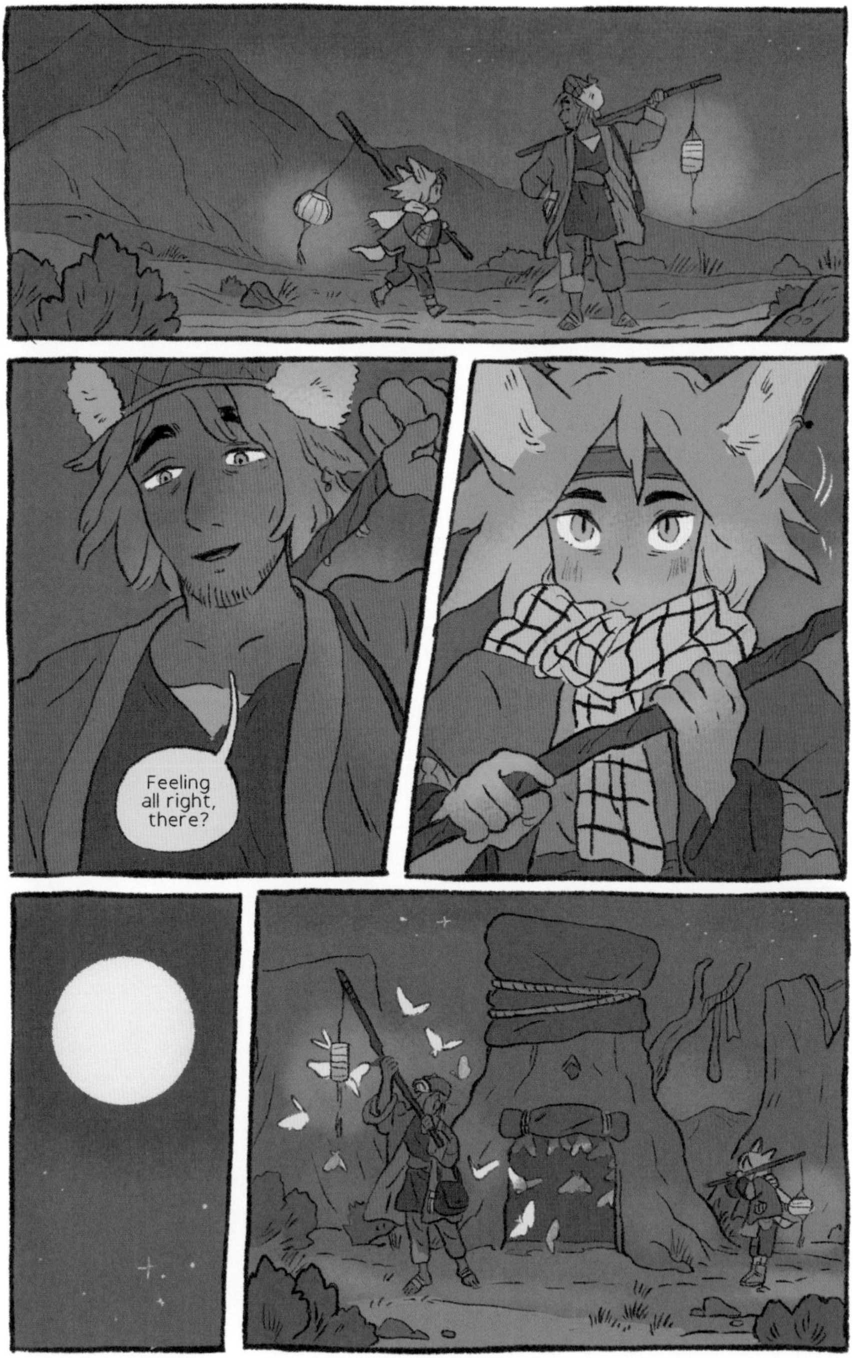
Feeling all right, there?

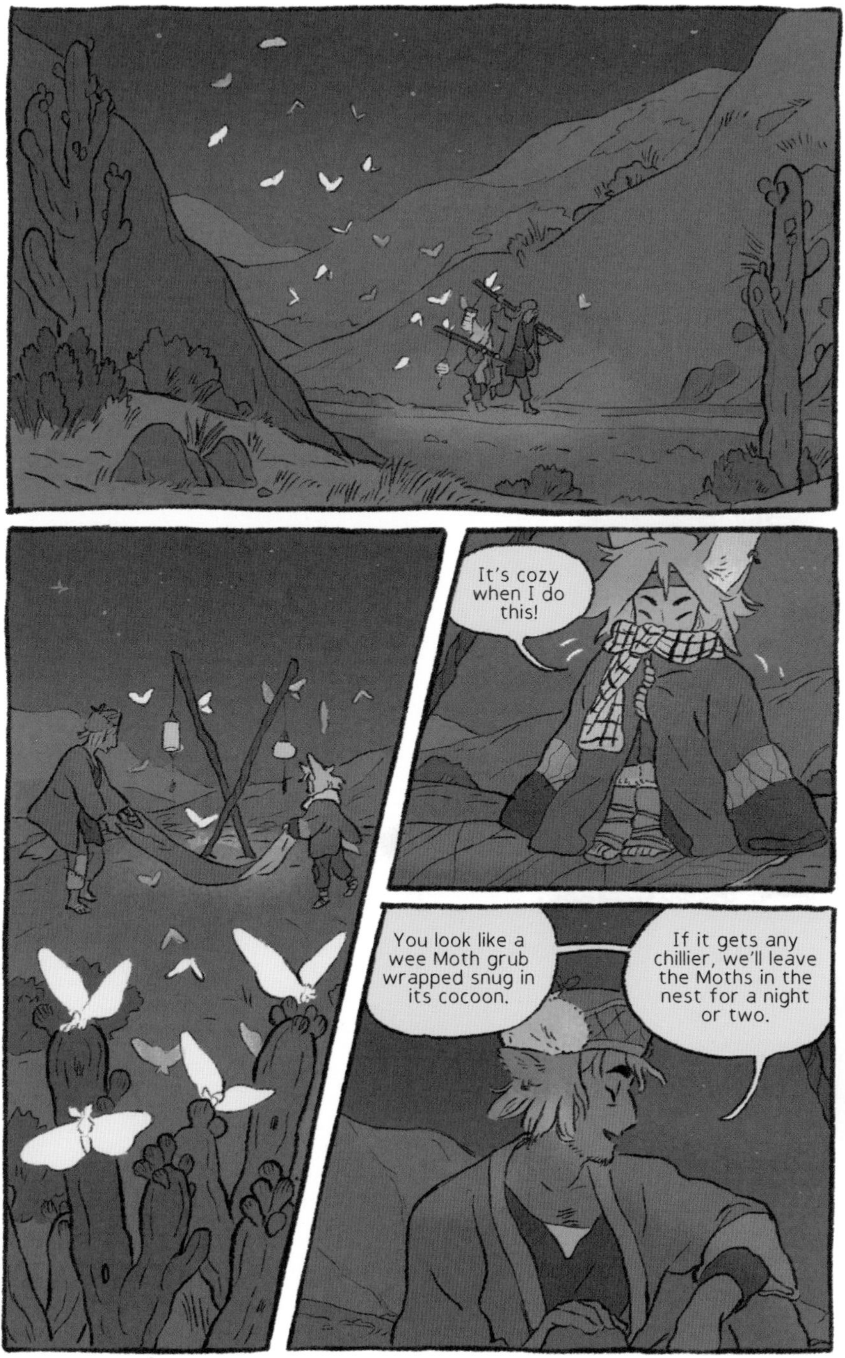

It's cozy when I do this!
You look like a wee Moth grub wrapped snug in its cocoon.
If it gets any chillier, we'll leave the Moths in the nest for a night or two.

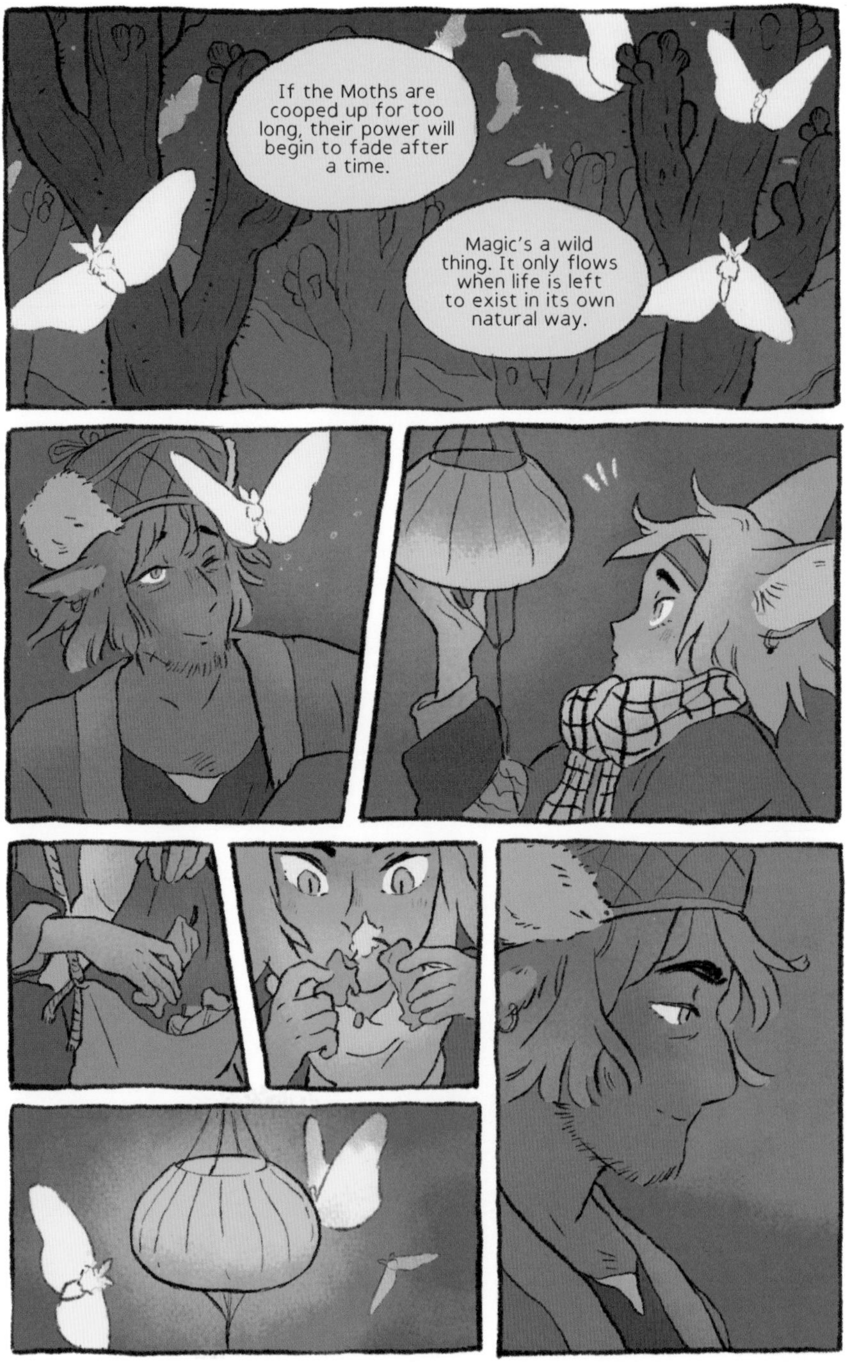
If the Moths are cooped up for too long, their power will begin to fade after a time.
Magic's a wild thing. It only flows when life is left to exist in its own natural way.

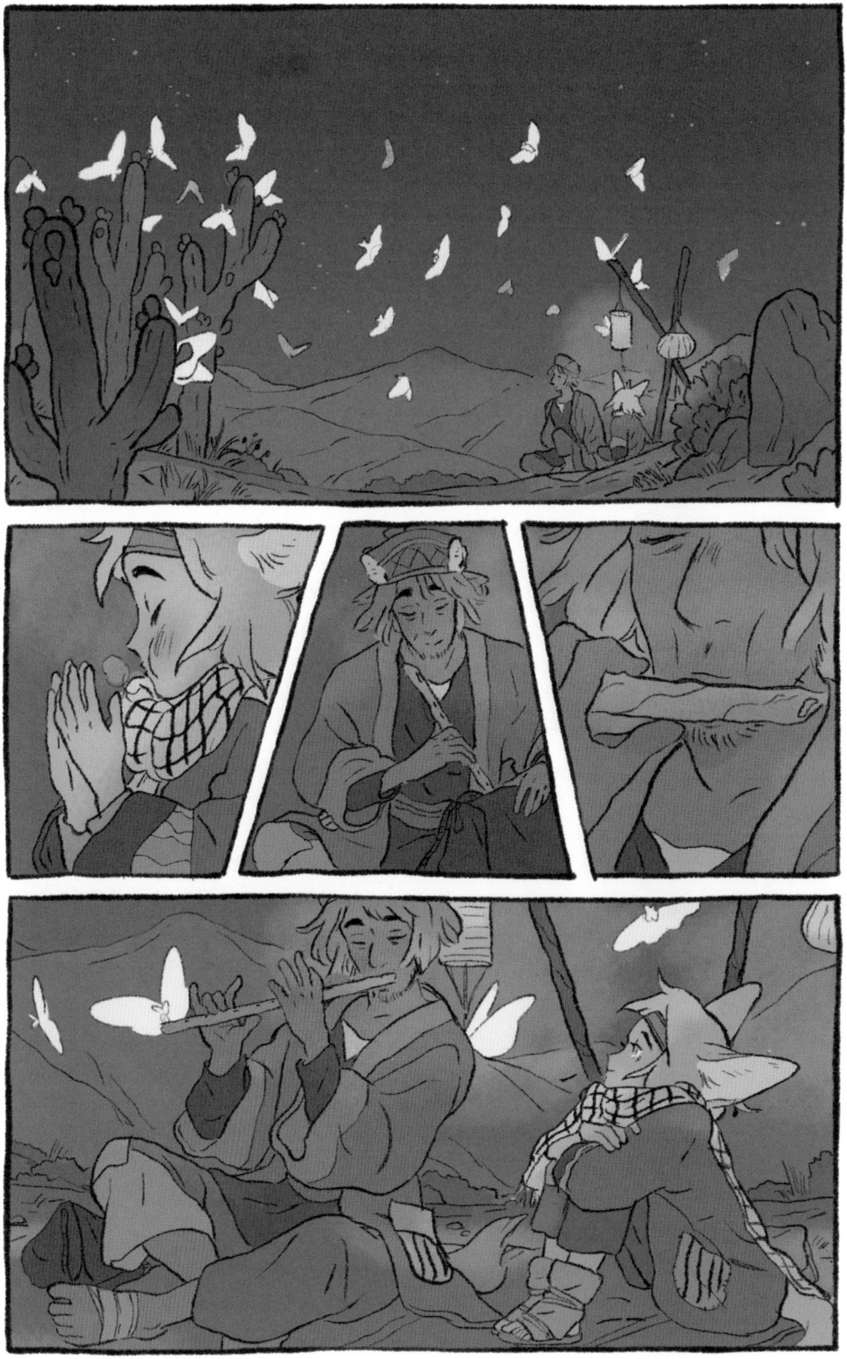

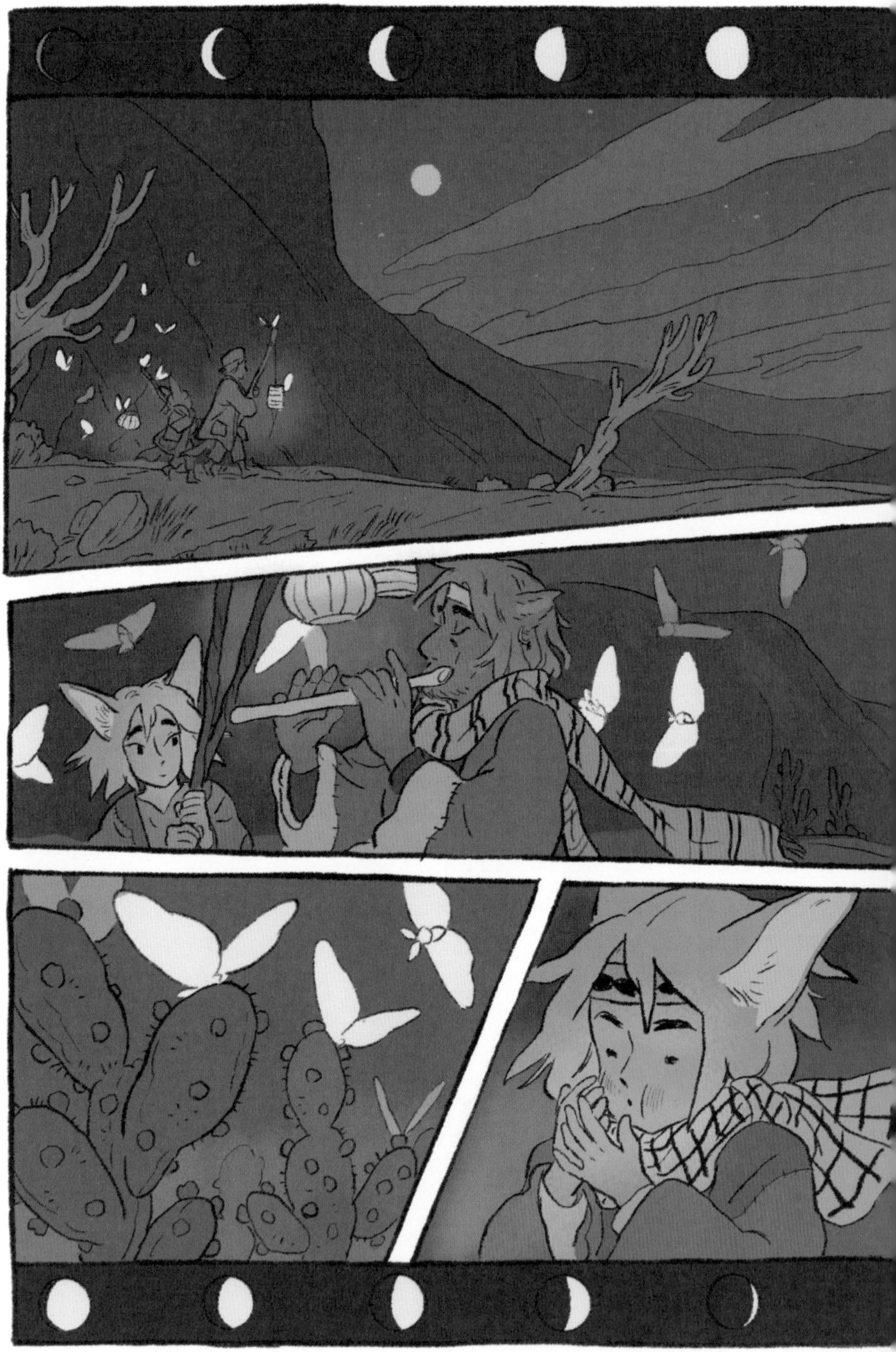

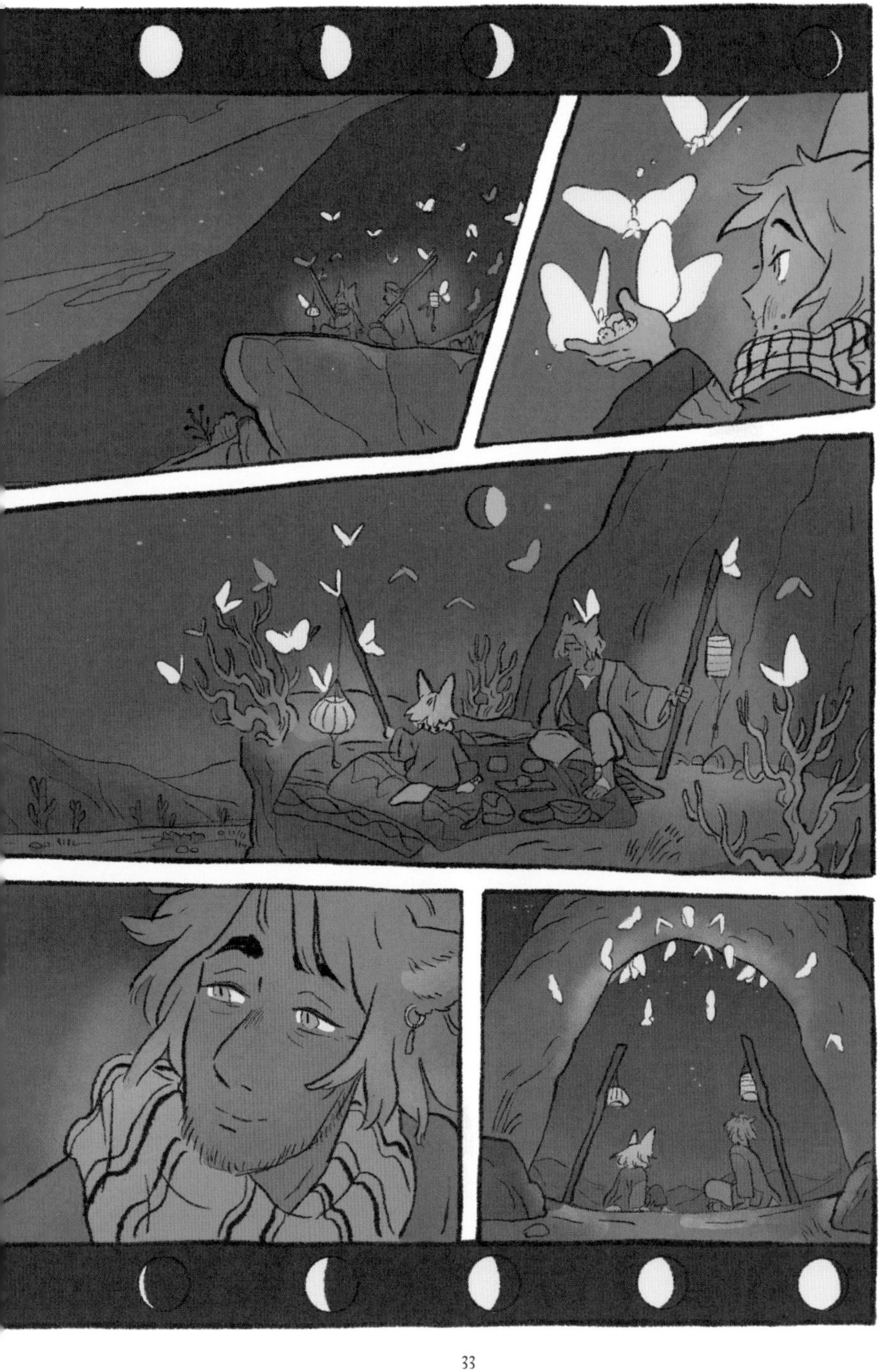

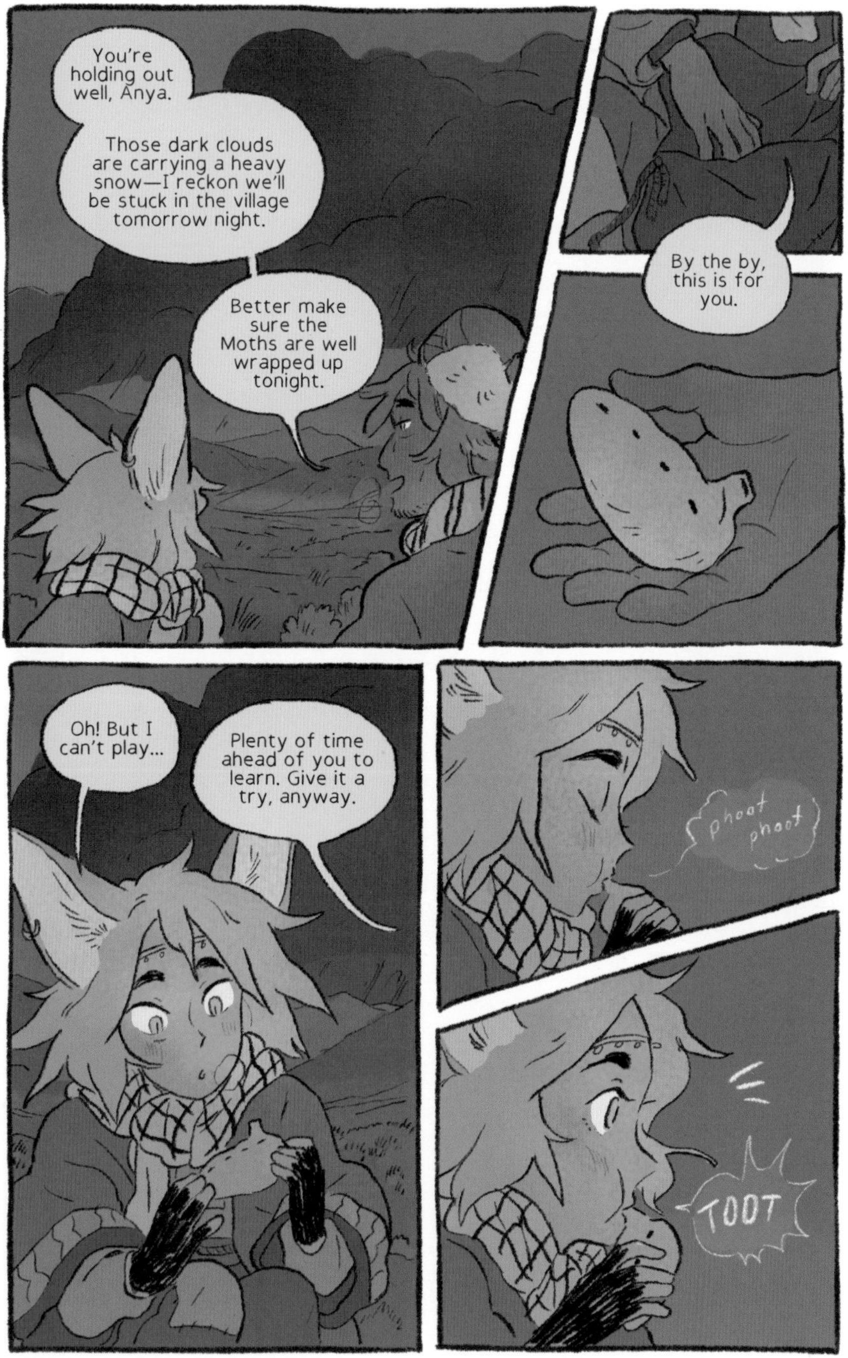
You're holding out well, Anya.
Those dark clouds are carrying a heavy snow—I reckon we'll be stuck in the village tomorrow night.
Better make sure the Moths are well wrapped up tonight.
By the by, this is for you.
Oh! But I can't play...
Plenty of time ahead of you to learn. Give it a try, anyway.
phoot phoot
TOOT

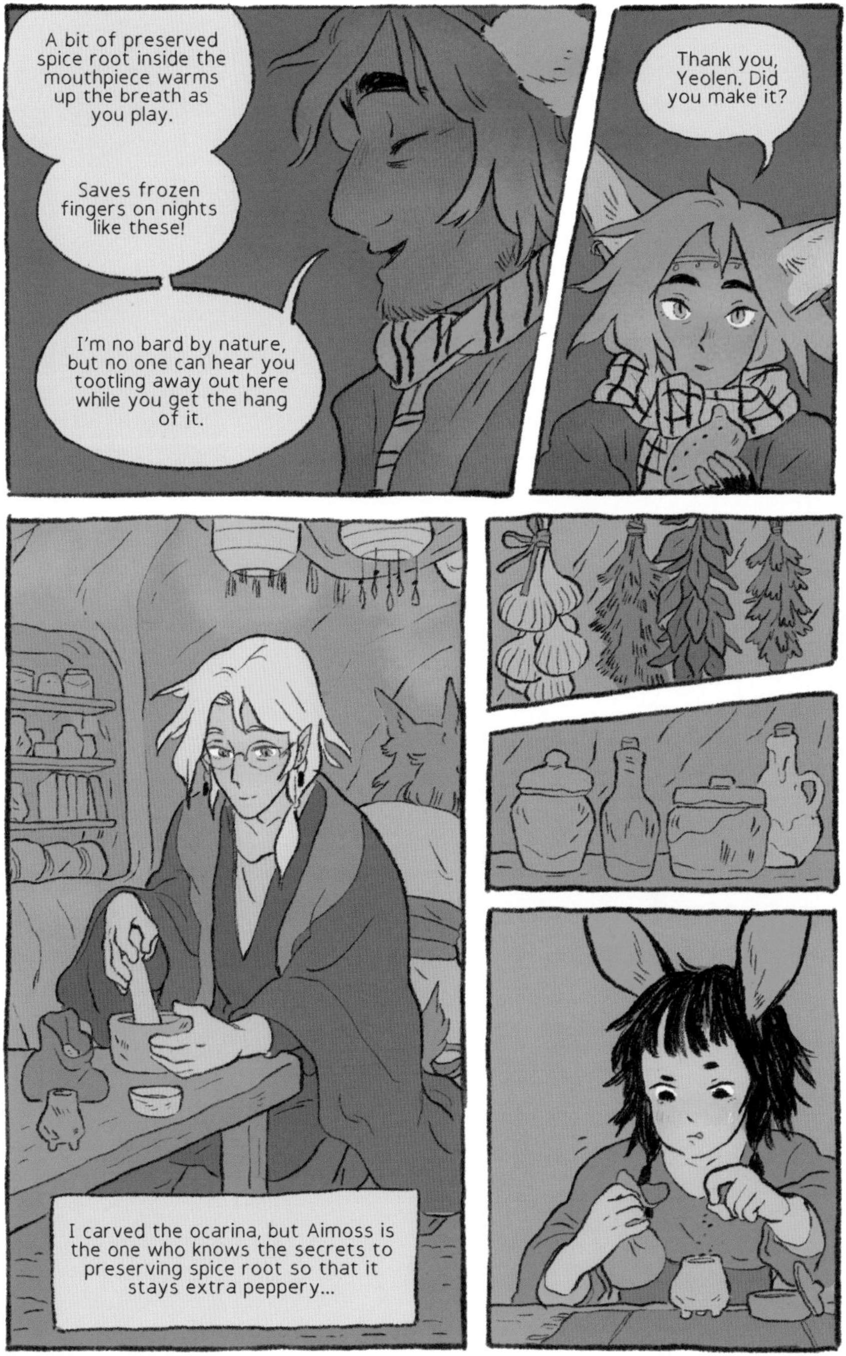
A bit of preserved spice root inside the mouthpiece warms up the breath as you play.
Saves frozen fingers on nights like these!
I'm no bard by nature, but no one can hear you tootling away out here while you get the hang of it.
Thank you, Yeolen. Did you make it?
I carved the ocarina, but Aimoss is the one who knows the secrets to preserving spice root so that it stays extra peppery...

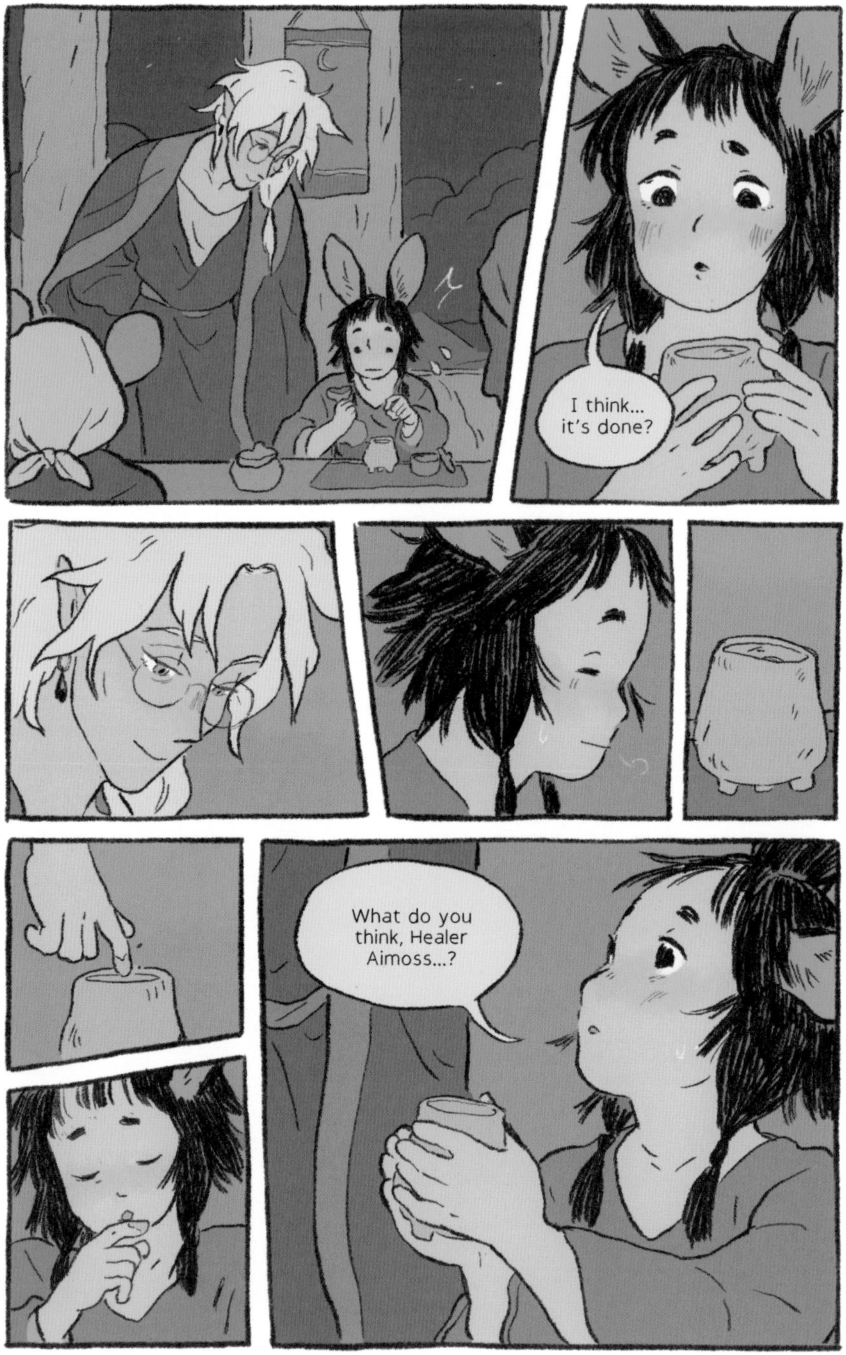
I think... it's done?
What do you think, Healer Aimoss...?

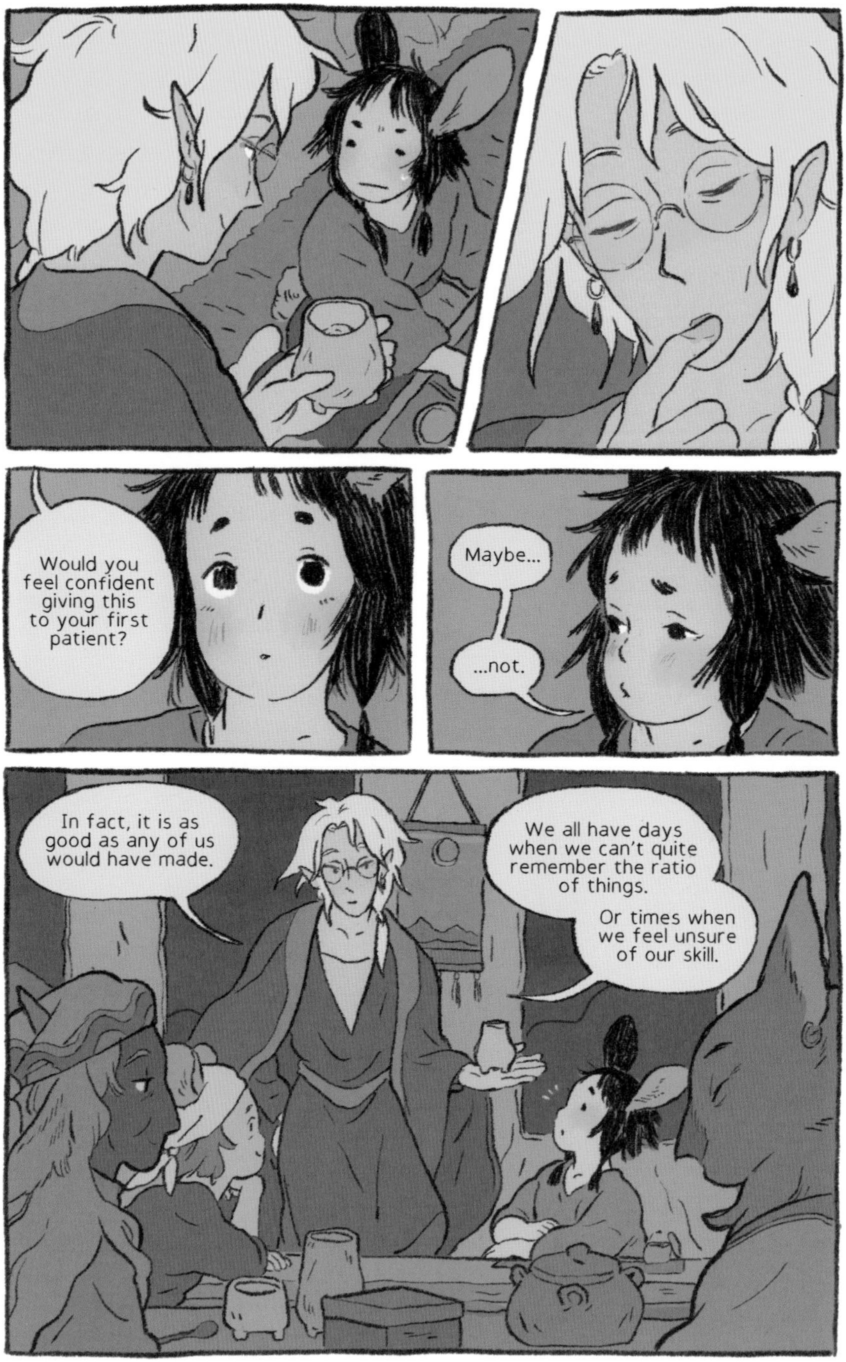
Would you feel confident giving this to your first patient?
Maybe...
...not.
In fact, it is as good as any of us would have made.
We all have days when we can't quite remember the ratio of things.
Or times when we feel unsure of our skill.

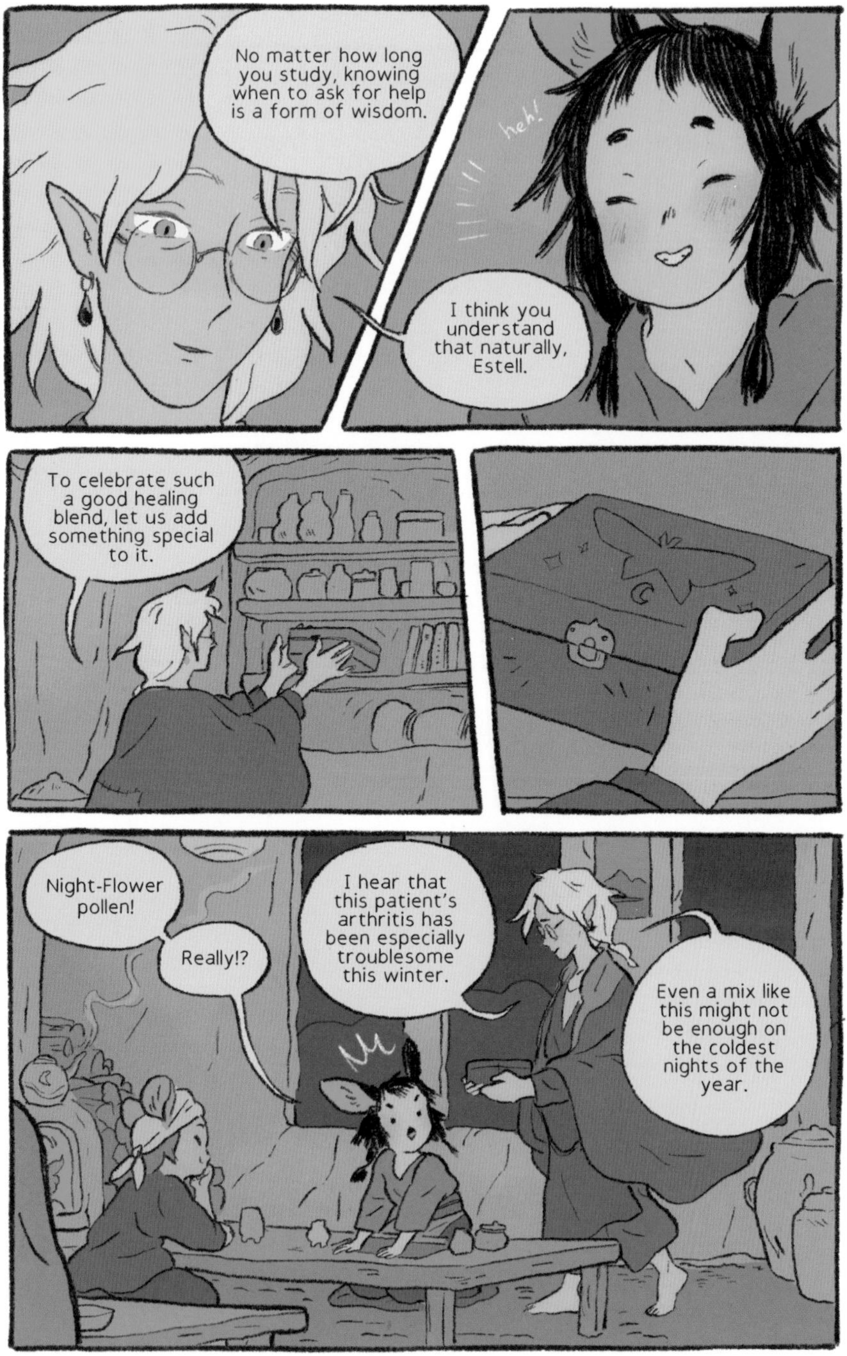
No matter how long you study, knowing when to ask for help is a form of wisdom.
heh!
I think you understand that naturally, Estell.
To celebrate such a good healing blend, let us add something special to it.
Night-Flower pollen!
Really!?
I hear that this patient's arthritis has been especially troublesome this winter.
Even a mix like this might not be enough on the coldest nights of the year.

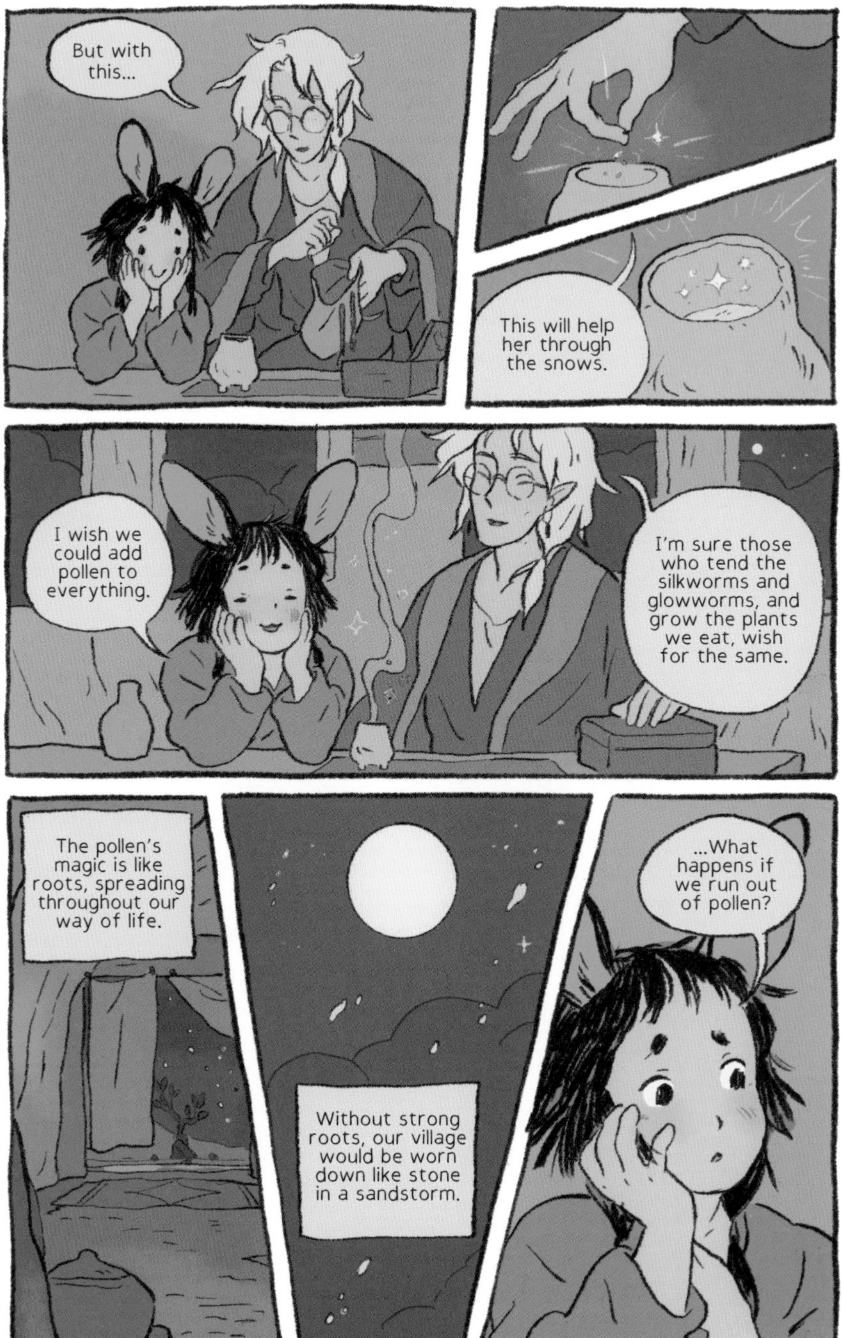

But with this...
This will help her through the snows.
I wish we could add pollen to everything.
I'm sure those who tend the silkworms and glowworms, and grow the plants we eat, wish for the same.
The pollen's magic is like roots, spreading throughout our way of life.
Without strong roots, our village would be worn down like stone in a sandstorm.
...What happens if we run out of pollen?

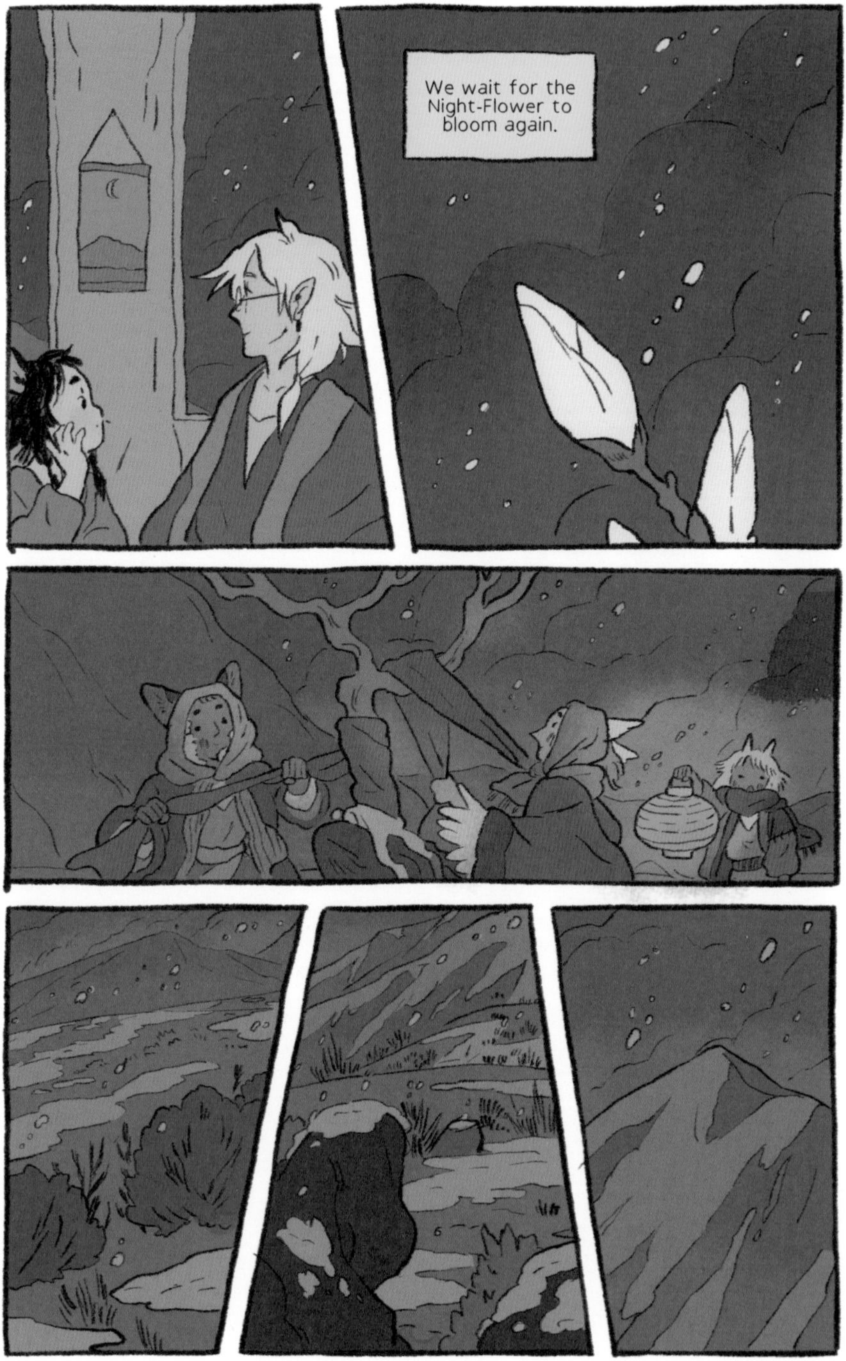
We wait for the Night-Flower to bloom again.

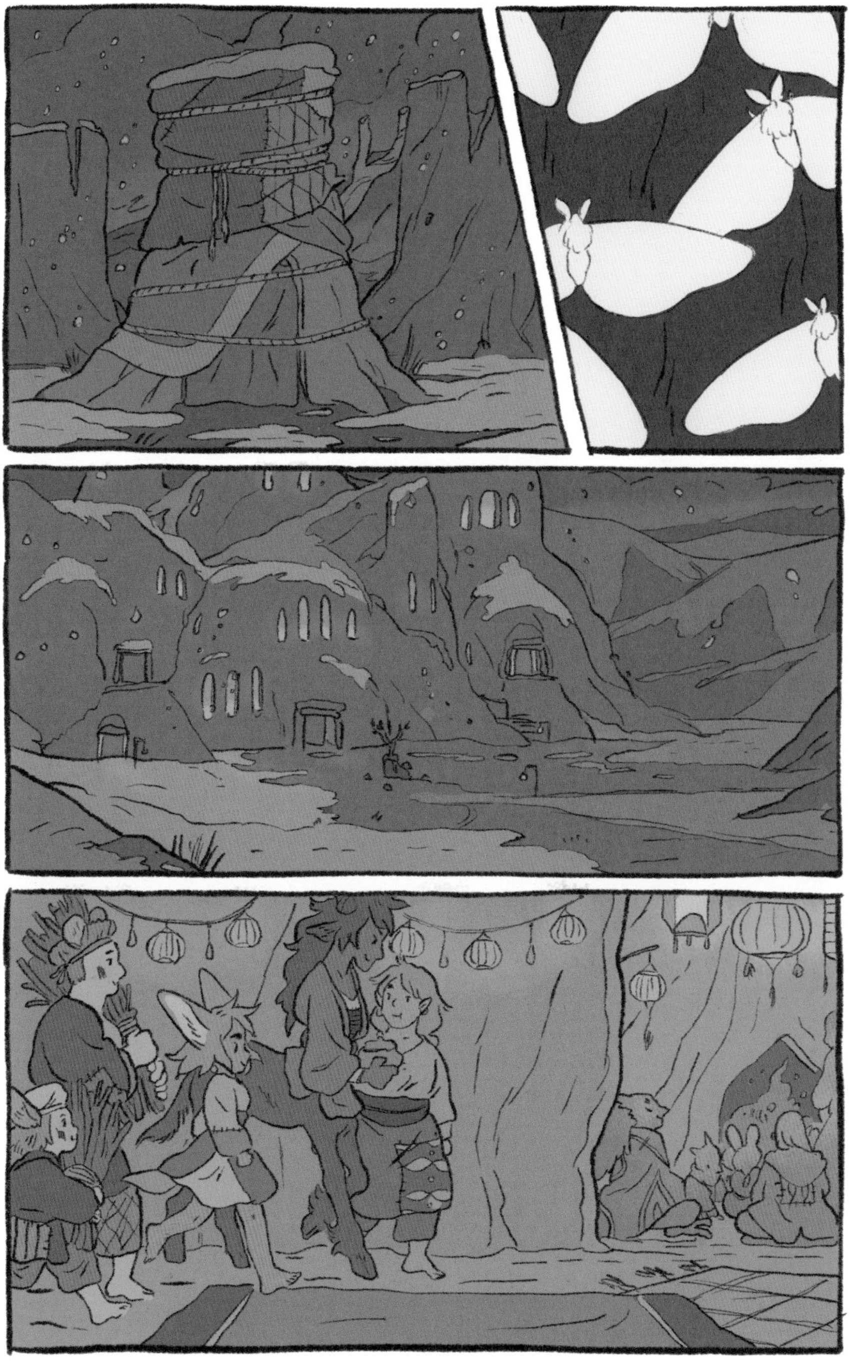

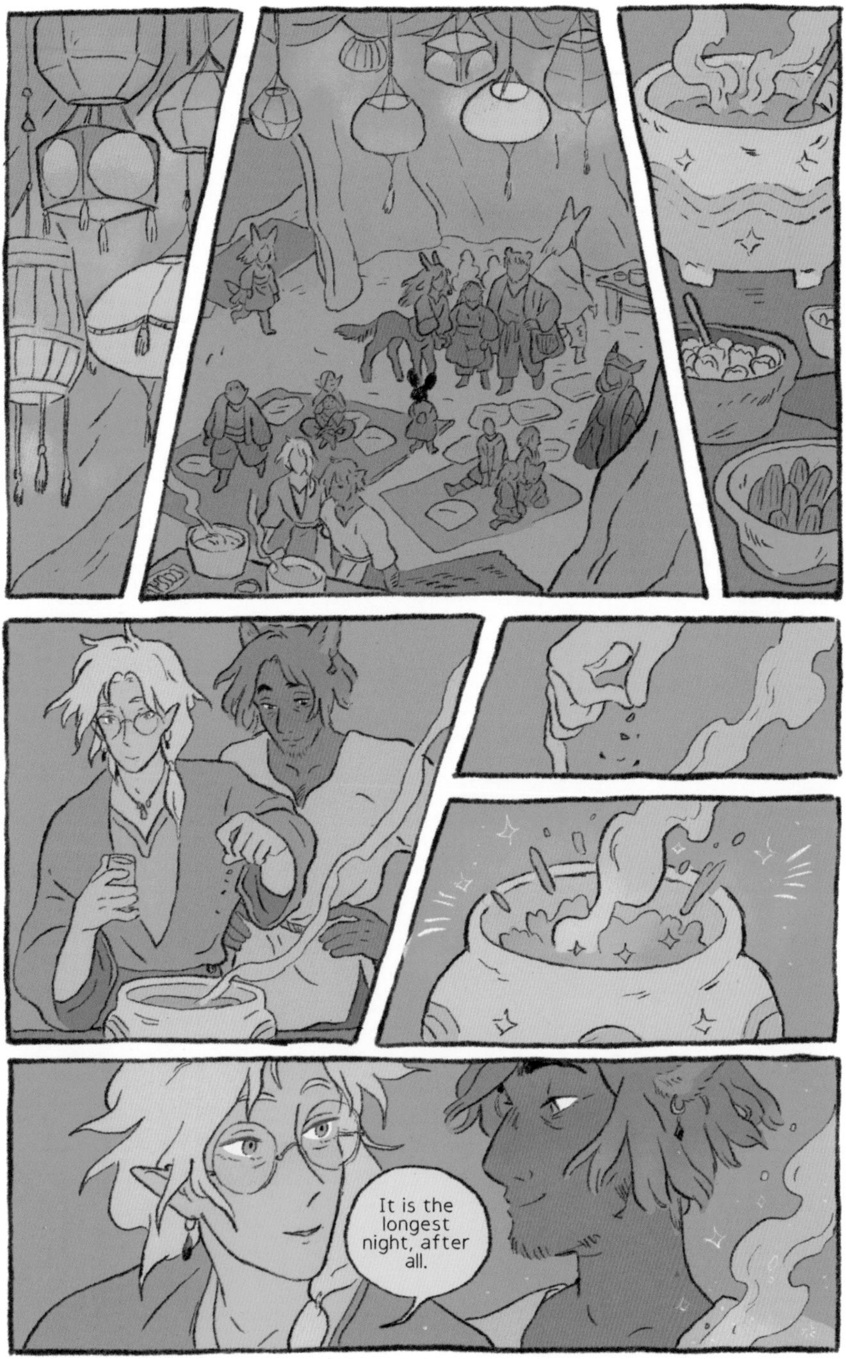
It is the longest night, after all.

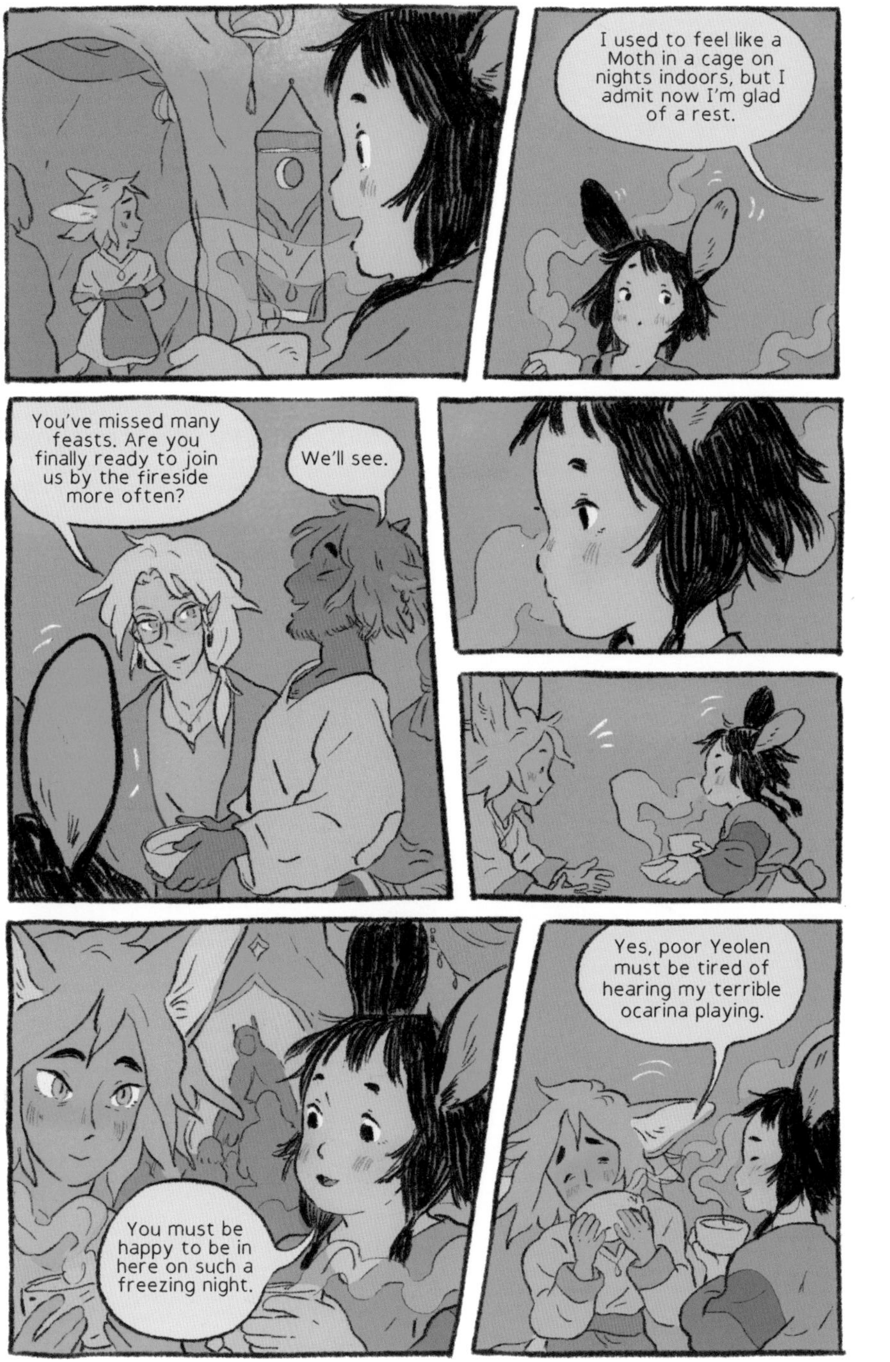
I used to feel like a Moth in a cage on nights indoors, but I admit now I'm glad of a rest.
You've missed many feasts. Are you finally ready to join us by the fireside more often?
We'll see.
You must be happy to be in here on such a freezing night.
Yes, poor Yeolen must be tired of hearing my terrible ocarina playing.

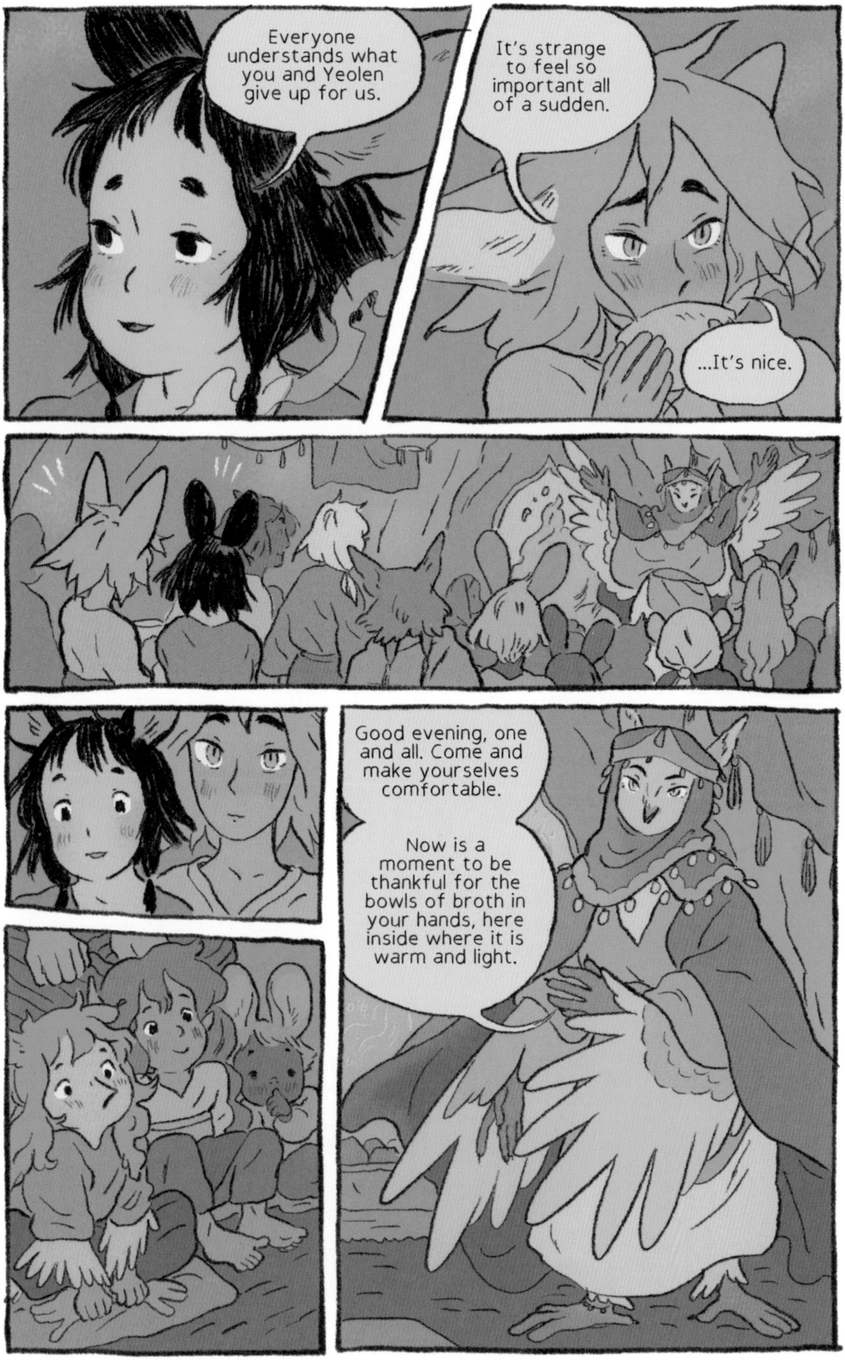
Everyone understands what you and Yeolen give up for us.
It's strange to feel so important all of a sudden.
...It's nice.
Good evening, one and all. Come and make yourselves comfortable.
Now is a moment to be thankful for the bowls of broth in your hands, here inside where it is warm and light.

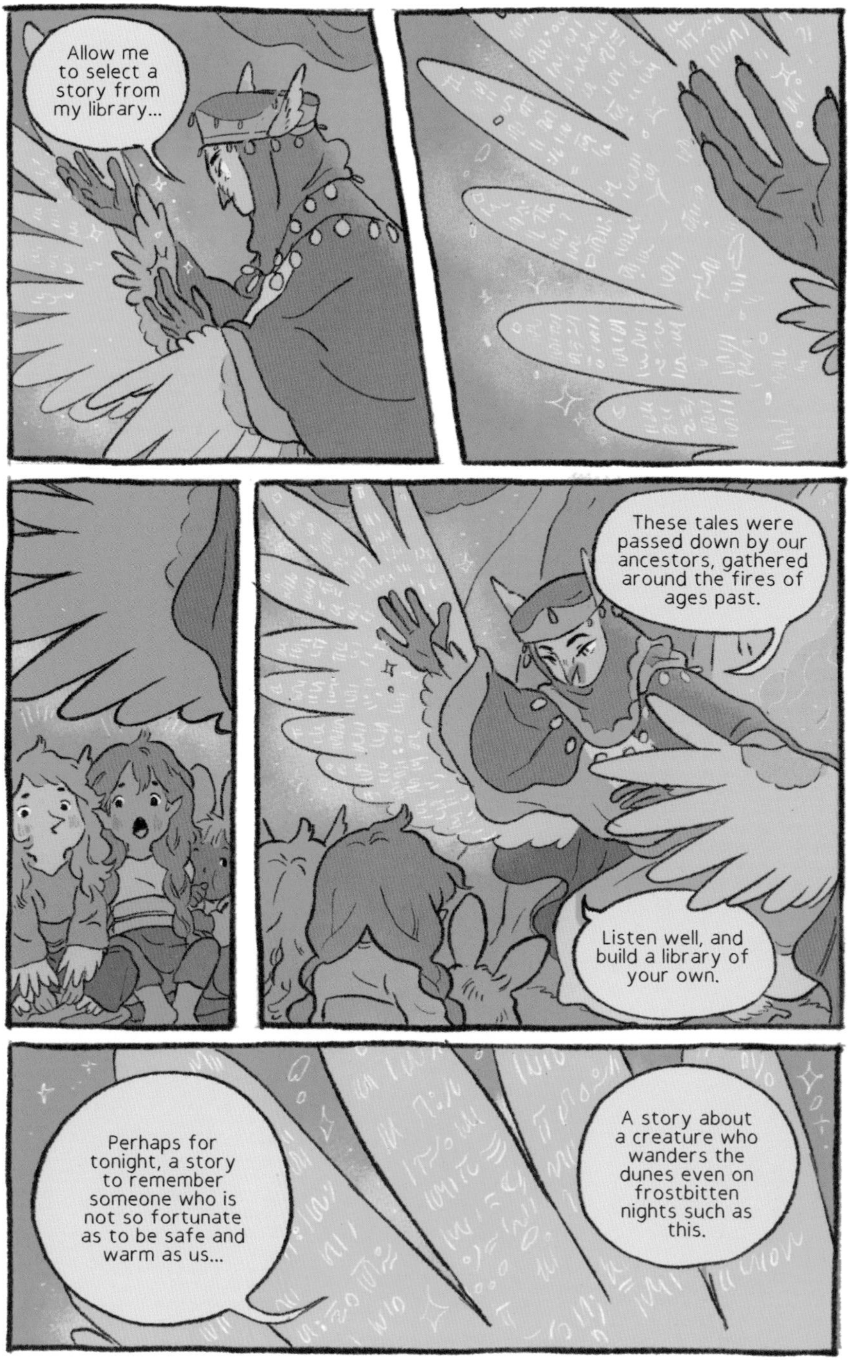
Allow me to select a story from my library...
These tales were passed down by our ancestors, gathered around the fires of ages past.
Listen well, and build a library of your own.
Perhaps for tonight, a story to remember someone who is not so fortunate as to be safe and warm as us...
A story about a creature who wanders the dunes even on frostbitten nights such as this.

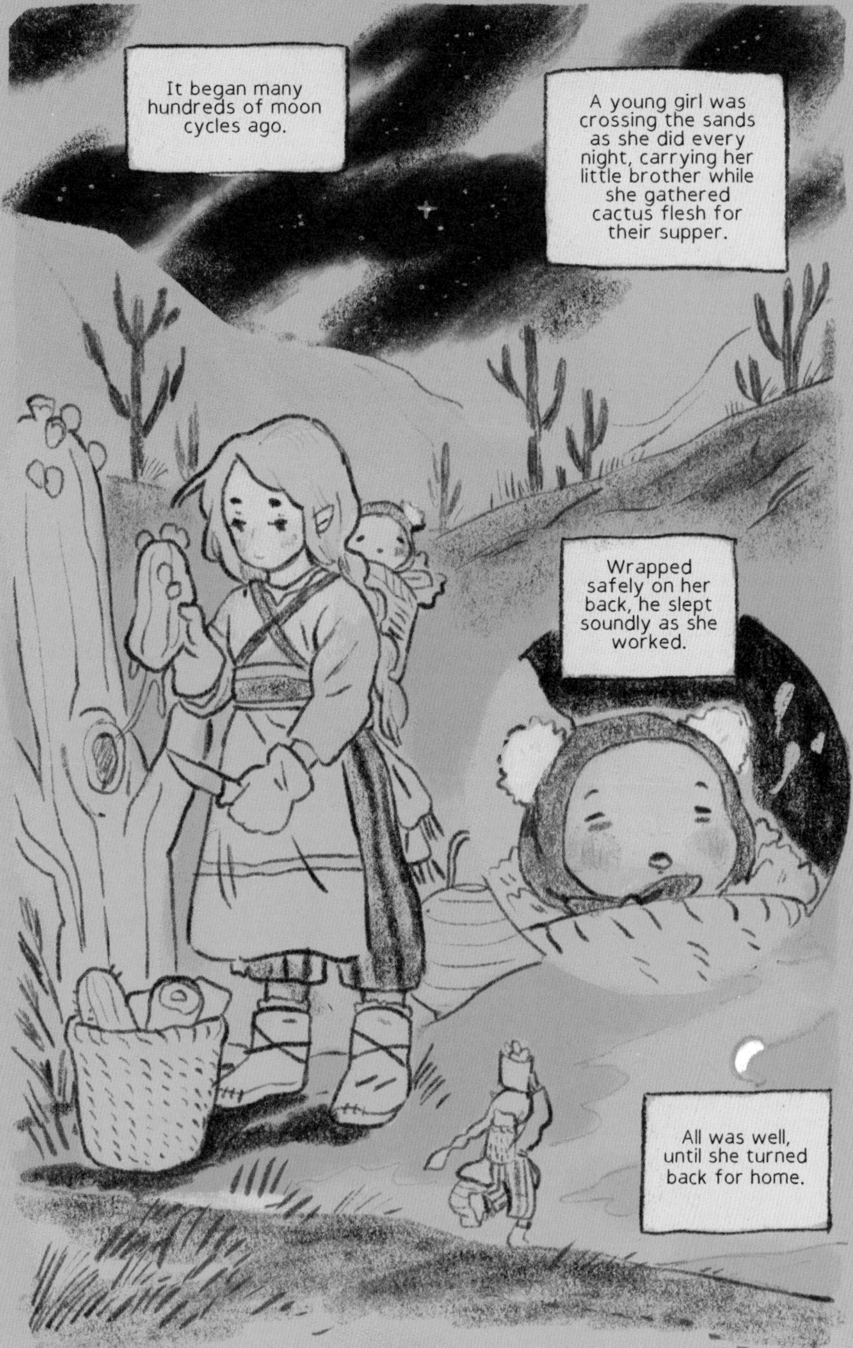
It began many hundreds of moon cycles ago.
A young girl was crossing the sands as she did every night, carrying her little brother while she gathered cactus flesh for their supper.
Wrapped safely on her back, he slept soundly as she worked.
All was well, until she turned back for home.

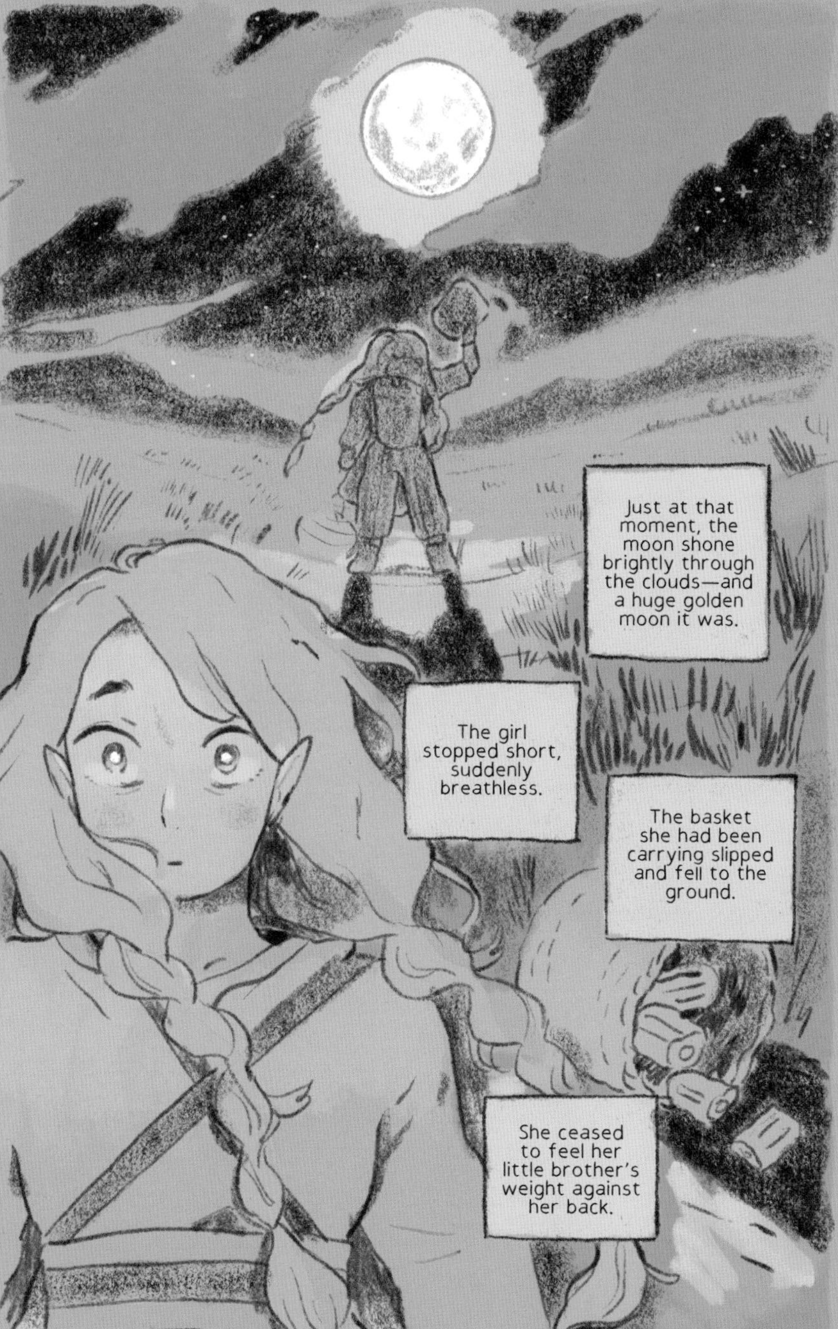
Just at that moment, the moon shone brightly through the clouds—and a huge golden moon it was.
The girl stopped short, suddenly breathless.
The basket she had been carrying slipped and fell to the ground.
She ceased to feel her little brother's weight against her back.

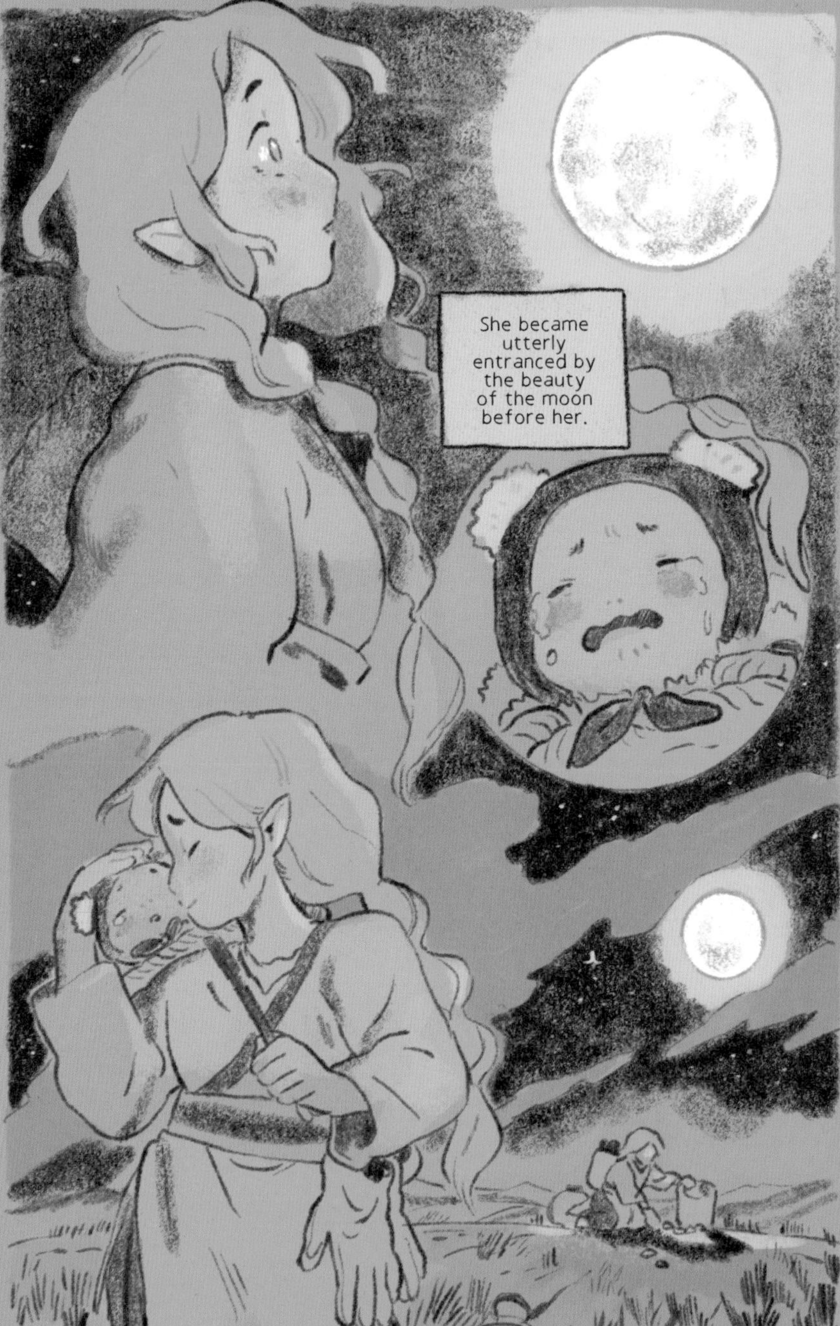
She became utterly entranced by the beauty of the moon before her.

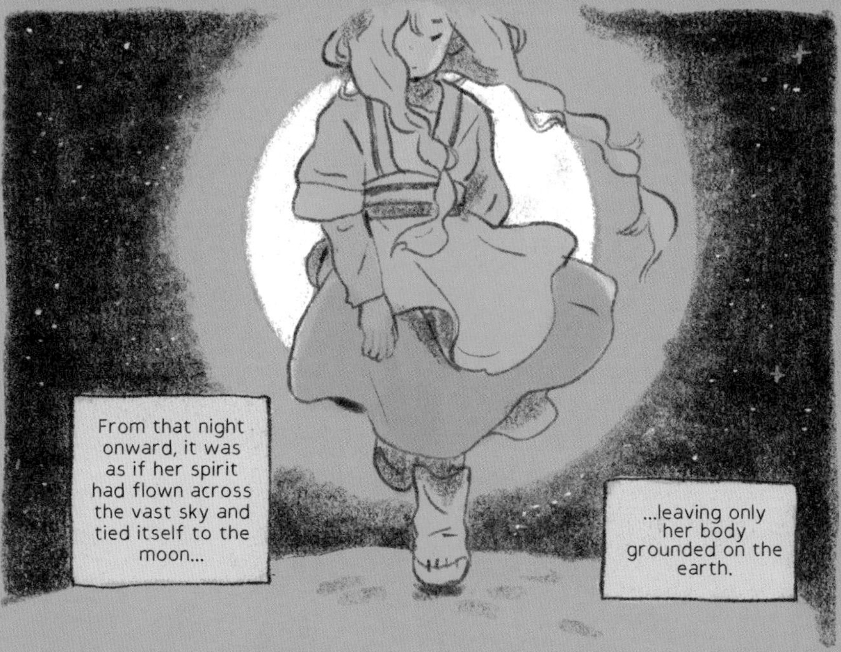
From that night onward, it was as if her spirit had flown across the vast sky and tied itself to the moon...
...leaving only her body grounded on the earth.

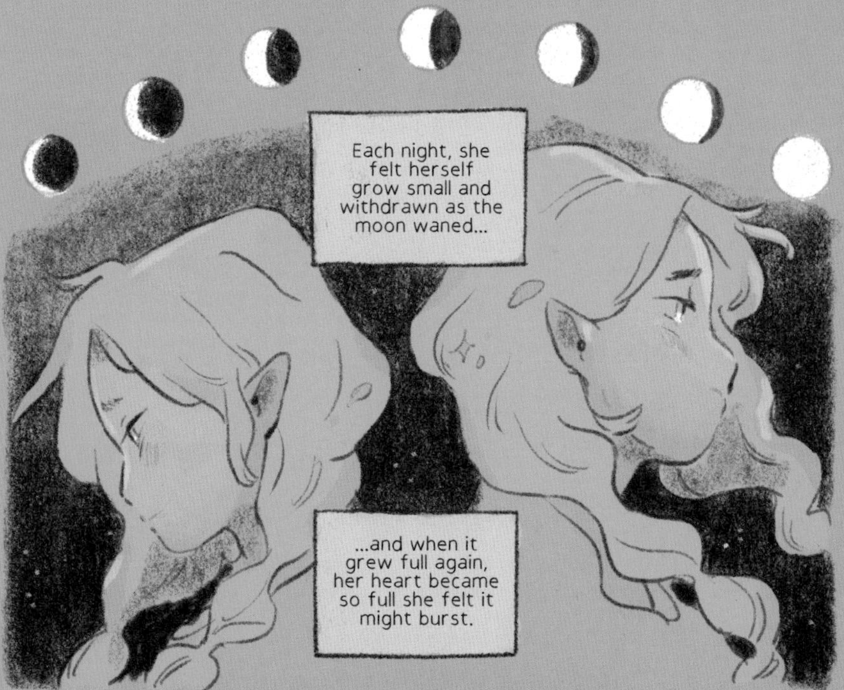
Each night, she felt herself grow small and withdrawn as the moon waned...
...and when it grew full again, her heart became so full she felt it might burst.

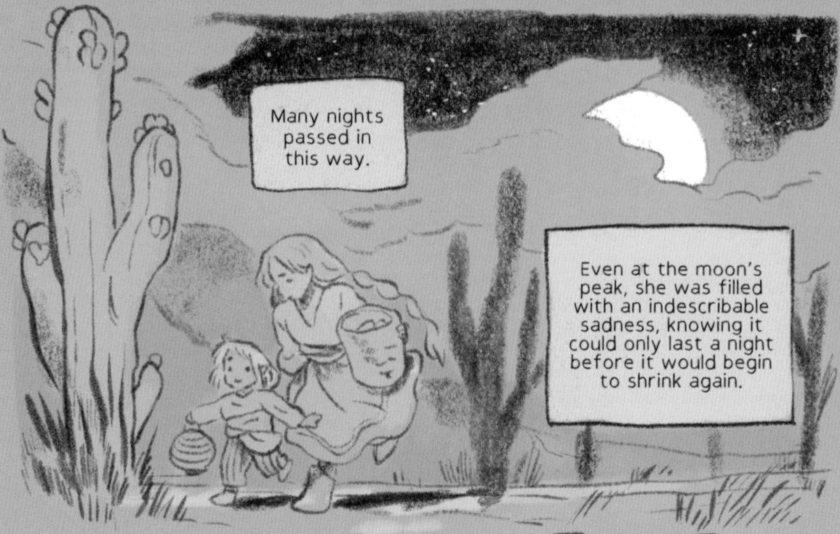
Many nights passed in this way.
Even at the moon's peak, she was filled with an indescribable sadness, knowing it could only last a night before it would begin to shrink again.

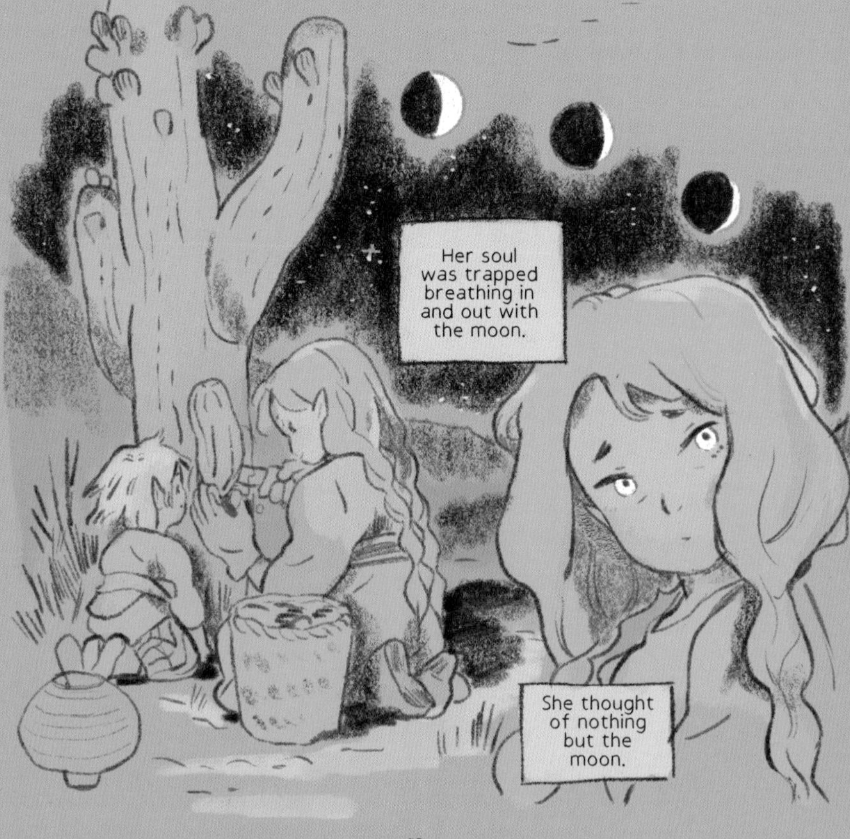
Her soul was trapped breathing in and out with the moon.
She thought of nothing but the moon.

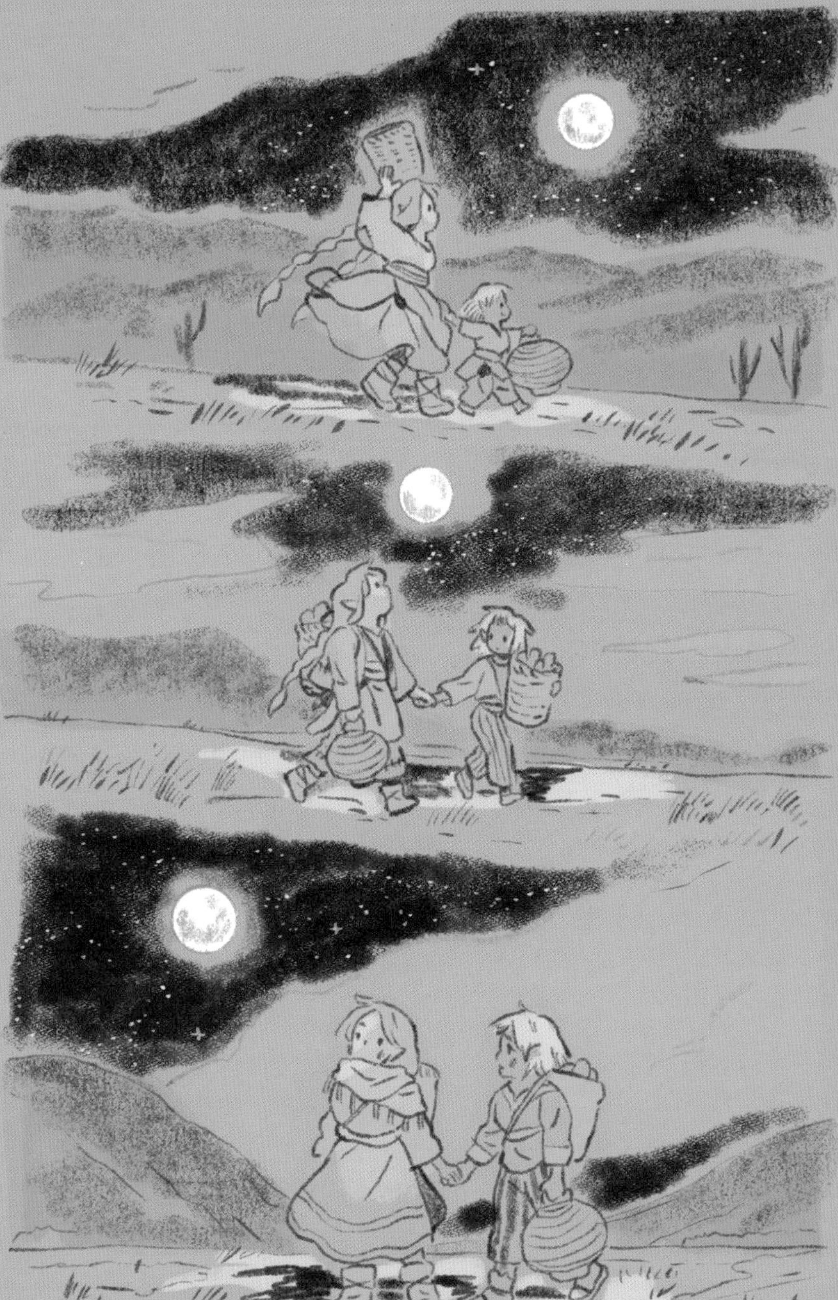

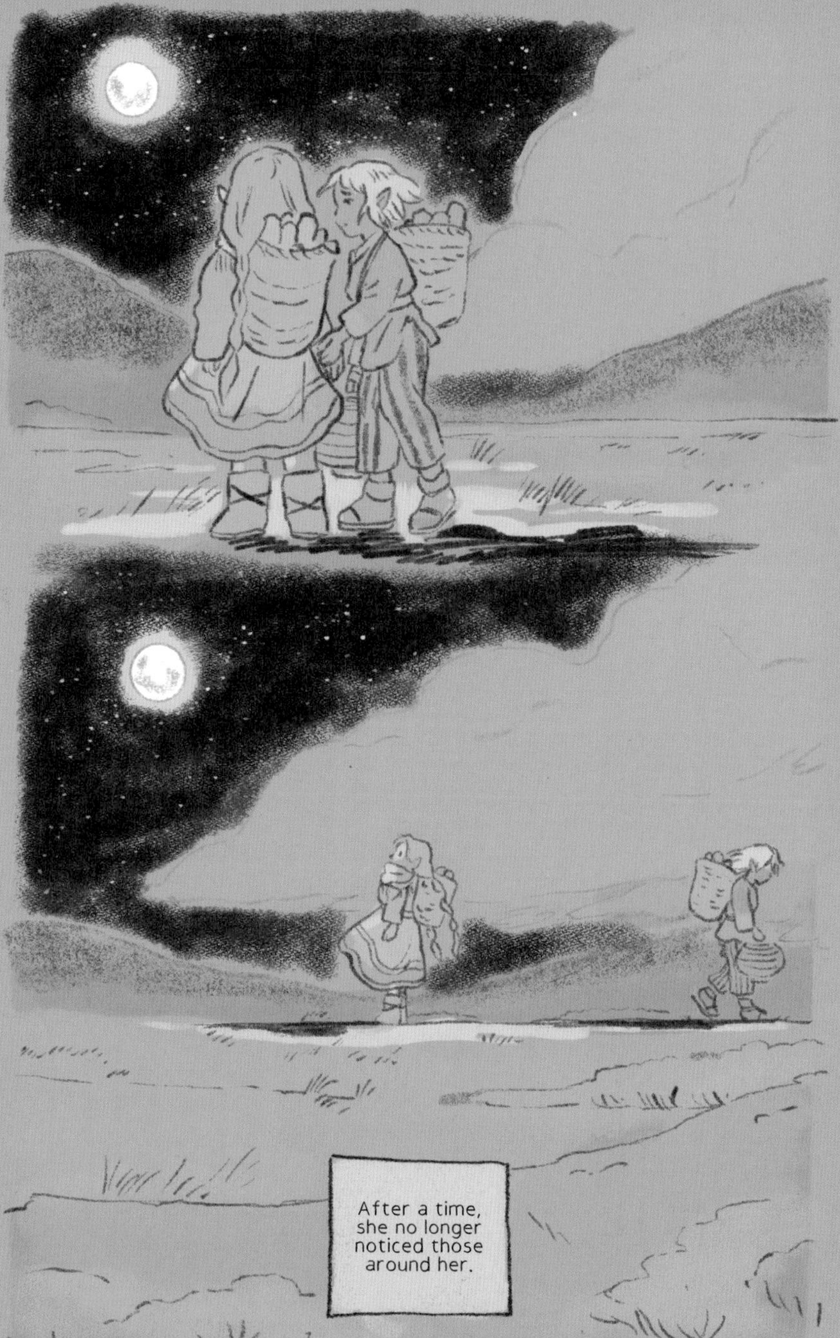
After a time, she no longer noticed those around her.

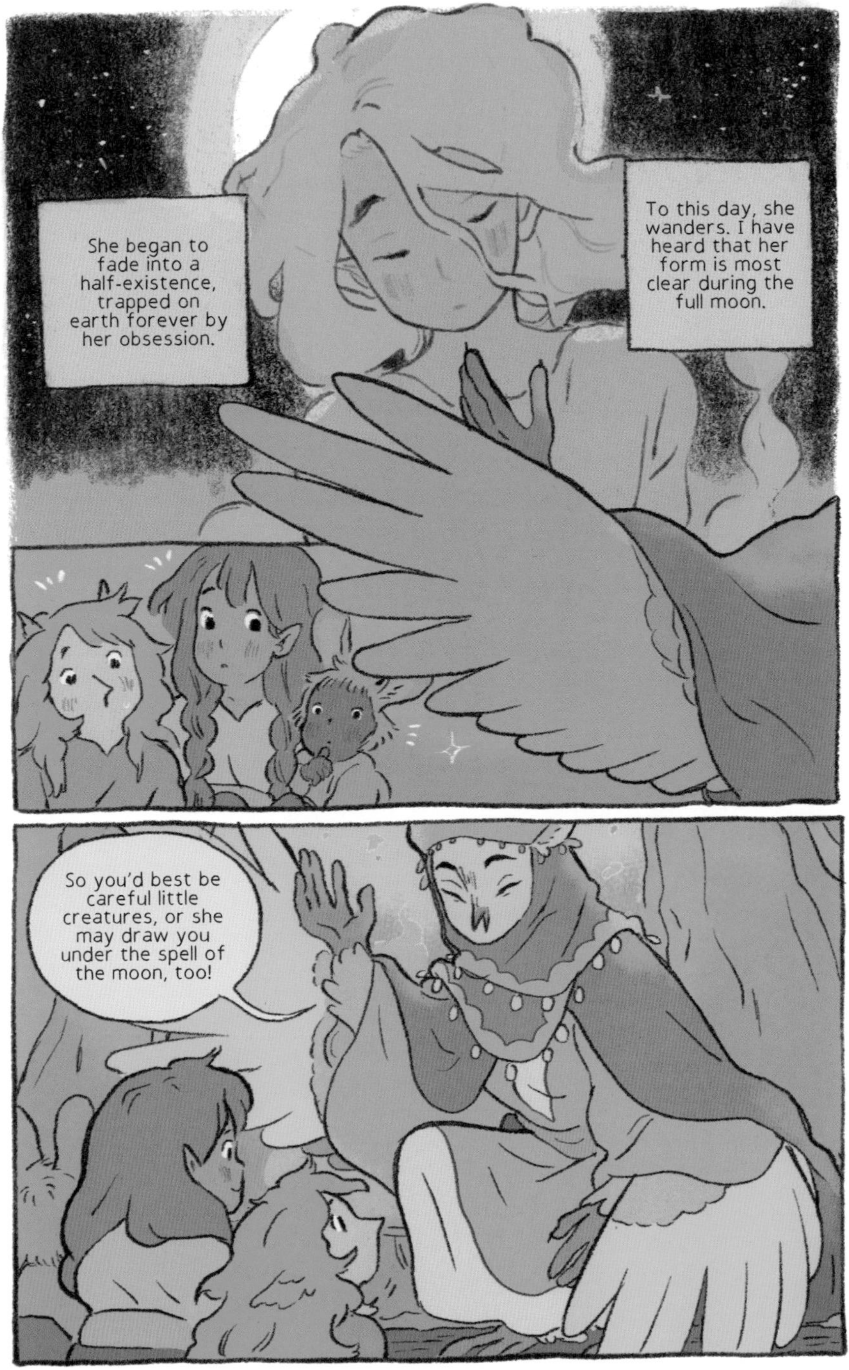
She began to fade into a half-existence, trapped on earth forever by her obsession.
To this day, she wanders. I have heard that her form is most clear during the full moon.
So you'd best be careful little creatures, or she may draw you under the spell of the moon, too!

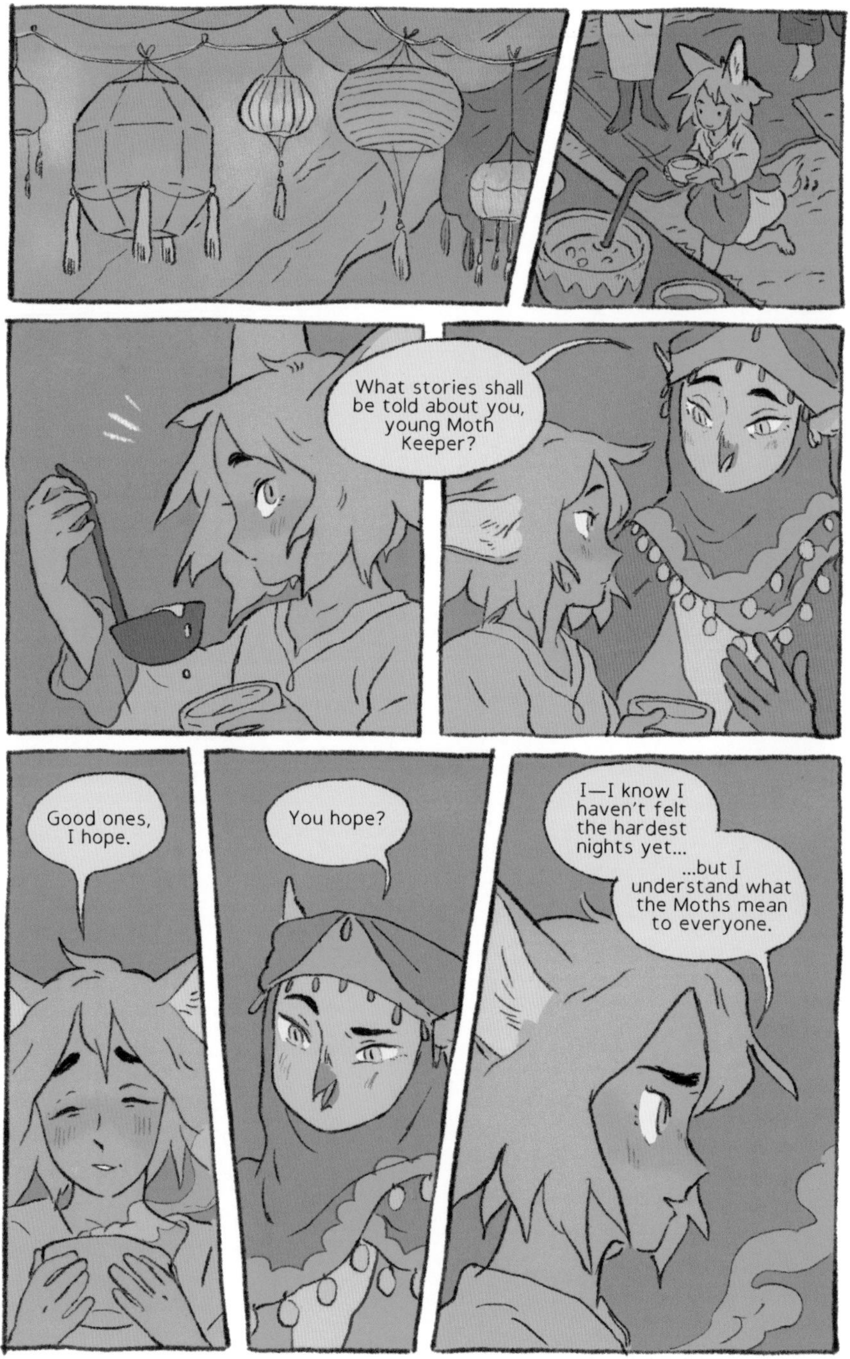
What stories shall be told about you, young Moth Keeper?
Good ones, I hope.
You hope?
I—I know I haven't felt the hardest nights yet...
...but I understand what the Moths mean to everyone.

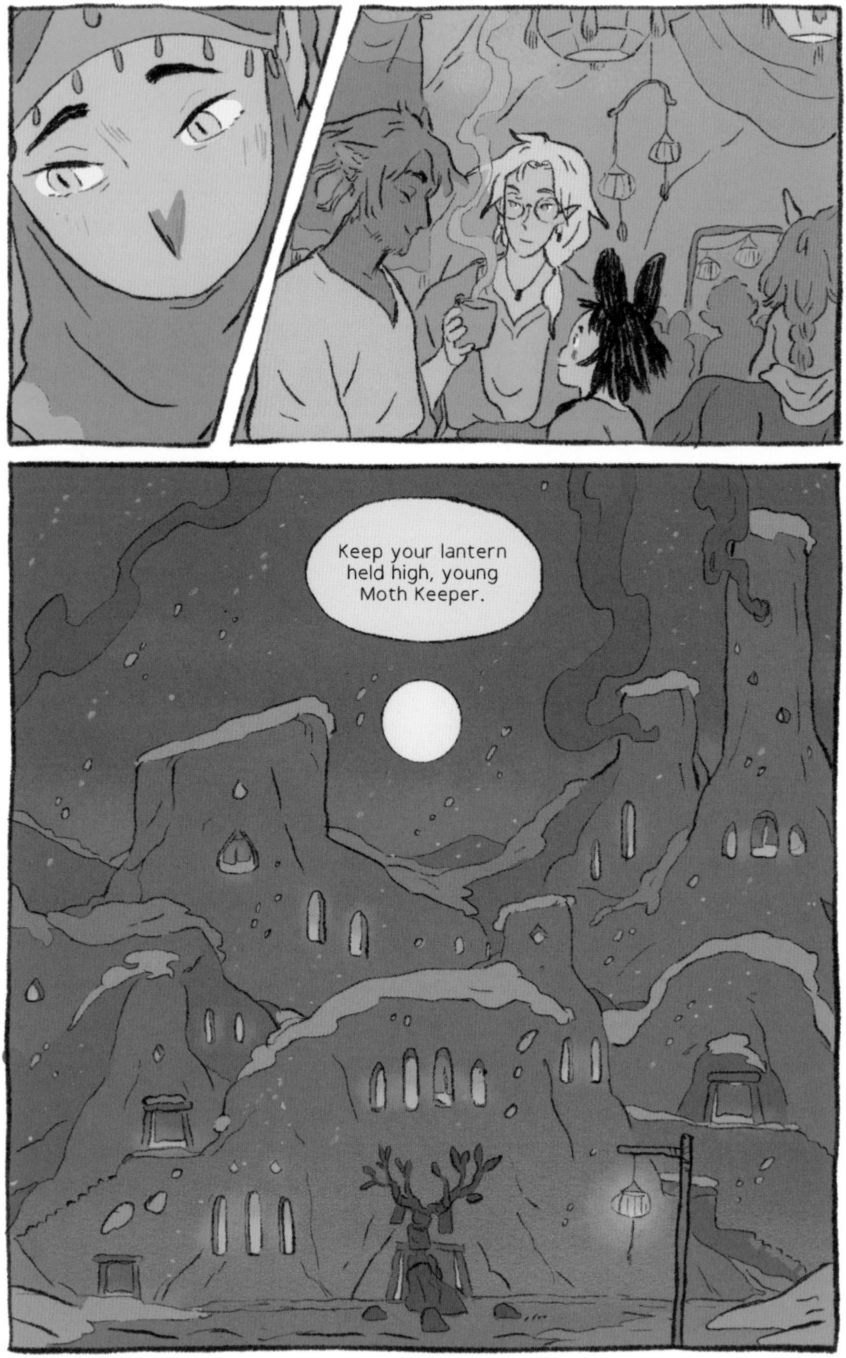
Keep your lantern
held high, young
Moth Keeper.

Chapter Three

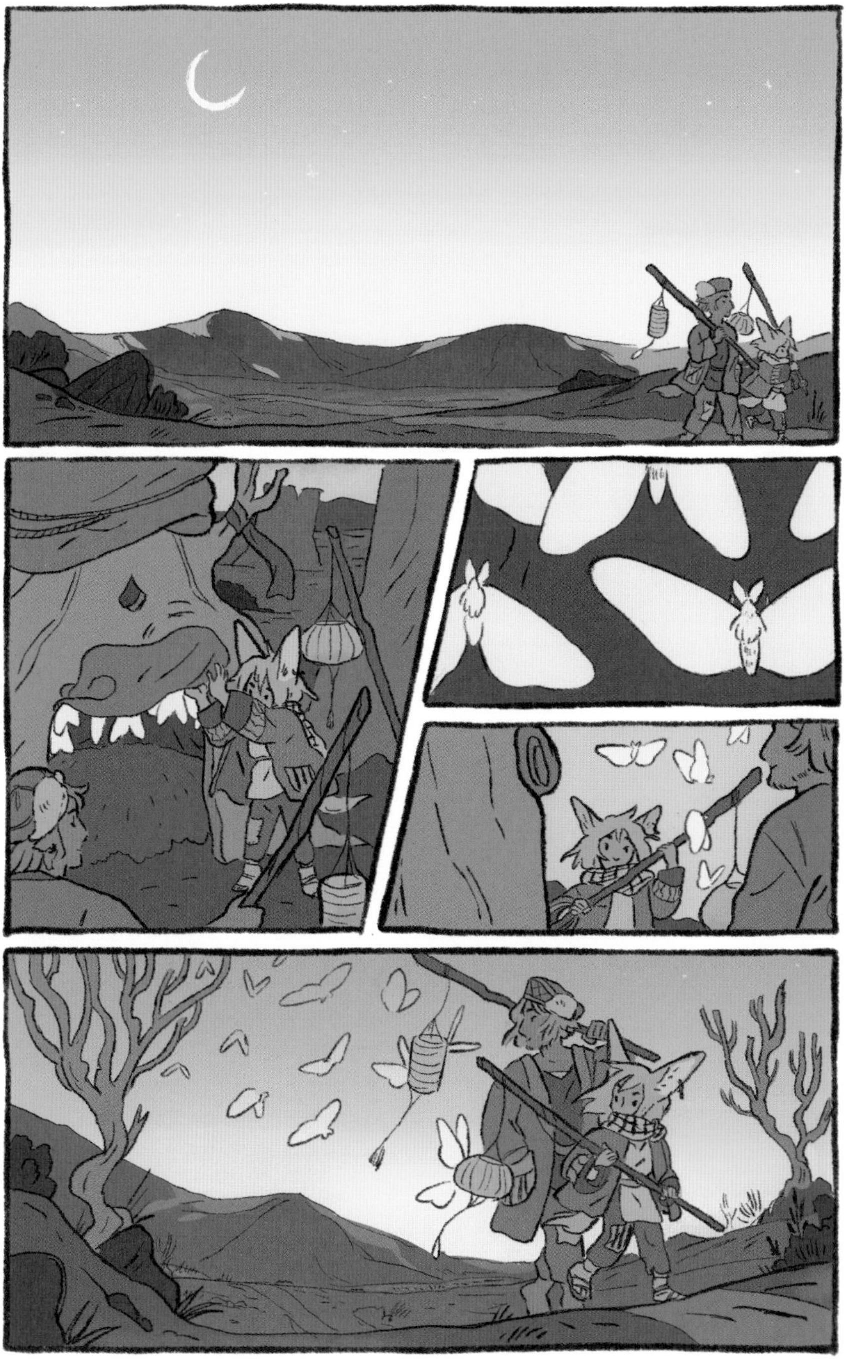

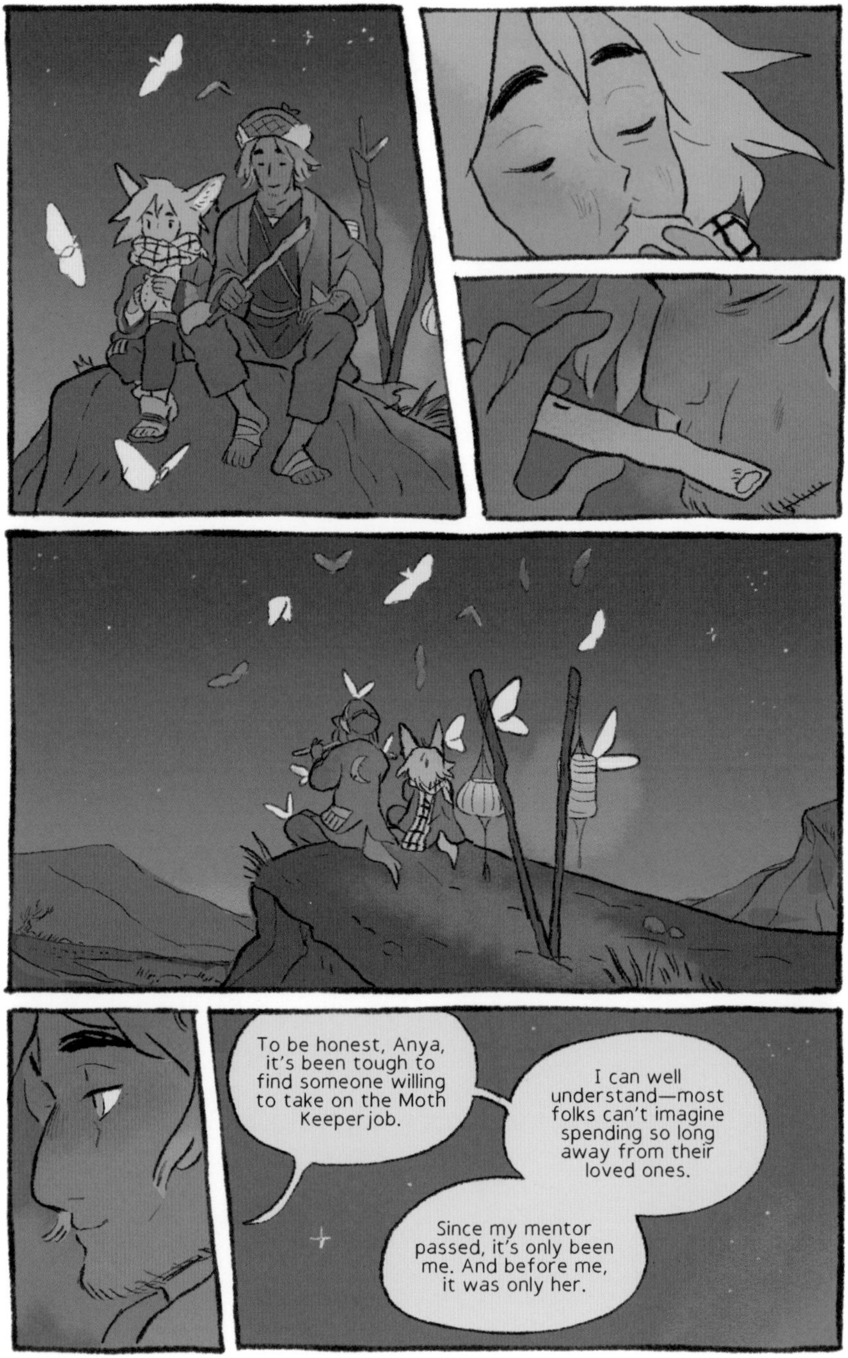
To be honest, Anya, it's been tough to find someone willing to take on the Moth Keeper job.
I can well understand—most folks can't imagine spending so long away from their loved ones.
Since my mentor passed, it's only been me. And before me, it was only her.

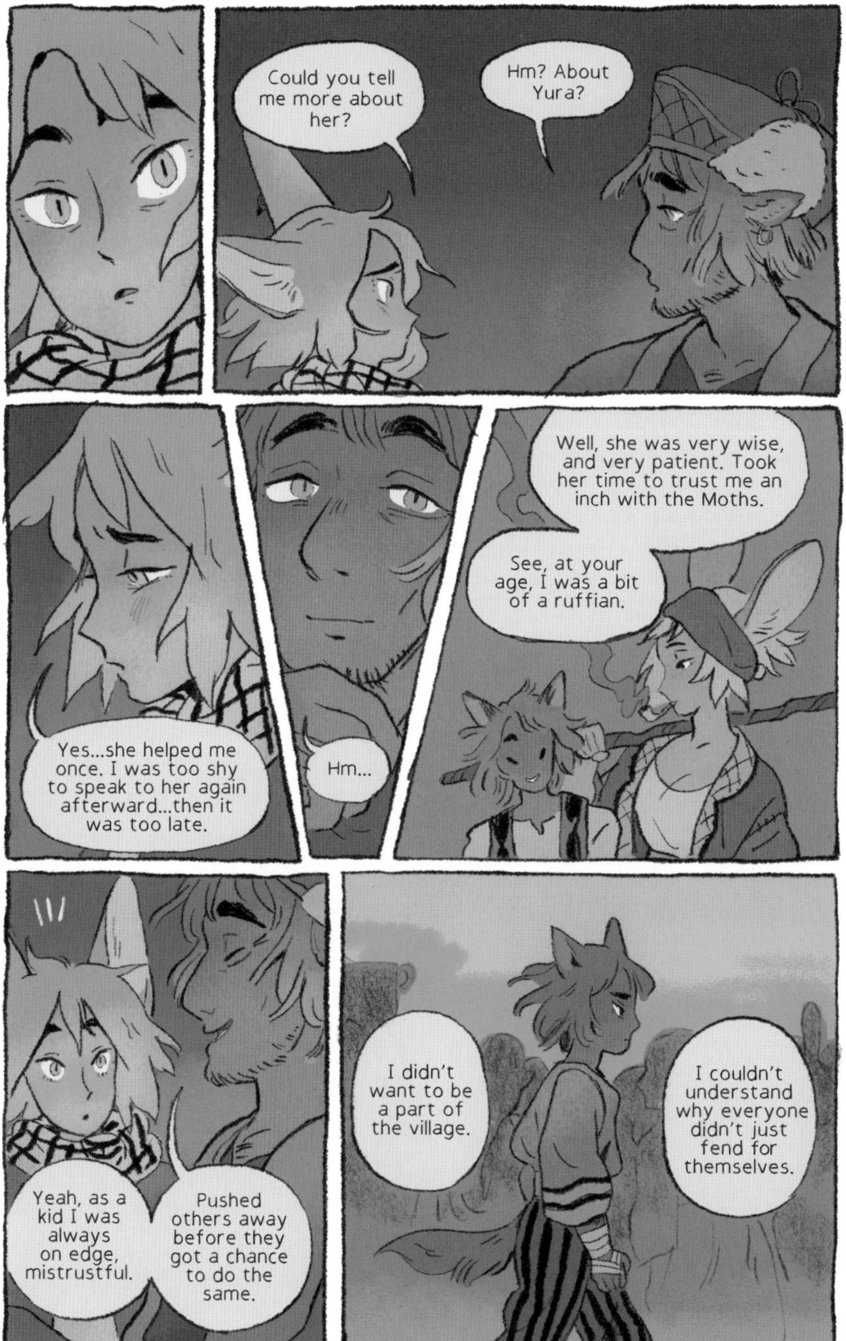
Could you tell me more about her?
Hm? About Yura?
Yes...she helped me once. I was too shy to speak to her again afterward...then it was too late.
Hm...
Well, she was very wise, and very patient. Took her time to trust me an inch with the Moths.
See, at your age, I was a bit of a ruffian.
Yeah, as a kid I was always on edge, mistrustful.
Pushed others away before they got a chance to do the same.
I didn't want to be a part of the village.
I couldn't understand why everyone didn't just fend for themselves.

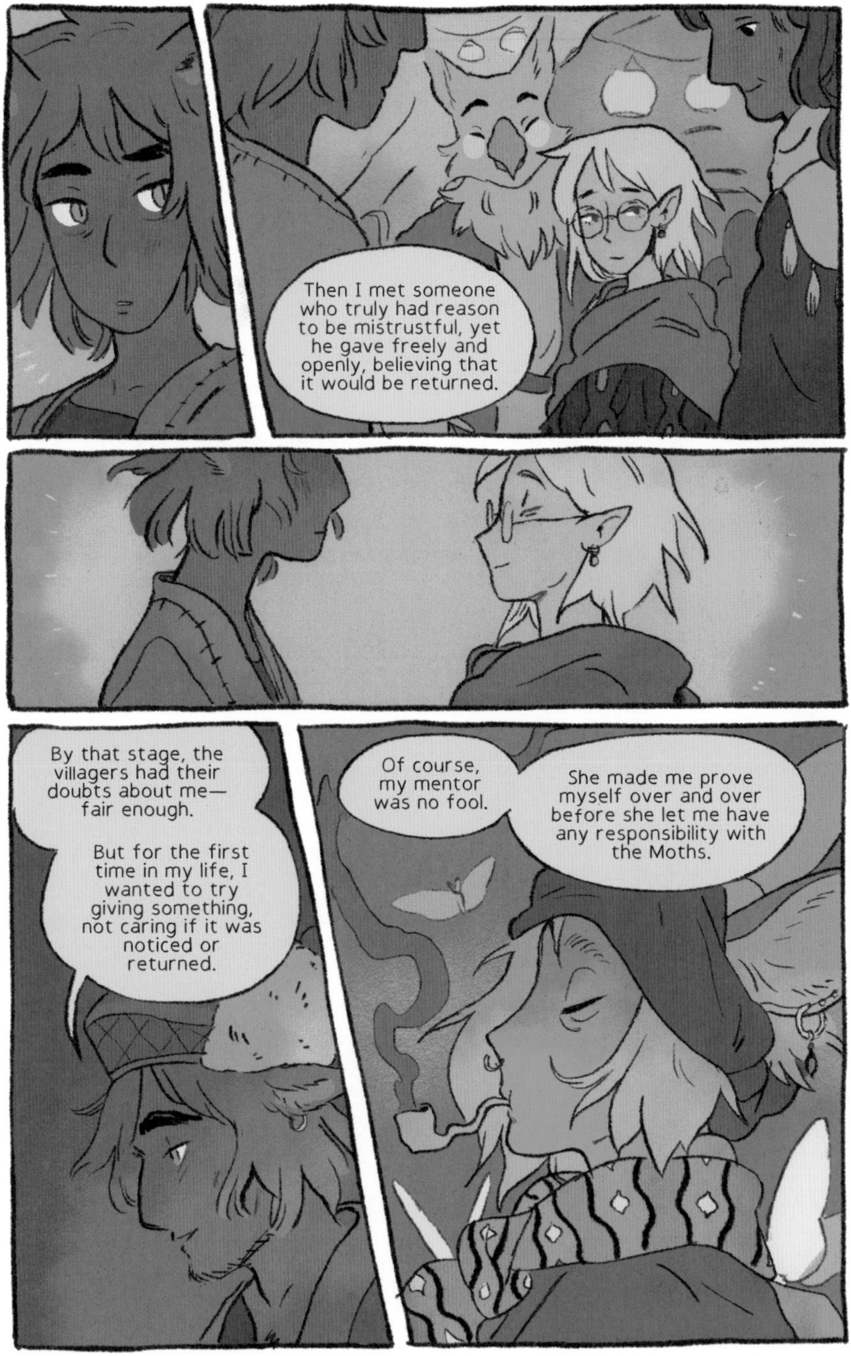
Then I met someone who truly had reason to be mistrustful, yet he gave freely and openly, believing that it would be returned.
By that stage, the villagers had their doubts about me—fair enough.
But for the first time in my life, I wanted to try giving something, not caring if it was noticed or returned.
Of course, my mentor was no fool.
She made me prove myself over and over before she let me have any responsibility with the Moths.

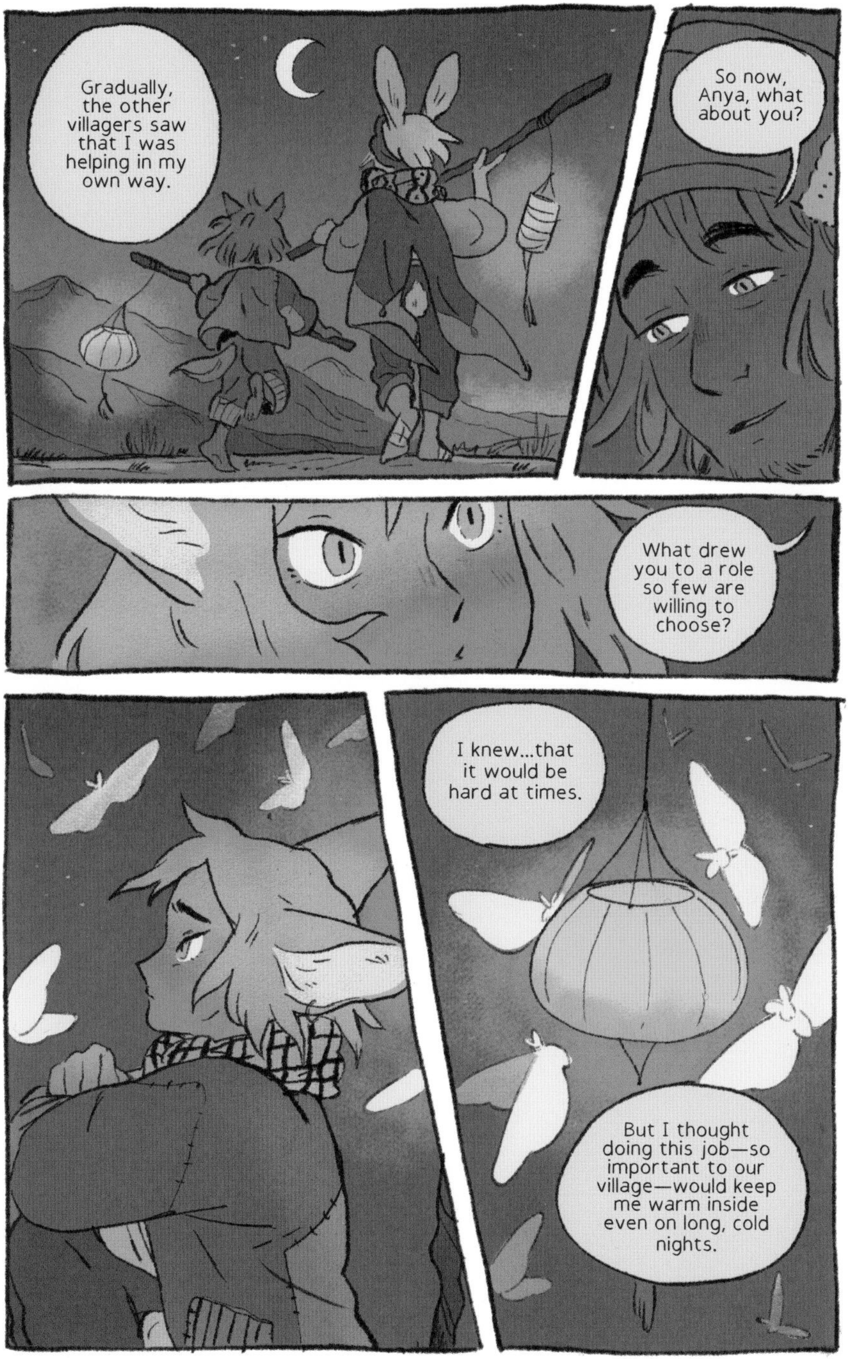
Gradually, the other villagers saw that I was helping in my own way.
So now, Anya, what about you?
What drew you to a role so few are willing to choose?
I knew...that it would be hard at times.
But I thought doing this job—so important to our village—would keep me warm inside even on long, cold nights.

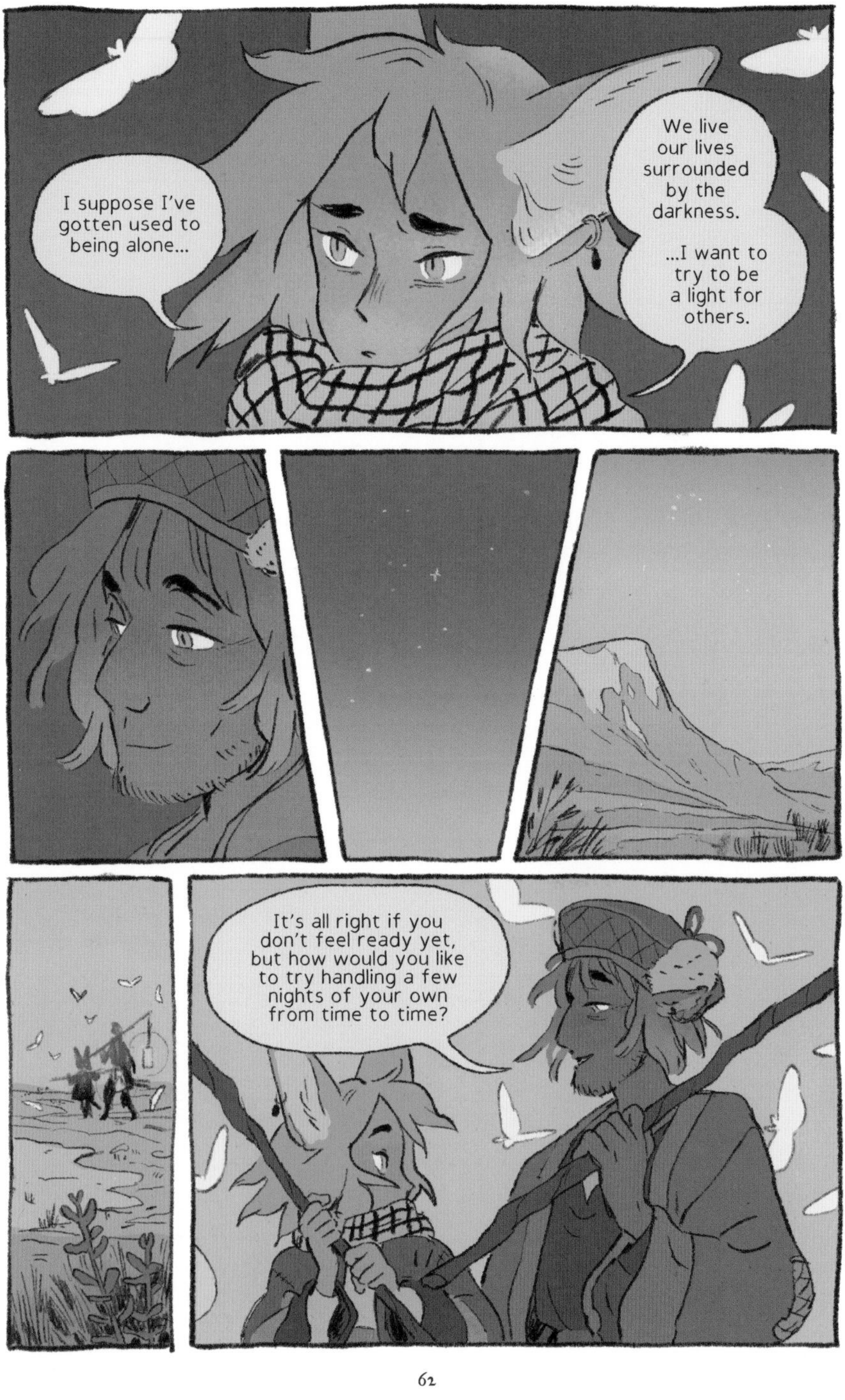
I suppose I've gotten used to being alone...
We live our lives surrounded by the darkness.
...I want to try to be a light for others.
It's all right if you don't feel ready yet, but how would you like to try handling a few nights of your own from time to time?

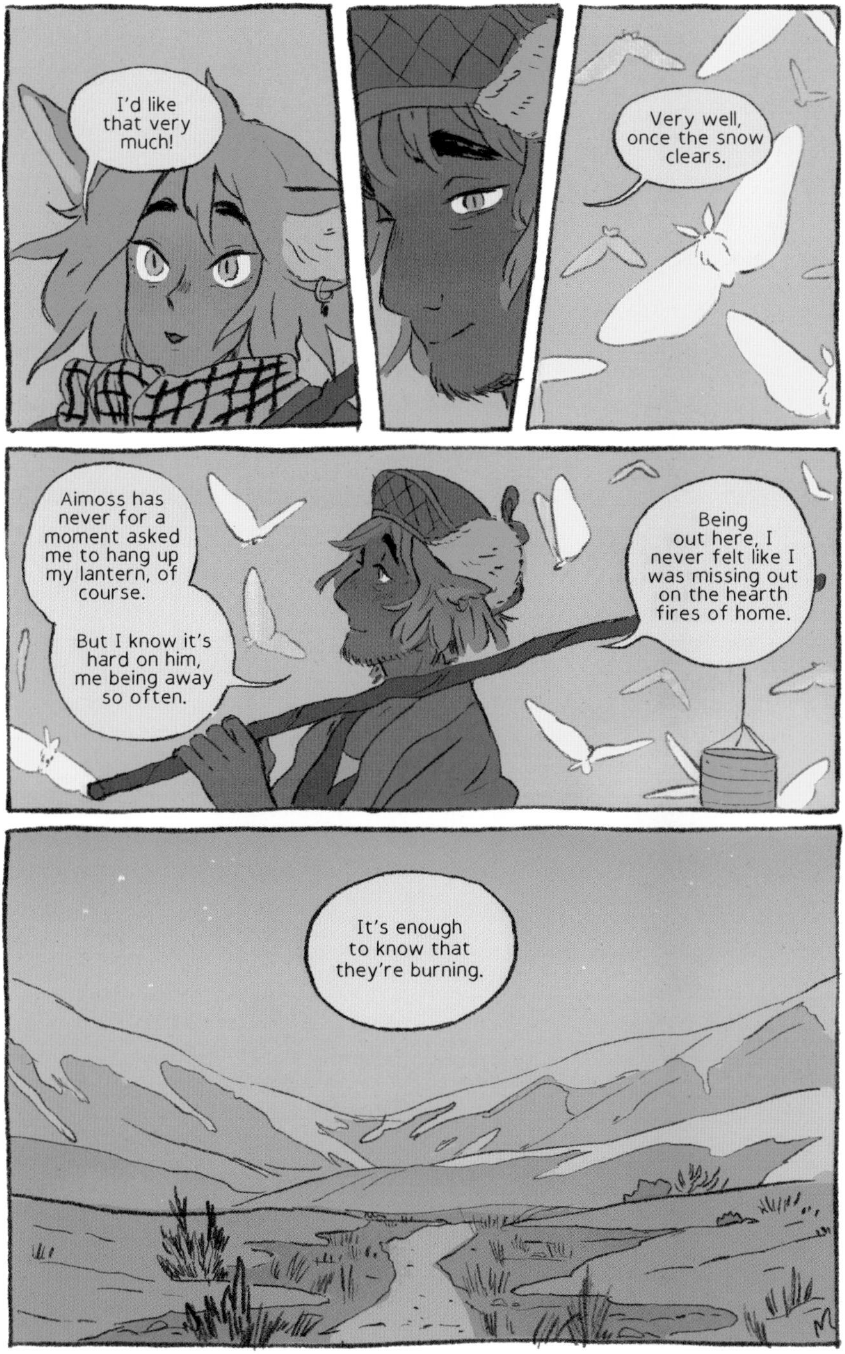
I'd like that very much!
Very well, once the snow clears.
Aimoss has never for a moment asked me to hang up my lantern, of course.
But I know it's hard on him, me being away so often.
Being out here, I never felt like I was missing out on the hearth fires of home.
It's enough to know that they're burning.

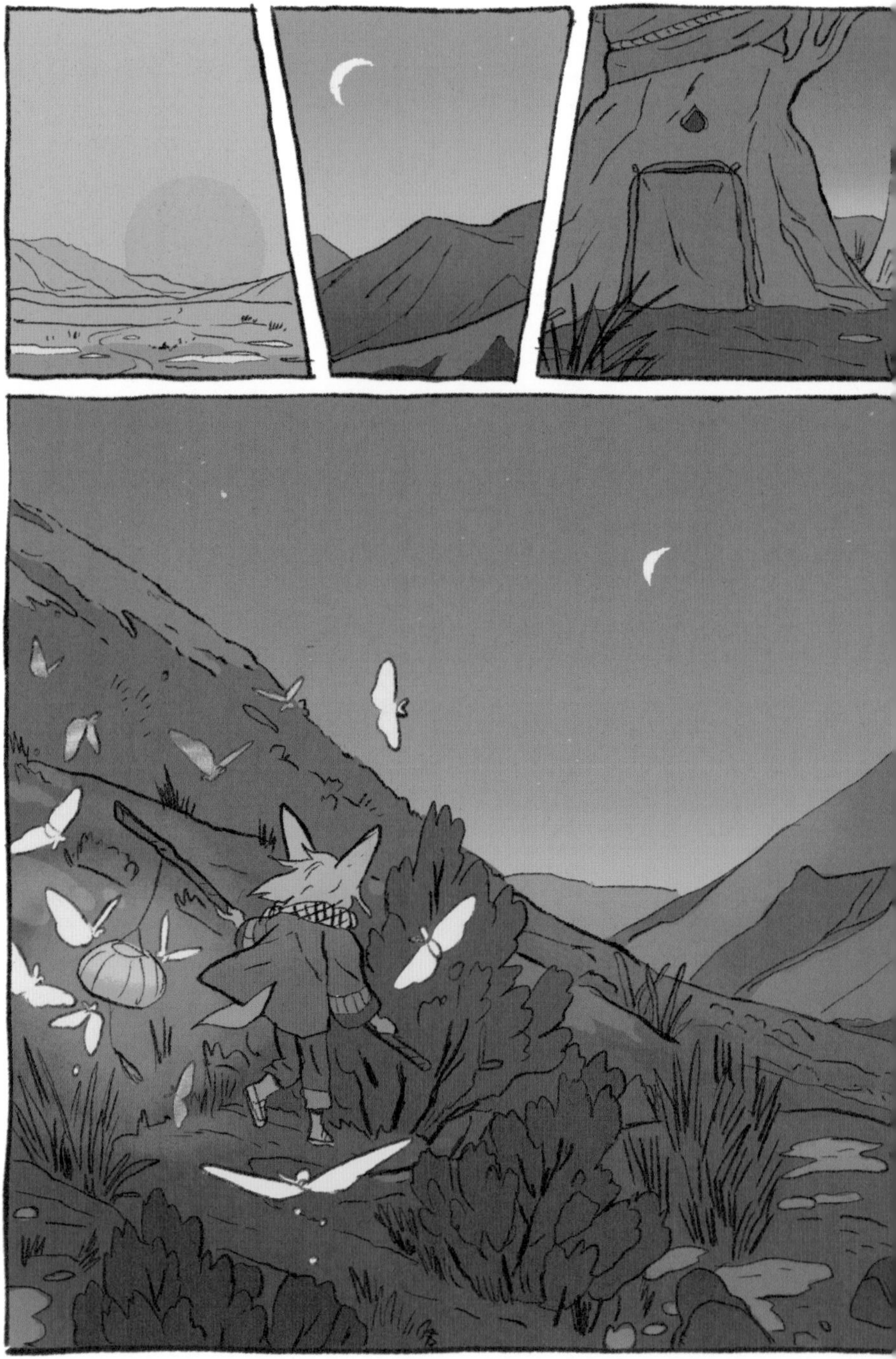

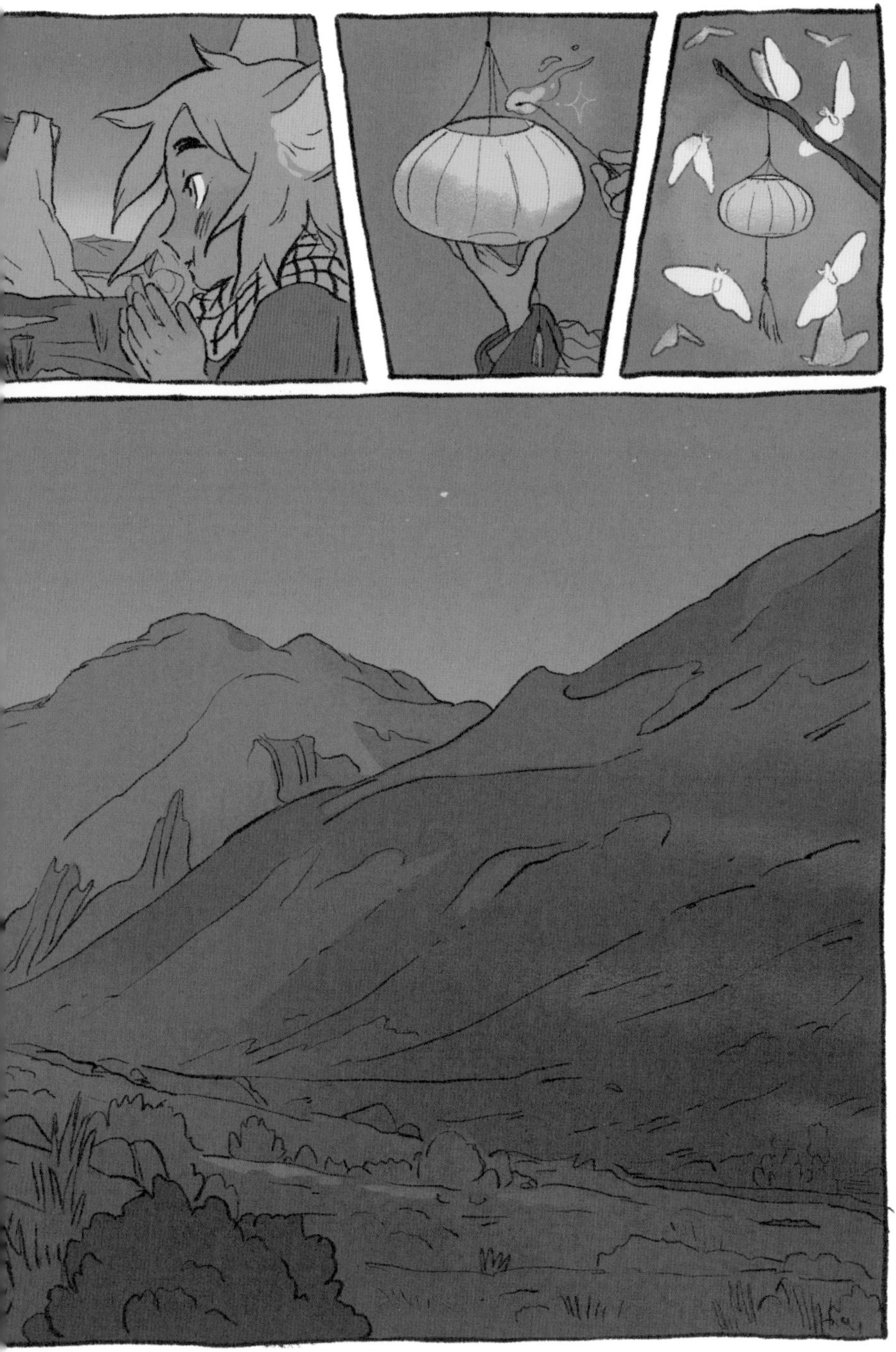

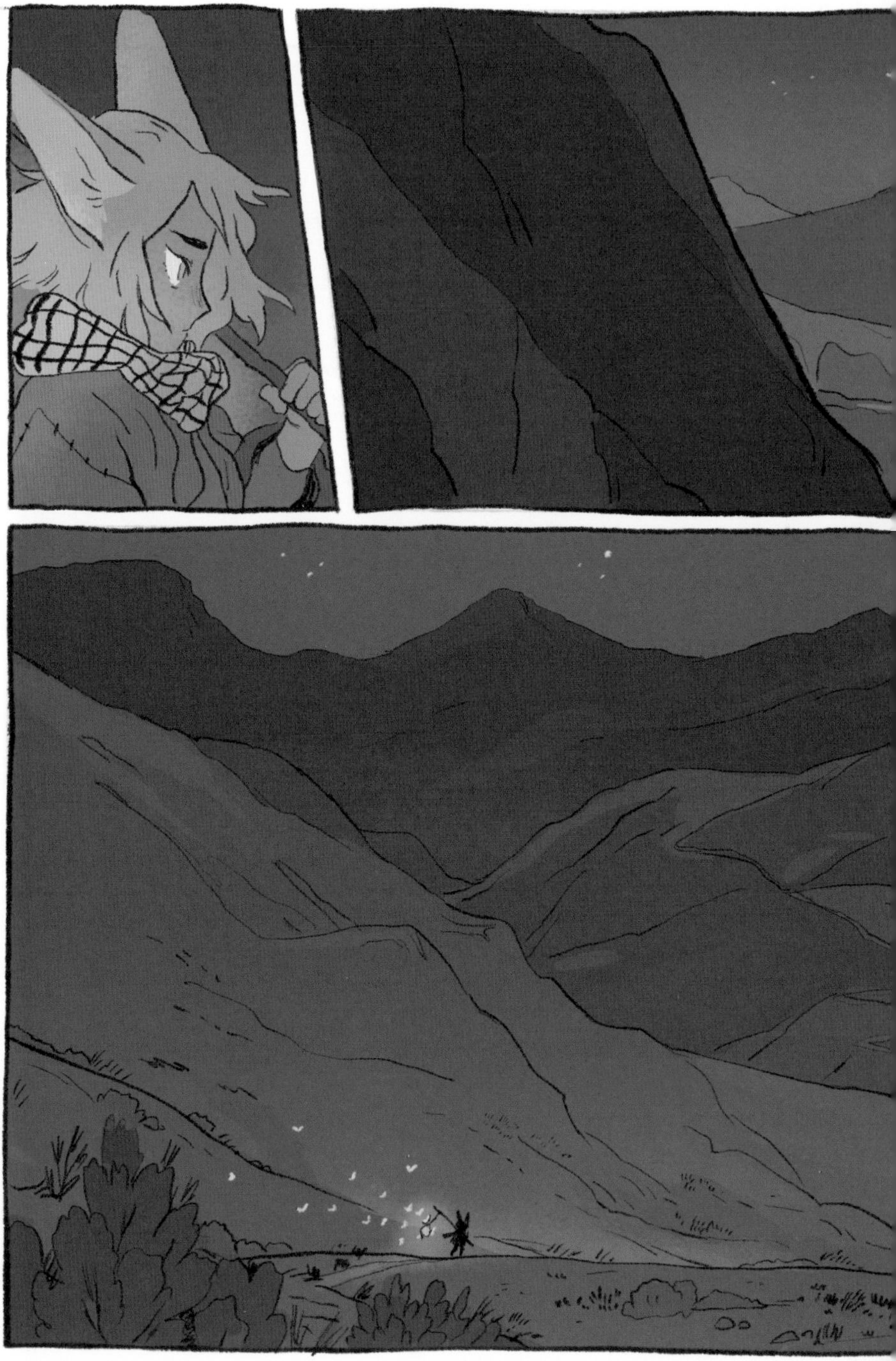

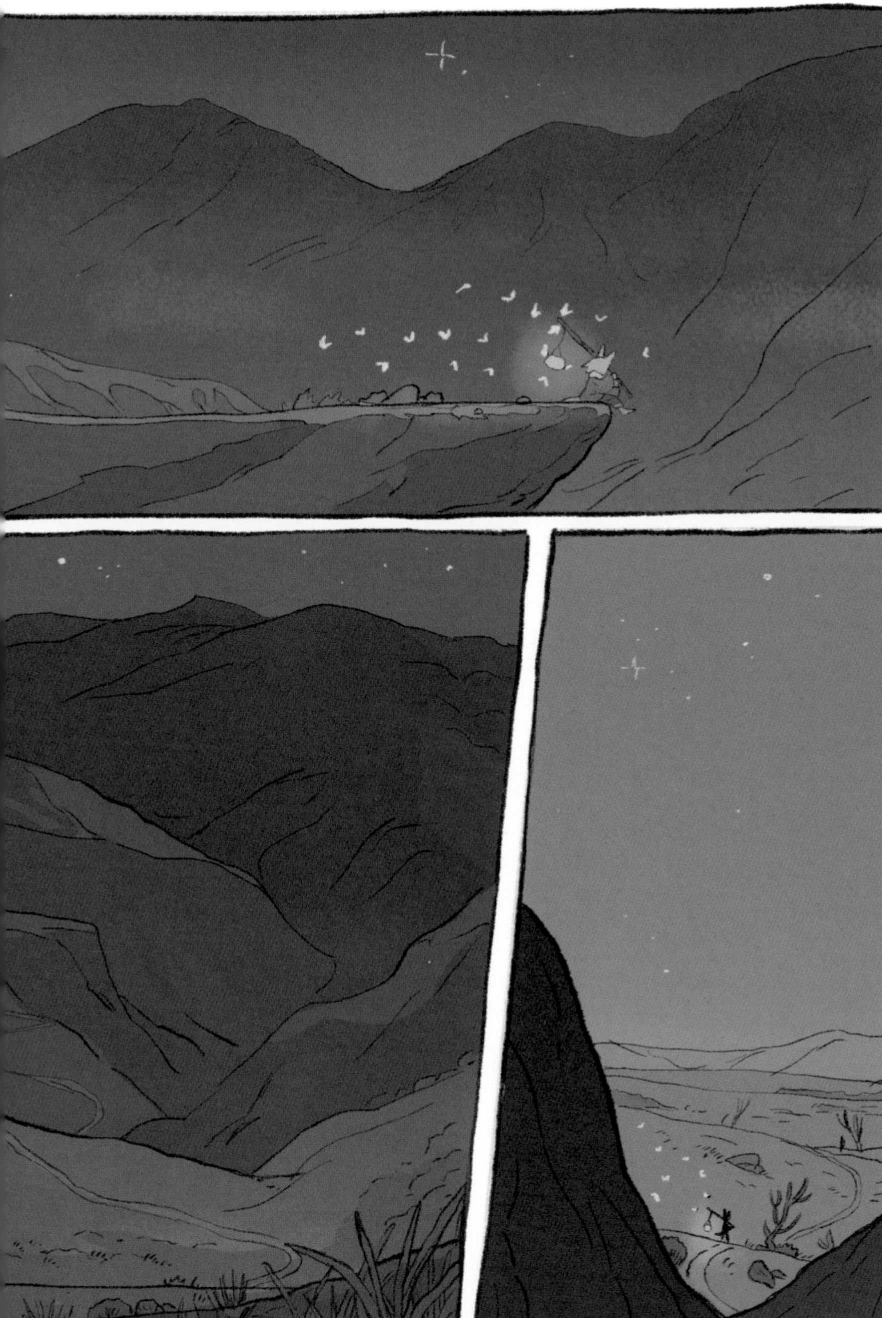

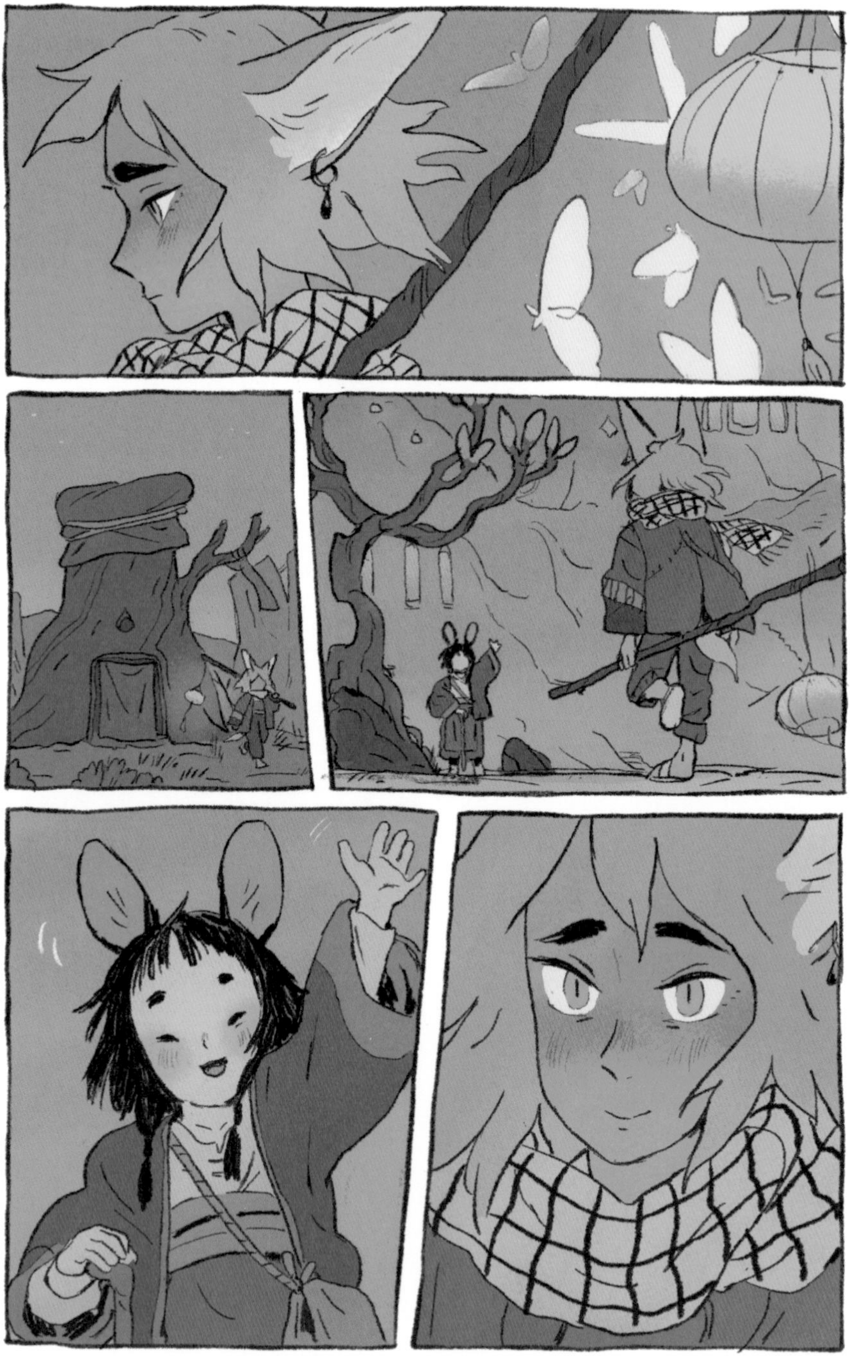

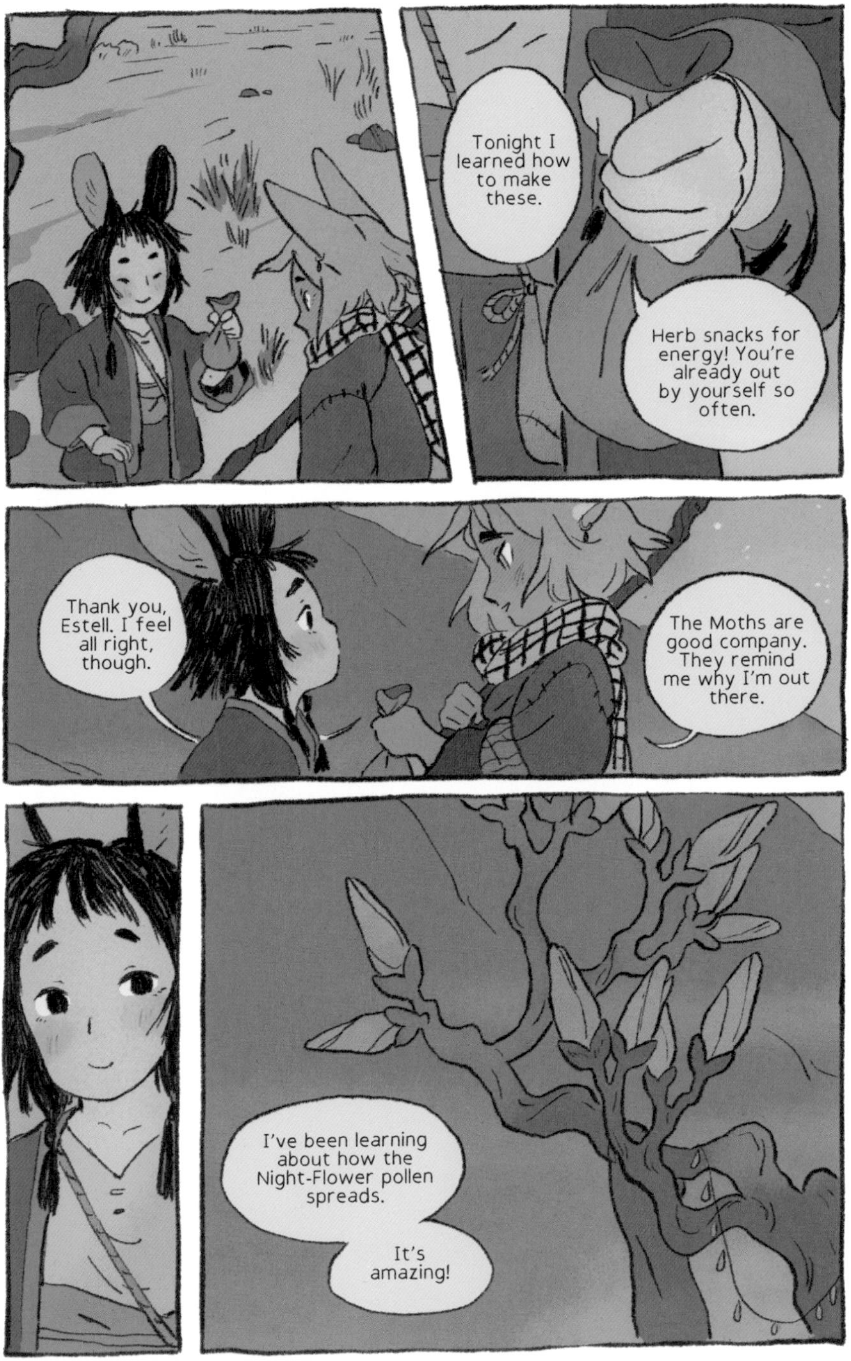
Tonight I learned how to make these.
Herb snacks for energy! You're already out by yourself so often.
Thank you, Estell. I feel all right, though.
The Moths are good company. They remind me why I'm out there.
I've been learning about how the Night-Flower pollen spreads.
It's amazing!

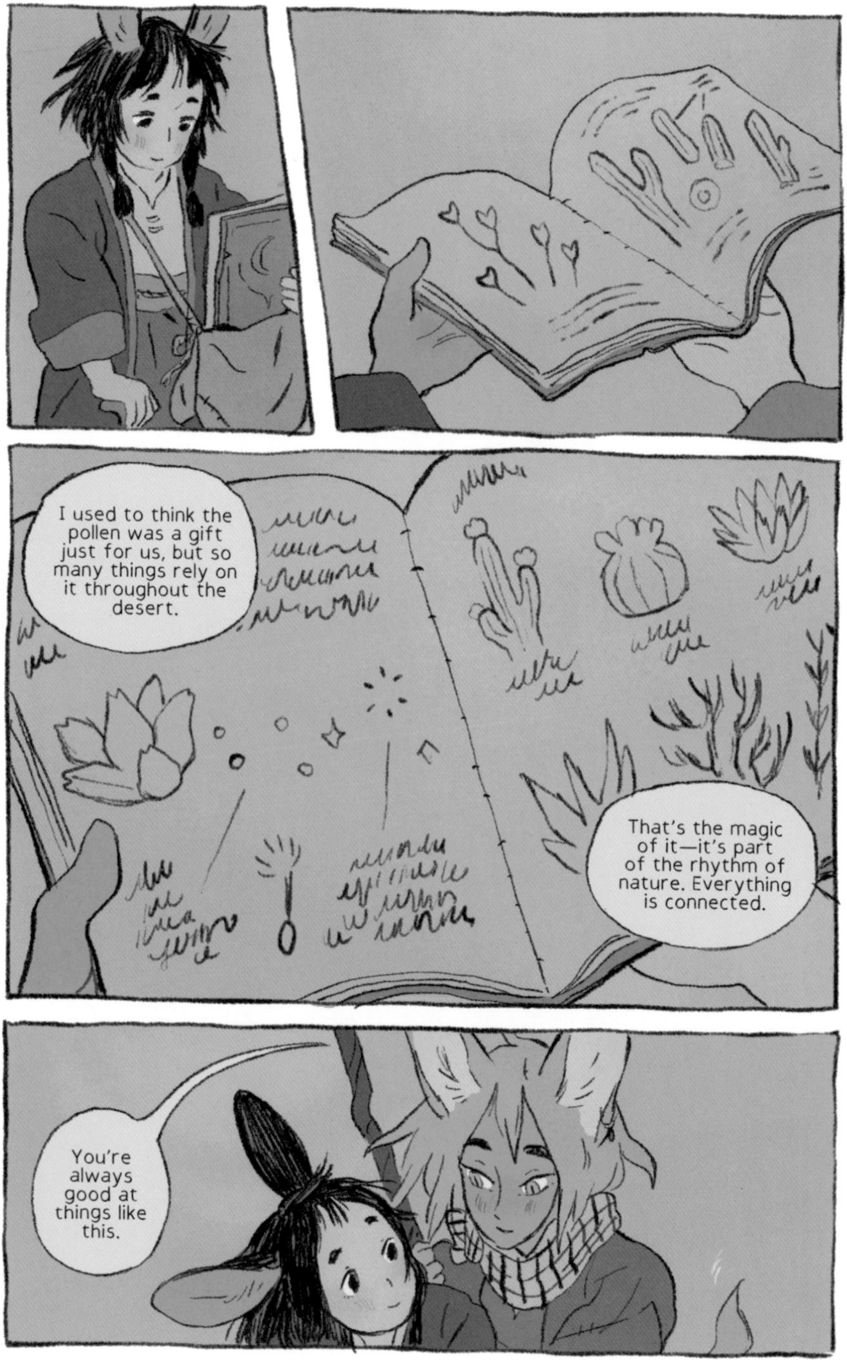
I used to think the pollen was a gift just for us, but so many things rely on it throughout the desert.
That's the magic of it—it's part of the rhythm of nature. Everything is connected.
You're always good at things like this.

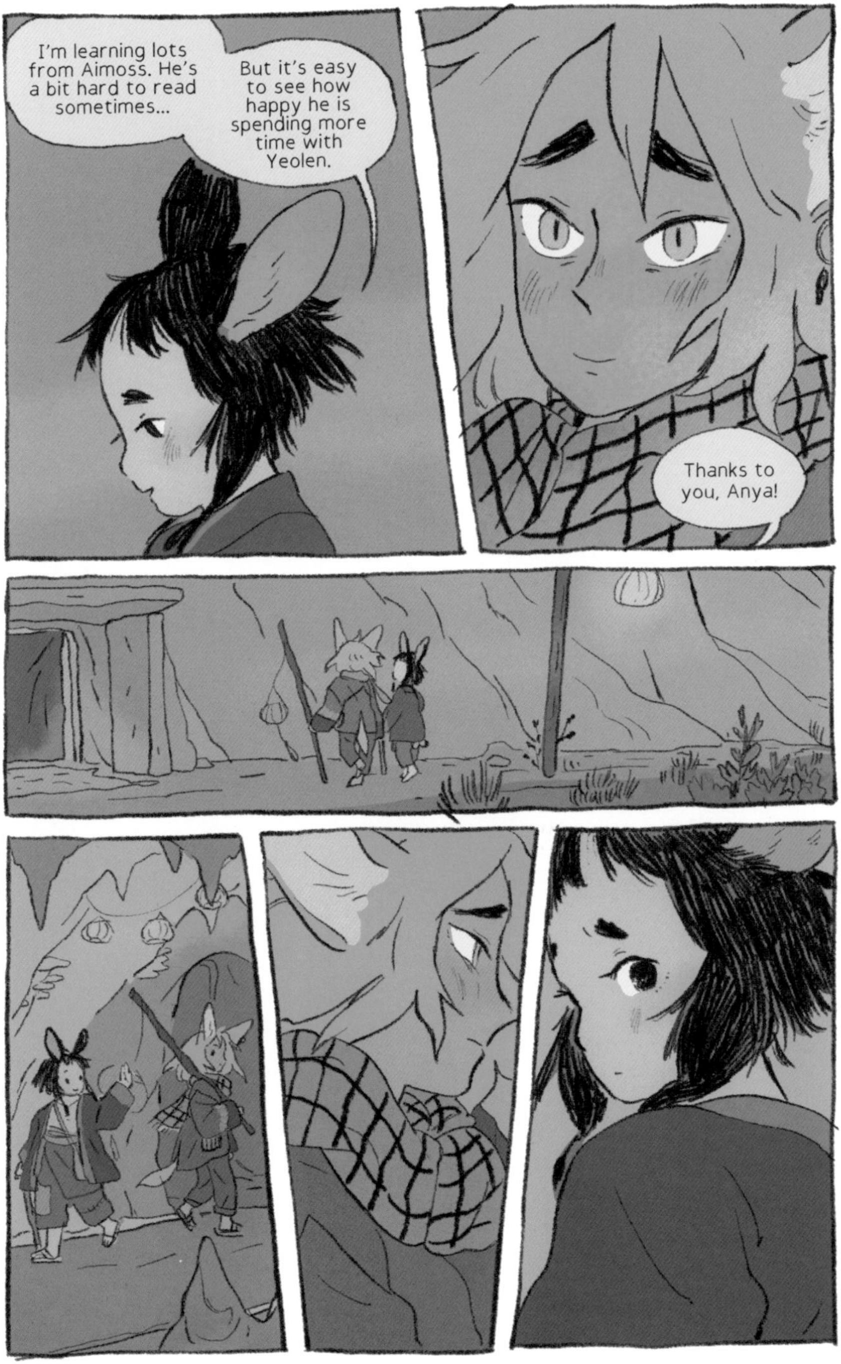
I'm learning lots from Aimoss. He's a bit hard to read sometimes...
But it's easy to see how happy he is spending more time with Yeolen.
Thanks to you, Anya!

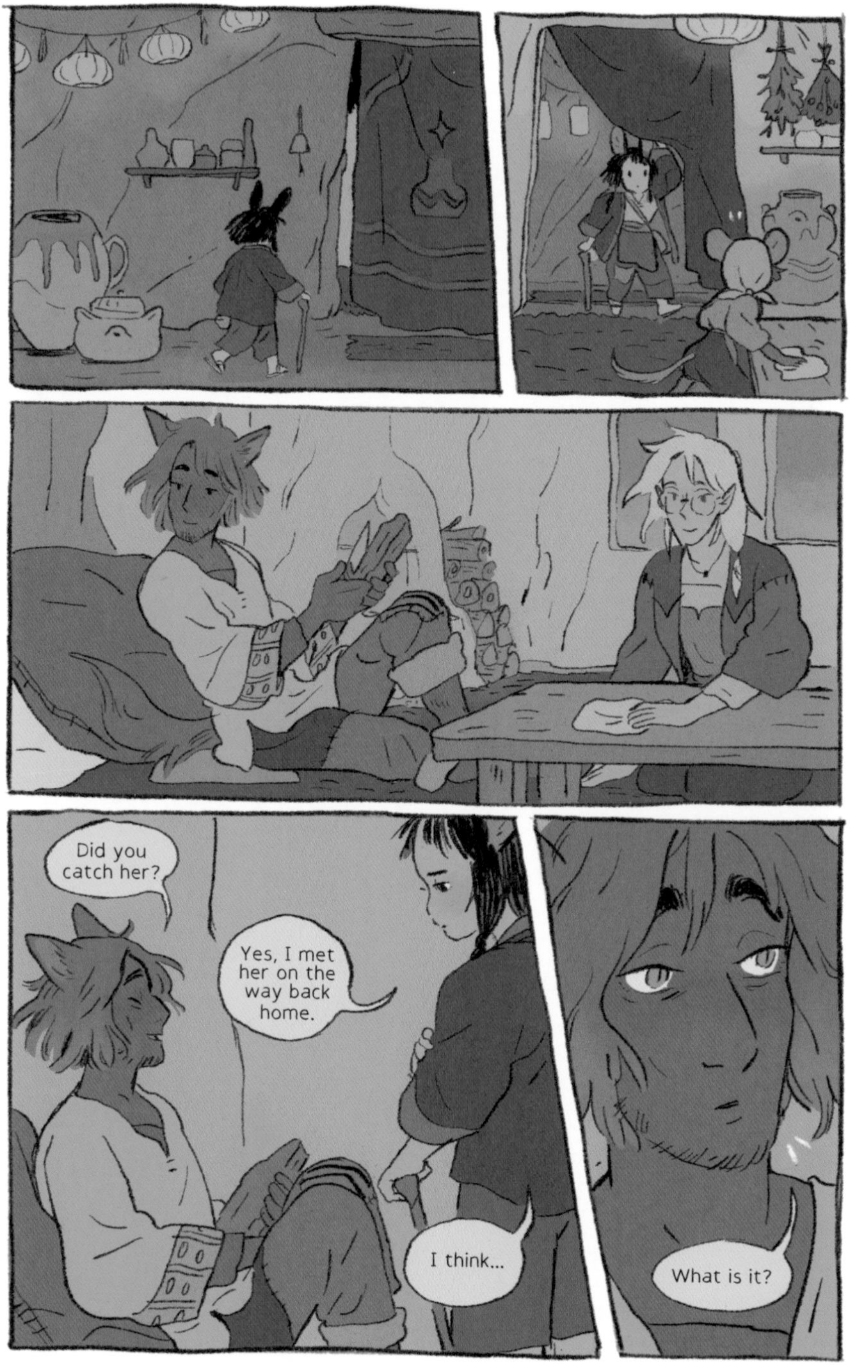
Did you catch her?
Yes, I met her on the way back home.
I think...
What is it?

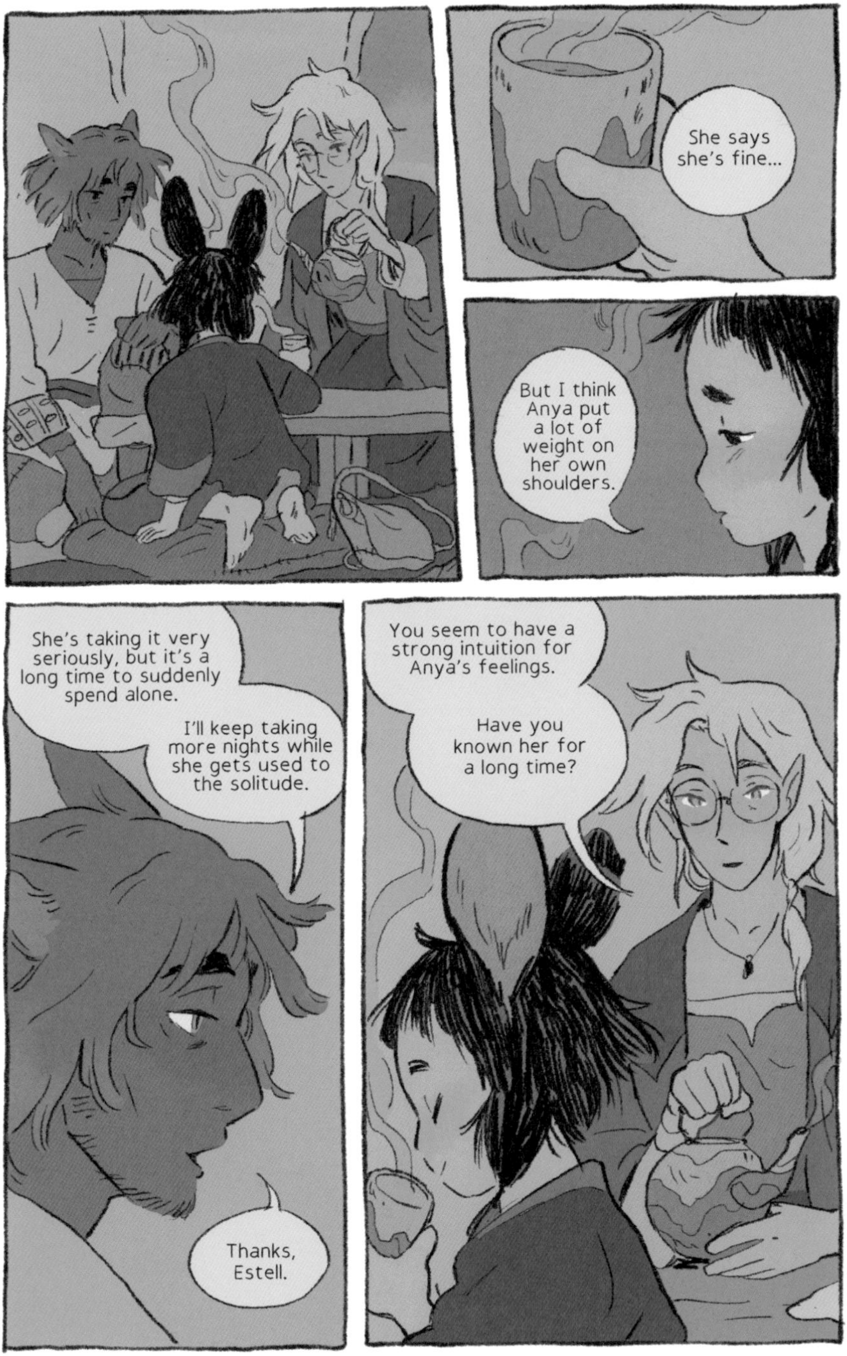
She says she's fine...
But I think Anya put a lot of weight on her own shoulders.
She's taking it very seriously, but it's a long time to suddenly spend alone.
I'll keep taking more nights while she gets used to the solitude.
Thanks, Estell.
You seem to have a strong intuition for Anya's feelings.
Have you known her for a long time?

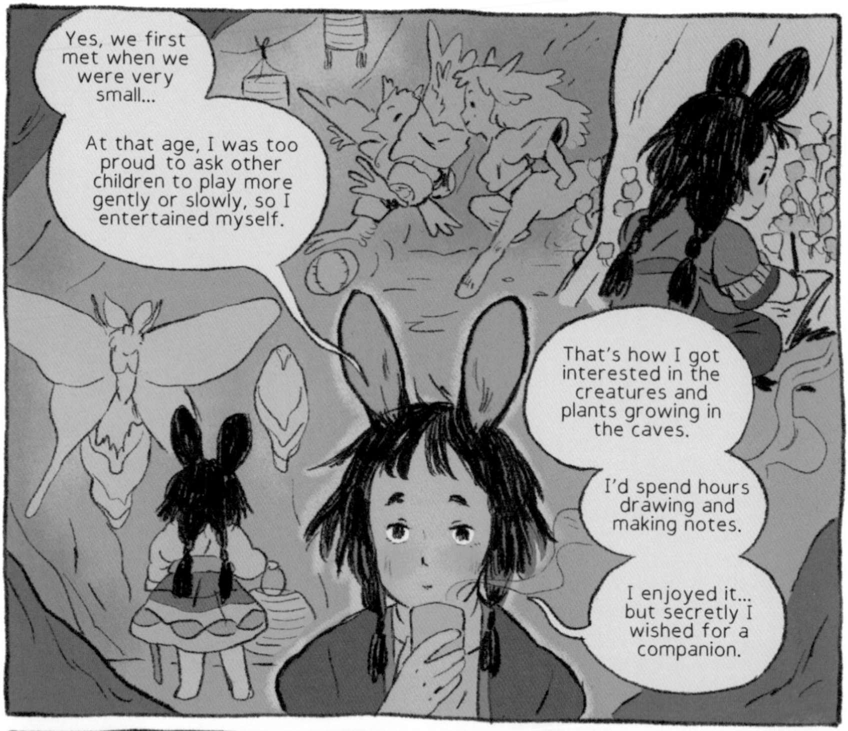
Yes, we first met when we were very small...
At that age, I was too proud to ask other children to play more gently or slowly, so I entertained myself.
That's how I got interested in the creatures and plants growing in the caves.
I'd spend hours drawing and making notes.
I enjoyed it... but secretly I wished for a companion.

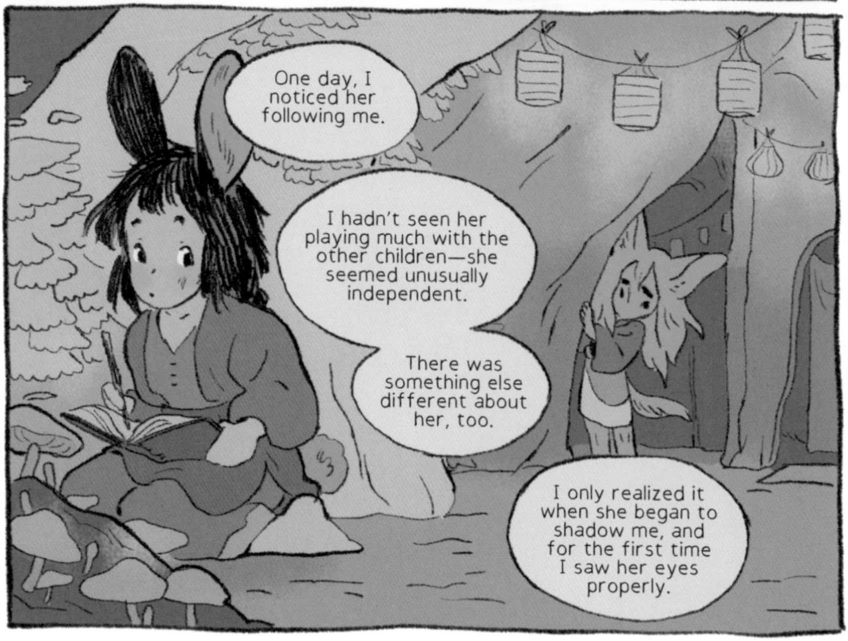
One day, I noticed her following me.
I hadn't seen her playing much with the other children—she seemed unusually independent.
There was something else different about her, too.
I only realized it when she began to shadow me, and for the first time I saw her eyes properly.

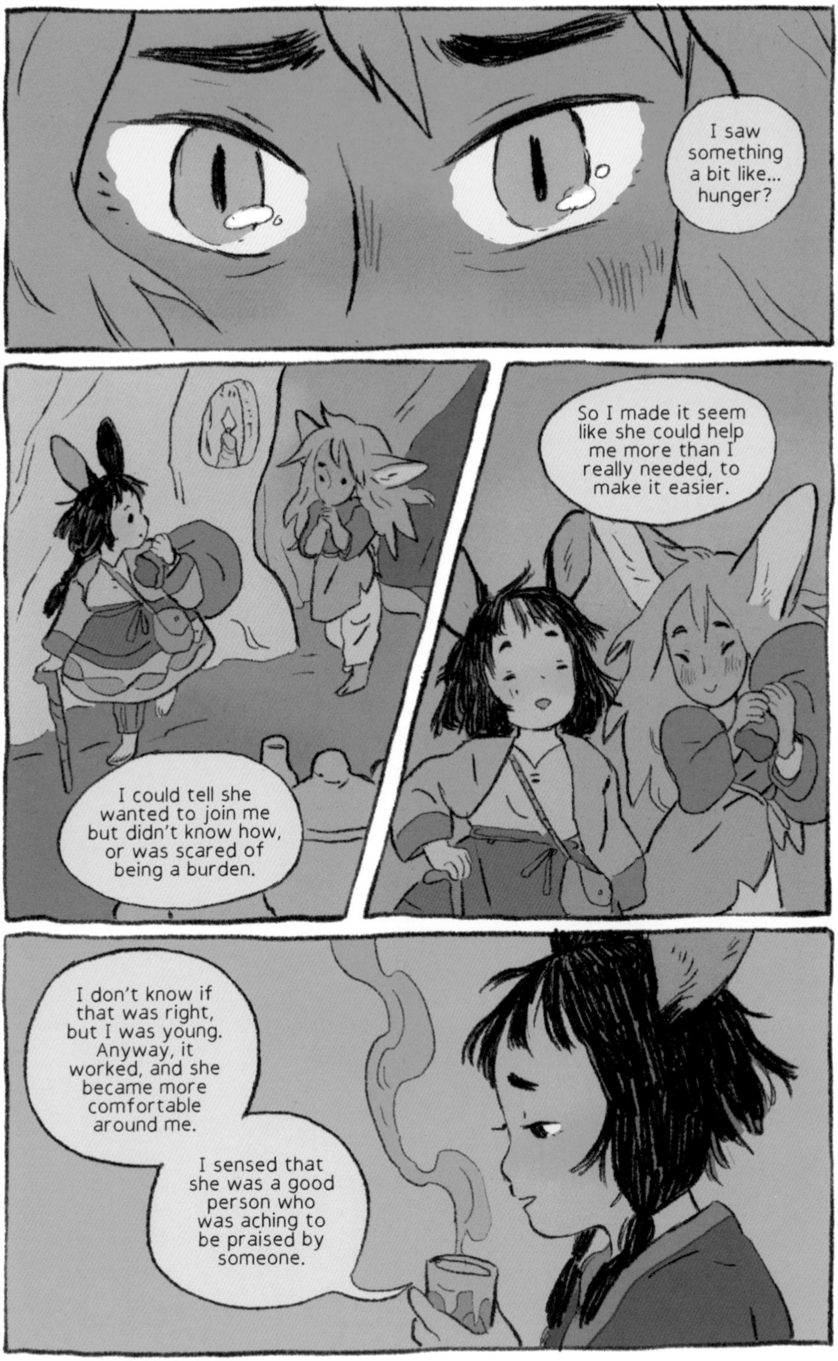
I saw something a bit like... hunger?
I could tell she wanted to join me but didn't know how, or was scared of being a burden.
So I made it seem like she could help me more than I really needed, to make it easier.
I don't know if that was right, but I was young. Anyway, it worked, and she became more comfortable around me.
I sensed that she was a good person who was aching to be praised by someone.

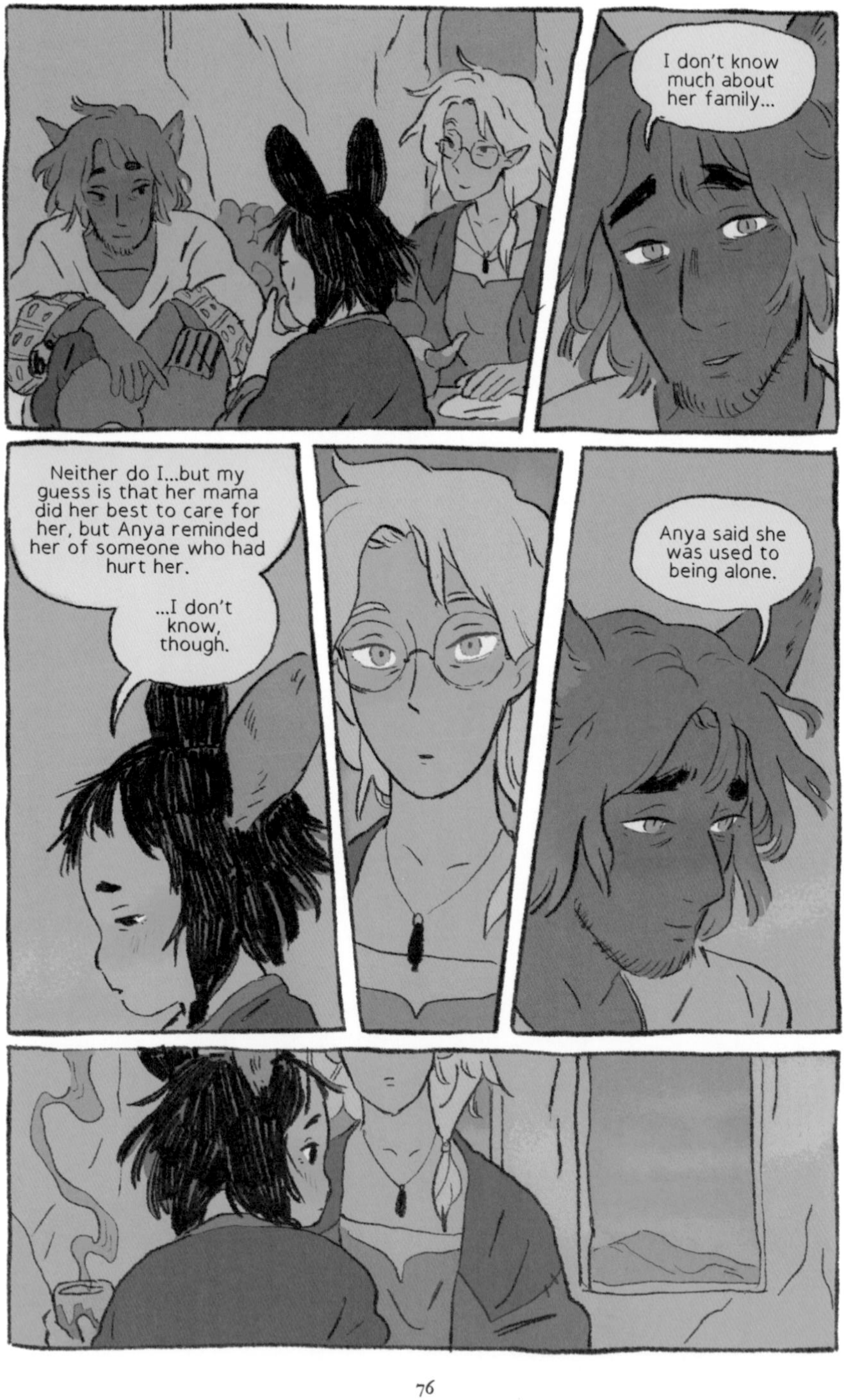
I don't know much about her family...
Neither do I...but my guess is that her mama did her best to care for her, but Anya reminded her of someone who had hurt her.
...I don't know, though.
Anya said she was used to being alone.

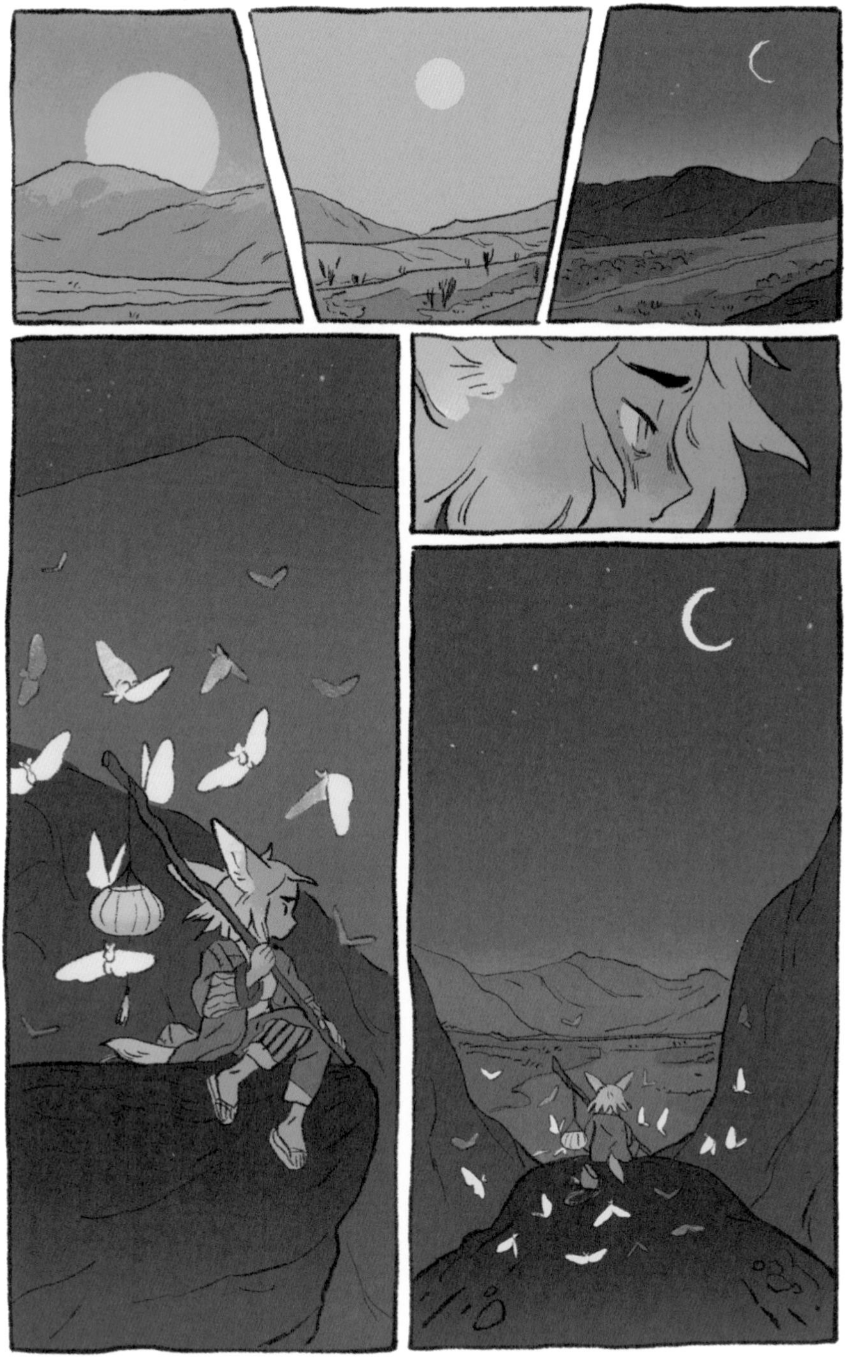

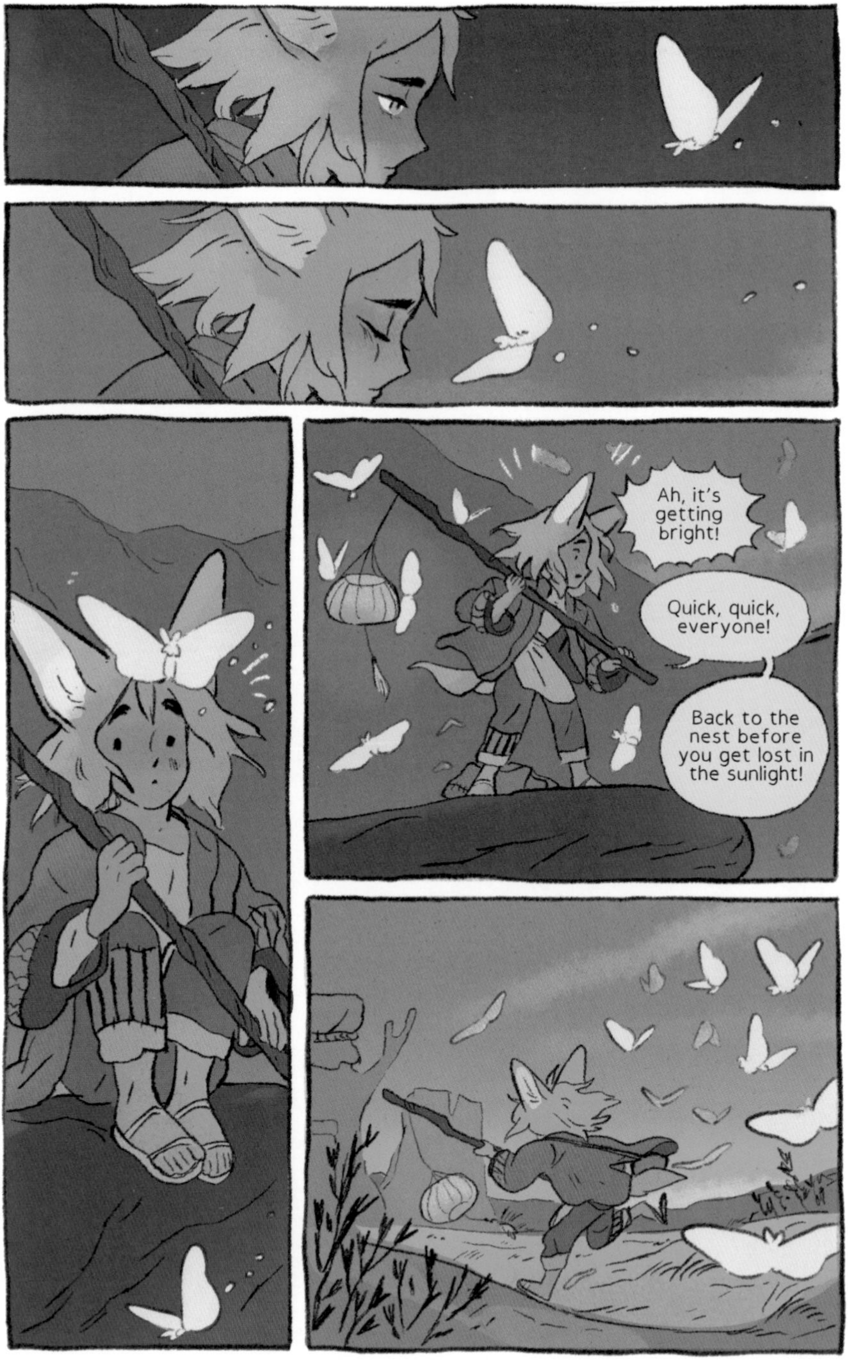
Ah, it's getting bright!
Quick, quick, everyone!
Back to the nest before you get lost in the sunlight!

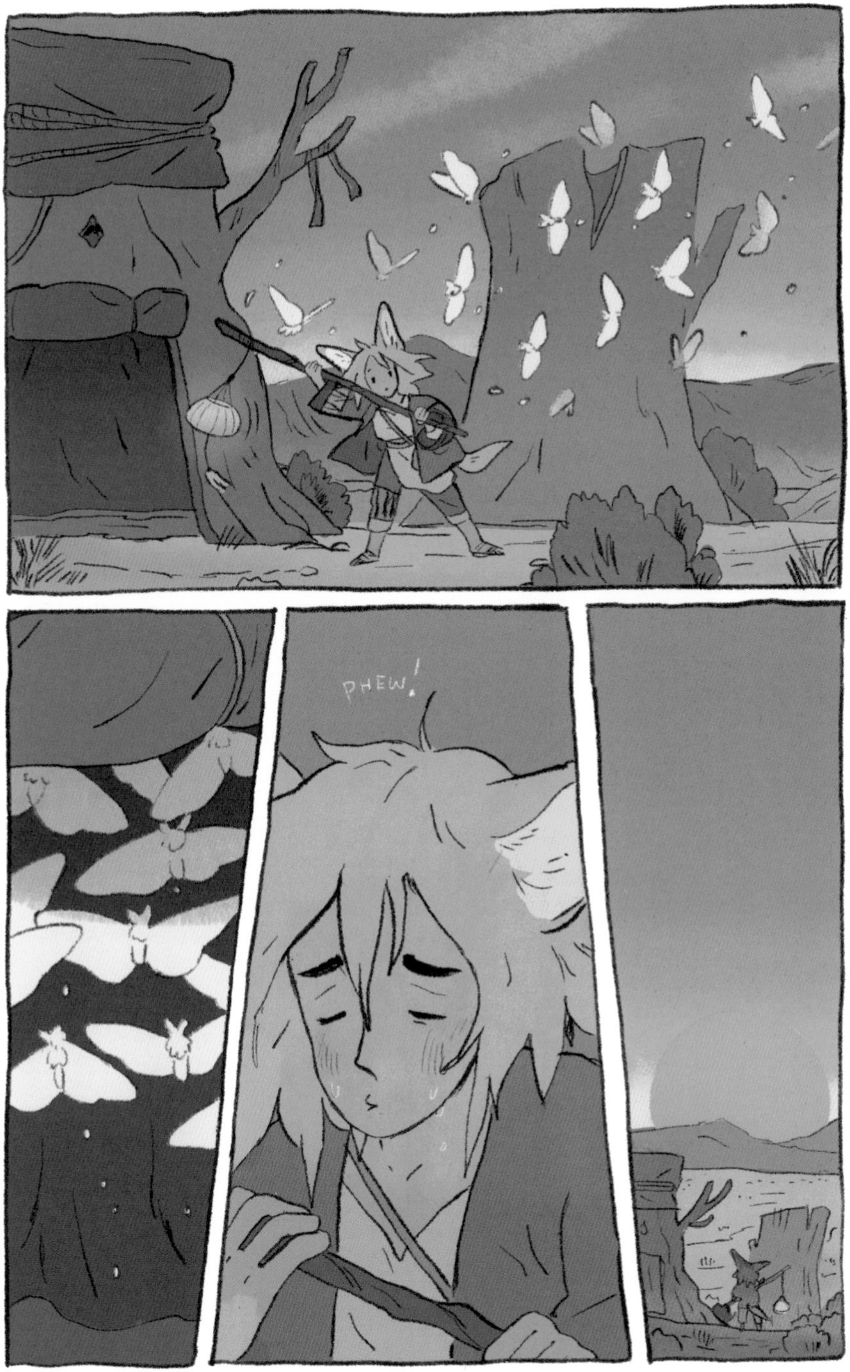
PHEW!

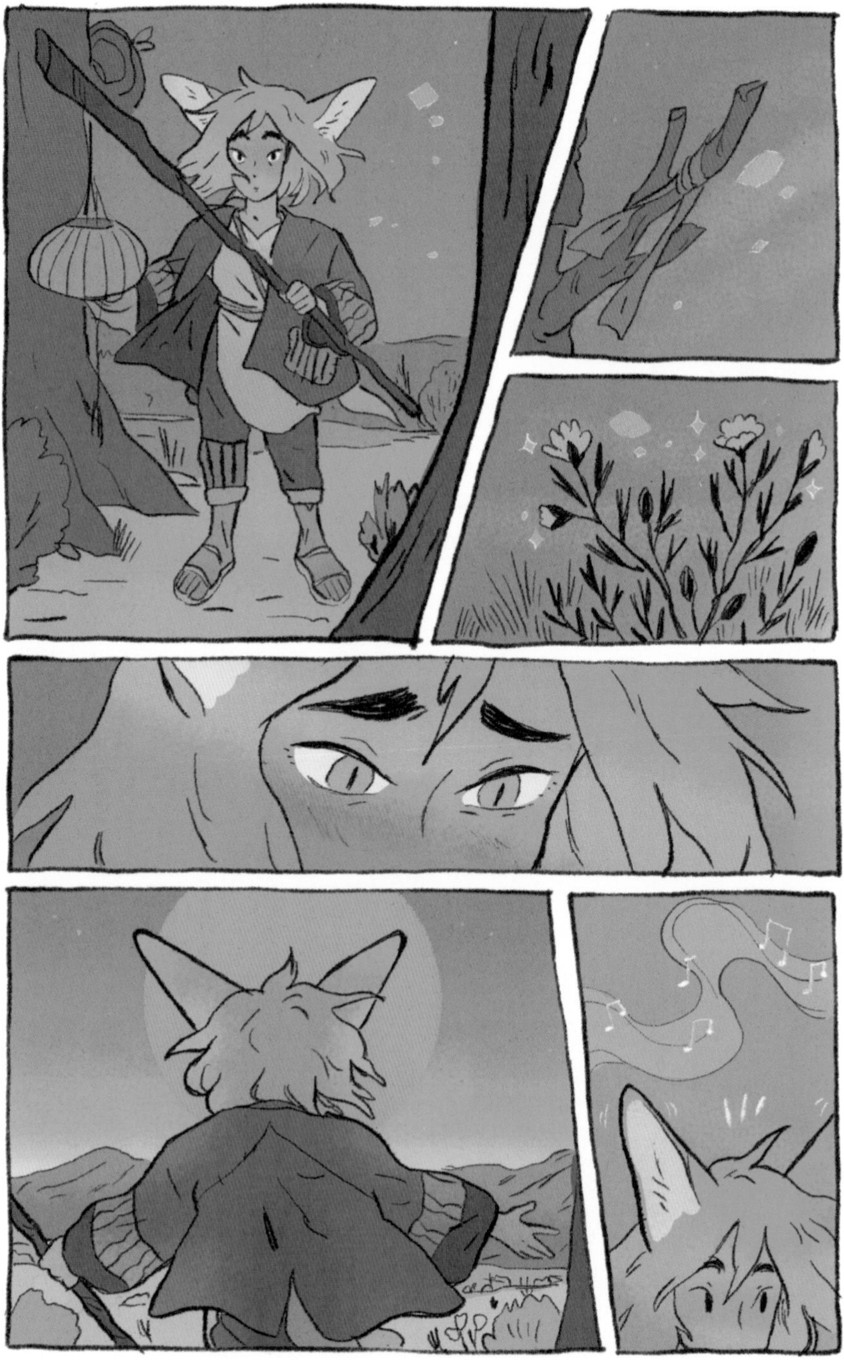

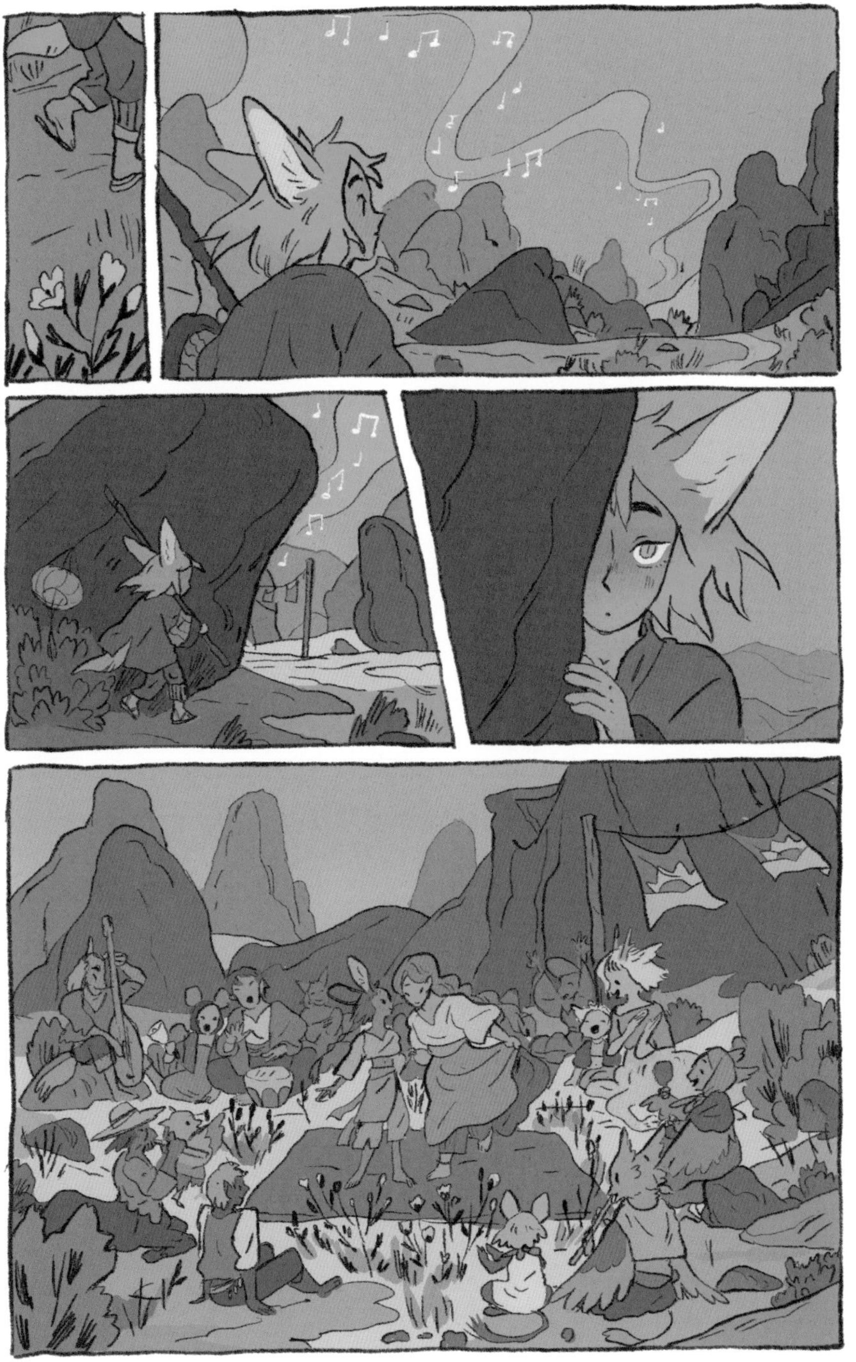

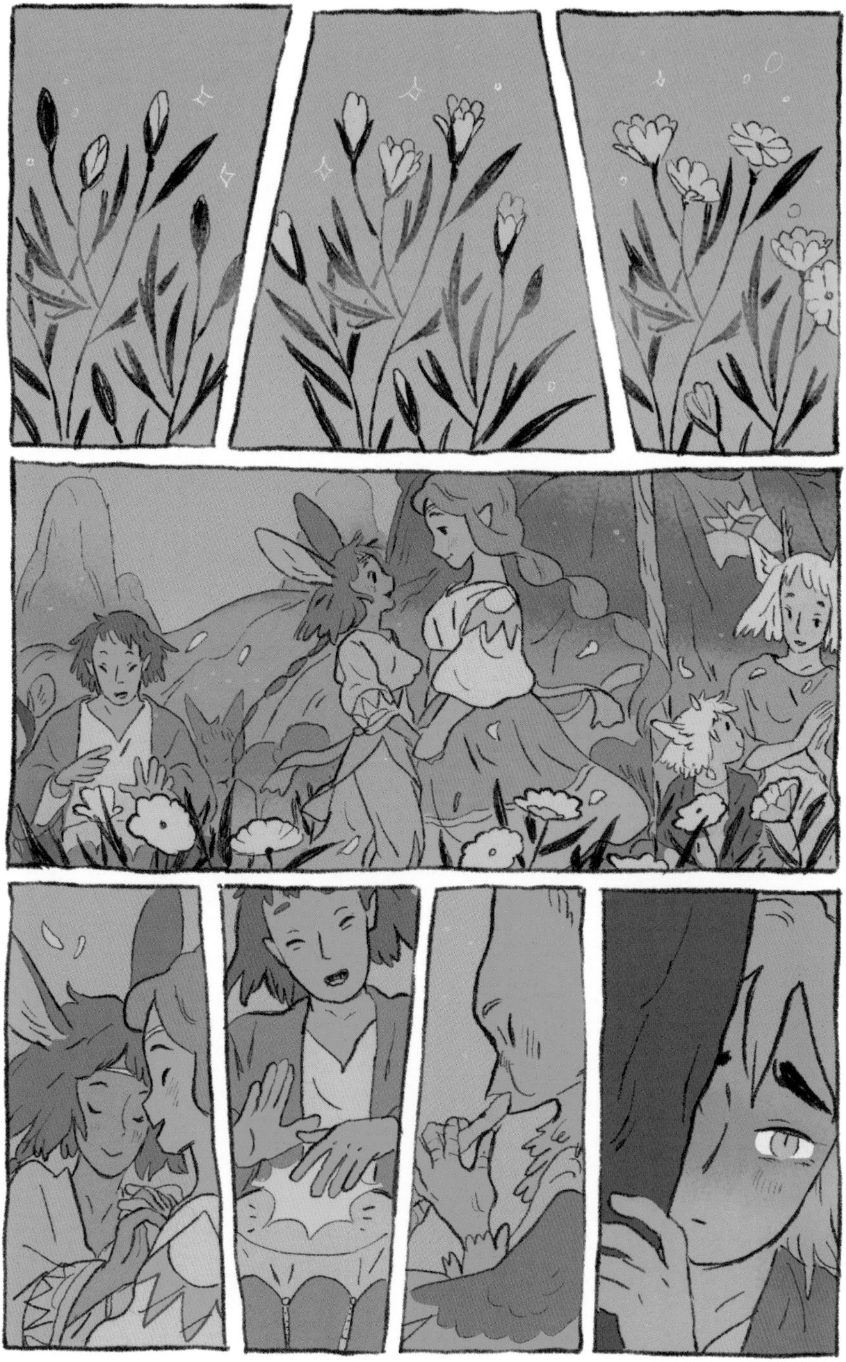

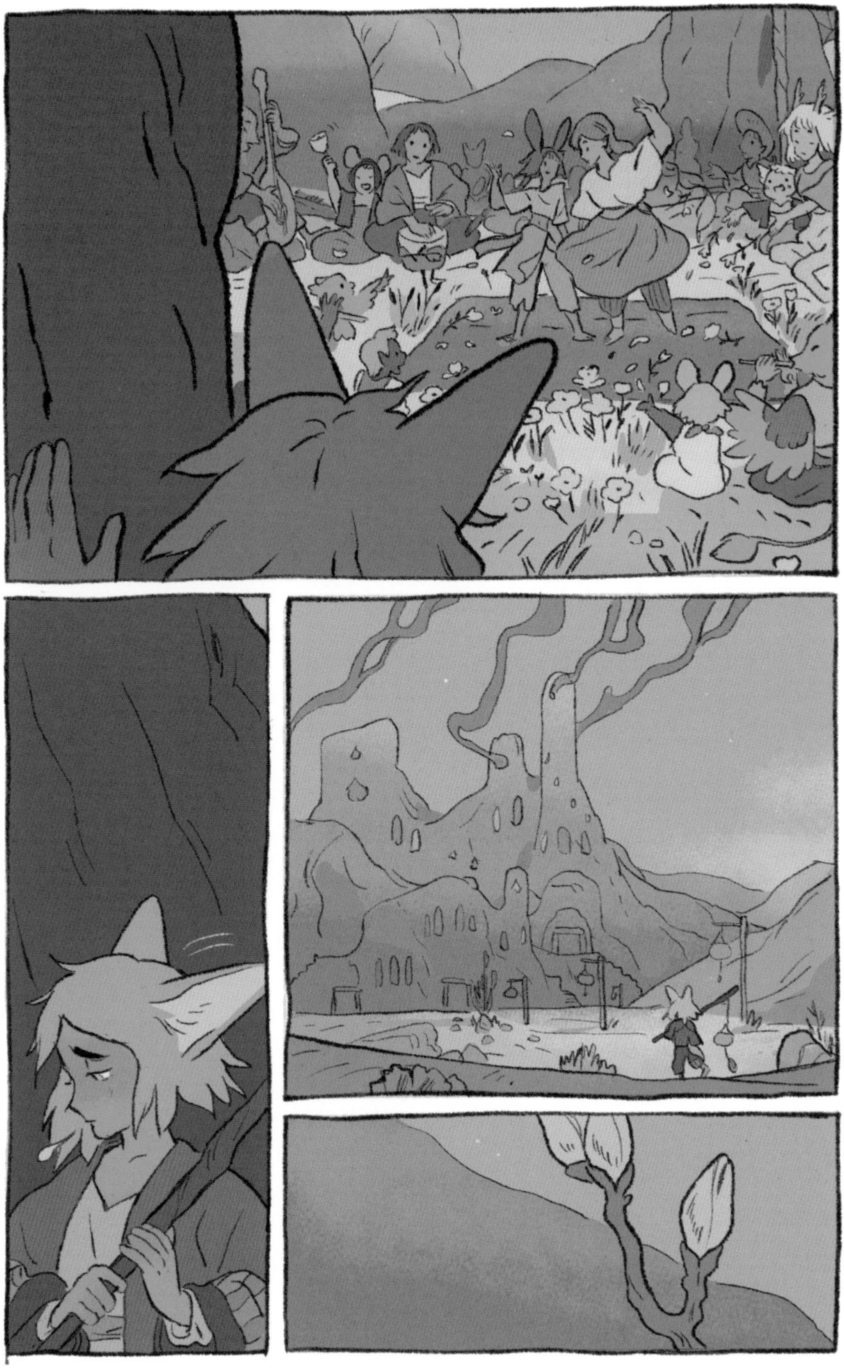

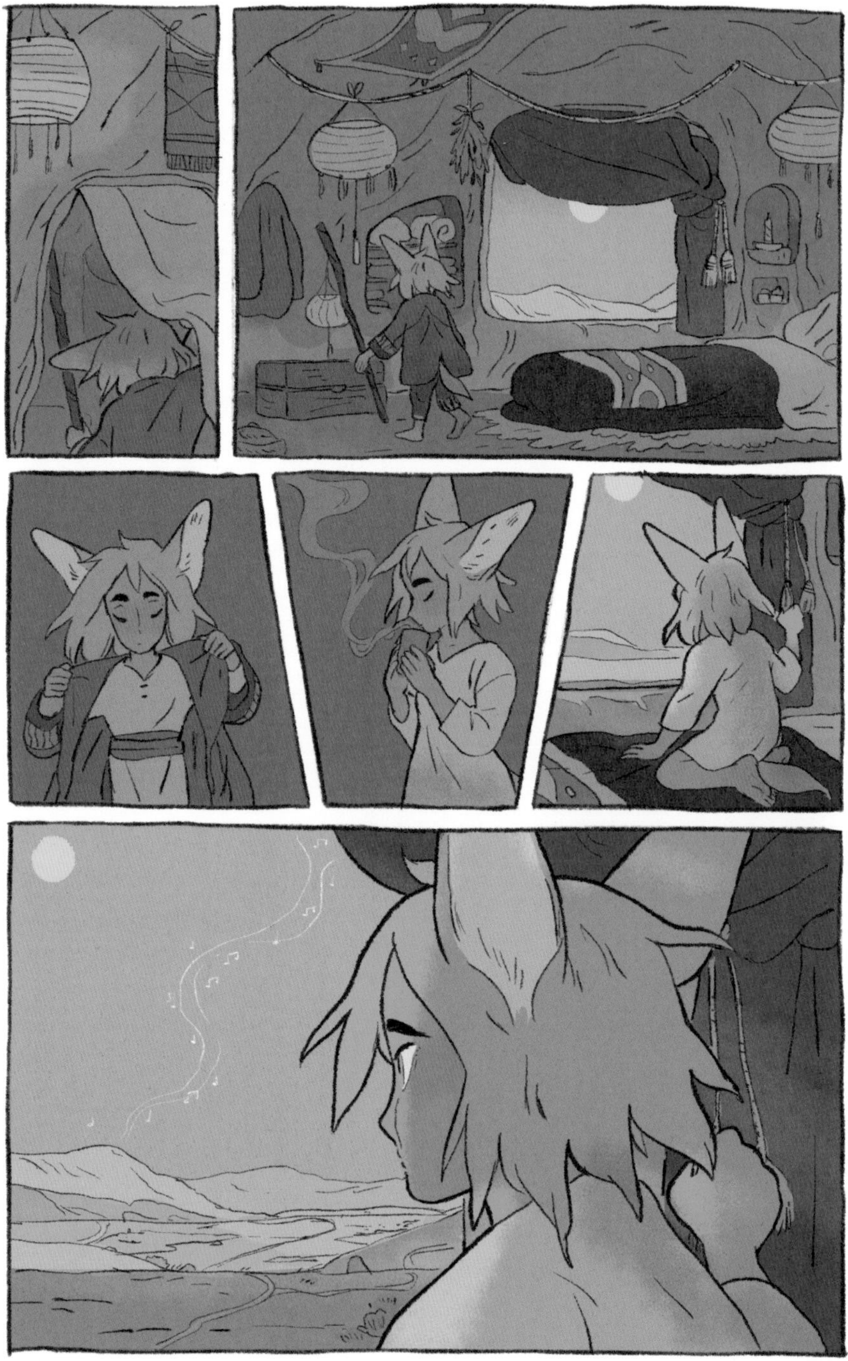

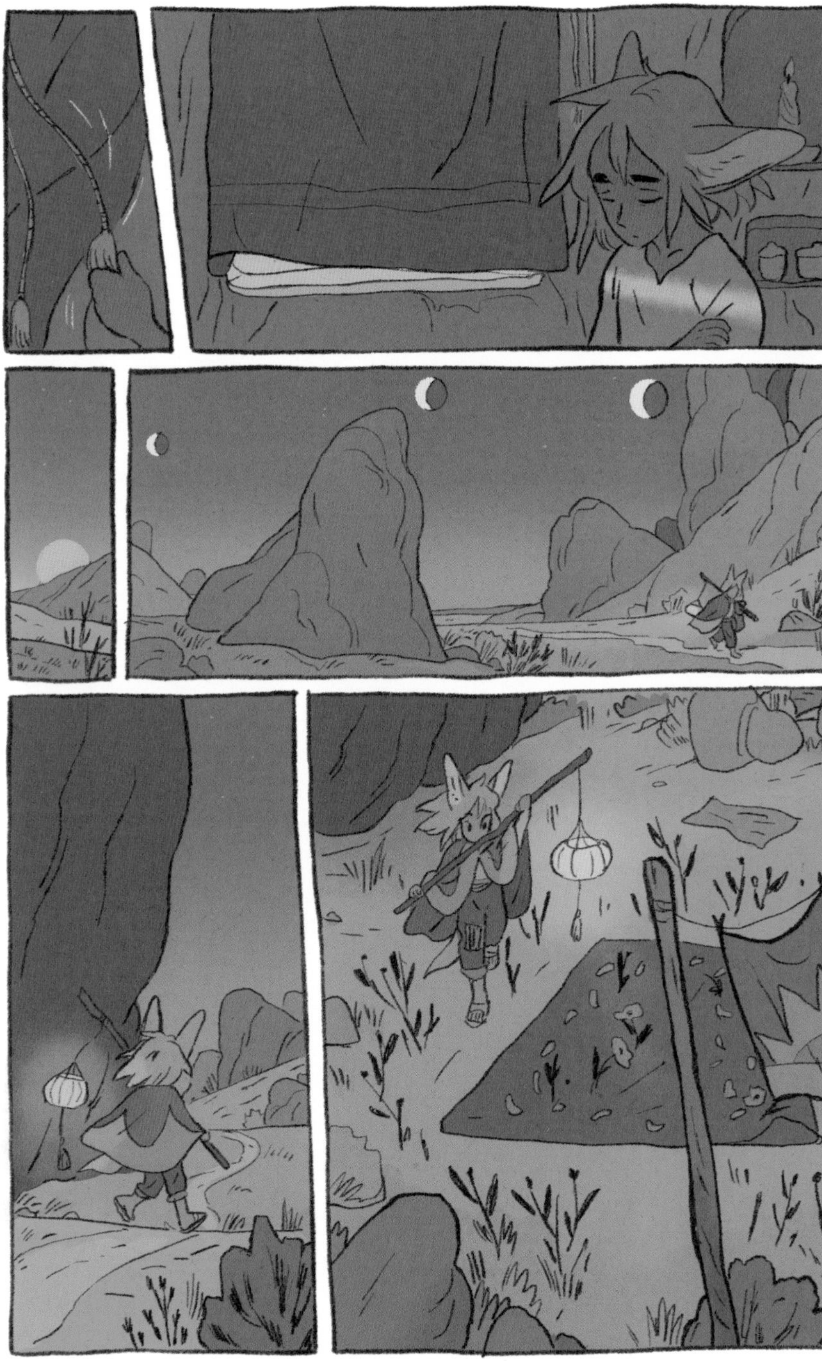

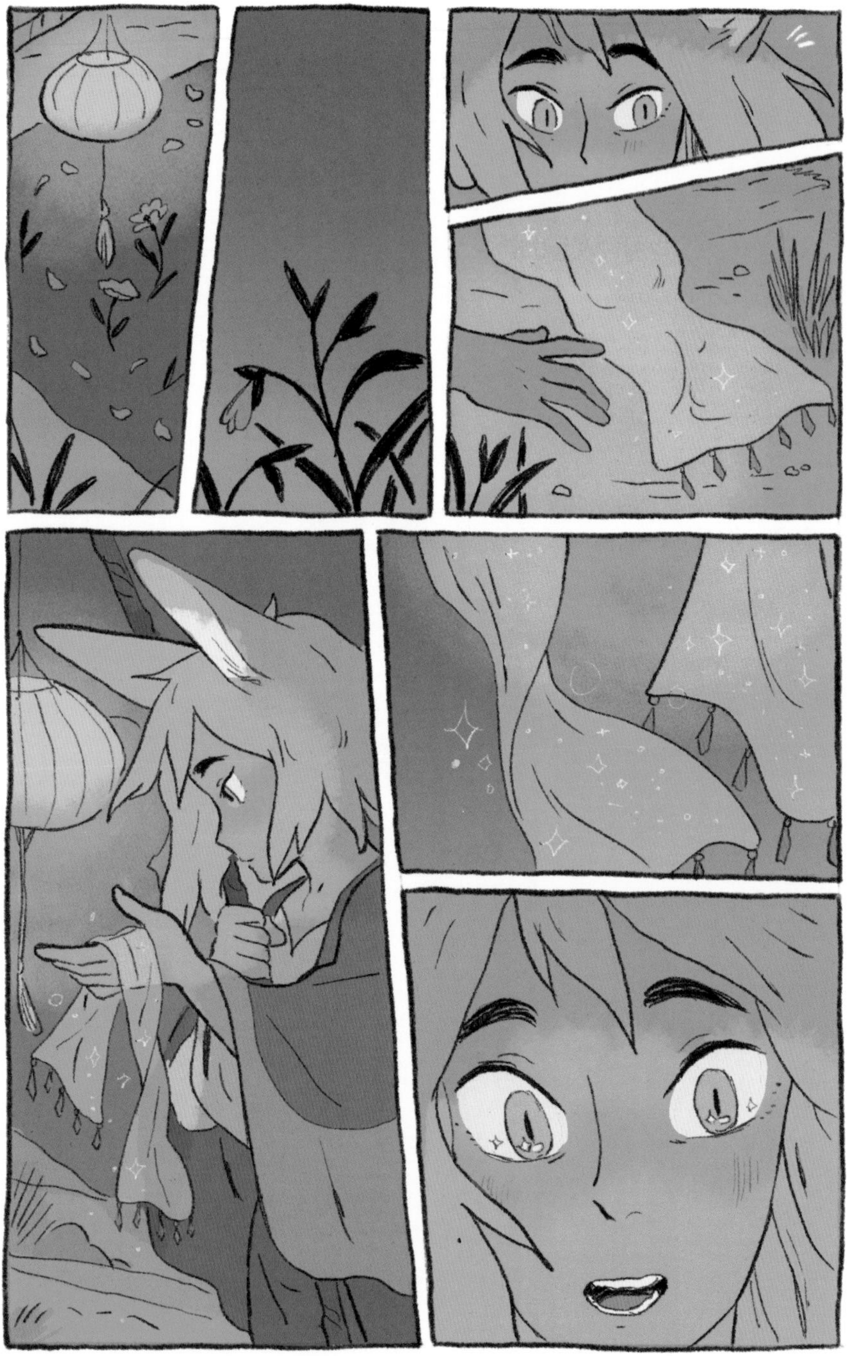

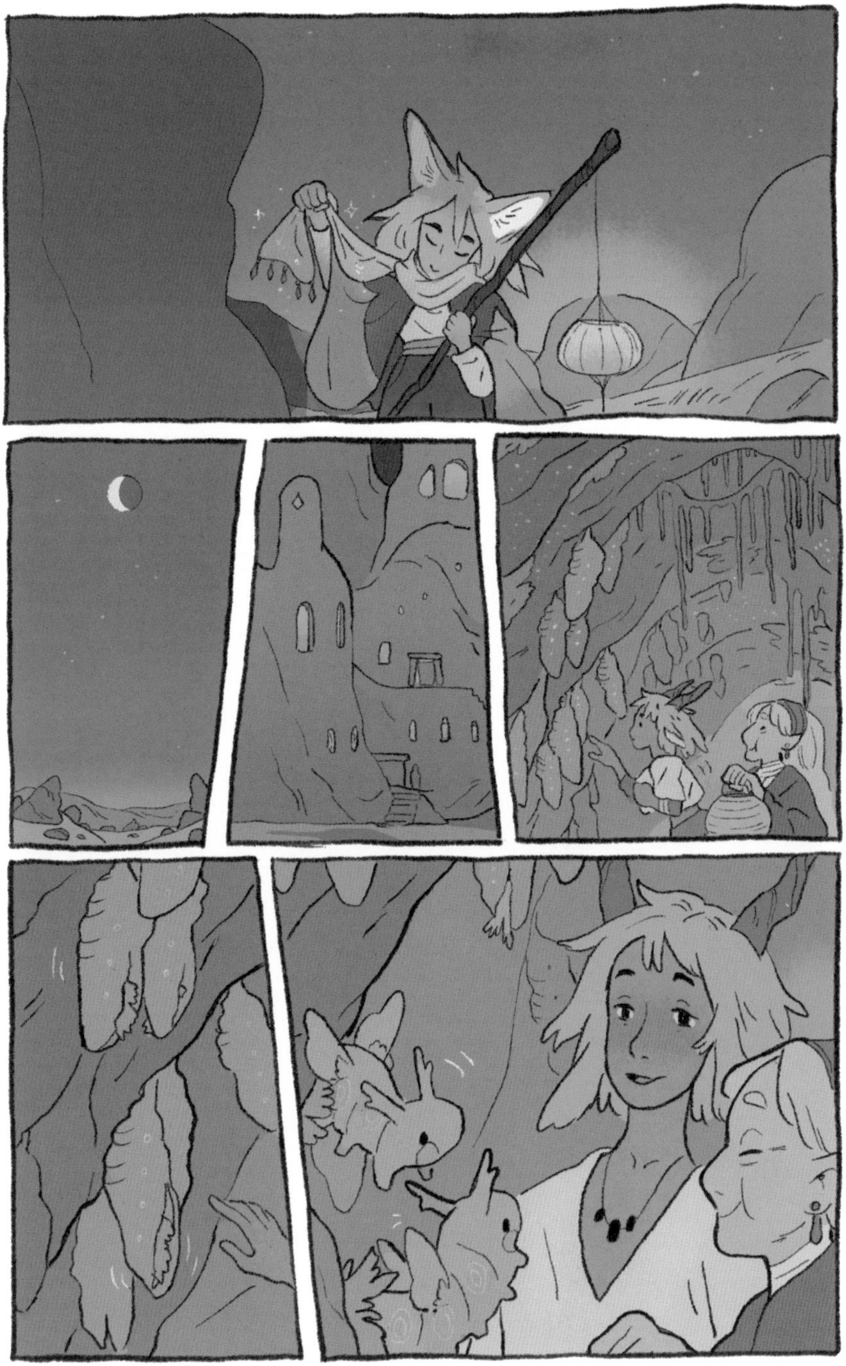

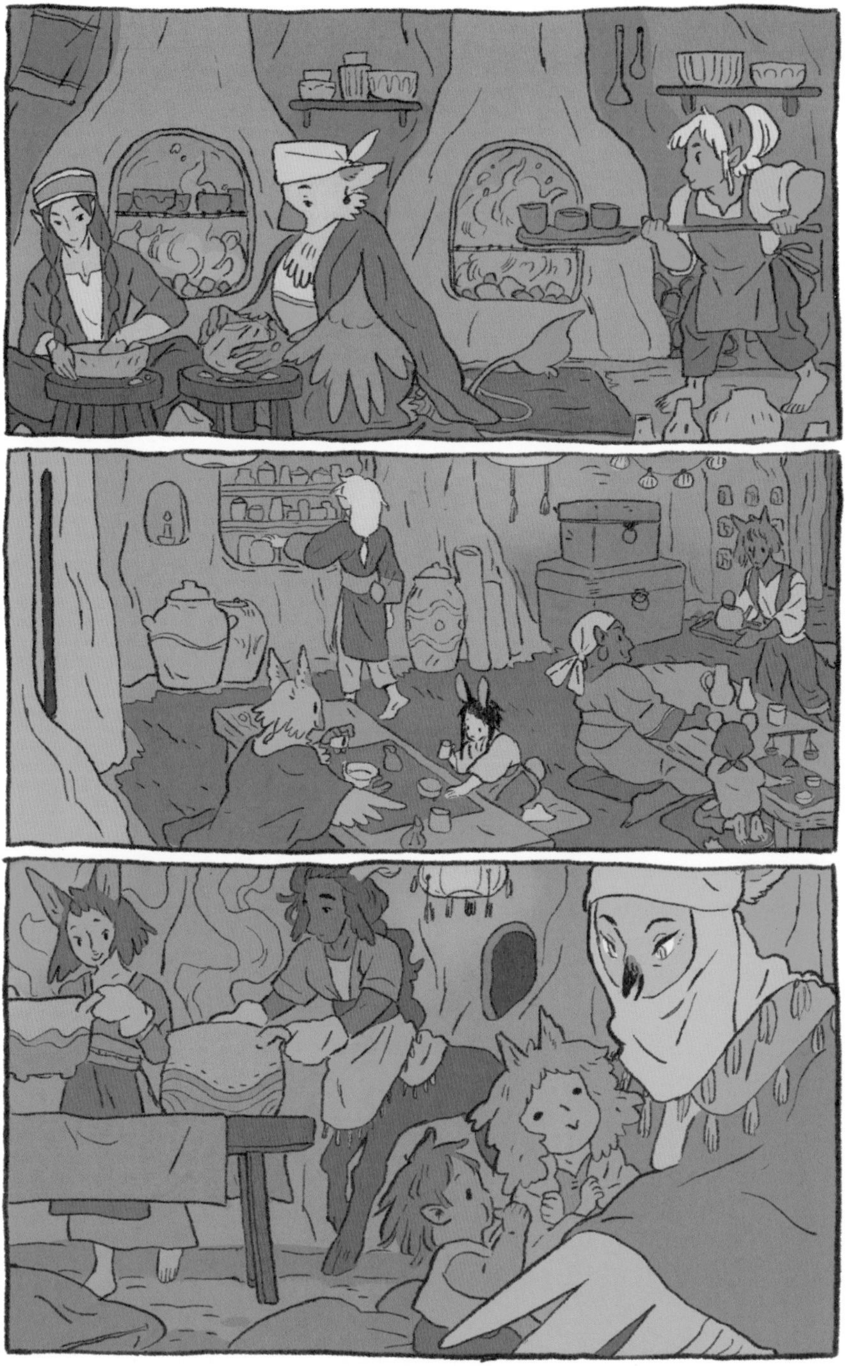

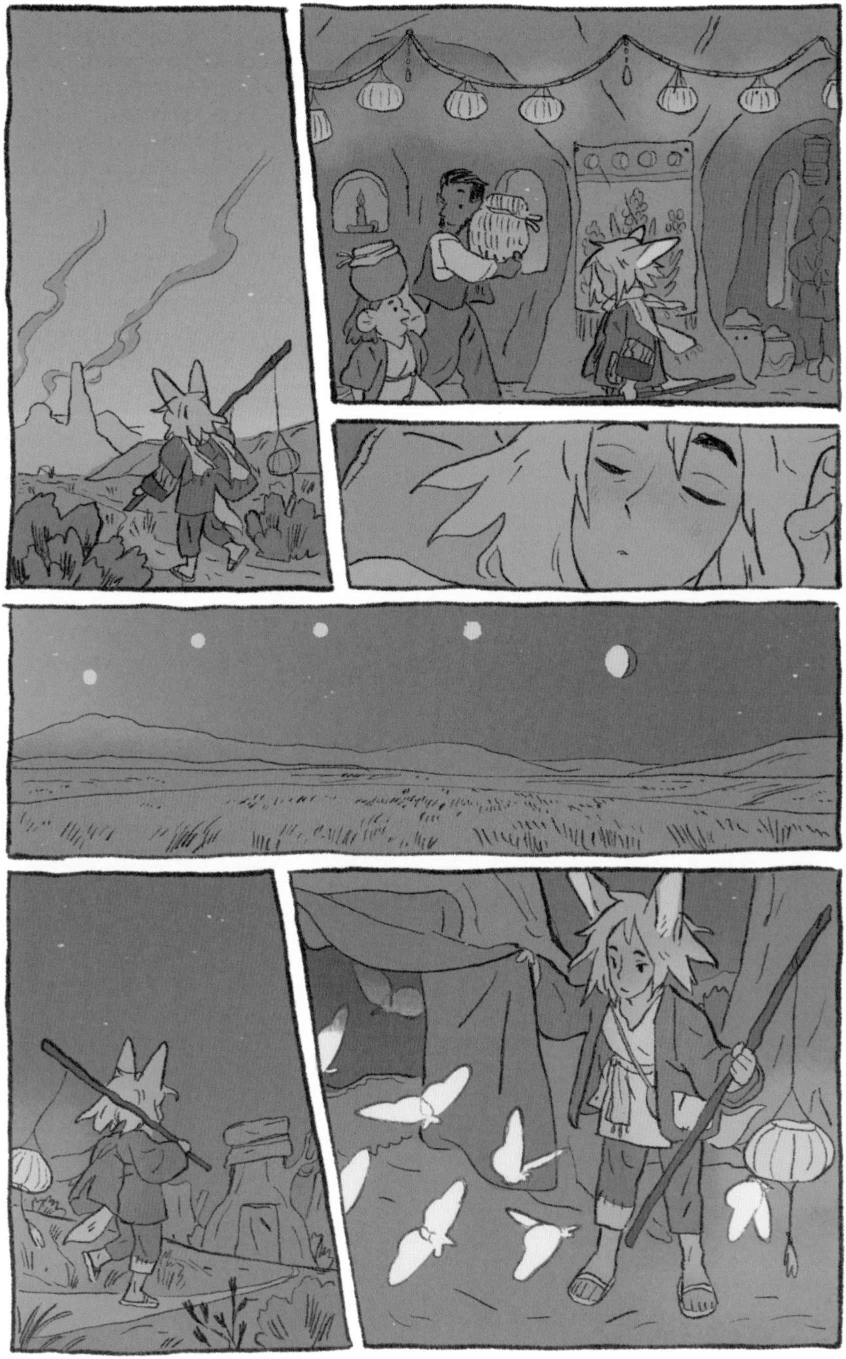

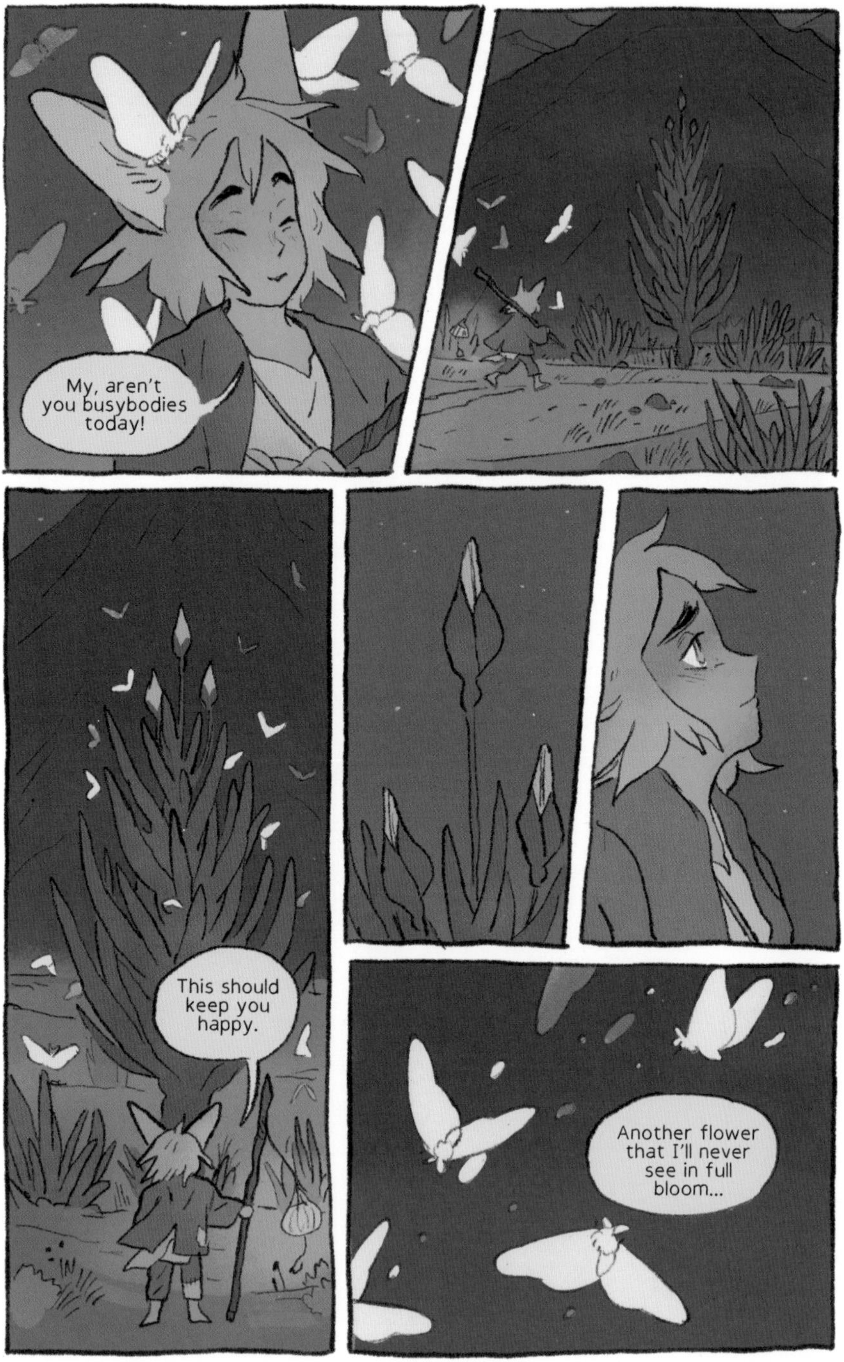
My, aren't you busybodies today!
This should keep you happy.
Another flower that I'll never see in full bloom...

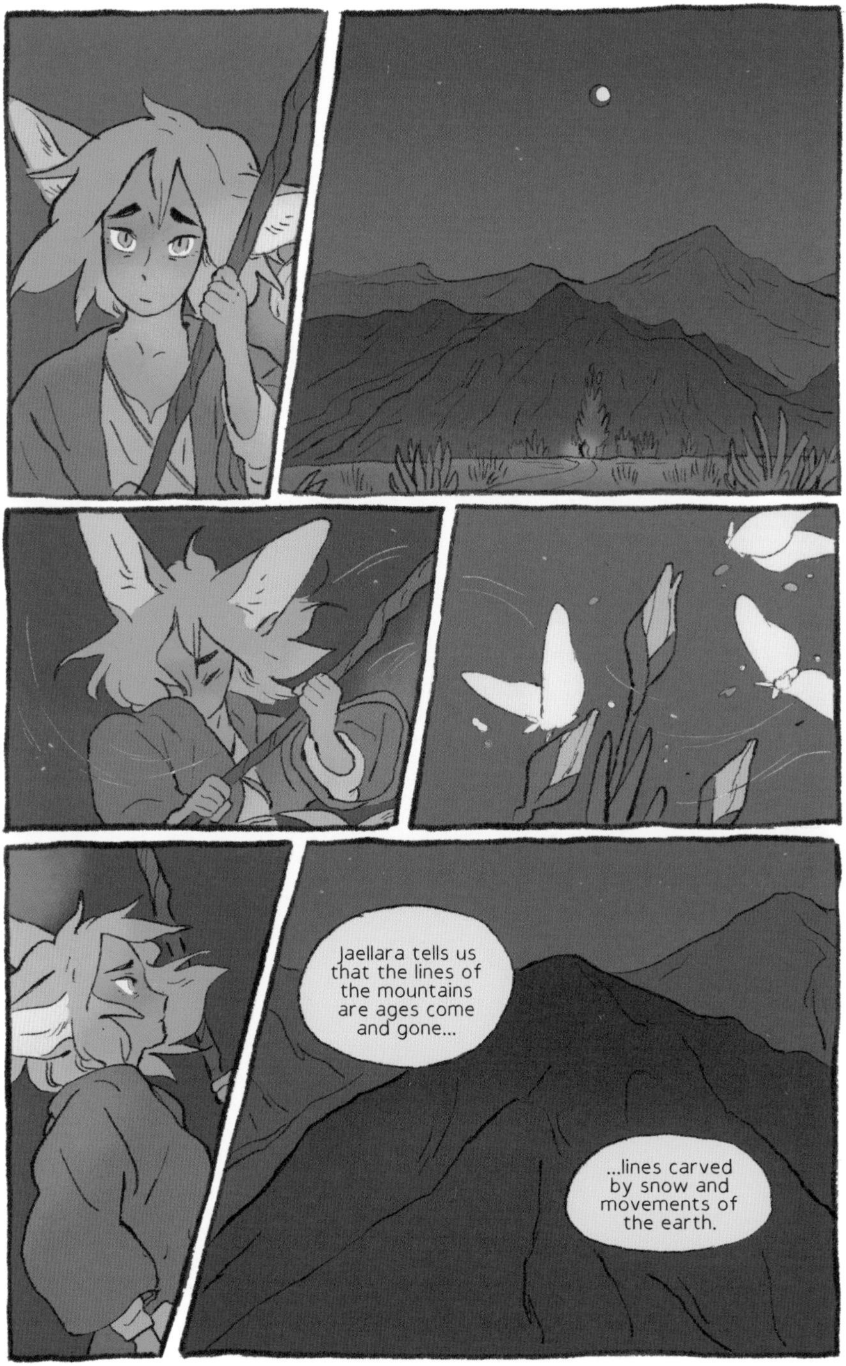
Jaellara tells us that the lines of the mountains are ages come and gone...
...lines carved by snow and movements of the earth.

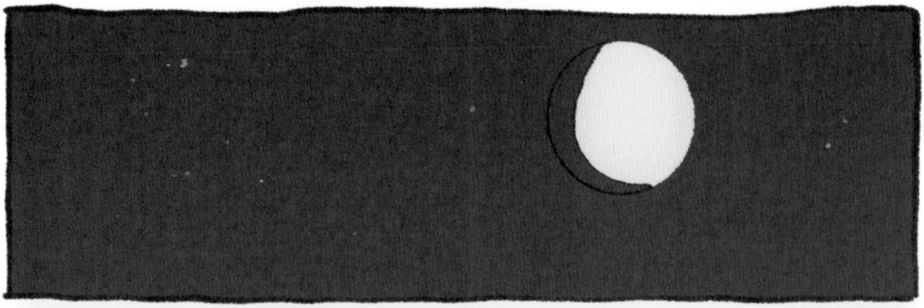

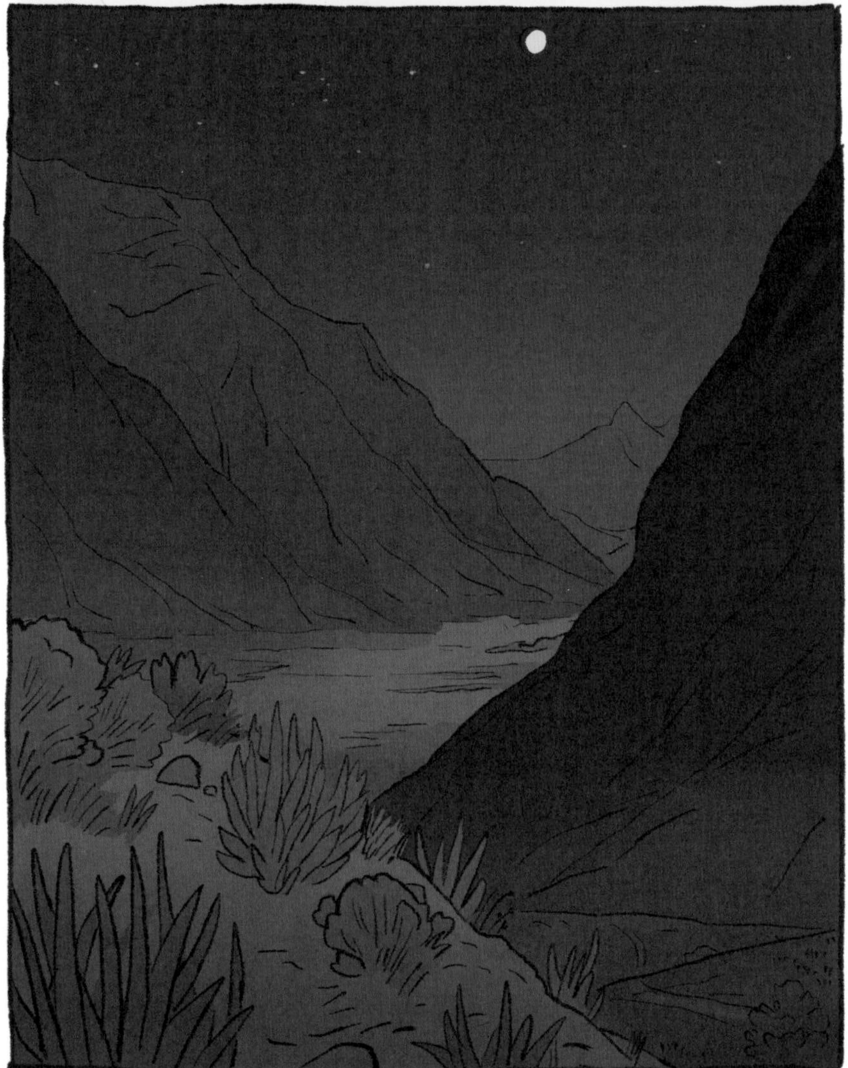

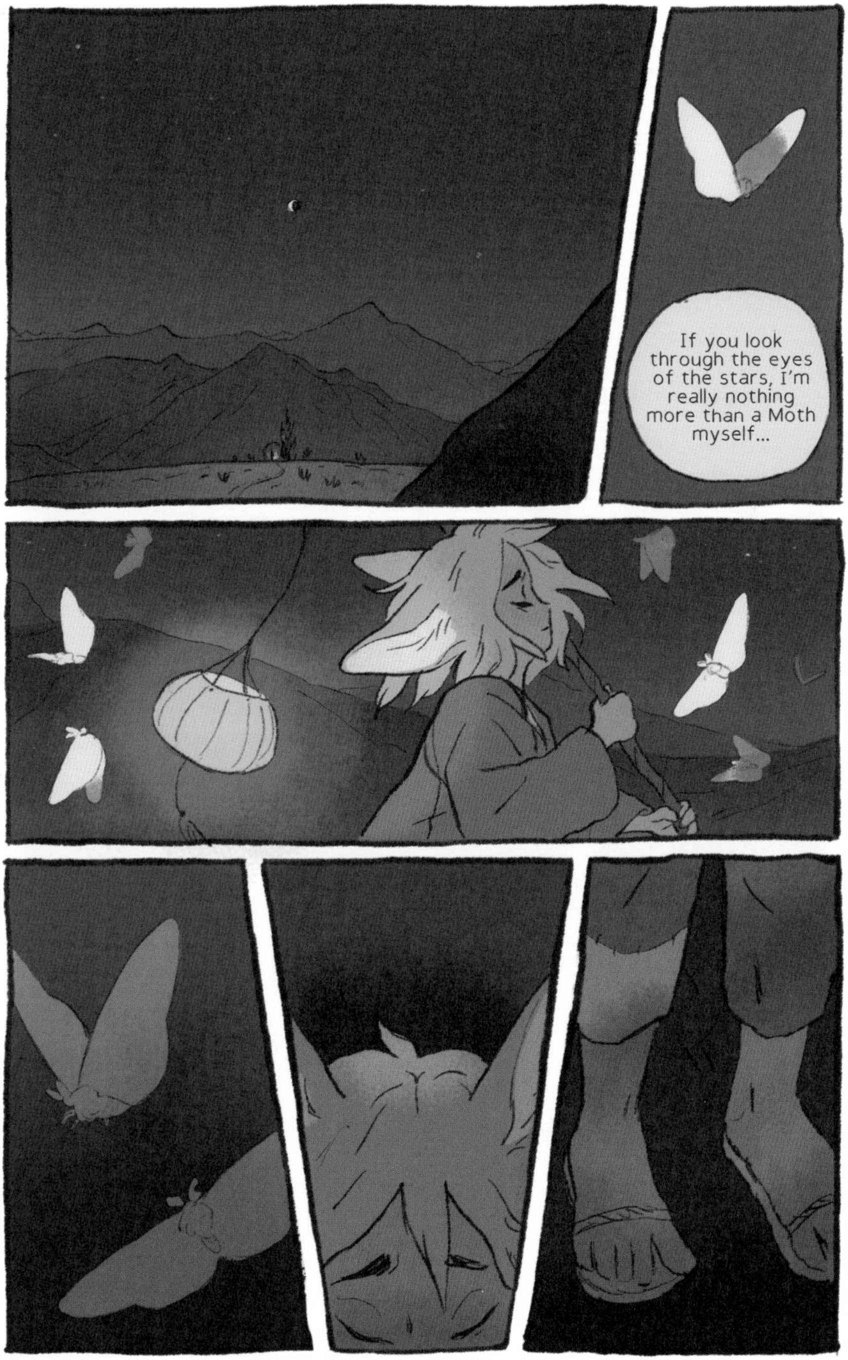
If you look through the eyes of the stars, I'm really nothing more than a Moth myself...

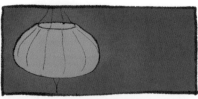

If my lantern went out right now...

...would I even exist anymore?

POF

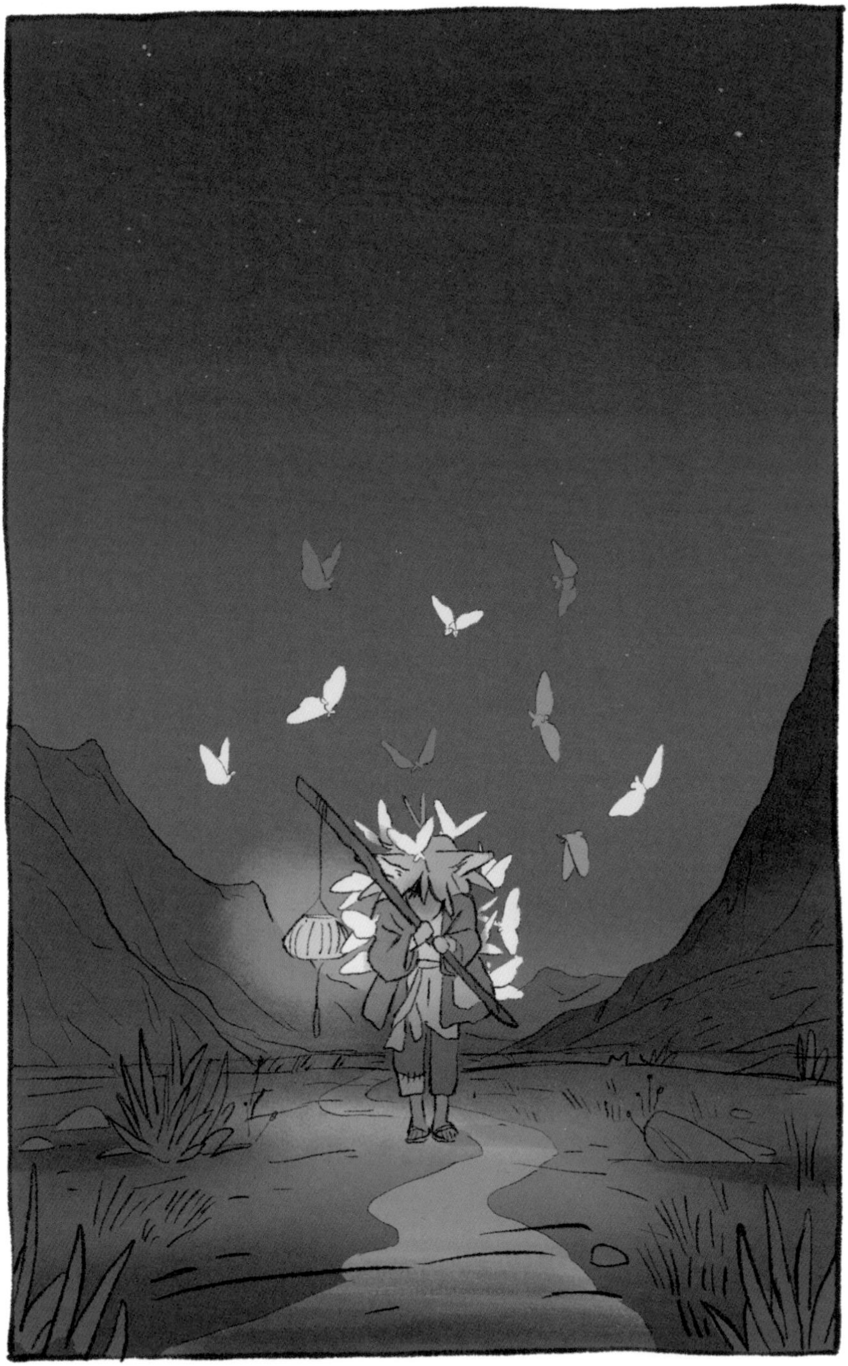

Chapter Four

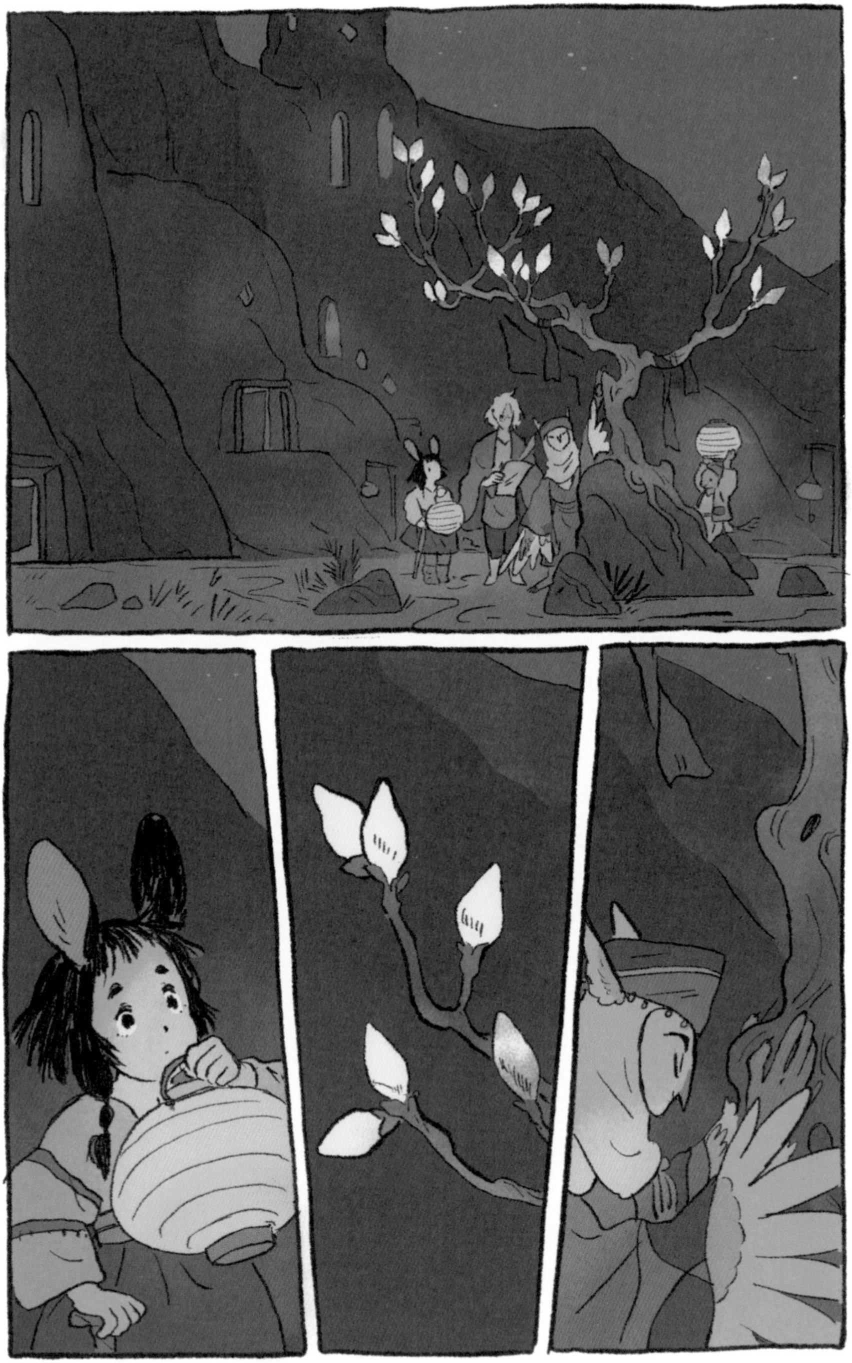

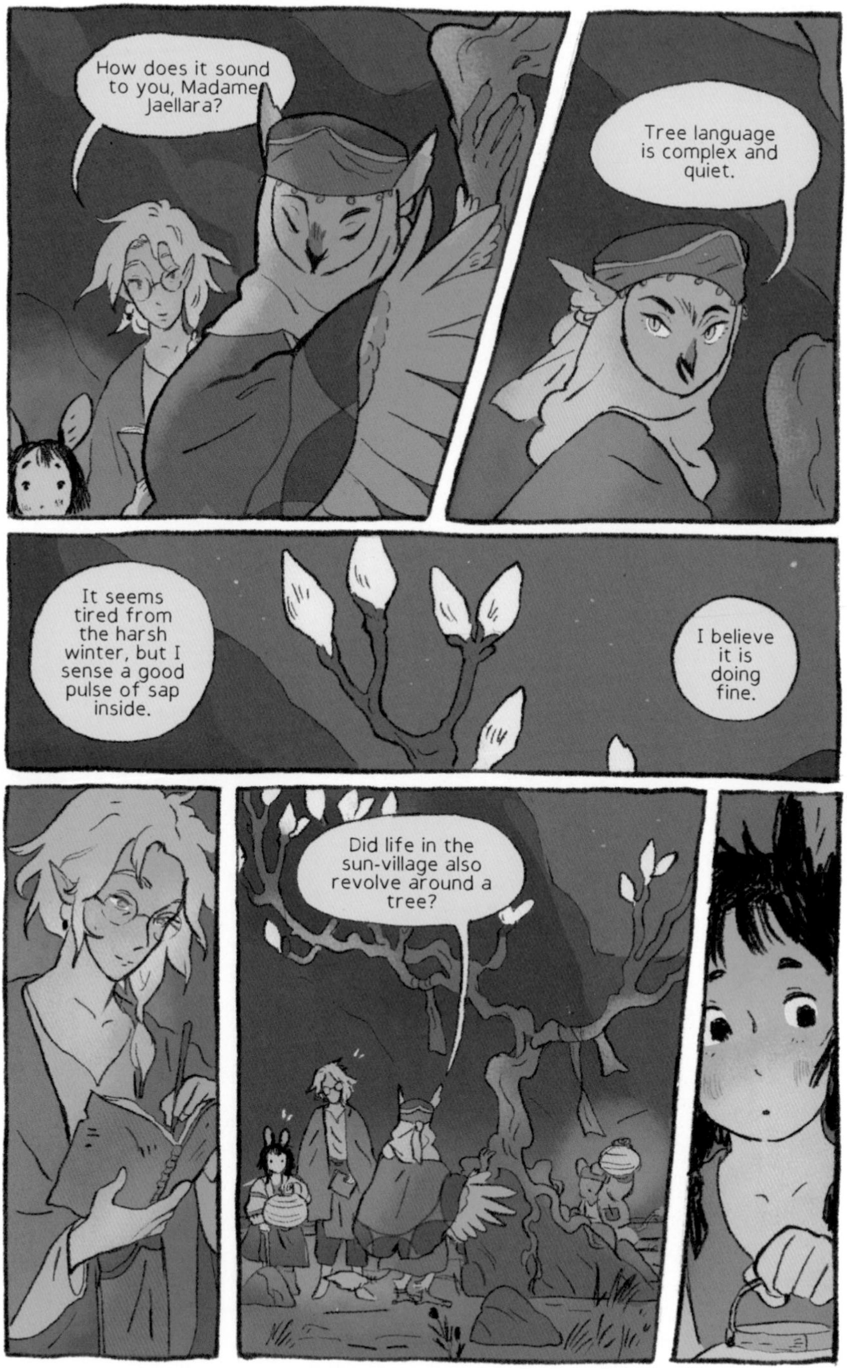
How does it sound to you, Madame Jaellara?
Tree language is complex and quiet.
It seems tired from the harsh winter, but I sense a good pulse of sap inside.
I believe it is doing fine.
Did life in the sun-village also revolve around a tree?

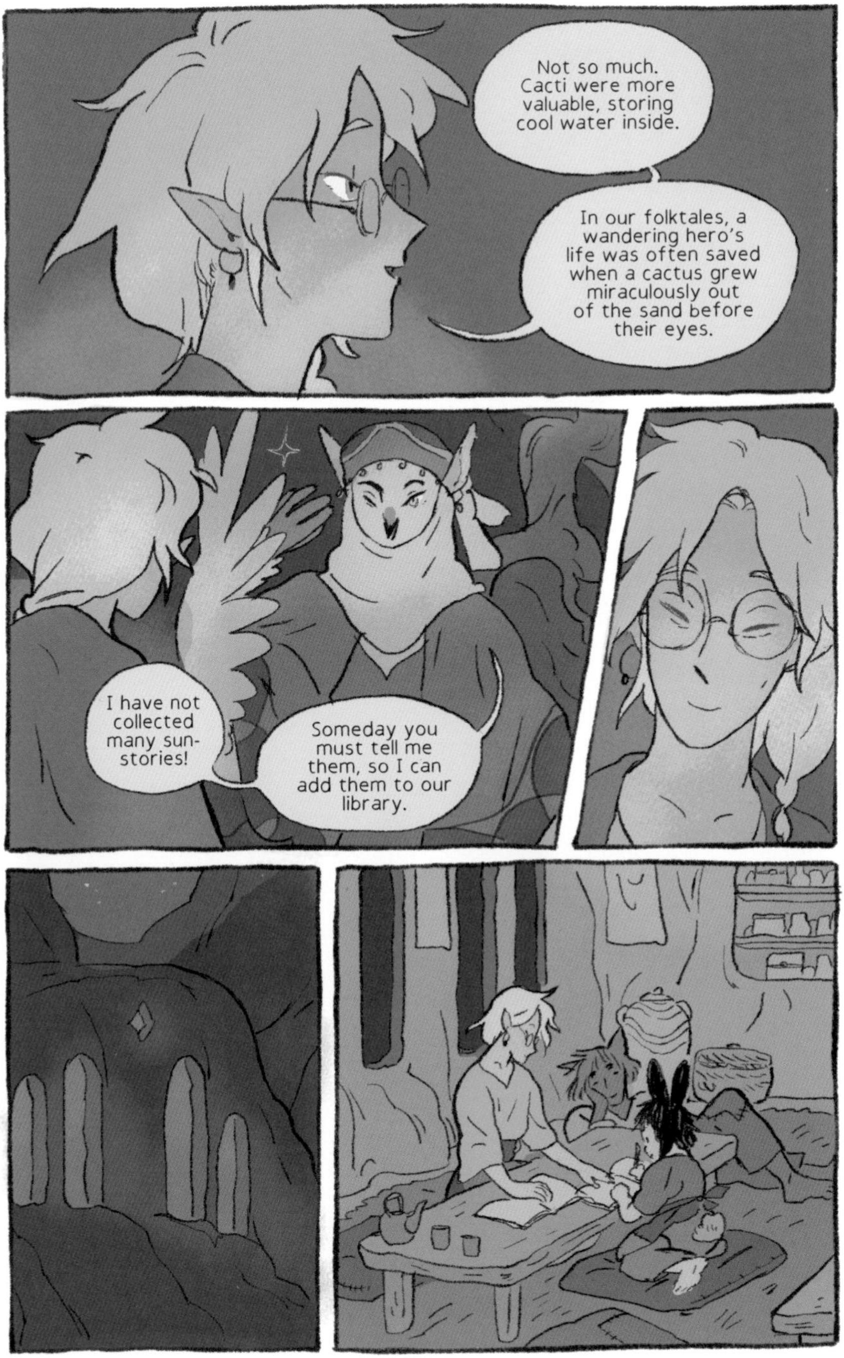
Not so much. Cacti were more valuable, storing cool water inside.
In our folktales, a wandering hero's life was often saved when a cactus grew miraculously out of the sand before their eyes.
I have not collected many sun-stories!
Someday you must tell me them, so I can add them to our library.

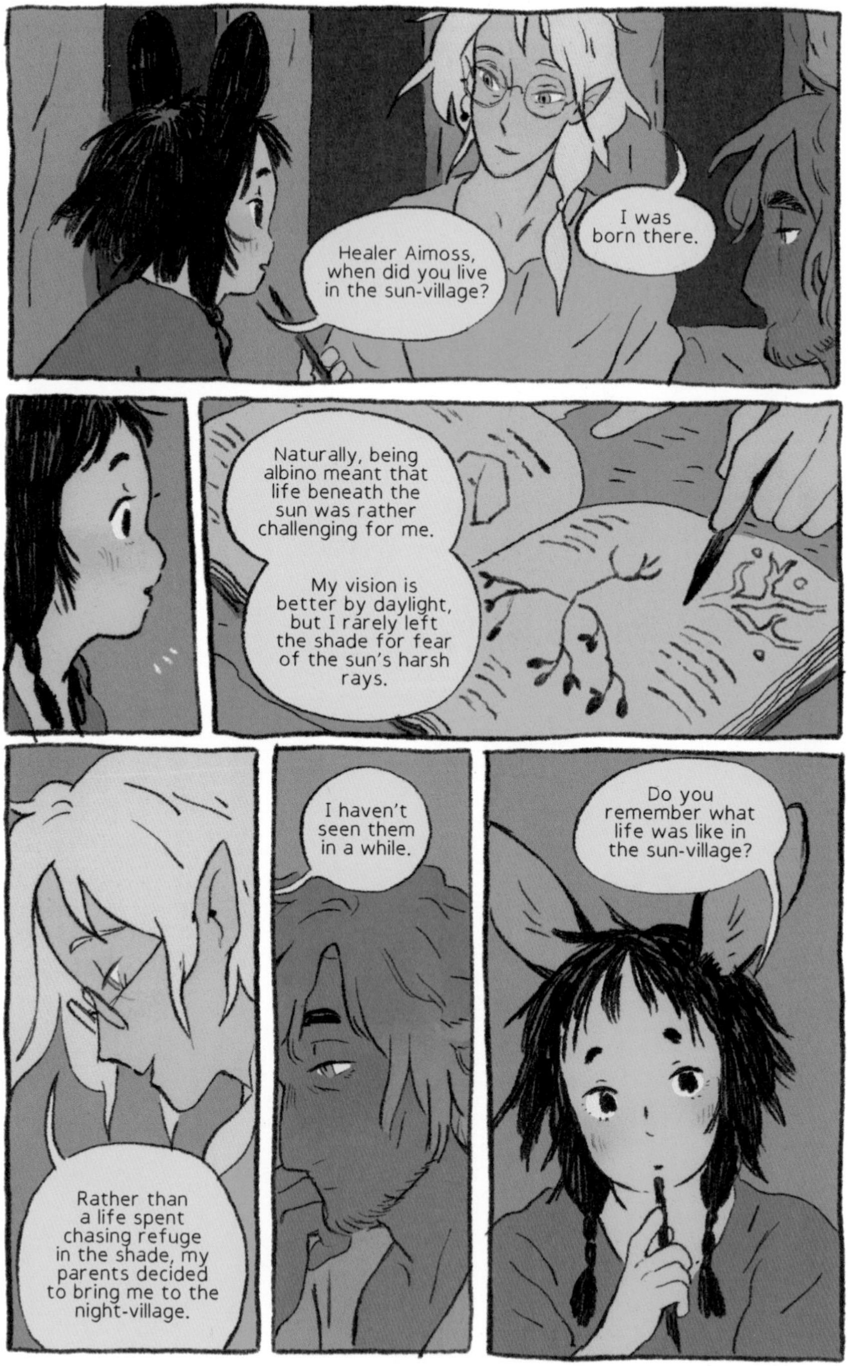
Healer Aimoss, when did you live in the sun-village?
I was born there.
Naturally, being albino meant that life beneath the sun was rather challenging for me.
My vision is better by daylight, but I rarely left the shade for fear of the sun's harsh rays.
Rather than a life spent chasing refuge in the shade, my parents decided to bring me to the night-village.
I haven't seen them in a while.
Do you remember what life was like in the sun-village?

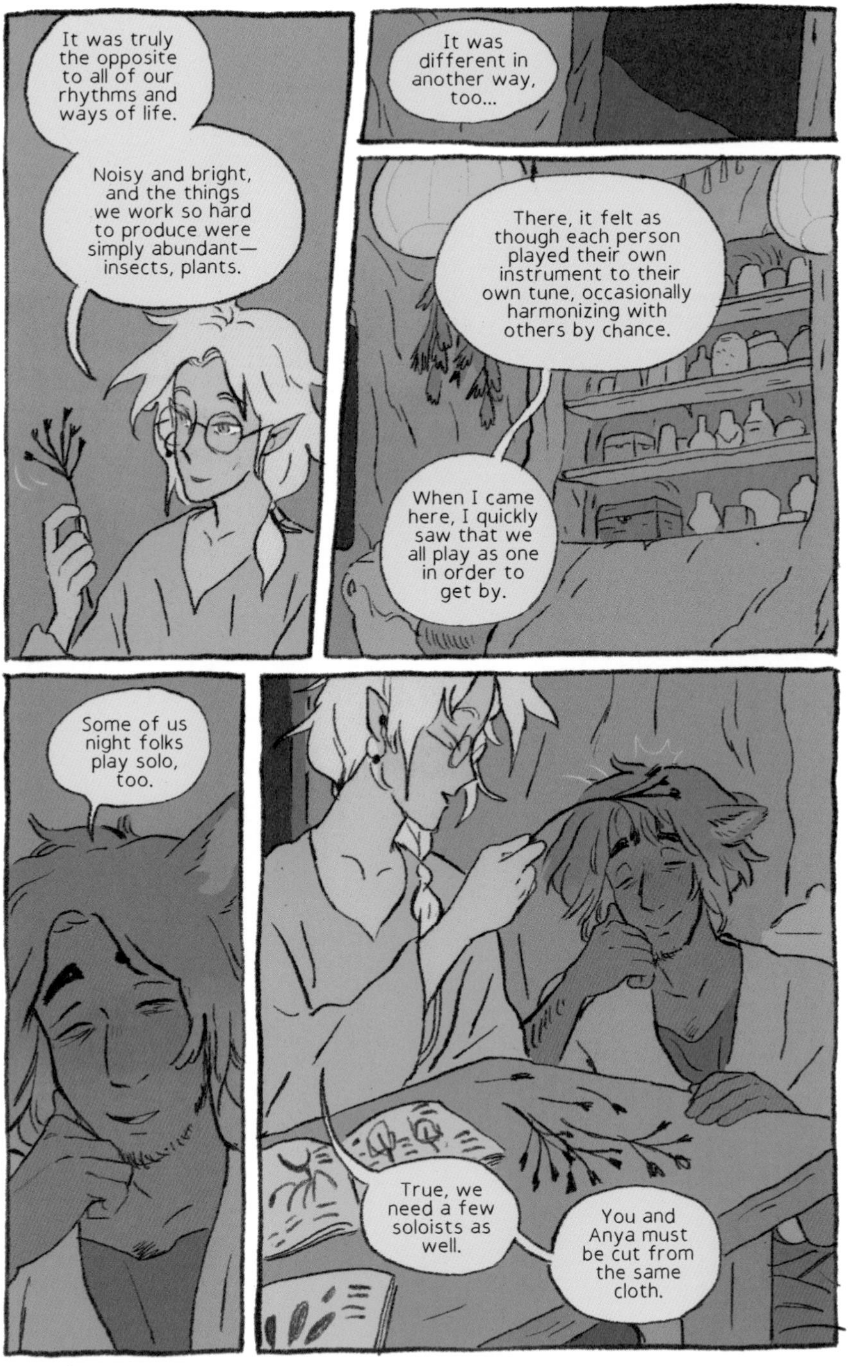
It was truly the opposite to all of our rhythms and ways of life.
Noisy and bright, and the things we work so hard to produce were simply abundant—insects, plants.
It was different in another way, too...
There, it felt as though each person played their own instrument to their own tune, occasionally harmonizing with others by chance.
When I came here, I quickly saw that we all play as one in order to get by.
Some of us night folks play solo, too.
True, we need a few soloists as well.
You and Anya must be cut from the same cloth.

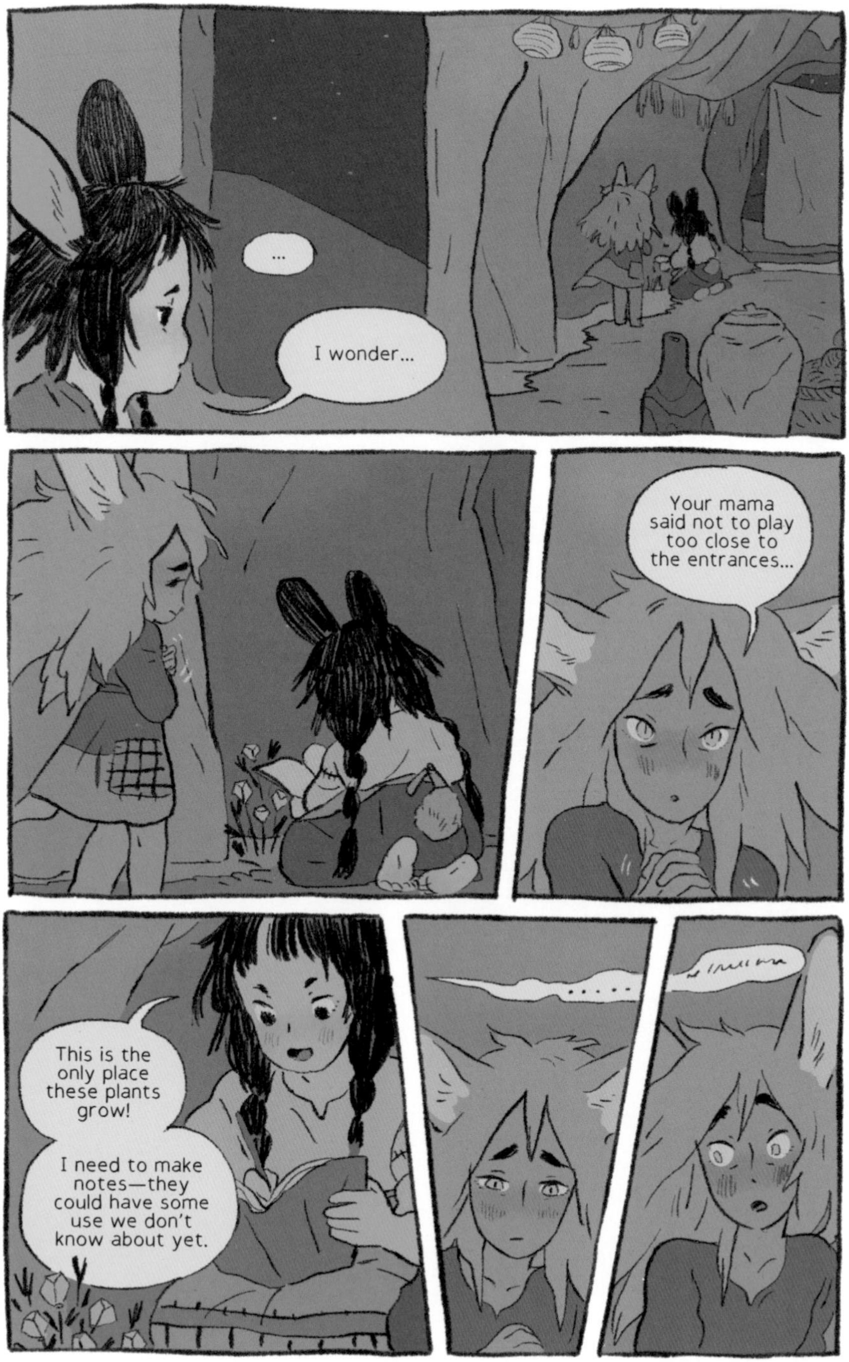
...
I wonder...
Your mama said not to play too close to the entrances...
This is the only place these plants grow!
I need to make notes—they could have some use we don't know about yet.
.....

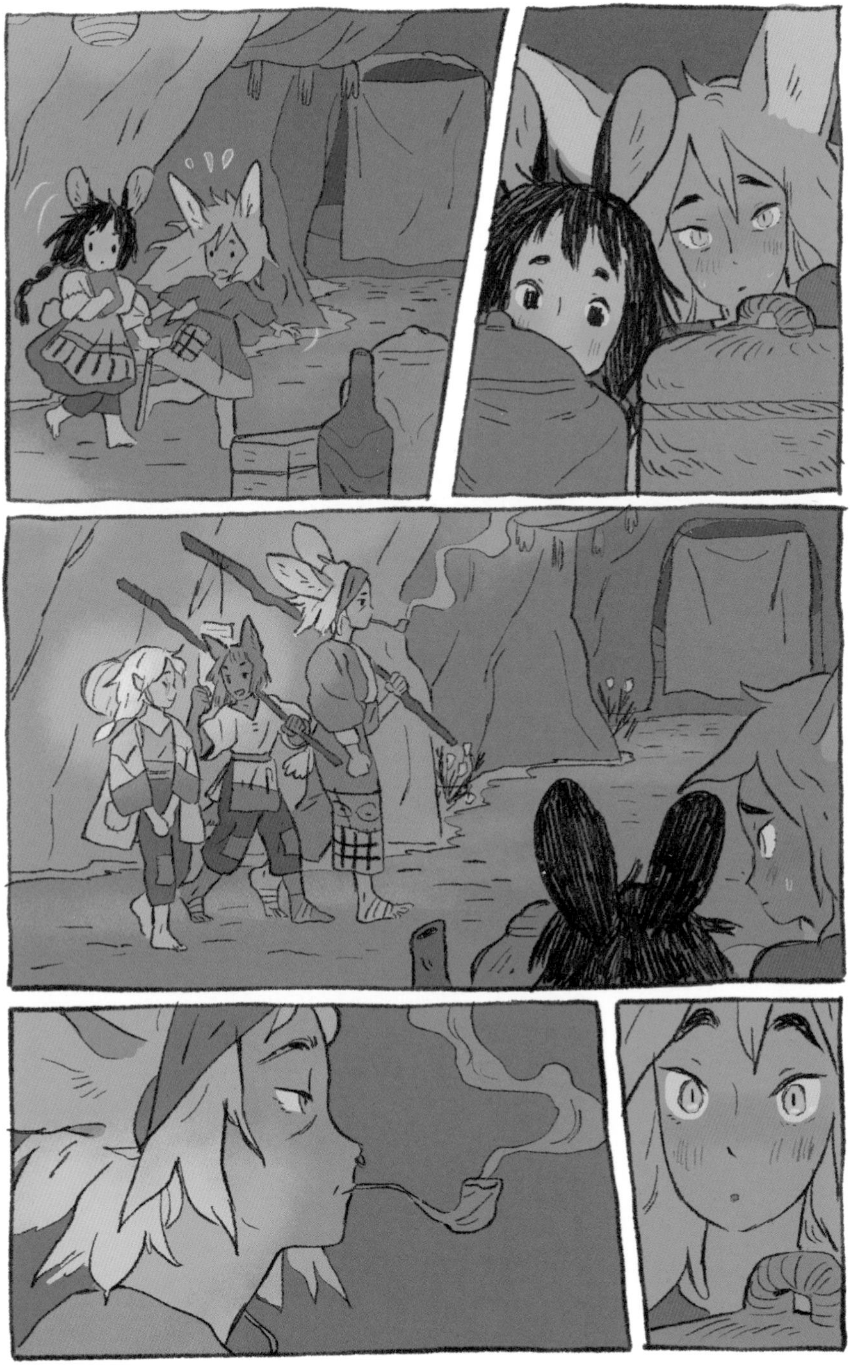

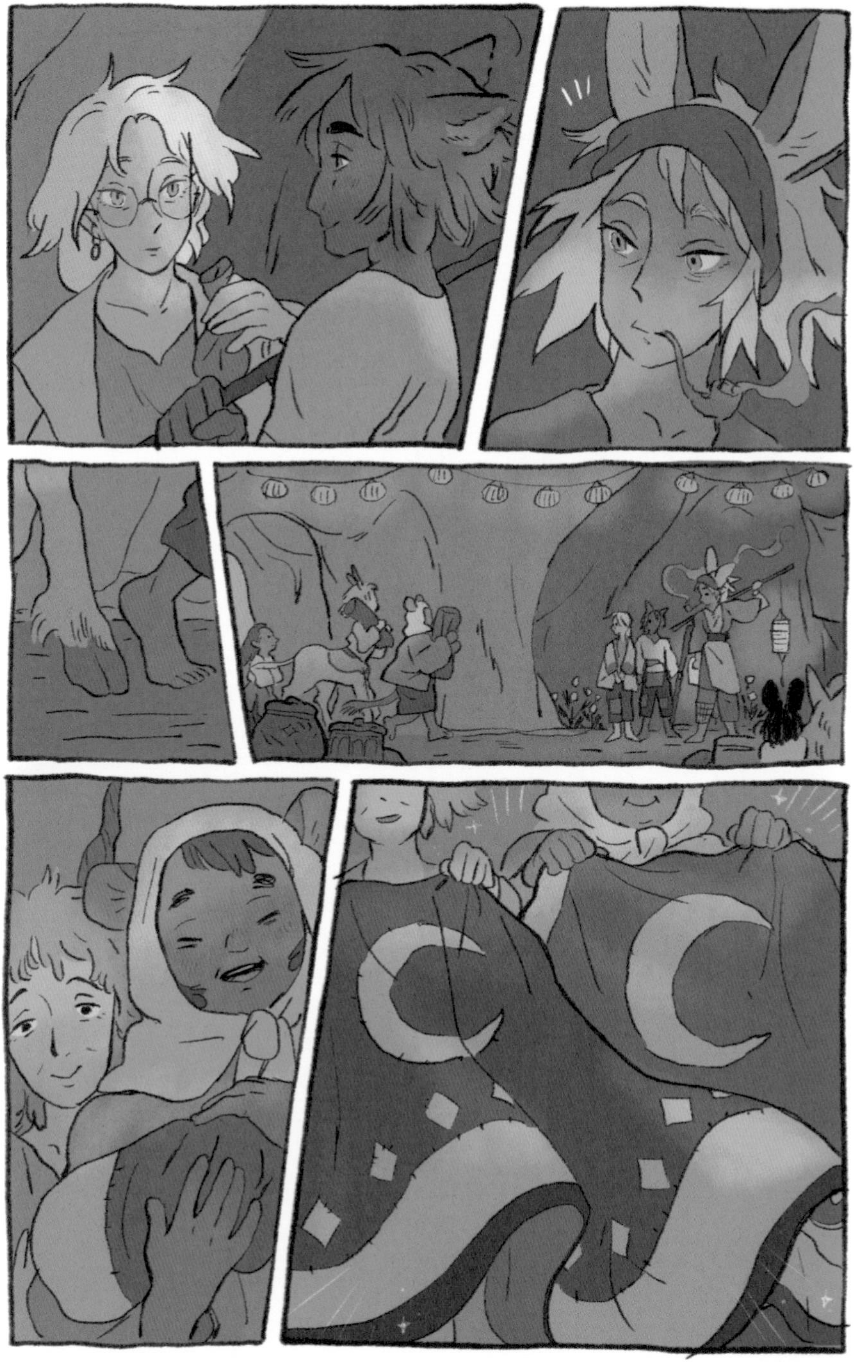

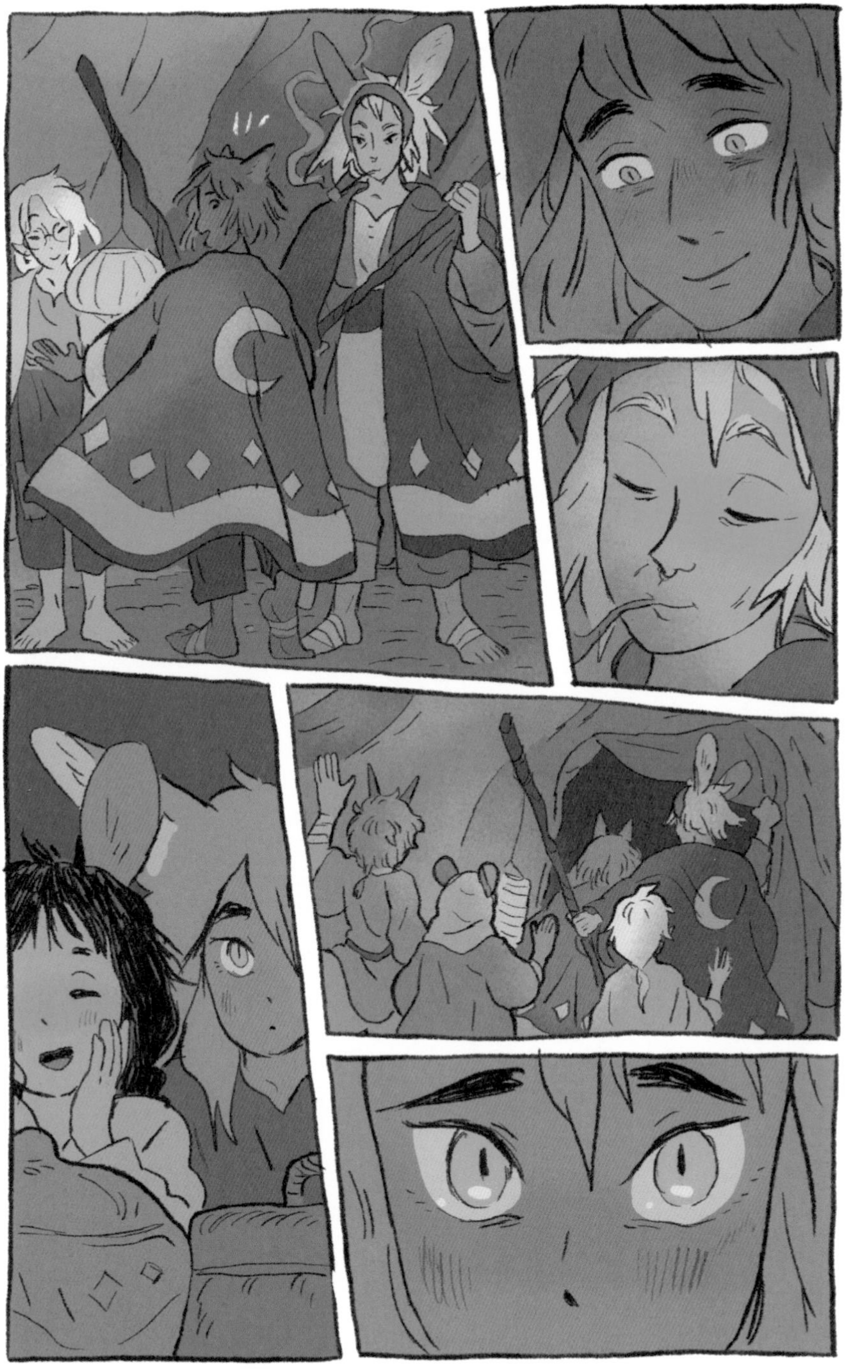

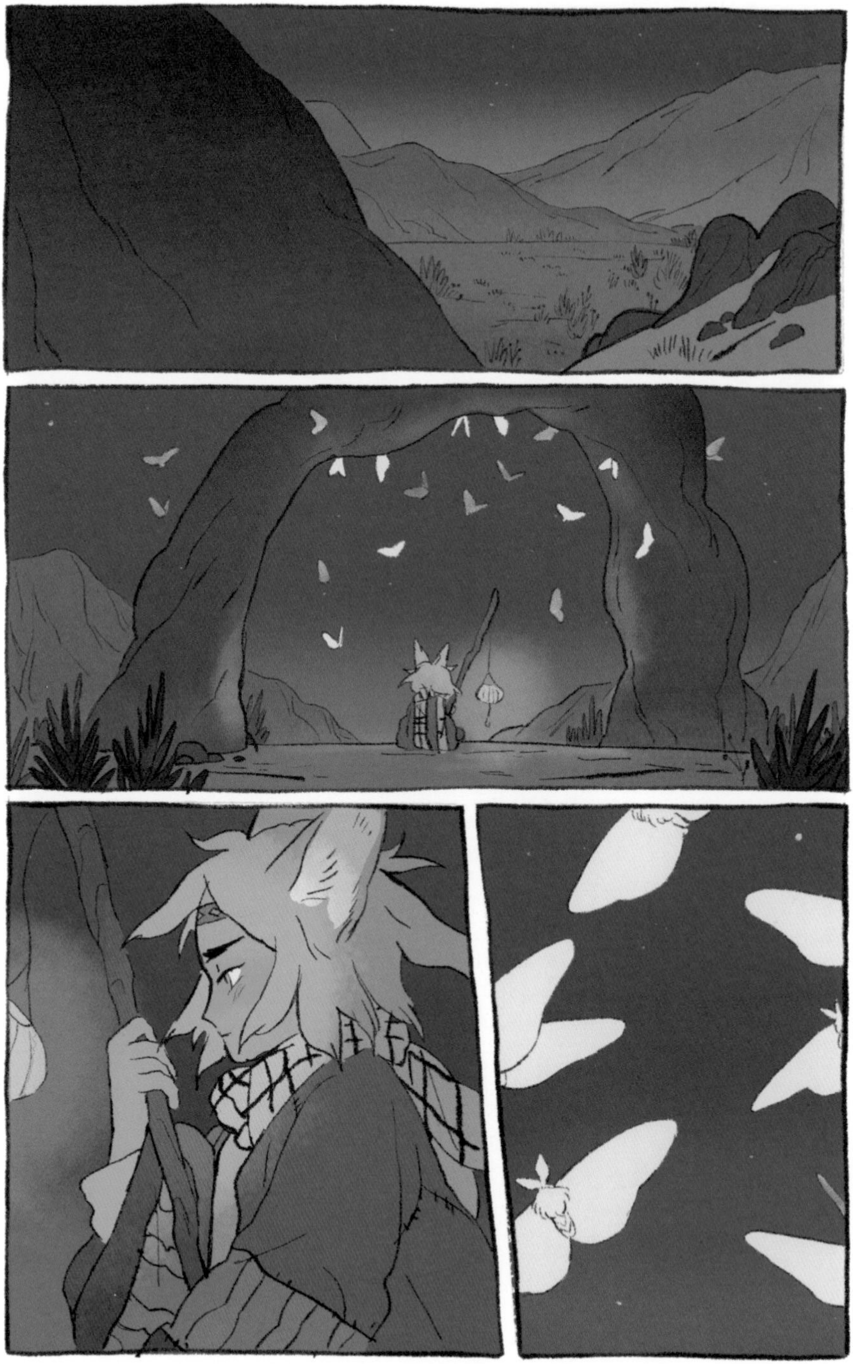

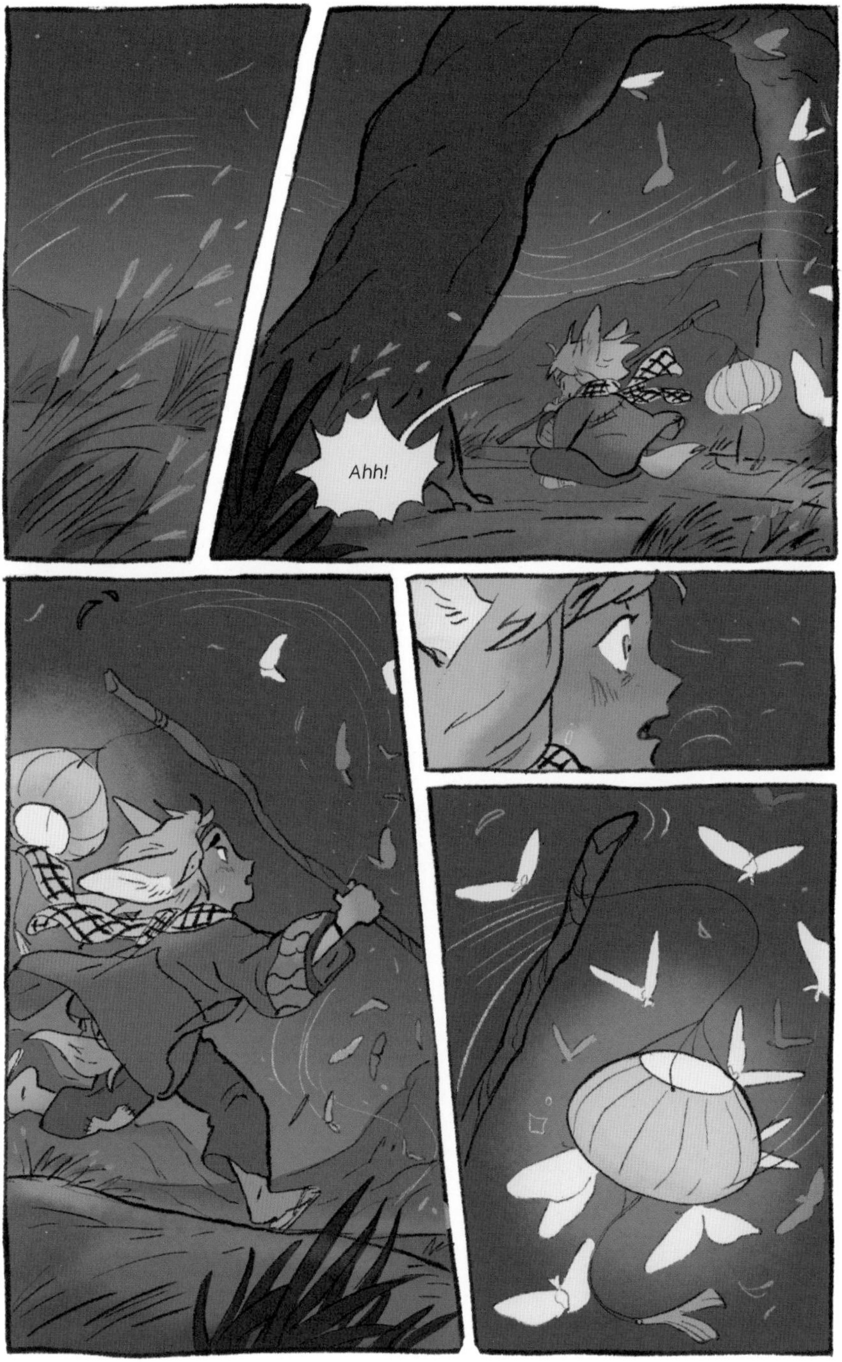
Ahh!

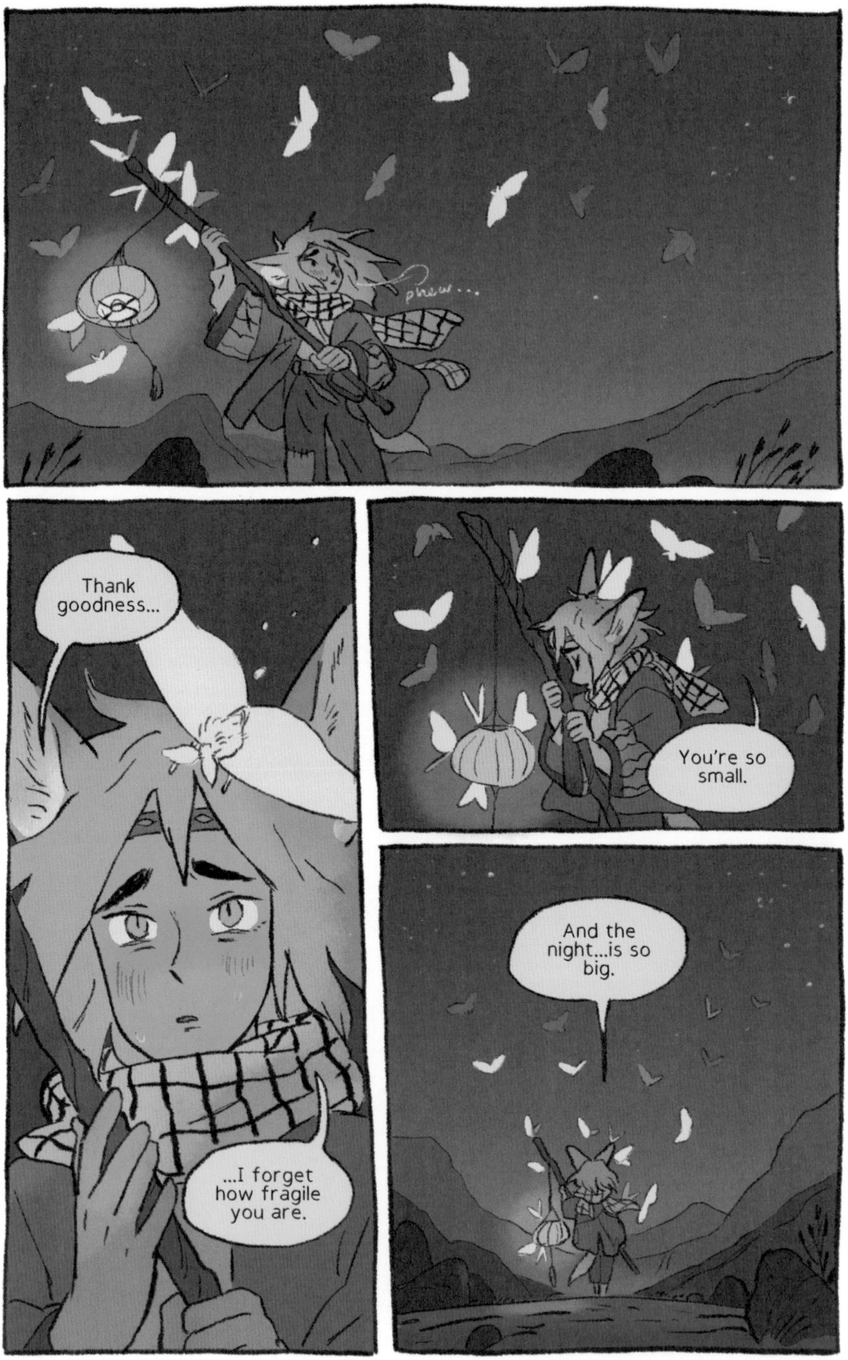
phew...
Thank goodness...
...I forget how fragile you are.
You're so small.
And the night...is so big.

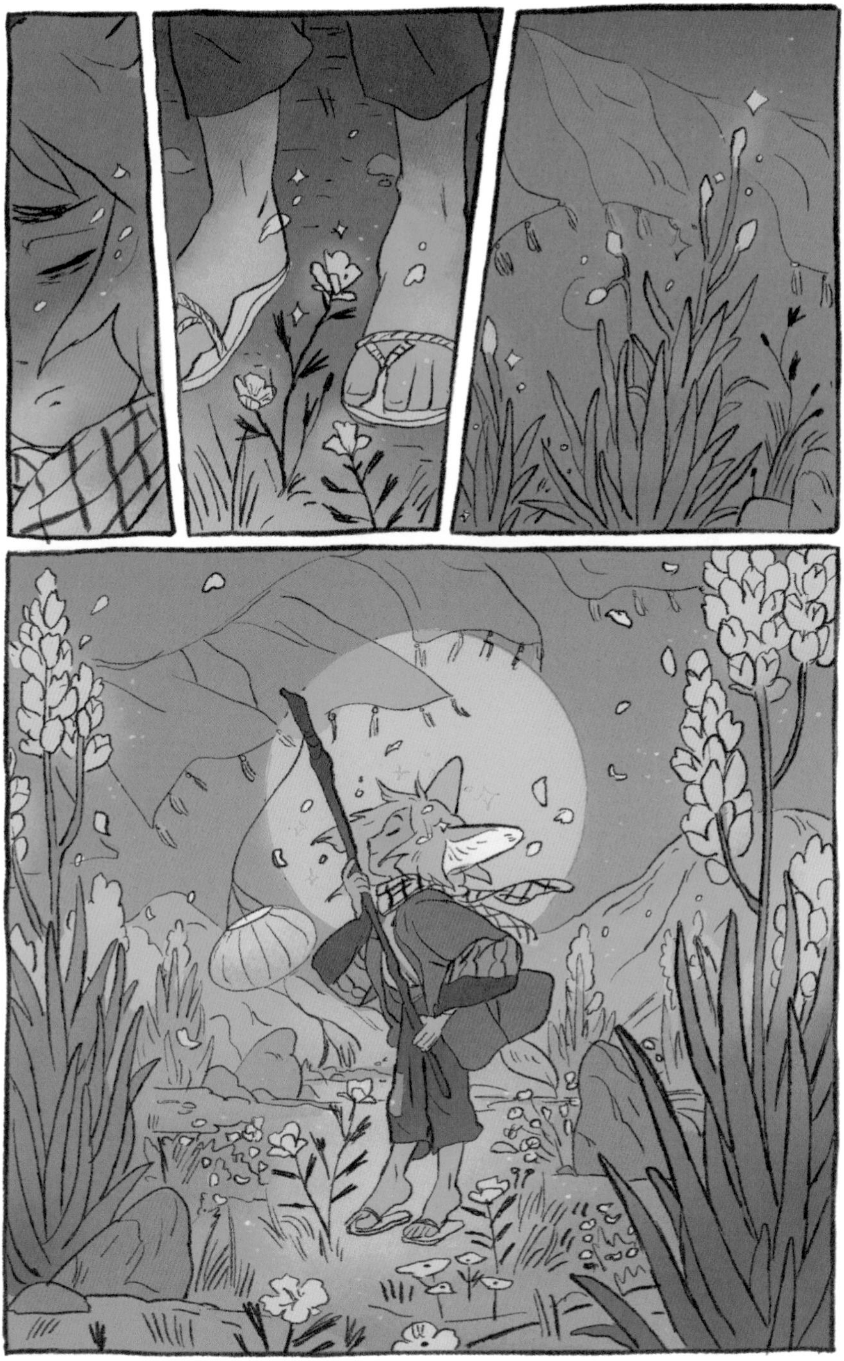

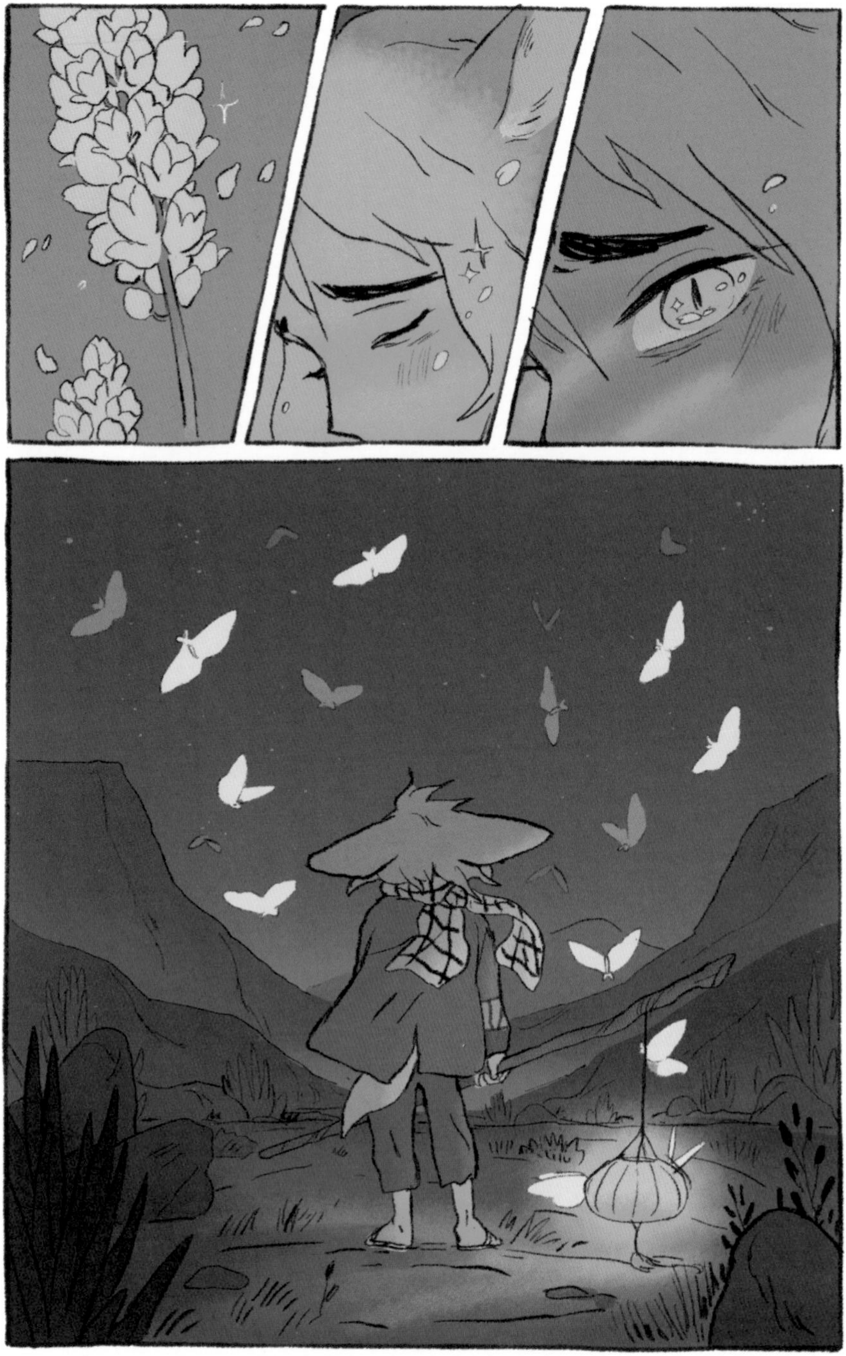

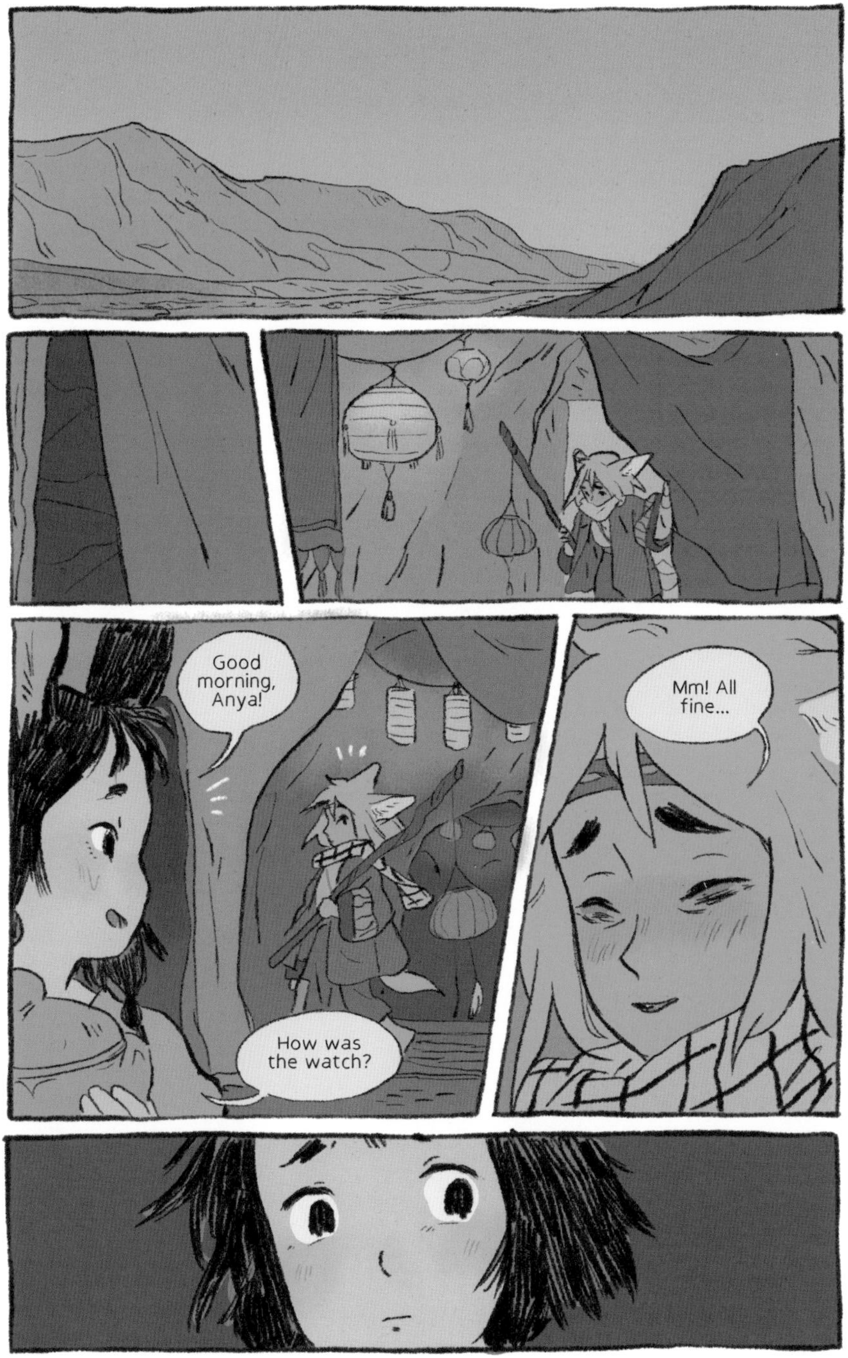
Good morning, Anya!
How was the watch?
Mm! All fine...

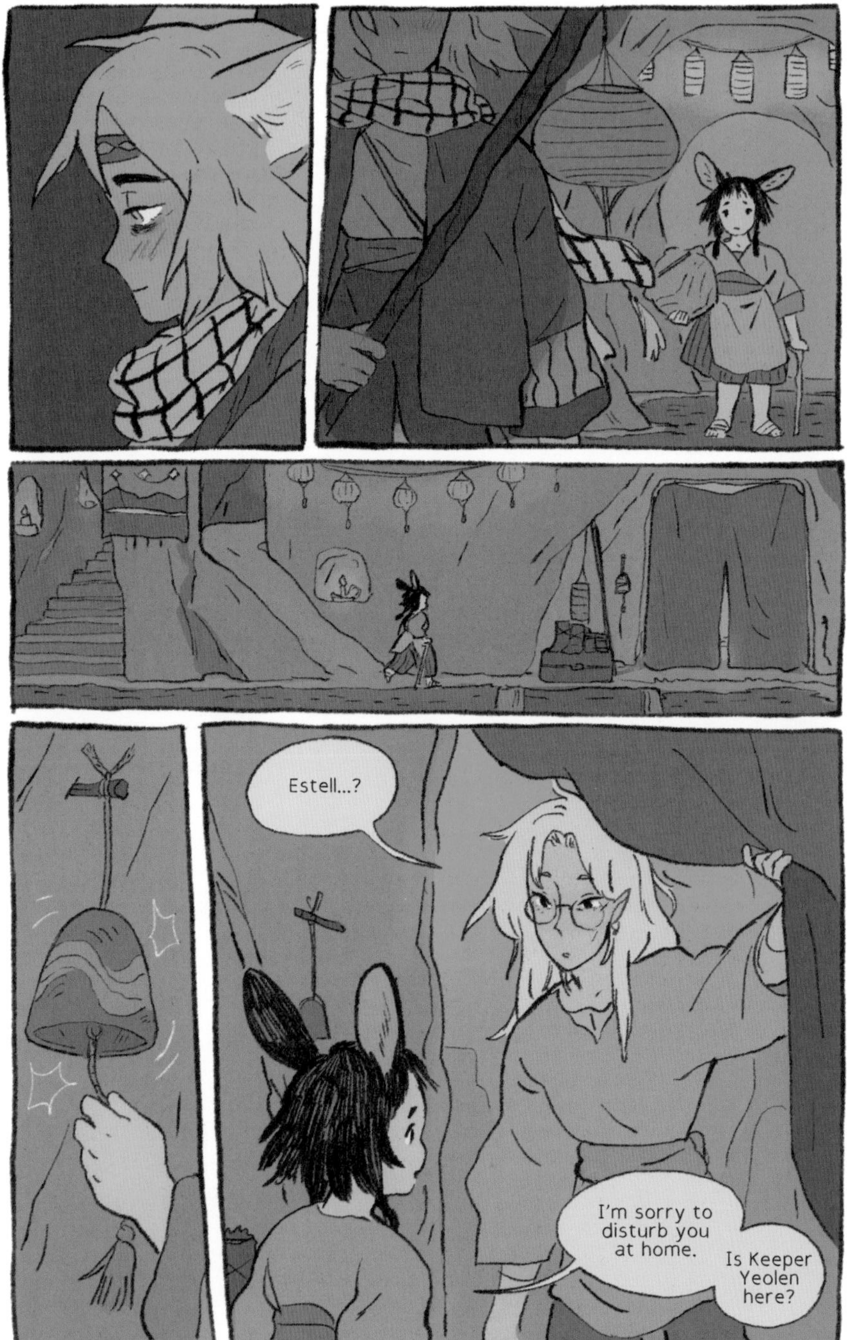
Estell...?
I'm sorry to disturb you at home.
Is Keeper Yeolen here?

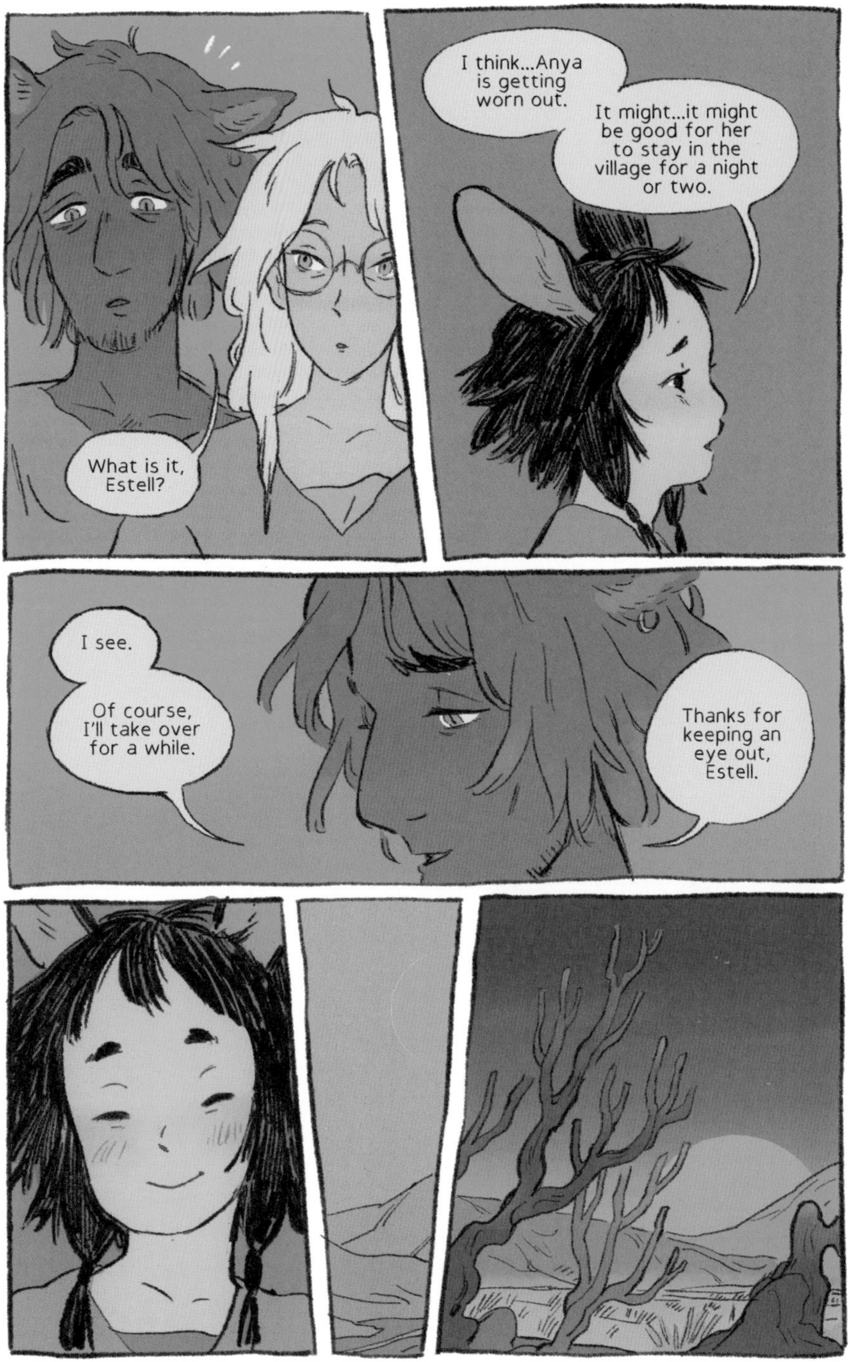
What is it, Estell?
I think...Anya is getting worn out.
It might...it might be good for her to stay in the village for a night or two.
I see.
Of course, I'll take over for a while.
Thanks for keeping an eye out, Estell.

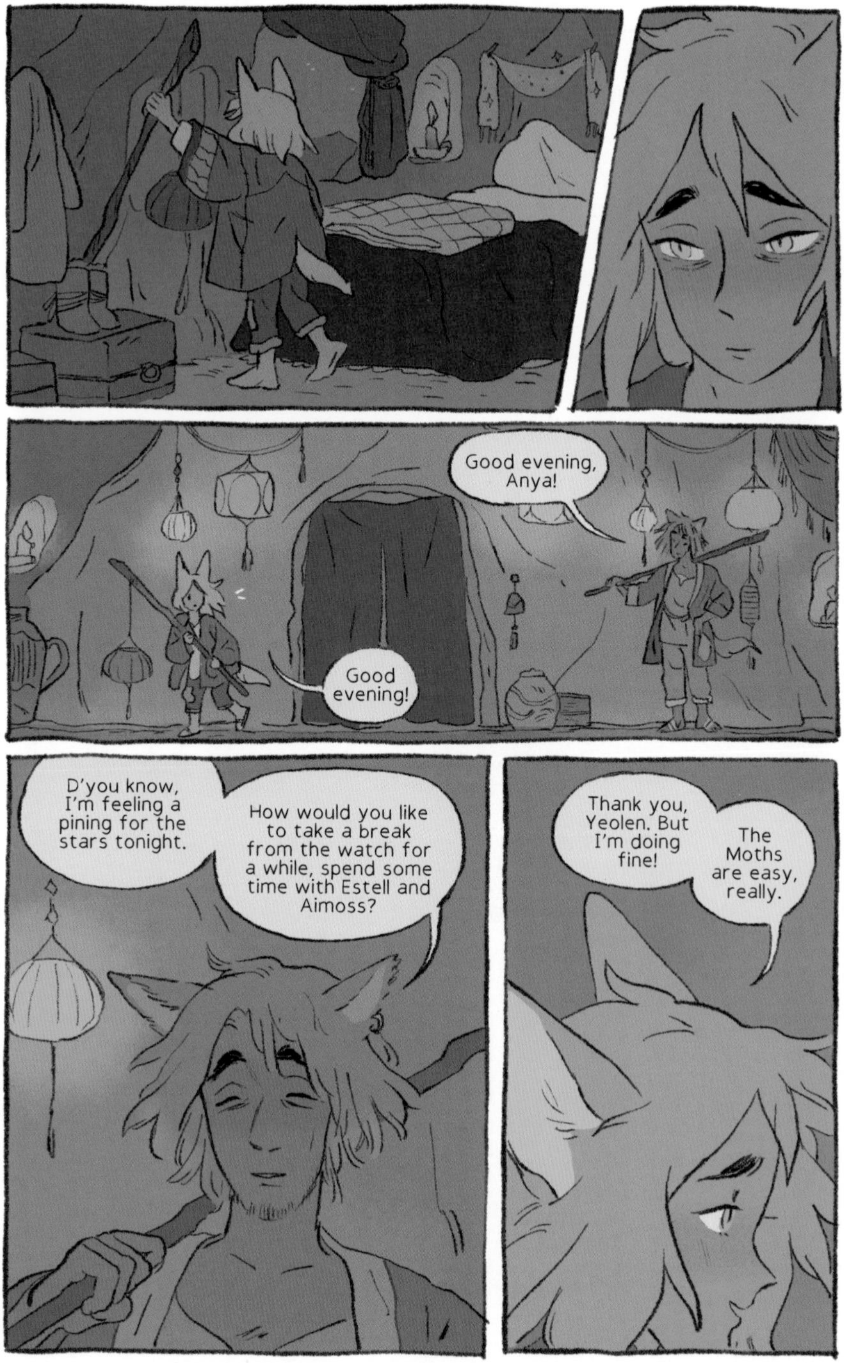
Good evening, Anya!
Good evening!
D'you know, I'm feeling a pining for the stars tonight.
How would you like to take a break from the watch for a while, spend some time with Estell and Aimoss?
Thank you, Yeolen. But I'm doing fine!
The Moths are easy, really.

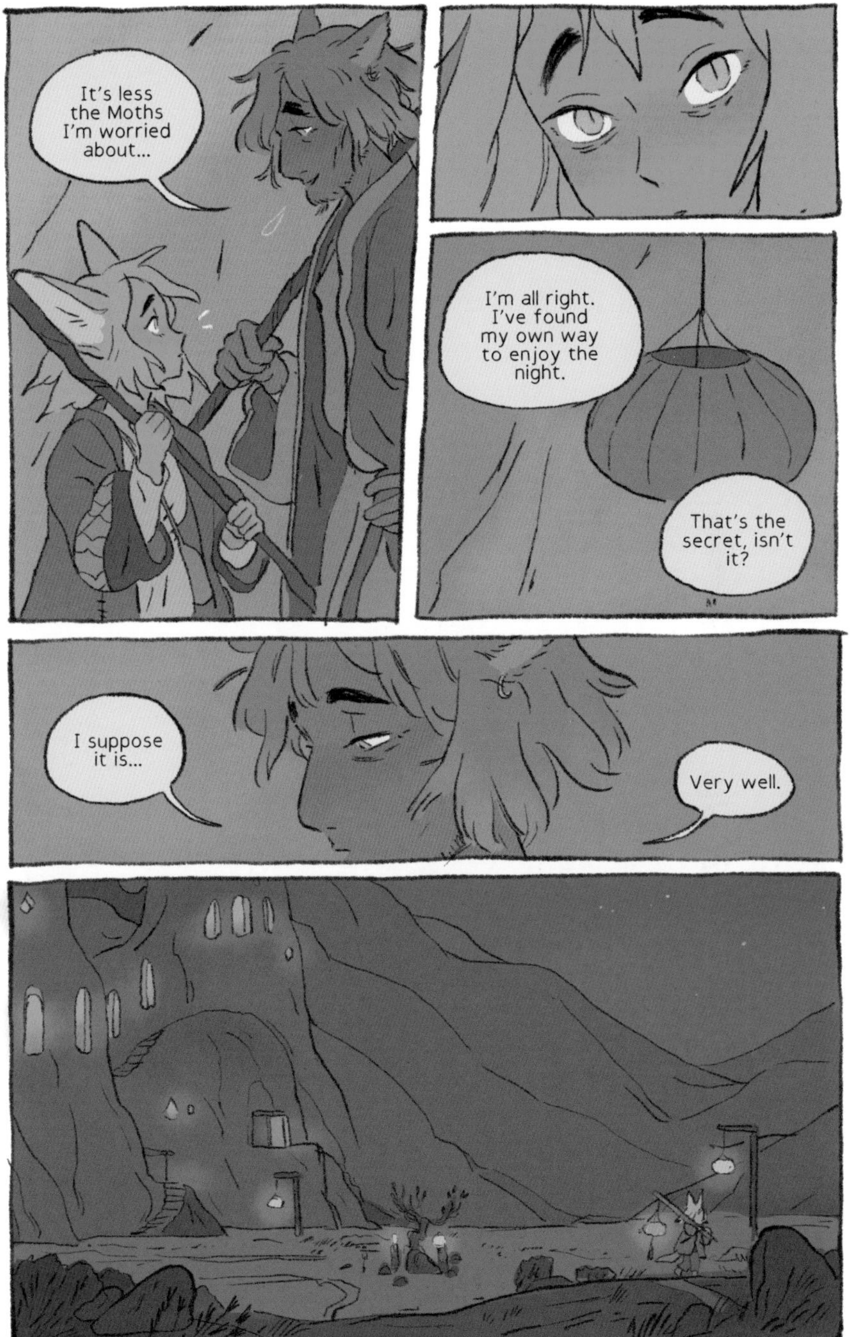
It's less the Moths I'm worried about...
I'm all right. I've found my own way to enjoy the night.
That's the secret, isn't it?
I suppose it is...
Very well.

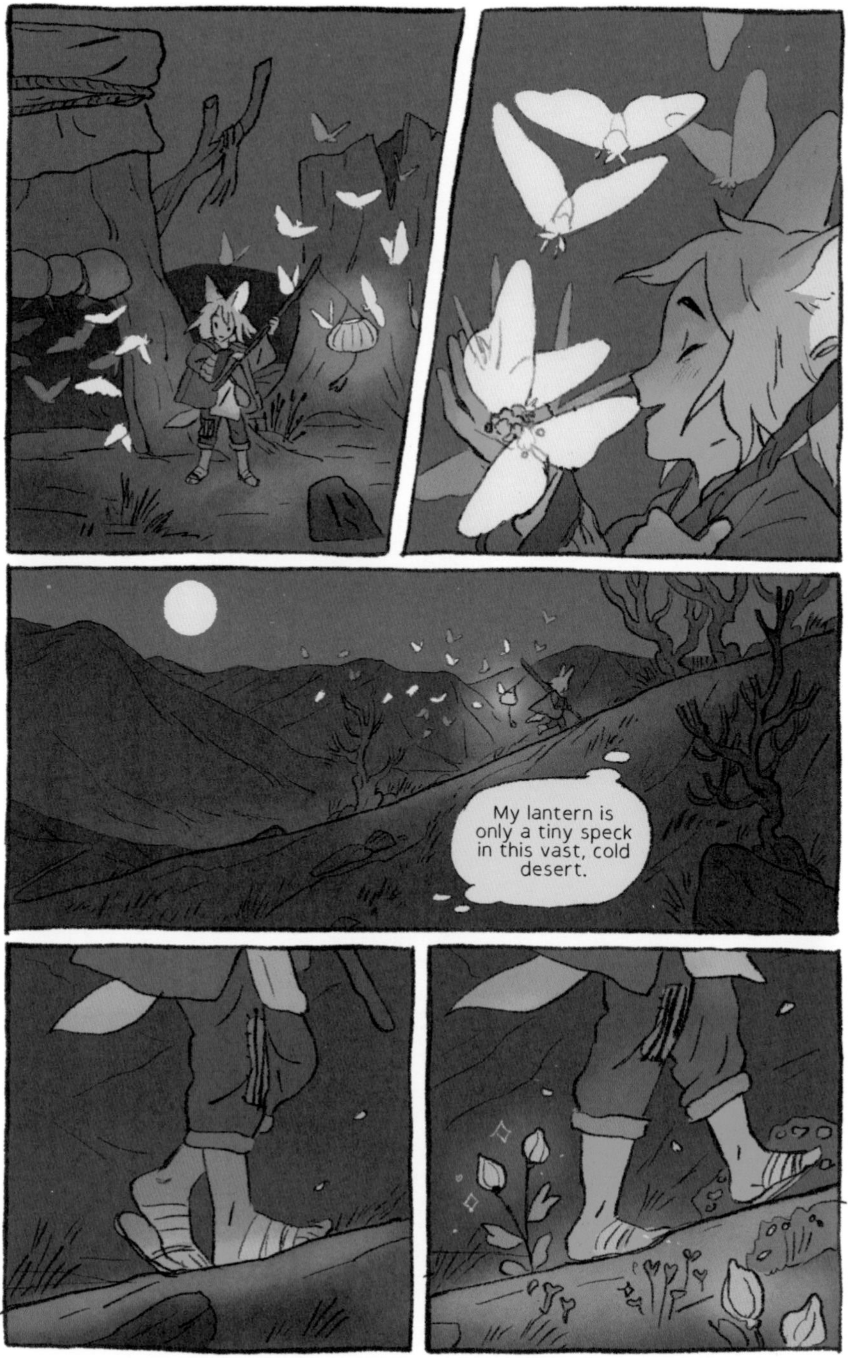
My lantern is only a tiny speck in this vast, cold desert.

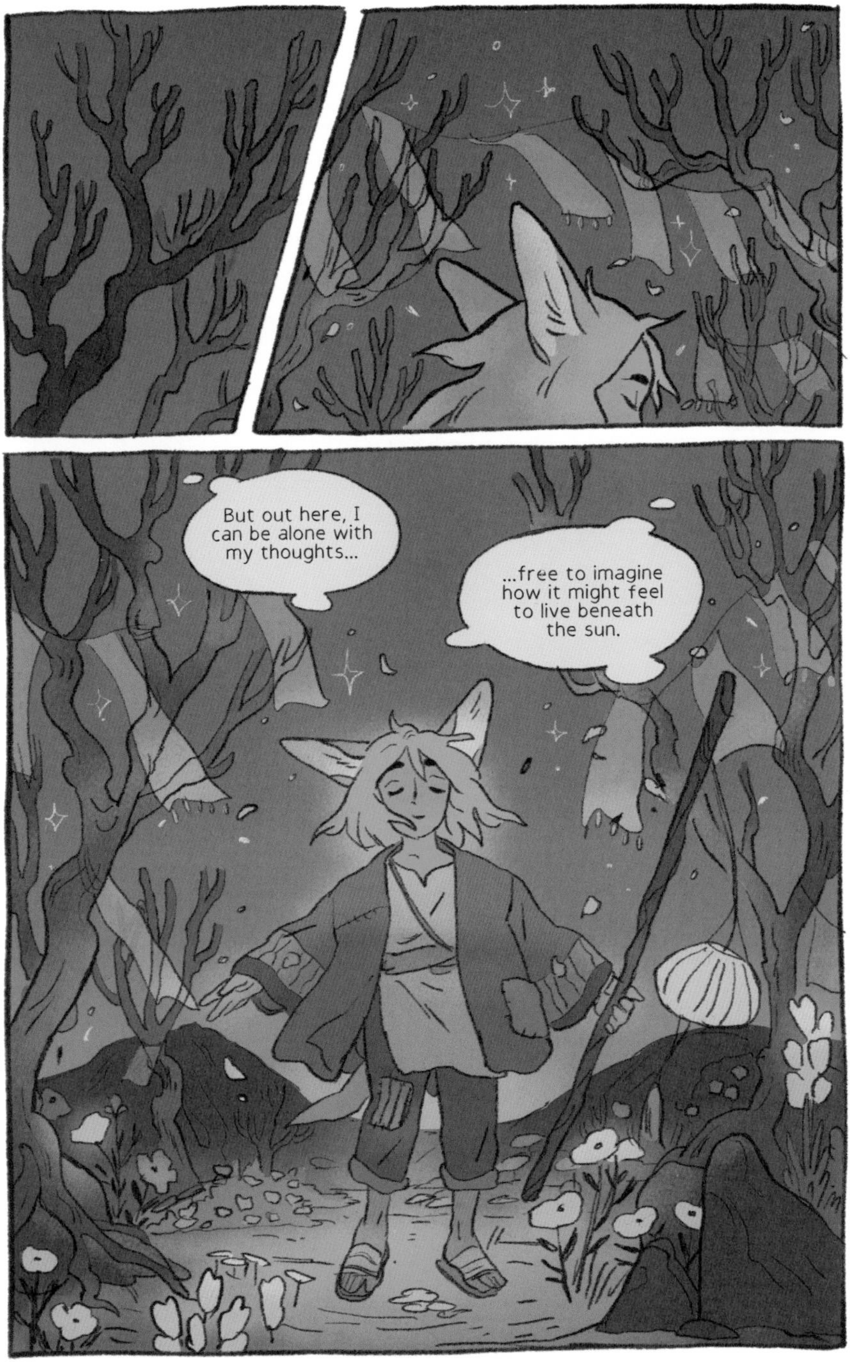
But out here, I can be alone with my thoughts...
...free to imagine how it might feel to live beneath the sun.

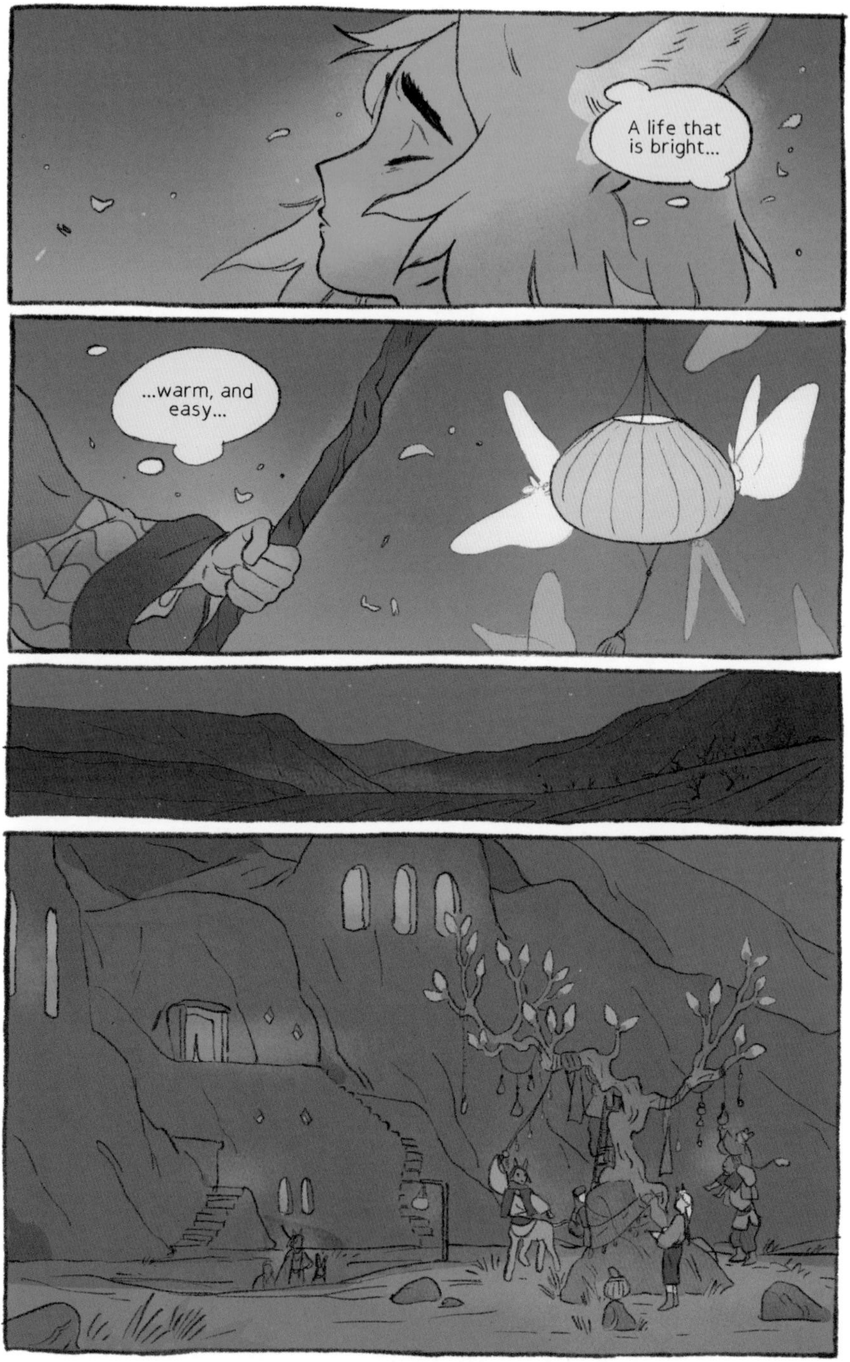
A life that is bright...
...warm, and easy...

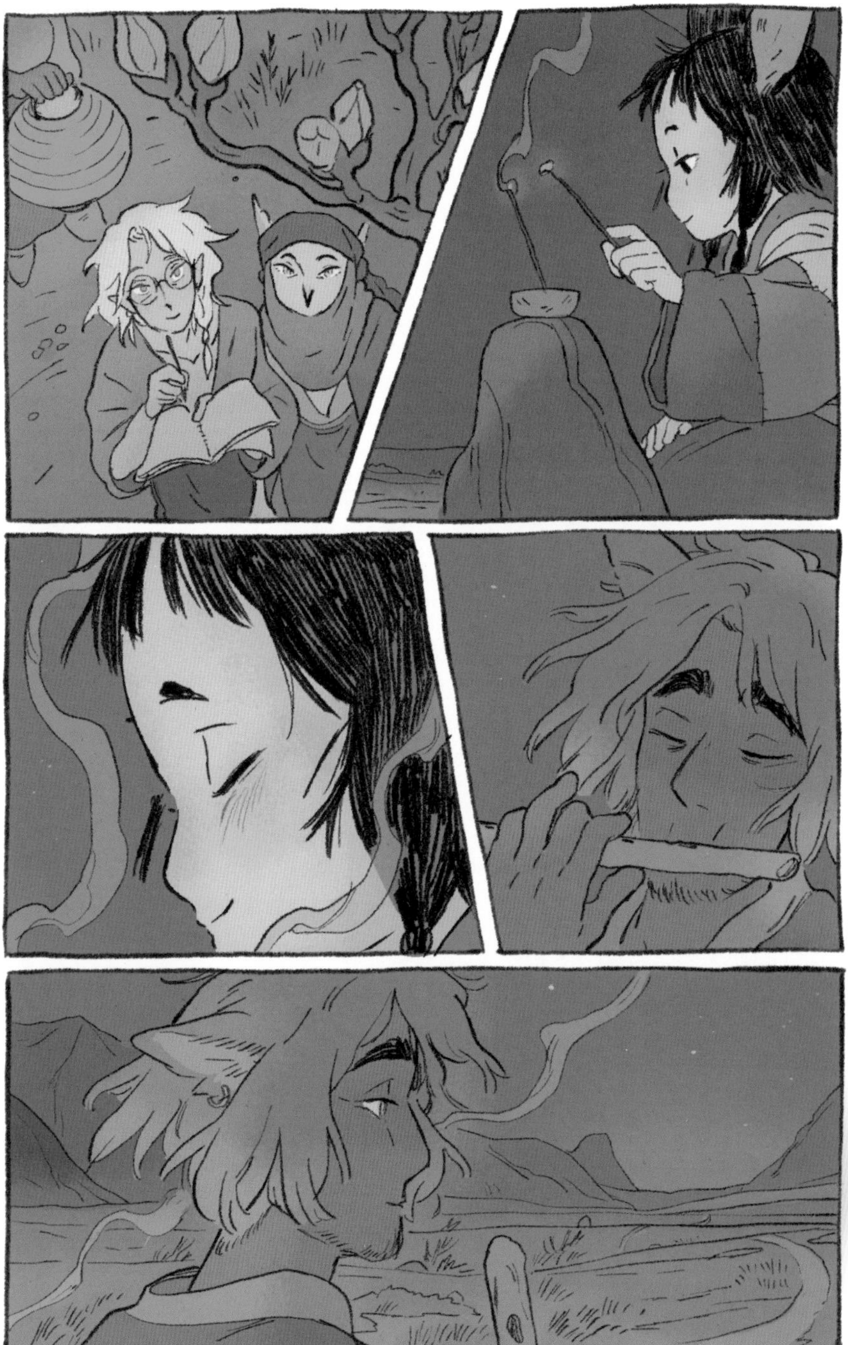

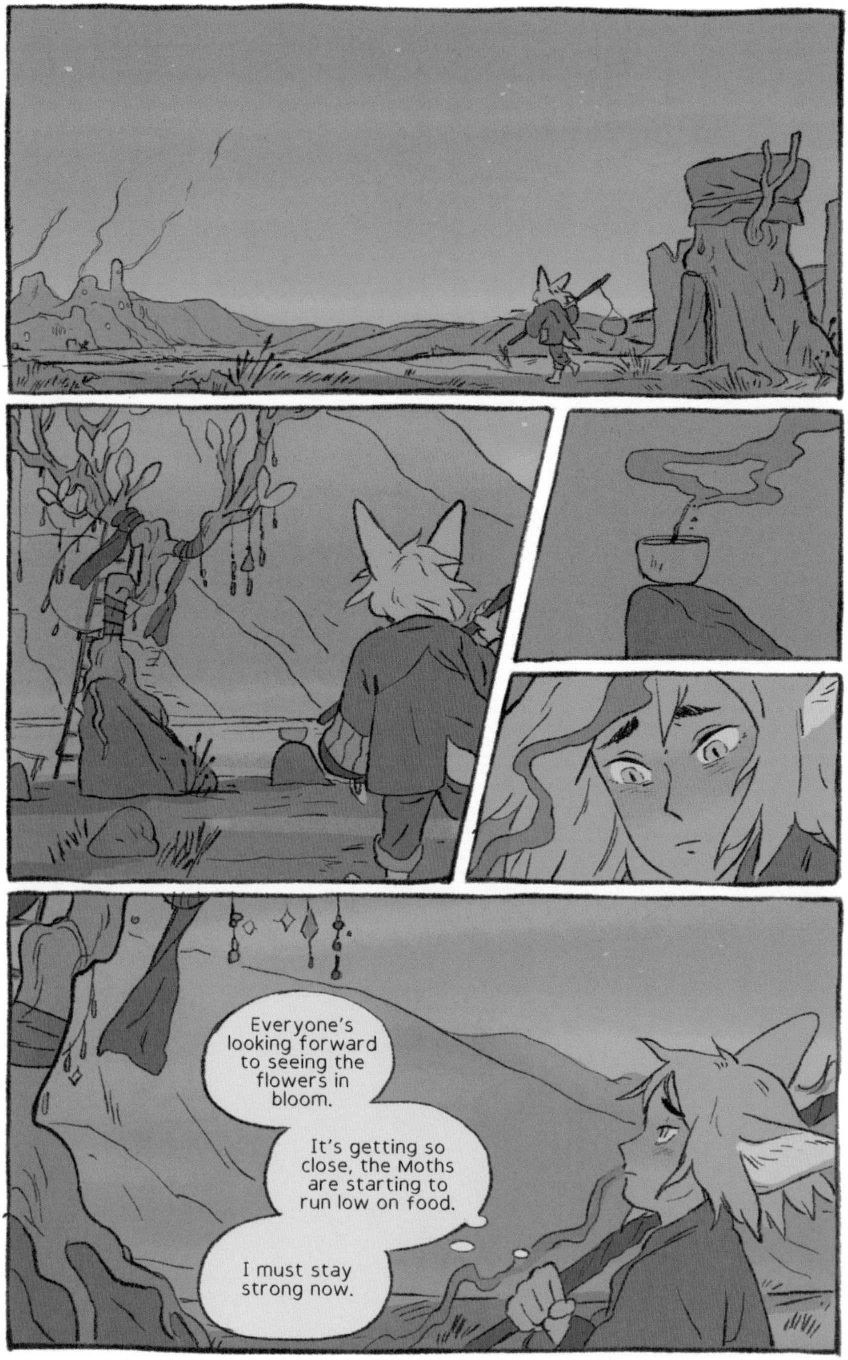
Everyone's looking forward to seeing the flowers in bloom.
It's getting so close, the Moths are starting to run low on food.
I must stay strong now.

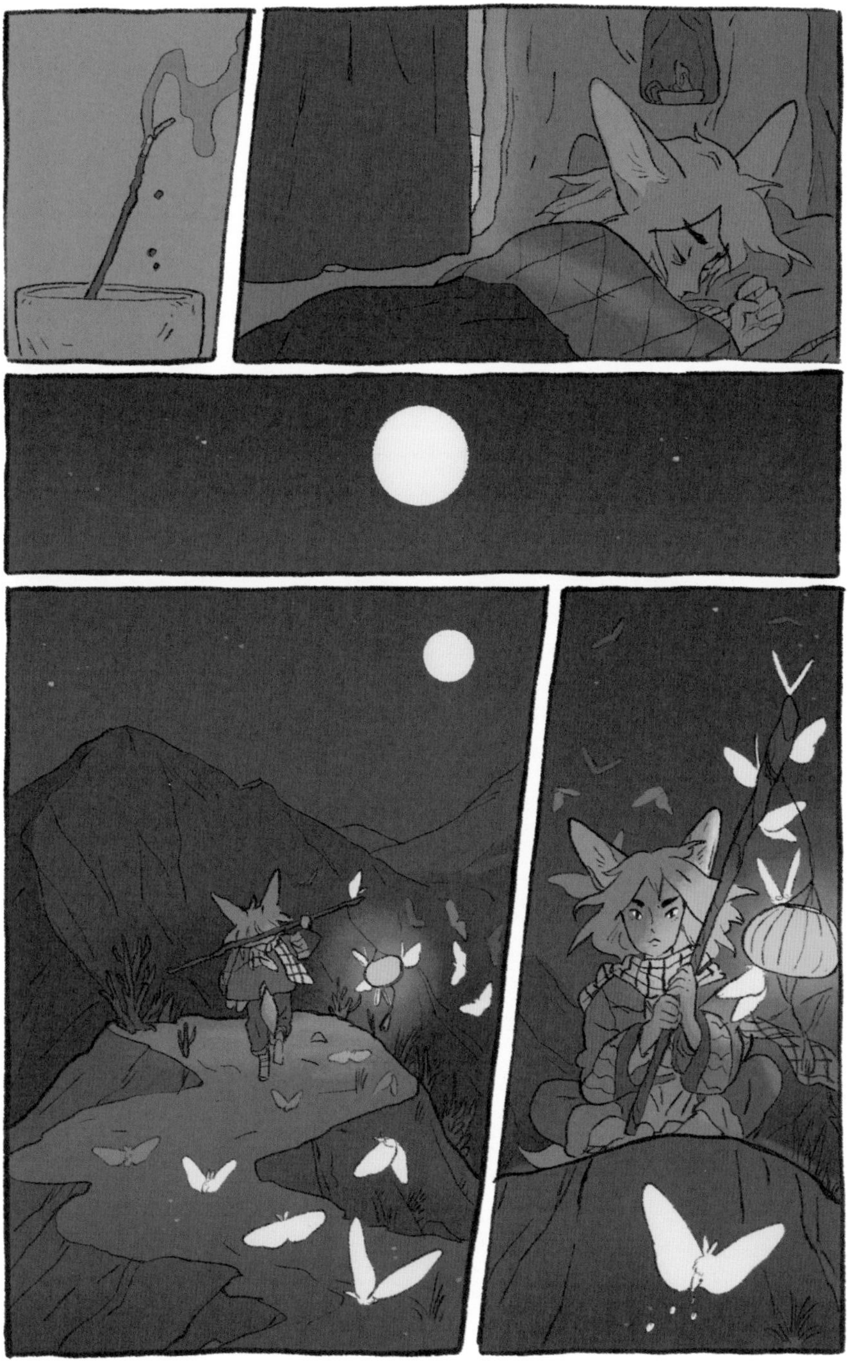

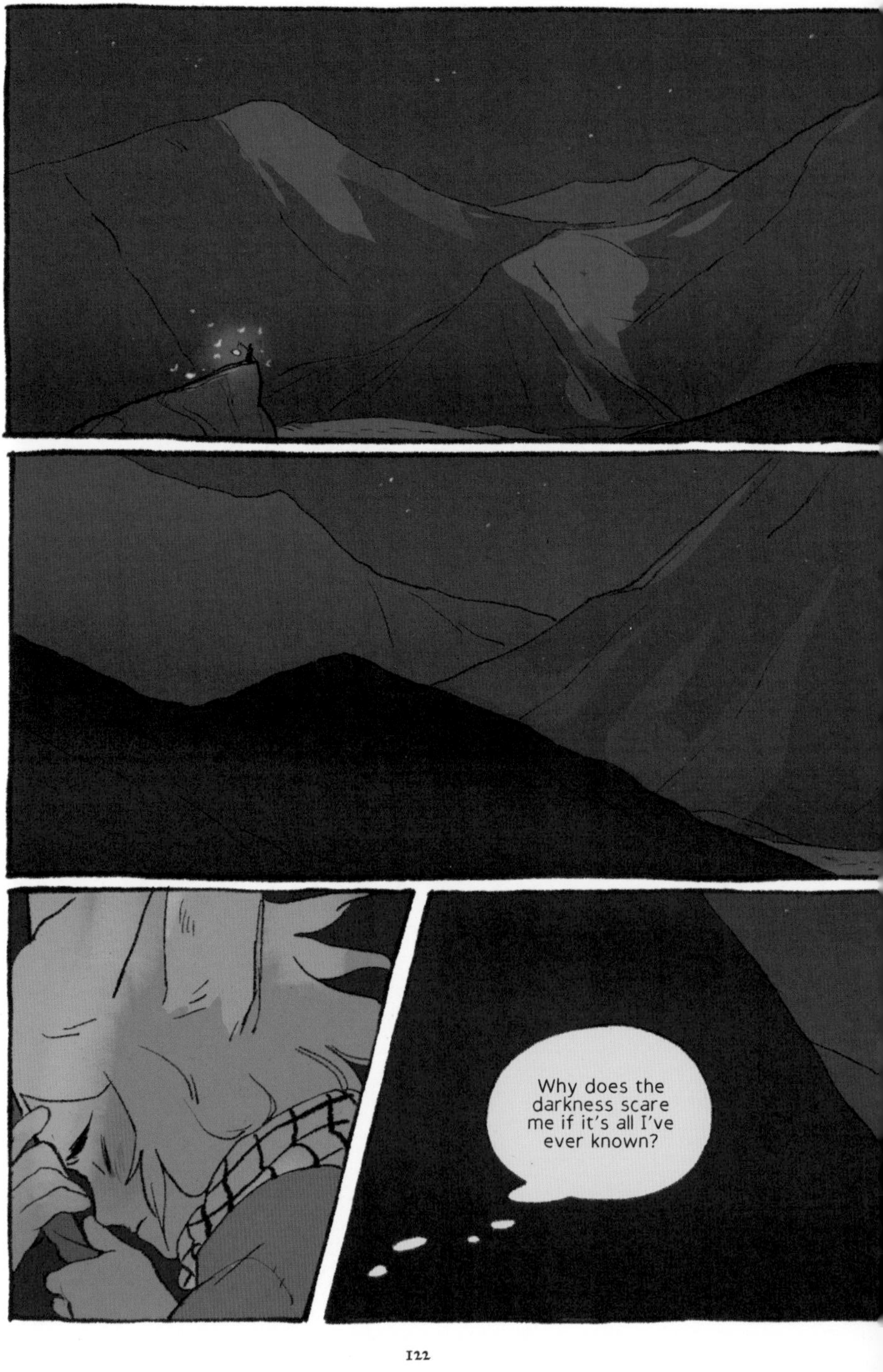
Why does the darkness scare me if it's all I've ever known?

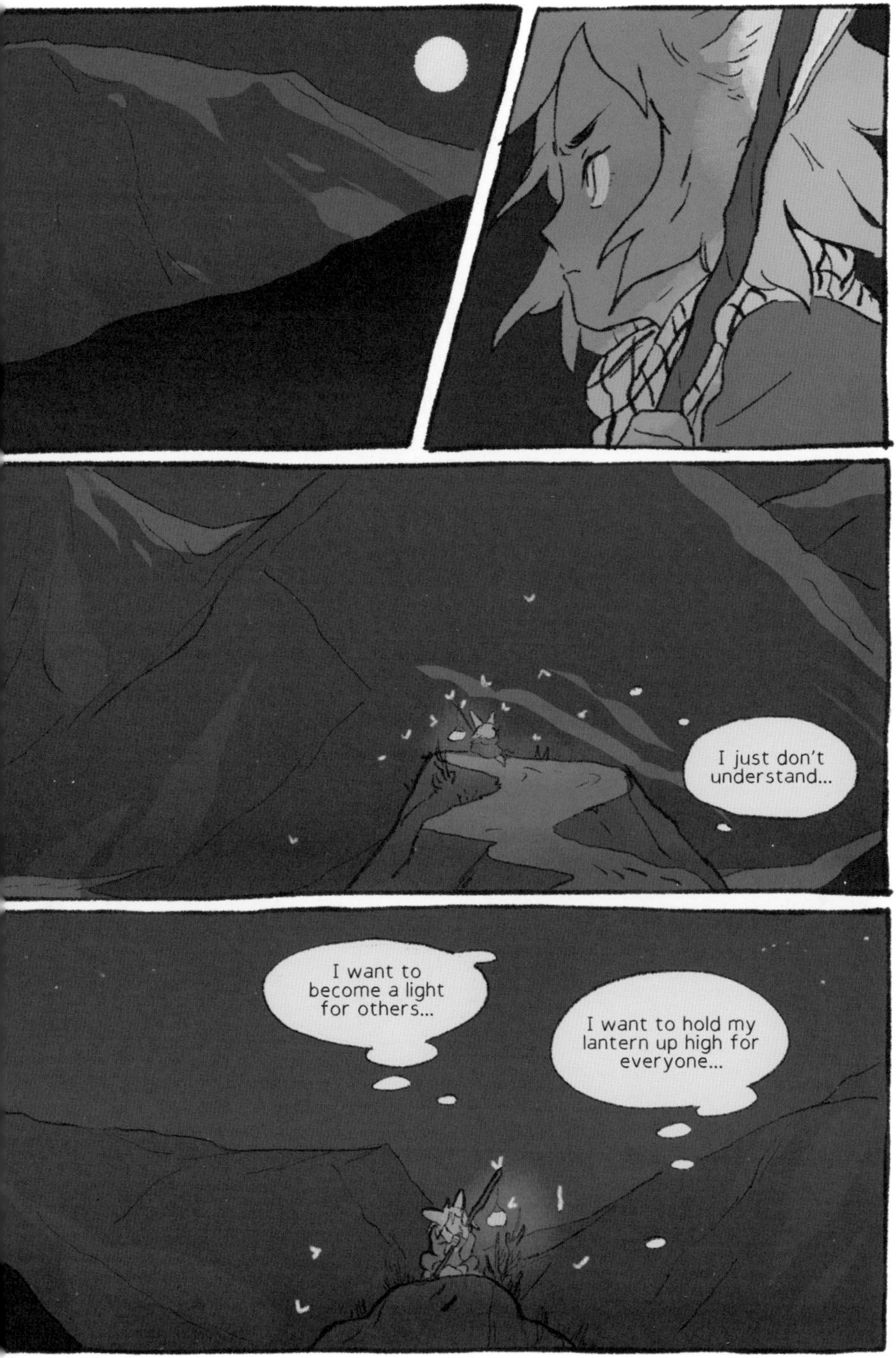
I just don't understand...
I want to become a light for others...
I want to hold my lantern up high for everyone...

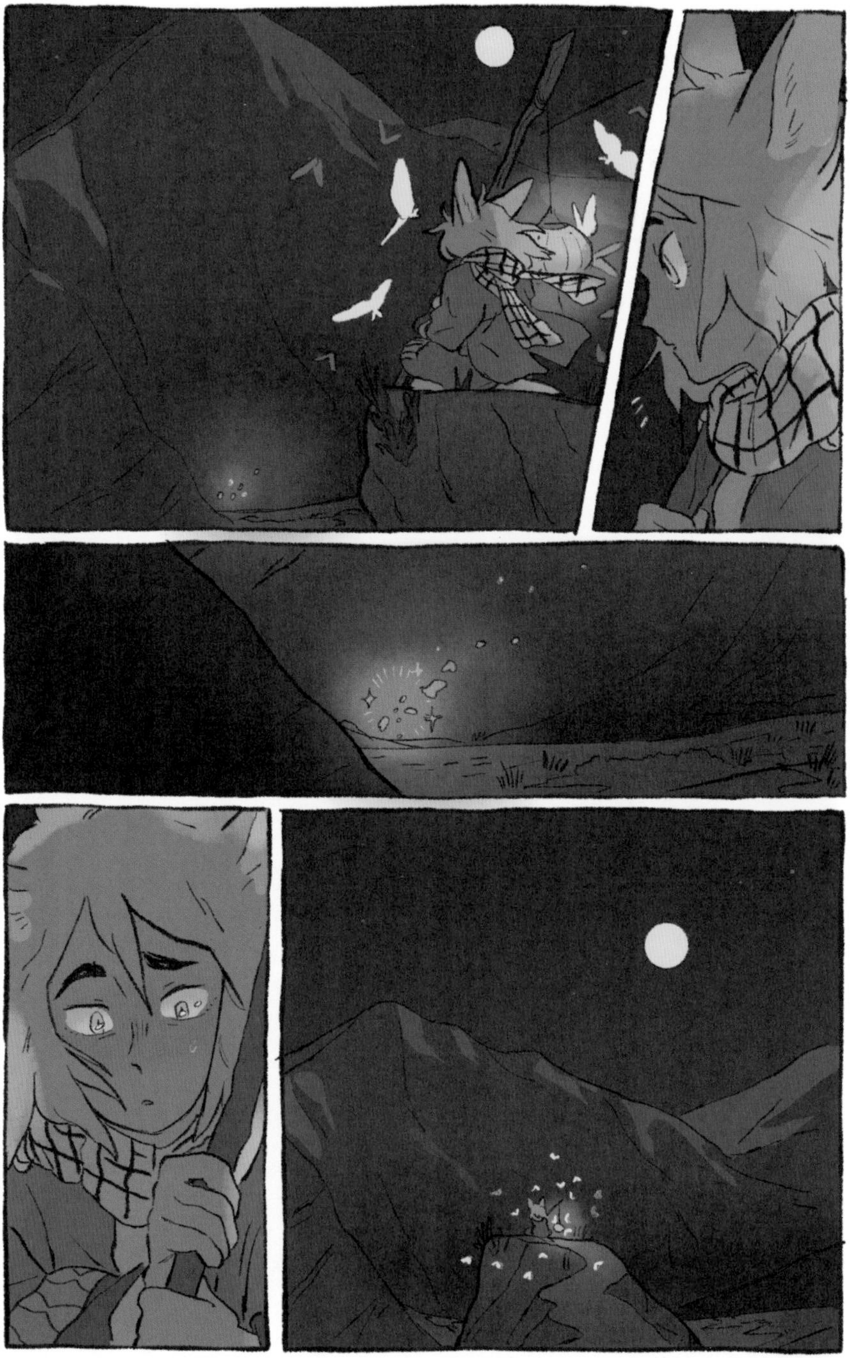

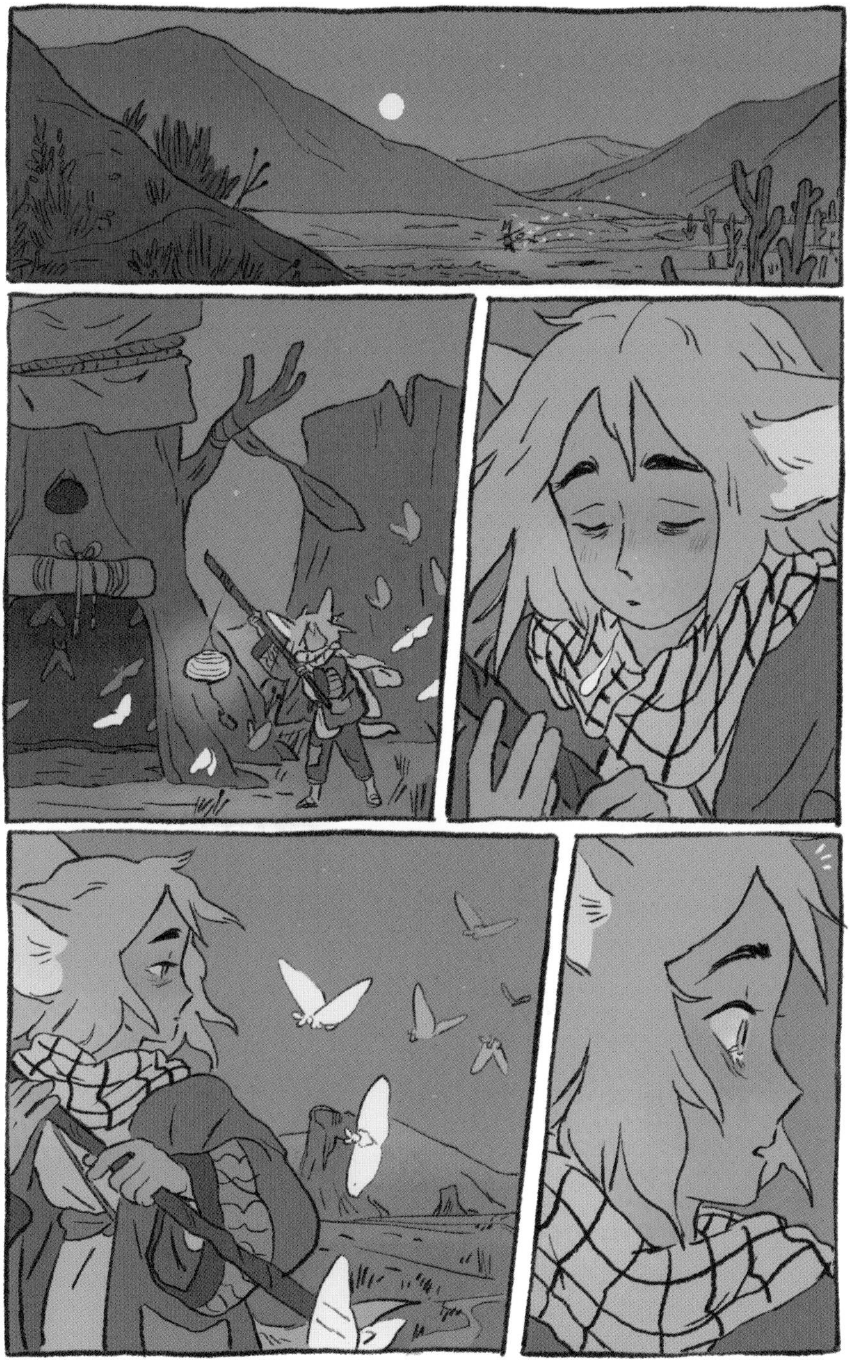

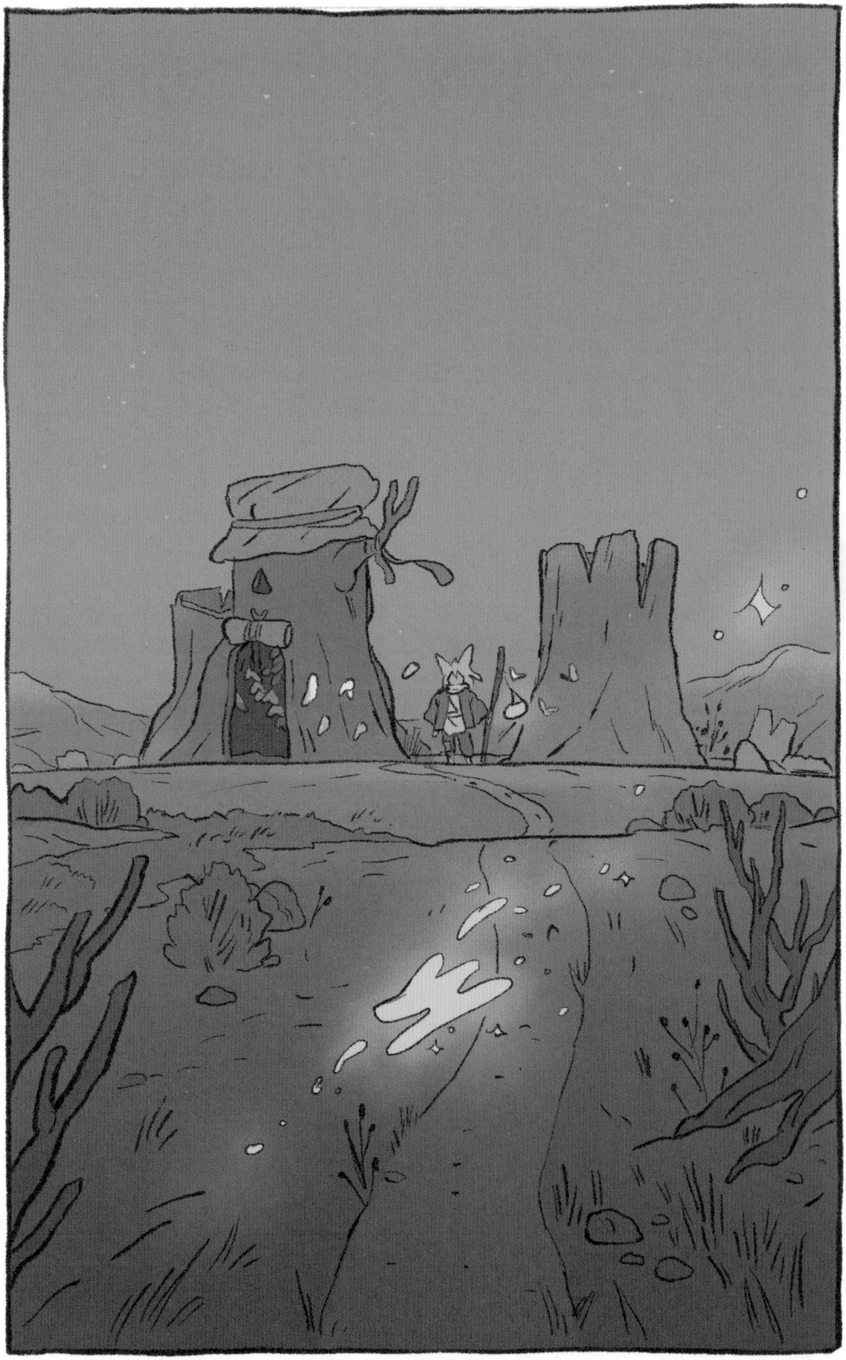

Chapter Five

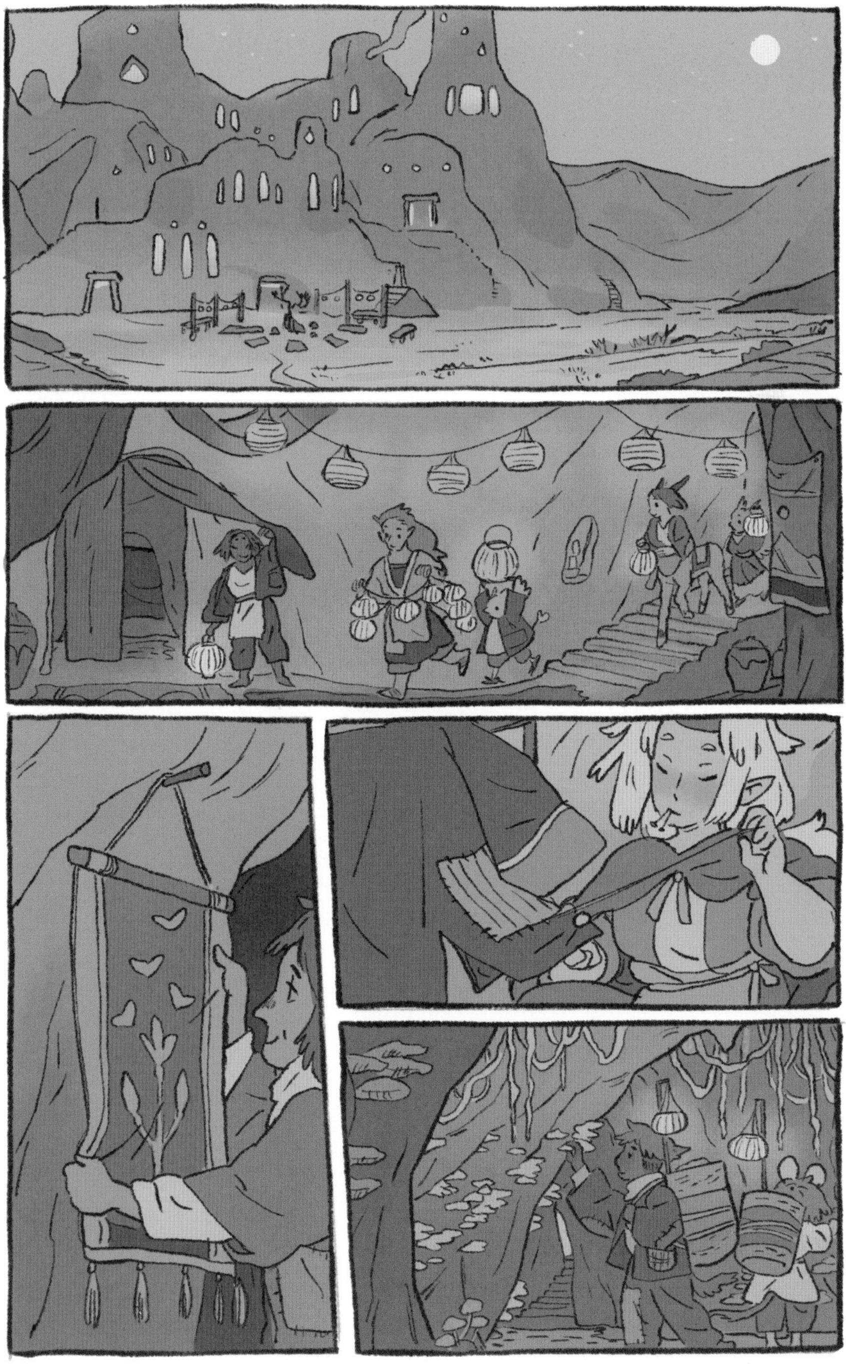

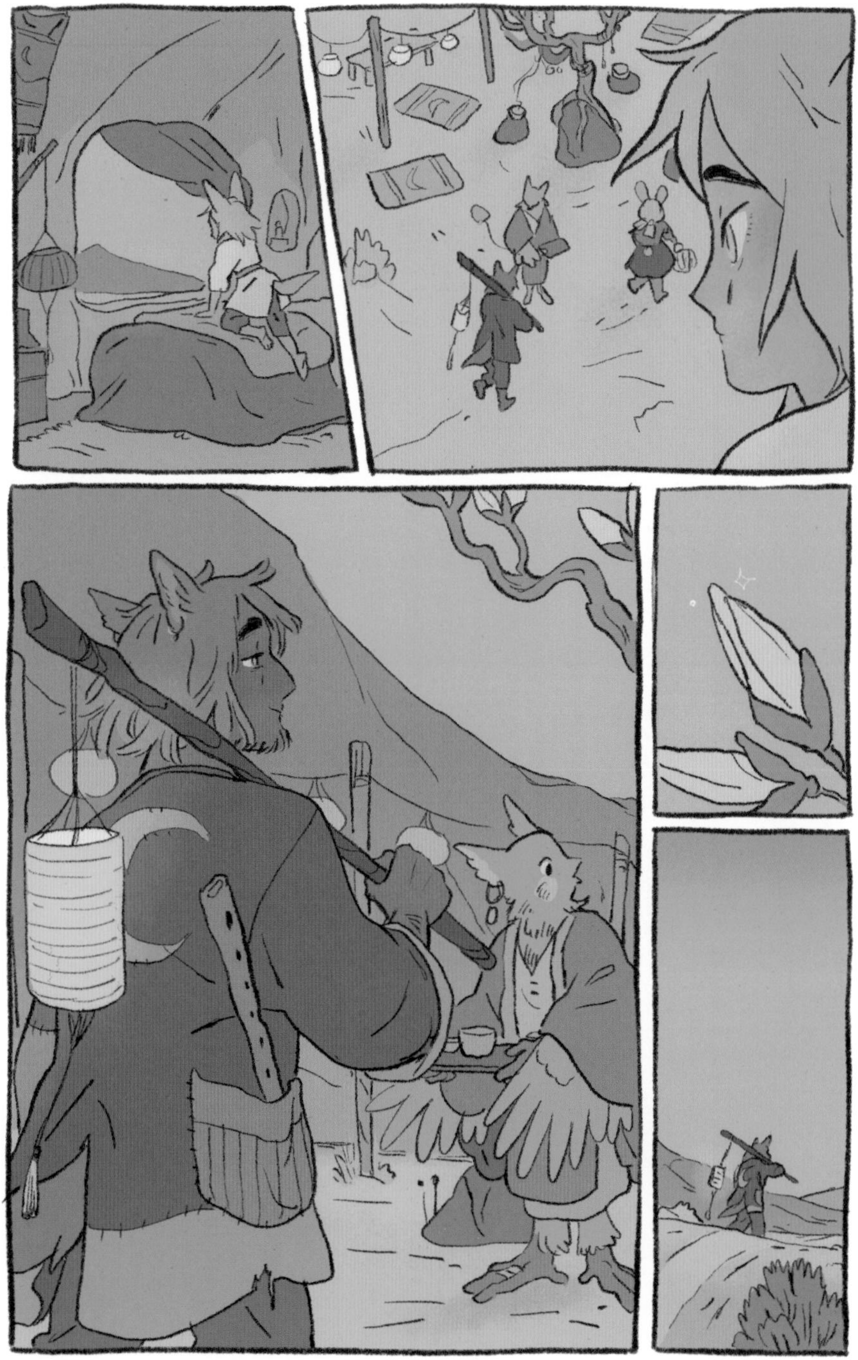

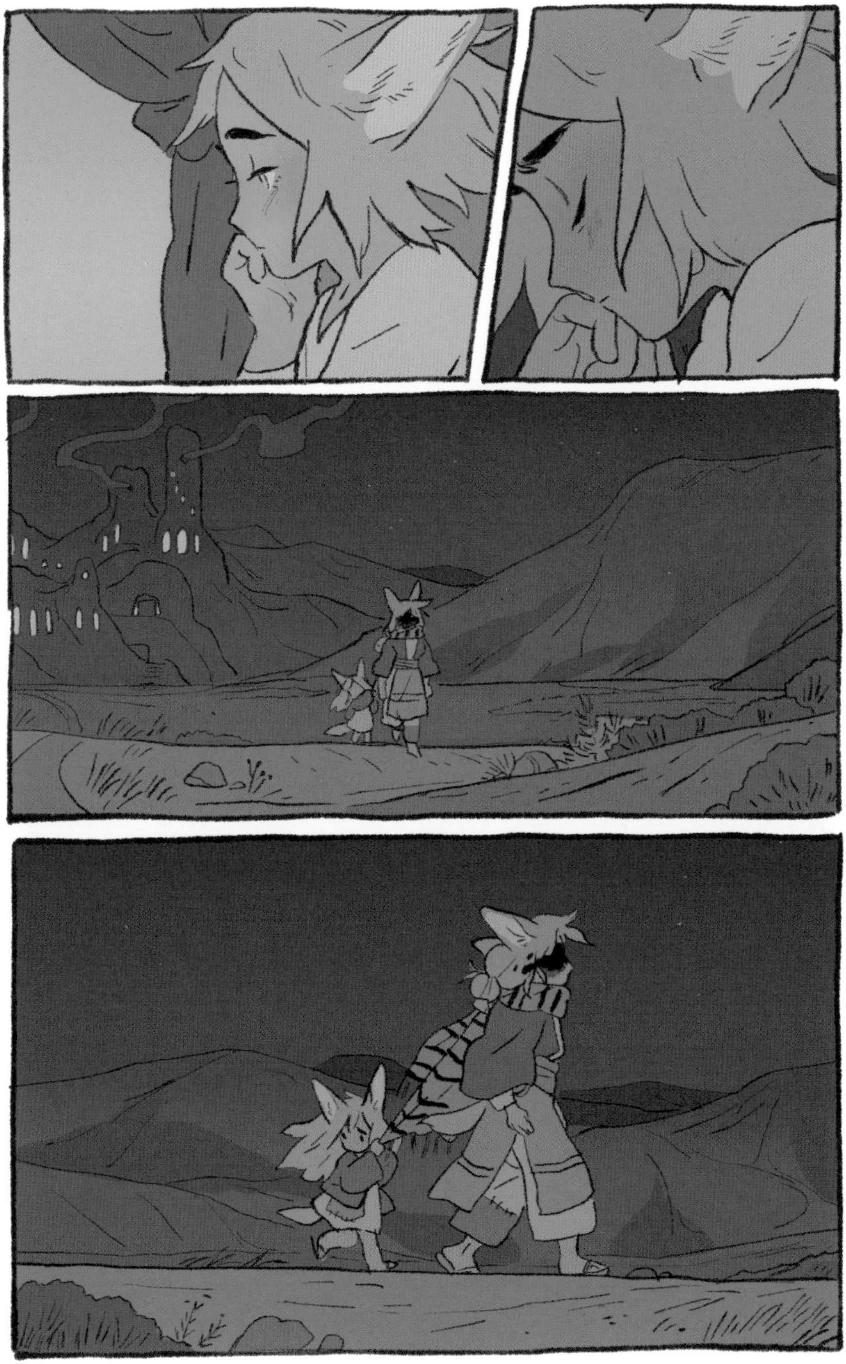

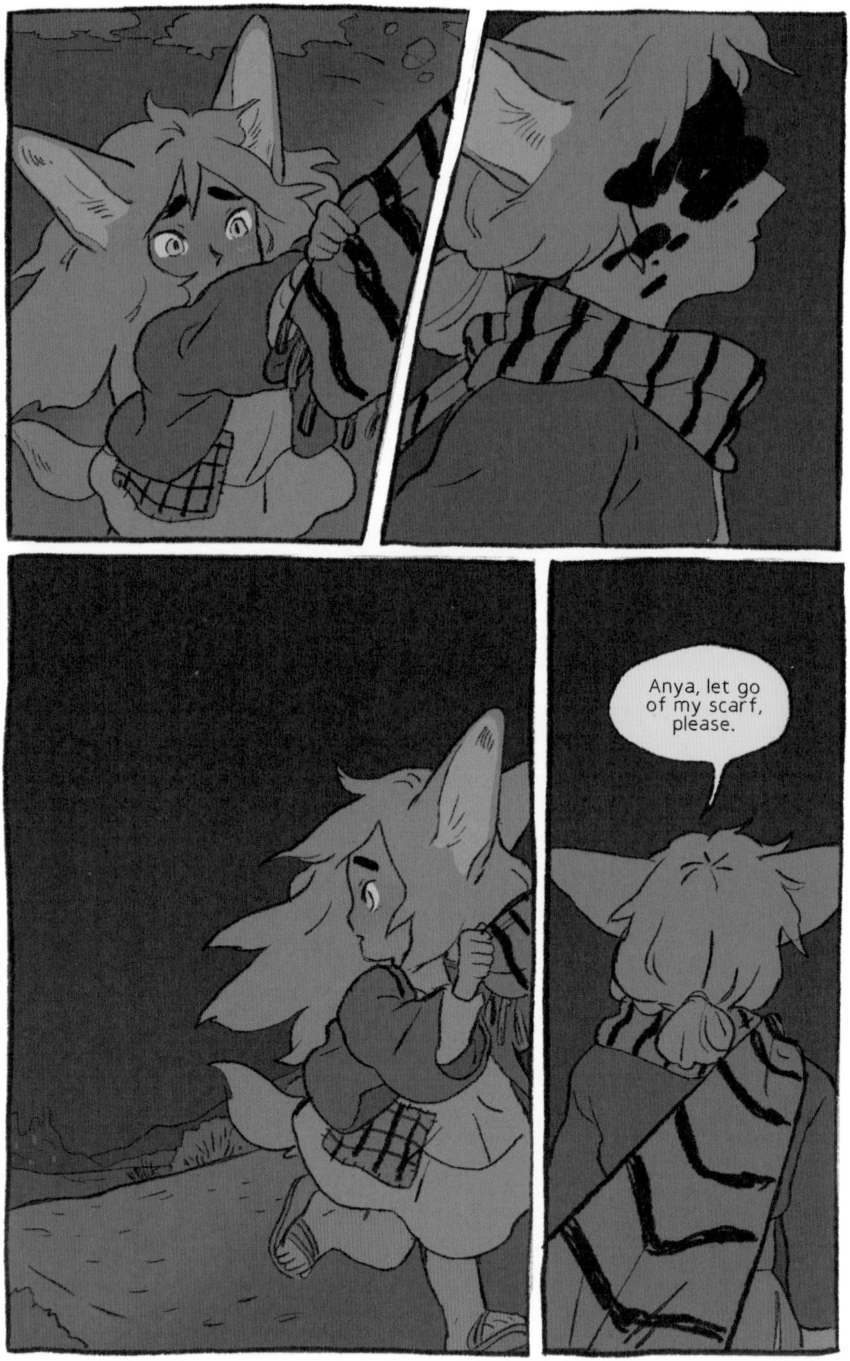
Anya, let go of my scarf, please.

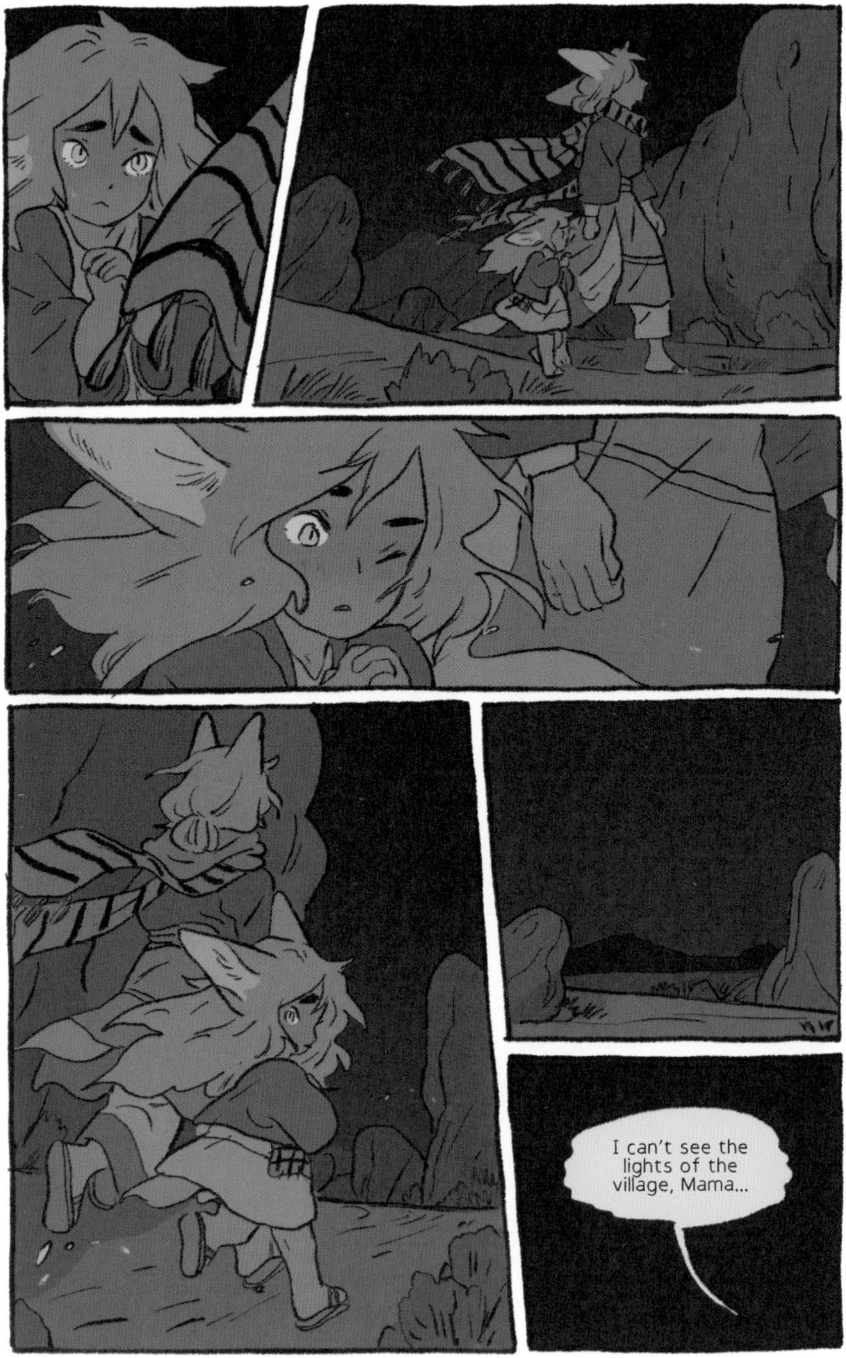
I can't see the
lights of the
village, Mama...

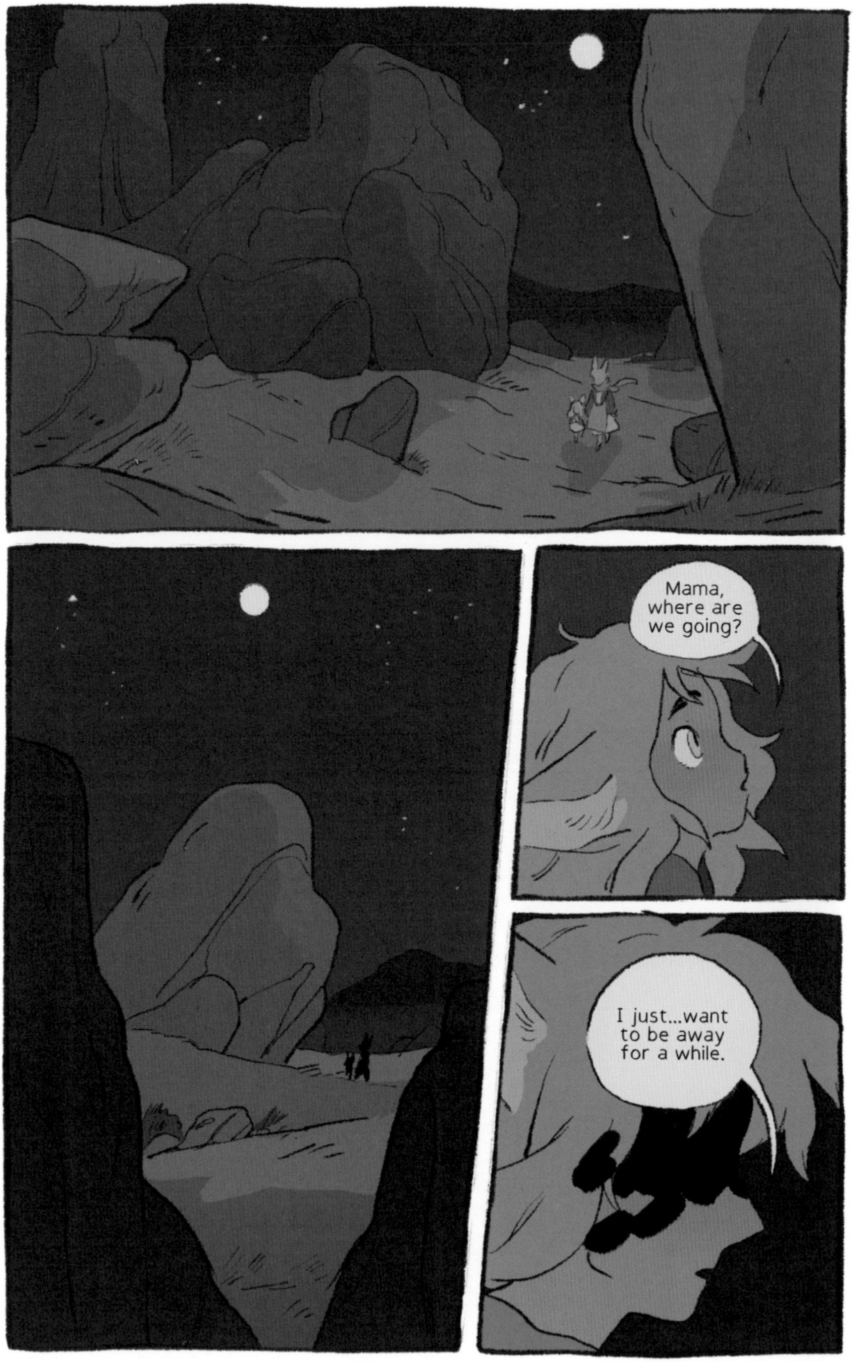
Mama, where are we going?
I just...want to be away for a while.

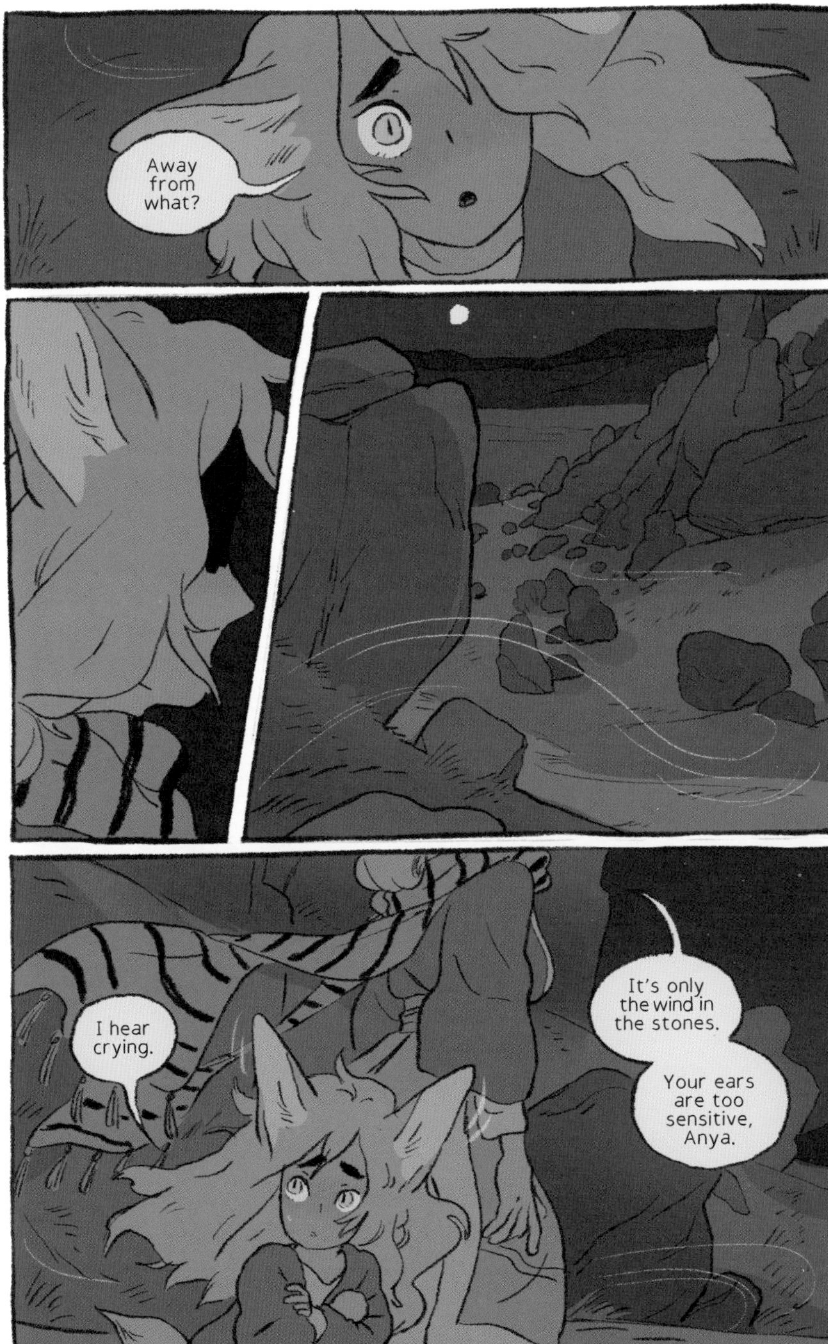

Away from what?
I hear crying.
It's only the wind in the stones.
Your ears are too sensitive, Anya.

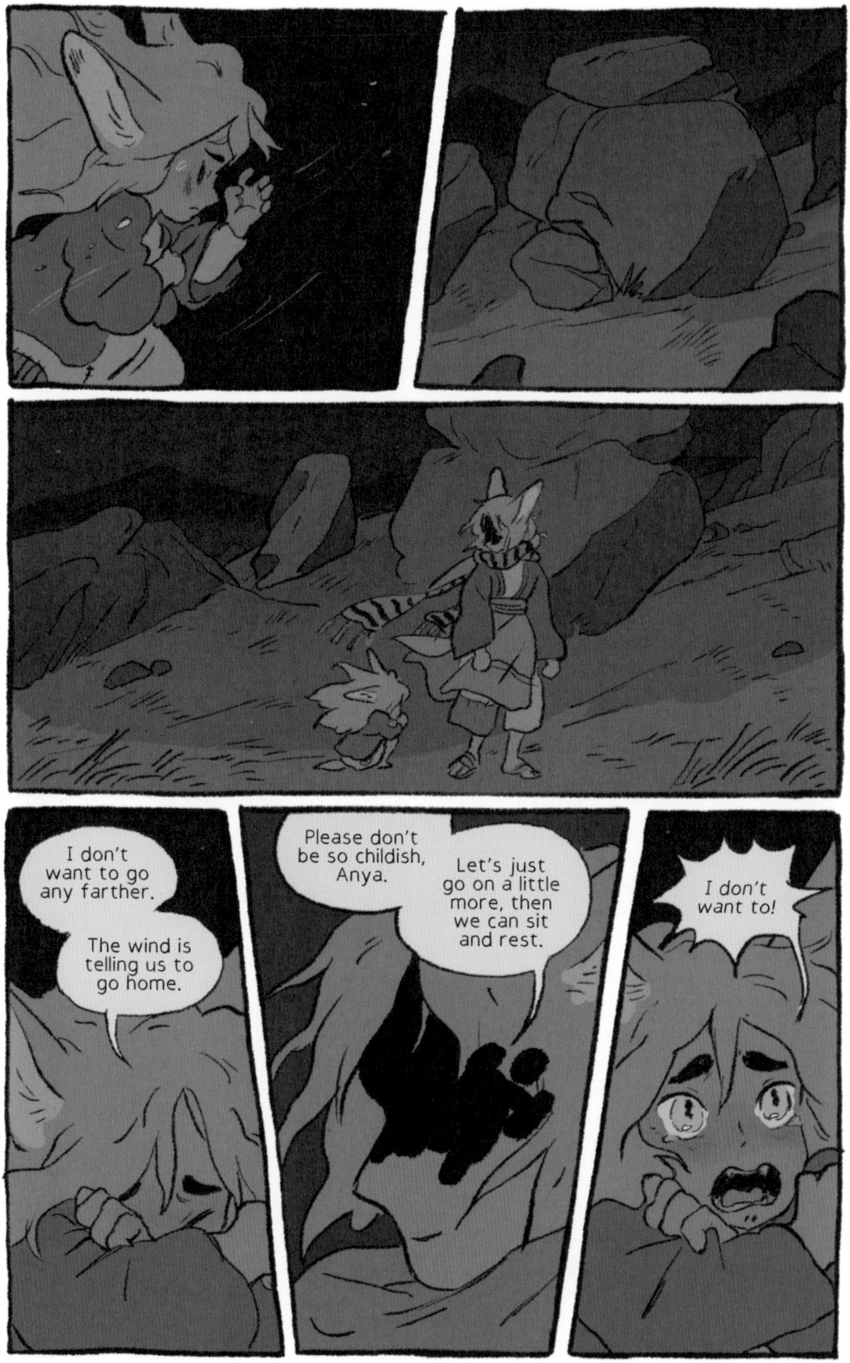
I don't want to go any farther.
The wind is telling us to go home.
Please don't be so childish, Anya.
Let's just go on a little more, then we can sit and rest.
I don't want to!

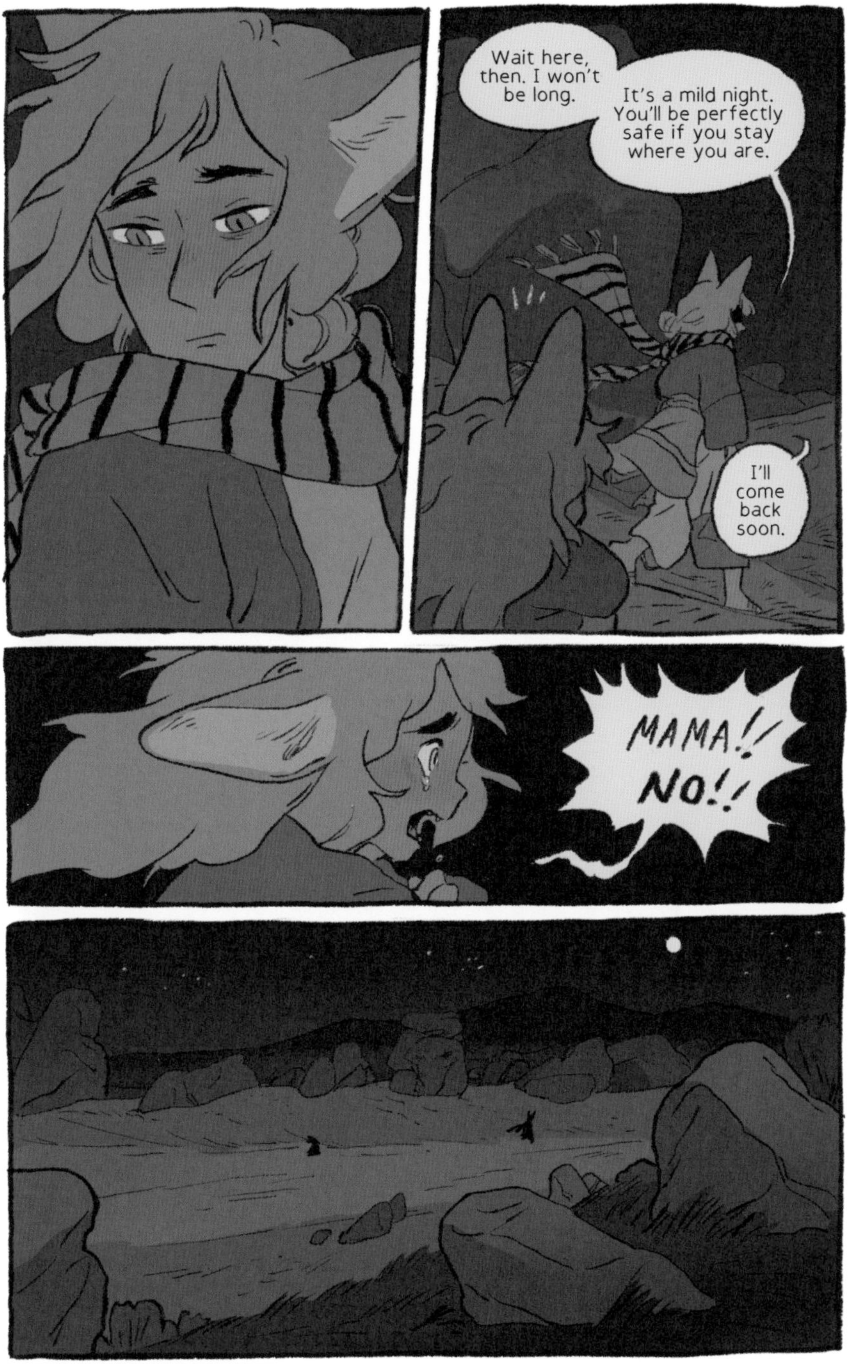
Wait here, then. I won't be long.
It's a mild night. You'll be perfectly safe if you stay where you are.
I'll come back soon.
MAMA!! NO!!

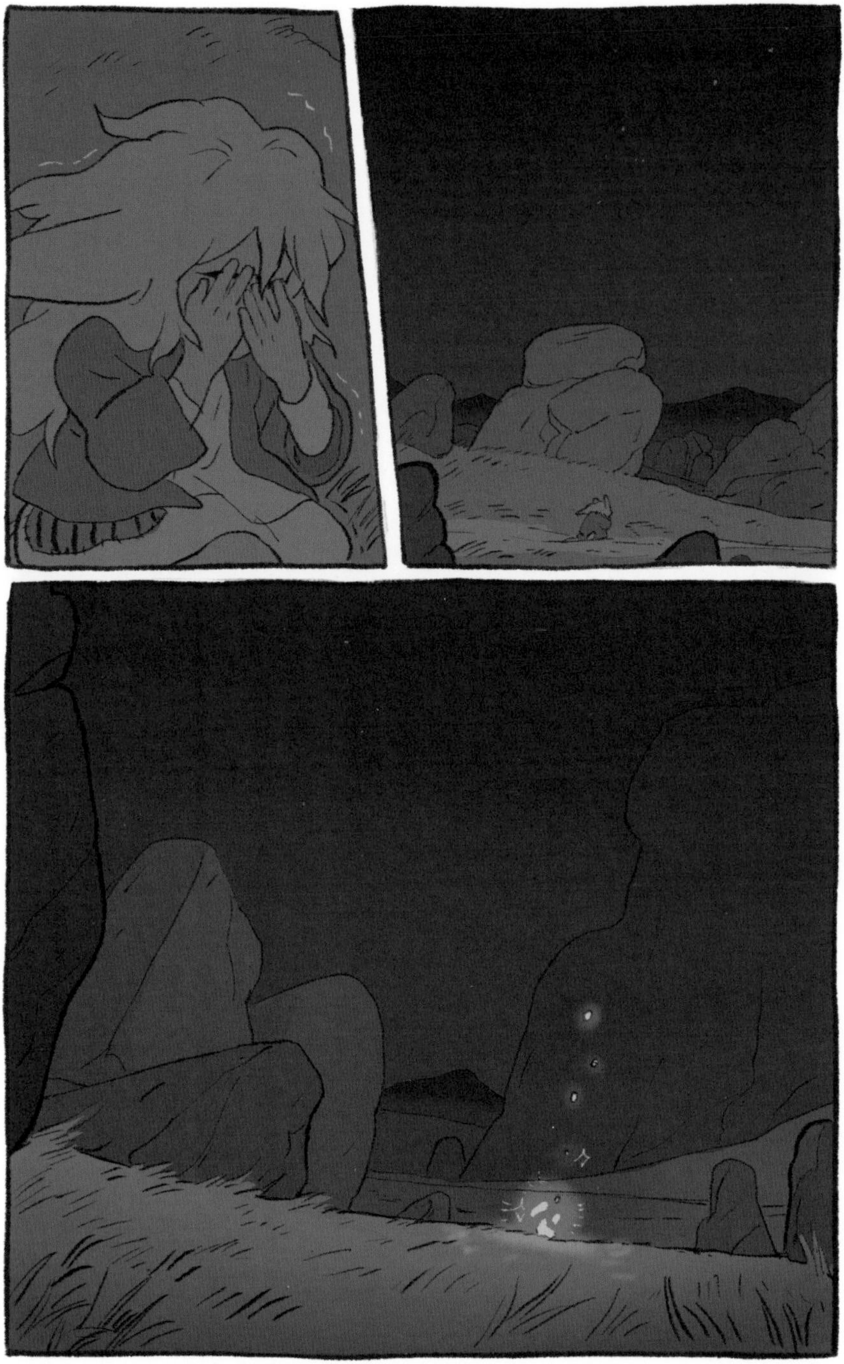

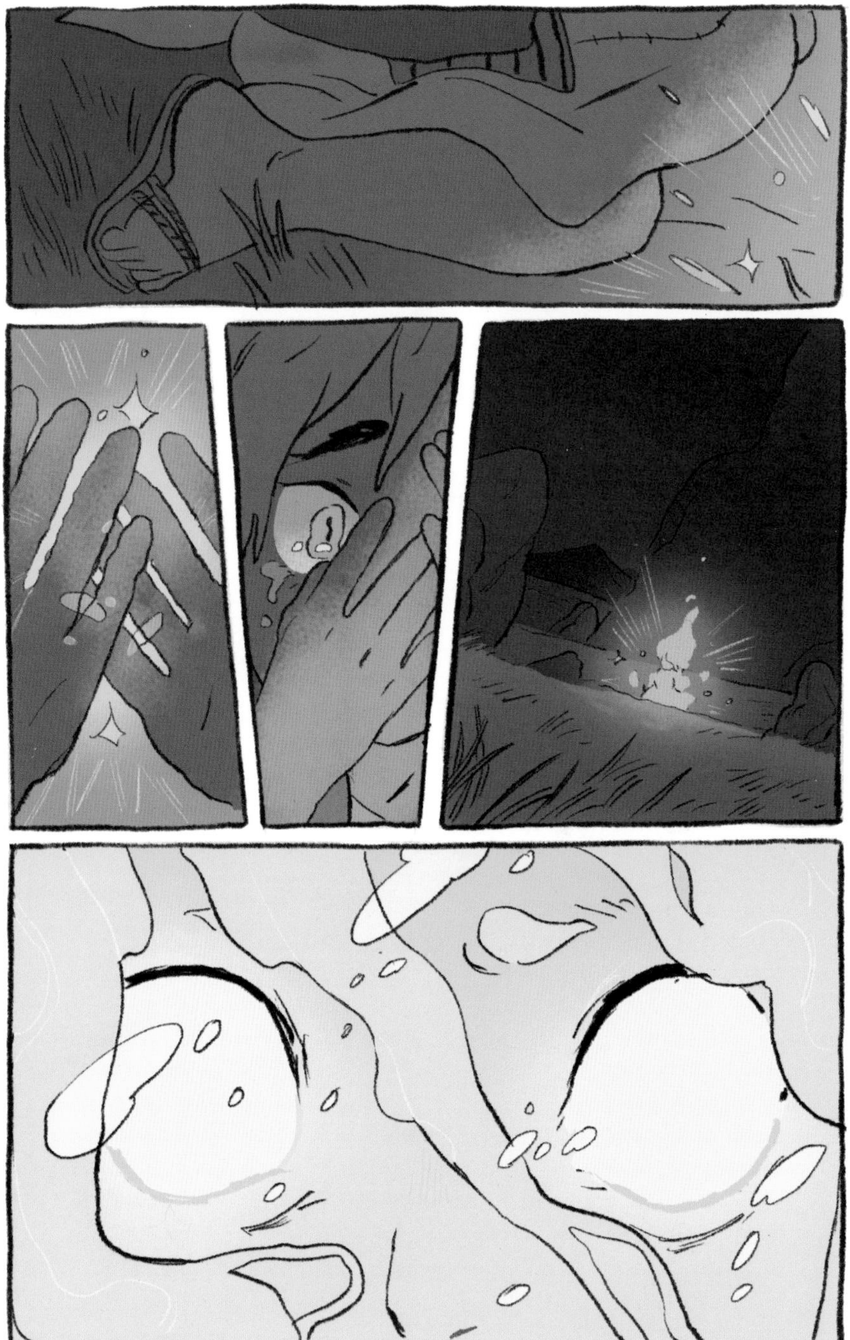

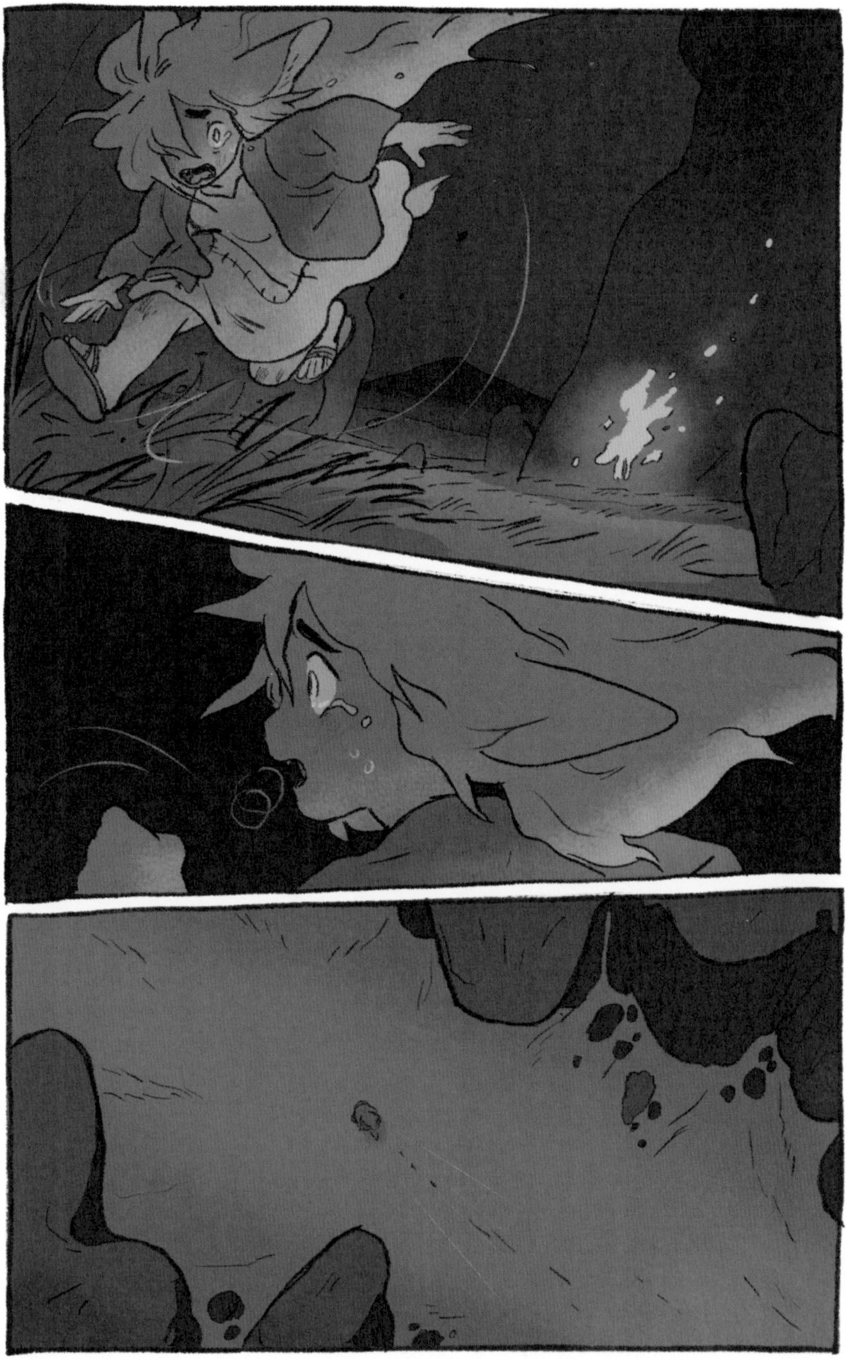

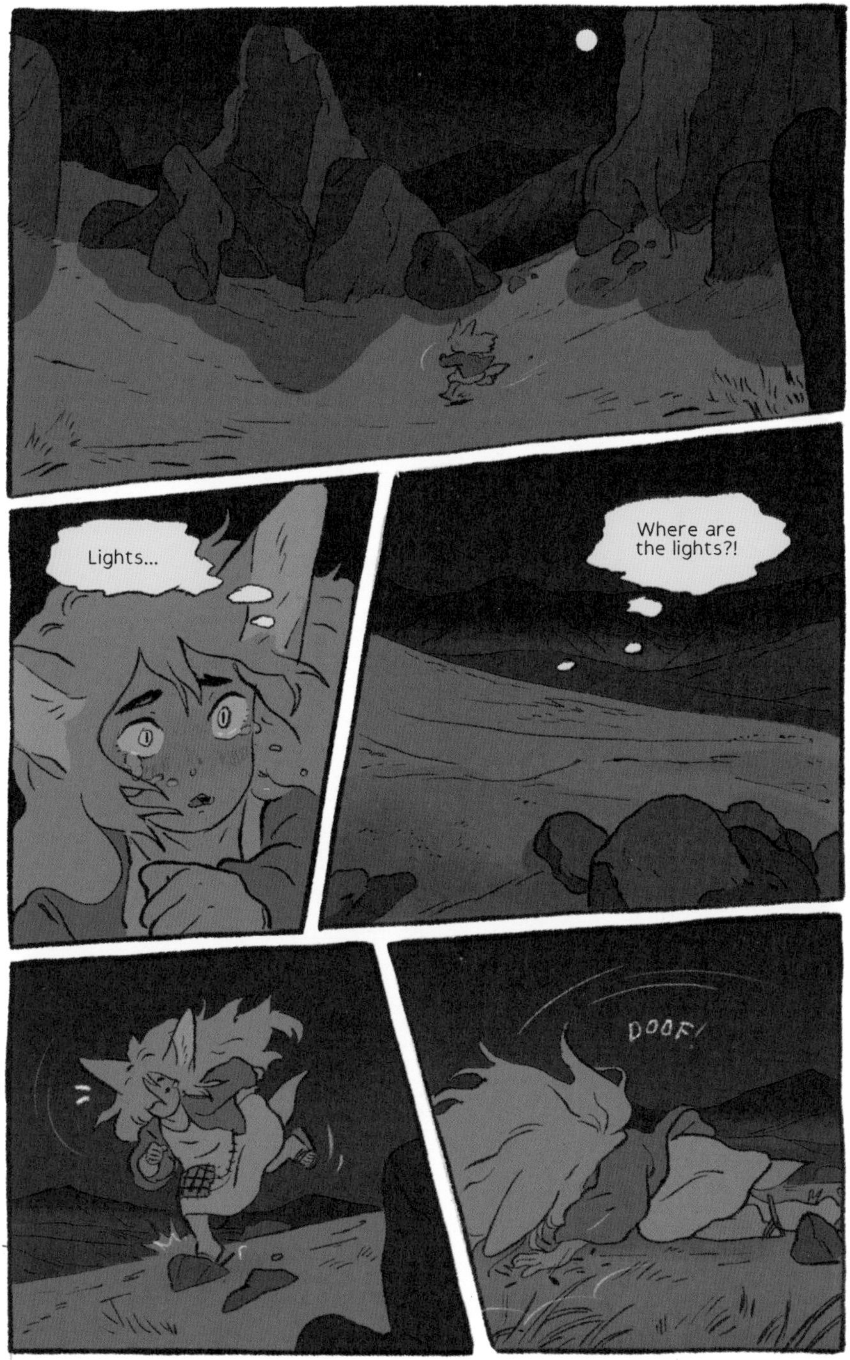
Lights...
Where are the lights?!
DOOF!

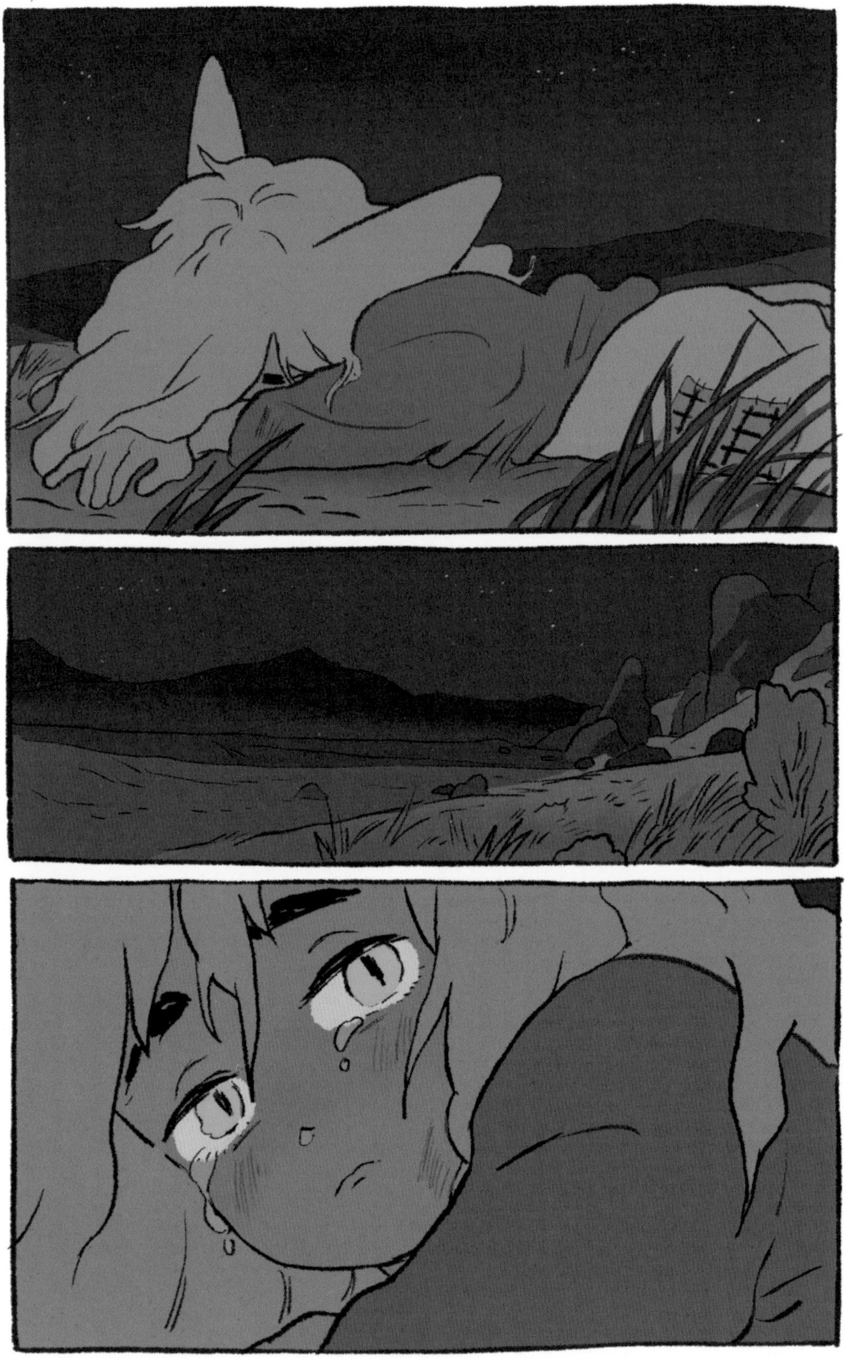

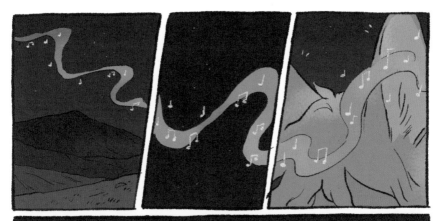

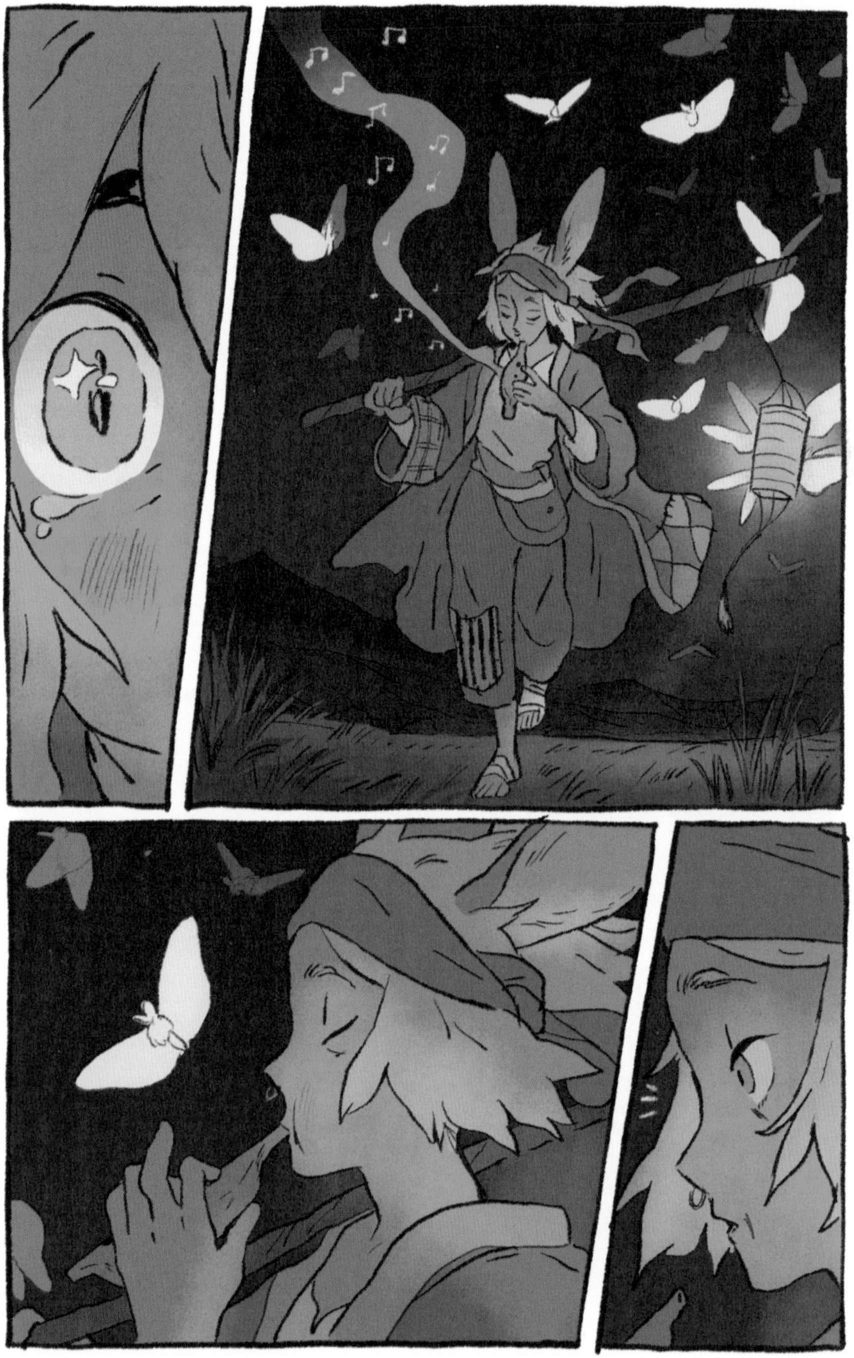

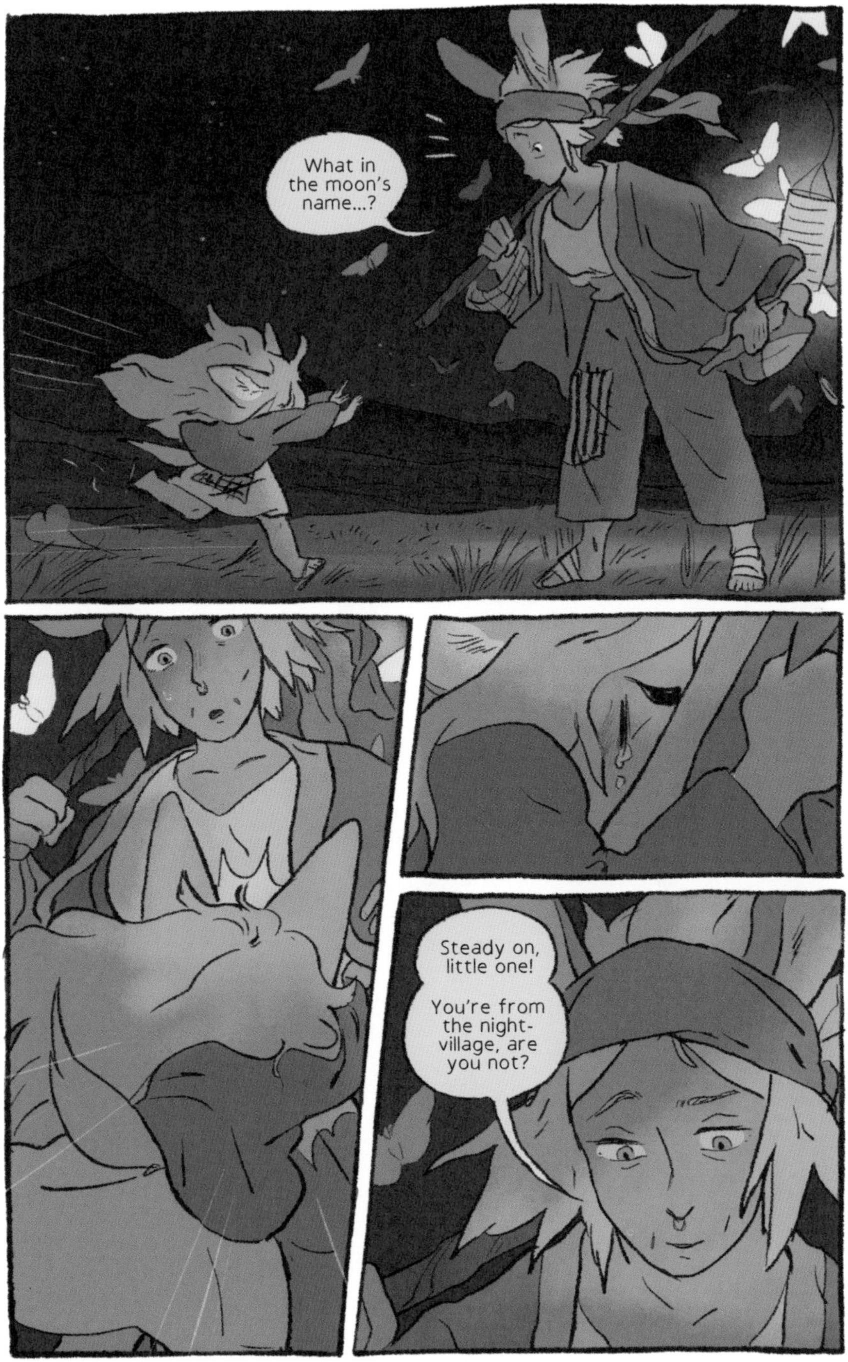
What in the moon's name...?
Steady on, little one!
You're from the night-village, are you not?

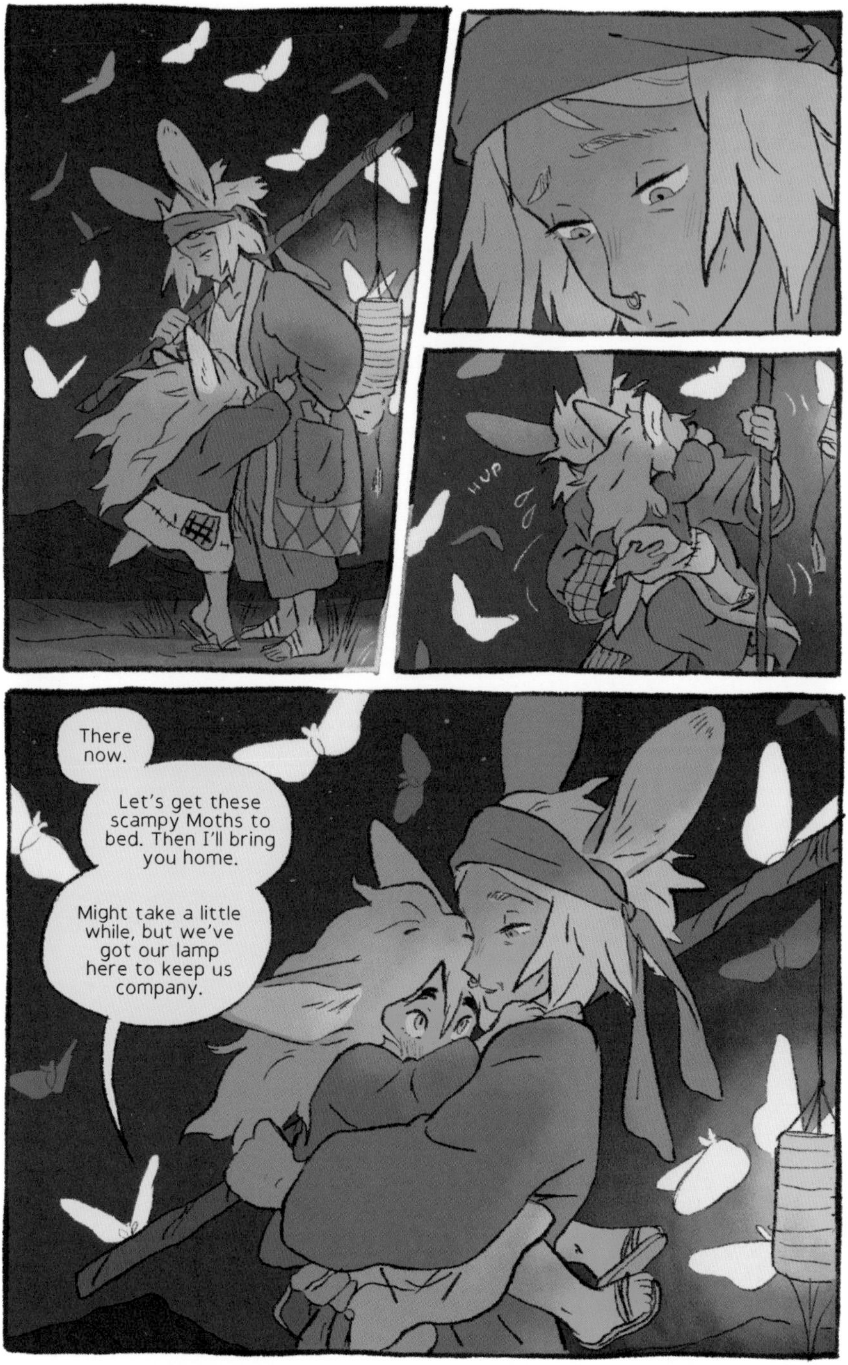
HUP
There now.
Let's get these scampy Moths to bed. Then I'll bring you home.
Might take a little while, but we've got our lamp here to keep us company.

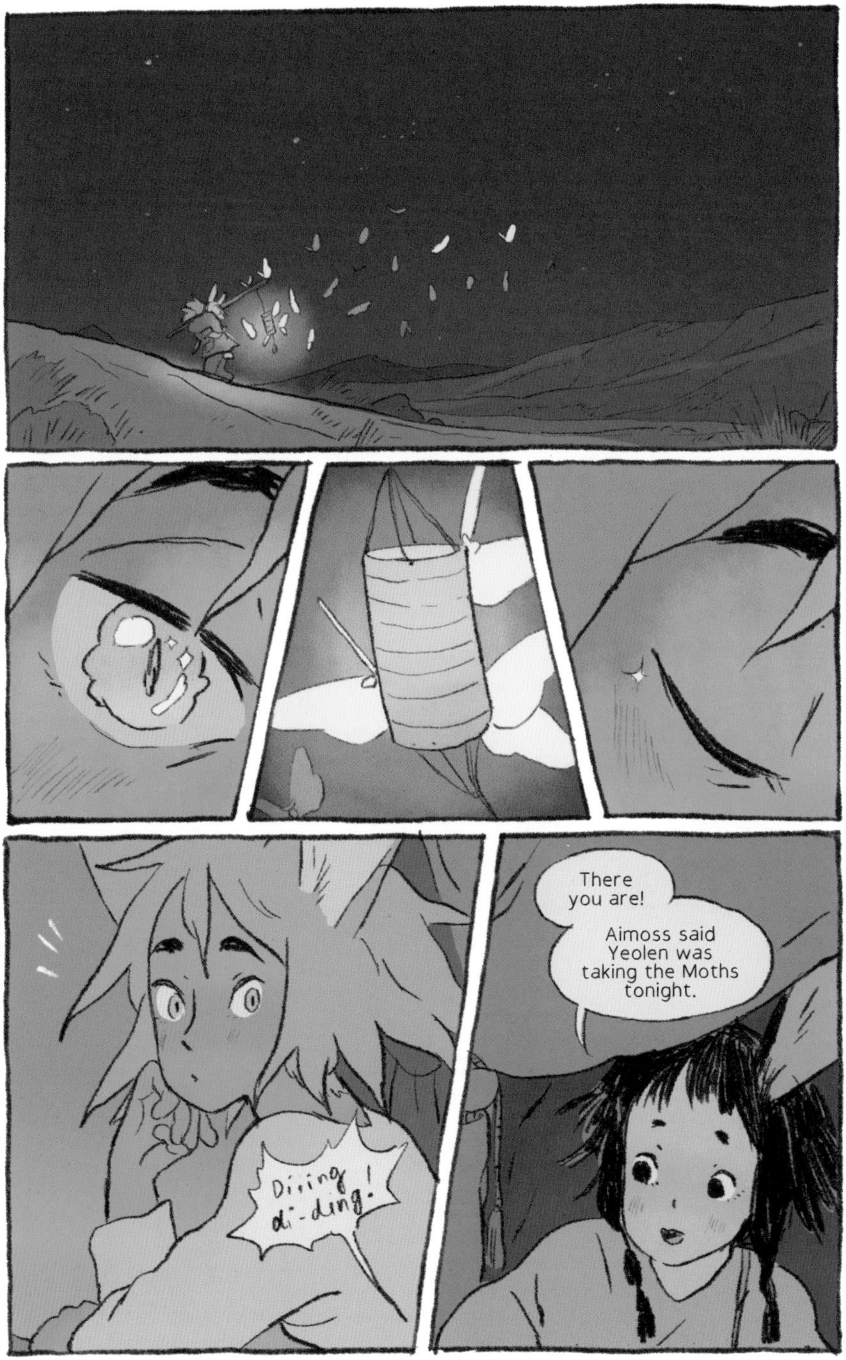
Diiing! di-ding!
There you are!
Aimoss said Yeolen was taking the Moths tonight.

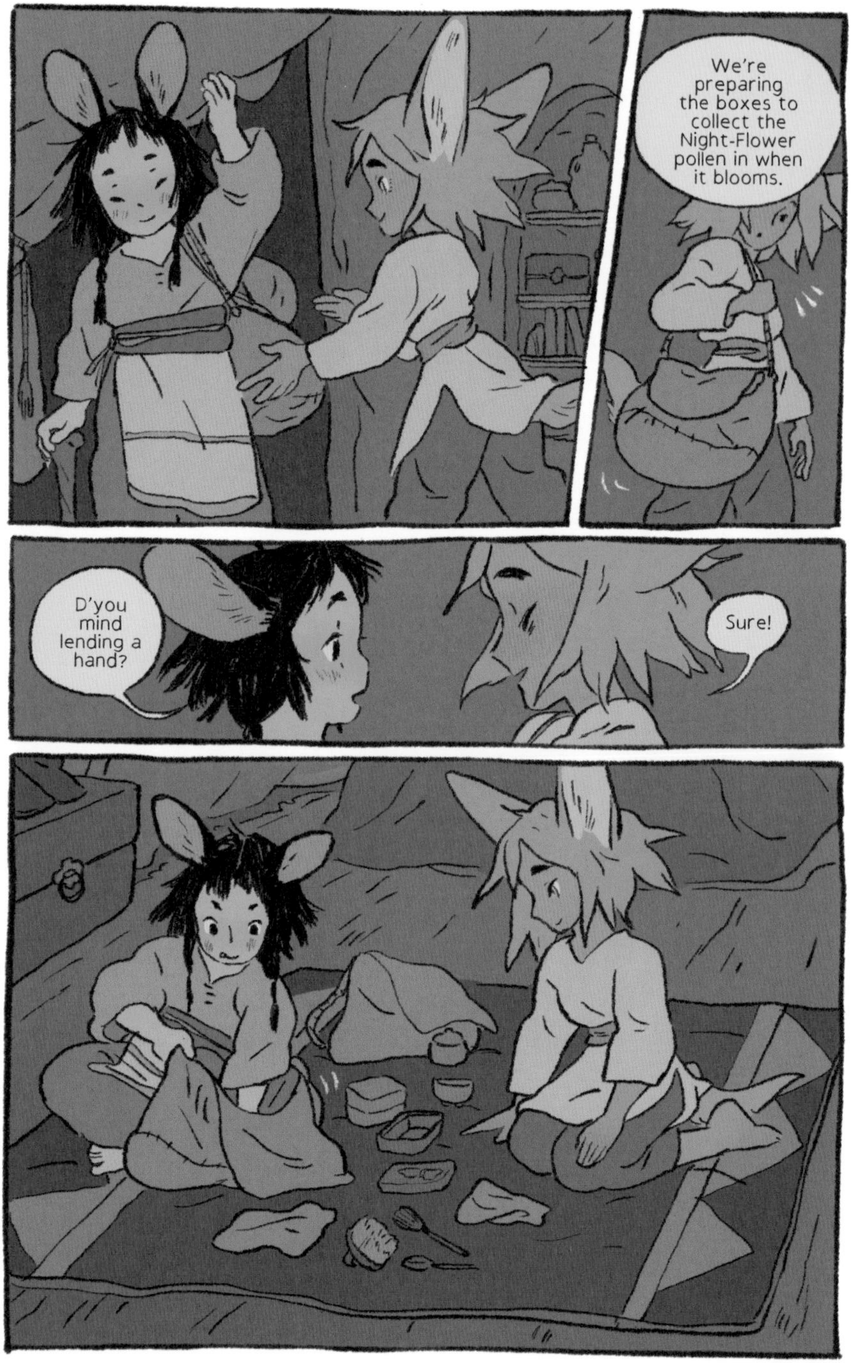
We're preparing the boxes to collect the Night-Flower pollen in when it blooms.
D'you mind lending a hand?
Sure!

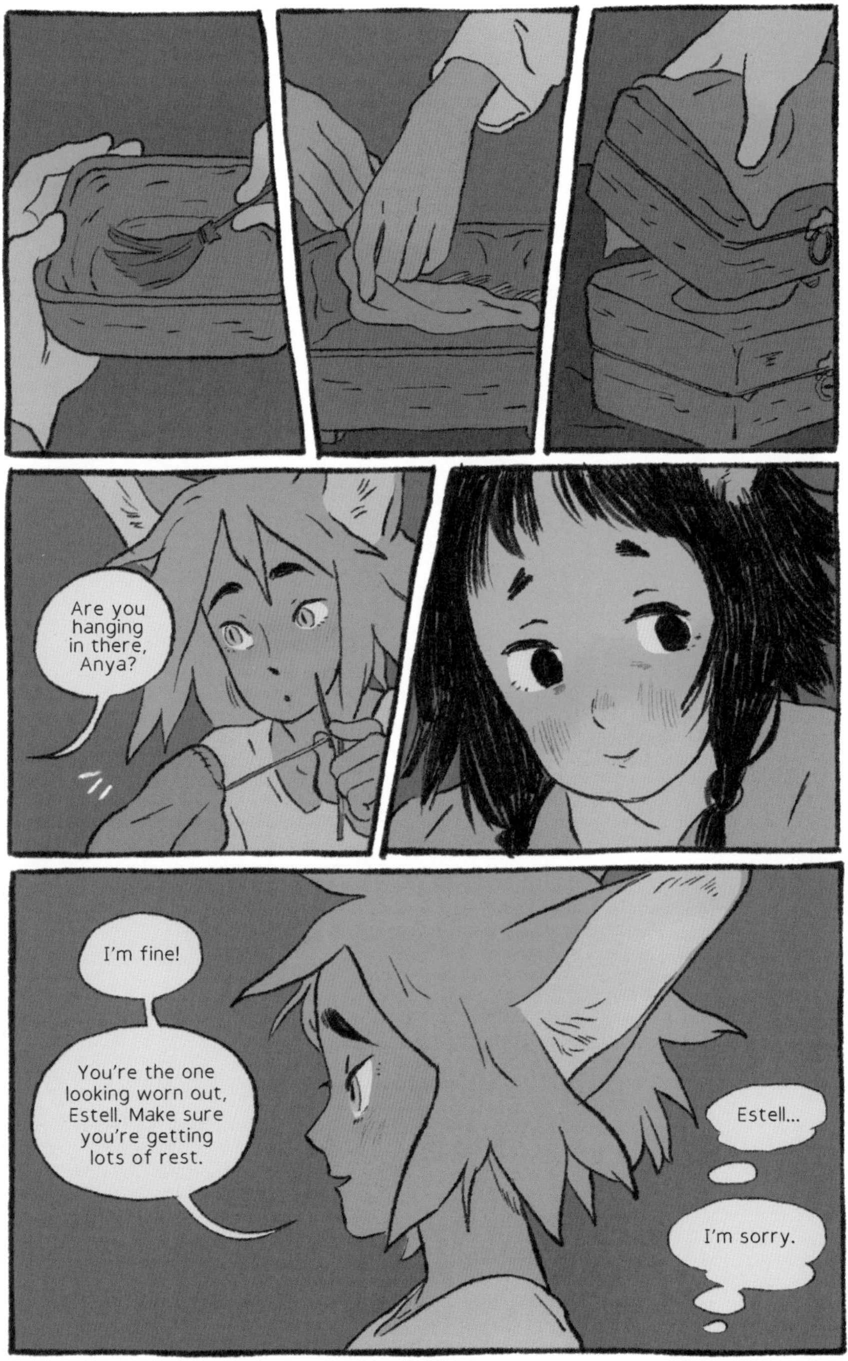
Are you hanging in there, Anya?
I'm fine!
You're the one looking worn out, Estell. Make sure you're getting lots of rest.
Estell...
I'm sorry.

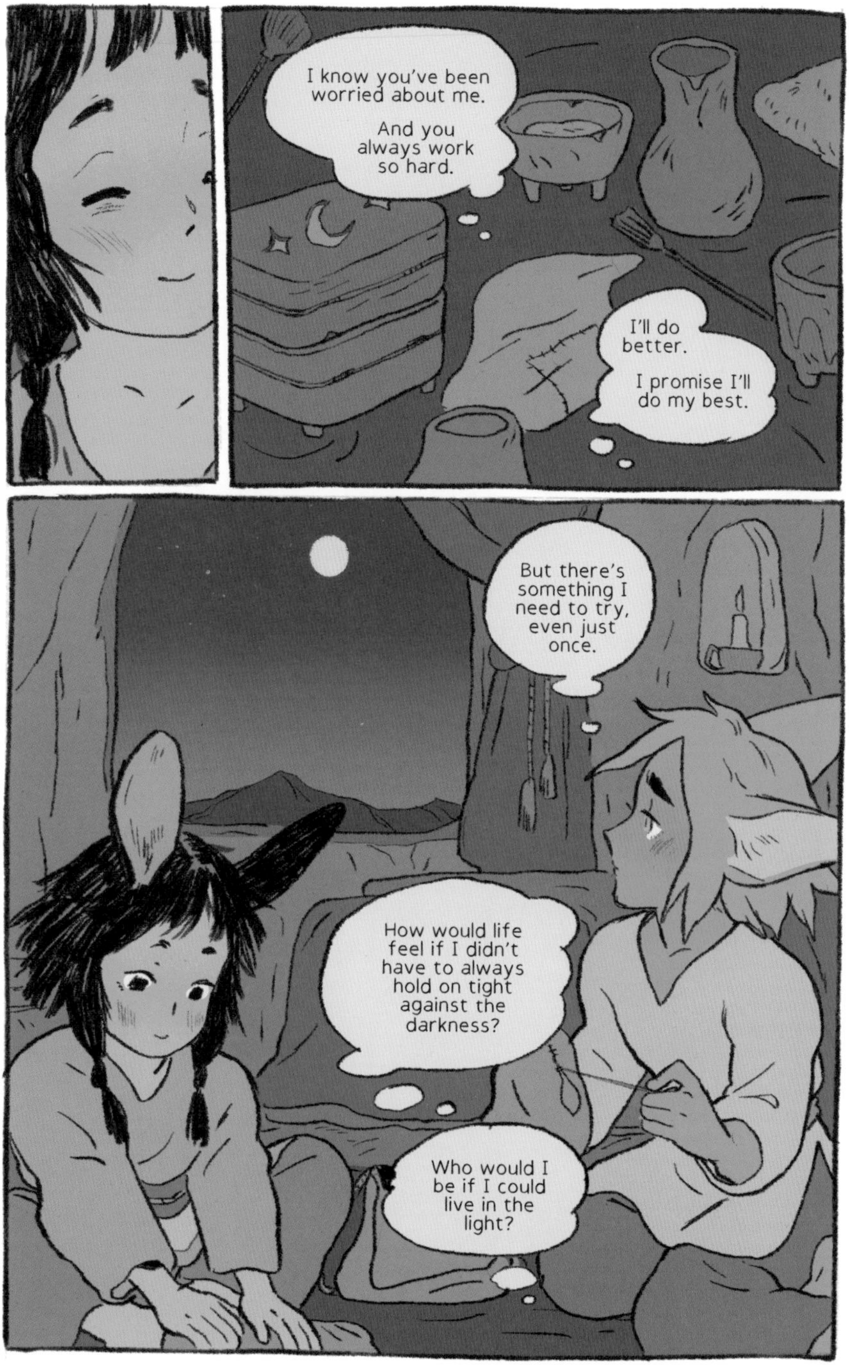
I know you've been worried about me.
And you always work so hard.
I'll do better.
I promise I'll do my best.
But there's something I need to try, even just once.
How would life feel if I didn't have to always hold on tight against the darkness?
Who would I be if I could live in the light?

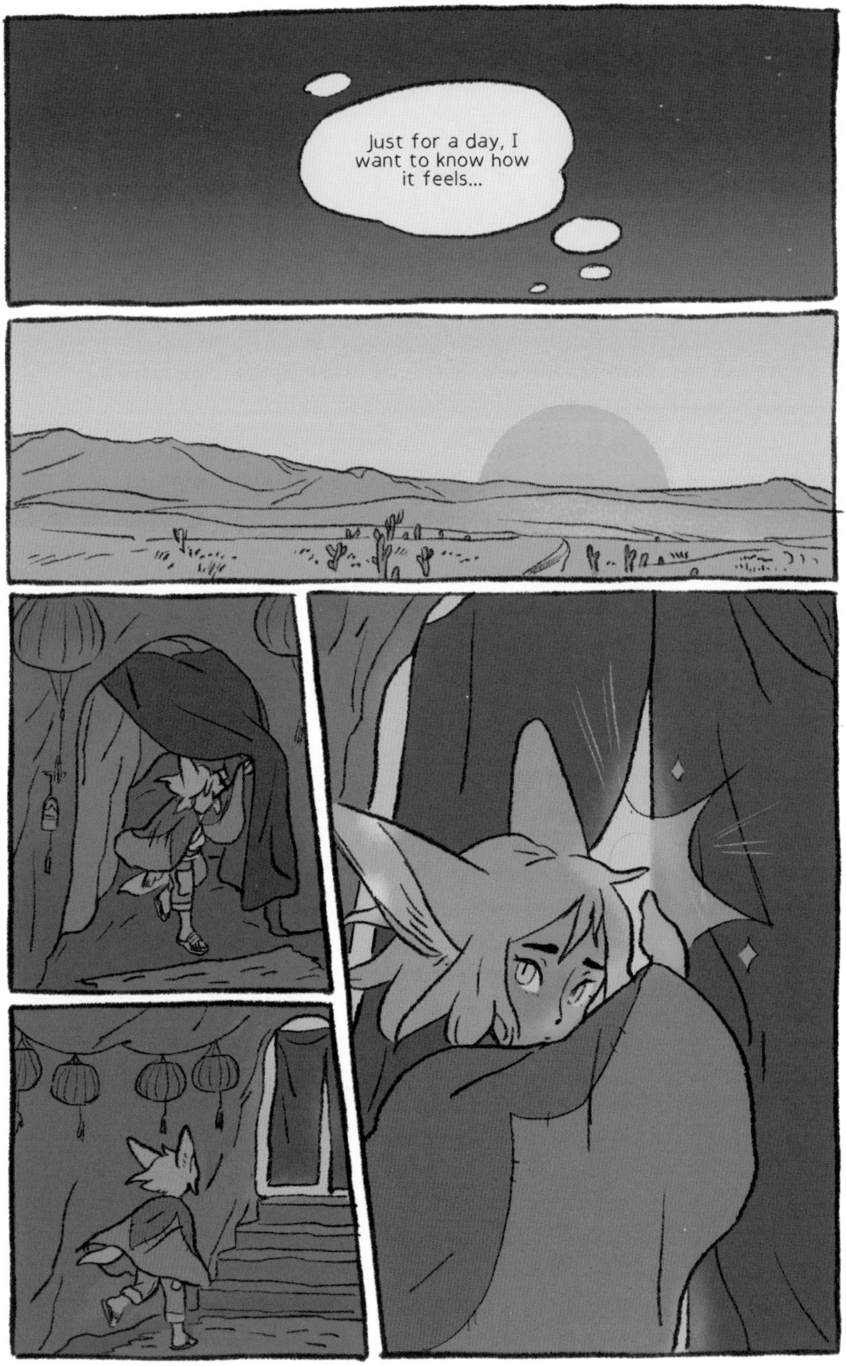
Just for a day, I want to know how it feels...

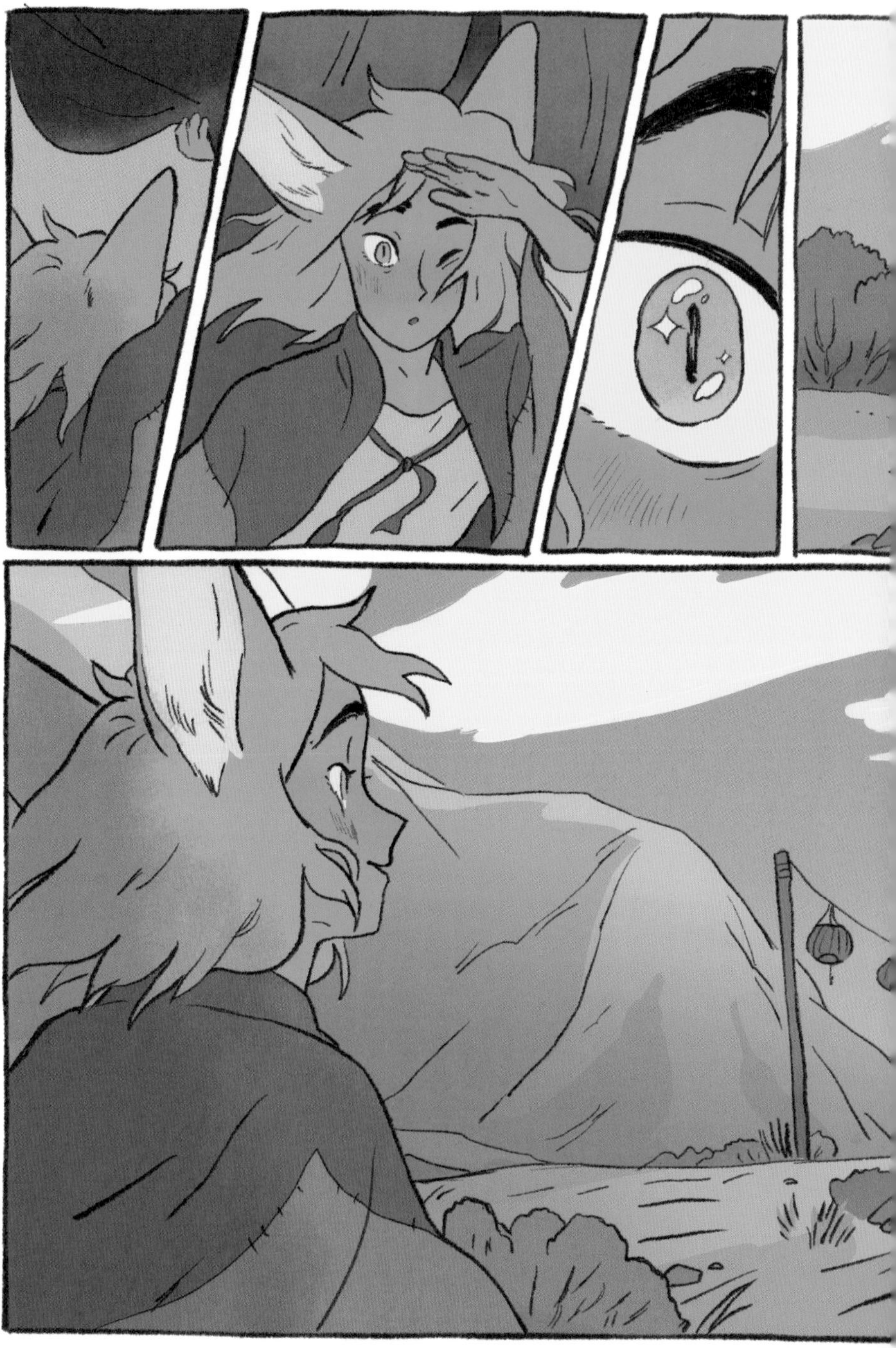

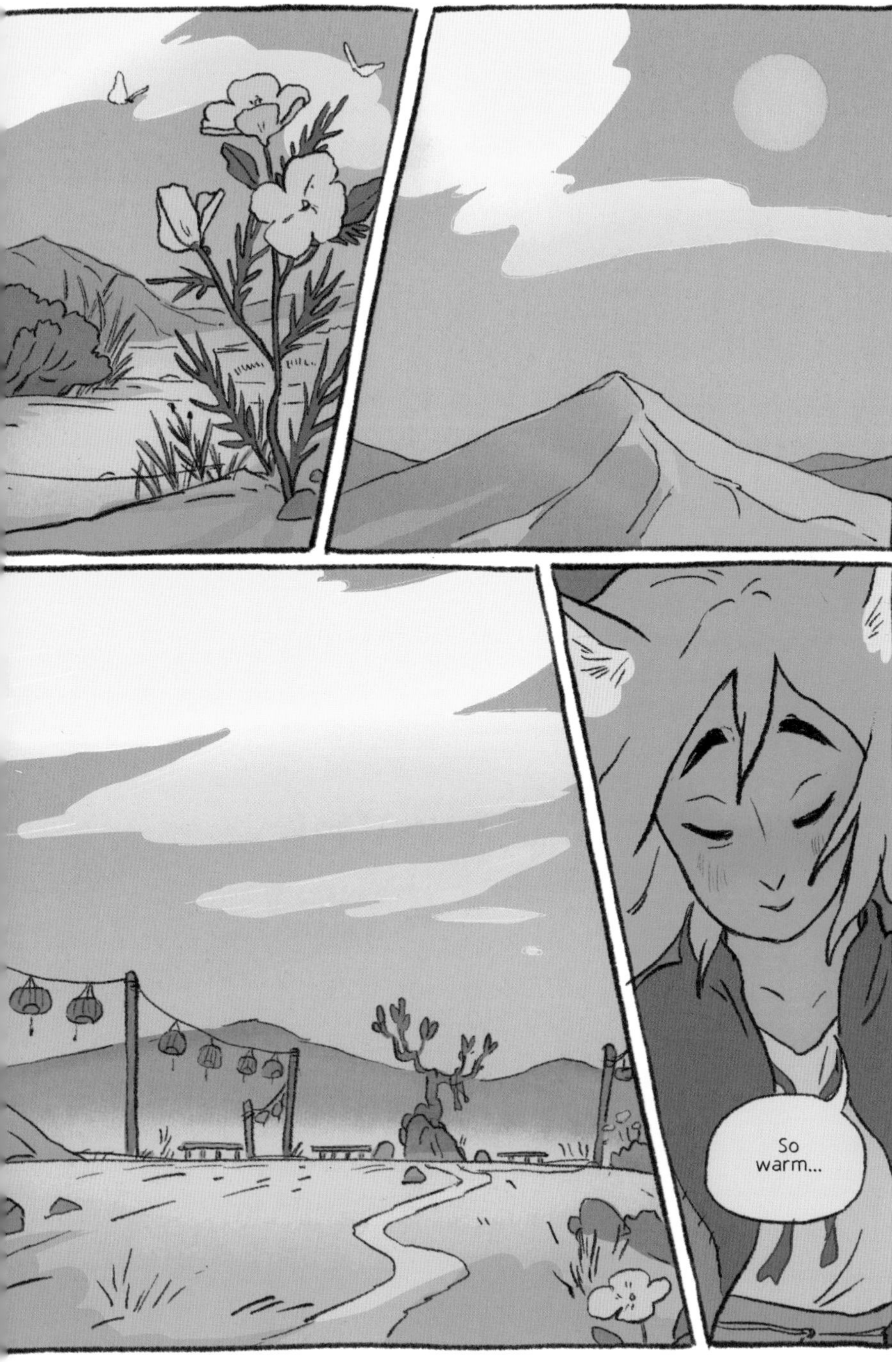
So warm...

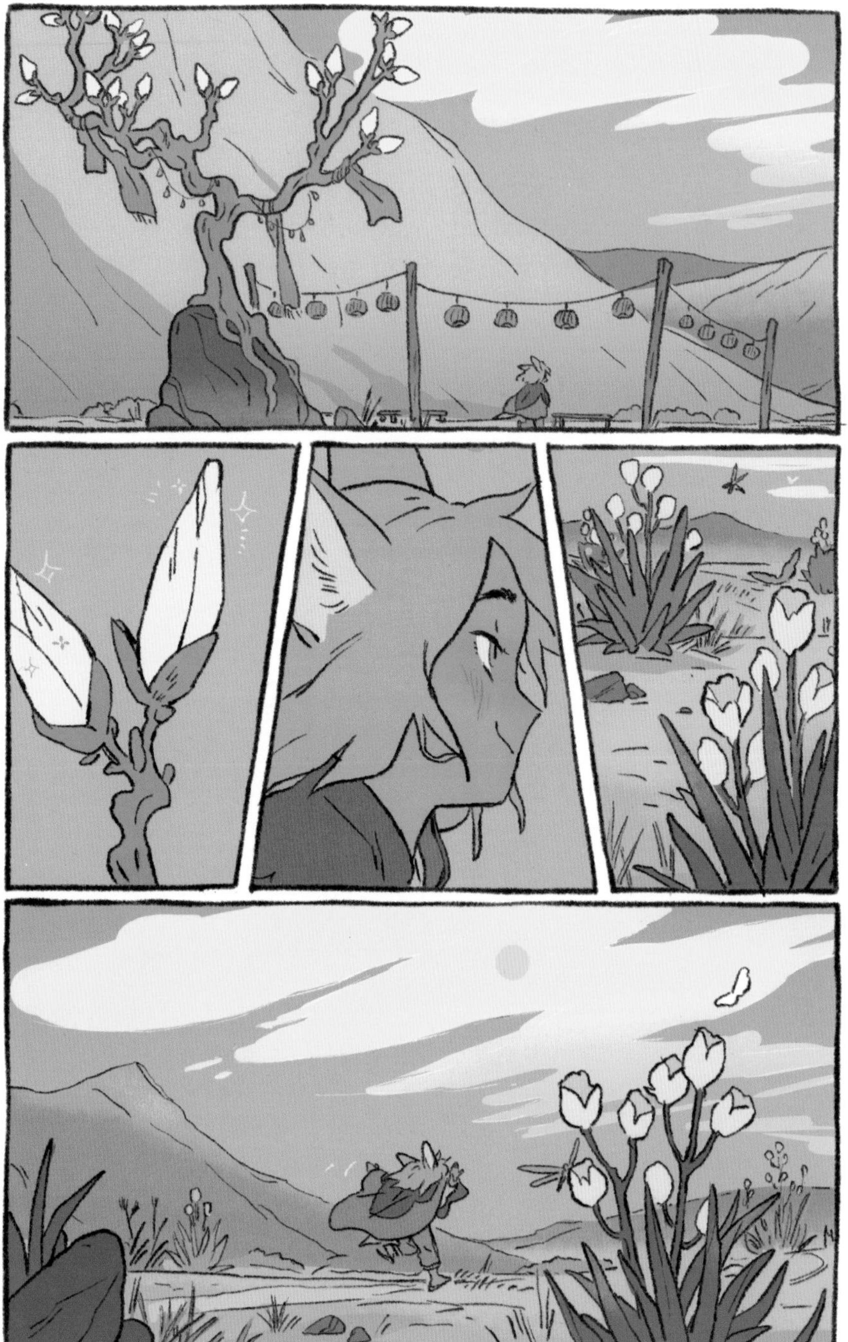

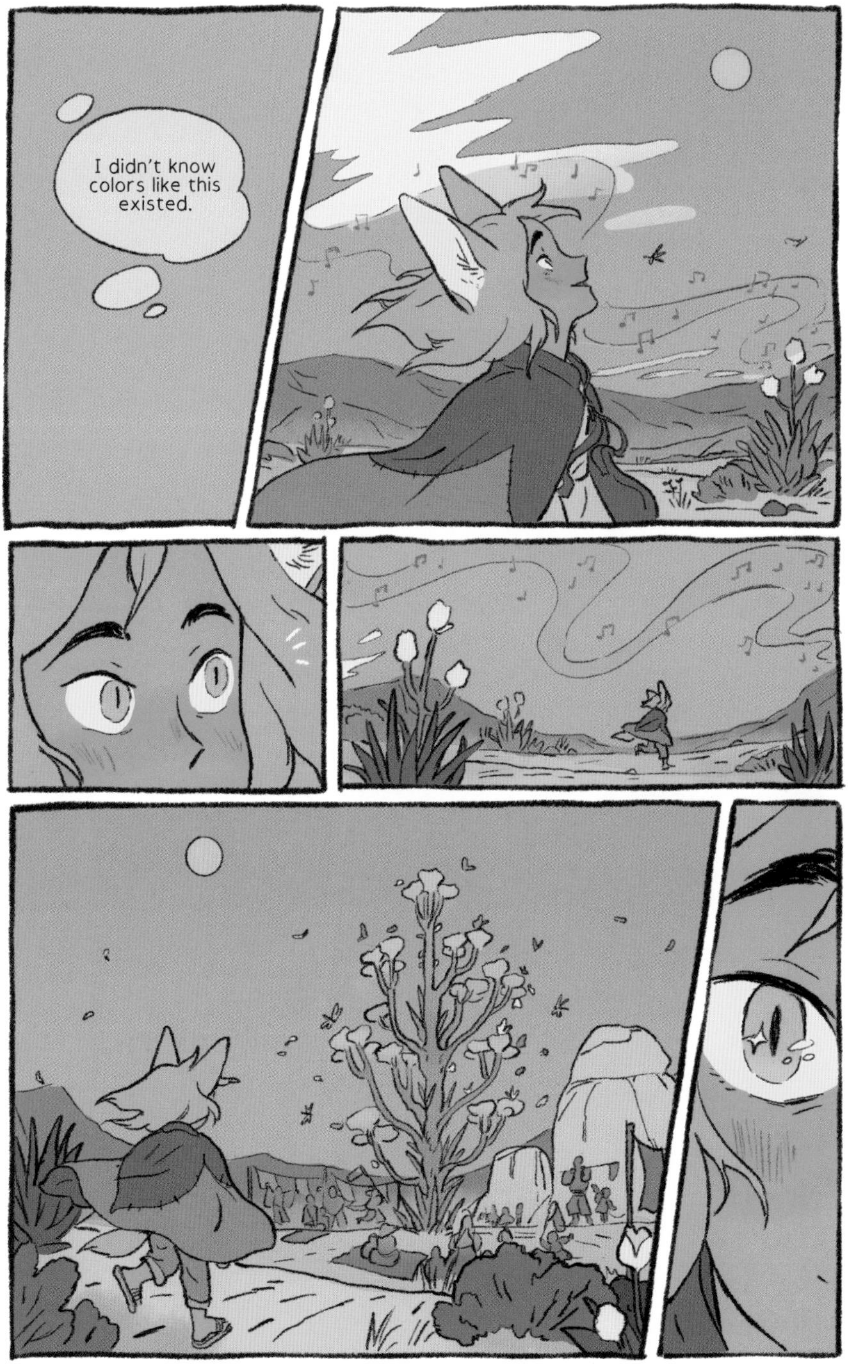
I didn't know colors like this existed.

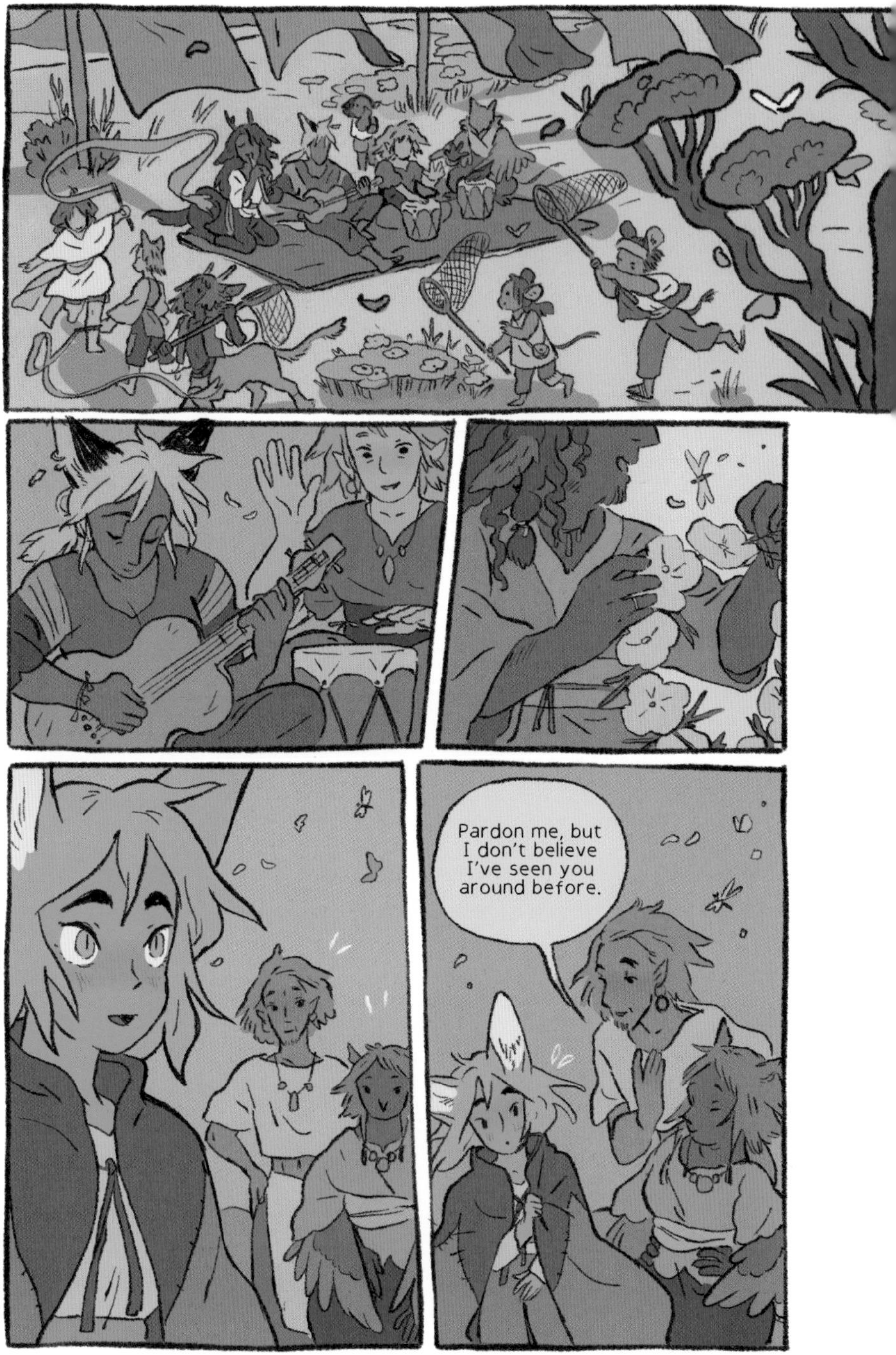
Pardon me, but I don't believe I've seen you around before.

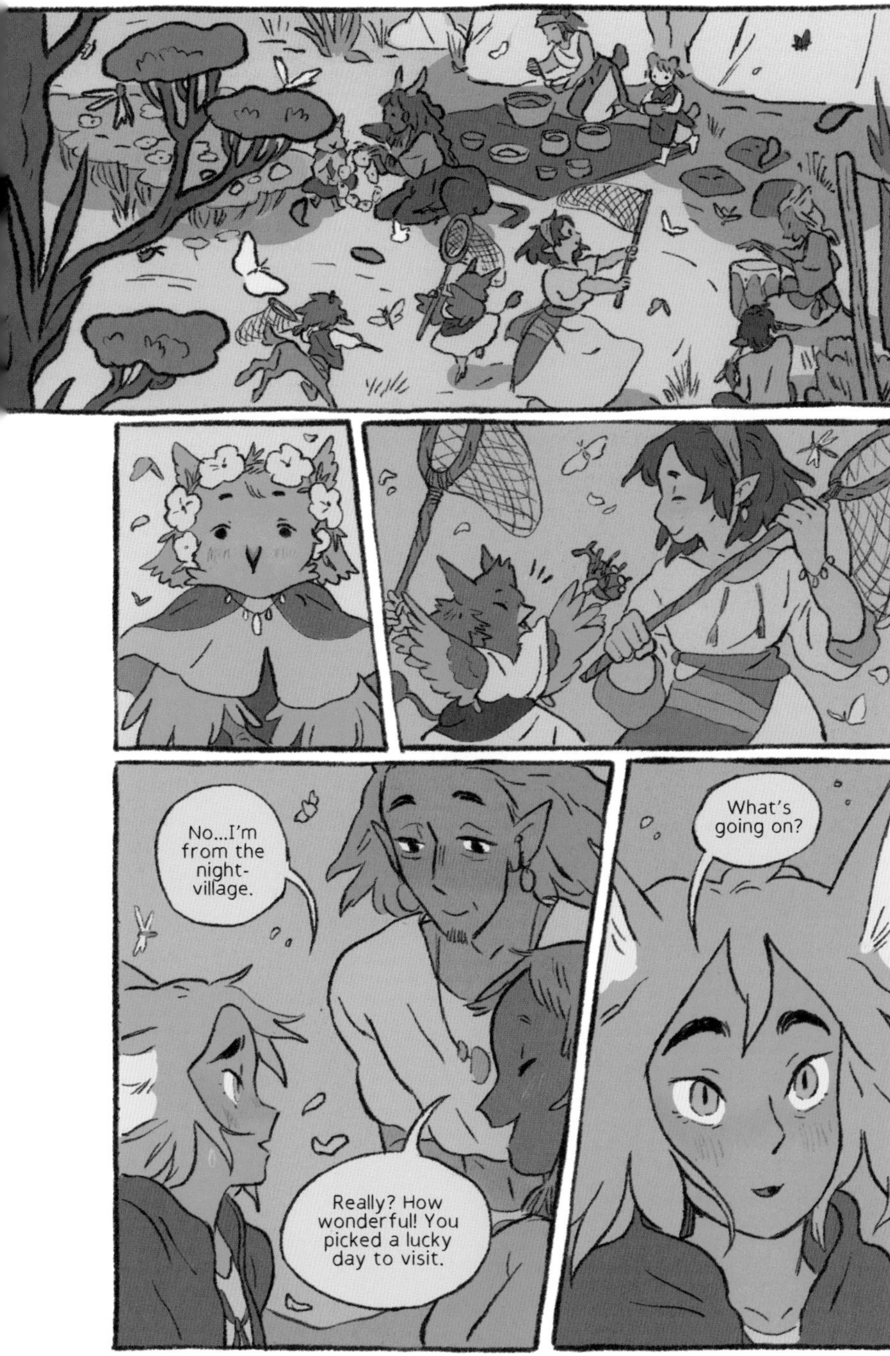
No...I'm from the night-village.
Really? How wonderful! You picked a lucky day to visit.
What's going on?

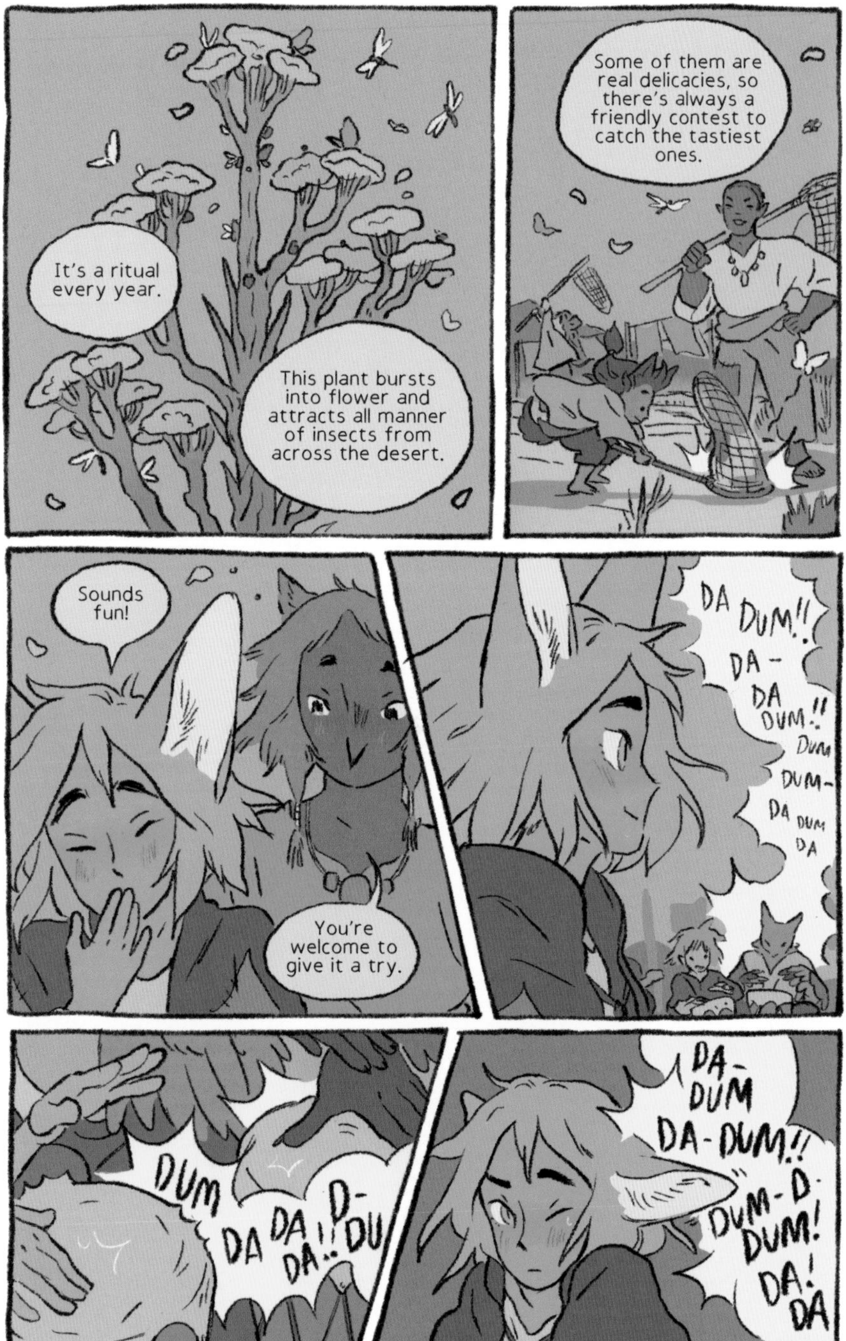
It's a ritual every year.
This plant bursts into flower and attracts all manner of insects from across the desert.
Some of them are real delicacies, so there's always a friendly contest to catch the tastiest ones.
Sounds fun!
You're welcome to give it a try.
DA DUM!! DA-DA DUM!! DUM DUM-DA DUM DA
DUM DA DA DA!! D-DU
DA-DUM DA-DUM!! DUM-D-DUM! DA! DA

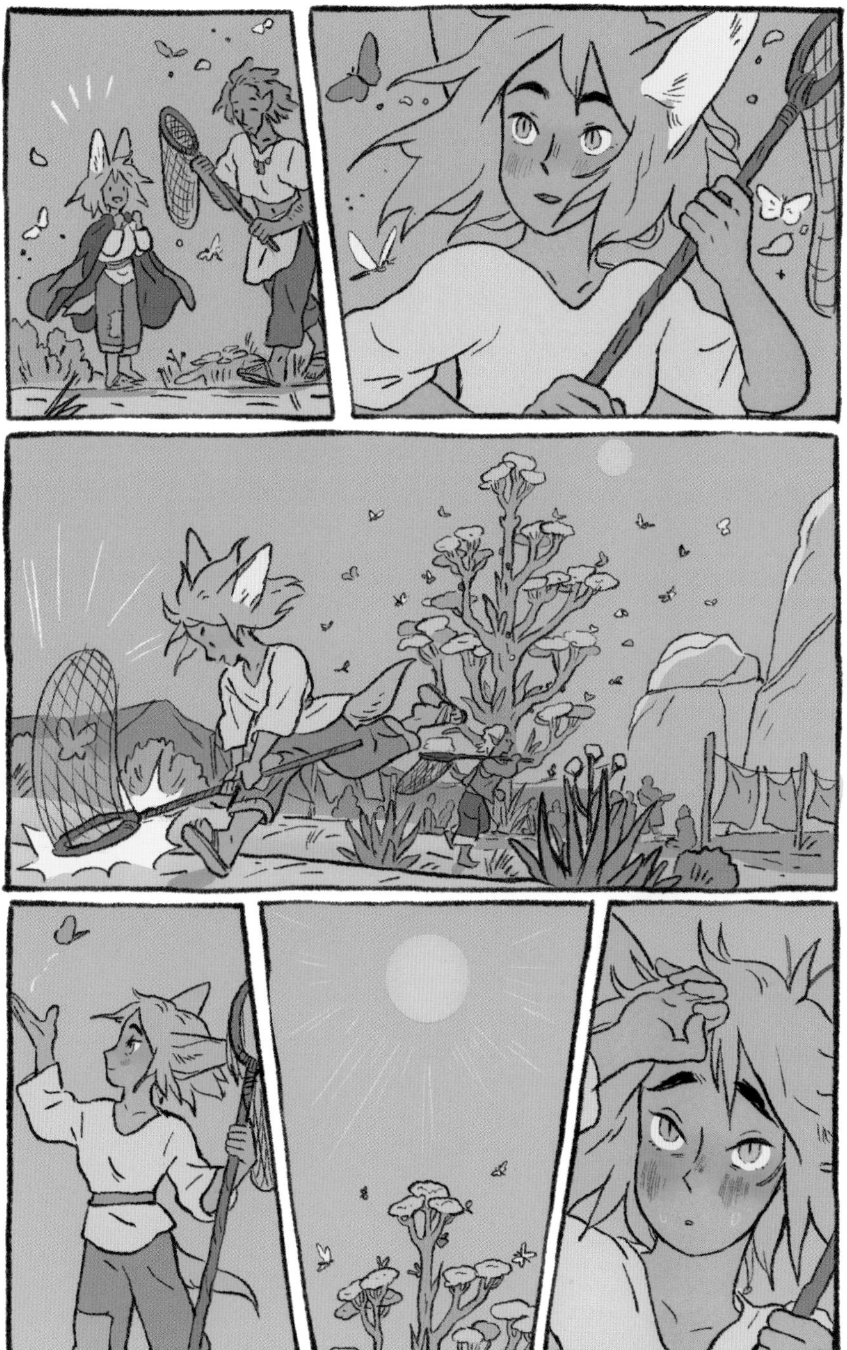

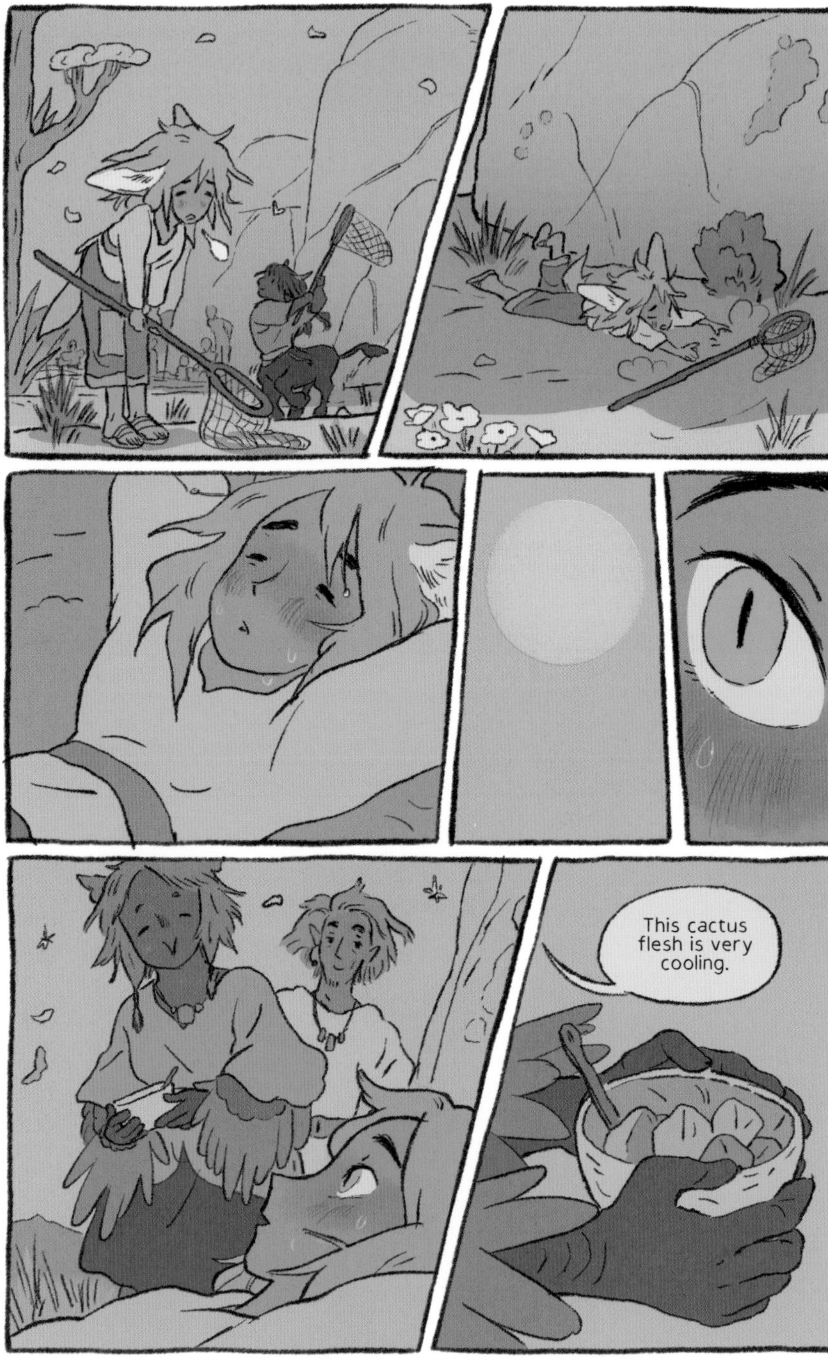
This cactus flesh is very cooling.

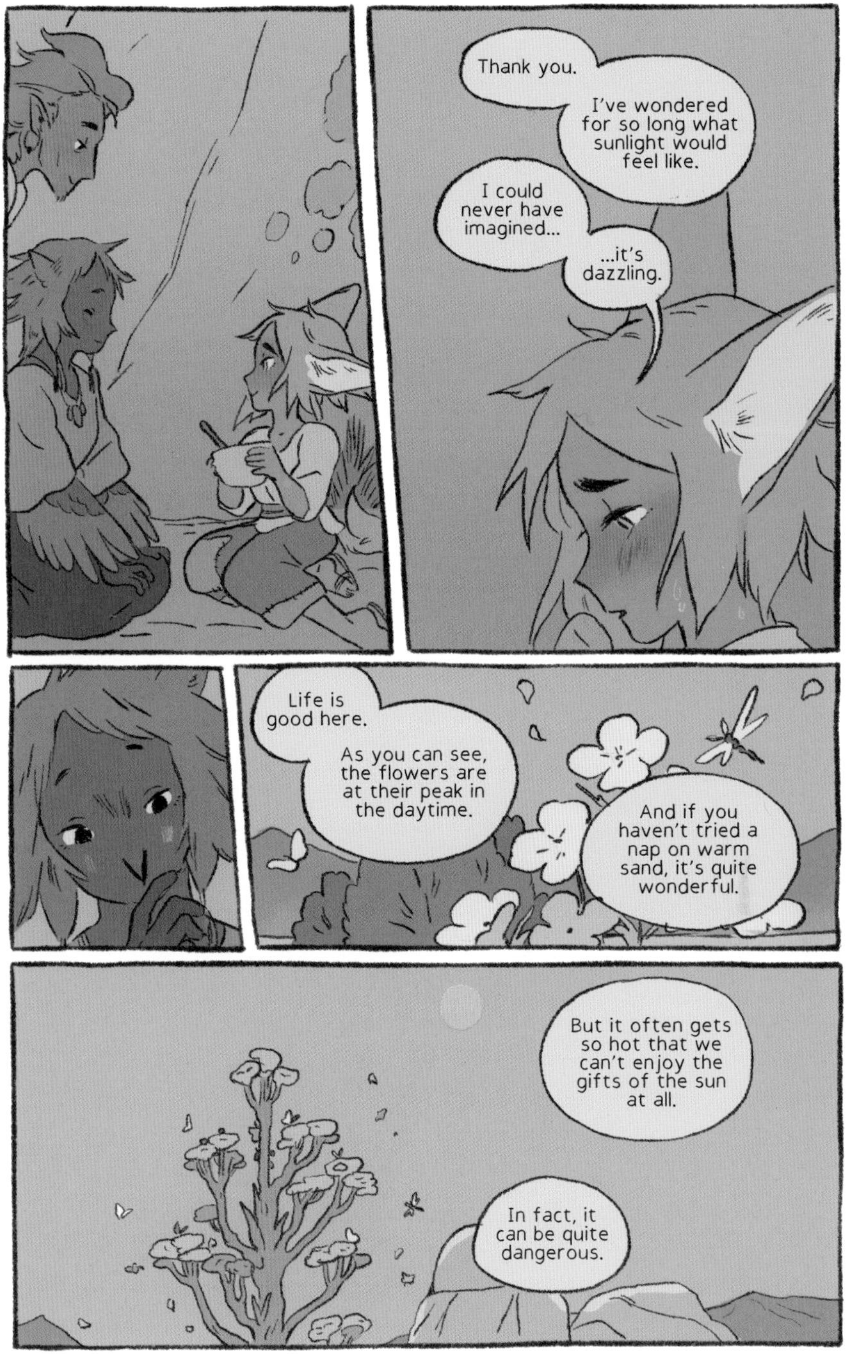
Thank you.
I've wondered for so long what sunlight would feel like.
I could never have imagined...
...it's dazzling.
Life is good here.
As you can see, the flowers are at their peak in the daytime.
And if you haven't tried a nap on warm sand, it's quite wonderful.
But it often gets so hot that we can't enjoy the gifts of the sun at all.
In fact, it can be quite dangerous.

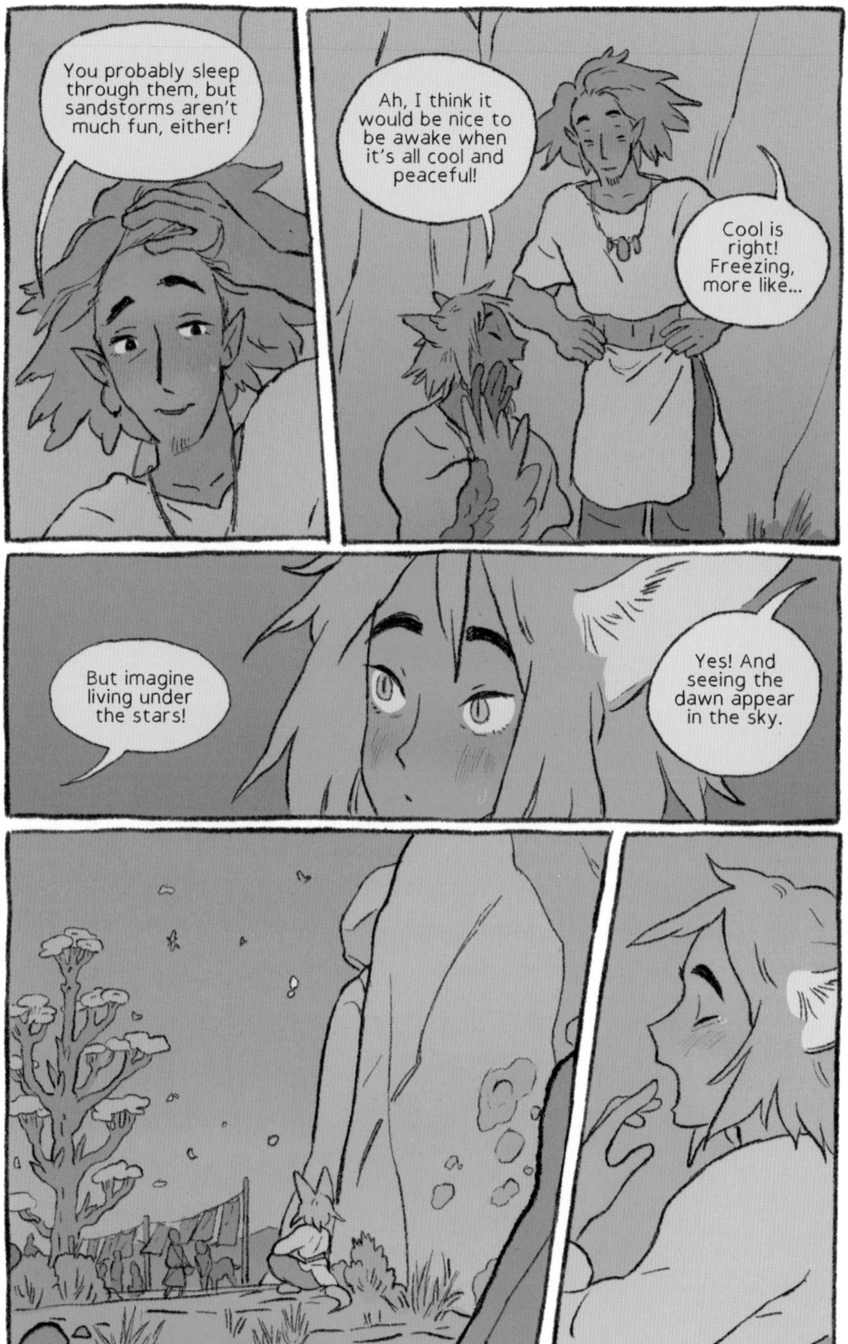
You probably sleep through them, but sandstorms aren't much fun, either!
Ah, I think it would be nice to be awake when it's all cool and peaceful!
Cool is right! Freezing, more like...
But imagine living under the stars!
Yes! And seeing the dawn appear in the sky.

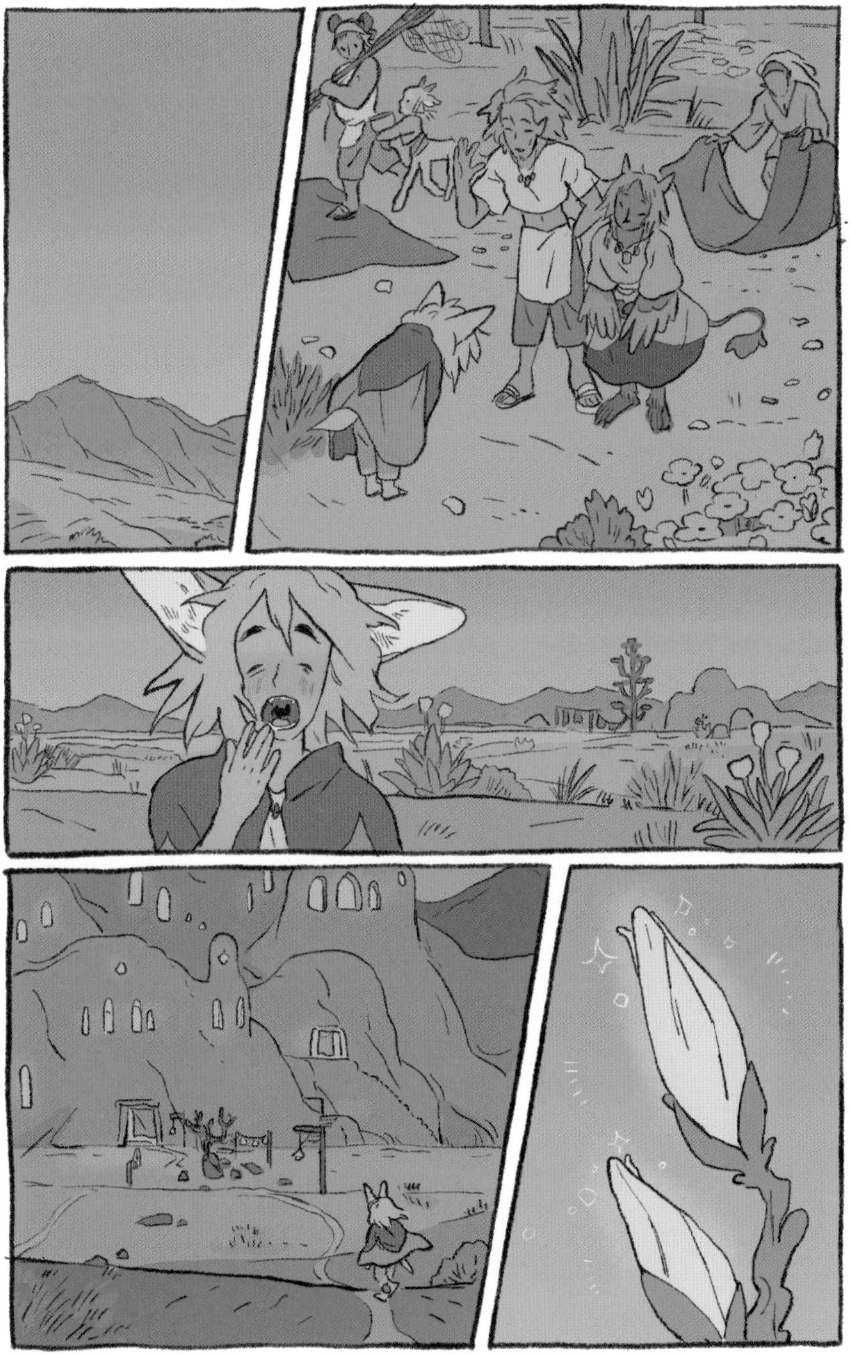

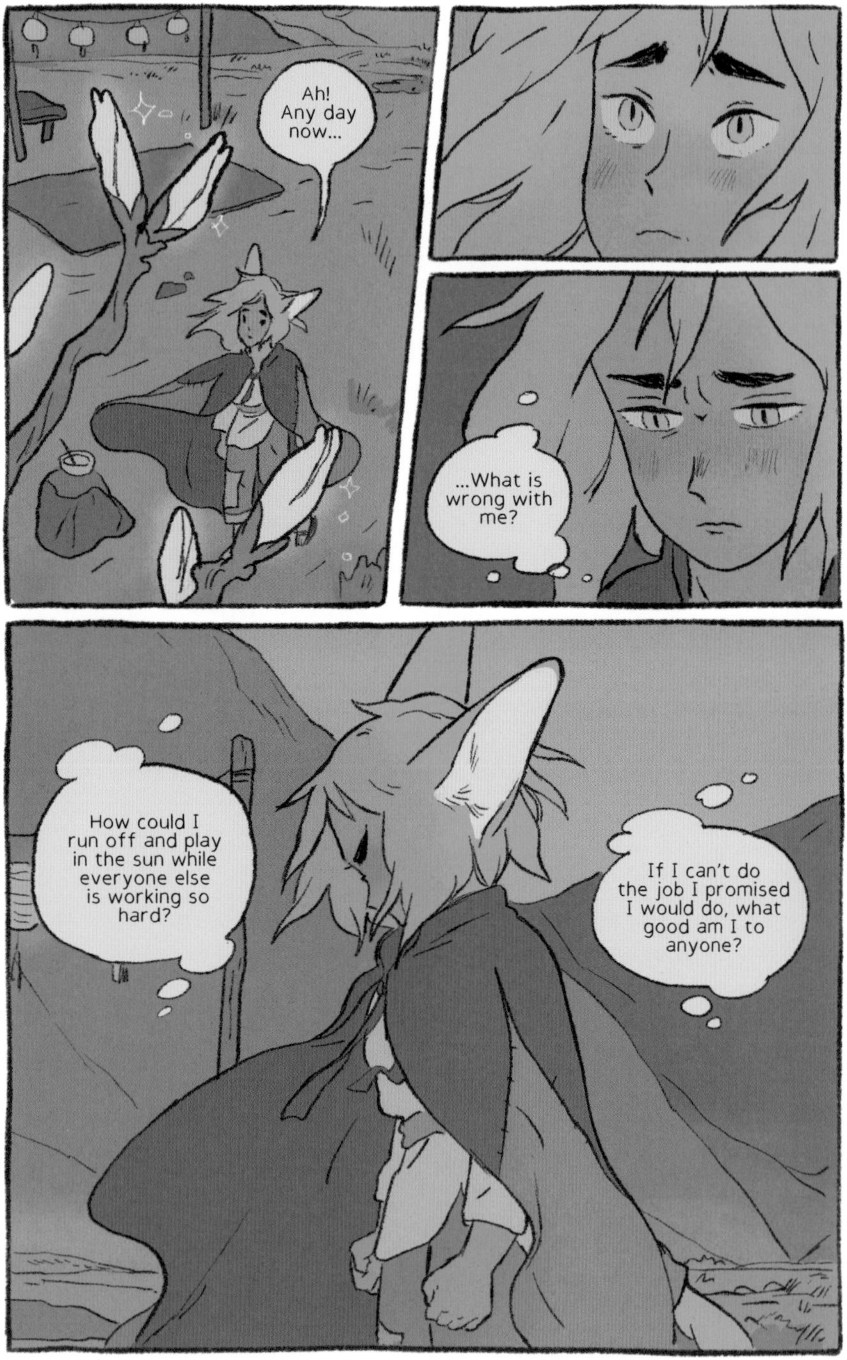
Ah! Any day now...
...What is wrong with me?
How could I run off and play in the sun while everyone else is working so hard?
If I can't do the job I promised I would do, what good am I to anyone?

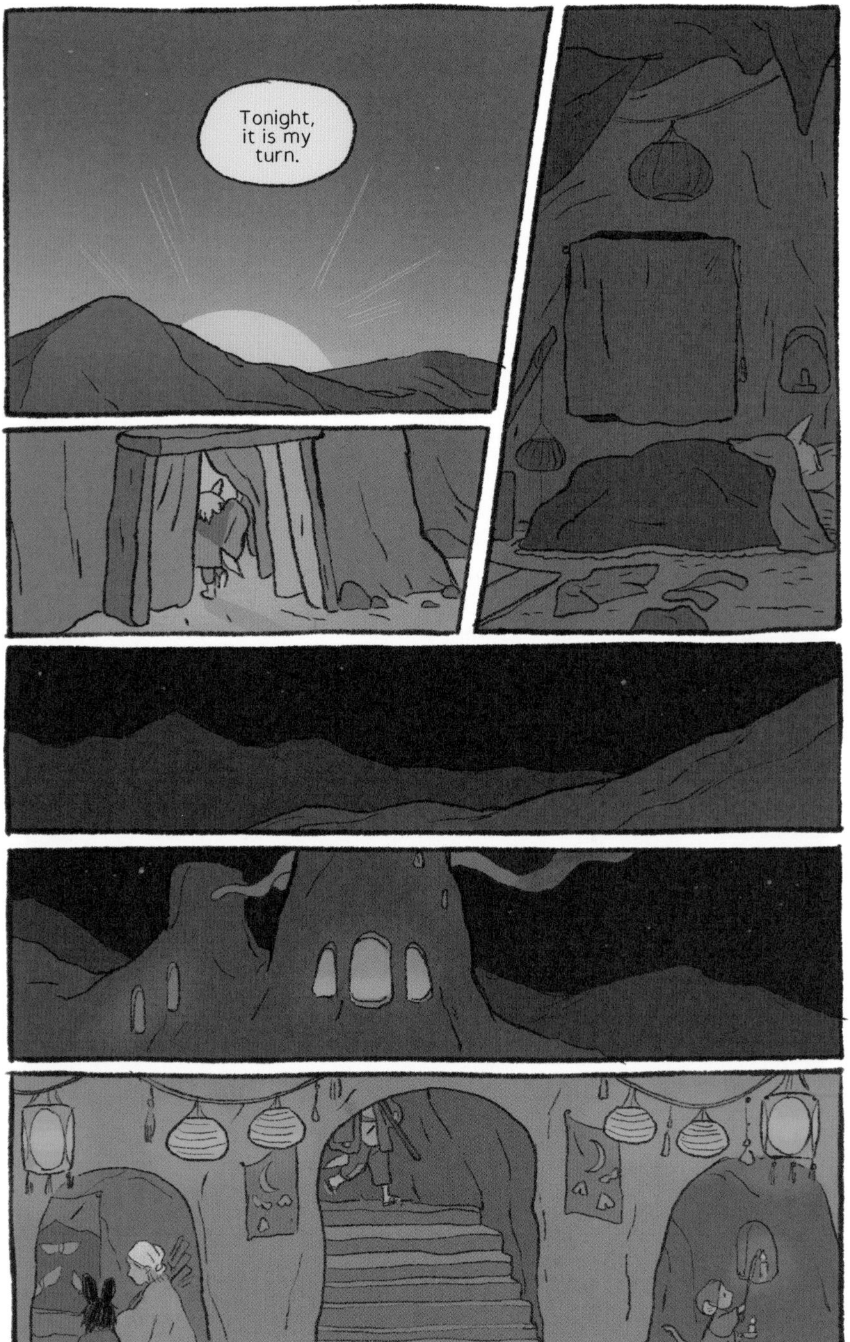
Tonight, it is my turn.

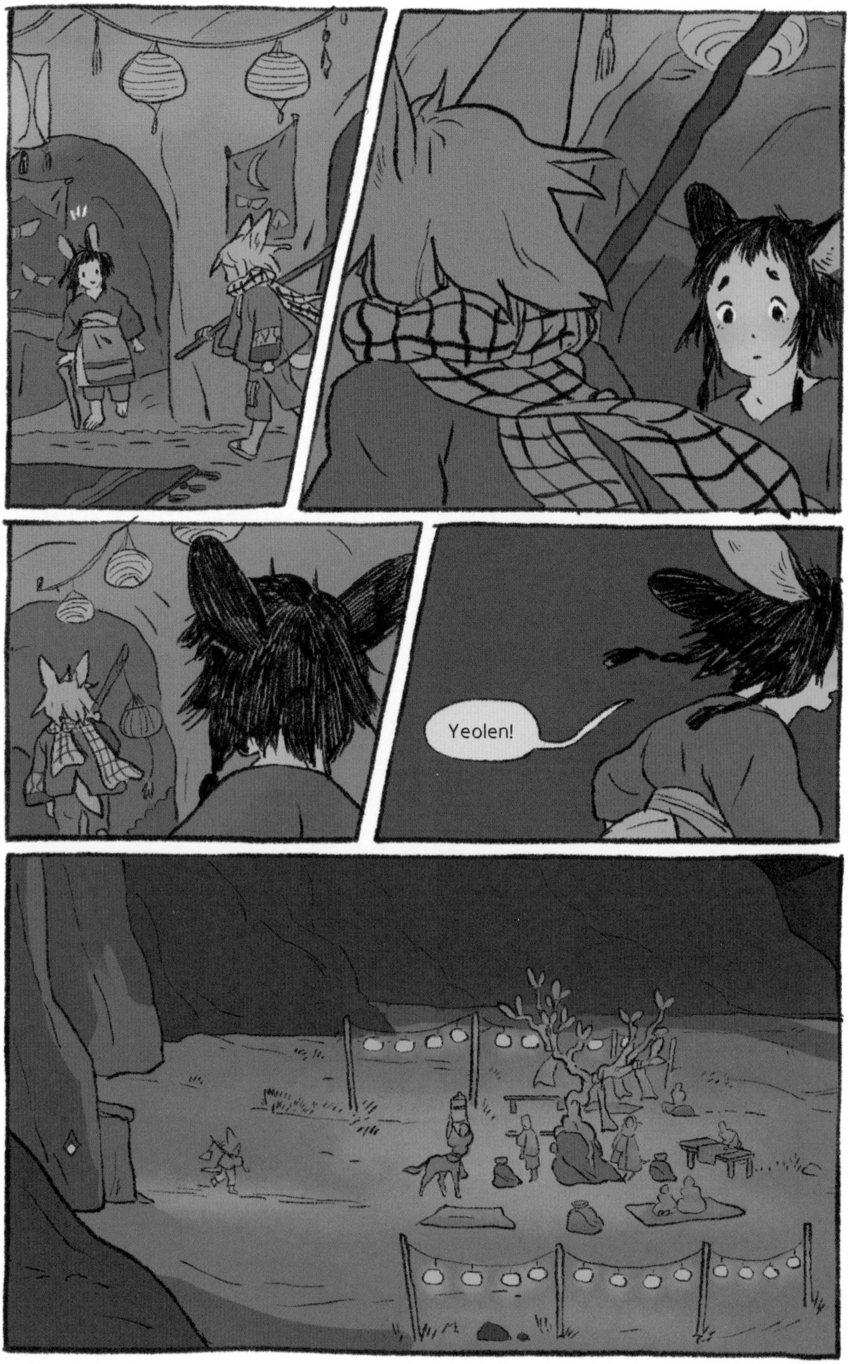
Yeolen!

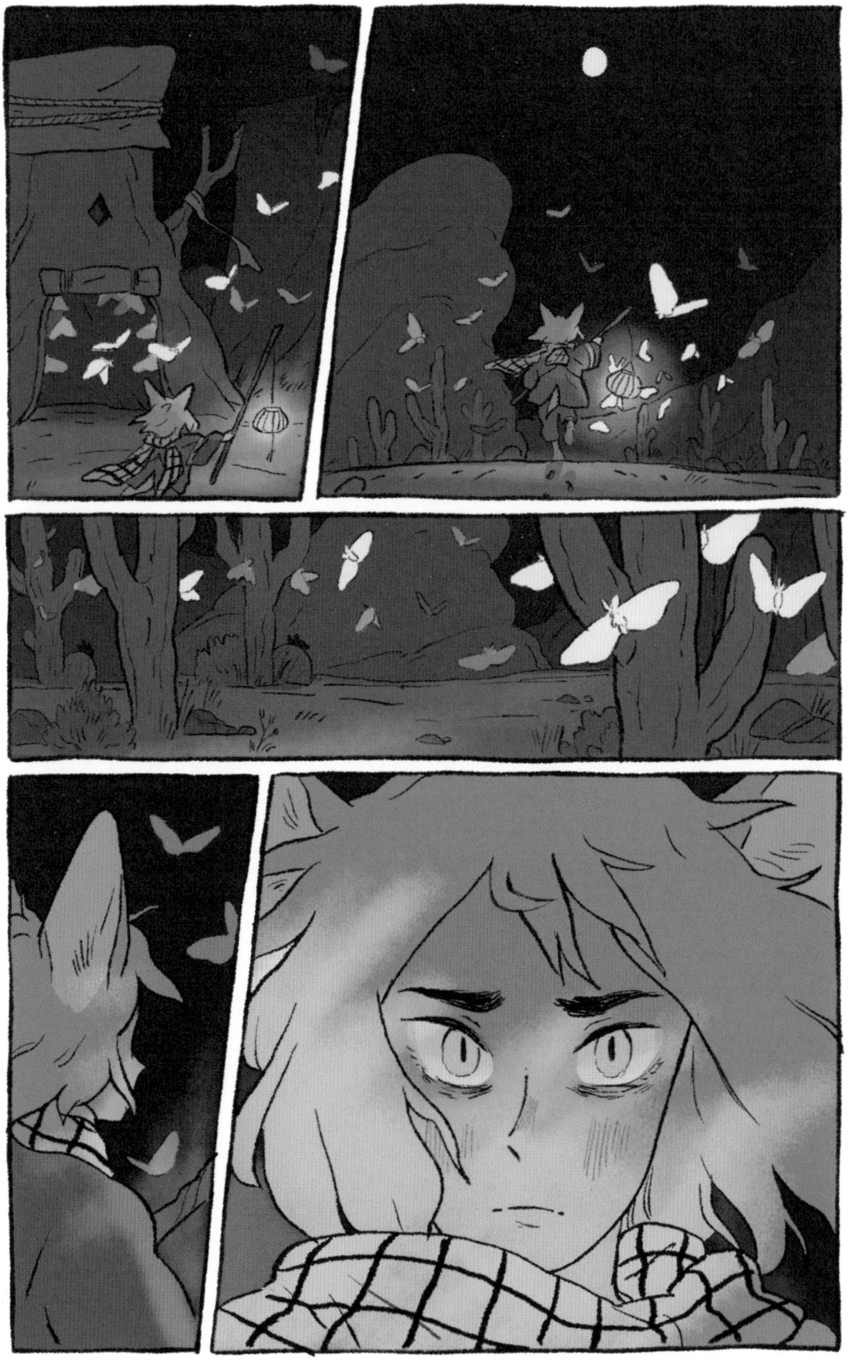

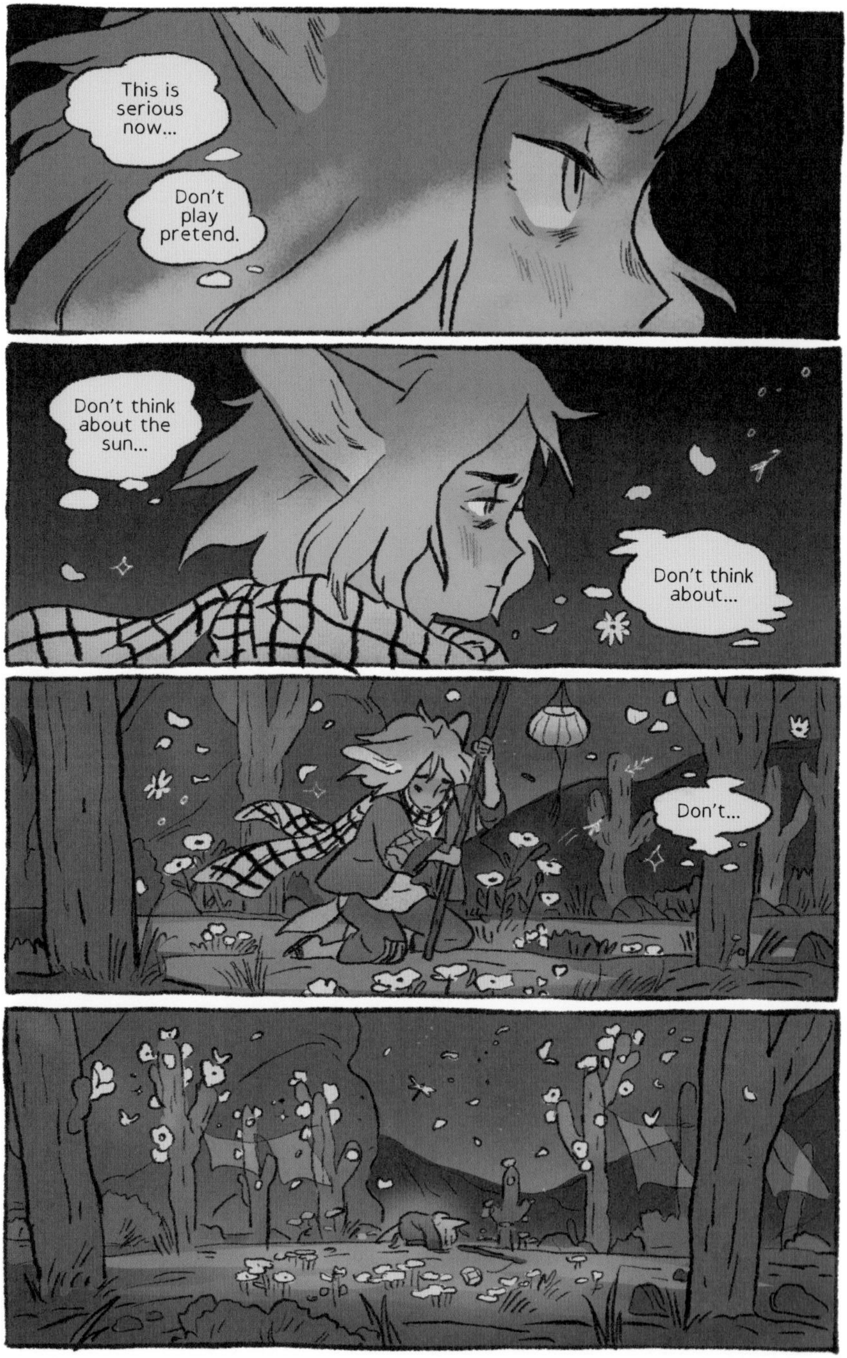
This is serious now...
Don't play pretend.
Don't think about the sun...
Don't think about...
Don't...

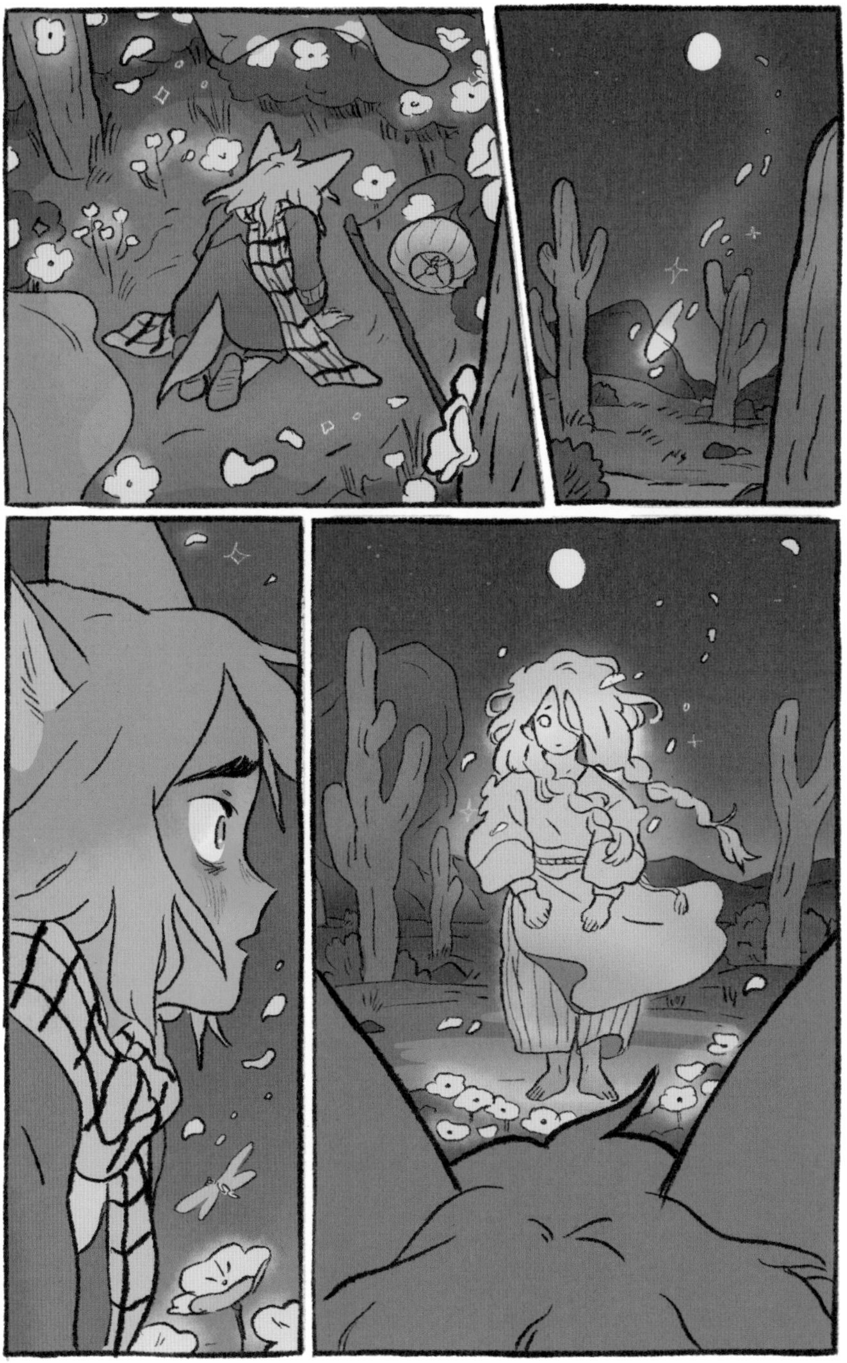

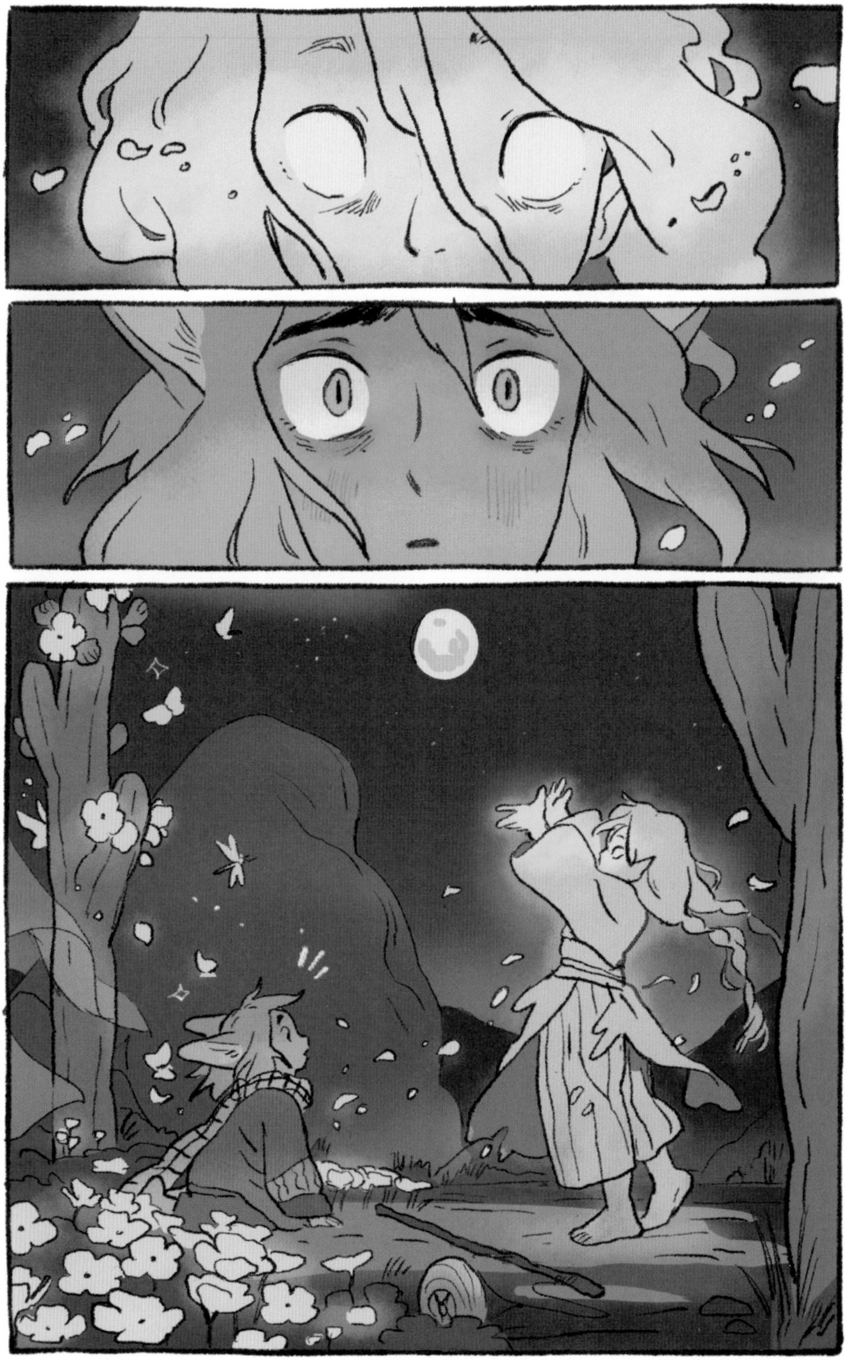

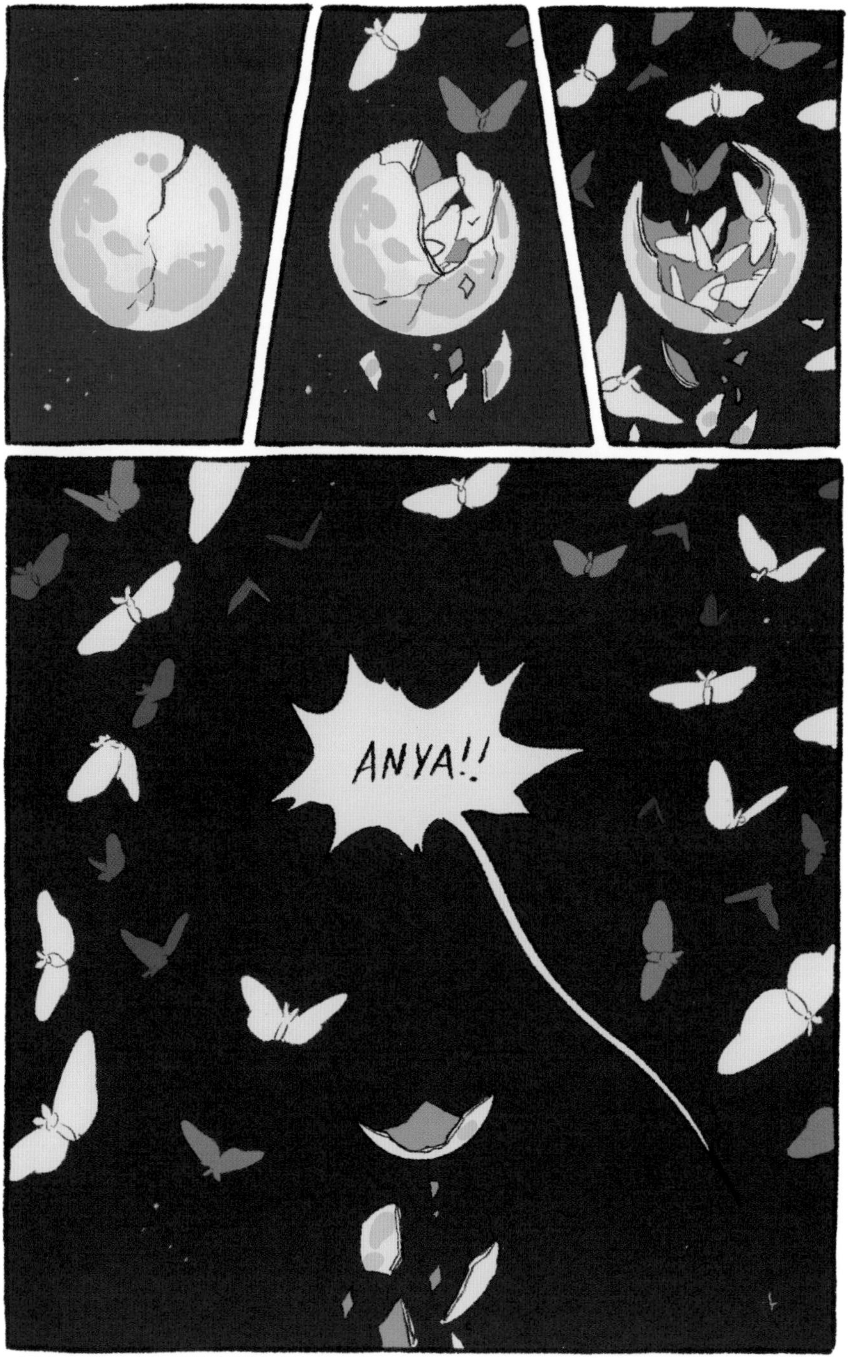
ANYA!!

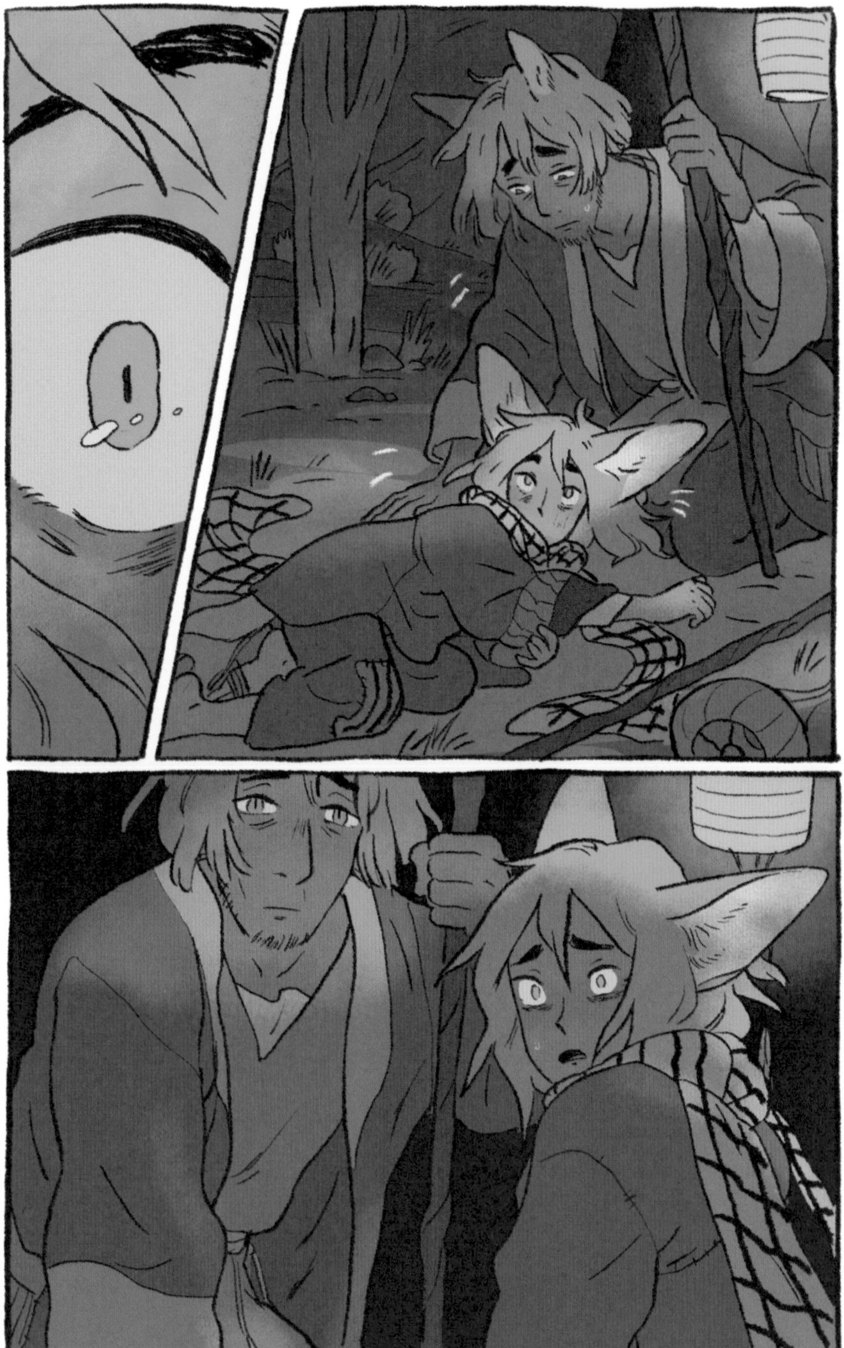

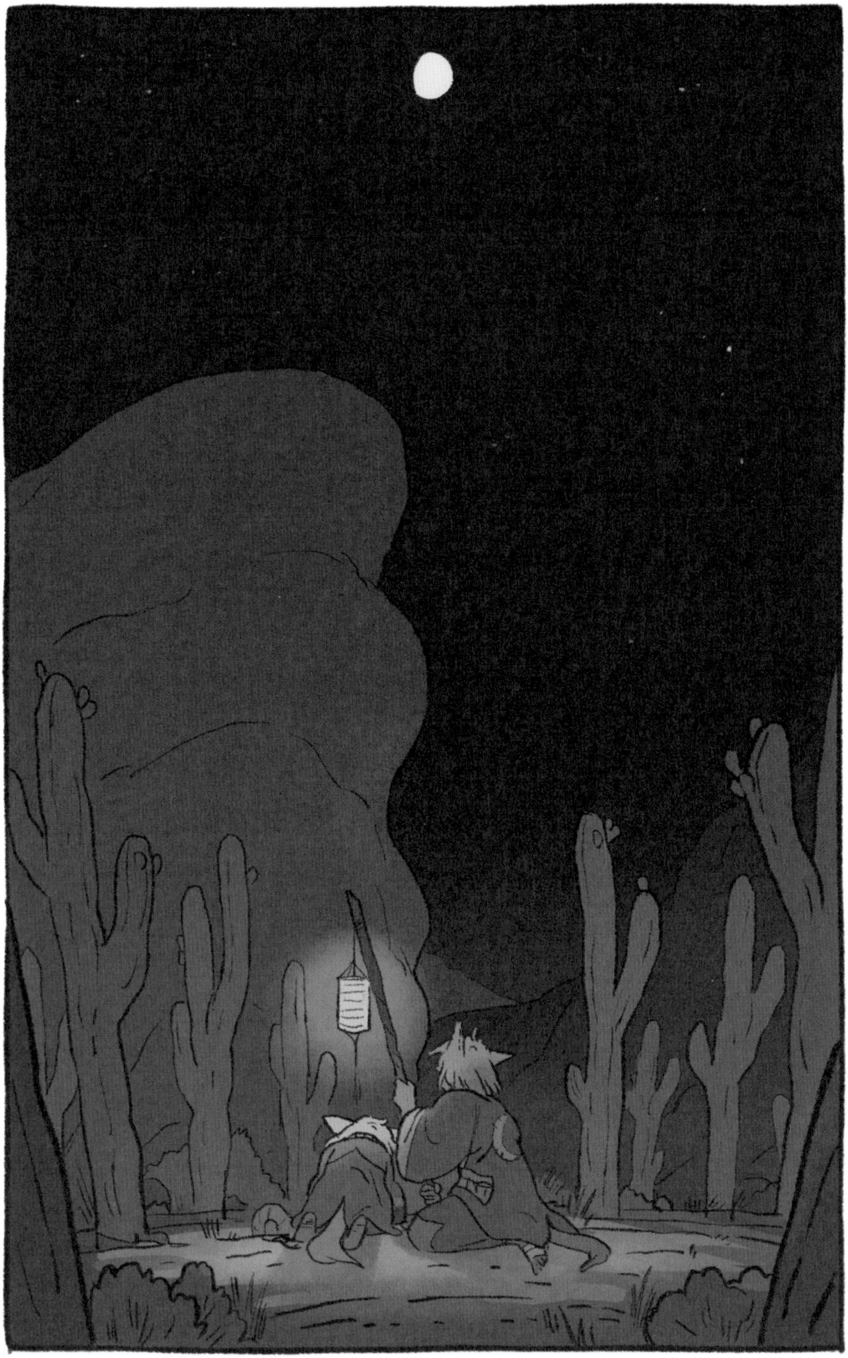

Chapter Six

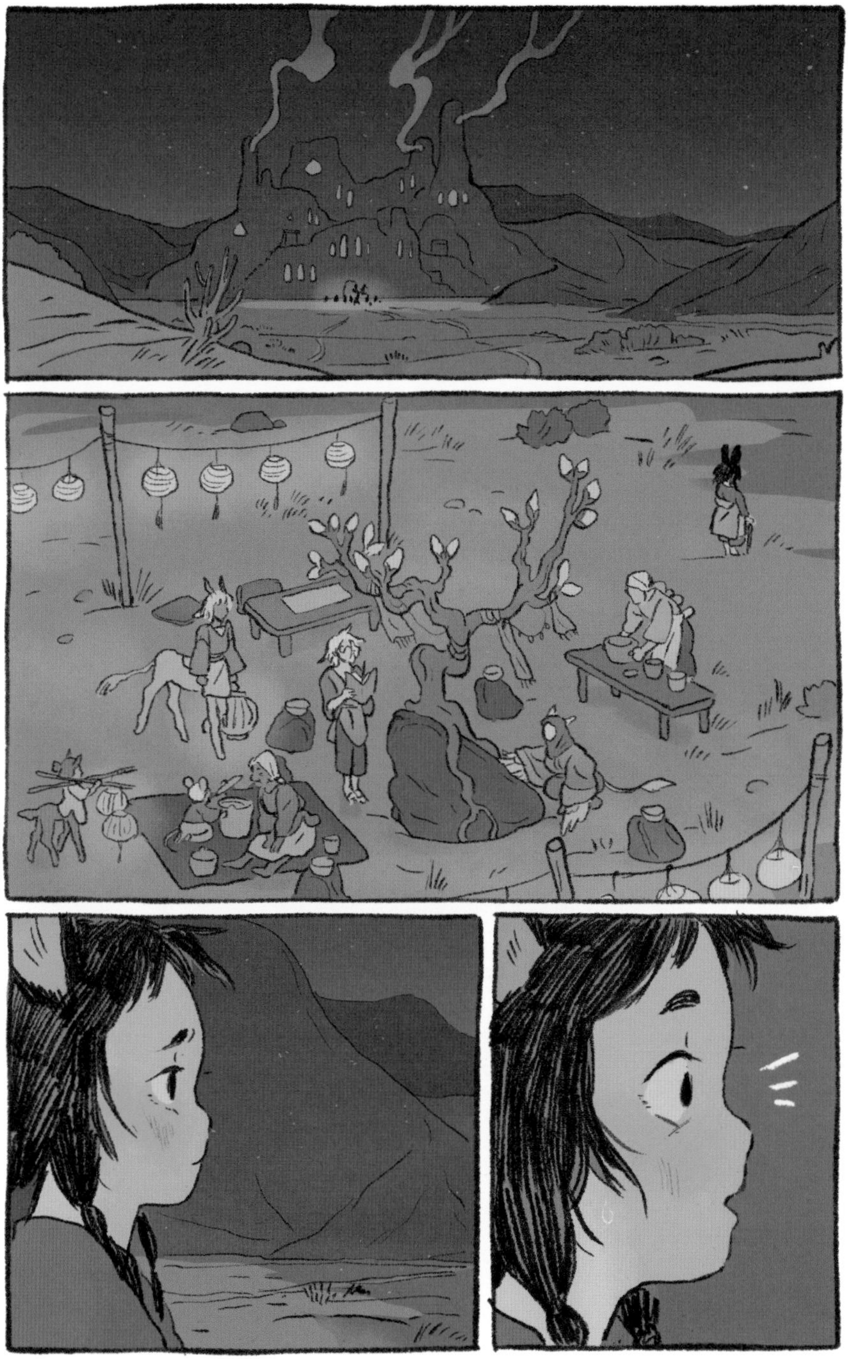

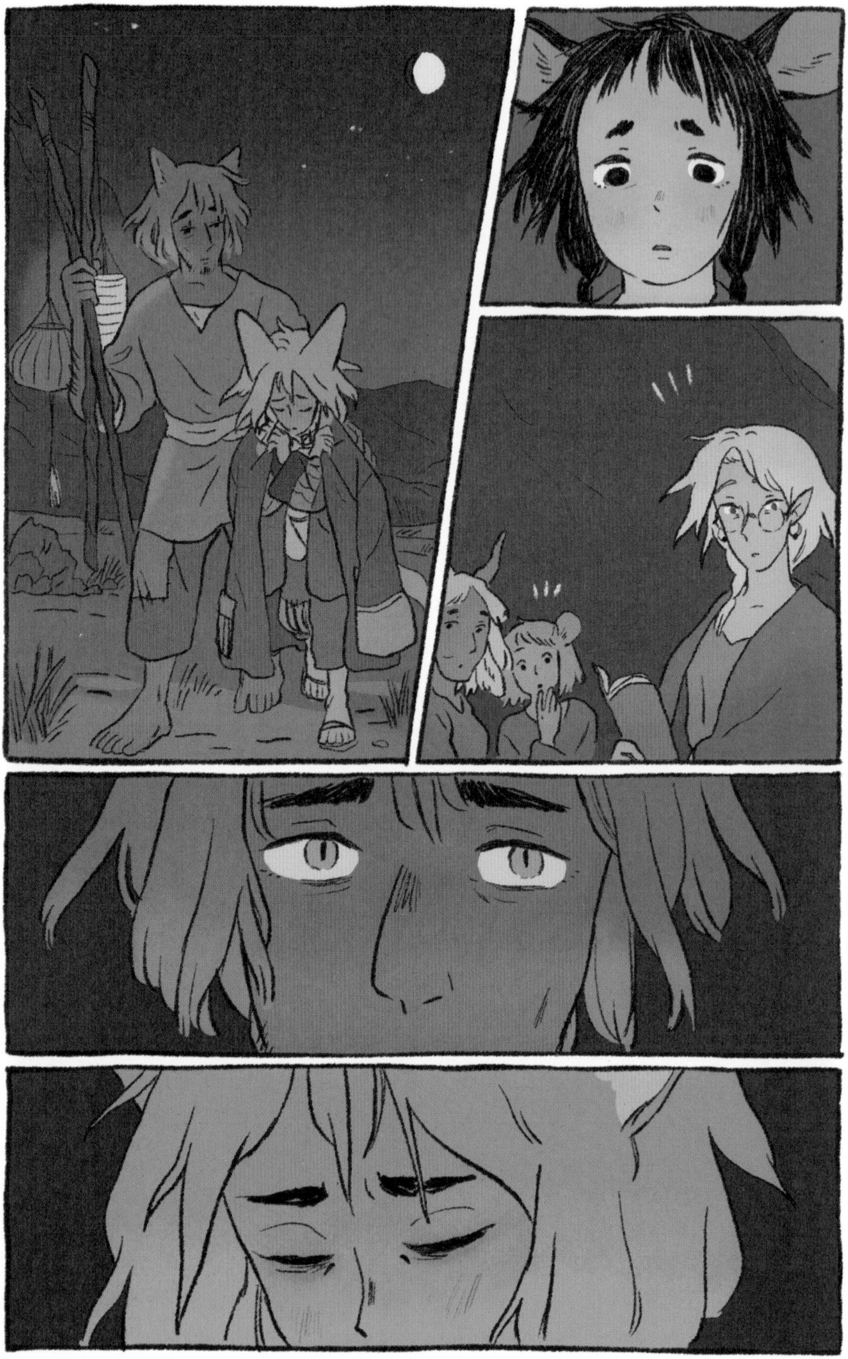

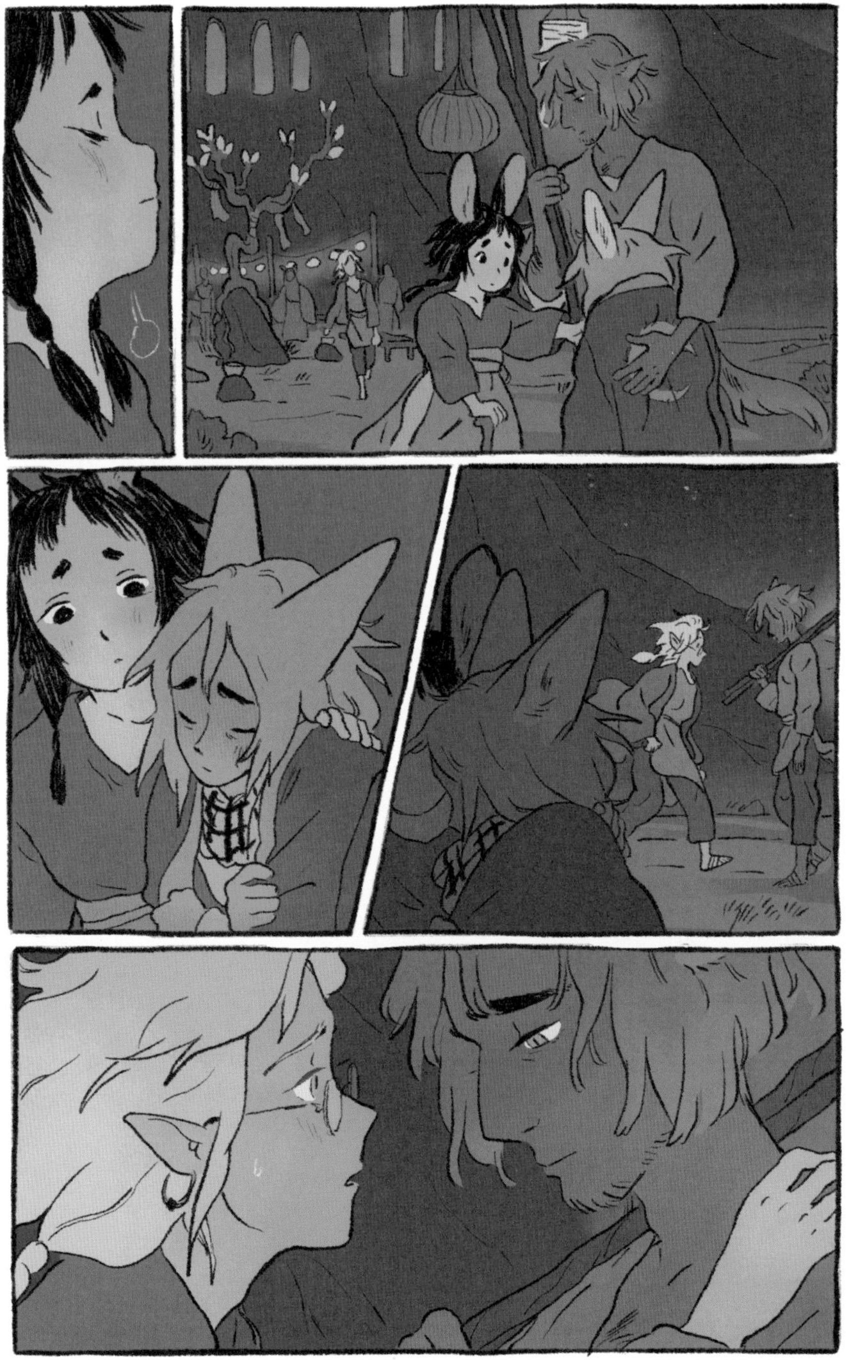

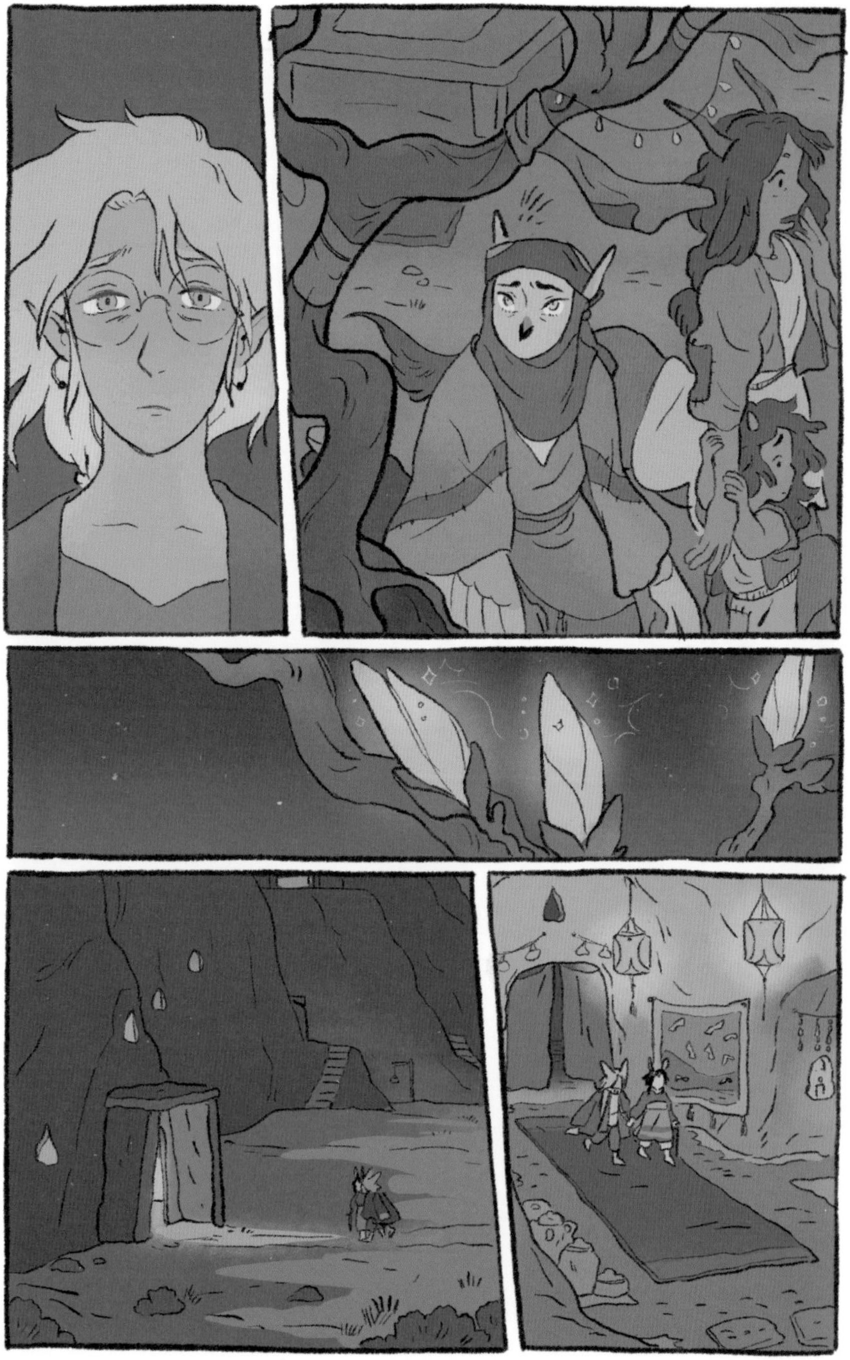

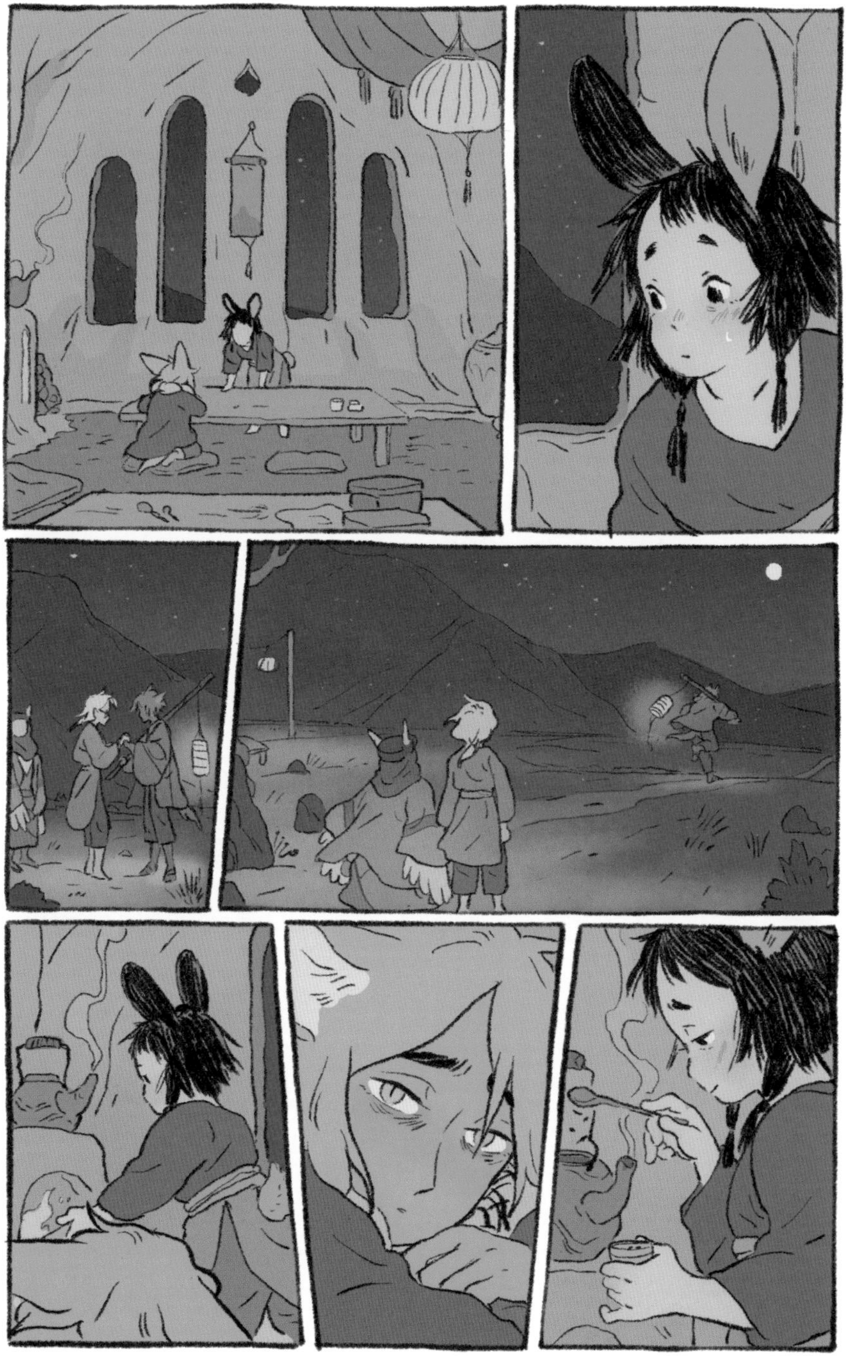

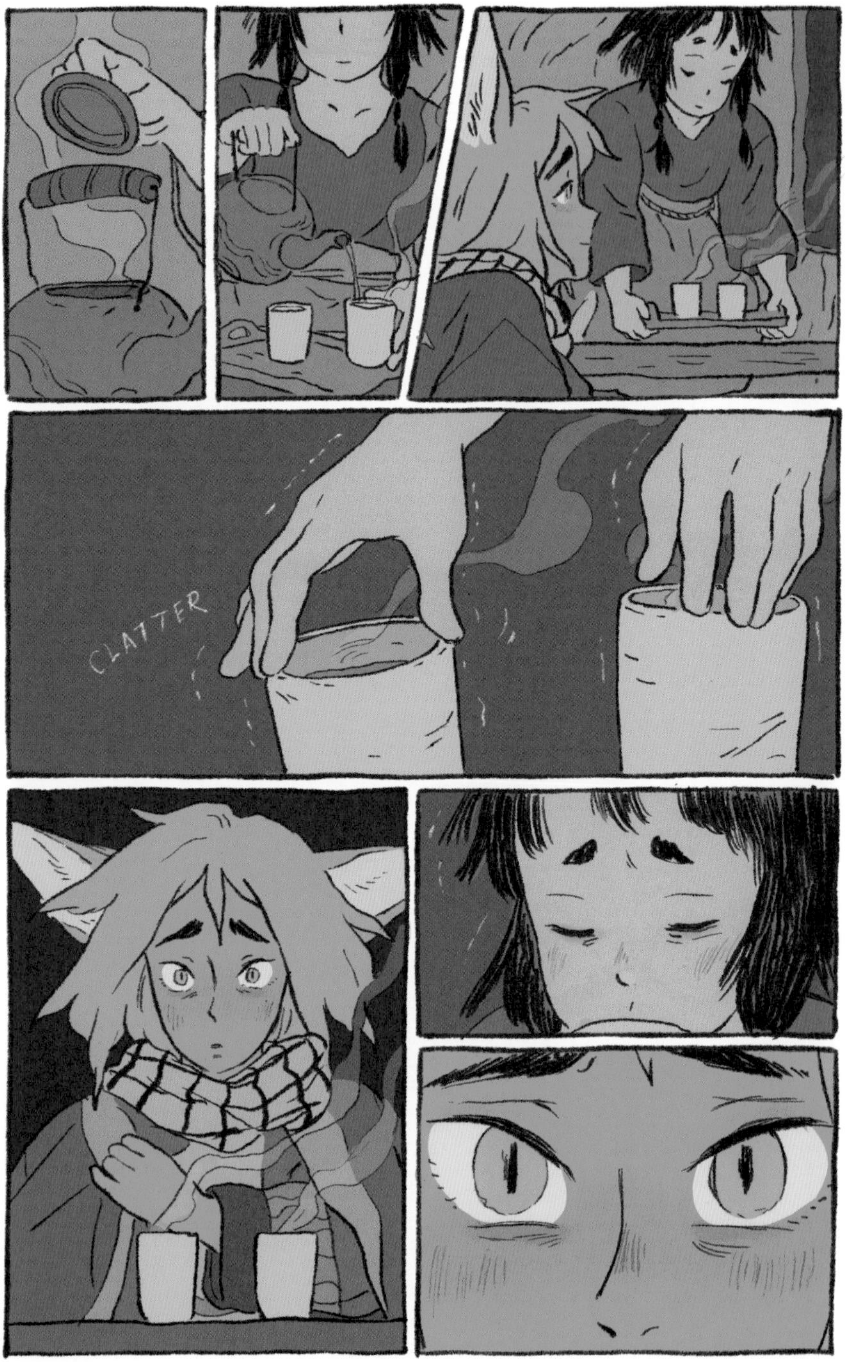
CLATTER

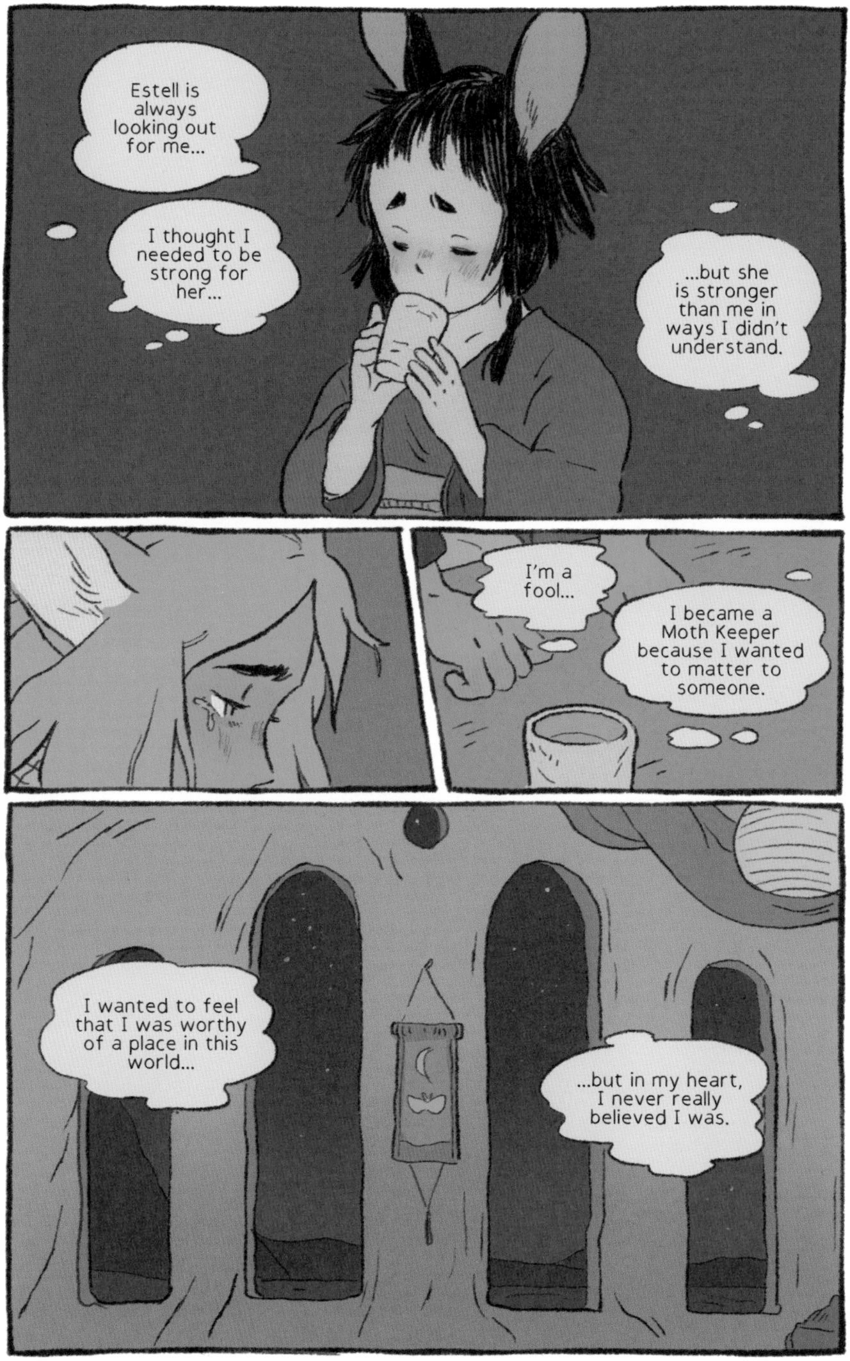
Estell is always looking out for me...
I thought I needed to be strong for her...
...but she is stronger than me in ways I didn't understand.
I'm a fool...
I became a Moth Keeper because I wanted to matter to someone.
I wanted to feel that I was worthy of a place in this world...
...but in my heart, I never really believed I was.

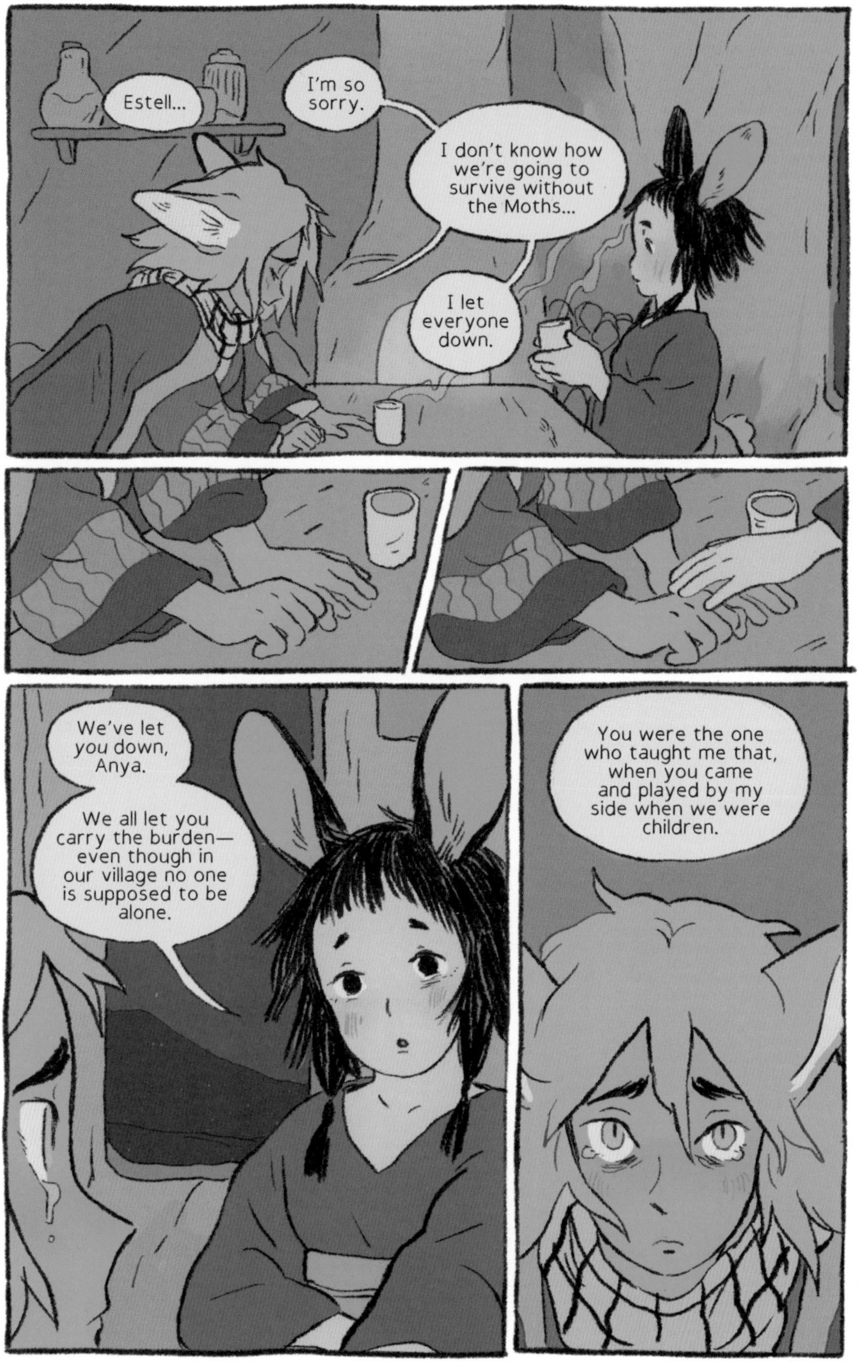
Estell...
I'm so sorry.
I don't know how we're going to survive without the Moths...
I let everyone down.
We've let *you* down, Anya.
We all let you carry the burden—even though in our village no one is supposed to be alone.
You were the one who taught me that, when you came and played by my side when we were children.

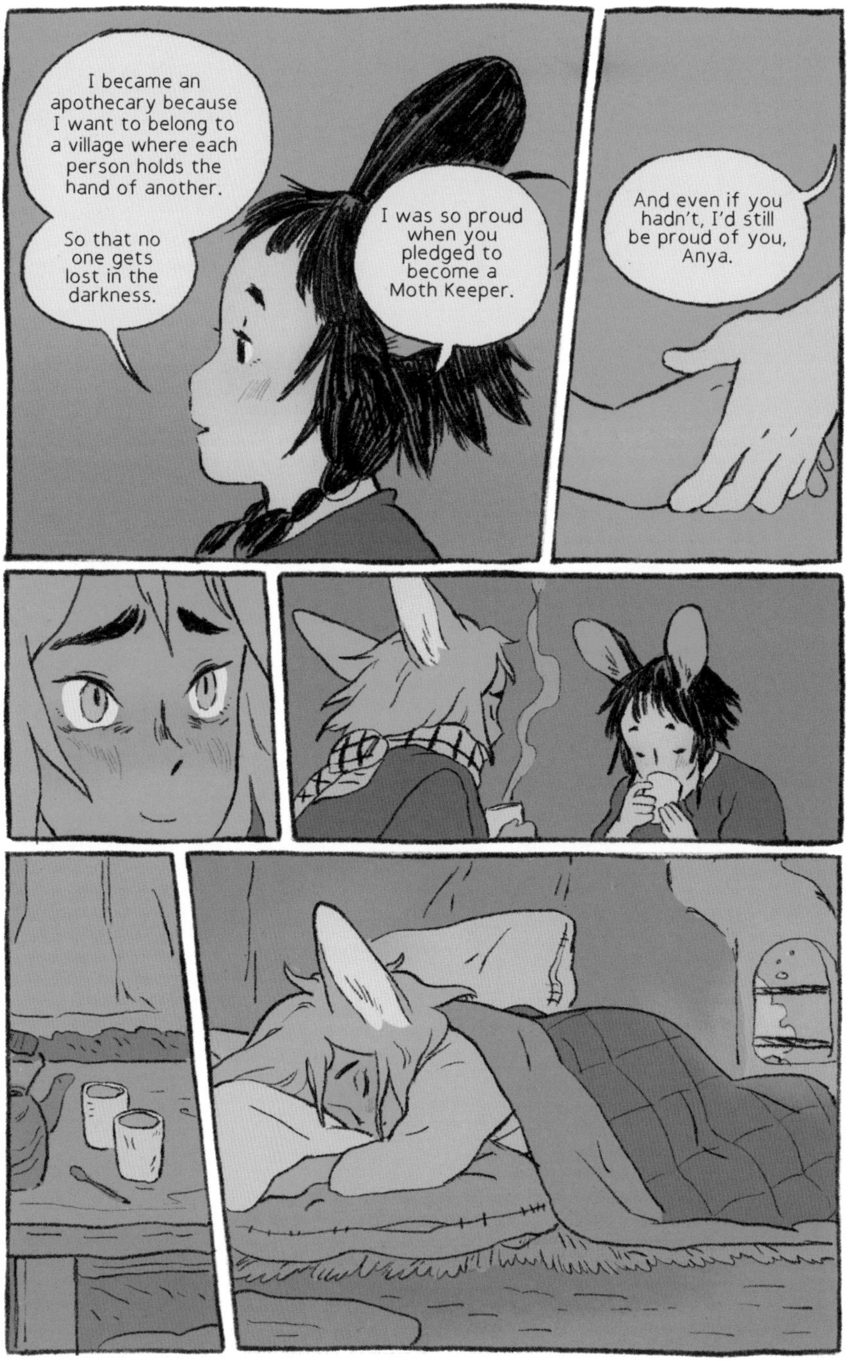

I became an apothecary because I want to belong to a village where each person holds the hand of another.
So that no one gets lost in the darkness.
I was so proud when you pledged to become a Moth Keeper.
And even if you hadn't, I'd still be proud of you, Anya.

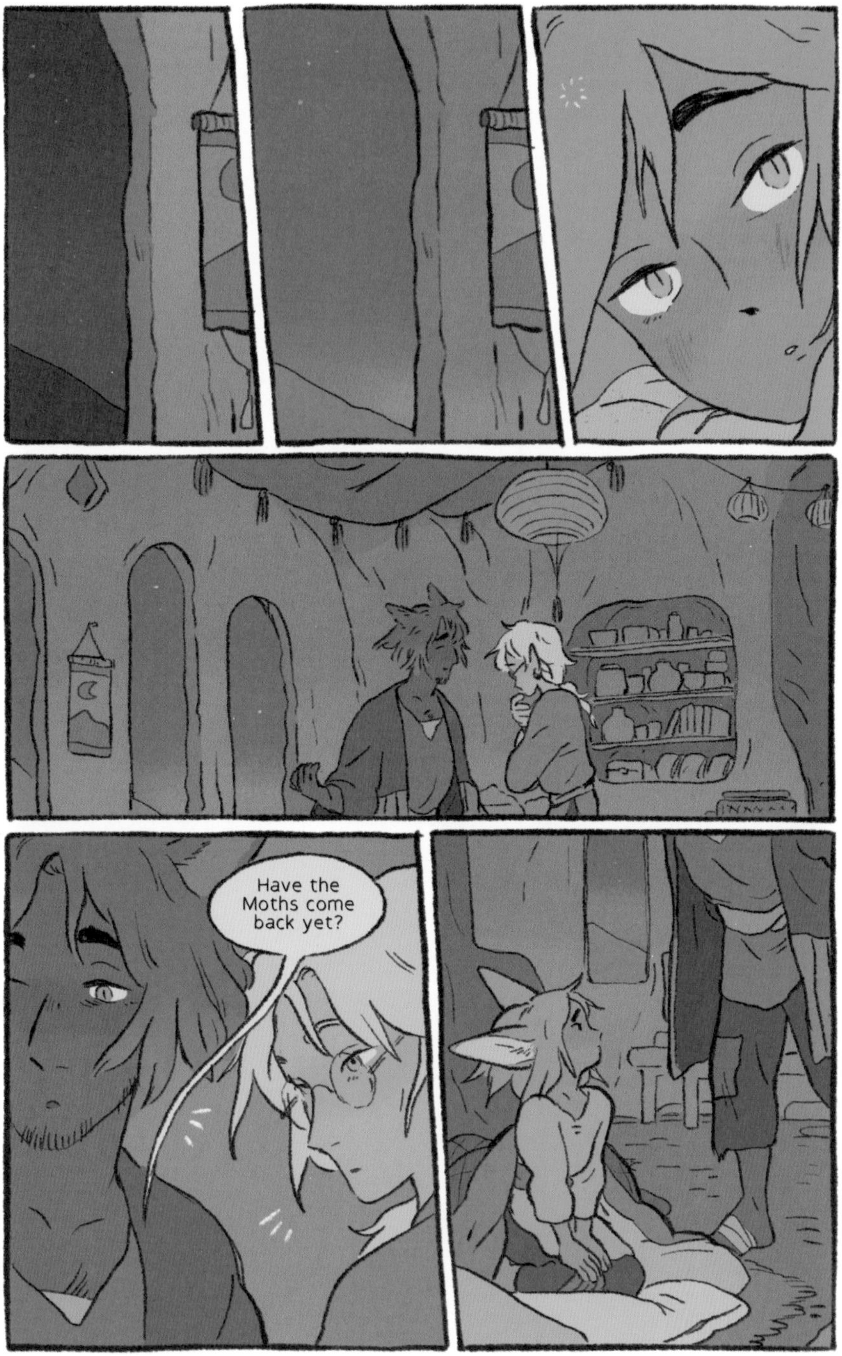
Have the Moths come back yet?

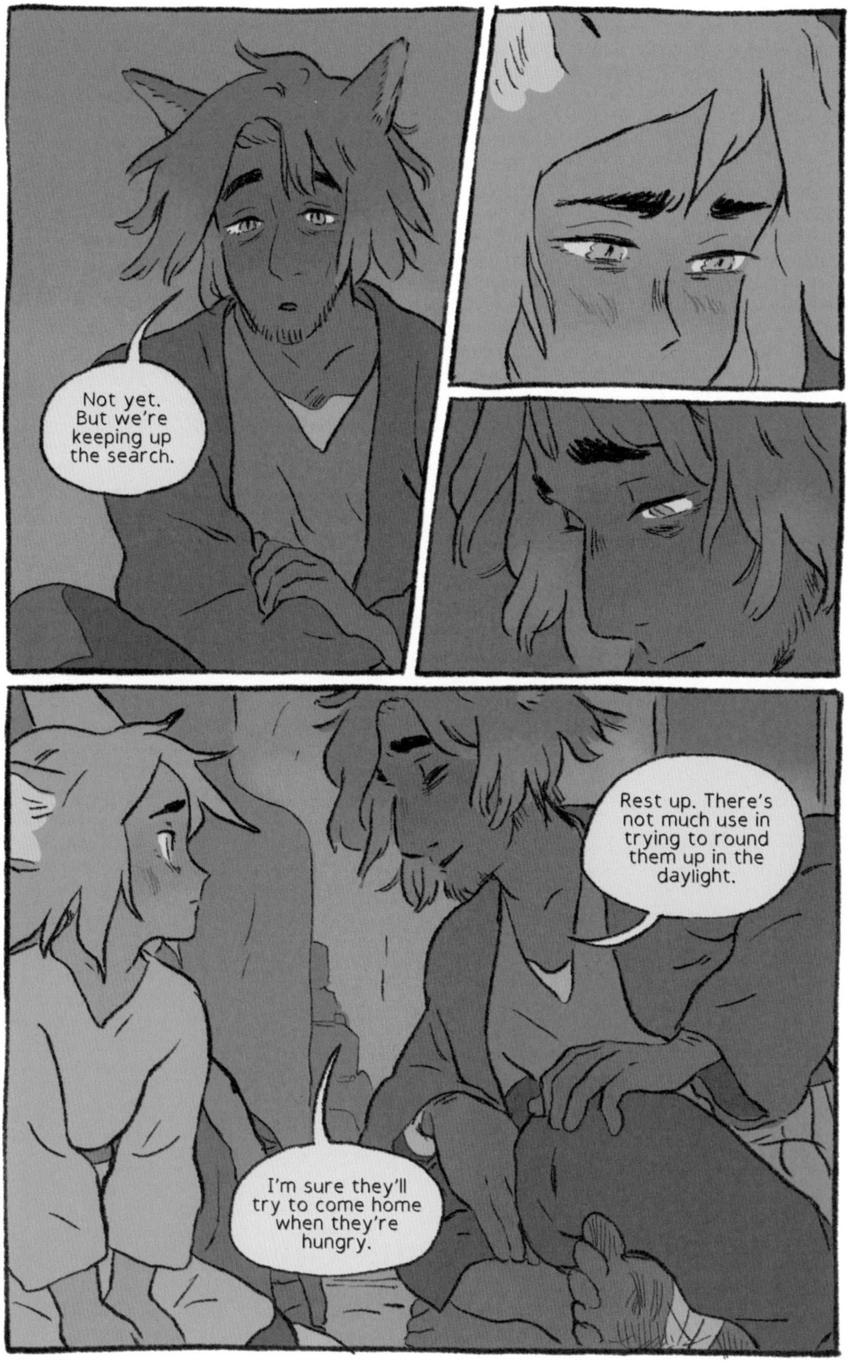

Not yet. But we're keeping up the search.
Rest up. There's not much use in trying to round them up in the daylight.
I'm sure they'll try to come home when they're hungry.

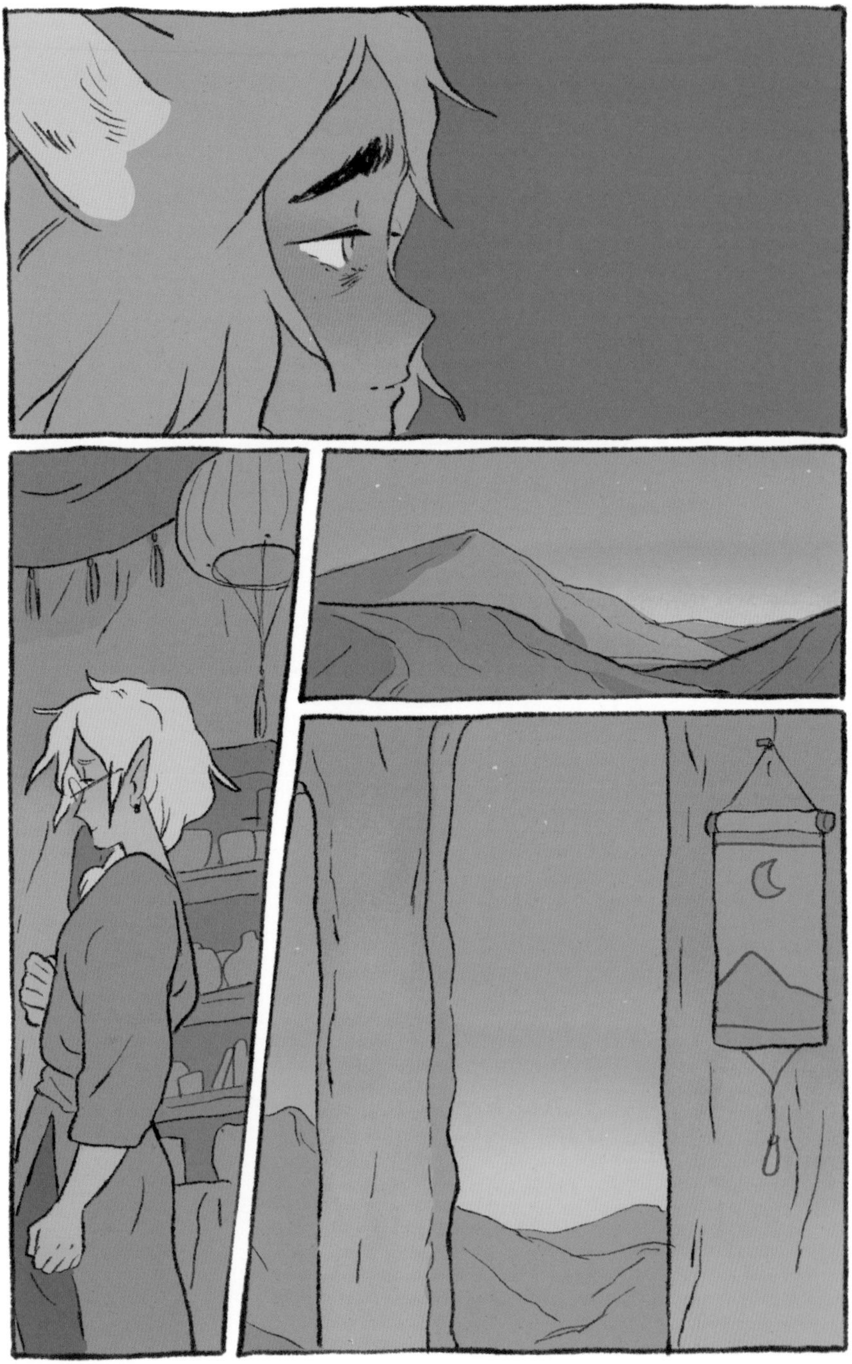

Chapter Seven

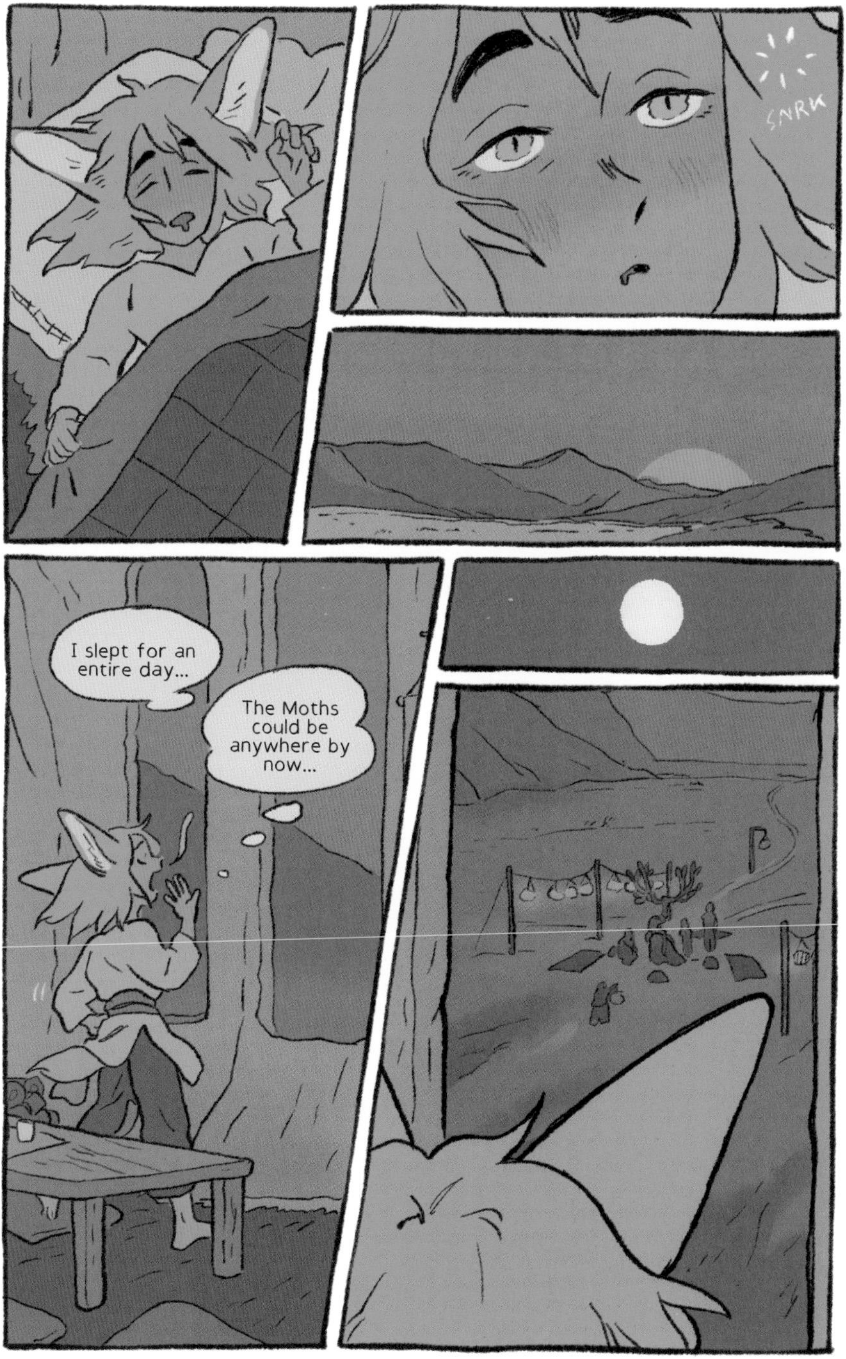
SNRK
I slept for an entire day...
The Moths could be anywhere by now...

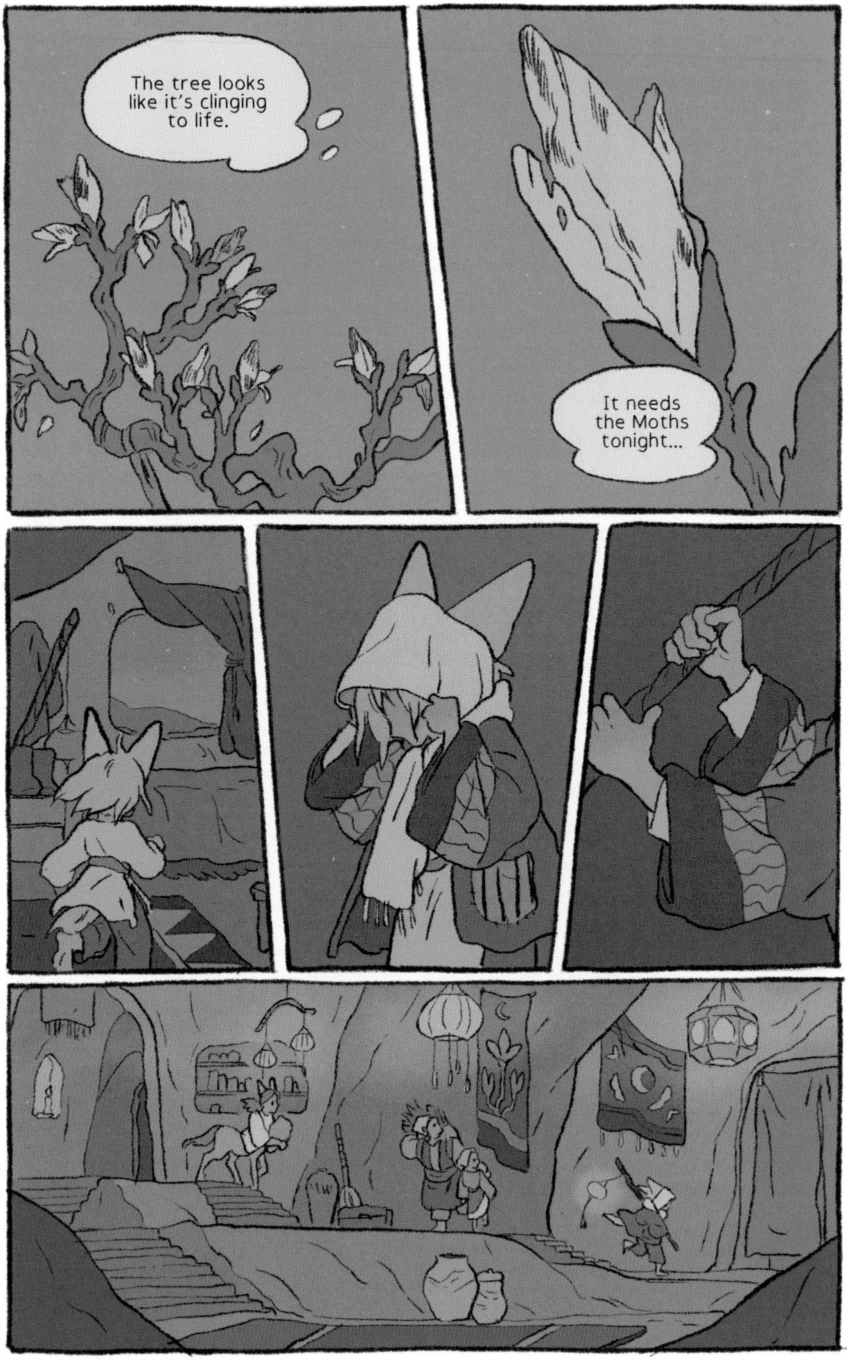
The tree looks like it's clinging to life.
It needs the Moths tonight...

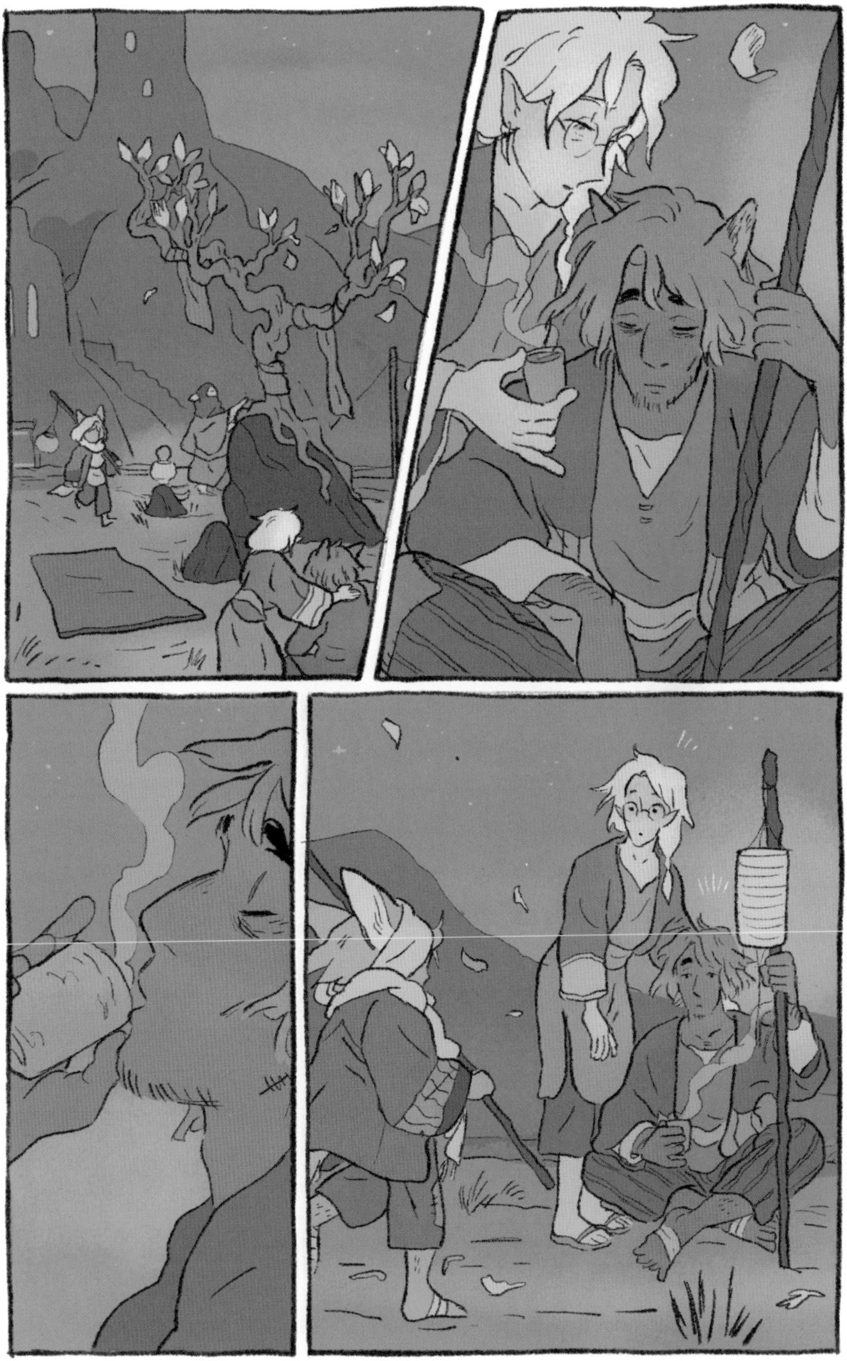

Yeolen...I'll go look for the Moths.

I've been looking all over, but I haven't seen so much as a flutter...

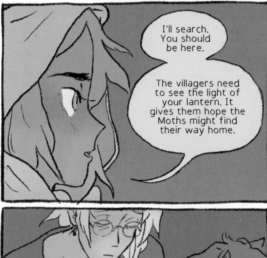

I'll search. You should be here.

The villagers need to see the light of your lantern. It gives them hope the Moths might find their way home.

I'll walk all night if I have to.

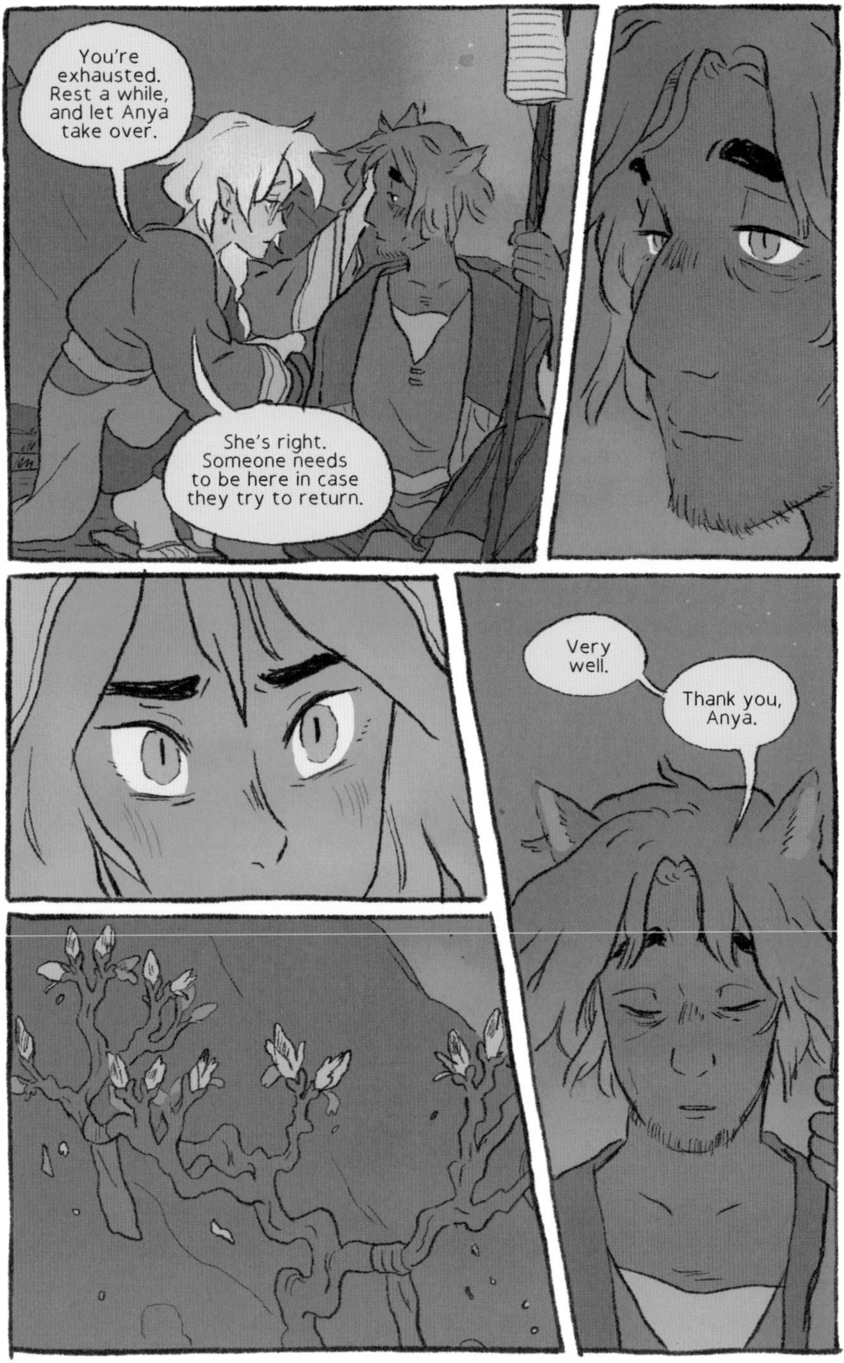
You're exhausted. Rest a while, and let Anya take over.
She's right. Someone needs to be here in case they try to return.
Very well.
Thank you, Anya.

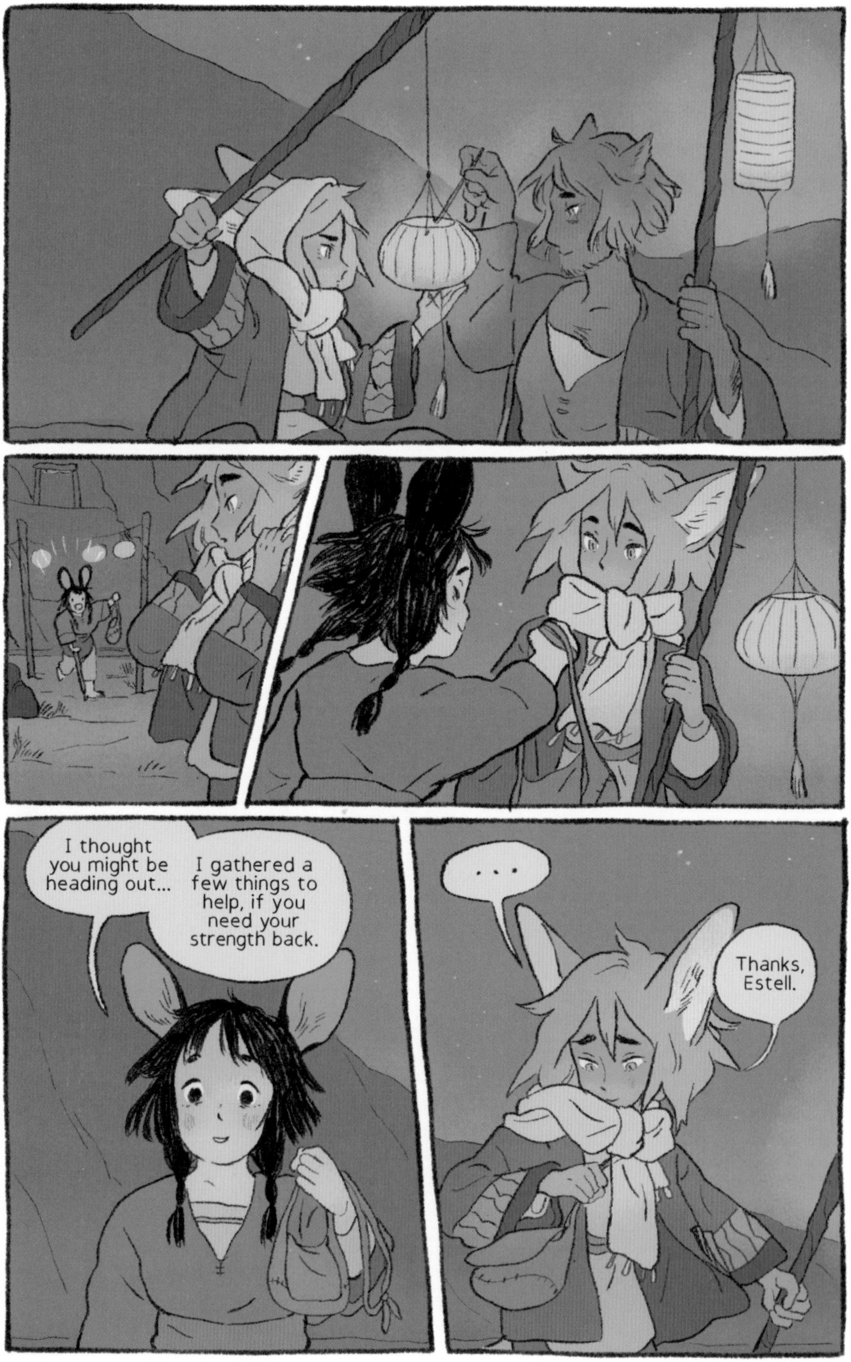
I thought you might be heading out...
I gathered a few things to help, if you need your strength back.
. . .
Thanks, Estell.

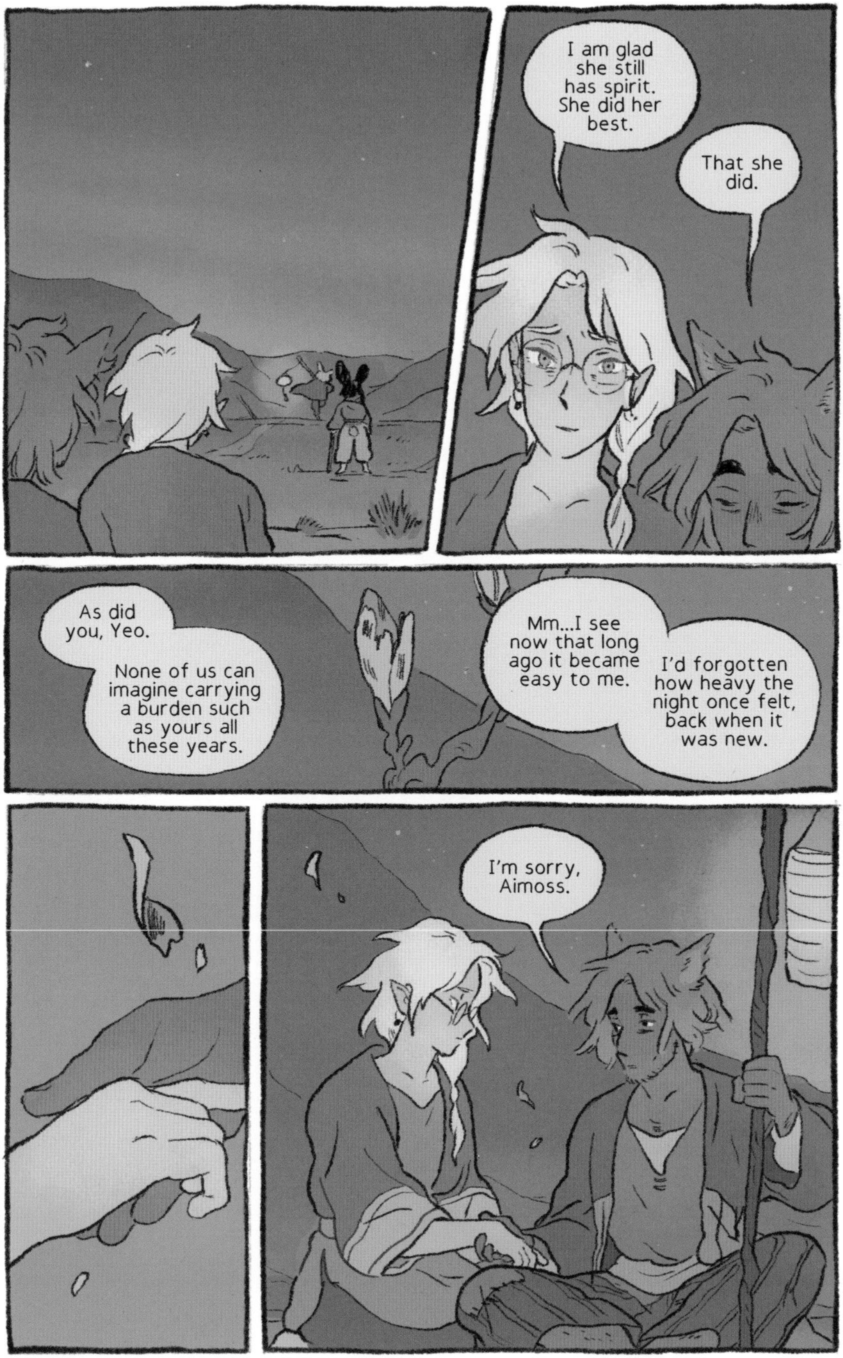
I am glad she still has spirit. She did her best.
That she did.
As did you, Yeo.
None of us can imagine carrying a burden such as yours all these years.
Mm...I see now that long ago it became easy to me.
I'd forgotten how heavy the night once felt, back when it was new.
I'm sorry, Aimoss.

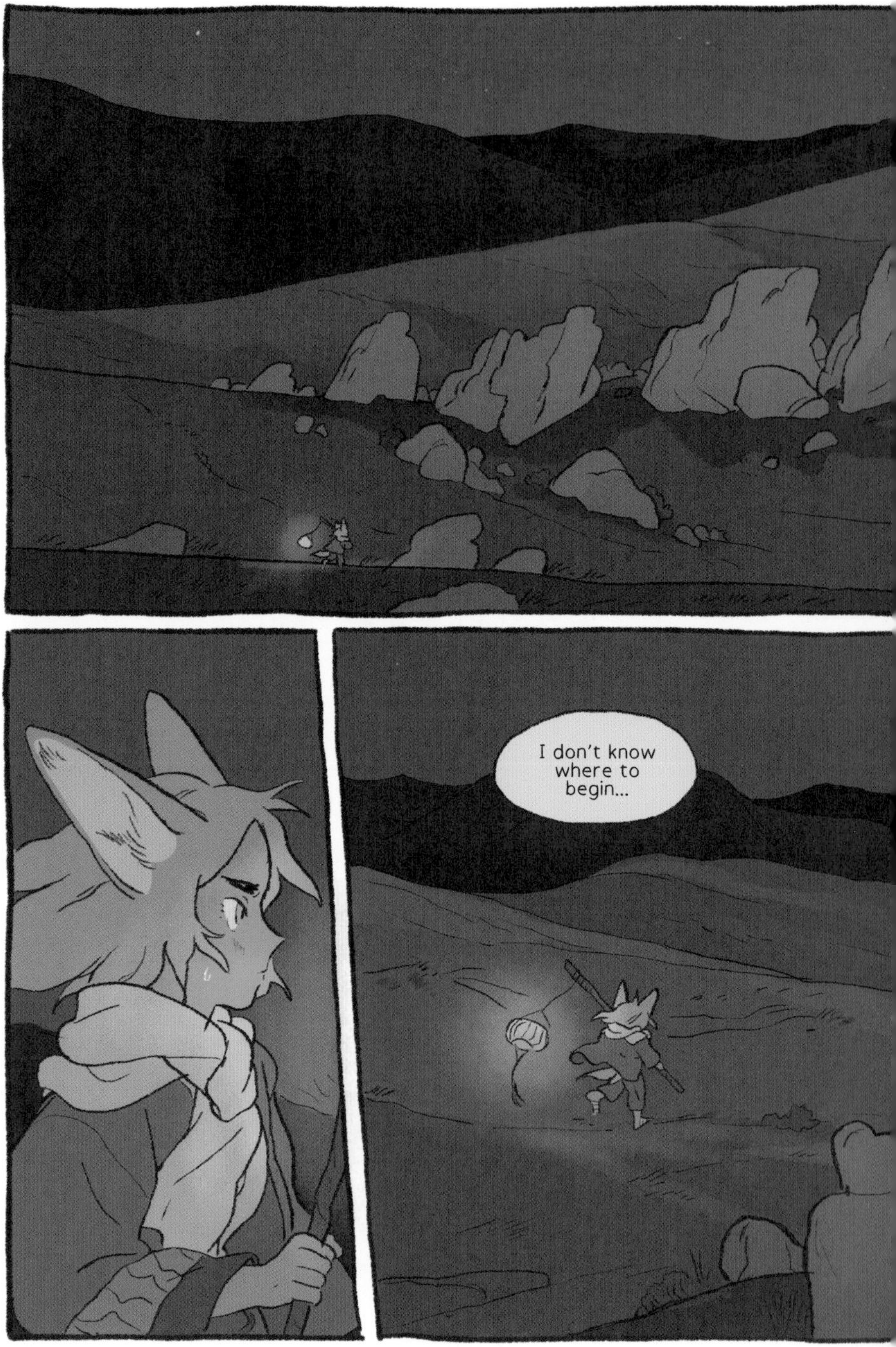
I don't know where to begin...

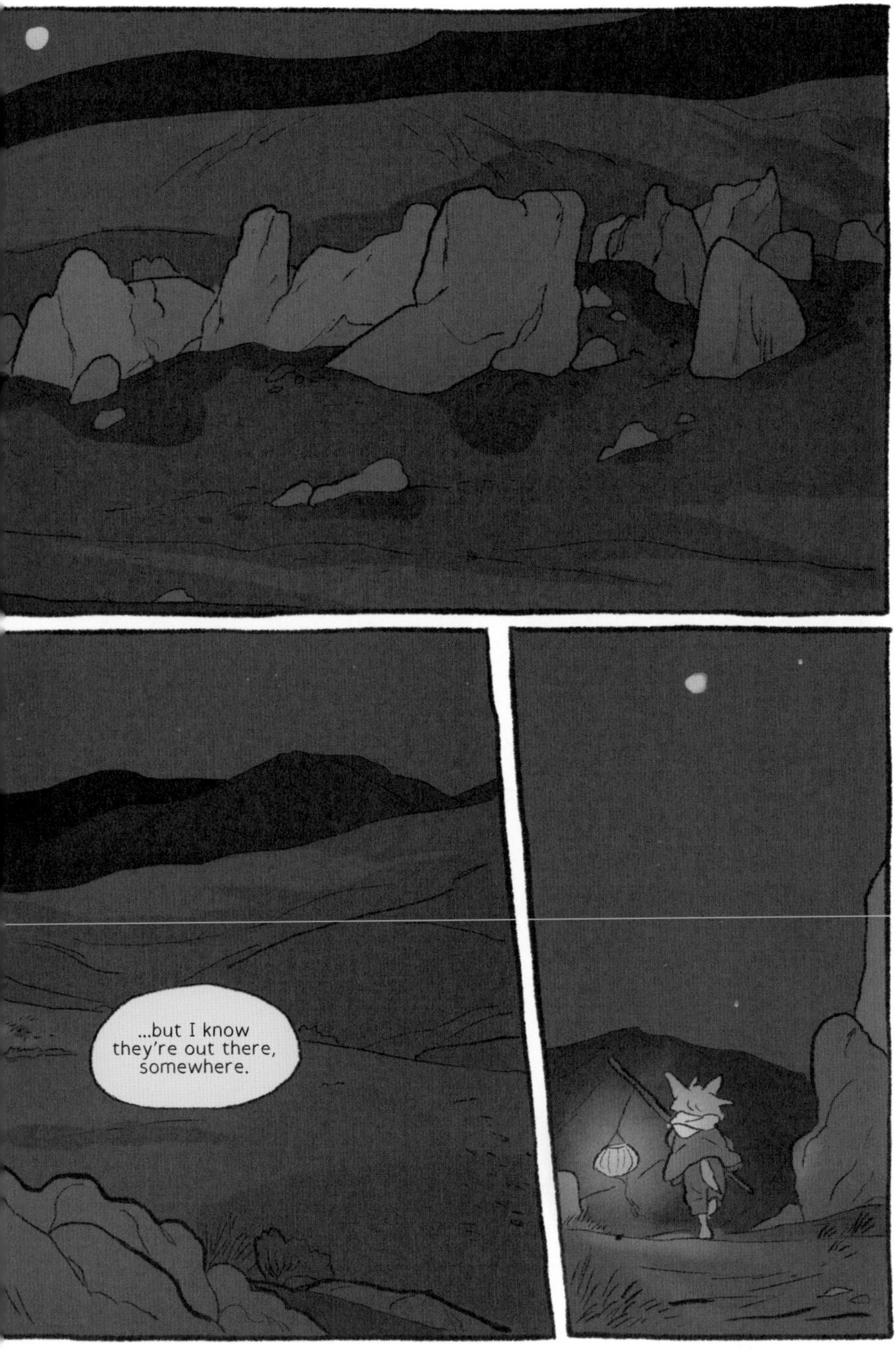
...but I know they're out there, somewhere.

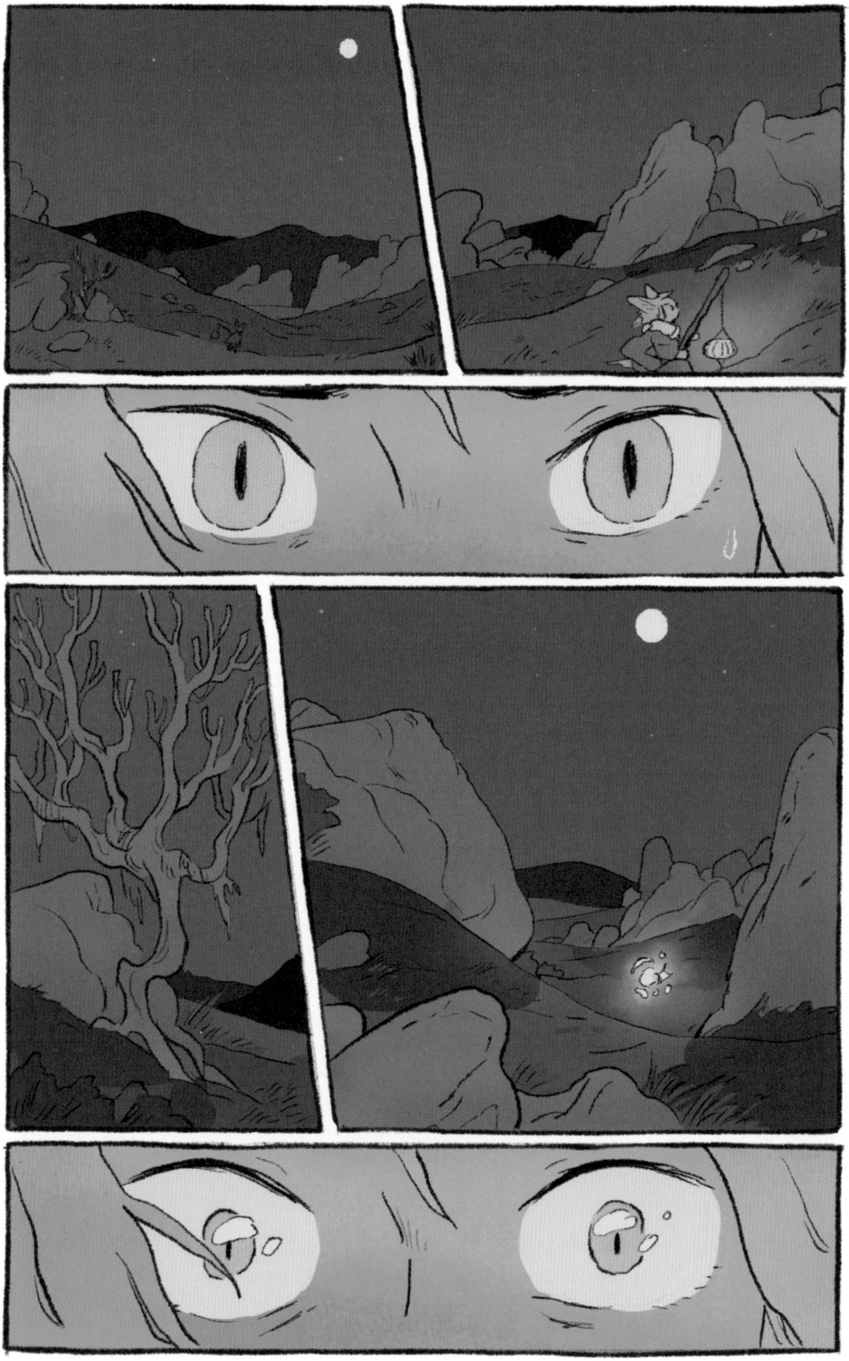

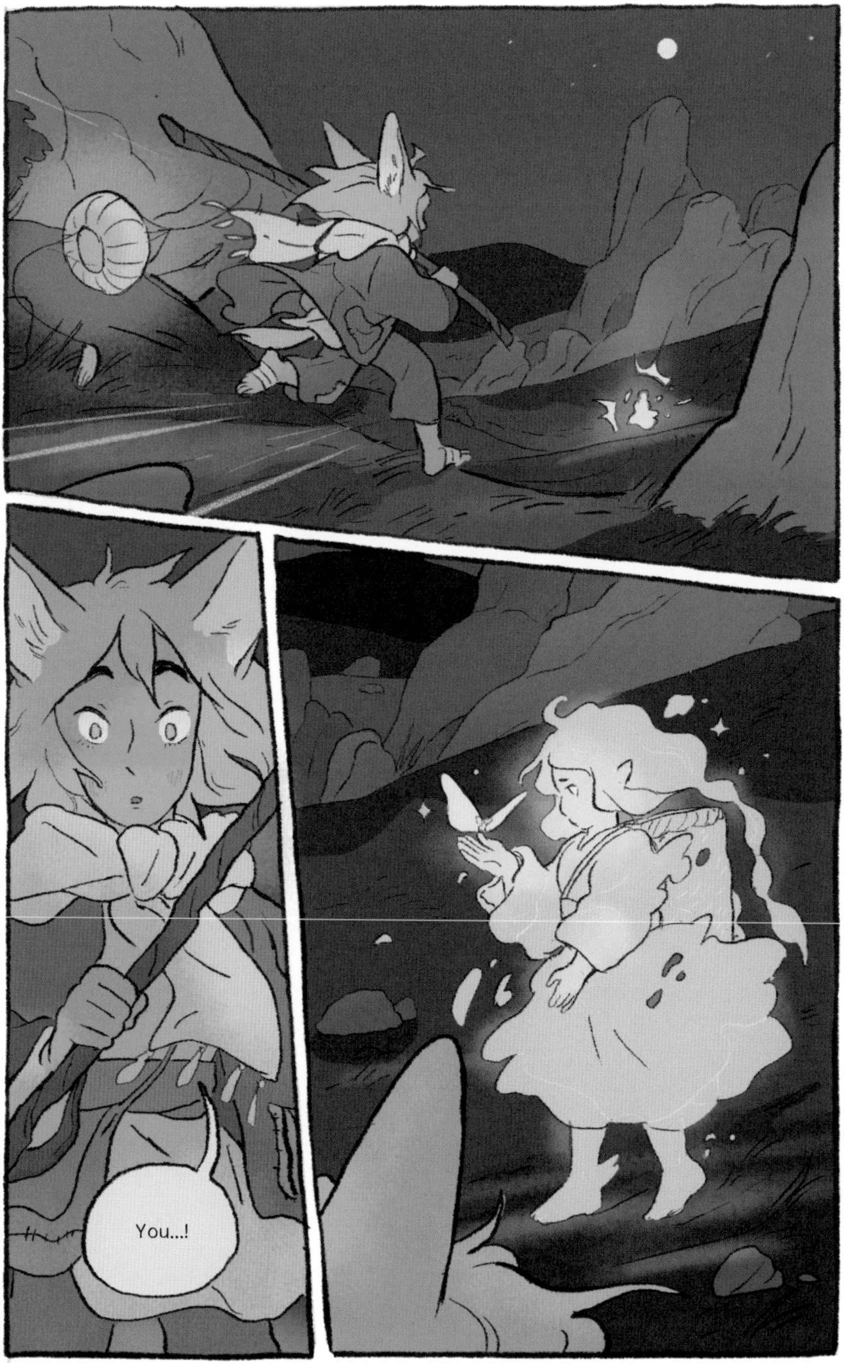
You...!

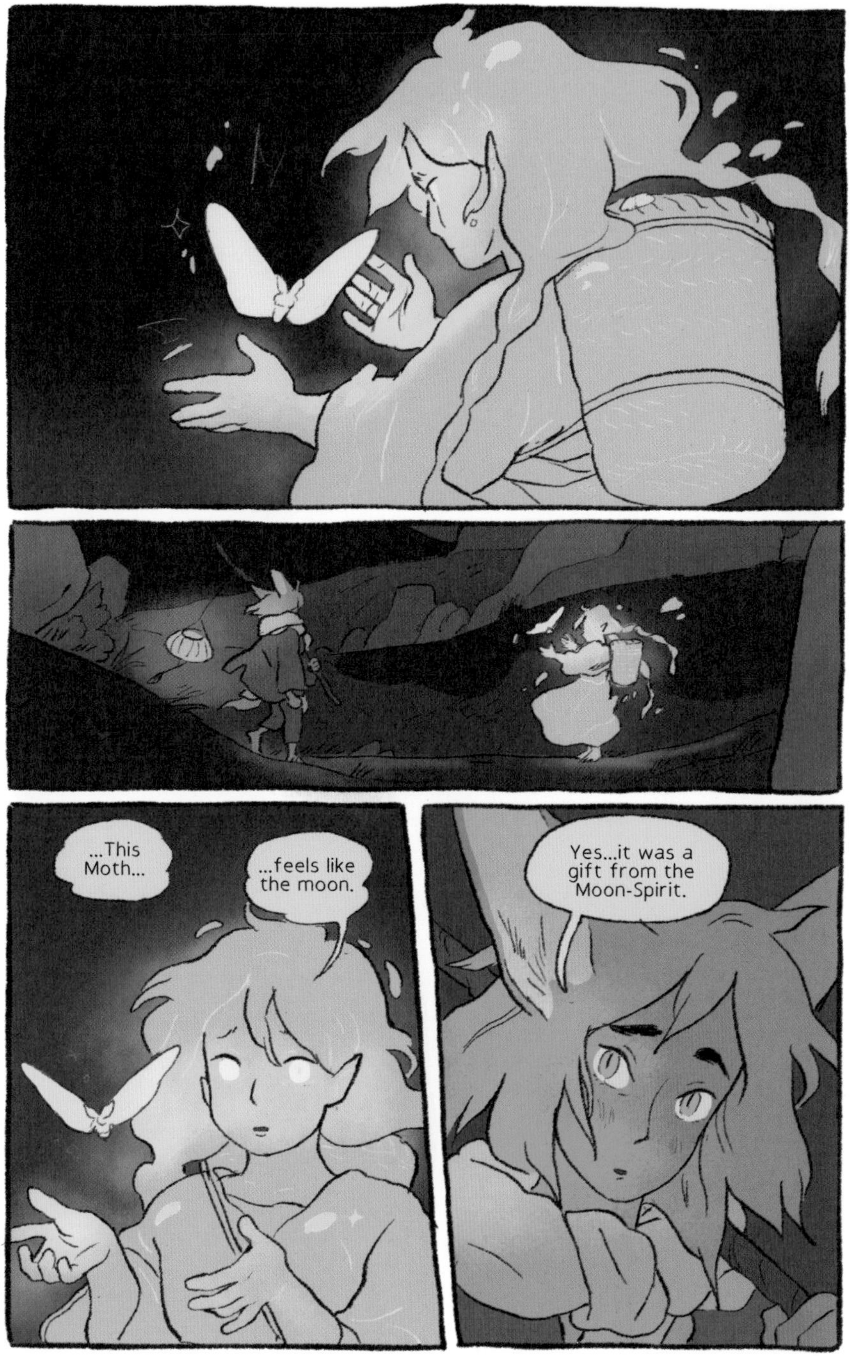
...This Moth...
...feels like the moon.
Yes...it was a gift from the Moon-Spirit.

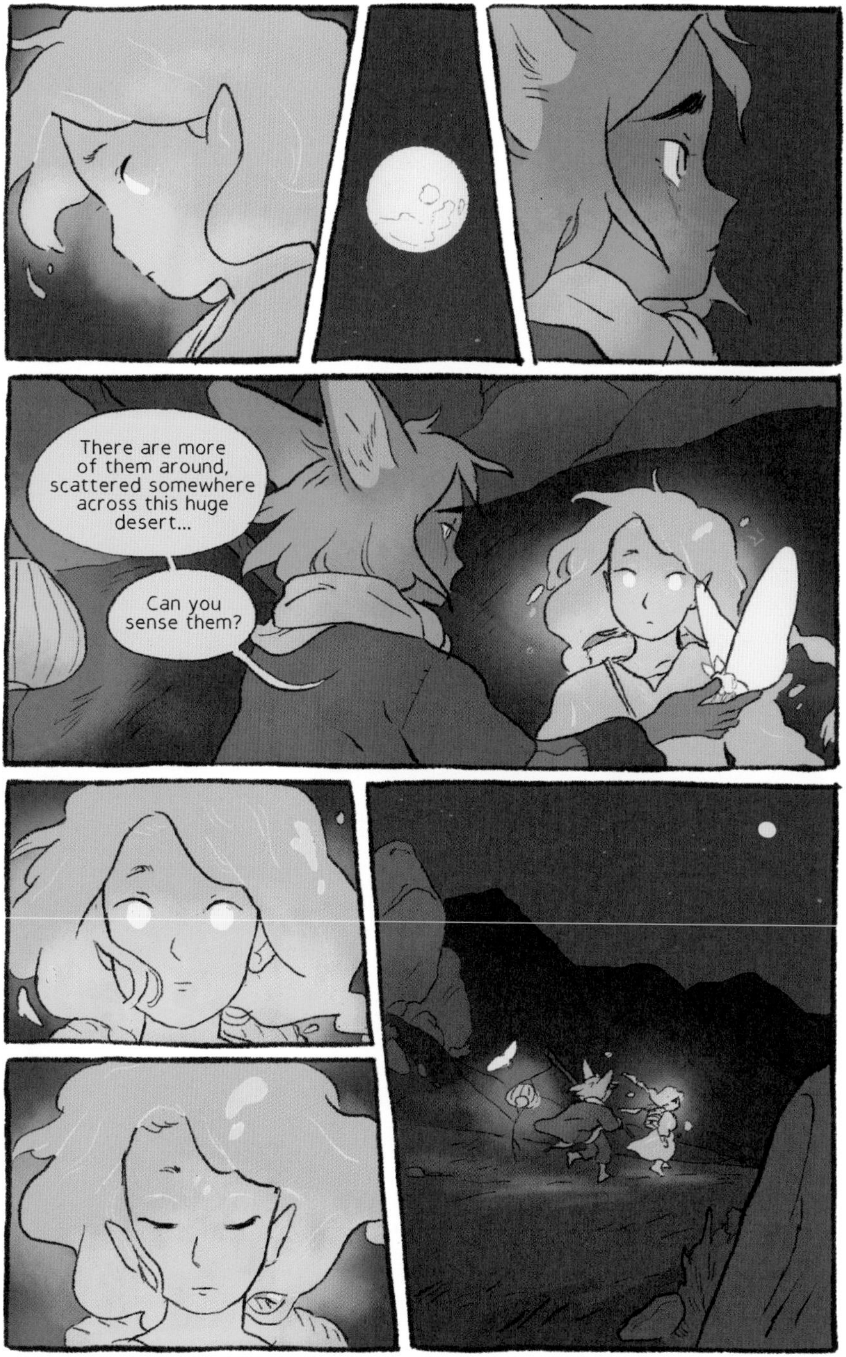
There are more of them around, scattered somewhere across this huge desert...
Can you sense them?

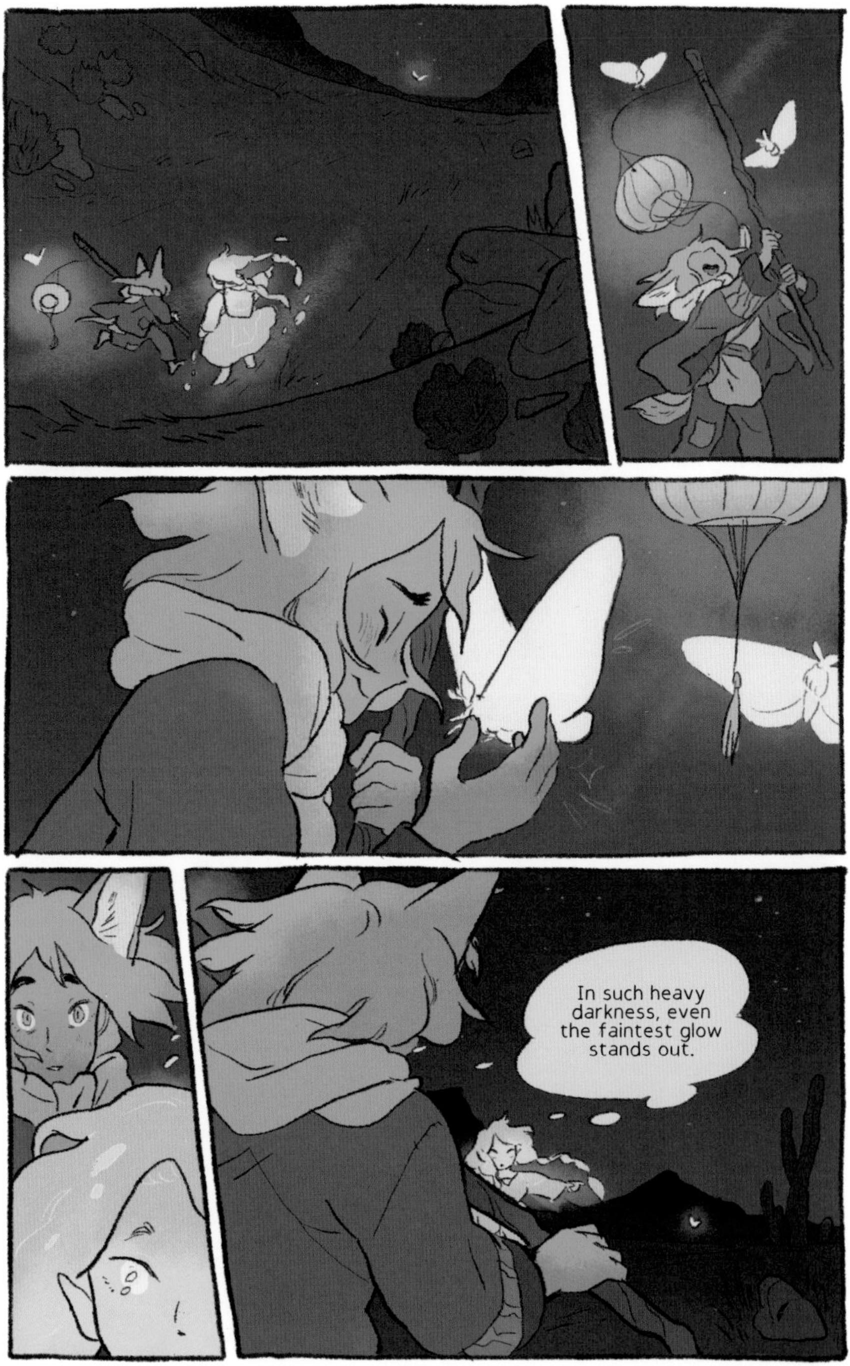
In such heavy darkness, even the faintest glow stands out.

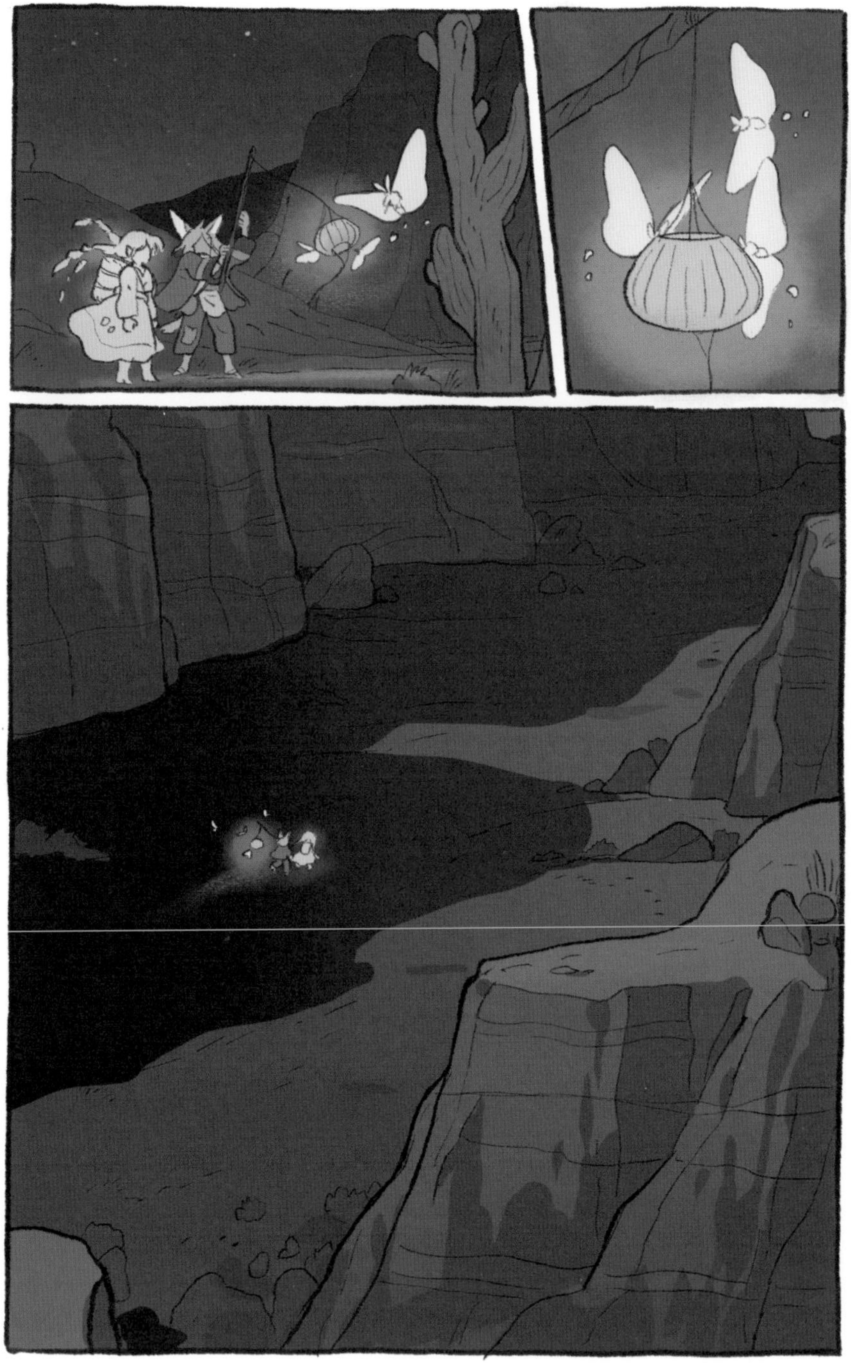

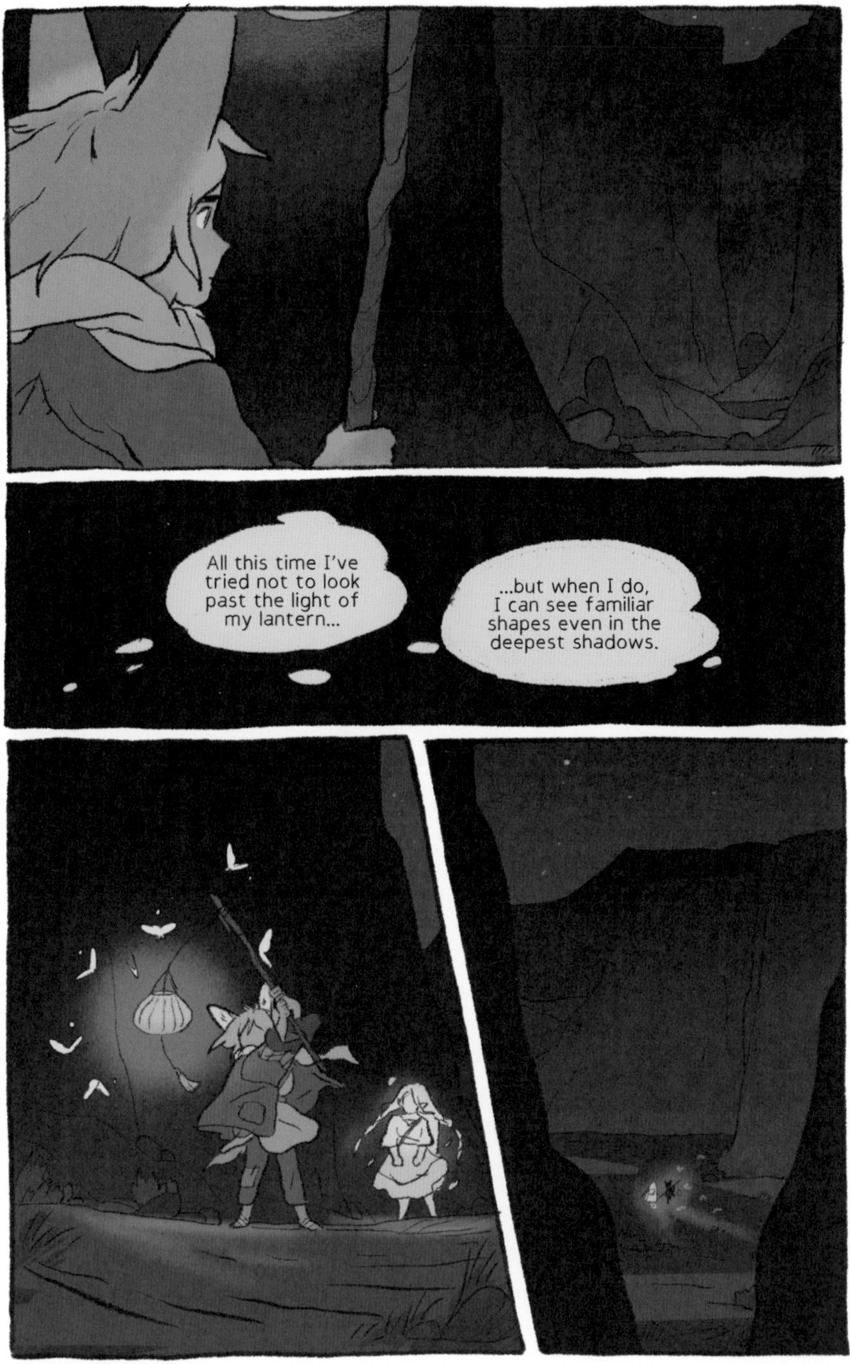
All this time I've tried not to look past the light of my lantern...
...but when I do, I can see familiar shapes even in the deepest shadows.

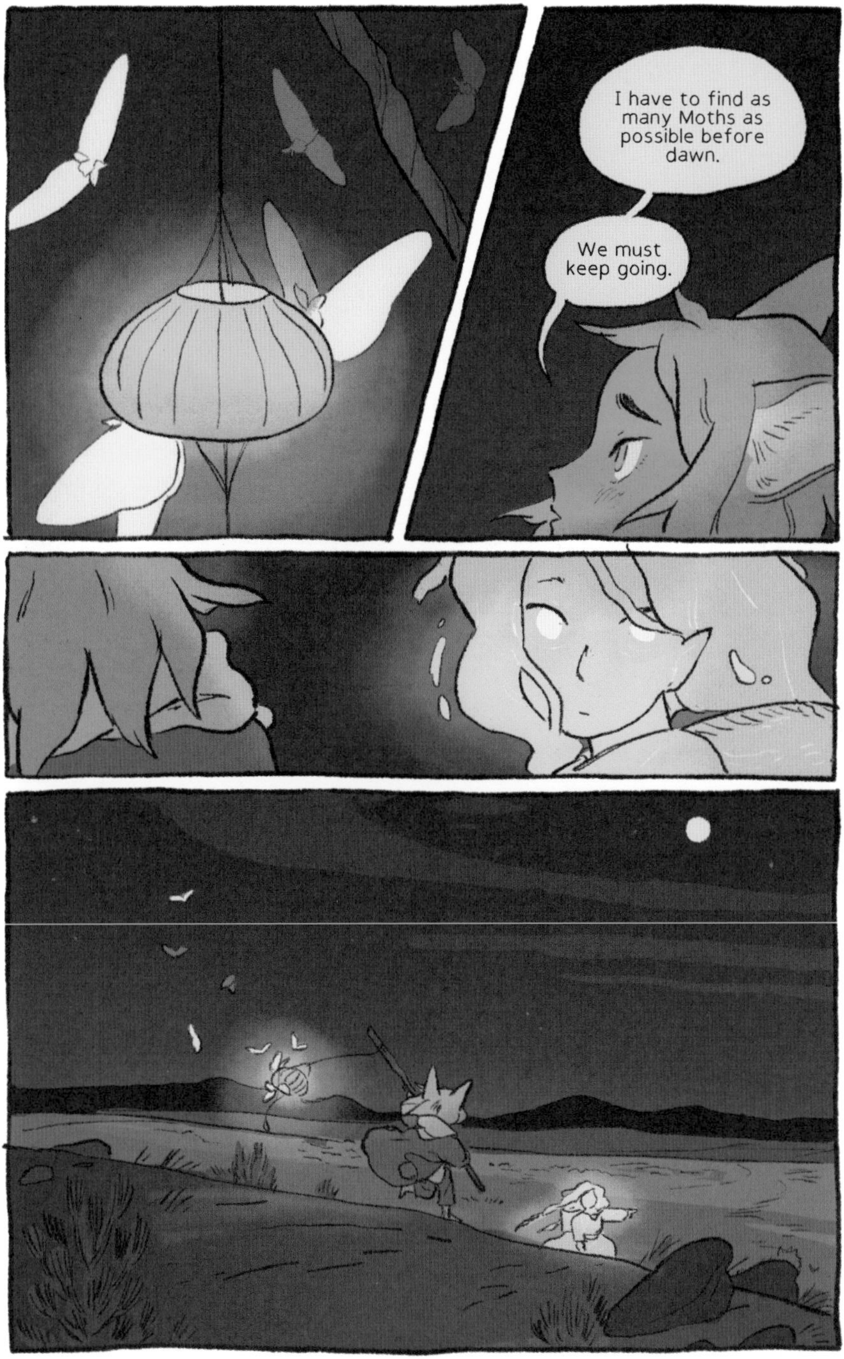
I have to find as many Moths as possible before dawn.
We must keep going.

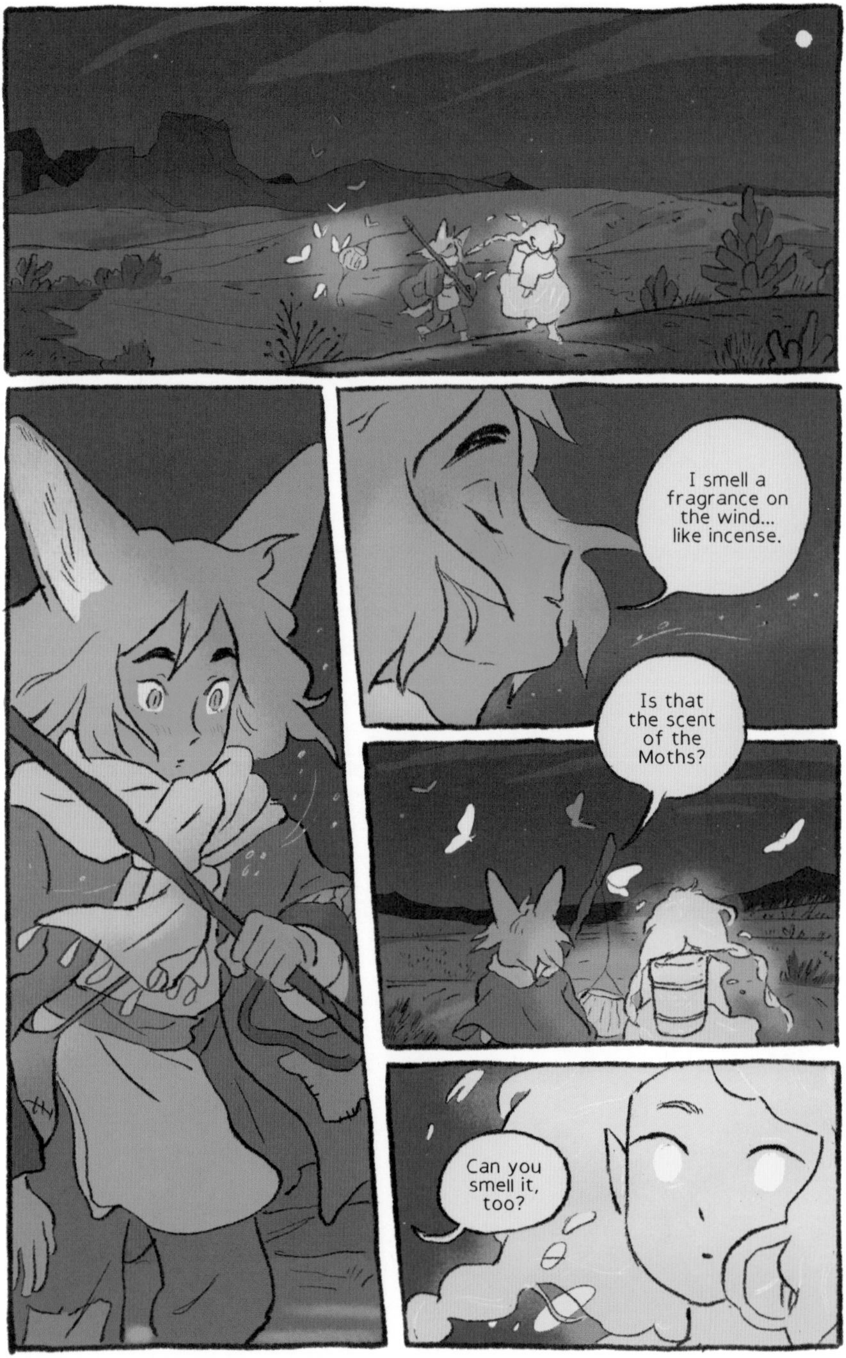
I smell a fragrance on the wind... like incense.
Is that the scent of the Moths?
Can you smell it, too?

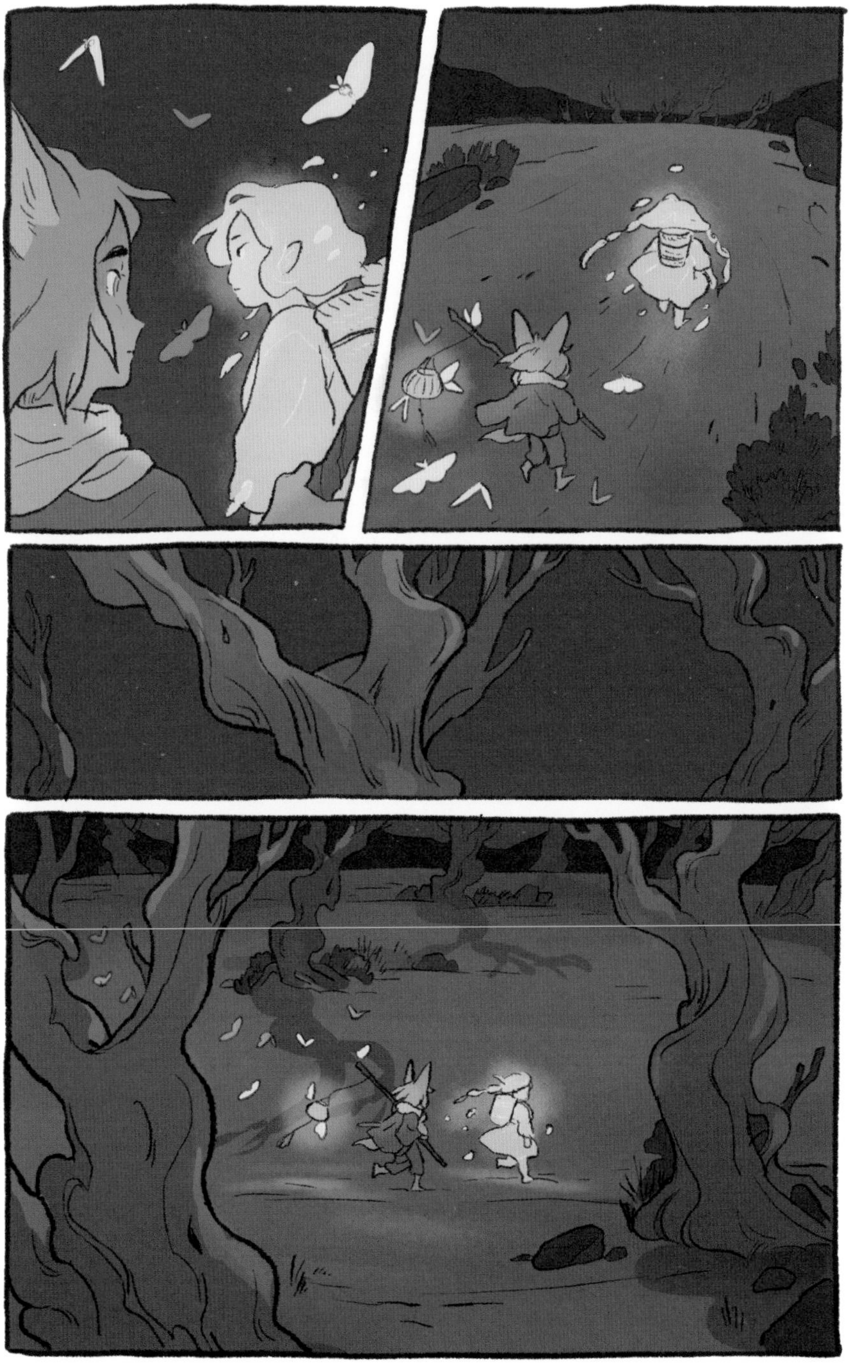

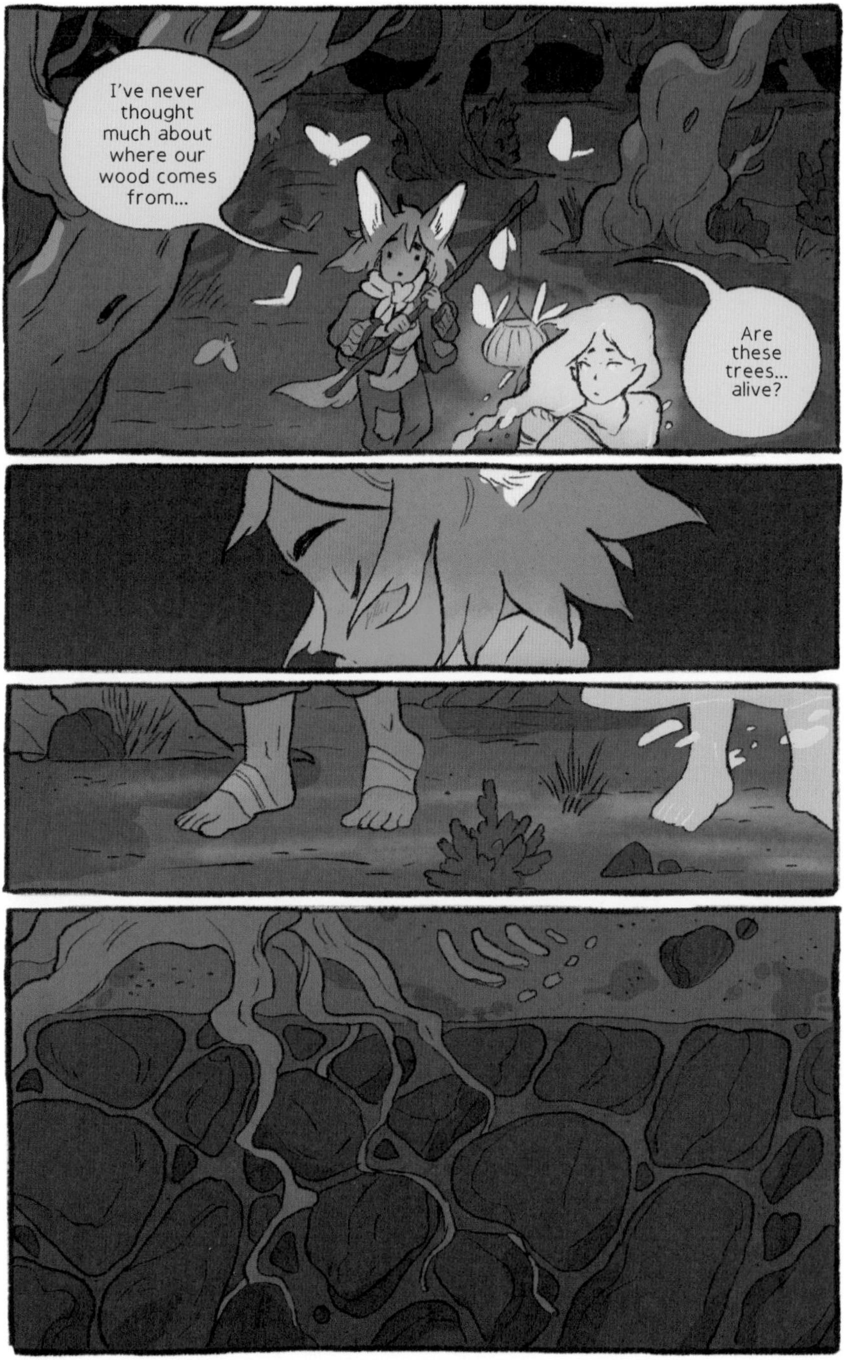
I've never thought much about where our wood comes from...
Are these trees... alive?

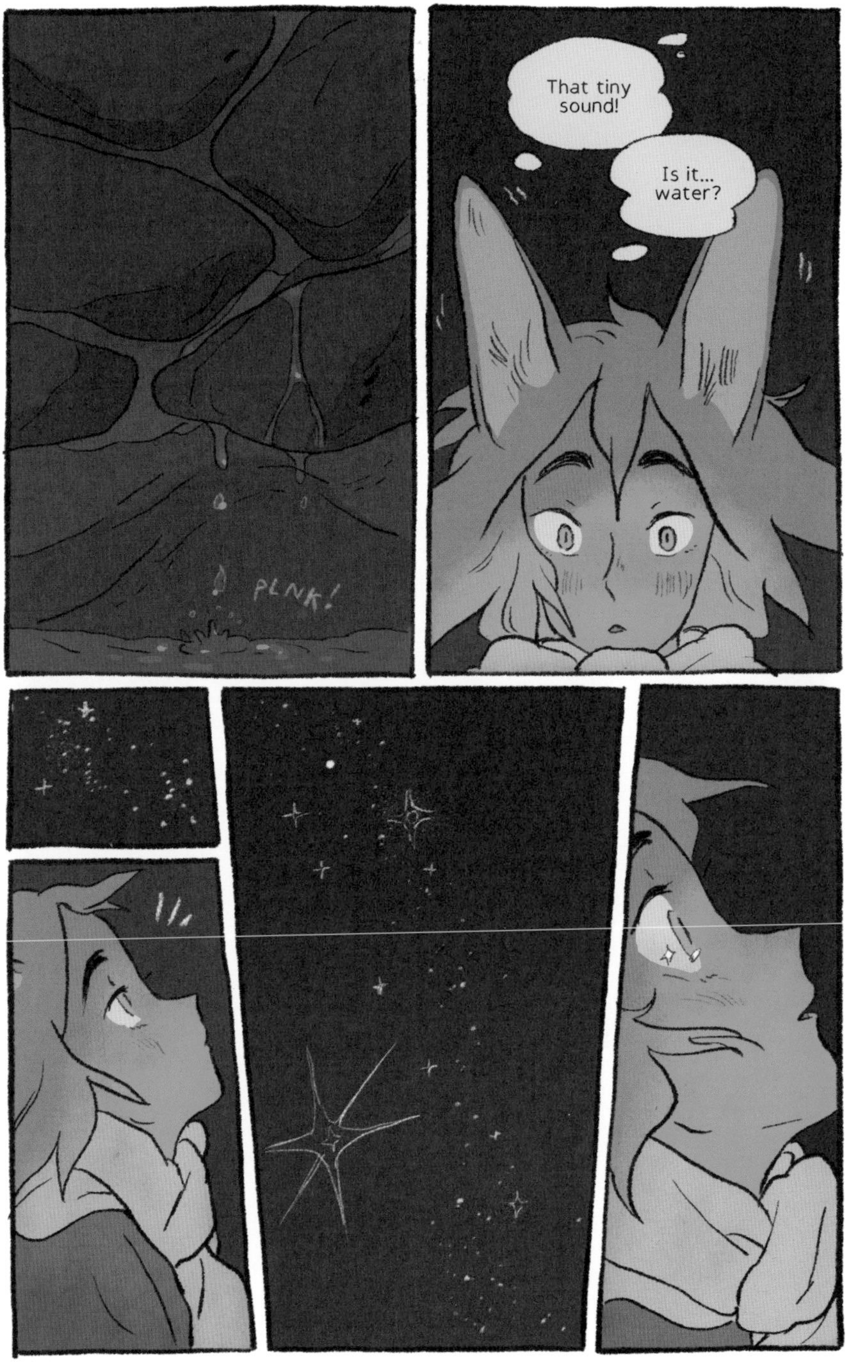
PLNK!
That tiny sound!
Is it... water?

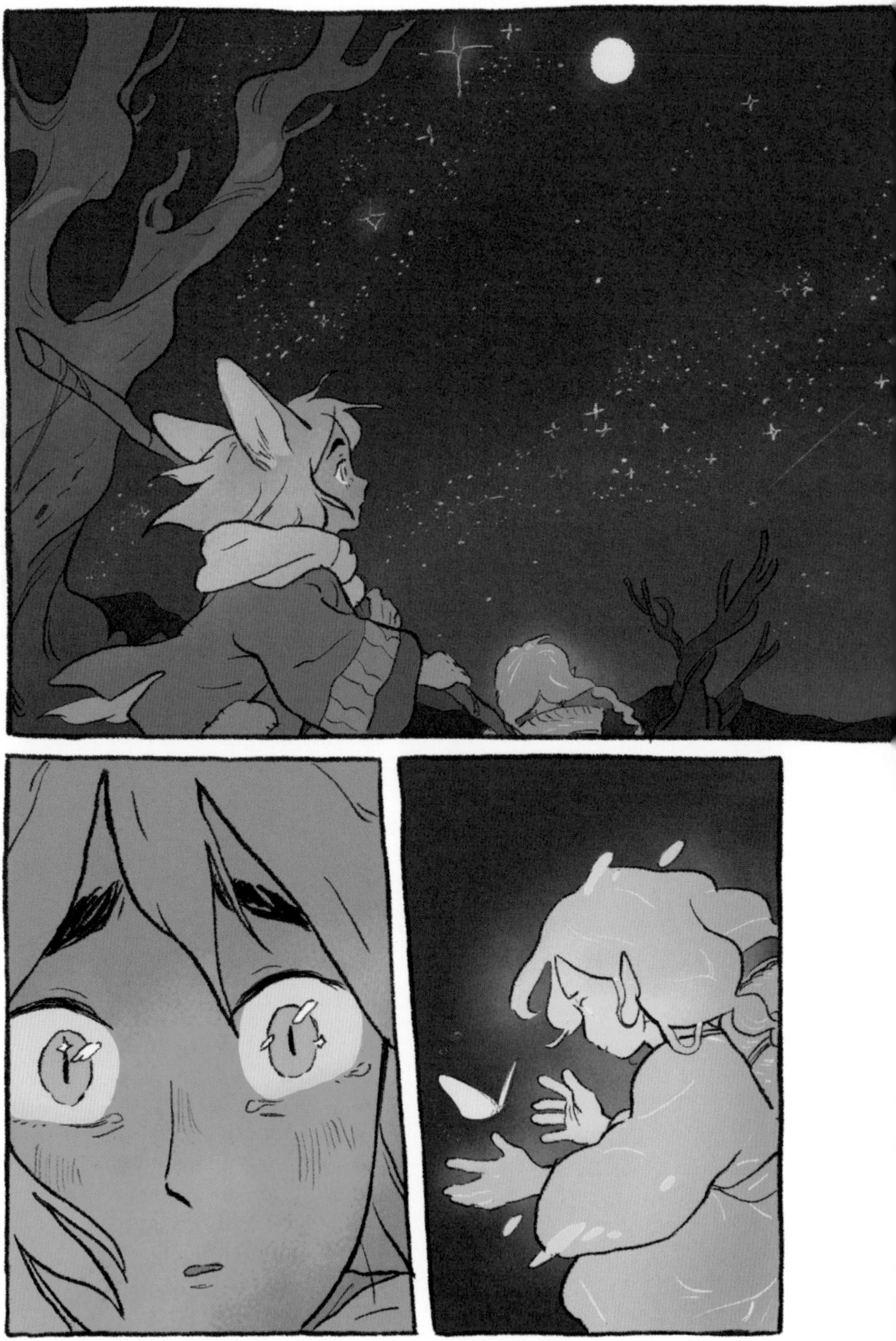

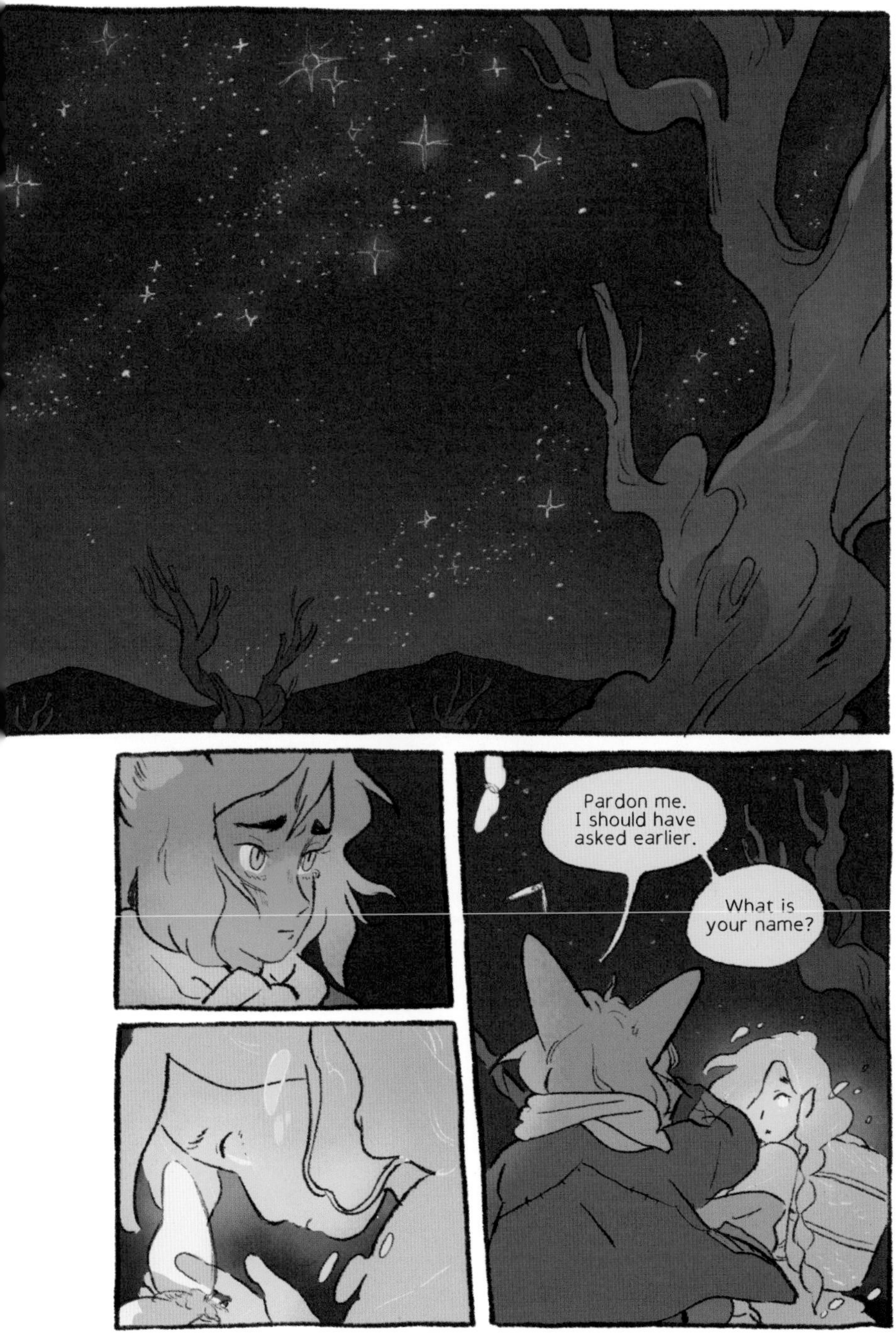
Pardon me. I should have asked earlier.
What is your name?

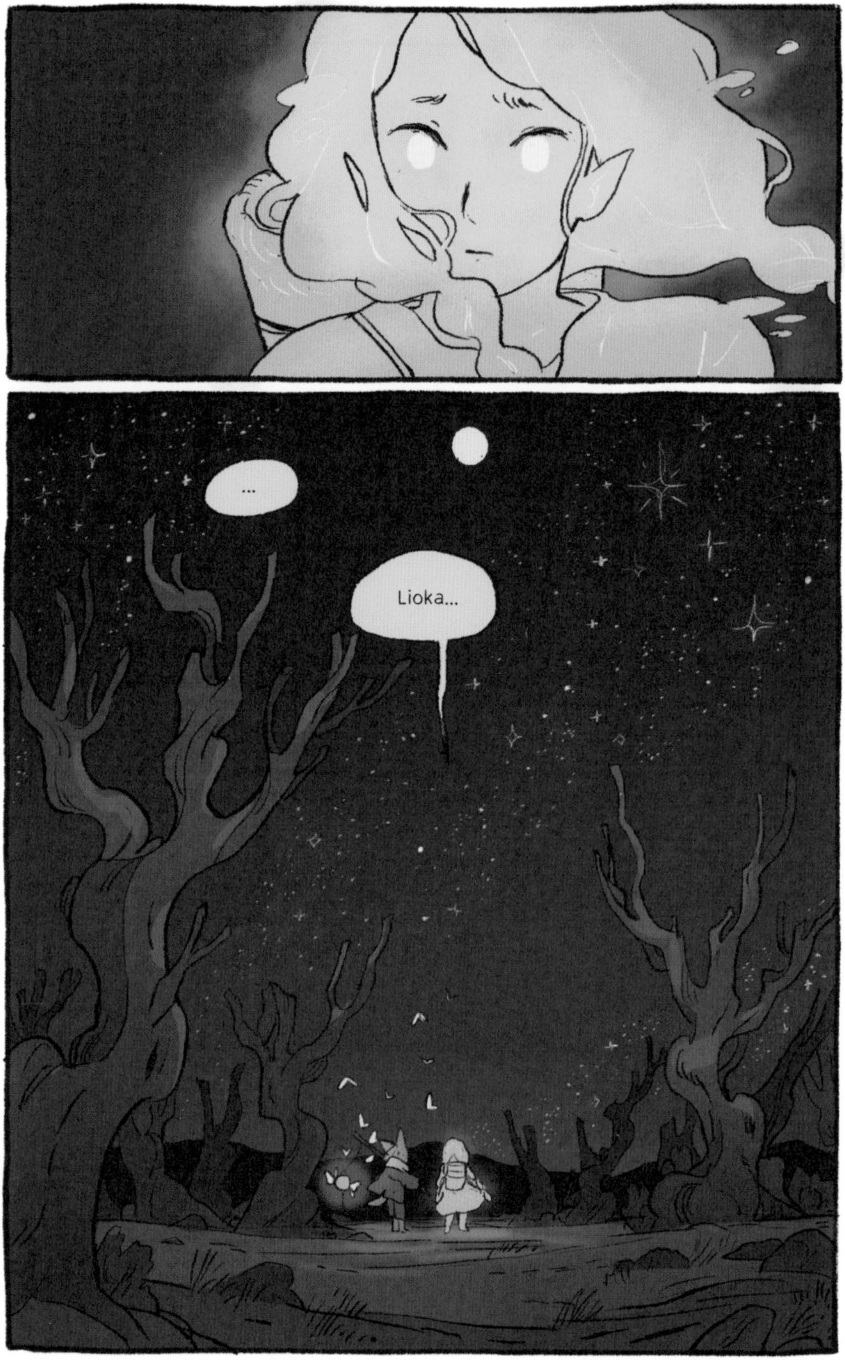
...
Lioka...

Chapter Eight

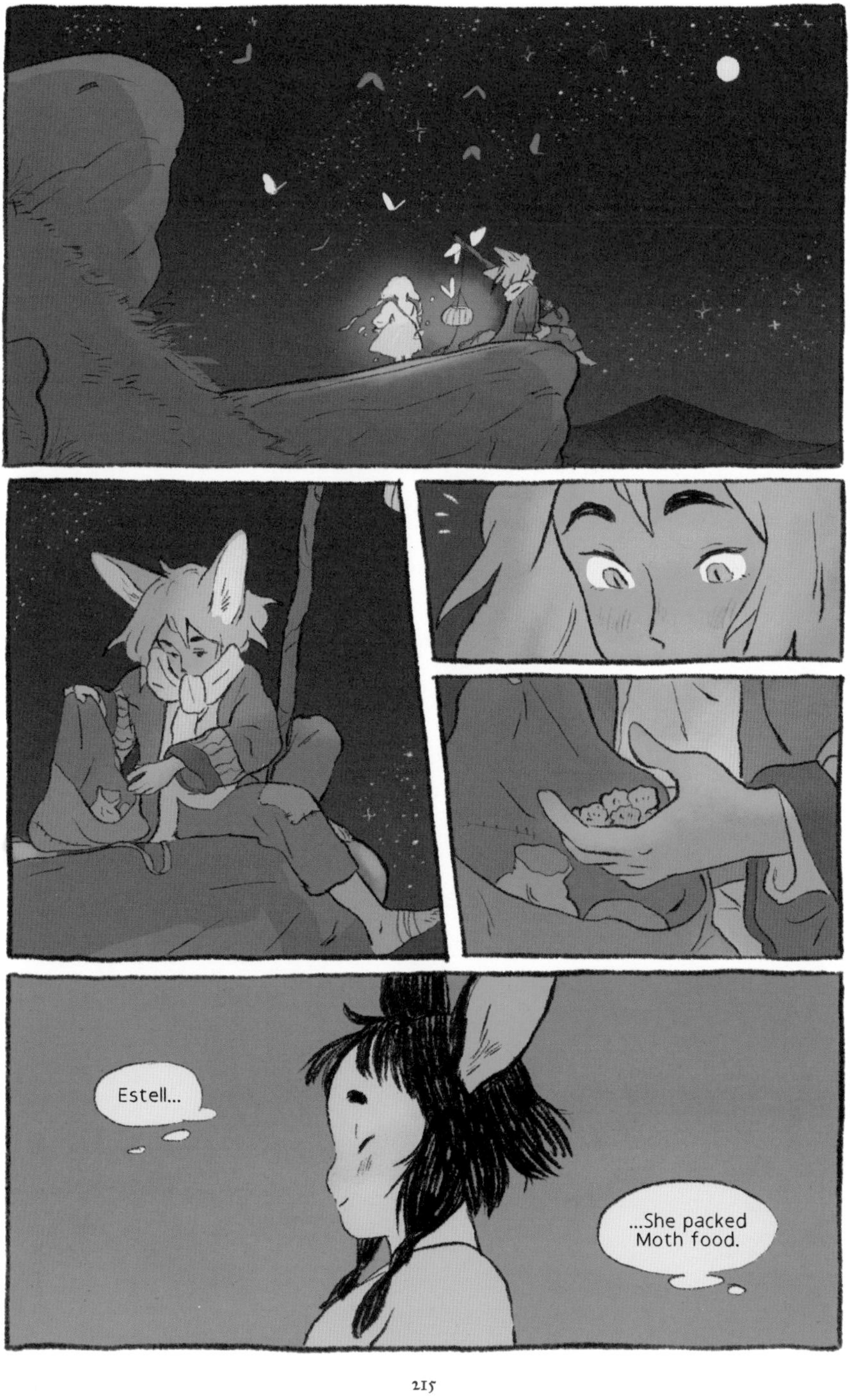
Estell...
...She packed Moth food.

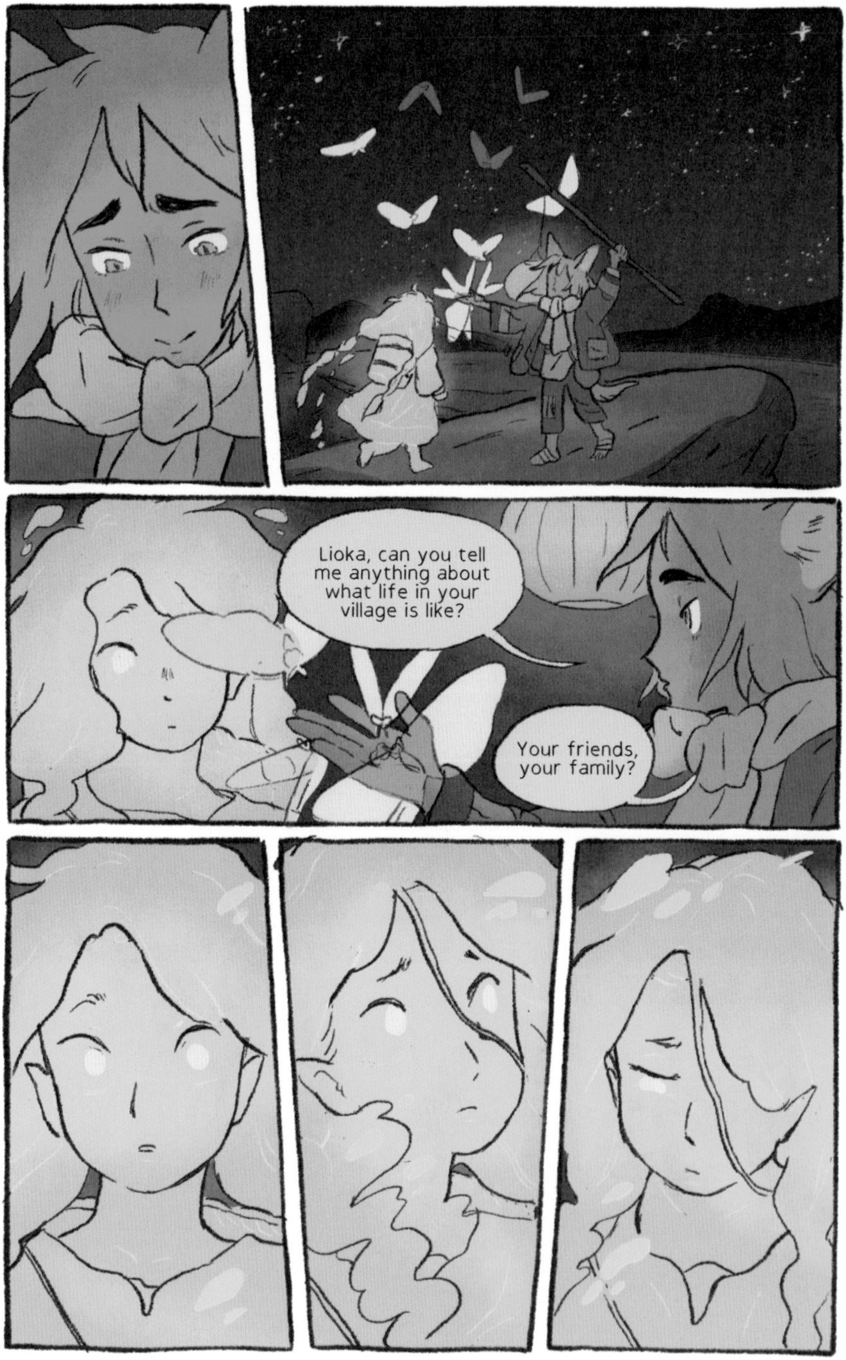
Lioka, can you tell me anything about what life in your village is like?
Your friends, your family?

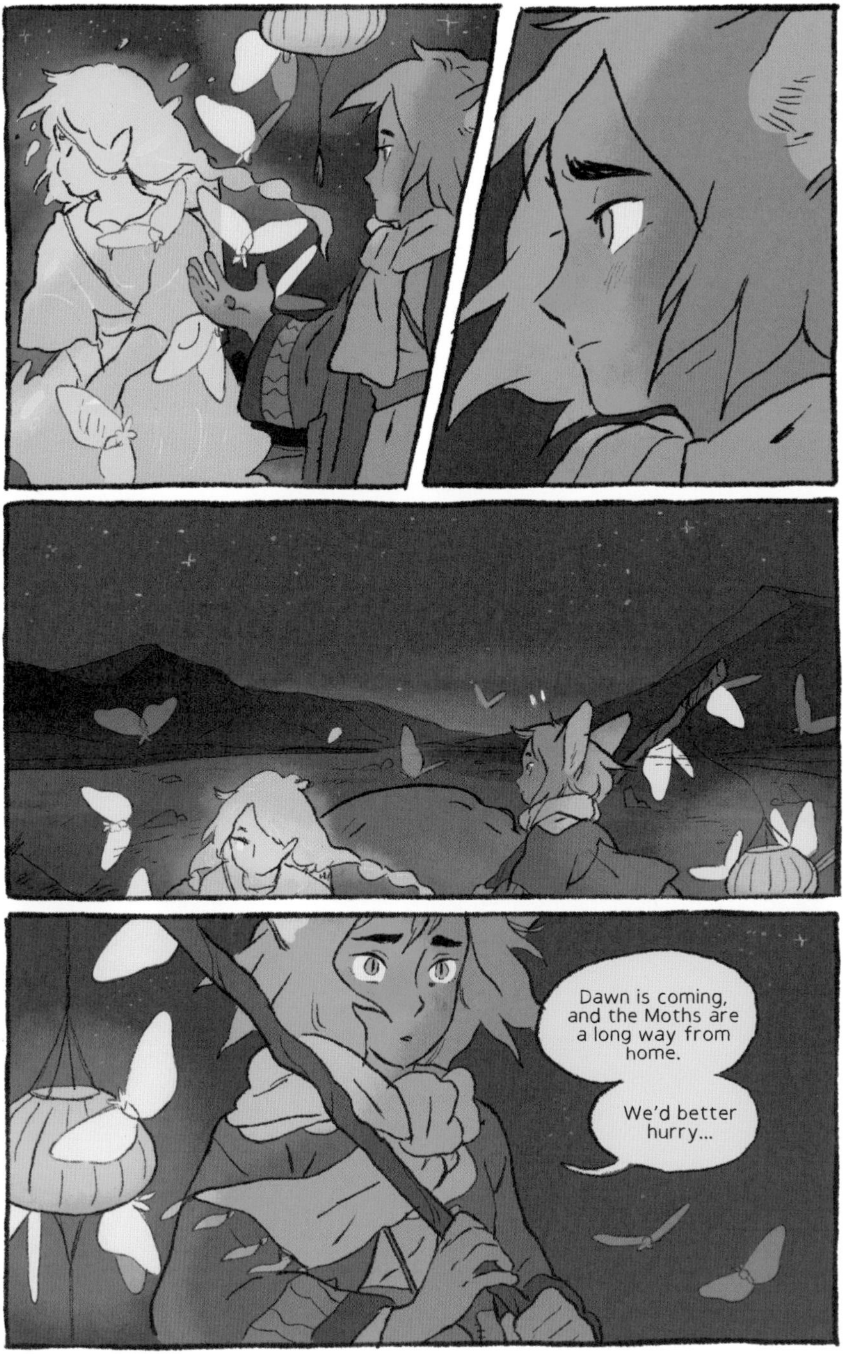
Dawn is coming, and the Moths are a long way from home.
We'd better hurry...

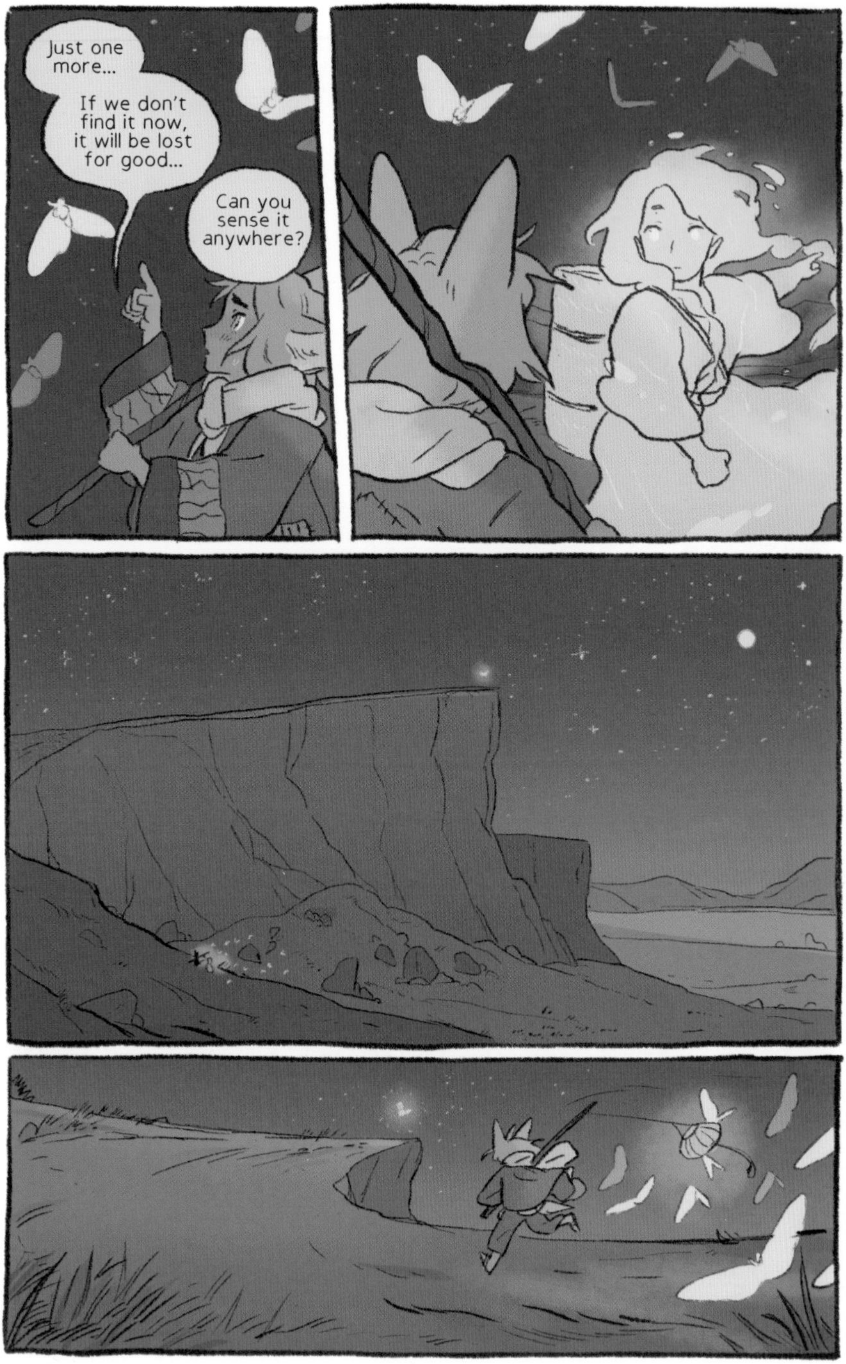
Just one more...
If we don't find it now, it will be lost for good...
Can you sense it anywhere?

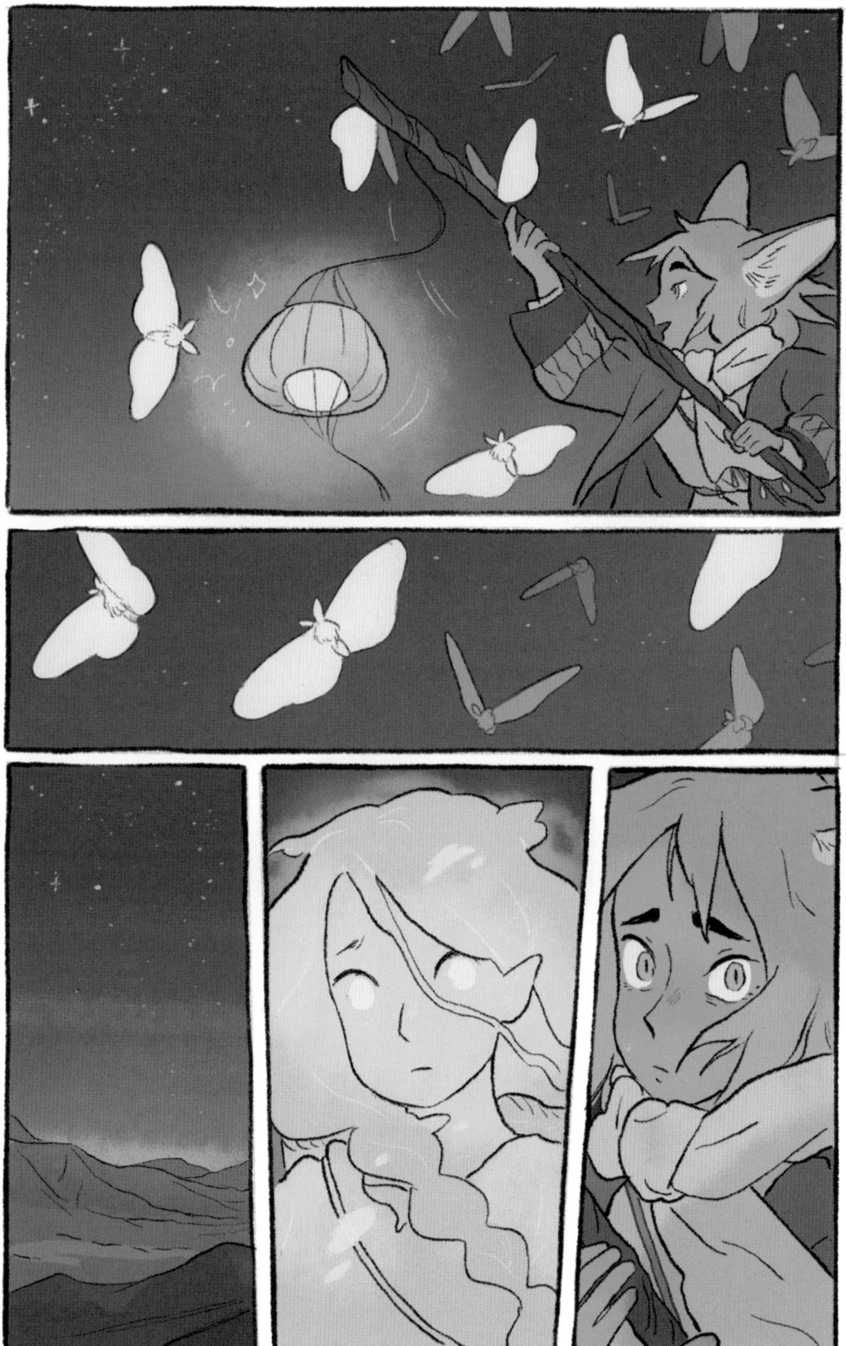

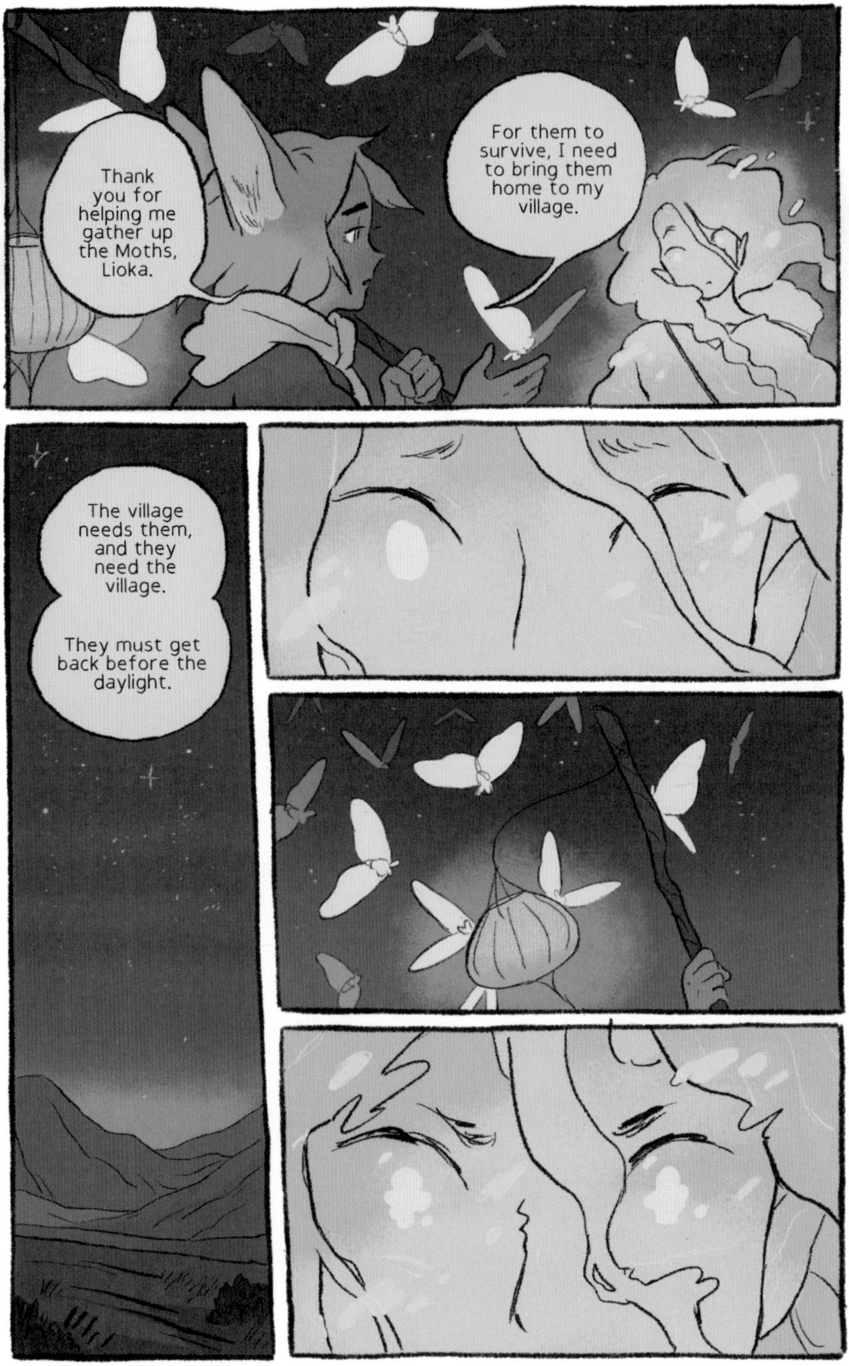
Thank you for helping me gather up the Moths, Lioka.
For them to survive, I need to bring them home to my village.
The village needs them, and they need the village.
They must get back before the daylight.

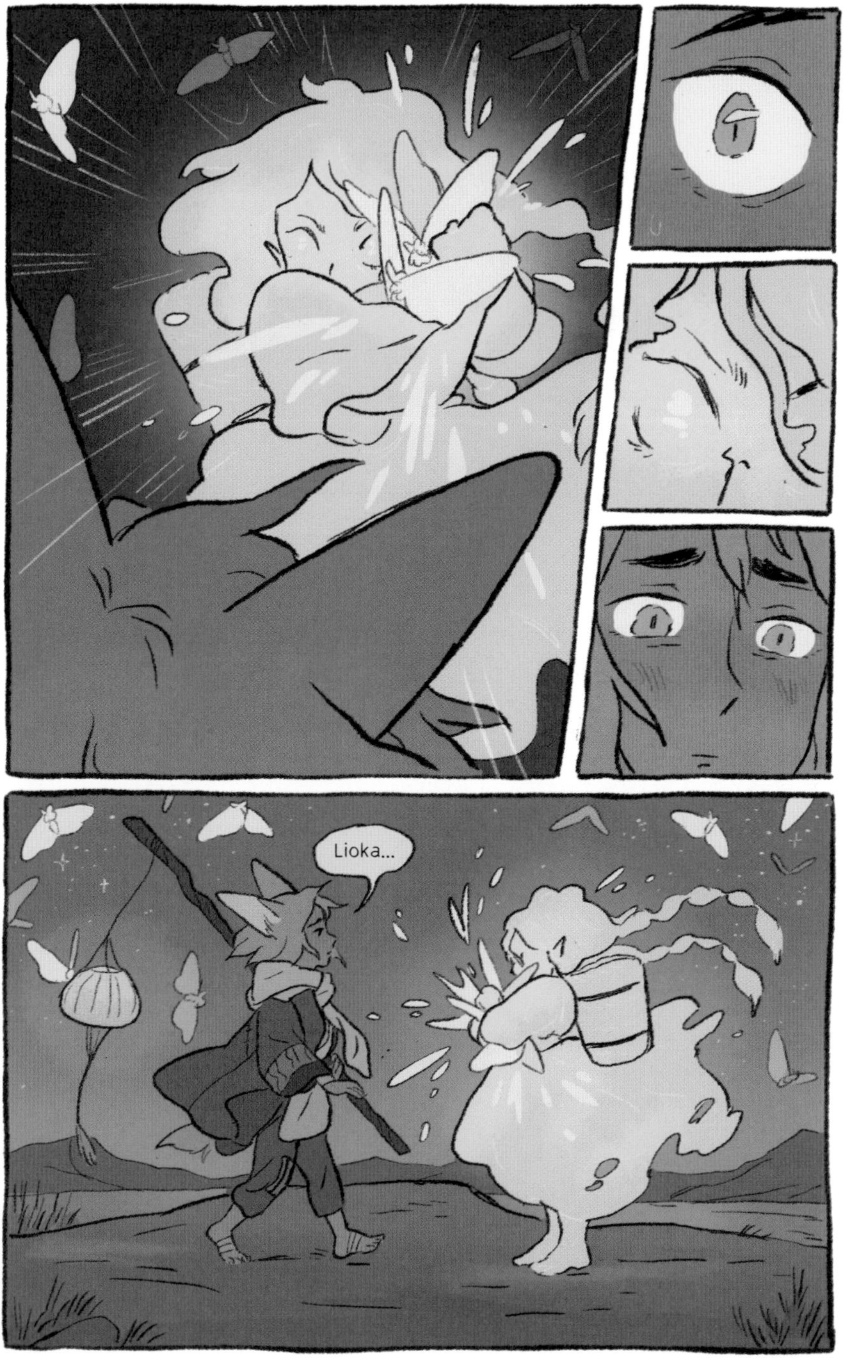
Lioka...

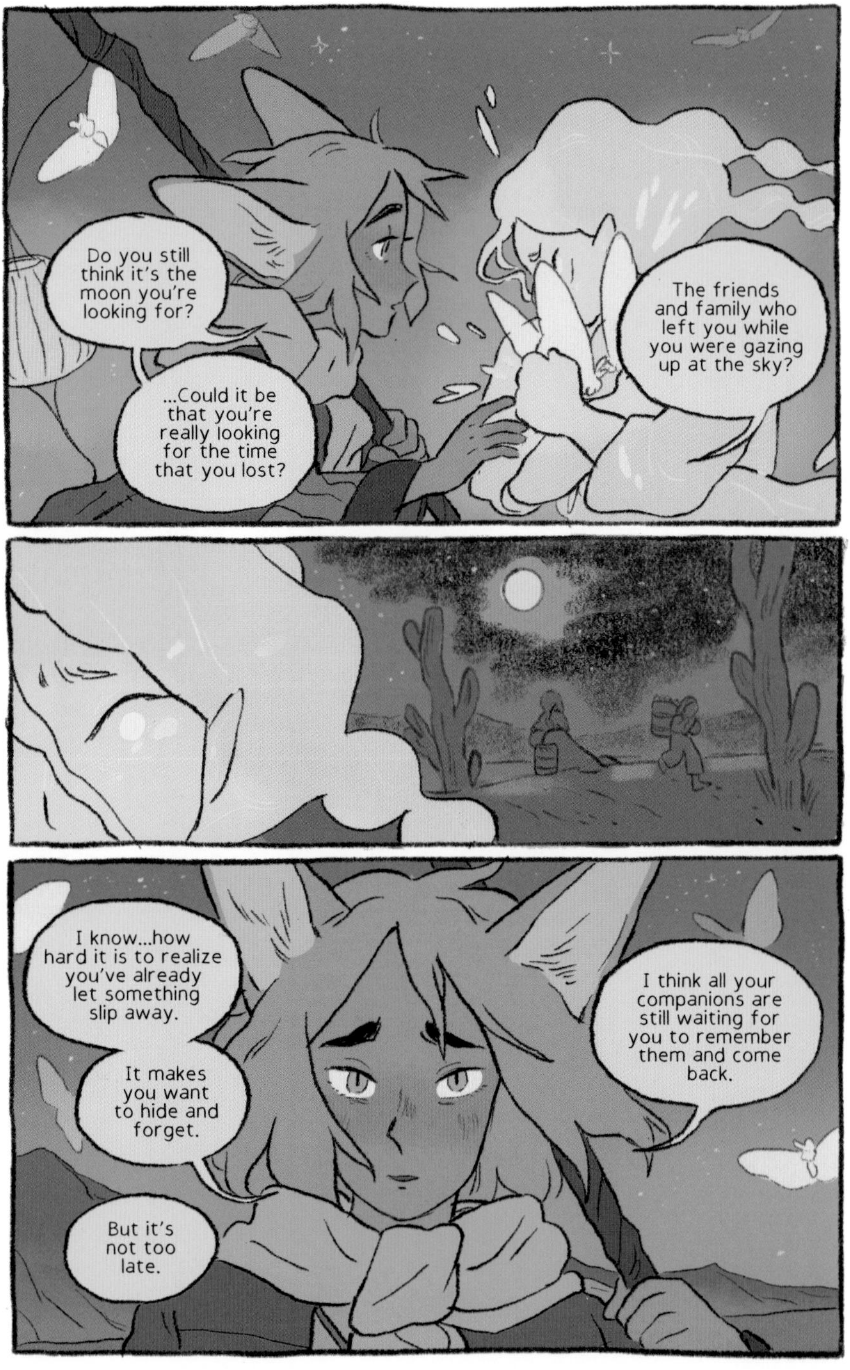
Do you still think it's the moon you're looking for?
...Could it be that you're really looking for the time that you lost?
The friends and family who left you while you were gazing up at the sky?
I know...how hard it is to realize you've already let something slip away.
It makes you want to hide and forget.
But it's not too late.
I think all your companions are still waiting for you to remember them and come back.

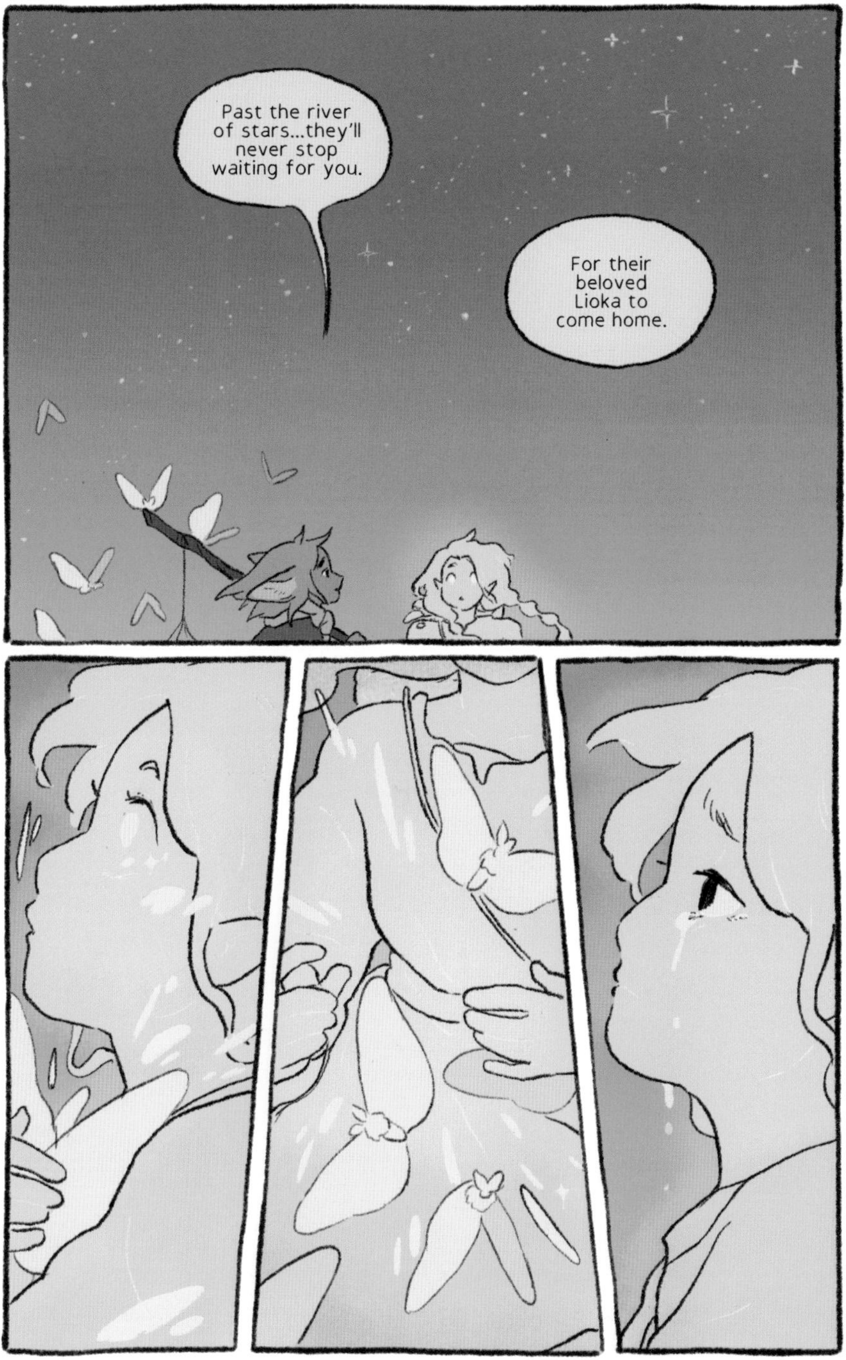
Past the river of stars...they'll never stop waiting for you.
For their beloved Lioka to come home.

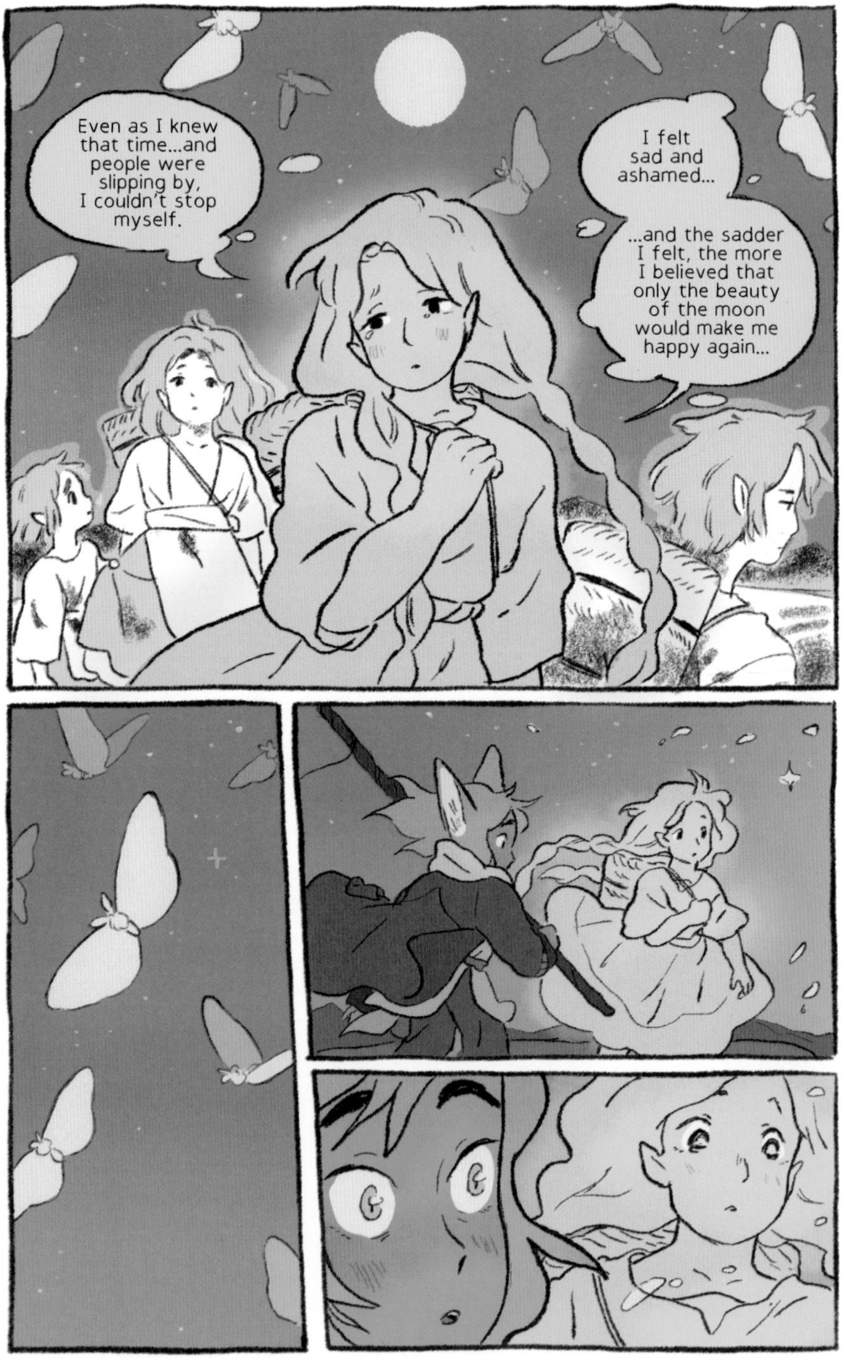
Even as I knew that time...and people were slipping by, I couldn't stop myself.
I felt sad and ashamed...
...and the sadder I felt, the more I believed that only the beauty of the moon would make me happy again...

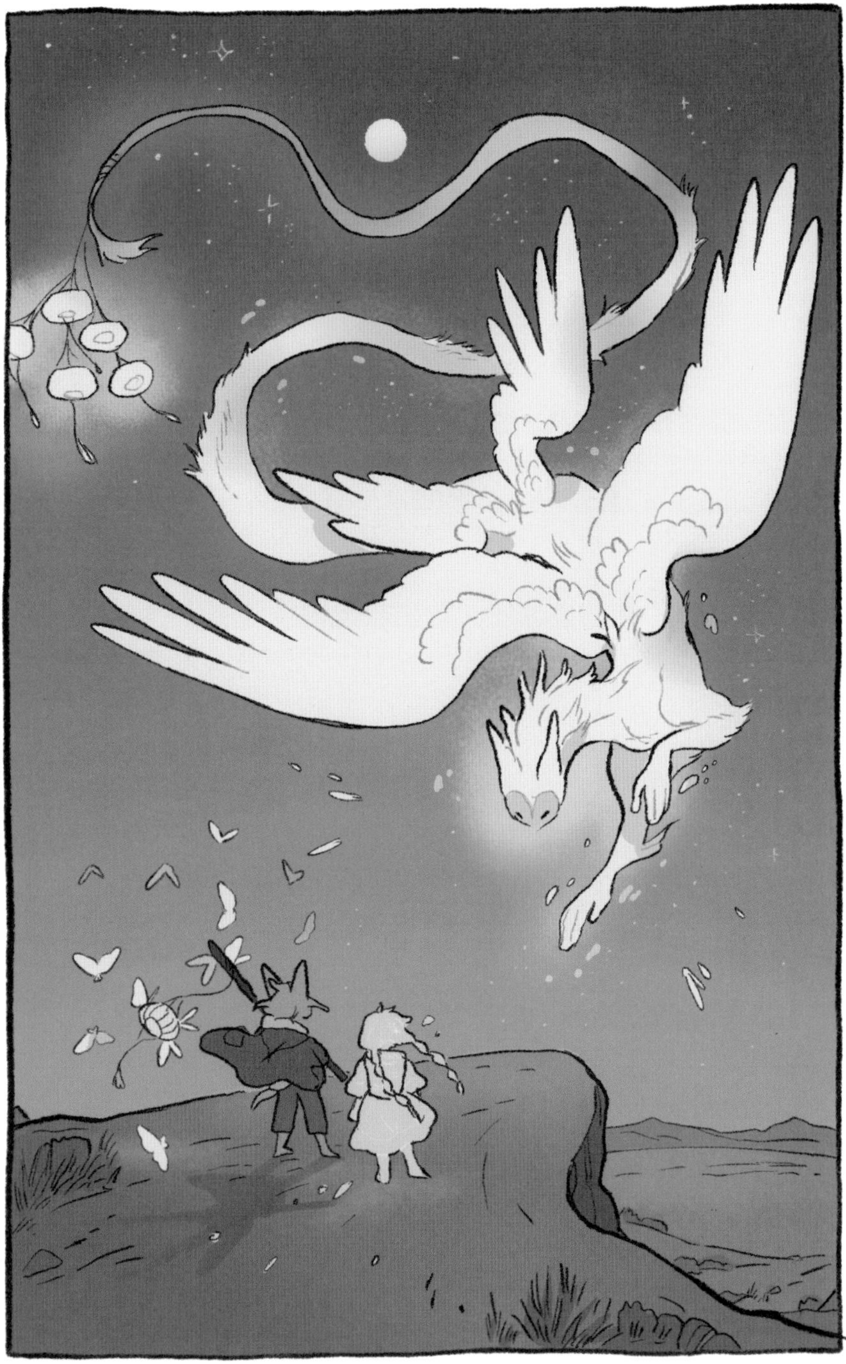

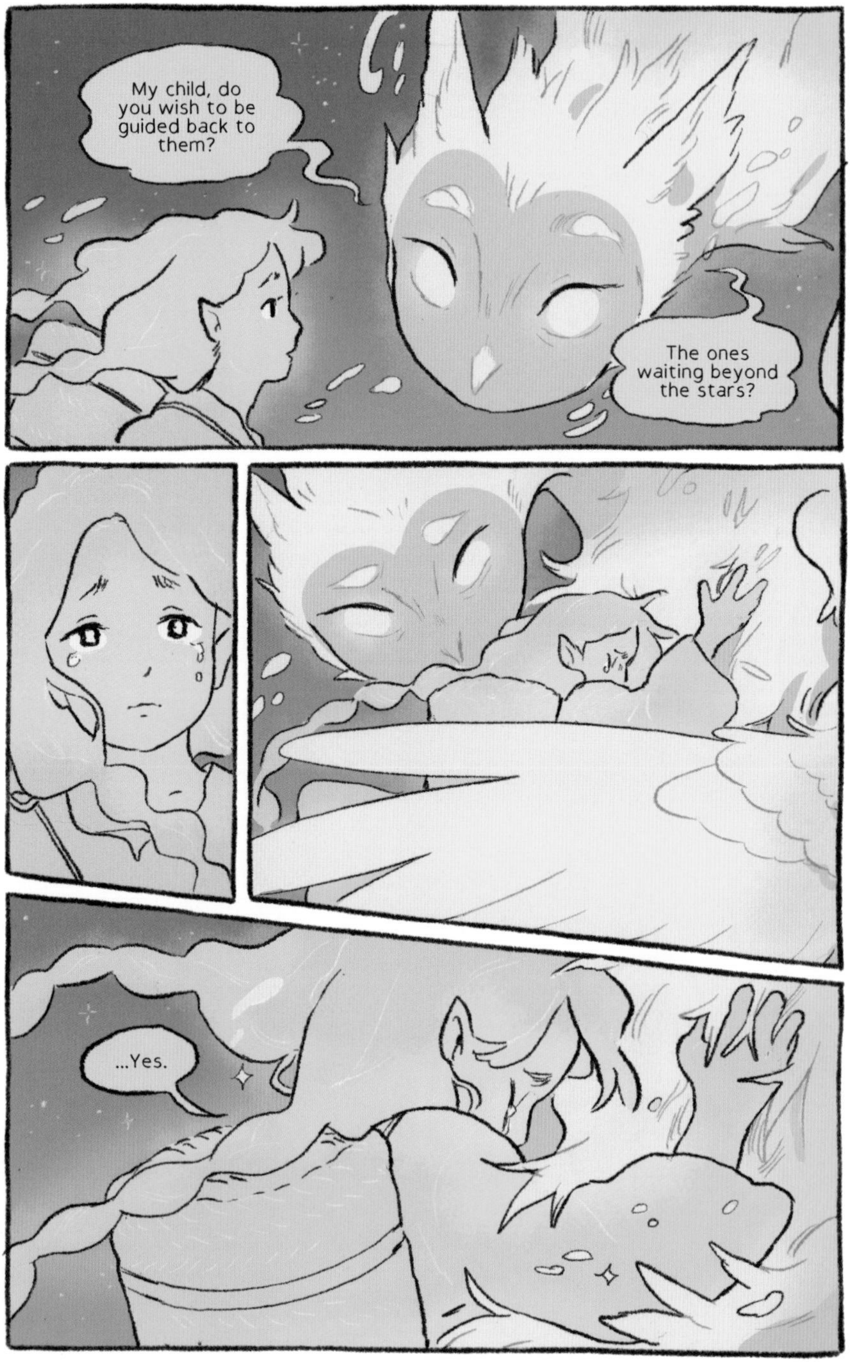
My child, do you wish to be guided back to them?
The ones waiting beyond the stars?
...Yes.

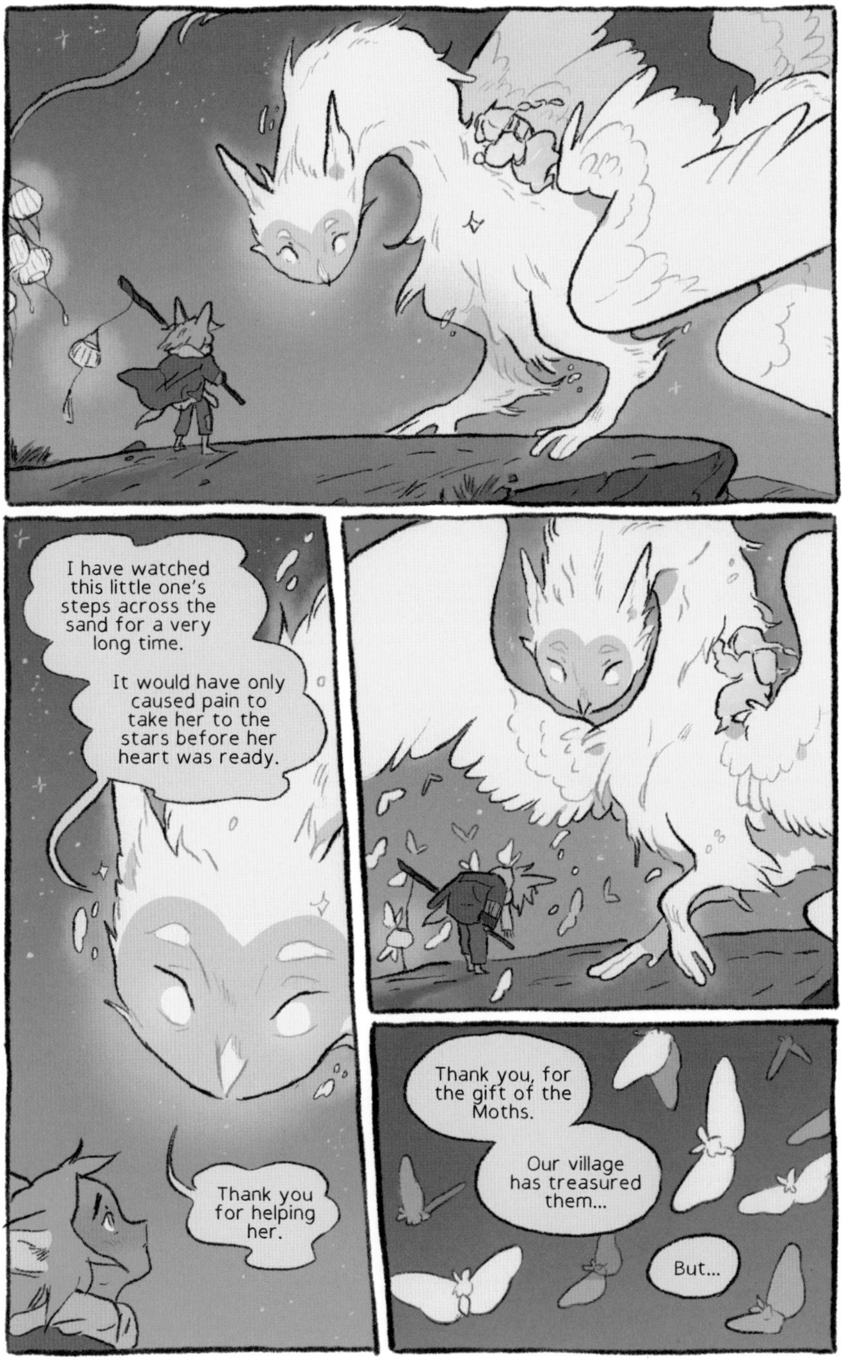
I have watched this little one's steps across the sand for a very long time.
It would have only caused pain to take her to the stars before her heart was ready.
Thank you for helping her.
Thank you, for the gift of the Moths.
Our village has treasured them...
But...

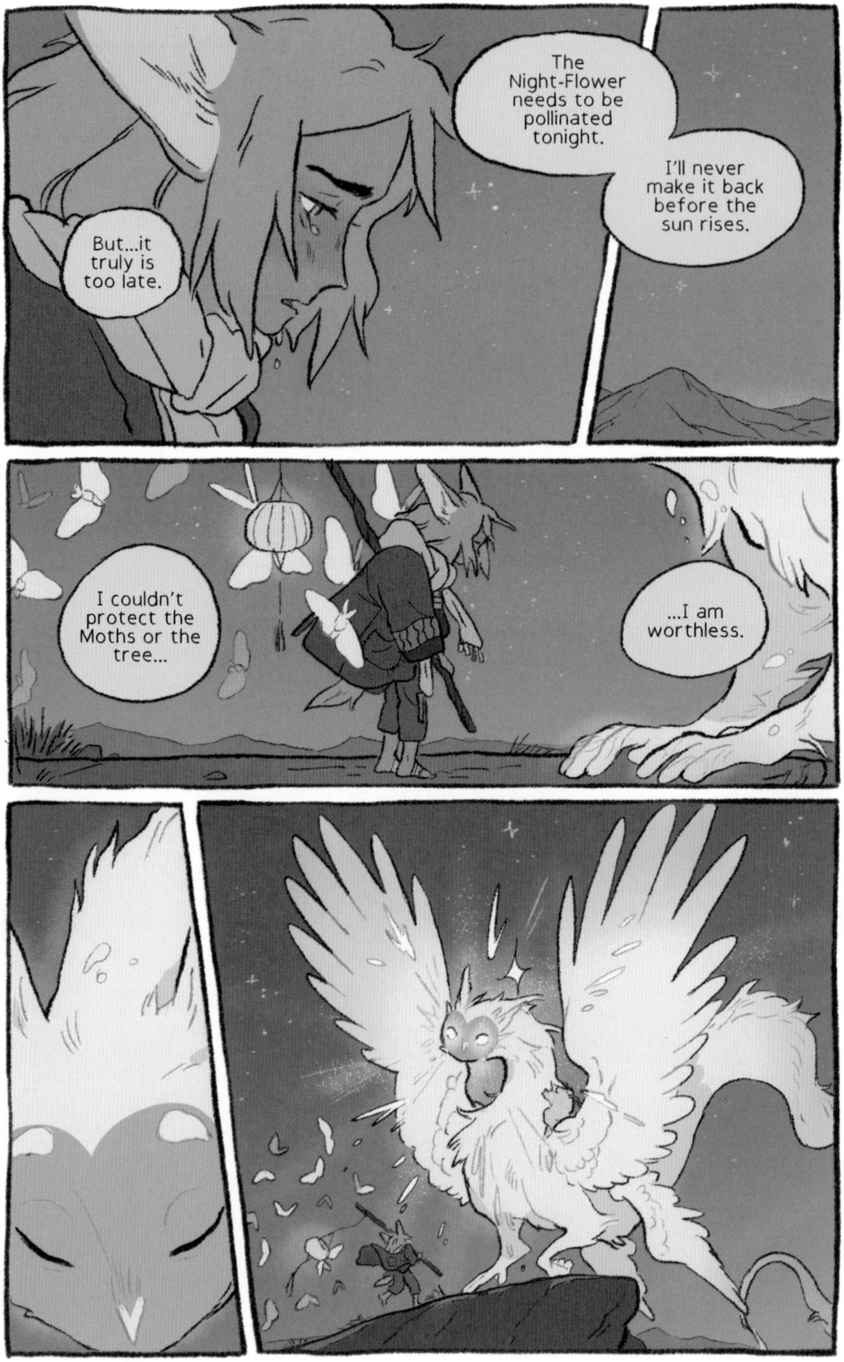
The Night-Flower needs to be pollinated tonight.
I'll never make it back before the sun rises.
But...it truly is too late.
I couldn't protect the Moths or the tree...
...I am worthless.

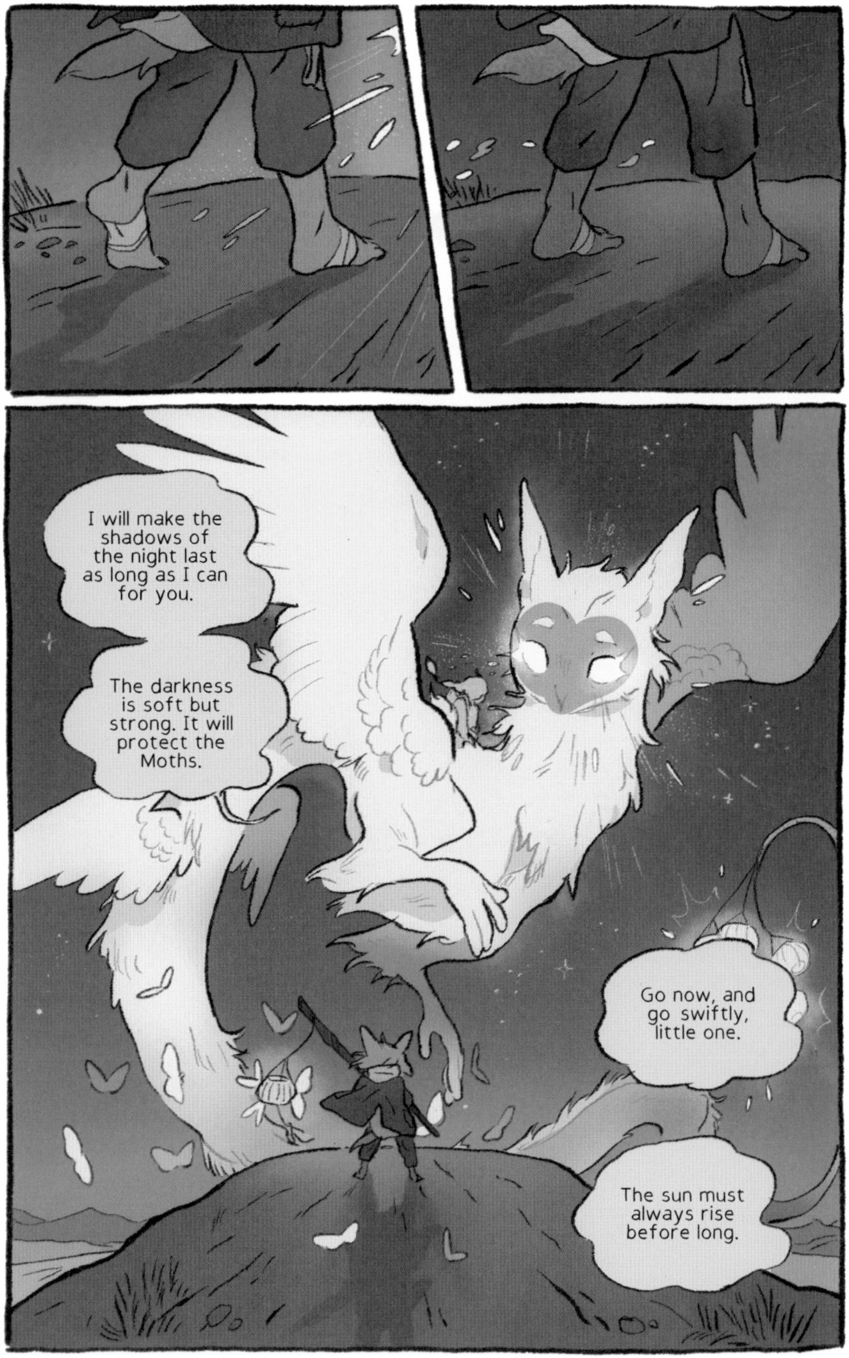
I will make the shadows of the night last as long as I can for you.
The darkness is soft but strong. It will protect the Moths.
Go now, and go swiftly, little one.
The sun must always rise before long.

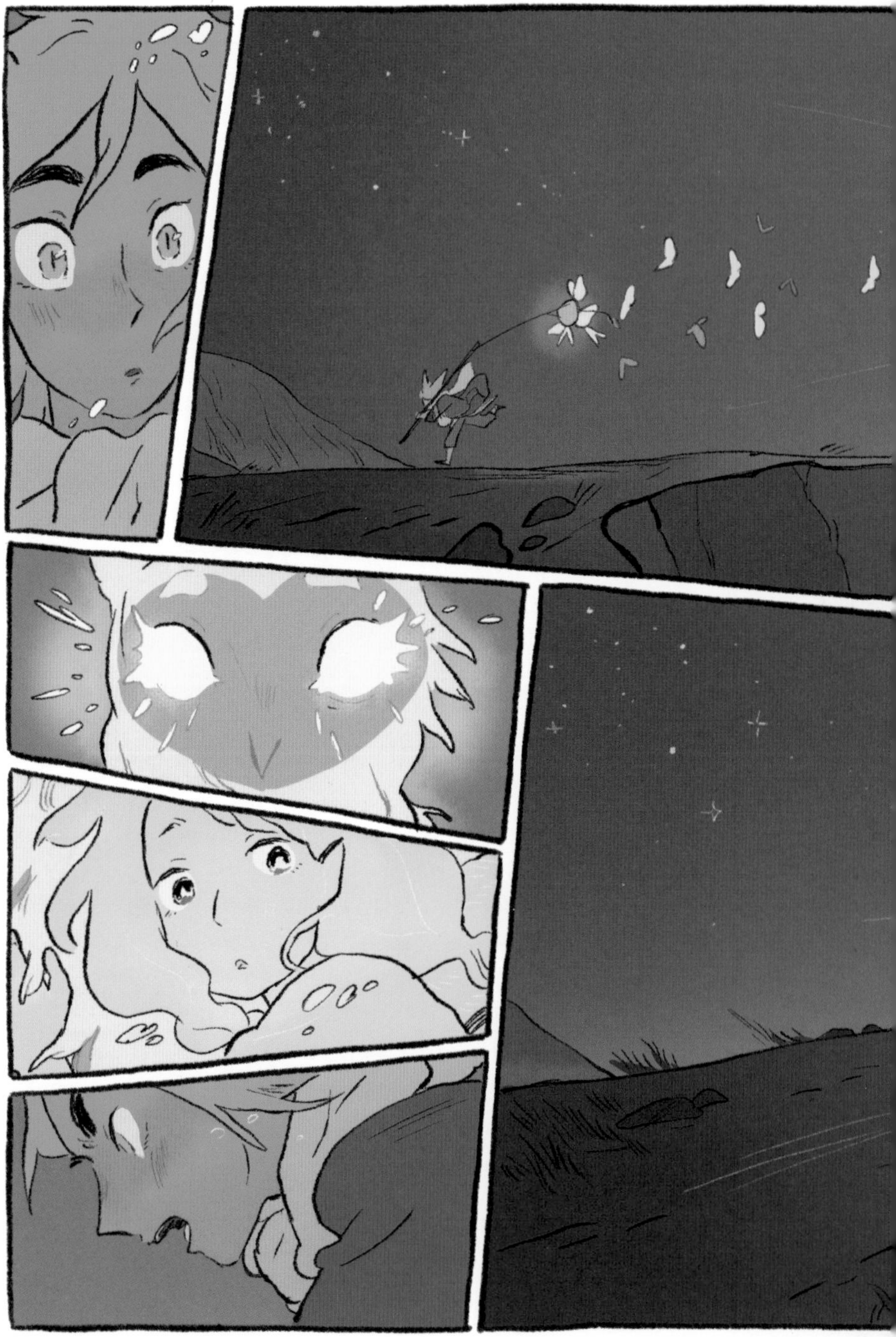

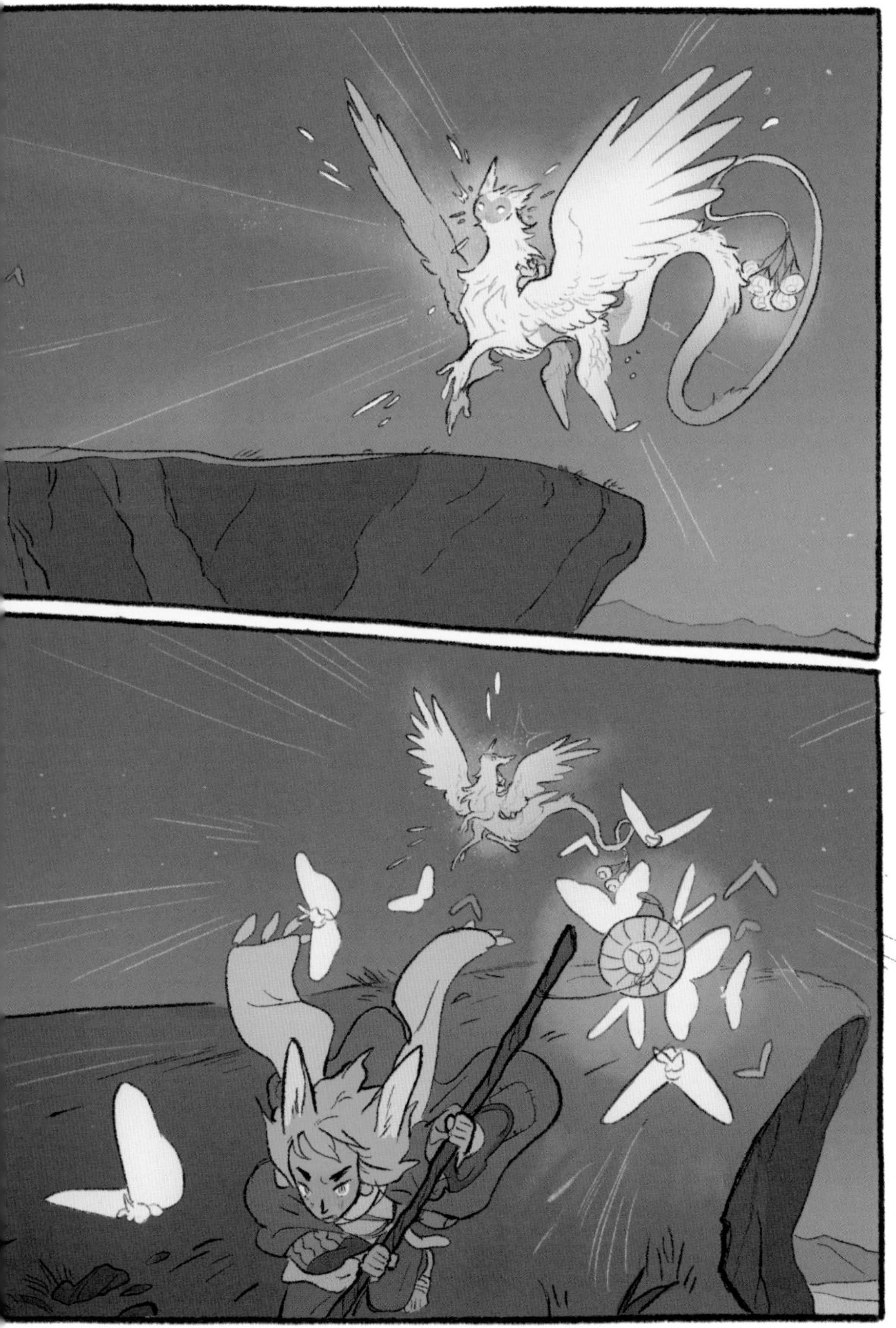

Chapter Nine

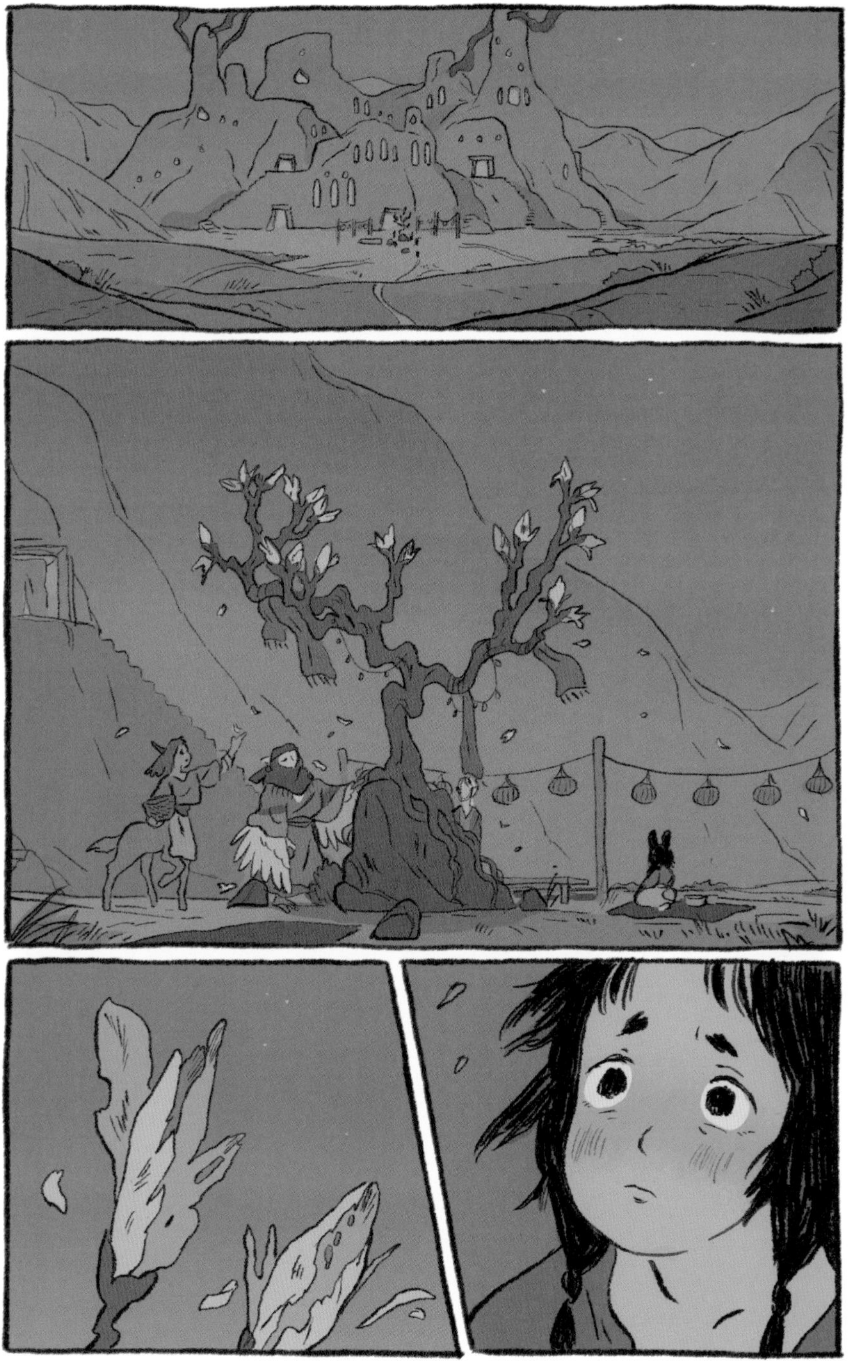

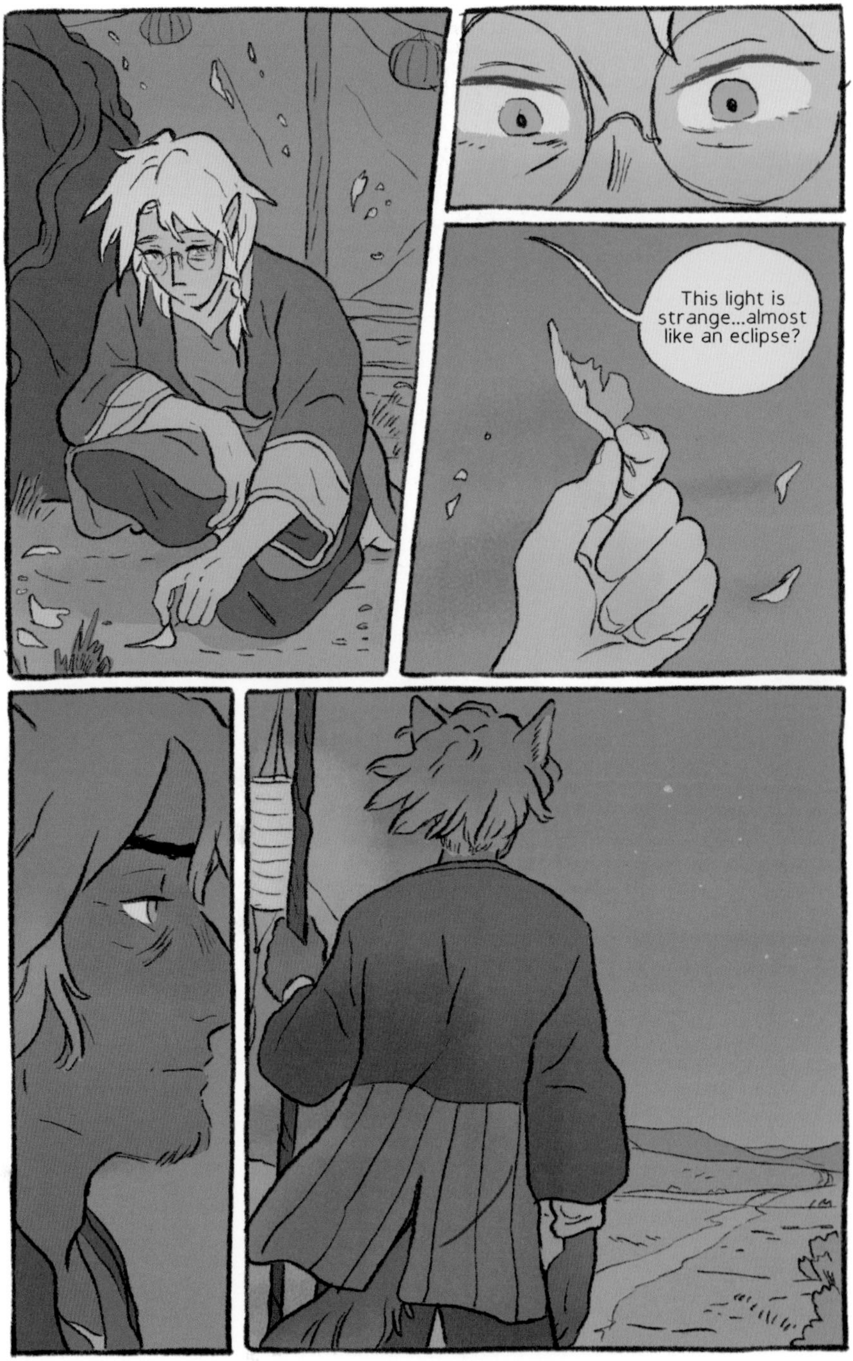
This light is strange...almost like an eclipse?

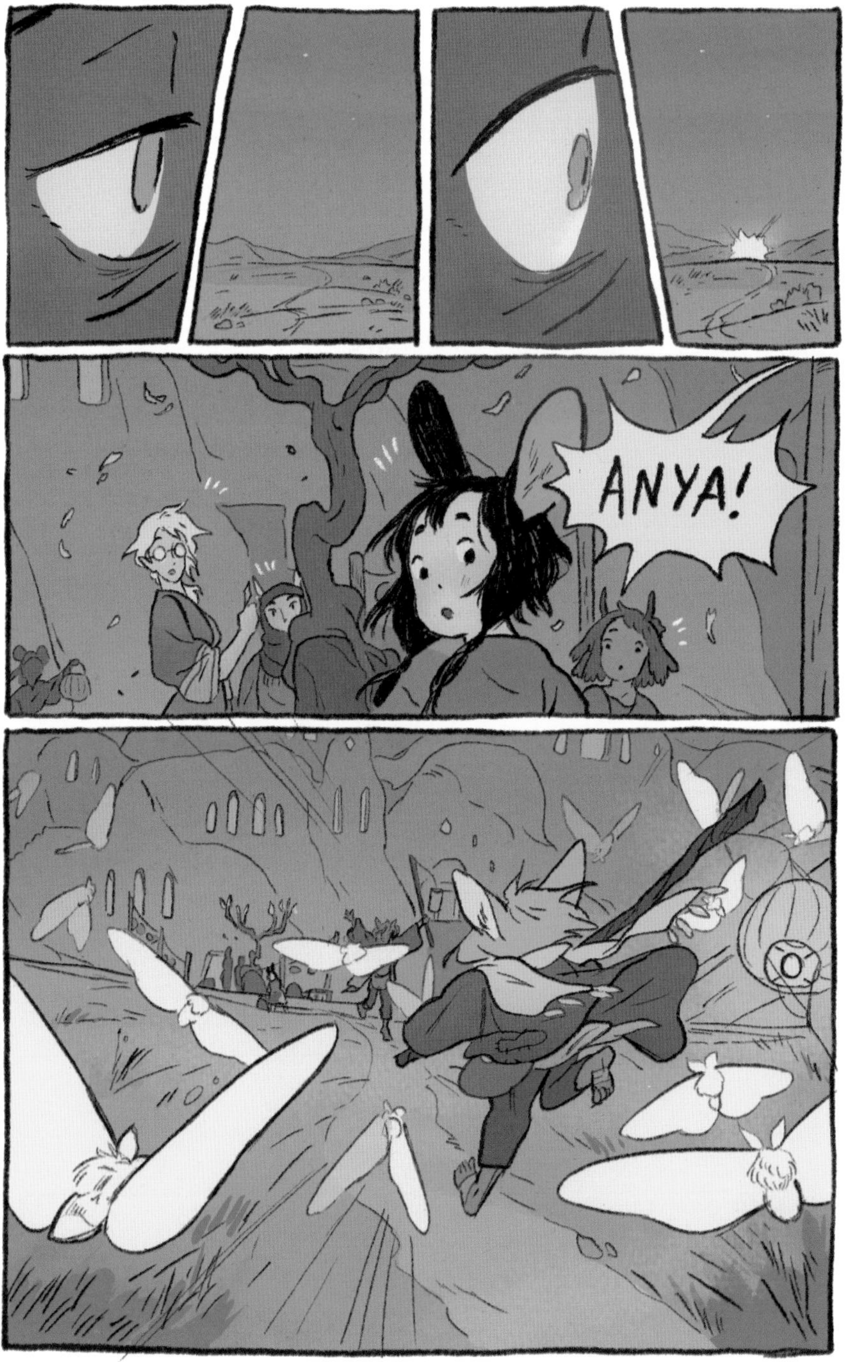
ANYA!

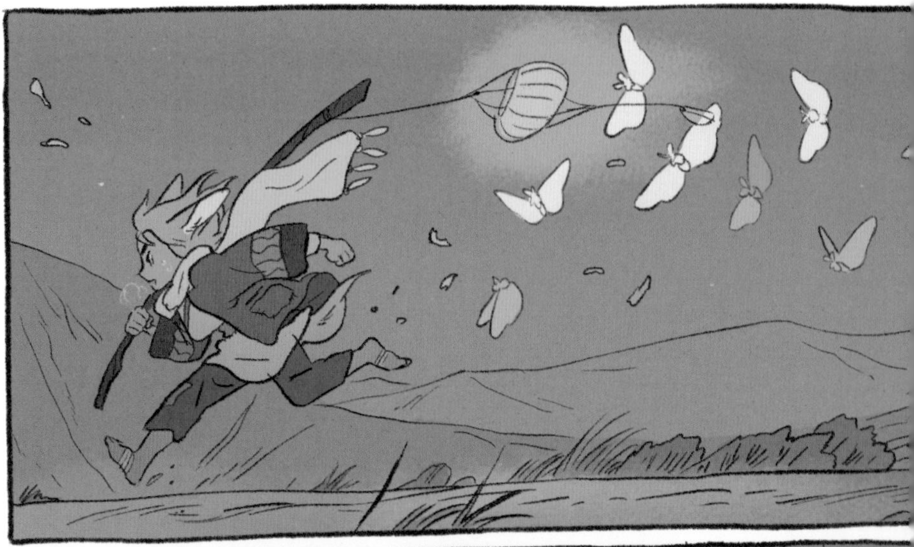

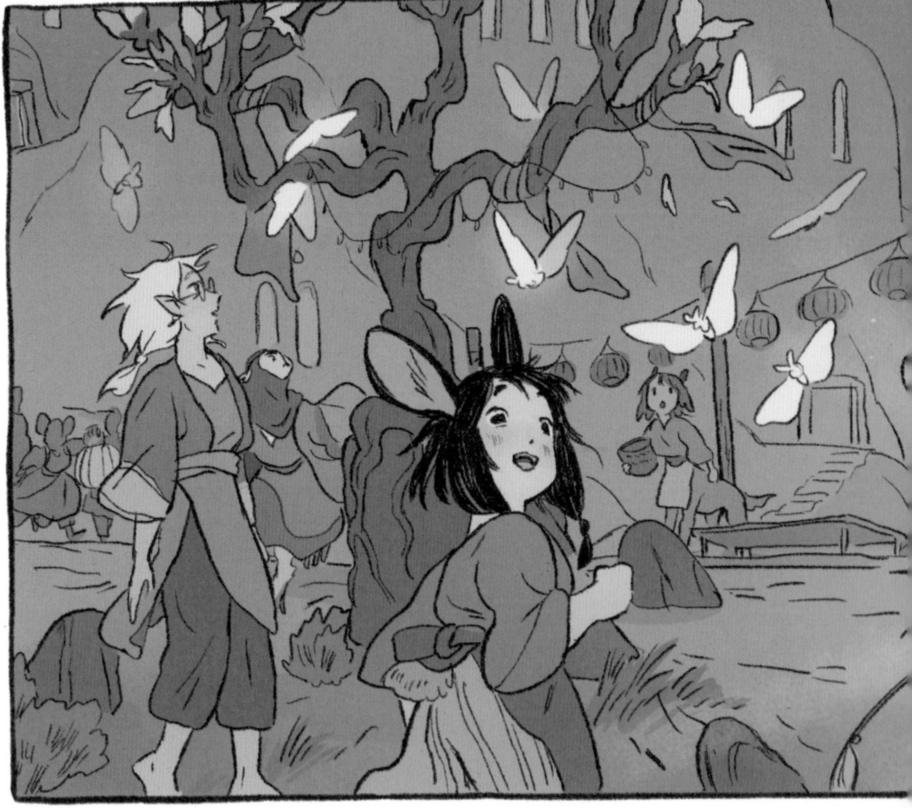

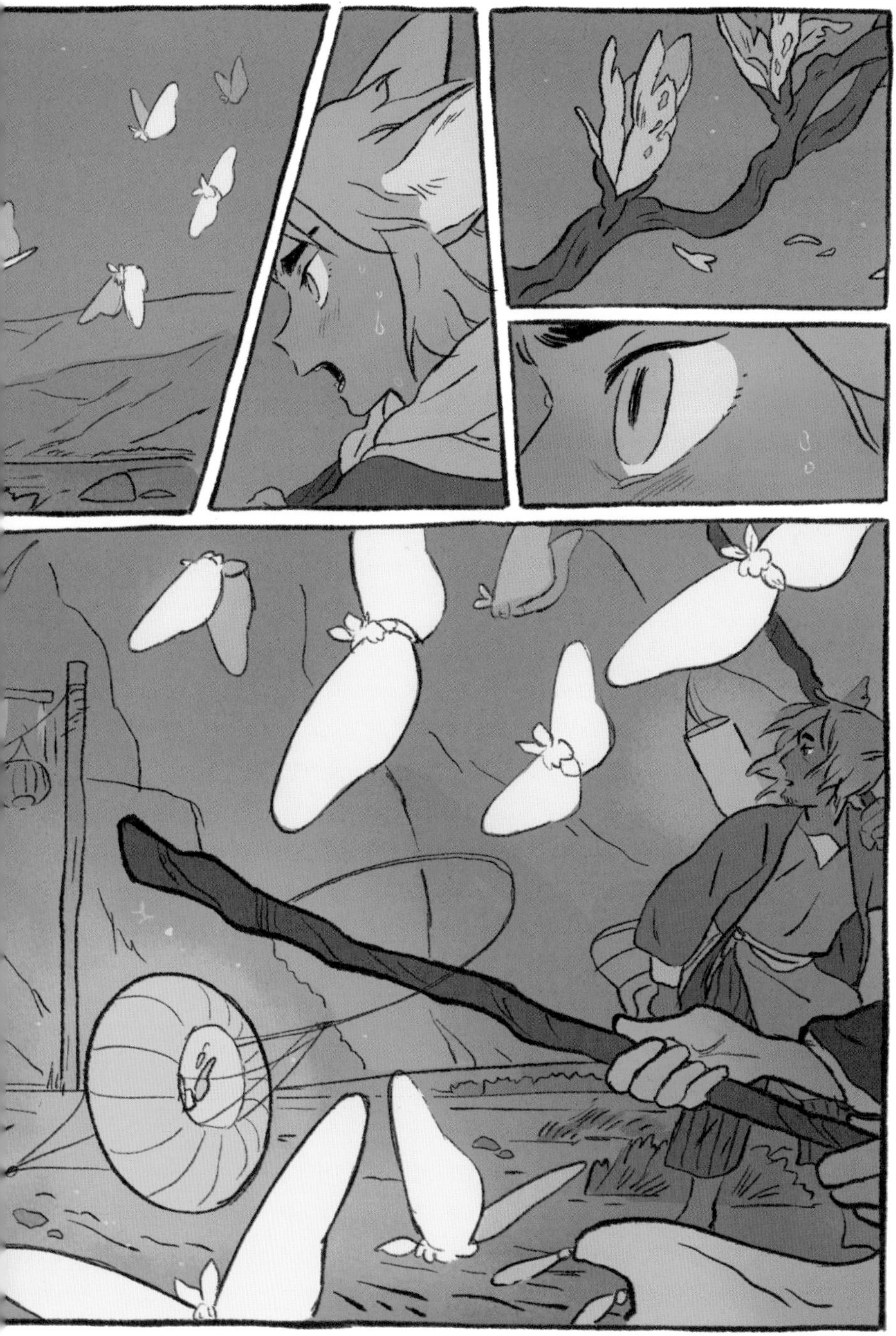

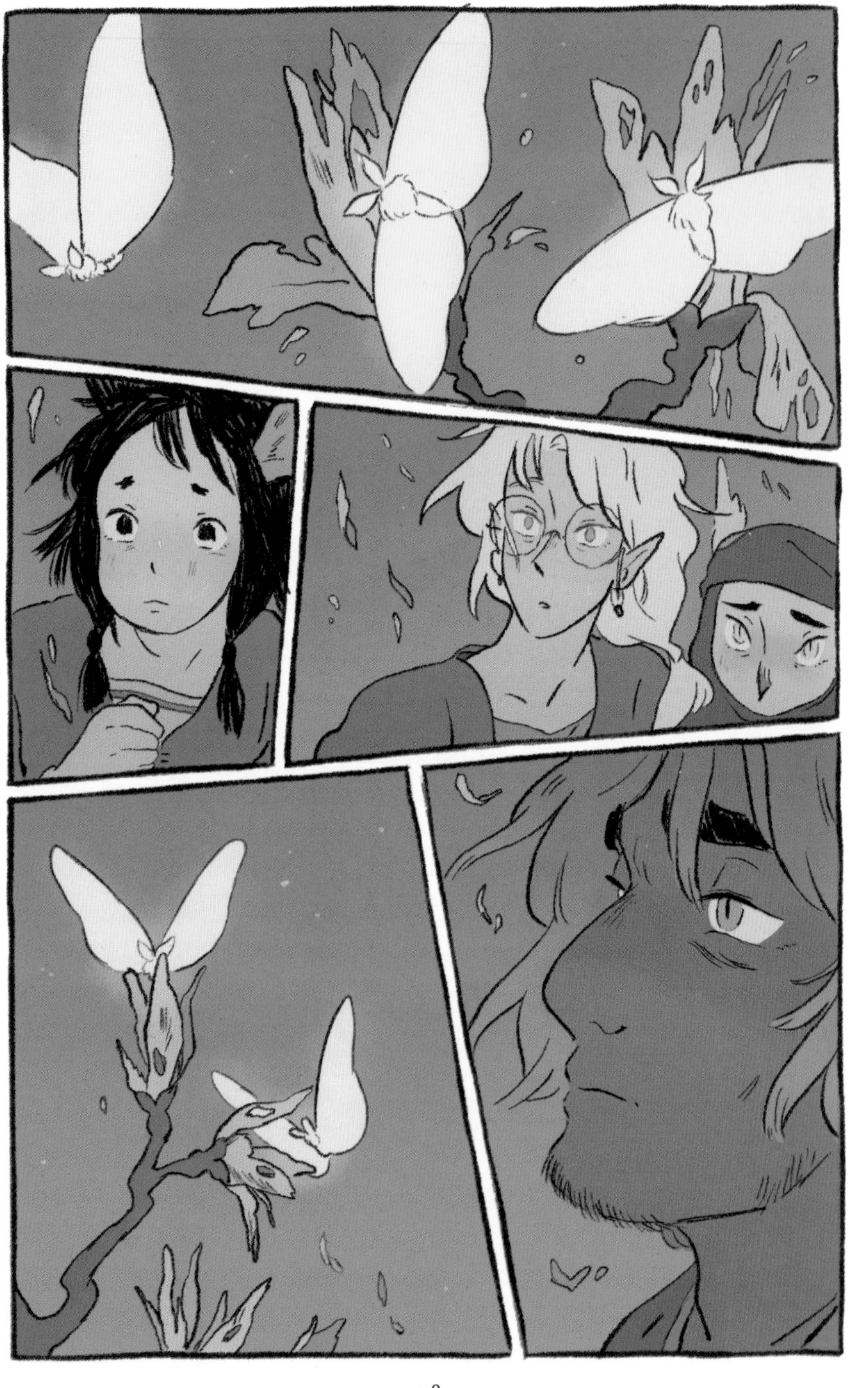

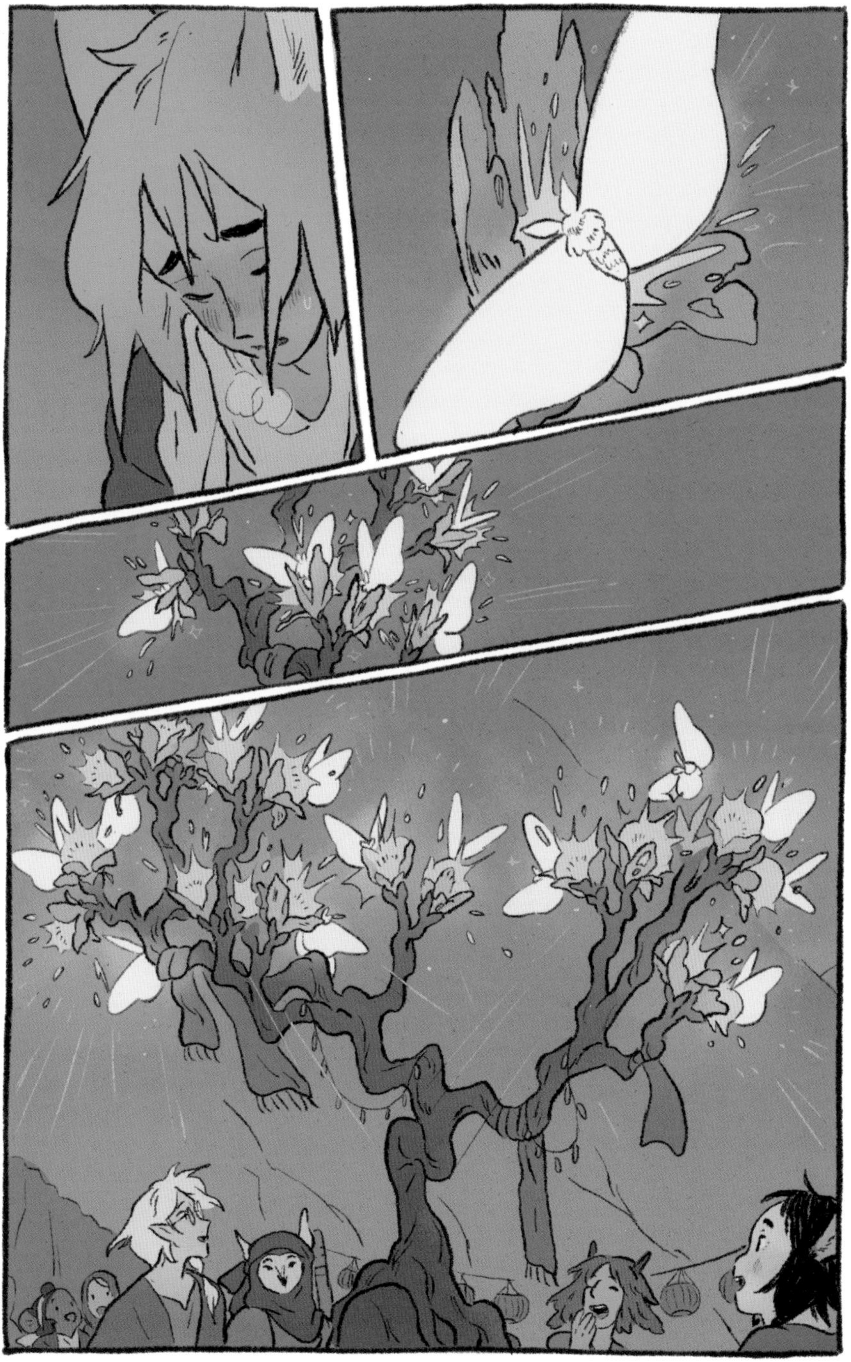

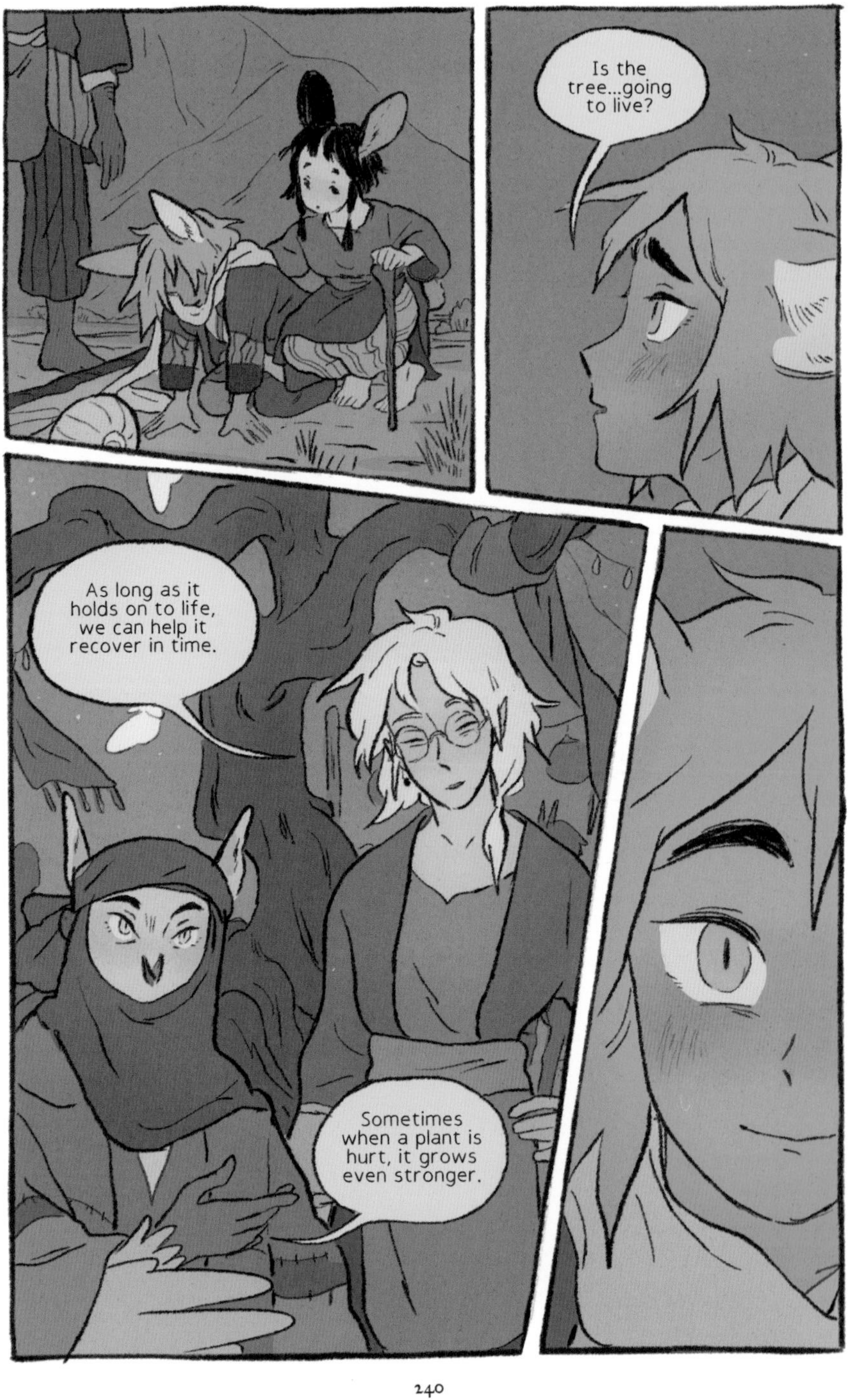
Is the tree...going to live?
As long as it holds on to life, we can help it recover in time.
Sometimes when a plant is hurt, it grows even stronger.

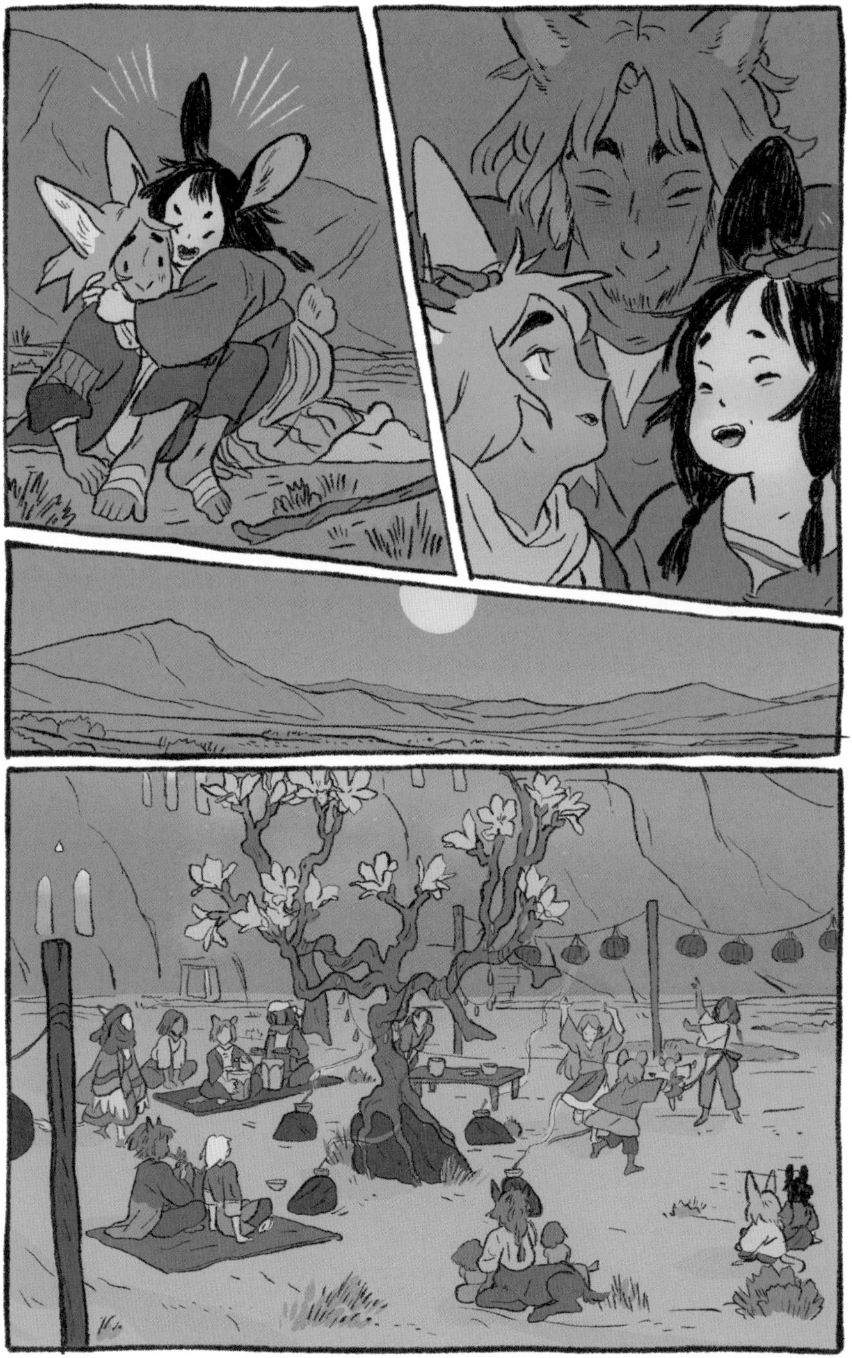

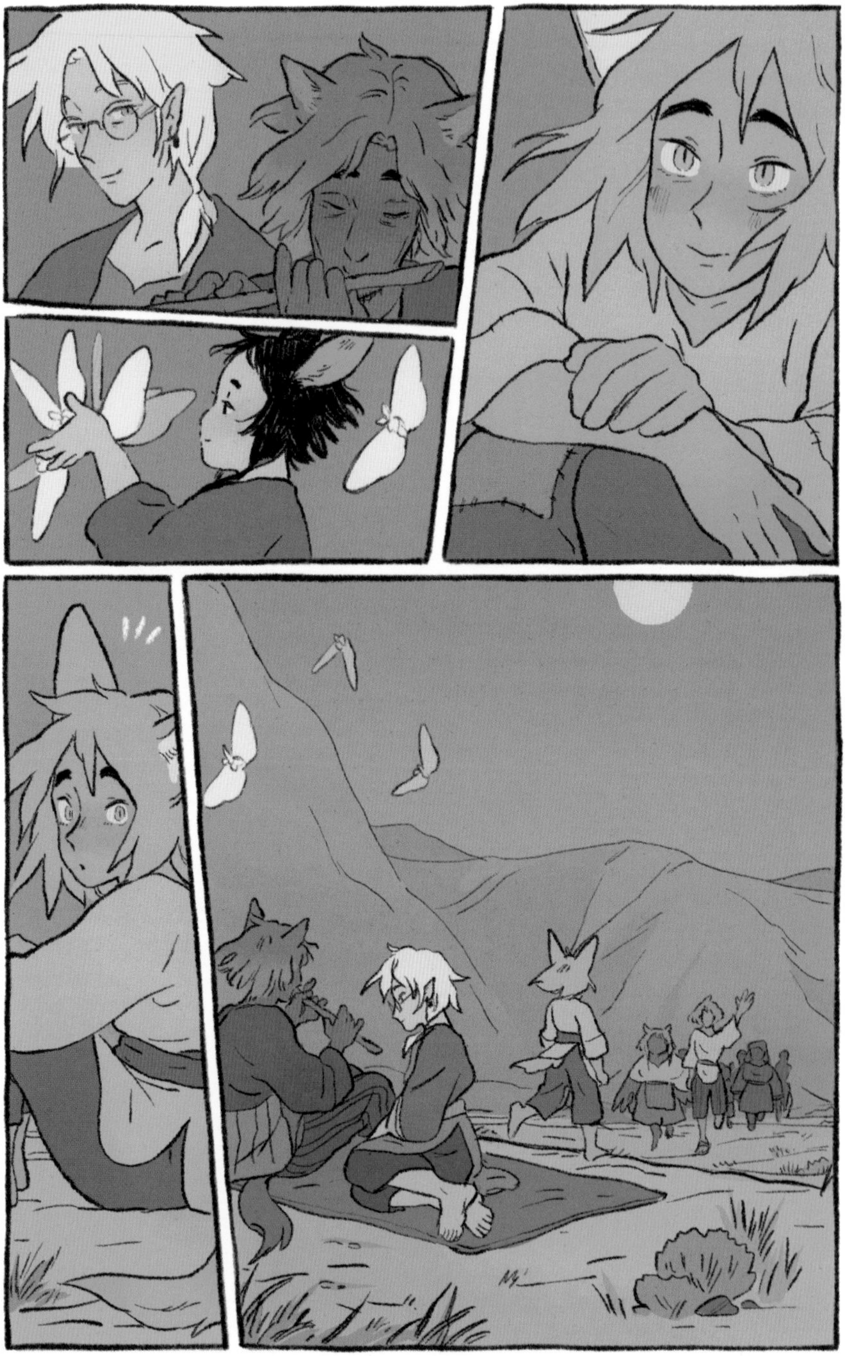

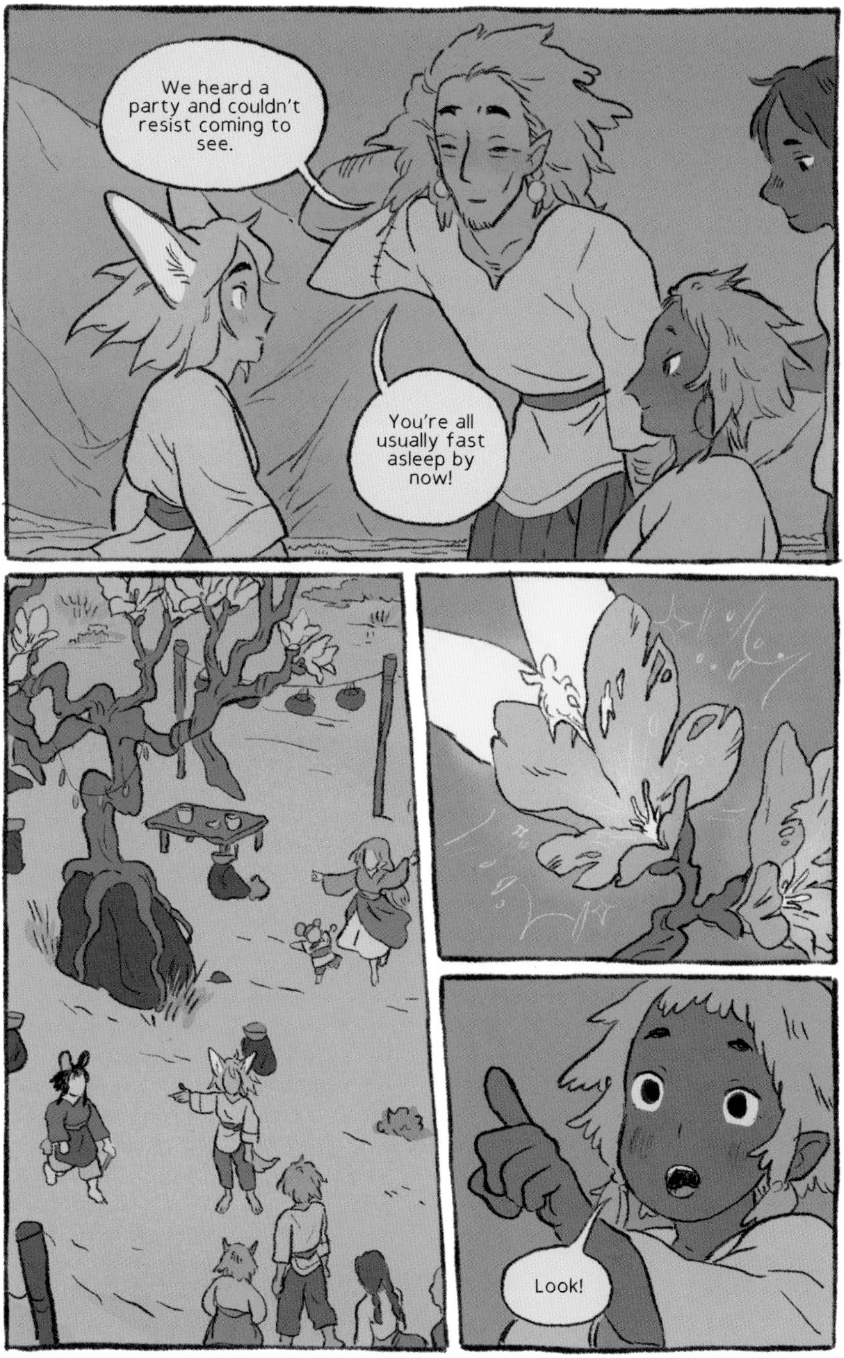
We heard a party and couldn't resist coming to see.
You're all usually fast asleep by now!
Look!

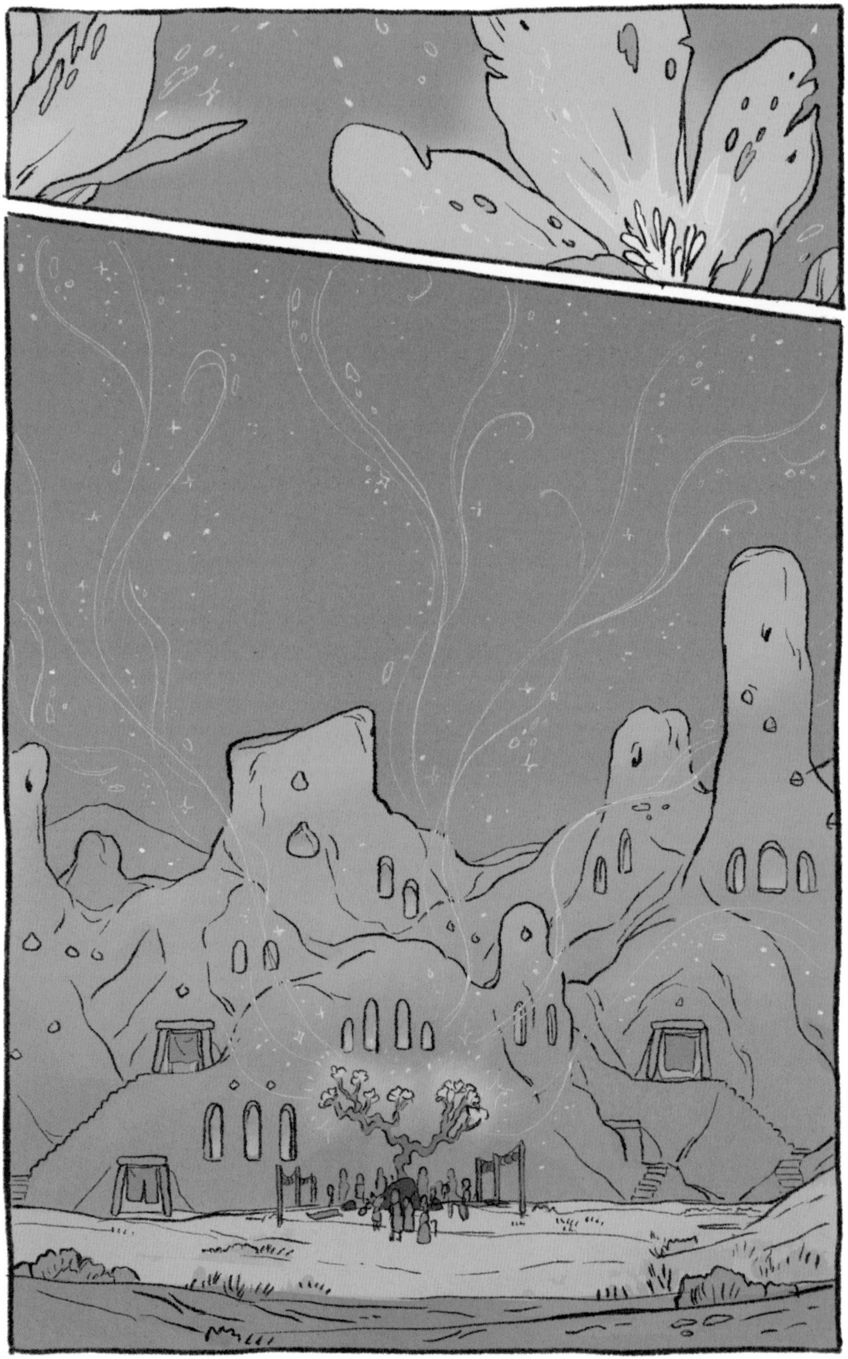

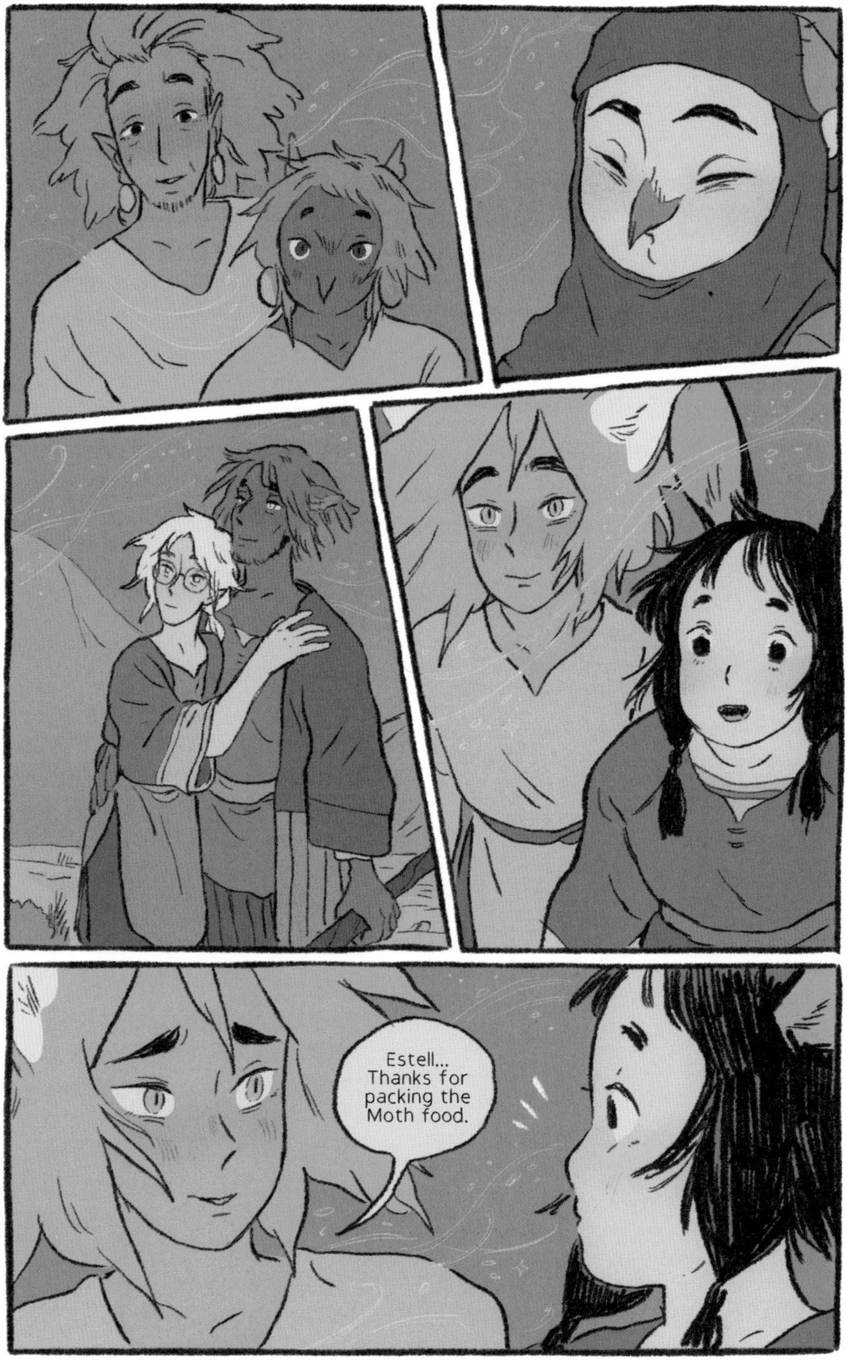
Estell... Thanks for packing the Moth food.

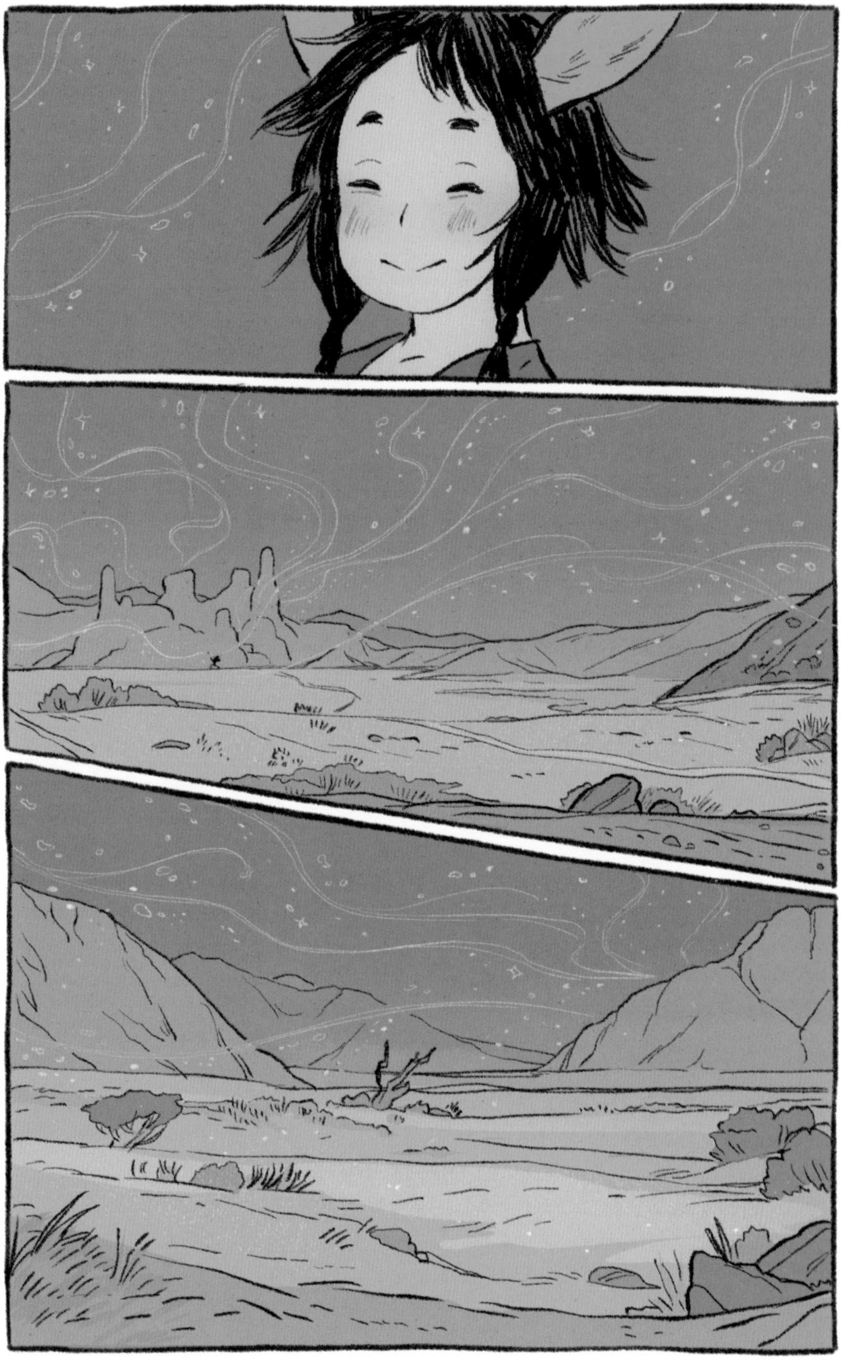

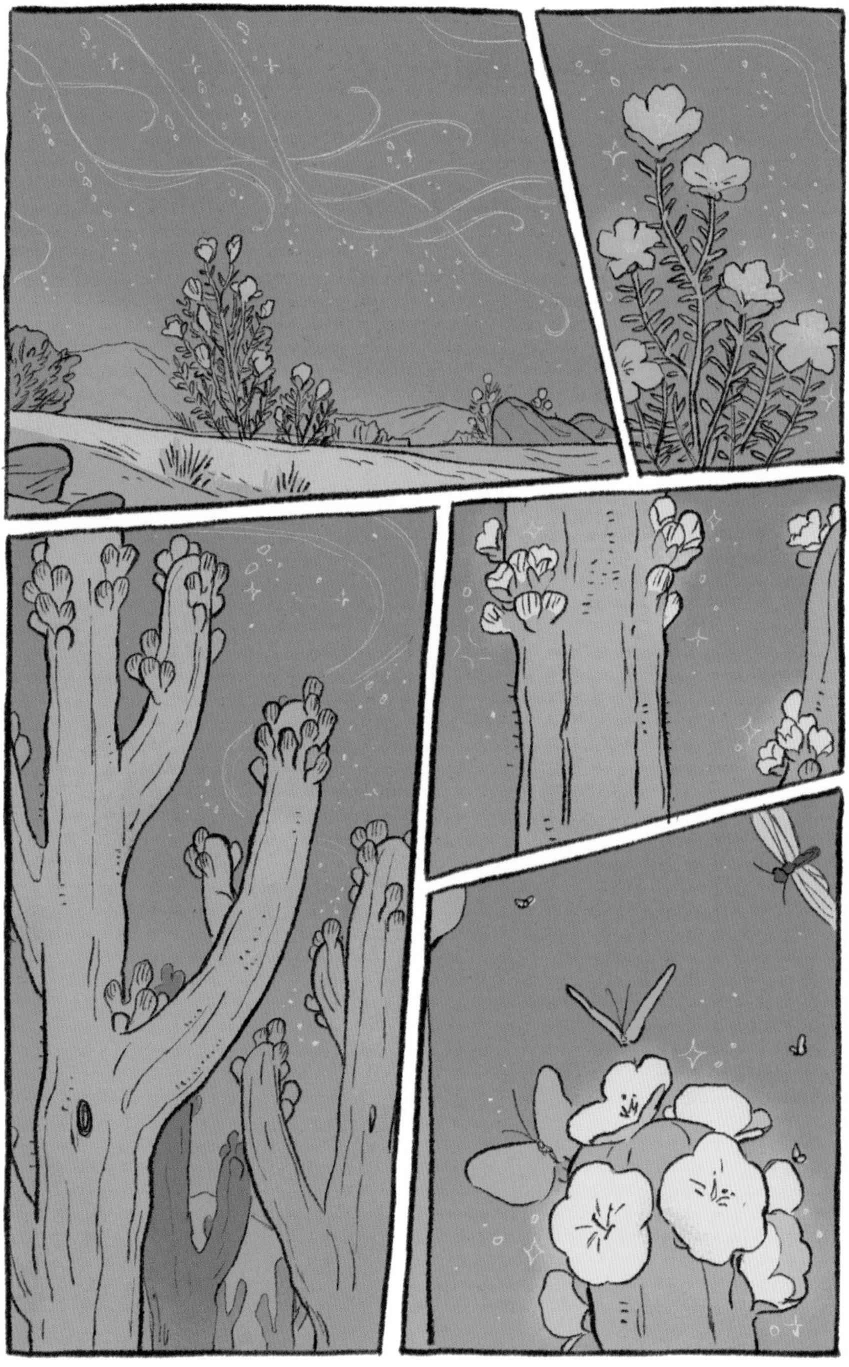

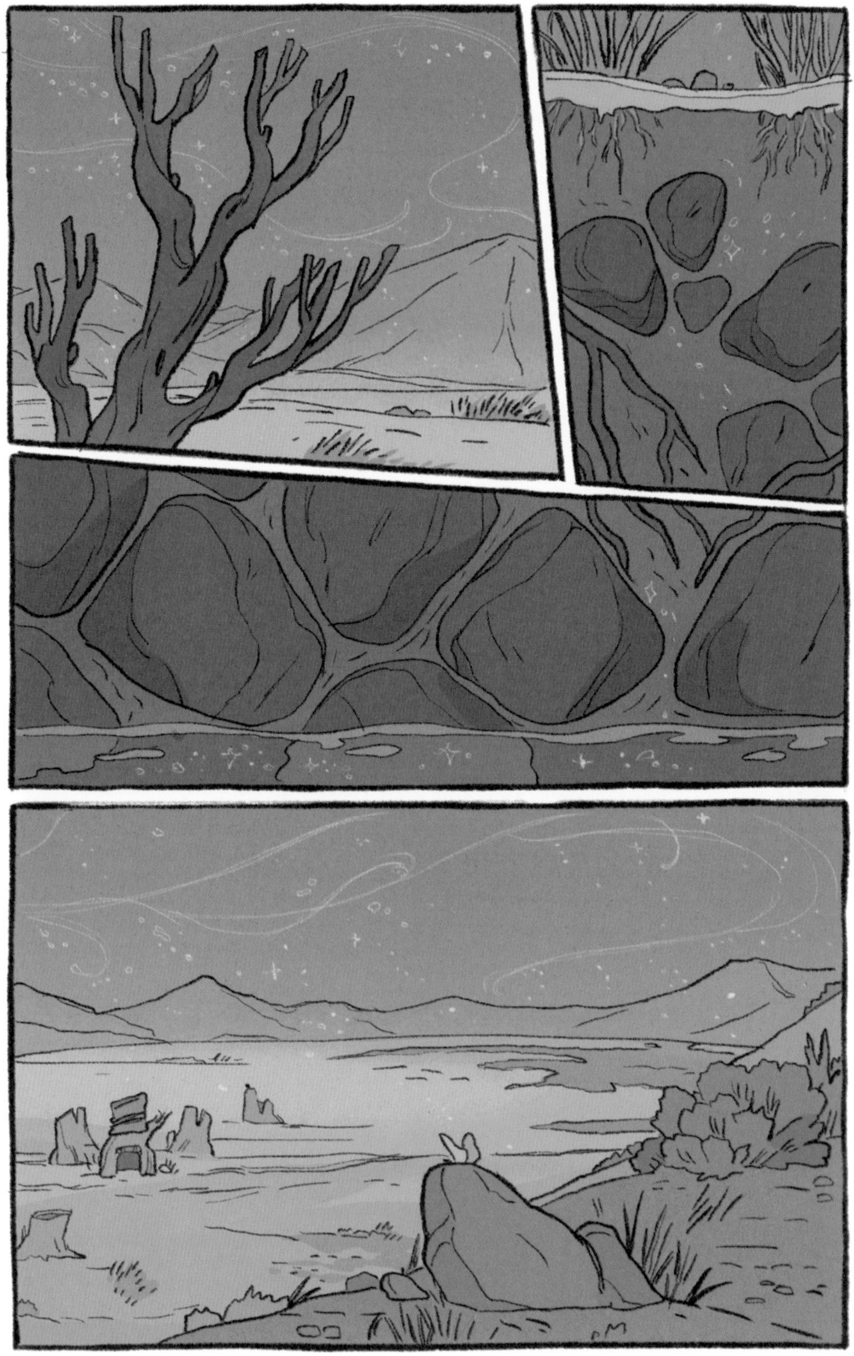

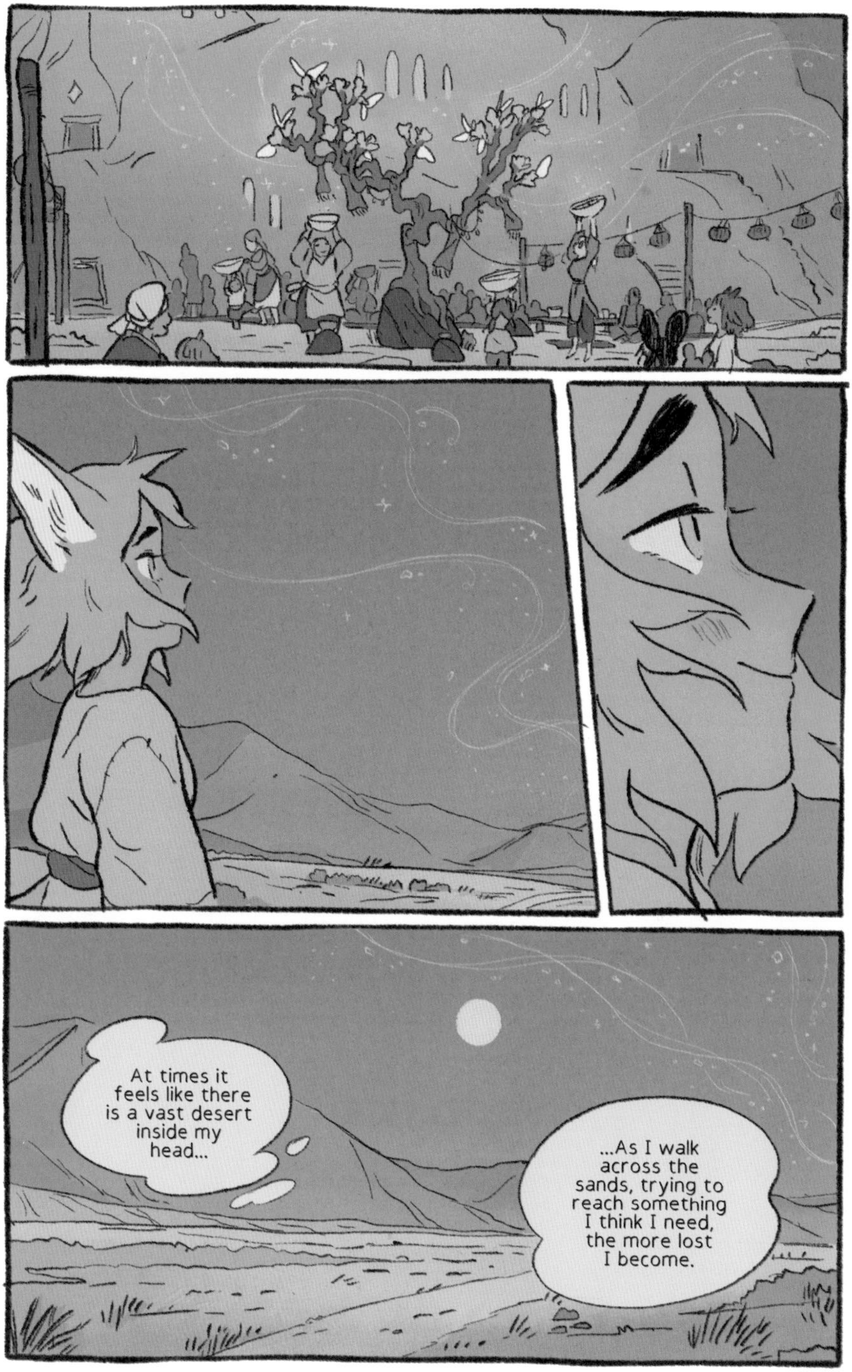
At times it feels like there is a vast desert inside my head...
...As I walk across the sands, trying to reach something I think I need, the more lost I become.

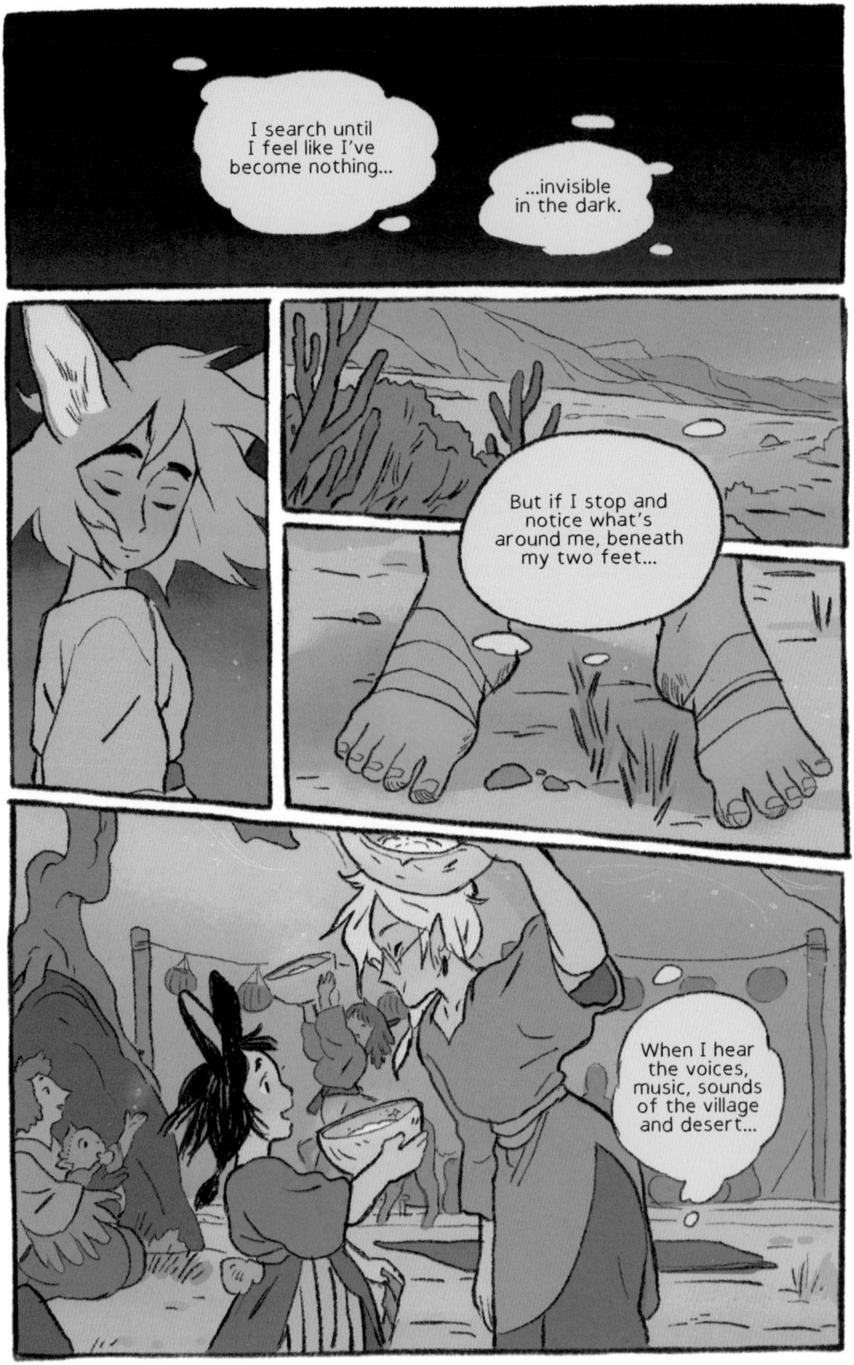
I search until I feel like I've become nothing...
...invisible in the dark.
But if I stop and notice what's around me, beneath my two feet...
When I hear the voices, music, sounds of the village and desert...

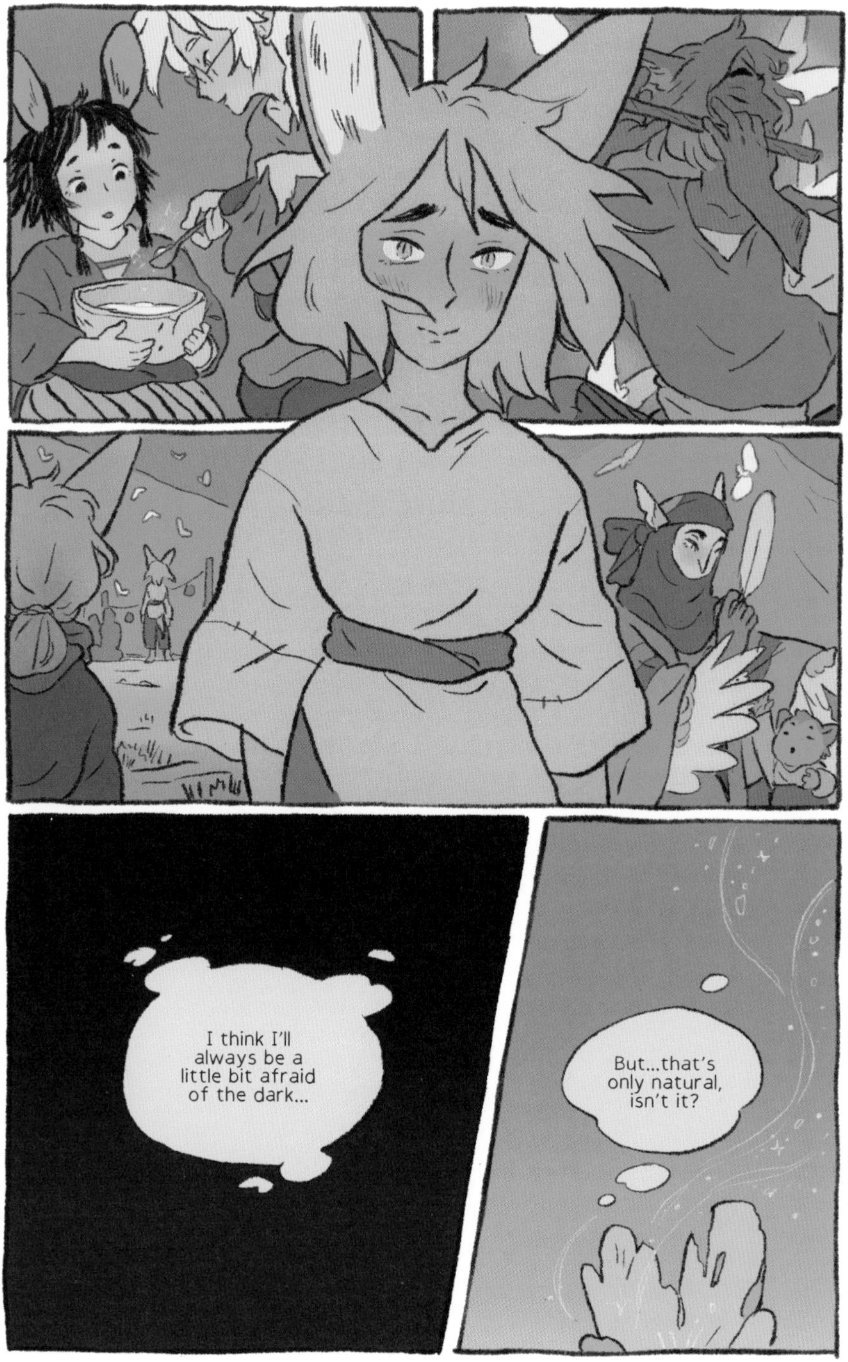
I think I'll always be a little bit afraid of the dark...
But...that's only natural, isn't it?

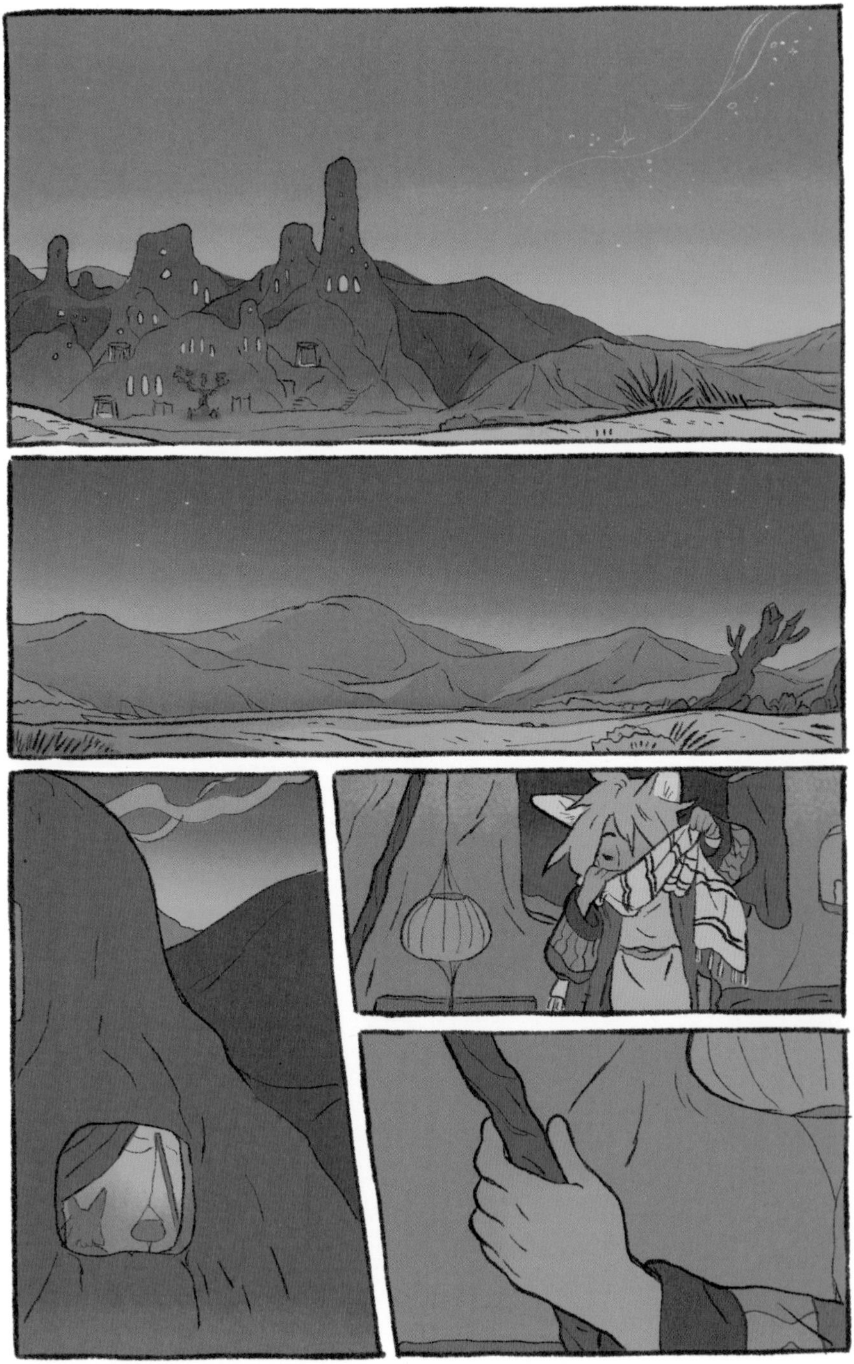

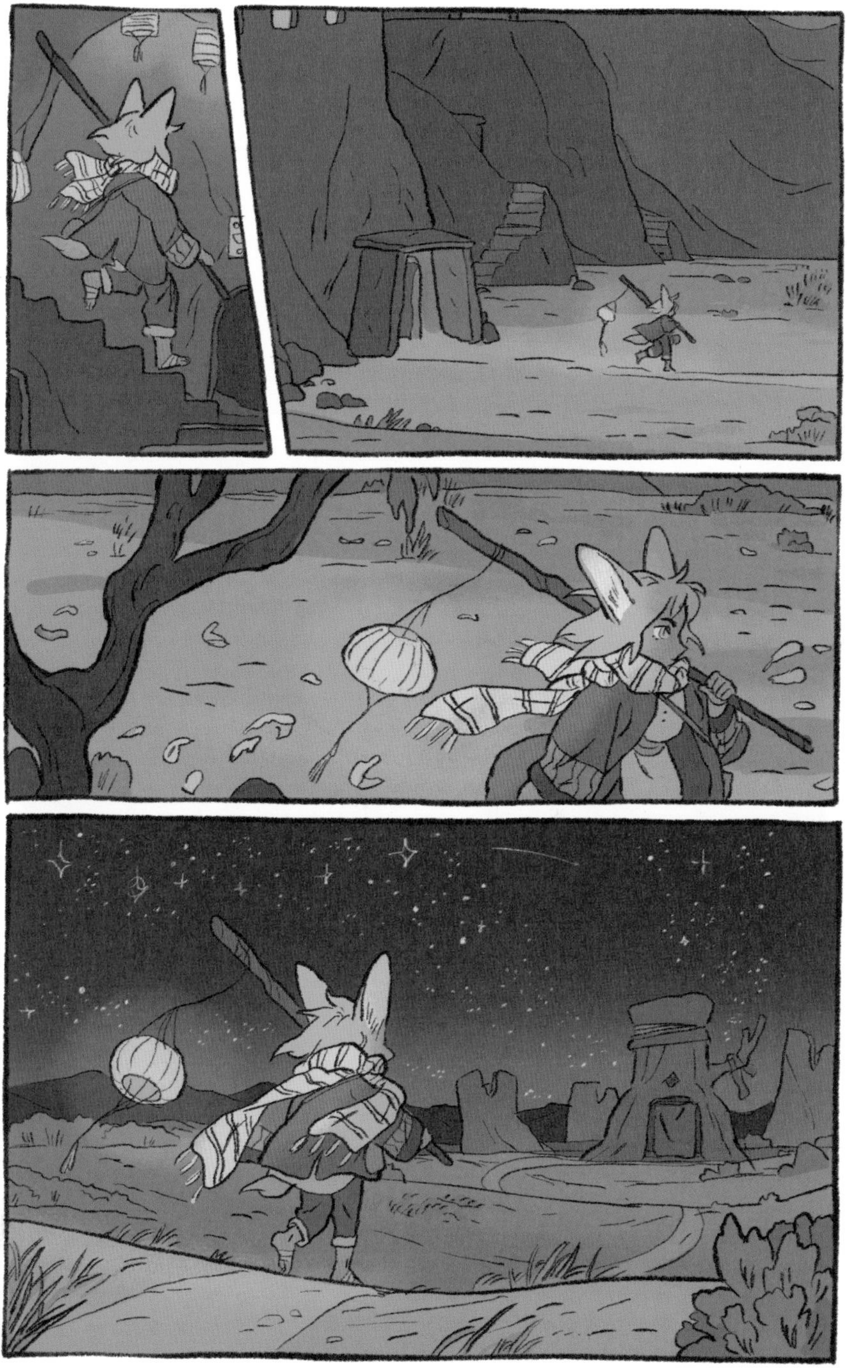

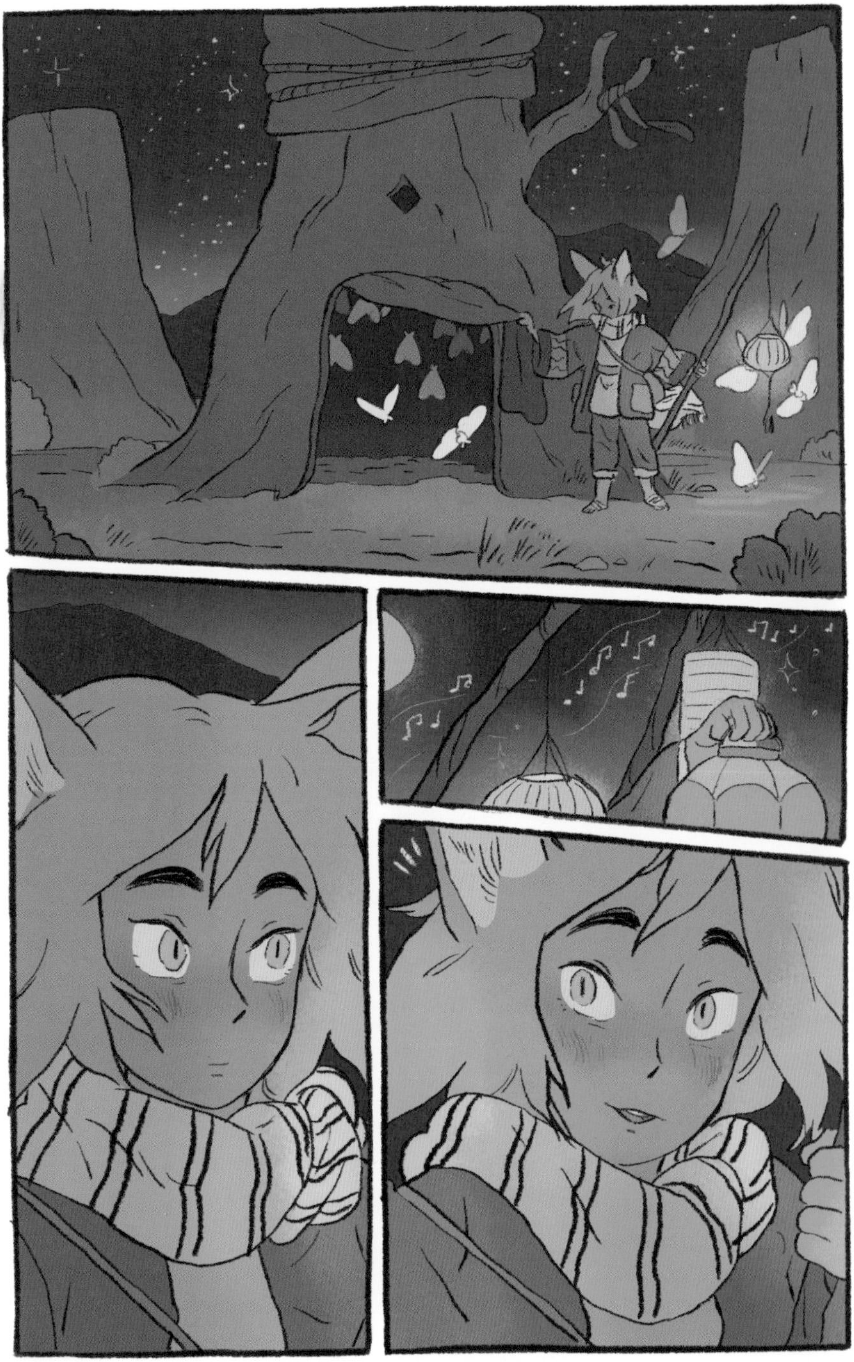

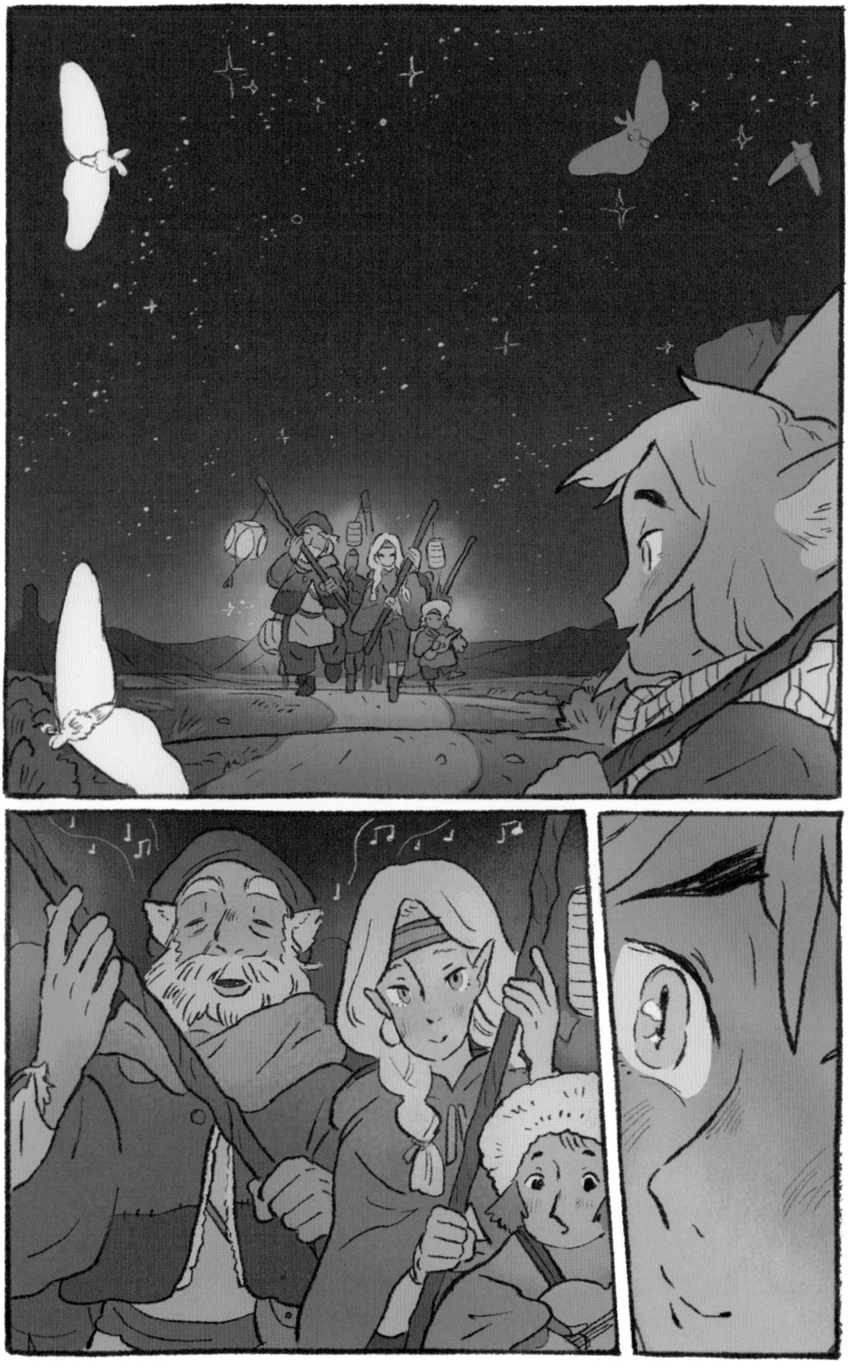

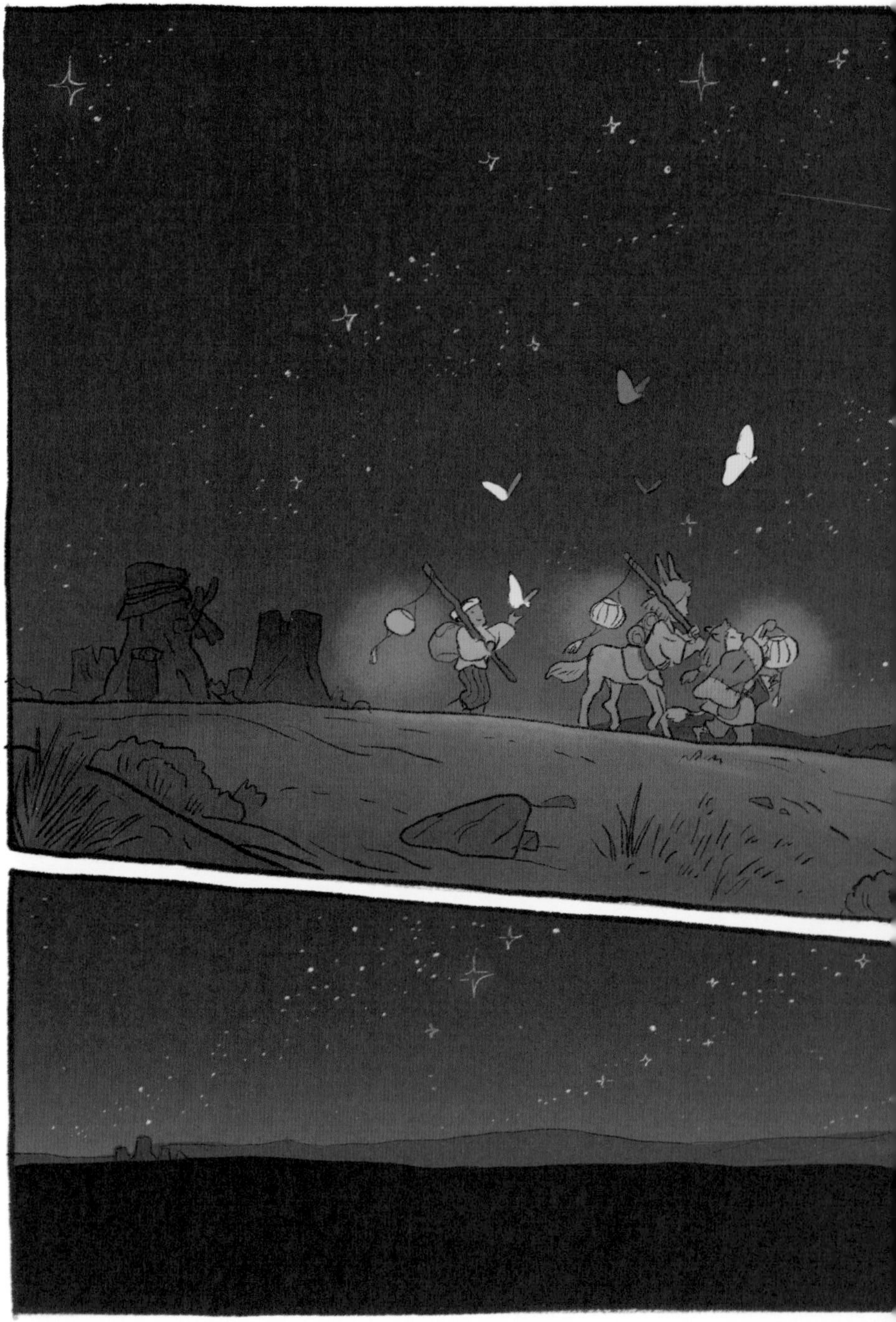

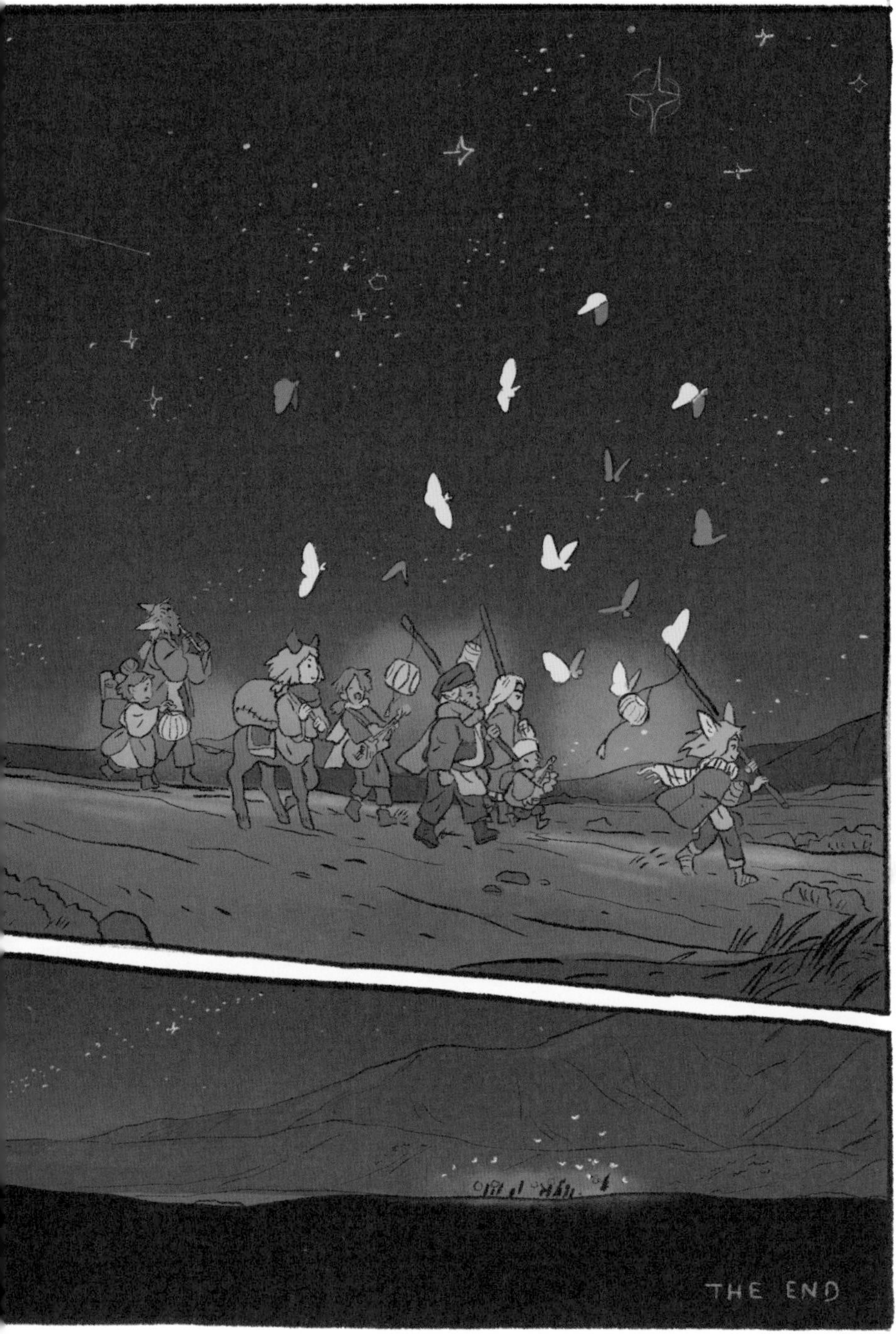
THE END

INSPIRATION

Although Aotearoa New Zealand doesn't have what you'd typically think of as a desert, the high alpine regions around the Tongariro National Park and Kā Tiritiri o te Moana (Southern Alps) are very dry, covered with beautiful tussock fields and stony scree slopes. I was inspired by the rolling, undulating landforms, the lines of the mountain ranges, the colors of the receding distance, and the small-ness one feels standing amid such scenery. Not far from my home-town, the dark sky reserve at Lake Tekapo, with its ocean of stars, also served as inspiration for this book.

Aotearoa, being made up of small islands isolated from other continents for millions and millions of years, has endless examples of highly specialized relationships between flora and fauna—plants and creatures that require one another to survive. There is a species of native moth that will only lay its larvae in a type of rush plant found in just a handful of wetland areas.

An example from the United States is the Joshua tree and the yucca moth. The Joshua tree flowers save their energy by producing only a small amount of pollen, which the moths have evolved to be able to carefully harvest and spread to other flowers. In the process, they lay batches of eggs inside that will eventually hatch and feast upon some of the pollinated seeds.

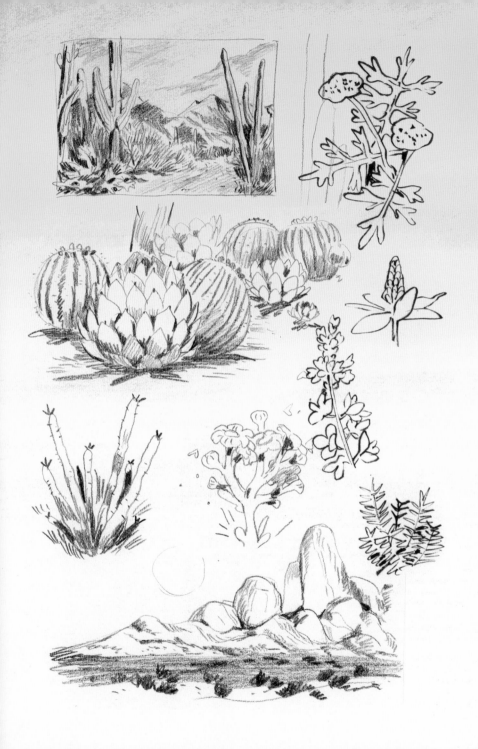

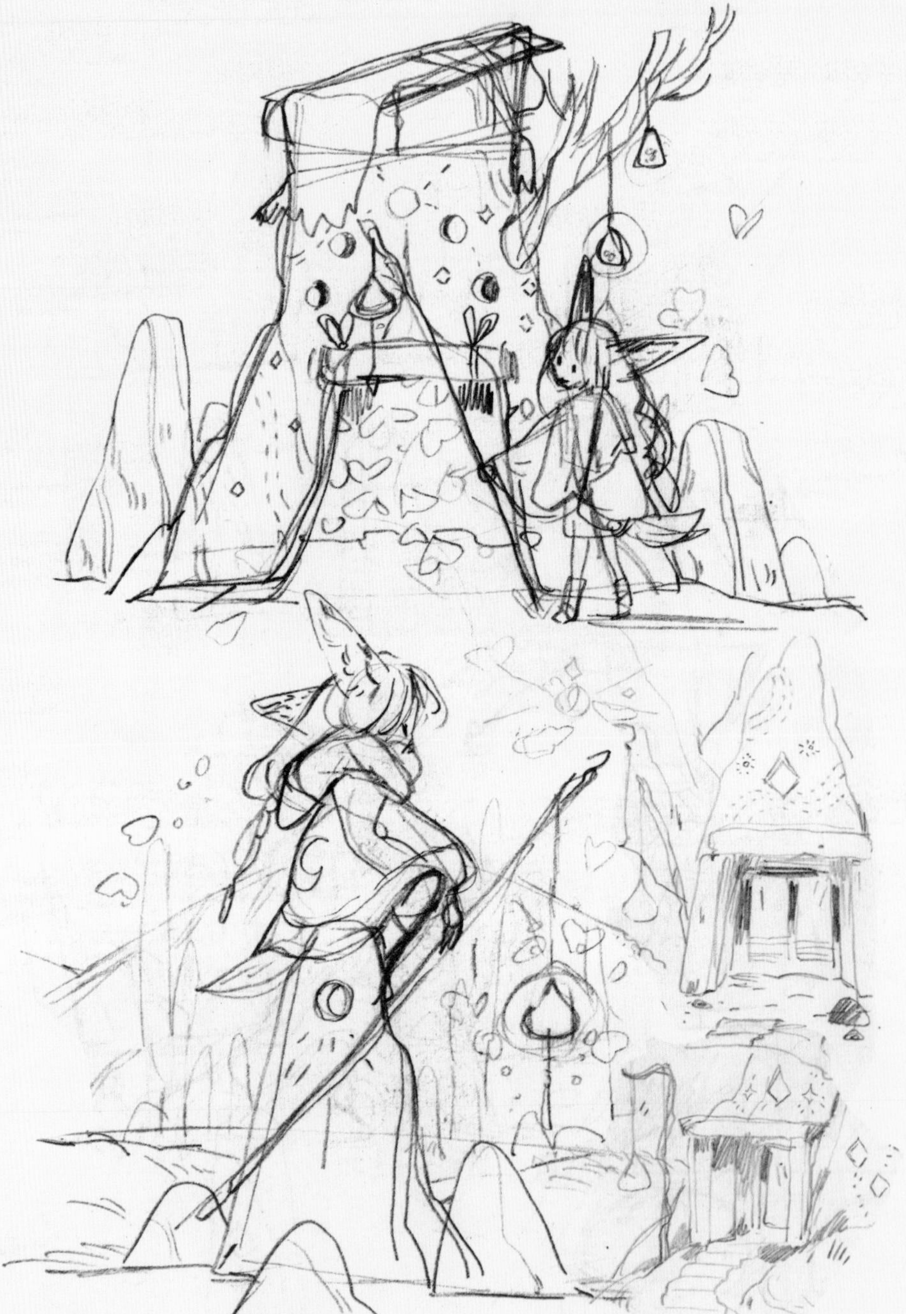

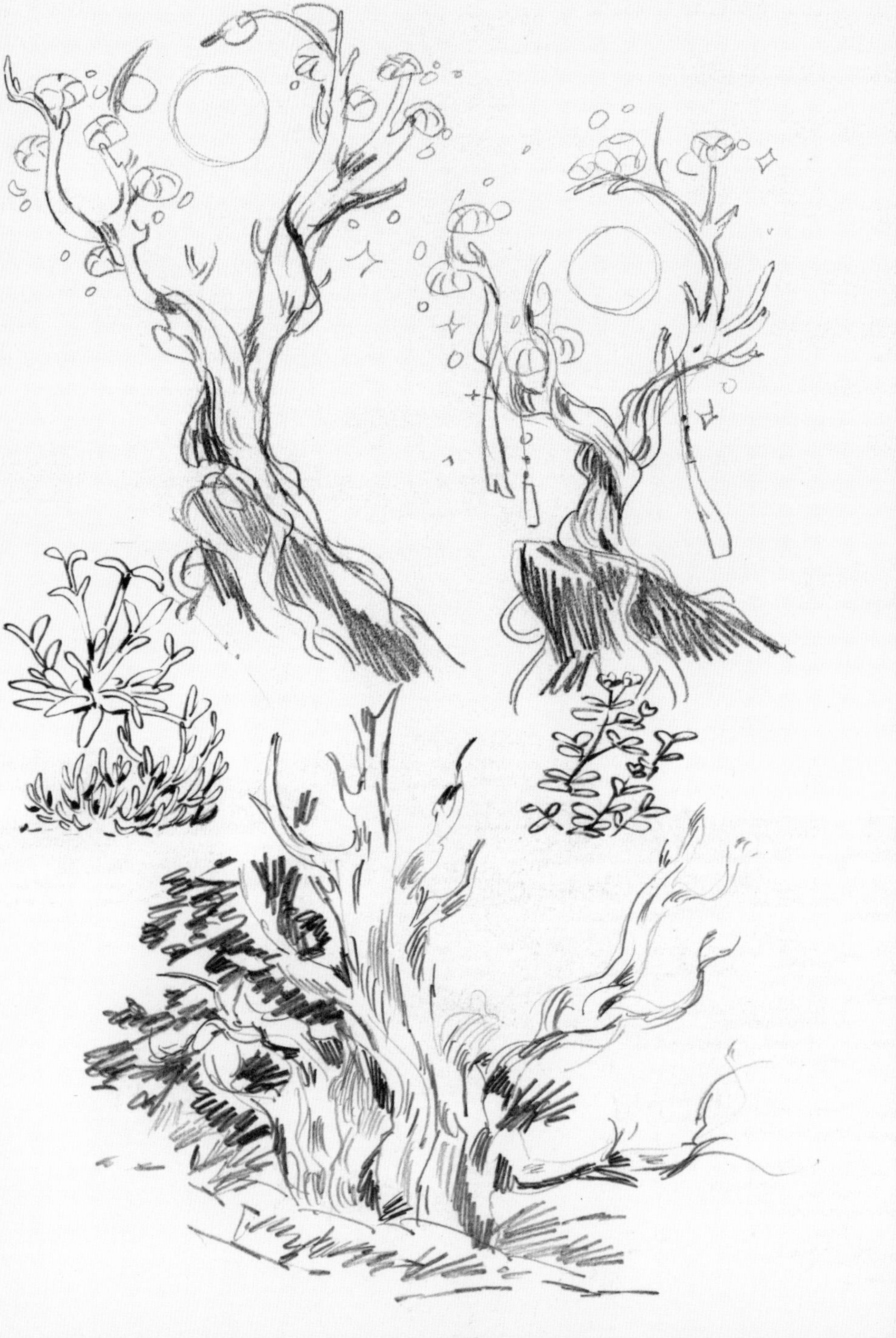

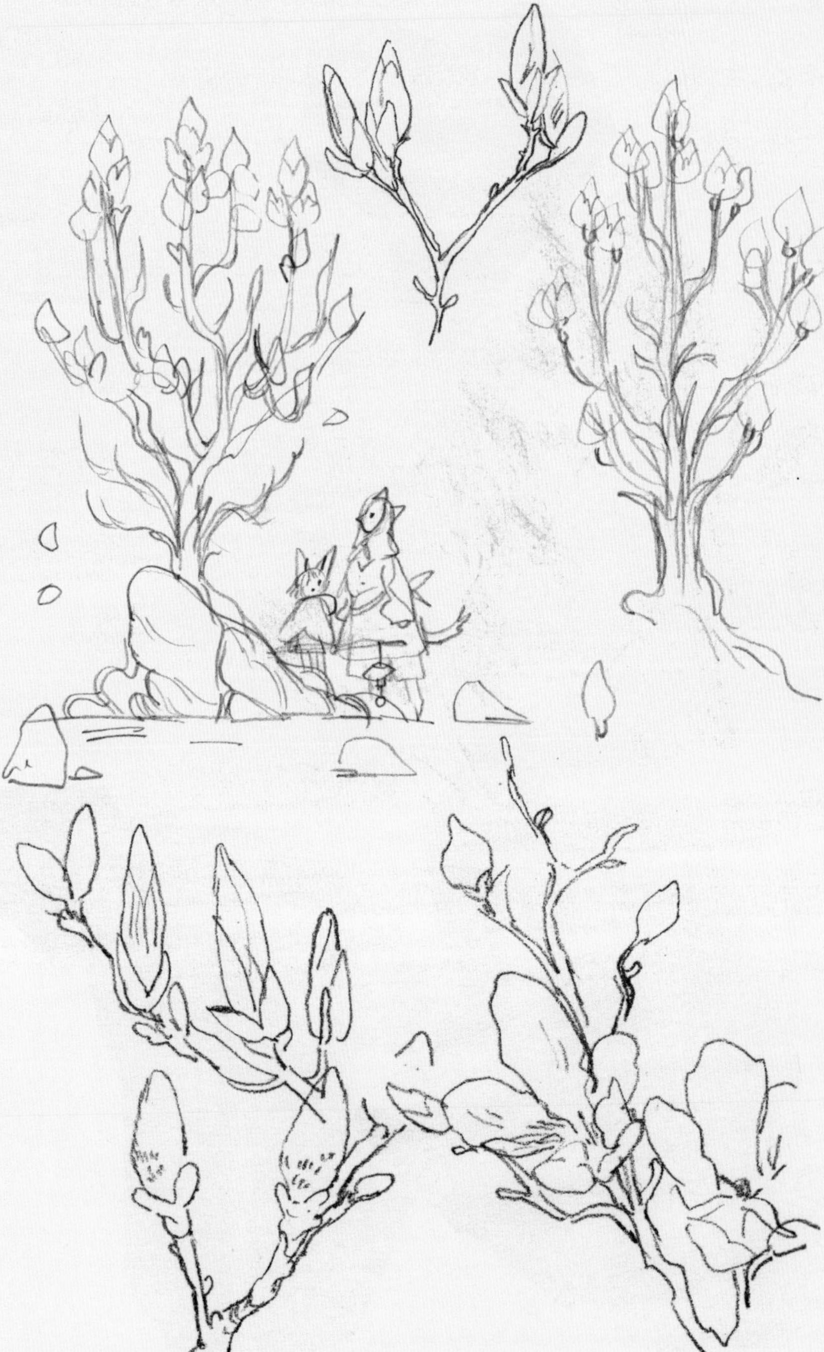

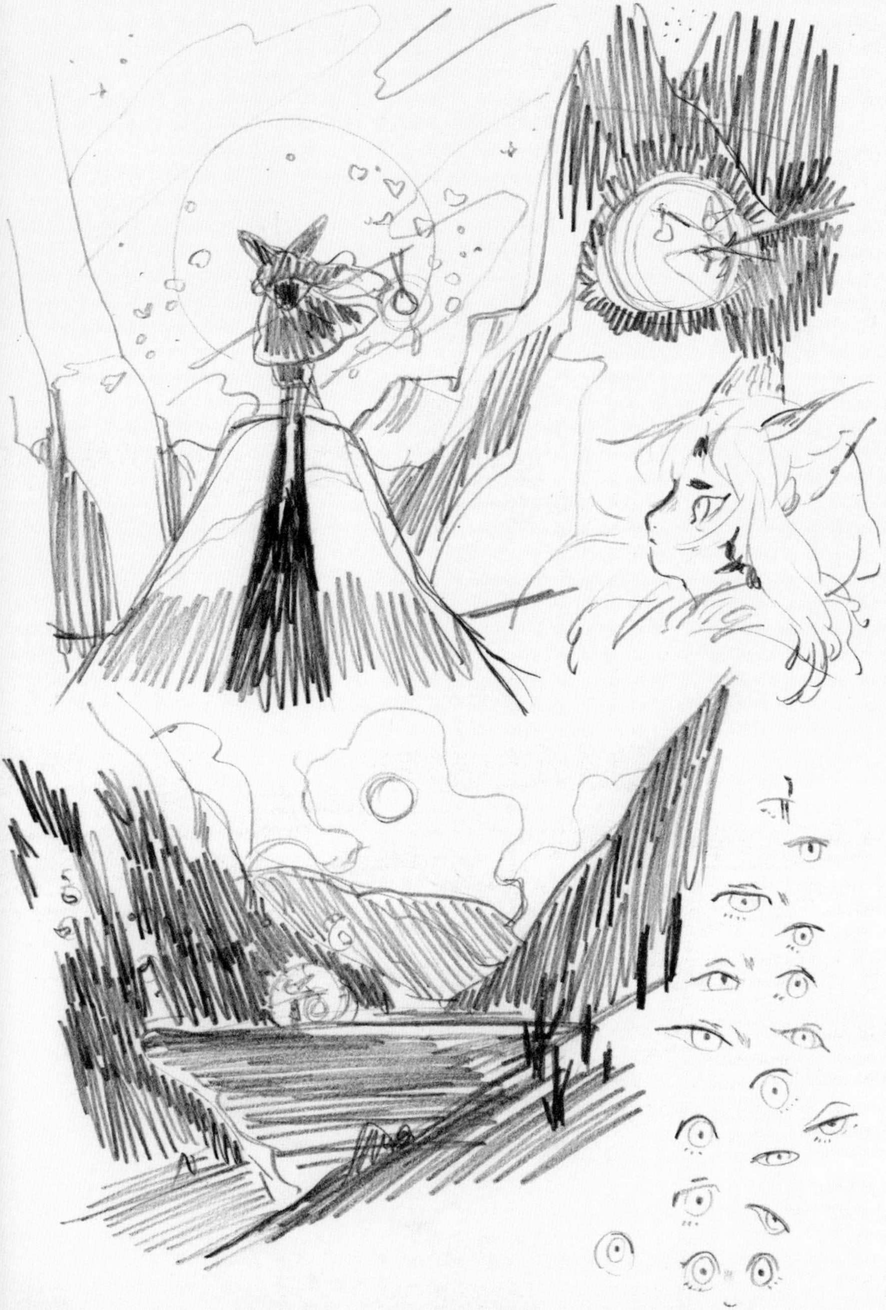

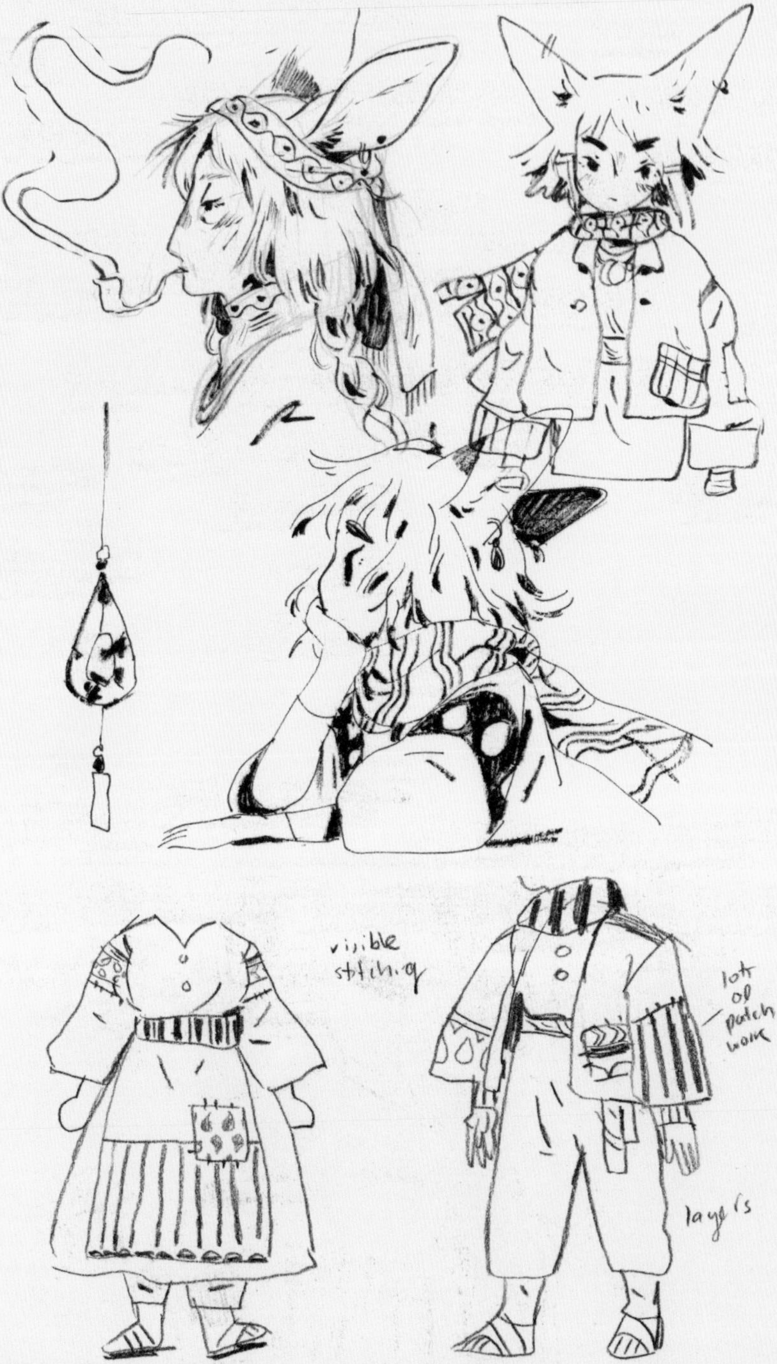
visible stiching
lots of patch work
layers

About the Creator

K. O'Neill is an author and illustrator based in Aotearoa New Zealand who is a lover of nature, tea, and growing things. They strive to make books with themes of kindness, inclusiveness, and well-being, creating worlds that children can play in and characters they can identify with and admire.

K.'s books *The Tea Dragon Society* and *Princess Princess Ever After* have garnered numerous awards, including Eisner Awards for Best Children's Comic and Webcomic, the Dwayne McDuffie Award, and the Harvey Award, and have been included on the ALA Rainbow and Amelia Bloomer Lists.

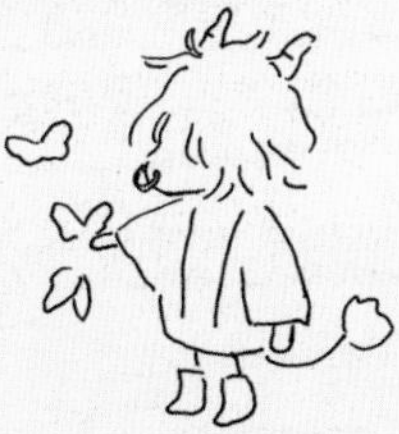

MAGIC AND ADVENTURE AWAIT!

One pig's perilous journey to find purpose and friendship
Ham Helsing
VAMPIRE HUNTER
RICH MOYER

"An action-packed page-turner with heart!" —DAV PILKEY, author of the DOG MAN series
NEW YORK TIMES BESTSELLING SERIES
HiLO
GINA AND THE BIG SECRET
BY JUDD WINICK

Grace NEEDS SPACE!
BENJAMIN A WILGUS
RII ABREGO

MAPMAKERS AND THE LOST MAGIC
CAMERON CHITTOCK
AMANDA CASTILLO

Meesh the BAD DEMON
MICHELLE LAM

From the Eisner-Winning Author of The Tea Dragon Society series
The Moth Keeper
K. O'Neill

PACEY PACKER UNICORN TRACKER
J. C. PHILLIPPS

Sophie Escabasse
WITCHES of BROOKLYN

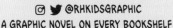